MW01616375

BEST
SHORT
NOVELS
2007

BEST
SHORT
NOVELS
2007

Edited by
Jonathan Strahan

SCIENCE
FICTION

For Richard Scriven,
who probably will never see it,
but without whom it could
never have happened.

There's little doubt that the volume you now hold in your hands wouldn't exist without the enthusiasm and determination of Charles N. Brown. When the going became rocky, he supported it above all others. I also can't thank my editor Andrew Wheeler enough for his support with this project. If the Best Short Novels project has been a collaboration, it's been a collaboration with him and his team at the SF Book Club. Thanks too to my agent Howard Morhaim, who has worked tirelessly on all of my projects, these past three years or so.

As I've said in previous years, a book like this takes a community of people to get done. As always I'd like to thank Pete Crowther and Nick Gevers of PS Publishing and Marty Halpern and Gary Turner at Golden Gryphon, who were all kind, gracious, and generous when they didn't have to be; Justin Ackroyd, who continues to be a vital supporter of my work and this anthology series; Jack Dann, anthology guru, pal, and confidante; and my *Locus* colleagues Nick Gevers and Rich Horton, who have always been there to discuss the best short fiction of the year when I needed it most. Thanks also to the following good friends and colleagues without whom this book would have been much poorer, and much less fun to do: Ellen Datlow, Kelly Link, Gavin Grant, Sean Wallace, Sean Williams, Jason Williams, and all of the book's contributors.

And, last but not least, the big ones. Extra special thanks to my three angels, Marianne, Jessica, and Sophie, who make every day an adventure and fill it with joy.

⇒ Contents ⇐

Introduction

by Jonathan Strahan

It is tempting to imagine that nearly sixty years ago, when Everett Bleiler and Ted Dikty sat down in the winter of 1949 to compile the first ever science fiction year's best, they had the world at their feet. The Golden Age of Science Fiction was almost over, but the pulp magazines were still ensuring a good volume of high quality fiction to choose from, and the quantity was small enough that they could easily read everything. At the very least, we can imagine that the sheer novelty of such a thing—who'd ever heard of a year's best science fiction anthology?—might have made their job fairly straightforward. With little science fiction being published between book covers, there was little competition for the reprint rights to stories, and being the first such book it's likely that many of the writers of the day would have been happy to see their stories collected in it.

Such is not the case in early 2007, as I write this introduction. Things have changed, in many ways for the better, but in some ways not. While we are no longer in that first great Golden Age, which arguably began in the late 1930s and was done by the mid-50s, we are in a new Golden Age of sorts. As I noted in the introduction to last year's volume, there are more stories being published in a wider variety of venues than ever before. Even though the numbers were down slightly in 2006, mostly due to the closure of a number of online publications, there were still somewhere between 2,500 and 3,000 original science fiction and fantasy stories published during the year. And, while that number is staggering enough, it's likely only a sampling of the true number. No matter what the exact figure might be, what is important is to realize that it's simply impossible for any one reader to read *everything* published during the year. Even if one reader could *find* everything, he or she would need to read more than half a dozen stories every day of the year. The compensation for all of that reading, though, is that the quality of the best work being published is extraordinary. The writers working today stand alongside the best to ever write short science fiction, and the best stories being written will be the classics of the future.

That makes for a tough but rewarding job when you sit down to compile a year's best annual. There are one or two more complications today that Bleiler and Dikty likely never even imagined, let alone experienced. First, the year's best annual has proliferated over the past two or three years in a way that science fiction has never seen before. Where twenty years ago there were maybe half a dozen year's best annuals being published, this year there will be at least sixteen annuals published according to the year's best website, Year's Best SF Info (www.yearsbestsf.info/). This isn't an entirely good or bad thing. Readers certainly have the chance to find an editor whose taste fits their own, and can allow them to help navigate the huge volume of new fiction. Writers, though, could be forgiven for finding the prospect of being published in a year's best a little less exciting than they once did. Publishing has also changed since 1949. It's now an enormous industry that publishes huge numbers of science fiction novels, collections, and anthologies every year. This year alone, according to trade journal *Locus*, 242 publishers produced 2,495 new books. The competition for rights to reprint fiction is fierce, especially with the recent trend towards high-priced small press gift editions of books, which are well liked by collectors, but can tie up rights for some time.

In short, unlike Bleiler and Dikty, it's not only hard these days to read everything, often you can't get what you want when you do. And that is something of a problem for science fiction, if you happen to agree that year's best annuals do more than just provide an entertaining afternoon or two's distraction. As I've said elsewhere, I think year's best annuals perform an important function. They are part of the process—not all of it, but an important part—of how the field identifies the new short fiction that will enter science fiction's canon of great works. Editors sift through millions of words of fiction, hopefully finding the best work of the year. They put it in a volume that's read by readers and writers. They help push those stories further into the conversation the field constantly has with itself. And, as time goes by, those annuals become a reference for readers looking back at the best we've done. I know, for example, that I turned to Bleiler and Dikty's half dozen annuals to explain the late '40s and early '50s, and followed Judith Merril, Terry Carr, Gardner Dozois, and others to better understand science fiction in the second half of the twentieth century.

What's the solution? Is a year's best truly a year's best if the editor hasn't read every story published, and can't necessarily get permission to publish what they think the best work is, even if they do? Well, mostly yes. Editors read an enormous amount, taste plays a significant part, and rights are still only occasionally a problem. But it's something we need to be aware of, need to discuss as openly as we can. I know, for example, that this year I read more novellas and novelettes to assemble the nearly 200,000 words of stories in this book than in any other year. There were more great stories than I could possibly include, and one or two that I couldn't get regardless. Charles Stross's "Missile Gap," for example, stands amongst the best novellas of the year. I would have included it here, if I could have. Instead, I'd exhort you to order Gardner Dozois's excellent anthology *One Million A.D.* from the SF Book Club, which includes that story and strong work by Alastair Reynolds, Greg Egan, and others. I'd also have added Alastair Reynolds "Nightingale" from his collection *Galactic North.* That too should be on your reading list. Does that make this a weaker book? No. Definitely not. The eight stories collected here are my choice for the best short novels of the year. Some will end up on awards ballots, some are likely to enter the field's canon of great works, all are going to amply repay the time you spend reading them. There's a lot more than just an afternoon or two of great reading here, though that too, would be a fine thing.

And, before you go on to the stories, a few thank yous. The book you're now holding very nearly didn't appear at all. I'd like to thank my editor Andrew Wheeler for his extraordinary faith in this series, and my agent Howard Morhaim for his work on making this possible. I'd also like to acknowledge Charles Brown of *Locus*, without whom this book would surely have died. I believe that there remains in the field a place for a book like this one: A book that brings together the best science fiction *and* the best fantasy short novels of the year in one single volume; a book that is aware of, but not trapped, by the history of the genre; a book that has both eyes on the future, but hasn't forgotten the past. I can only hope you'll agree.

And on to the stories. Here are some of the best and brightest science fiction and fantasy writers of our time doing what they do best, creating unforgettable stories. I hope you enjoy them as much as I did, and that you'll join me here again next year.

Jonathan Strahan
February 2007
Perth, Western Australia

BEST
SHORT
NOVELS
2007

WHERE THE GOLDEN APPLES GROW

by Kage Baker

Kage Baker was born in Hollywood, California, in 1952. She worked as an actor, director, artist, insurance clerk, and teacher of Elizabethan English, before becoming a full-time writer. Her first professional sale was the story "Noble Mold" in 1997, first in her romantic SF Company series, which now includes eight novels and two collections. Her novels include In the Garden of Iden, Sky Coyote, *and the non-series fantasy* The Anvil of the World. *In addition to the Company collections* Black Projects, White Knights, *and* Gods and Pawns, *her short fiction has been collected in* Mother Ægypt and Other Stories *and* Dark Mondays. *Her novella "The Empress of Mars" won the Theodore Sturgeon Memorial Award, and "Son Observe the Time" was nominated for the Hugo Award. She is currently working on a new fantasy novel,* The House of the Stag.

ONE

He WAS THE third boy born on Mars.

He was twelve years old now, and had spent most of his life in the cab of a freighter. His name was Bill.

Bill lived with his dad, Billy Townsend. Billy Townsend was a Hauler. He made the long runs up and down Mars, to Depot North and Depot South, bringing ice back from the ends of the world. Bill had always gone along on the runs, from the time he'd been packed into the shotgun seat like a little duffel bag to now, when he sat hunched in the far corner of the cab with his Gamebuke, ignoring his dad's loud and cheerful conversation.

There was no other place for him to be. The freighter was the only home he had ever known. His dad called her Beautiful Evelyn.

As far as Bill knew, his mum had passed on. That was one of the answers his dad had given him, and it might be true; there were a lot of things to die from on Mars, with all the cold and dry and blowing grit, and so little air to breathe. But it was just as likely she had gone back to Earth, to judge from other things his dad had said. Bill tried not to think about her, either way.

He didn't like his life very much. Most of it was either boring— the long, long runs to the Depots, with nothing to look at but the monitor screens showing miles of red rocky plain—or scary, like the times they'd had to run through bad storms, or when Beautiful Evelyn had broken down in the middle of nowhere.

Better were the times they'd pull into Mons Olympus. The city on the mountain had a lot to see and do (although Bill's dad usually went straight to the Empress of Mars Tavern and stayed there); there were plenty of places to eat, and shops, and a big public data terminal where Bill could download school programs into his Buke. But what Bill liked most about Mons Olympus was that he could look down through its dome and see the Long Acres.

The Long Acres weren't at all like the city, and Bill dreamed of living there. Instead of endless cold red plains, the Long Acres had warm expanses of green life, and actual canals of water for crop irrigation, stretching out for kilometers under vizio tunnels. Bill had heard that from space, it was supposed to look like green lines crossing the lowlands of the planet.

People stayed put in the Long Acres. Families lived down there and worked the land. Bill liked that idea.

His favorite time to look down the mountain was at twilight. Then the lights were just coming on, shining through the vizio panels, and the green fields were empty; Bill liked to imagine families sitting down to dinner together, a dad and a mum and kids in their home, safe in one place from one year to the next. He imagined that they saved their money, instead of going on spending sprees when they hit town, like Bill's dad did. They never forgot things, like birthdays. They never made promises and forgot to keep them.

● ● ●

"Payyyydayyyy!" Billy said happily, beating out a rhythm on the console as he drove. "Gonna spend my money free! Yeah! We'll have us a good time, eh, mate?"

"I need to buy socks," said Bill.

"Whatever you want, bookworm. Socks, boots, buy out the whole shop."

"I just need socks," said Bill. They were on the last stretch of the High Road, rocketing along under the glittering stars, and ahead of them he could see the high-up bright lights of Mons Olympus on the monitor. Its main dome was luminous with colors from the neon signs inside; even the outlying Tubes were lit up, from all the psuit-lights of the people going to and fro. It looked like pictures he had seen of circus tents on Earth. Bill shut down his Gamebuke and slid it into the front pocket of his psuit, and carefully zipped the pocket shut.

"Time to put your mask on, Dad," he said. If Billy wasn't reminded, he tended to just take a gulp of air, jump from the cab and sprint for the Tube airlocks, and one or twice he had tripped and fallen, and nearly killed himself before he'd got his mask on.

"Sure thing," said Billy, fumbling for the mask. He had managed to get it on his face unassisted by the time Beautiful Evelyn roared into the freighter barn, and backed into the unloading bay. Father and son climbed from the cab and walked away together toward the Tube, stiff-legged after all those hours on the road.

At this moment, walking side by side, they really did look like father and son. Bill had Billy's shock of wild hair that stuck up above the mask, and though he was small for a Mars-born kid, he was lean and rangy like Billy. Once they stepped through the airlocks and into the Tube, they pushed up their masks, and then they looked different; for Billy had bright crazy eyes in a lean wind-red face, and a lot of wild red beard. Bill's eyes were dark, and there was nothing crazy about him.

"Payday, payday, got money on my mind," sang Billy as they walked up the hill toward the freight office. "Bam! I'm gonna start with a big plate of scramble with gravy, and then *two* slices of duff, and then it's hello Ares Amber Lager. What'll you do, kiddo?"

"I'm going to buy socks," said Bill patiently. "Then I guess I'll go to the public terminal. I need my next lesson plan, remember?"

"Yeah, right." Billy nodded, but Bill could tell he wasn't paying attention.

Bill went into the freight office with his dad, and waited in the lobby while Billy went in to present their chits. As he waited, he took out his Buke and thumbed it on, and accessed their bank account. He watched the screen until it flashed and updated, and checked the bank balance against what he thought it should be; the amount was correct.

He sighed and relaxed. For a long while last year, the paycheck had been short every month; money was taken out by the civil court to pay off a fine Billy had incurred for beating up another guy. Billy was easygoing and never started fights, even when he drank, but he had a long reach and no sense of fear, so he tended to win them. The other Haulers never minded a good fight; this one time, though, the other guy had been a farmer from the MAC, and he had sued Billy.

Billy came out of the office now whistling, with the look in his eyes that meant he wanted to go have fun.

"Come on, bookworm, the night's young!" he said. Bill fell into step beside him as they went on up the Tube, and out to Commerce Square.

Commerce Square was the biggest single structure on the planet. Five square miles of breathable air! The steel beams soared in an unsupported arch, holding up Permavizio panes through which the stars and moons shone down. Beneath it rose the domes of houses and shops, and the spiky towers of the Edgar Allan Poe Memorial Center for the Performing Arts. It was built in an Old Earth style called *Gothic*. Bill had learned that just last term.

"Right!" Billy stretched. "I'm off to the Empress. Where you going?"

"To buy socks, remember?" said Bill.

"Okay," said Billy. "See you round, then." He wandered off into the crowd.

Bill sighed. He went off to the general store.

You could get almost anything at Prashant's; this was the only one on Mars and it had been here a whole year now, but Bill still caught his breath when he stepped inside. Row upon row of shiny things in brilliant colors! Cases of fruit juice, electronics, furniture, tools, clothing, tinned delicacies—and all of it imported from Earth. A whole aisle of download stations selling music, movies, books and games. Bill, packet of cotton socks in hand, approached the aisle furtively.

Should he download more music? It wasn't as though Billy would ever notice or care, but the downloads were expensive. All the same . . .

Bill saw that Earth Hand had a new album out, and that decided him. He plugged in his Buke and ordered the album, and twenty minutes later was sneaking out of the store, feeling guilty. He went next to the public terminal and downloaded his lesson plan; that, at least, was free. Then he walked on up the long steep street, under the flashing red and green and blue signs for the posh hotels. His hands were cold, but rather than put his gloves back on he simply jammed his fists in his psuit pockets.

At the top of the street was the Empress of Mars. It was a big place, a vast echoing tavern with a boarding house and restaurant opening off one side and a bathhouse opening off the other. All the Haulers came here. Mother, who ran the place, didn't mind Haulers. They weren't welcome in the fancy new places, which had rules about noise and gambling and fighting, but they were always welcome at the Empress.

Bill stepped through the airlock and looked around. It was dark and noisy in the tavern, with only a muted golden glow over the bar and little colored lights in the booths. It smelled like spilled beer and frying food, and the smell of the food made Bill's mouth water. Haulers sat or stood everywhere, and so did con-

struction workers, and they were all eating and drinking and talking at the top of their lungs.

But where was Billy? Not in his usual place at the bar. Had he
decided to go for a bath first? Bill edged his way through the
crush to the bathhouse door, which was already so clouded with
steam he couldn't see in. He opened the door and peered at the
row of psuits hung up behind the attendant, but Billy's psuit
wasn't one of them.

"Young Bill?" said someone, touching him on the shoulder.
He turned and saw Mother herself, a solid little middle-aged lady
who spoke with a thick PanCeltic accent. She wore a lot of jewelry; she was the richest lady on Mars, and owned most of Mons
Olympus. "What do you need, my dear?"

"Where's my dad?" Bill shouted, to be heard above the din.

"Hasn't come in yet," Mother replied. "What, was he to meet
you here?"

Bill felt the familiar stomach ache he got whenever Billy went
missing. Mother, looking into his eyes, patted his arm.

"Like as not just stopped to talk to somebody, I'm sure. He's
friendly, our Billy, eh? Would start a conversation with any stone
in the road, if he thought he recognized it. Now, you come and sit
in the warm, my dear, and have some supper. Soygold strip with
gravy and sprouts, that's your favorite, yes? And we've barley-
sugar duff for afters. Let's get you some tea . . ."

Bill let her settle him in a corner booth and bring him a mug
of tea. It was delicious, salty-sweet and spicy, and the warmth of
the mug felt good on his hands; but it didn't unclench the knot in
his stomach. He sipped tea and watched the airlock opening and
closing. He tried raising Billy on the psuit comm, but Billy
seemed to have forgotten to turn it on. Where was his dad?

TWO

He was the second boy born on Mars, and he was six years old.

In MAC years, that is.

The Martian year was twenty-four months long, but most of
the people in Mons Olympus and the Areco administrative cen-

ter had simply stuck to reckoning time in twelve-month-long Earth years. That way, every other year, Christmas fell in the Martian summer, and those years were called Australian years. A lot of people on Mars had emigrated from Australia, so it suited them fine.

When the Martian Agricultural Collective had arrived on Mars, though, they'd decided to do things differently. After all (they said), it was a new world; they were breaking with Earth and her traditions forever. So they set up a calendar with twenty-four months. The twelve new months were named Stothart, Engels, Hardie, Bax, Blatchford, Pollitt, Mieville, Attlee, Bentham, Besant, Hobsbawm and Quelch.

When a boy had been born to Mr. and Mrs. Marlon Thurkettle on the fifth day of the new month of Blatchford, they named their son in honor of the month. His friends, such of them as he had, called him Blatt.

He disliked his name because he thought it sounded stupid, but he *really* disliked Blatt, because it led to another nickname that was even worse: Cockroach.

Martian cockroaches were of the order *Blattidae,* and they had adapted very nicely to all the harsh conditions that had made it such a struggle for humans to settle Mars. In fact, they had mutated, and now averaged six inches in length and could survive outside the Tubes. Fortunately they made good fertilizer when ground up, so the Collective had placed a bounty of three Martian Pence on each insect. MAC children hunted them with hammers and earned pocket money that way. They knew all about cockroaches, and so Blatchford wasn't even two before Hardie Stubbs started calling him Cockroach. All the other children thought it was the funniest thing they'd ever heard.

He called himself Ford.

He lived with his parents and his brothers and sisters, crowded all together in an allotment shelter. He downloaded lesson programs and studied whenever he'd finished his chores for the day, but now that he was as tall as his dad and his brother Sam, his dad had begun to mutter that he'd had all the schooling he needed.

There was a lot of work for an able-bodied young man to do,

after all: milking the cows, mucking out their stalls, spreading muck along the rows of sugar beets and soybeans. There was cleaning the canals, repairing the vizio panels that kept out the Martian climate, working in the methane plant. There was work from before the dim sun rose every morning until after the little dim moons rose at night. The work didn't stop for holidays, and it didn't stop if you got sick or got old or had an accident and were hurt.

The work had to be done, because if the MAC worked hard enough, they could turn Mars into another Earth; only one without injustice, corruption or poverty. Every MAC child was supposed to dream of that wonderful day, and do his or her part to make it arrive.

But Ford liked to steal out of the shelter at night, and look up through the vizio at the foot of Mons Olympus, where its city shone out across the long miles of darkness. That was where he wanted to be! It was full of lights. The high-beam lights of the big freighters rocketed along the High Road toward it, roaring out of the dark and cold, and if you watched you could see them coming and going from the city all night. They came back from the far poles of the world, and went out there again.

The Haulers drove them. The Haulers were the men and women who rode the High Road through the storms, through the harsh dry places nobody else dared to go, but they went because they were brave. Ford had heard lots of stories about them. Ford's dad said Haulers were all scum, and half of them were criminals. They got drunk, they fought, they made huge sums in hazard pay and gambled it away or spent it on rich food. They had adventures. Ford thought he'd like to have an adventure someday.

As he grew up, though, he began to realize that this wasn't very likely to happen.

⌣ ⌣ ⌣

"Will you be taking Blatchford?" asked his mum, as she shaved his head.

Ford nearly jumped up in his seat, he was so startled. But the habit of long years kept him still, and he only peered desperately into the mirror to see his dad's face before the reply. *Yes please, yes please, yes please!*

His dad hesitated a moment, distracted from bad temper.

"I suppose so," he said. "Time he saw for himself what it's like up there."

"I'll pack you another lunch, then," said his mum. She wiped the razor and dried Ford's scalp with the towel. "There you go, dear. Your turn, Baxine."

Ford got up as his little sister slid into his place, and turned to face his dad. He was all on fire with questions he wanted to ask, but he knew it wasn't a good idea to make much noise when his dad was in a bad mood. He sidled up to his older brother Sam, who was sitting by the door looking sullen.

"Never been up there," he said. "What's it like, eh?"

Sam smiled a little.

"You'll see. There's this place called the Blue Room, right? Everything's blue in there, with holoes of the Sea of Earth, and lakes too. I remember lakes! And they play sounds from Earth like rain—"

"You shut your face," said his dad. "You ought to be ashamed of yourself, talking like that to a kid."

Sam turned a venomous look on their dad.

"Don't start," said their mum, sounding more tired than angry. "Just go and do what you've got to do."

Ford sat quietly beside Sam until it was time to go, when they all three pulled on their stocking caps and facemasks, slid on their packs, and went skulking up the Tube.

They skulked because visiting Mons Olympus was frowned upon. There was no need to go up there, or so the Council said; everything a good member of the Collective might need could be found in the MAC store, and if it couldn't, then you probably didn't need it, and certainly shouldn't want it.

The problem was that the MAC store didn't carry boots in Sam's size. Ford's dad had tried to order them, but there was endless paperwork to fill out, and the store clerk had looked at Sam as though it was his fault for having such big feet, as though a *good* member of the Collective would have sawed off a few toes to make himself fit the boots the MAC store stocked.

But Prashant's up in Mons Olympus carried all sizes, so every time Sam wore out a pair of boots, that was where Ford's dad had to go.

As though to make up for the shame of it, he lectured Ford the whole way up the mountain, while Sam stalked along beside them in resentful silence.

"This'll be an education for you, Blatchford, yes indeed. You'll get to see thieves and drunks and fat cats living off the sweat of others. Everything we left Earth to get away from! Shops full of vanities to make you weak. Eating places full of poisons. It's a right cesspool, that's what it is."

"What'll happen to it when we turn Mars into a paradise?" asked Ford.

"Oh, it'll be gone by then," said his dad. "It'll collapse under its own rotting weight, you mark my words."

"I reckon I'll have to go home to Earth to buy boots then, won't I?" muttered Sam.

"Shut up, you ungrateful lout," said his dad.

They came out under the old Settlement dome, where the Areco offices and the MAC store were, as well as the spaceport and the Ephesian Church. This was the farthest Ford had ever been from home, and up until today the most exotic place he had ever seen. There was a faint sweet incense wafting out from the Church, and the sound of chanting. Ford's dad hurried them past the Ephesian Tea Room with a disdainful sniff, ignoring the signs that invited wayfarers in for a hot meal and edifying brochures about the Goddess.

"Ignorance and superstition, that is," he told Ford. "Another thing we left behind when we came here, but you can see it's still putting out its tentacles, trying to control the minds of the people."

He almost ran them past the MAC store, and they were panting for breath as they ducked up the Tube that led to Mons Olympus.

Ford stared around. The Tube here was much wider, and much better maintained, than where it ran by his parents' allotment. The vizio used was a more expensive kind, for one thing: it was almost as transparent as water. Ford could now see clearly across the mountainside, the wide cinnamon-colored waste of rocks and sand. He gazed up at Mons Olympus, struck with awe at its sheer looming size. He turned and looked back on the lowlands, and for the first time saw the green expanse of the Long Acres that had been his whole world until now, stretching out in domed lines to the horizon. He walked backwards a while, gaping, until he stumbled and his dad caught him.

"It's hard to look away from, isn't it?" said his dad. "Don't worry. We'll be going home soon enough."

"Soon enough," Sam echoed in a melancholy sort of way.

Once past the airlock from the spaceport the Tube became crowded, with suited strangers pushing past them, dragging baggage, or walking slow and staring as hard as Ford was staring: he realized they must be immigrants from Earth, getting their first glimpse of a new world.

But Ford got his new world when he stepped through the last airlock and looked into Commerce Square.

"Oh . . ." he said.

Even by daylight, it glittered and shone. Along the main street was a double line of actual *trees,* like on earth; there was a green and park-like place immediately to the left, where real flowers grew. Ford thought he recognized roses, from the images in his lessons. Their scent hung in the air like music. There were other good smells, from spicy foods cooking in a dozen little stalls and wagons along the Square, and big stores breathing out a perfume of expensive wares.

And there were *people!* More people, and more kinds of people, than Ford had even known existed. There were Sherpa contract laborers and Incan construction workers, speaking to one another in languages Ford couldn't understand. There were hawkers selling souvenirs and cheap nanoprocessors from handcarts. There were Ephesian missionaries talking earnestly to thin people in ragged clothes.

There were Haulers—Ford knew them at once, big men and women in their psuits, and their heads were covered in long hair and the men had beards. Some had tattooed faces. All had bloodshot eyes. They talked loudly and laughed a lot, and they looked as though they didn't care what anyone thought of them at all. Ford's dad scowled at them.

"Bloody lunatics," he told Ford. "Most of 'em were in Hospital on Earth, did you know that, Blatchford? Certifiable. The only ones Areco could find who were reckless enough for that kind of work. Exploitation, I call it."

Sam muttered something. Their dad turned on him.

"What did you say, Samuel?" he demanded.

"I said we're at the shop, all right?" said Sam, pointing at the neon sign.

Ford gasped as they went in, as the warmed air and flowery scent wrapped around him. It was nothing like the MAC store, which had rows of empty shelves, and what merchandise was there, was dusty; everything here looked clean and new. He didn't even know what most of it was for. Sleek, pretty people smiled from behind the counters.

He smiled back at them, until he passed a counter and came face to face with three men skulking along—skinny scarecrows with shaven heads, with canal mud on their boots. He blushed scarlet to realize he was looking into a mirror. Was *he* that gawky person between his dad and Sam? Did his ears really stick out like that? Ford pulled his cap down, so mortified he wanted to run all the way back down the mountain.

But he kept his eyes on the back of his dad's coat instead, following until they came to the Footwear Department. There he was diverted by the hundreds and hundreds of shoes on the walls, apparently floating in space, turning so he could see them better. They were every color there was, and they were clearly never designed to be worn while shoveling muck out of the cowsheds.

He came close and peered at them, as his dad and Sam argued with one of the beautiful people, until he saw the big-eyed boy staring back at him from beyond the dancing shoes. Another mirror; did he really have his mouth hanging open like that? And, oh, look at his nose, pinched red by the cold, and look at those watery blue eyes all rimmed in red, and those gangling big hands with the red chapped knuckles!

Ford turned around, wishing he could escape from himself. There were his dad and Sam, and they looked just like him, except his dad was old. Was he, Ford, going to look just like that, when he was somebody's dad? How mean and small his dad looked, trying to sound posh as he talked to the clerk:

"Look, we don't want this fancy trim and we don't want your shiny brass, thank you *very* much, we just want plain decent waders the lad can do a day's honest work in! Now, you can understand that much, can't you?"

"I like the brass buckles, Dad," said Sam.

"Well, you don't need 'em—they're only a vanity," said their dad. Sam shut his mouth like a box.

Ford stood by, cringing inside, as more boots were brought, until at last a pair was found that was plain and cheap enough to suit their dad. More embarrassment followed then, as their dad pulled out a wad of MAC scrip and tried to pay with it, before remembering that scrip could only be used at the MAC store. Worse still, he then pulled out a wrinkly handful of Martian paper money. Both Ford and Sam saw the sales clerks exchange looks; what kind of people didn't have credit accounts? Sam tried to save face by being sarcastic.

"We're all in the Stone Age down the hill, you know," he said loudly, accepting the wrapped boots and tucking them under his arm. "I reckon we'll get around to having banks one of these centuries."

"Banks are corrupt institutions," said their dad like a shot, rounding on him. "How'd you get so tall without learning anything, eh? What have I told—"

"Sam?" A girl's voice stopped him. Ford turned in astonishment and saw one of the beautiful clerks hurrying toward them, smiling as though she meant it. "Sam, where were you last week? We missed you at the party—I wanted to show you my new . . ." She faltered to a stop, looking from Sam to their dad and Ford. Ford felt his heart jump when she looked at him. She had silver-gold hair, and wore makeup, and smelled sweet.

"I . . . er . . . Is this your family? How nice to meet you—" she began lamely, but their dad cut her off.

"Who's *this* painted cobweb, then?" he demanded of Sam. Sam's face turned red.

"Don't you talk that way about her! Her name is Galadriel,

and–it so happens we're dating, not that it's any of your business."

"You what?" Outraged, their dad clenched his knobby fists. "So you've been sneaking up here at night to live the high life, have you? No wonder you're no bloody use in the mornings! MAC girls not good enough for you? Fat lot of use a little mannequin like that's going to be when you settle down! Can she drive a tractor, eh?"

Sam threw down the boots. "Got a wire for you, Dad," he shouted. "I'm not settling down on Mars! I *hate* Mars, I've hated it since the day you dragged me up here, and the *minute* I come of age I'm off back to Earth! Get it?"

Sam leaving? Ford felt a double shock, of sadness and betrayal. Who'd tell him stories if Sam left?

"You self-centered great twerp!" their dad shouted back. "Of all the ungrateful–when the MAC's fed you and clothed you all these years–Just going to walk out on your duty, are you?"

Galadriel was backing away into the crowd, looking as though she wished she were invisible, and Ford wished he could be invisible too. People all over the store had stopped what they were doing to turn and stare.

"I never asked to join the MAC, you know," said Sam. "Nobody's ever given a thought to what *I* wanted at all!"

"That's because there are a few more important things in the world than what one snotty-nosed brat wants for himself!"

"Well, I'm telling you now, Dad–if you think I'm going to live my life doing the same boring thing every day until I get old like you, you're sadly mistaken!"

"Am I then?" Their dad jumped up and grabbed Sam by the ear, wringing tight. "I'll sort you out–"

Sam, grimacing in pain, socked their dad. Ford bit his knuckles, terrified. Their dad staggered back, his eyes wide and furious.

"Right, that's it! You're no son of mine, do you hear me? You're disowned! The Collective doesn't need a lazy, backsliding traitor like you!"

"Don't you call me a traitor!" said Sam. He put his head down and ran at their dad, and their dad jumped up and butted heads with him. Sam's nose gushed blood. They fell to the ground, punching each other. Sam was sobbing in anger.

Ford backed away from them. He was frightened and miserable, but there was a third emotion beginning to float up into his consciousness: a certain sense of wonder. Could Sam really stop being his father's son? Was it really possible just to become somebody else, to drop all the obligations and duties of your old life and step into a new life? Who would he, Ford, be, if he had the chance to be somebody else?

Did he *have* to be that red-nosed farm boy with muddy boots?

People were gathering around, watching the fight with amusement and disgust. Someone shouted, "You can't take the MAC anyplace nice, can you?" Ford's ears burned with humiliation.

Then someone else shouted, "Here come Mother's Boys!"

Startled, Ford looked up and saw several big men in Security uniforms making their way through the crowd. Security!

The police are a bunch of brutes, his dad had told him. *They like nothing better than to beat the daylights out of the likes of you and me, son!*

Ford's nerve broke. He turned and fled, weaving and dodging his way through the crowd until he got outside the shop, and then he ran for his life.

He had no idea where he was going, but he soon found himself in a street that wasn't nearly as elegant as the promenade. It was an industrial district, dirty and shabby, with factory workers and energy plant techs hurrying to and fro. If the promenade with its gardens was the fancy case of Mons Olympus, this was its circuit board, where the real works were. Feeling less out of place, Ford slowed to a walk and caught his breath. He wandered on, staring around him.

He watched for a long moment through the open door of a machine shop, where a pair of mechanics were repairing a quaddy. Their welding tools shot out fiery-bright stars that bounced harmlessly to the ground. There were two other men watching too, though as the minutes dragged by they began watching Ford instead. Finally they stepped close to him, smiling.

"Hey, Collective. You play cards?" said one of them.

"No," said Ford.

"That's okay," said the other. "This is an easy game." He opened his coat and Ford saw that he had a kind of box strapped to his chest. It had the word NEBULIZER painted on it, but when the man pressed a button, the front of the box swung down and open like a tray. The other man pulled a handful of cards from his back pocket.

"Here we go," he said. "Just three cards. Ace, deuce, Queen of Diamonds. See 'em? I'm going to shuffle them and lay them out, one, two, three." He laid them out face down on the tray. "See? Now, which one's the queen? Can you find her?"

Ford couldn't believe what a dumb game this was. Only three cards? He turned over the queen.

"Boy, it's hard to fool *you*," said the man with the tray. "You've got natural luck, kid. Want to go again?" The other man had already swept the three cards up and was shuffling them.

"Okay," said Ford.

"Got any money? Want to place a bet?"

"I don't have any money," said Ford.

"No money? That's too bad," said the man with the tray, closing it up at once. "A lucky guy like you, you could win big. But they don't get rich down there in the Collective, do they? Same dull work every day of your life, and nothing to show for it when it's all over. That's what I hear."

Ford nodded sadly. It wasn't just Sam, he realized; everybody laughed at the MAC.

"What would you say to a chance at something better, eh?" said the man with the cards. In one smooth movement he made the cards vanish and produced instead a text plaquette. Its case was grubby and cracked, but the screen was bright with a lot of very small words.

"Know what I have here? This is a deal that'll set you up as a diamond prospector. Think of that! You could make more with one lucky strike than you'd make working the Long Acres the whole rest of your life. Now, I know what you're going to say—you don't have any tools and you don't have any training. But, you know what you have got? You're *young*. You're in good shape, and you can take the weather Outside.

"So here's the deal: Mr. Agar has the tools and the training, but he ain't young. You agree to go to work for him, and he'll provide what you need. You pay him off out of your first big diamond strike, and then you're in business for yourself. Easiest way to get rich there is! And all you have to do is put your thumbprint right there. What do you say?" He held out the plaquette to Ford.

Ford blinked at it. He had heard stories of the people who dug red diamonds out of the clay—why, Mons Olympus had been founded by a lady who'd got rich like that! He was reaching for the plaquette when a voice spoke close to his ear.

"Can you read, kid?"

Ford turned around. A Hauler was looking over his shoulder, smiling.

"Well—I read a little—"

"Get lost!" said the man with the plaquette, looking angry.

"I can't read," the Hauler went on, "but I know these guys. They're with Agar Steelworks. You know what they're trying to get you to thumb? That's a contract that'll legally bind you to work in Agar's iron mines for fifteen years."

"Like you'd know, jackass!" said the man with the plaquette, slipping it out of sight. He brought out a short length of iron bar and waved it at the Hauler meaningfully. The Hauler's red eyes sparkled.

"You want to fight?" he said, smacking his fists together. "Yeah! You think I'm afraid of you? You lousy little street-corner hustler! C'mere!"

The man took a swipe at him with the bar, and the Hauler dodged it and grabbed it out of his hand. The other two broke and ran, vanishing down an alley. The Hauler grinned after them, tossing the bar into the street.

"Freakin' kidnappers," he said to Ford. "You're, what, twelve? I have a kid your age."

"Thank you," Ford stammered.

"That's okay. You want to watch out for Human Resourcers, though, kid. They work that con on a lot of MAC boys like you. Diamond prospectors! Nobody but Mother ever got rich that way." The Hauler yawned and stretched. "You head off to the nearest Security post and report 'em now, okay?"

"I can't," said Ford, and to his horror he felt himself starting to shake. "I–they–there was this fight, and–Security guys came and–I have to hide."

"You in trouble?" The Hauler leaned down and looked at Ford closely. "Fighting? Mother's Boys don't allow no fighting, that's for sure. You need a place to hide? Maybe get out of town until it all blows over?" He gave Ford a conspiratorial wink.

"Yes, please," said Ford.

"You come along with me, then. I got a safe place," said the Hauler. Without looking back to see if Ford was following him, he turned and loped off up the street. Ford ran after him.

"Please, who are you?"

The Hauler glanced over his shoulder. "Billy Townsend," he said. "But don't tell me who *you* are. Safer that way, right?"

"Right," said Ford, falling into step beside him. He looked up at his rescuer. Billy was tall and gangly, and lurched a little when he walked, but he looked as though he wasn't the least bit worried what people thought of him. His face and dreadlocked hair and beard were all red, the funny bricky red that came from years of going Outside and having the red dust get everywhere, until it became so deeply engrained water wouldn't wash it off. There were scars all over his face and hands, too. On the back of his psuit someone had painted white words in a circle.

"What's it say on your back?" Ford asked him.

"Says BIPOLAR BOYS AND GIRLS," said Billy. "On account of we go Up and Down there, see? And because we're nutcases, half of us."

"What's it like in the ice mines?"

"Cold," said Billy, chuckling. "Get your face mask on, now. Here we go! Here's our Beautiful Evelyn."

They stepped out through the airlock, and the cold bit into Ford. He gulped for air and followed Billy into a vast echoing building like a hangar. It was the car barn for the ice processing plant. Just now it was deserted, but over by the loading chute sat a freighter. Ford caught his breath.

He had never seen one up close before, and it was bigger than he had imagined. Seventy-five meters long, set high on big knobbed ball tires. Its steel tank had been scoured to a dull gleam by the wind and sand. At one end was a complication of hatches and lenses and machinery that Ford supposed must be the driver's cab. Billy reached up one long arm and grabbed a lever. The foremost hatch hissed, swung open and a row of steps clanked down into place.

"There you go," said Billy. "Climb on up! Nobody'll think to look for you in there. I'll be back later. Make yourself at home."

Ford scrambled up eagerly. He looked around as the hatch squeezed shut behind him, and air rushed back in. He pulled down his mask.

He was in a tiny room with a pair of bunks built into one side. The only light came from a dim panel set in the ceiling. There was nothing else in the room, except for a locker under the lower bunk and three doors in the wall opposite. It was disappointingly plain and spotless.

Ford opened the first door and beheld the tiniest lavatory he had ever seen, so compact he couldn't imagine how to use it. He tried the second door and found a kitchen built along similar lines, more a series of shelves than a room. The third door opened into a much larger space. He crawled through and found himself in the driver's cab.

Timidly, he edged his way farther in and sat down at the console. He looked up at the instrument panels, at the big screens that ran all around the inside of the cab. They were blank and blind now, but what would it be like to sit here when the freighter was roaring along the High Road?

On the panel above the console was a little figurine, glued in place. It was a cheap-looking thing, of cast red stone like the souvenirs he had seen for sale on the handcarts in Commerce Square. It represented a lady, leaning forward as though she were running, or perhaps flying. The sculptor had given her hair that streamed back in an imaginary wind. She was grinning crazily, as the Haulers all did. She had only one eye, of red cut glass; Ford guessed the matching one had fallen off. He looked on the floor of the cab, but didn't see it. Ford grinned too and, because no one was there to see him, he put his hands on the wheel. "Brrrrroooom," he whispered, and looked up at the screens as though to check on his location. He felt a little stupid.

But in every one of the screens, his reflection was smiling back at him. Ford couldn't remember when he'd been so happy.

THREE

Bill's dinner had gone cold, though he stuffed a forkful in his mouth every now and then when he noticed Mother watching him. He couldn't keep his eyes away from the door much. *Where was Billy?*

He might have gotten in a fight, and Mother's Boys might have hauled him off to the Security Station; if that were the case, sooner or later Mother would come over to Bill with an apologetic cough and say something like, "Your dad's just had a bit of an argument, dear, and I think you'd best doss down here tonight until he, er, wakes up. We'll let him out tomorrow." And Bill would feel his face burning with shame, as he always did when that happened.

Or Billy might have met someone he knew, and forgotten about the time . . . or he might have gone for a drink somewhere else . . . or . . .

Bill was so busy imagining all the places Billy might be that he got quite a shock when Billy walked through the airlock. Before Billy had spotted him and started making his way across the room, the cramping worry had turned to anger.

"Where were you?" Bill shouted. "You were supposed to be here!"

"I had stuff to do," said Billy vaguely, sliding into the booth. He waved at Mother, who acknowledged him with a nod and sent one of her daughters over to take his order. Bill looked him over suspiciously. No cuts or bruises on his face, nothing broken on his psuit. Not fighting, then. Maybe he had met a girl. Bill relaxed just a little, but his anger kept smoldering.

When Billy's beer had been brought, Bill said:

"I wondered where you were. How come you had the comm turned off?"

"Is it off?" Billy groped for the switch in his shoulder. "Oh.

Wow. Sorry, kiddo. Must have happened when I took my mask off."

He had a sip of beer. Bill gritted his teeth. He could tell that, as far as Billy was concerned, the incident was over. It had just been a mistake, right? What was the point of getting mad about it? Never mind that Bill had been scared and alone . . .

Bill exhaled forcefully and shoveled down his congealing dinner.

"I got my socks," he said loudly.

"That's nice," said Billy. Lifting his glass for another sip, his attention was taken by the holo playing above the bar. He stared across at it. Bill turned around in his seat to look. There was the image of one of Mother's Boys, a sergeant from his uniform, staring into the foremost camera as he made some kind of announcement. His lips moved in silence, though, with whatever he was saying drowned out by the laughter and the shouting in the bar.

Bill looked quickly back at Billy. Why was he watching the police report? Had he been in some kind of incident after all? Billy snorted with laughter, watching, and then pressed his lips shut to hide a smile. Why was he doing that?

Bill looked back at the holo, more certain than ever that Billy was in trouble, but now saw holofootage of two guys fighting. Was either one of them Billy? No; Bill felt his anger damp down again as he realized it was only a couple of MAC colonists, kicking and punching each other as they rolled in the street. Bill was appalled; he hadn't thought the Collective ever did stupid stuff like that.

Then there was a closeup shot of a skinny boy, with a shaven head—MAC, Bill supposed. He shrugged and turned his attention back to his plate.

Billy's food was brought and he dug into it with gusto.

"Think we'll head out again tonight," he said casually.

"But we just got back in!" Bill said, startled.

"Yeah. Well . . ." Billy sliced off a bit of Grilled Strip, put it in his mouth and chewed carefully before going on. "There's . . . mm . . . this big bonus right now for CO_2, see? MAC's getting a crop of something or other in the ground and they've placed like this humungous order for it. So we can earn like double what we just deposited if I get a second trip in before the end of the month."

Bill didn't know what to say. It was the sort of thing he nagged at his dad to do, saving more money; usually Billy spent it as fast as he had it. Bill looked at him with narrowed eyes, wondering if he had gotten into trouble after all. But he just shrugged again and said, "Okay."

"Hey, Mona?" Billy waved at the nearest of Mother's daughters. "Takeaway order too, okay, sweetheart? Soygold nuggets and sprouts. And a bottle of batch."

"Why are we getting takeaway?" Bill asked him.

"Er . . ." Billy looked innocent. "I'm just way hungry, is all. Think I'll want a snack later. I'll be driving all night."

"But you drove for twelve hours today!" Bill protested. "Aren't you ever going to sleep?"

"Sleep is for wusses," said Billy. "I'll just pop a Freddie."

Bill scowled. Freddies were little red pills that kept you awake and jittery for days. Haulers took them sometimes when they needed to be on the road for long runs without stopping. It was stupid to take them all the time, because they could kill you, and Bill threw them away whenever he found any in the cab. Billy must have stopped to buy some more. So *that* was where he'd been.

Night had fallen by the time they left the Empress and headed back down the hill. Cold penetrated down through the Permavizio; Bill shivered, and his psuit's thermostat turned itself up. There were still people in the streets, though fewer of them, and some of the lights had been turned out. Usually by this time, when they were in off the road, Bill would be soaking in a stone tub full of hot water, and looking forward to a good night's sleep someplace warm for a change. The thought made him grumpy as they came round the corner into the airlock.

"Masks on, Dad," Bill said automatically. Billy nodded, shifting the stoneware bucket of takeaway to his other hand as he reached for his mask. They went out to Beautiful Evelyn.

Bill was climbing up to open the cab when Billy grabbed him and pulled him back.

"Hang on," he said, and reached up and knocked on the hatch. "Yo, kid! Mask up, we're coming in!"

"What?" Bill staggered back, staring at Billy. "Who's in there?"

Billy didn't answer, but Bill heard a high-pitched voice calling *Okay* from inside the cab, and Billy swung the hatch open and climbed up. Bill scrambled after him. The hatch sealed behind them and the air whooshed back. Bill pulled off his mask as the lights came on to reveal a boy, pulling off his own mask. They stared at each other, blinking.

Billy held out the bucket of takeaway. "Here you go, kid. Hot dinner!"

"Oh! Thank you," said the other, as Bill recognized him for the MAC boy from the holofootage he'd watched.

"What's *he* doing here?" he demanded.

"Just, you know, sort of laying low," said Billy. "Got in a little trouble and needs to go off someplace until things cool down. Thought we could take him out on the run with us, right? No worries." He stepped sidelong into the cab and threw himself into the console seat, where he proceeded to start up Beautiful Evelyn's drives.

"But–but–!" said Bill.

"Er . . . Hi," said the other boy, avoiding his eyes. He was taller than Bill but looked younger, with big wide eyes and ears that stuck out. His shaven head made him look even more like a baby.

"Who're you?" said Bill.

"I'm, ah–" said the other boy, just as Billy roared from the cab:

"No names! No names! The less we know, the less they can beat out of us!" And he whooped with laughter. The noise of the drives powering up drowned out anything else he might have said. Bill clenched his fists and stepped close to Ford, glaring up into his eyes.

"What's going on? What'd my dad do?"

"Nothing!" Ford took a step backward.

"Well then, what'd *you* do? You must have done something,

because you were on the holo. I saw you! You were fighting, huh?"

Ford gulped. His eyes got even wider and he said, "Er–yeah. Yeah, I punched out these guys. Who were trying to trick me into working into the mines for them. And, uh, I ran because, because the Security Fascists were going to beat the daylights out of me. So Billy let me hide in here. What's your name?"

"Bill," he replied. "You're with the MAC, aren't you? What were you fighting for?"

"Well–the other guys started it," said Ford. He looked with interest at the takeaway. "This smells good. It was really nice of your dad to bring it for me. Is there anywhere I can sit down to eat?"

"In there," said Bill in disgust, pointing into the cab.

"Thank you. You want some?" Ford held out the bucket timidly.

"No," said Bill. "I want to go to sleep. Go on, clear out of here!"

"Okay," said Ford, edging into the cab. "It's nice meeting you, Billy."

"Bill!" said Bill, and slammed the door in his face.

Muttering to himself, he dimmed down the lights and lay down in his trunk. He threw the switch that inflated the mattress, and its contours puffed out around him, cradling him snugly as the freighter began to move. He didn't know why he was so angry, but somehow finding Ford here had been the last straw.

He closed his eyes and tried to send himself to sleep in the way he always had, by imagining he was going down the tube to the long Acres, step by step, into green, warm, quiet places. Tonight, though, he kept seeing the two MAC colonists from the holo, whaling away at each other like a couple of clowns while the city people looked on and laughed.

⊖ ⊖ ⊖

Ford, clutching his dinner, sat down in the cab and looked around. With all the screens lit up there was plenty of light by which to eat.

"Is it okay if I sit in here?" he asked Billy, who waved expansively.

"Sure, kid. Don't mind li'l Bill. He's cranky sometimes."

Ford opened the bucket and looked inside. "Do you have any forks?"

"Yeah. Somewhere. Try the seat pocket."

Ford groped into the pocket and found a ceramic fork that was, perhaps, clean. He was too hungry to care whether it was or not, and ate quickly. He wasn't sure what he was eating, but it tasted wonderful.

As he ate, he looked up at the screens. Some had just figures on them, data from the drives and external sensors. Four of them had images from the freighter's cameras, mounted front and rear, right and left. There was no windscreen—even Ford knew that an Earth-style glass windscreen would be scoured opaque by even one trip through the storms of sand and grit along the High Road, unless a forcefield was projected in front of it, and big forcefields were expensive, and unlikely to deflect blowing rocks anyhow. Easier and cheaper to fix four little forcefields over the camera lenses.

The foremost screen fascinated him. He saw the High Road itself, rolling out endlessly to the unseen night horizon under the stars. It ran between two lines of big rocks, levered into place over the years by Haulers to make it easier to find the straightest shot to the pole.

Every now and then Ford caught a glimpse of carving on some of the boulders as they flashed by—words, or figures. Some of them had what looked like tape wrapped around them, streaming out in the night wind.

"Are those . . ." Ford sought to remember his lessons about Earth roads. "Are those road signs? With, er, kilometer numbers and all?"

"What, on the boulders? Nope. They're shrines," said Billy.

"What's a shrine?"

"Place where somebody died," said Billy. "Or where somebody should have died, but didn't, because Marswife saved their butts." He reached out and tapped the little red lady on the console.

Ford thought about that. He looked at the figurine. "So . . . she's like, that Goddess the Ephesians are always on about?"

"No!" Billy grinned. "Not our Marswife. She was just this sheila, see. Somebody from Earth who came up here like the rest of us, and she was crazy. Same as us. She thought Mars, was, like, her husband or something. And there was this big storm and she went out into it, without a mask. And they say she didn't die! Mars got her and changed her into something else so she could live Outside. That's what they say, anyway."

"Like, she mutated?" Ford stared at the little figure.

"I guess so."

"But really she died, huh?"

"Well, you'd think so," Billy said, looking at him sidelong. "Except that there are guys who swear they've seen her. She lives on the wind. She's red like the sand and her eye is a ruby, and if you're lost sometimes you'll see a red light way off, which is her eye, see? And if you follow it, you'll get home again safe. And I *know* that's true, because it happened to me."

"Really?"

Billy held up one hand, palm out. "No lie. It was right out by Two-Fifty-K. There was a storm swept through so big, it was able to pick up the road markers and toss 'em around, see? And Beautiful Evelyn got thrown like she was a feather by the gusts, and my nav system went out. It was just me and li'l Bill, and he was only a baby then, and I found myself so far off the road I had no clue, *no clue* where I was, and I was sure we were going to die out there. But I saw that red light and I figured, that's somebody who knows where they are, anyway. I set off after it. Hour later the light blinks out and there's Two-Fifty-K Station right in front of me on the screen, but there's no red lights anyplace."

"Whoa," said Ford, wondering what Two-Fifty-K station was.

"There's other stories about her, too. Guys who see her riding the storm, and when she's there they know to make for a bunker, because there's a Strawberry coming."

"What's a Strawberry?"

"It's this kind of cyclone. Big *big* storm full of sand and rocks. Big red cone dancing across the ground. One took out that temple the Ephesians built, when they first got up here, and tore open half the tubes. They don't come up Tharsis way much, but when they do—" Billy shook his head. "People die, man. Some of your people died, that time. You never heard that story?"

"No," said Ford, "But we're not supposed to talk about bad stuff after it happens."

"Really?" Billy looked askance.

"Because we can't afford to be afraid of the past," said Ford, half-quoting what he remembered from every Council Meeting he'd ever been dragged to. "Because fear will make us weak, but working fearlessly for the future will make us strong." He chanted the last line, unconsciously imitating his dad's intonation.

"Huh," said Billy. "I guess that's a good idea. You can't go through life being scared of everything. That's what I tell Bill."

Ford looked into the takeaway bucket, surprised he had eaten his way to the bottom so quickly.

"It's good to hear stories, though," he said. "Sam, that's my brother, he gets into trouble for telling stories."

"Heh! Little white lies?"

"No," Ford said, "Real stories. Like about Earth. He remembers Earth. He says everything was wonderful there. He wants to go back."

"Back?" Billy looked across at him, startled. "But kids can't go back. I guess if he was old enough when he came up, maybe he might make it. I hear it's tough, though, going back down. The gravity's intense."

"Would you go back?"

Billy shook his head. "All I remember of Earth is the insides of rooms. Who needs that? Nobody up here to tell me what to do, man. I can just point myself at the horizon and go, and go, as far and as fast as I want. Zoom! I can think what I want, I can feel what I want, and you know what? The sand and the rocks don't care. The horizon don't care. The wind don't care.

"That's why they call this *space*. No, no way I'd ever go back."

Ford looked up at the screens, and remembered the nights he had watched for the long light-beams coming in from the darkness. It had given him an aching feeling for as long as he could remember, and now he understood why.

He had wanted space.

FOUR

They drove all night, and at some point Billy's stories of storms and fights and near-escapes from death turned into confusion, with Sam there somehow, and a room that ran blue with water. Then abruptly Ford was sitting up, staring around at the inside of the cab.

"Where are we?" he asked. The foremost screen showed a spooky gray distance, the High Road rolling ahead between its boulders to . . . what? A pale void full of roaming shadows.

"Almost to Five-Hundred-K Station," said Billy, from where he hunched over the wheel. "Step pretty soon."

"Can Security follow us out here?"

Billy just laughed and shook his head. "No worries, kiddo. There's no law out here but Mars's."

The door into the living space opened abruptly, and Bill looked in at them.

"Morning, li'l Bill!"

"Good morning," said Bill in a surly voice. "You never stopped once all night. Are you ever going to pull us off somewhere so you can sleep?"

"At Five-Hundred-K," Billy promised. "How about you fix a bite of scran, eh?"

Bill did not reply. He stepped back out of sight and a moment later Ford felt the warmth in the air that meant that water was steaming. He could almost taste it, and realized that he was desperately thirsty. He crawled from his seat and followed the vapor back to where Bill had opened the kitchen and was shoving a block of something under heating coils.

"Are you fixing tea?"

"Yeah," said Bill, with a jerk of his thumb at the tall can that steamed above a heat element.

"Can I have a cup, when it's ready?"

Bill frowned, but he got three mugs from a drawer.

"Do you fight much, in the Collective?" he asked. Ford blinked in surprise.

"No," he said. "It wasn't me fighting, actually. It was just my dad and my brother. They hate each other. But my mum won't let them fight in the house. Sam said he was deserting us and my dad went off on him about it. I ran when the Security came."

"Oh," said Bill. He seemed to become a little less hostile, but he said: "Well, that was pretty bloody stupid. They'd only have taken you to Mother's until your dad sobered up. You'd be safe home by now."

Ford shrugged.

"So, what's your name, really?"

"Ford."

"Like that guy in *The Hitchhiker's Guide to the Galaxy*?" Bill smiled for the first time.

"What's that?"

"It's a book I listen to all the time. Drowns out Billy singing." Bill's smile went away again. The tea can beeped to signal it was hot enough, and Bill turned and pulled it out. He poured dark bubbling stuff into the three mugs, and, reaching in a cold-drawer, took out a slab of something yellow on a dish. He spooned out three lumps of it, one into each mug, and presented one to Ford.

"Whoa." Ford stared into his mug. "That's not sugar."

"It's butter," said Bill, as though that were obvious. He had a gulp of tea and, not wanting to seem picky, Ford took a gulp too. It wasn't as nasty as he had expected. In fact, it wasn't nasty at all. Bill, watching his face, said:

"You've never had this before?"

Ford shook his head.

"But you guys are the ones who make the butter up here," said Bill. "This is MAC butter. What do you drink, if you don't drink this?"

"Just . . . batch, and tea with sugar sometimes," said Ford, wondering why this should matter. He had another gulp of the tea. It tasted even better this time.

"And the sugar comes from the sugar beets you grow?" Bill persisted.

"I guess so," said Ford. "I never thought about it."

"What's it like, living down there?"

"What's it like?" Ford stared at him. Why in the world would anybody be curious about the Long Acres? "I don't know. I muck out cow sheds. It's boring, mostly."

"How could it be *boring*?" Bill demanded. "It's so beautiful down there! Are you crazy?"

"No," said Ford, taking a step backward. "But if you think a big shovelful of cowshite and mega-roaches is beautiful, *you're* crazy."

Billy shouted something from the front of the cab and a second later Beautiful Evelyn swerved around. Both boys staggered a little at the shift in momentum, glaring at each other, and righted themselves as forward motion ceased.

"We're at Five-Hundred-K Station," Bill guessed. There was another beep. He turned automatically to pull the oven drawer open as Billy came staggering back into the living area.

"Mons Olympus to Five-Hundred-K in one night," he chortled. "That is some righteous driving! Where's the tea?"

They crowded together in the cramped space, sipping tea and eating something brown and bubbly that Ford couldn't identify. Afterward Billy climbed into his bunk with a groan, and yanked the cord that inflated his mattress.

"I am so ready for some horizontal. You guys go up front and talk about stuff, okay?"

"Whatever," said Bill, picking up his Gamebuke and stalking out. Billy, utterly failing to notice the withering scorn to which he had just been subjected, smiled and waved sleepily at Ford. Ford smiled back, but his smile faded as he turned, shut the door behind him and followed Bill, whom he had decided was a nasty little know-it-all.

Bill was sitting in one corner, staring into the screen of his Gamebuke. He had put on a pair of earshells and was listening to something fairly loud. He ignored Ford, who sat and looked up at the screens in puzzlement.

"Is this the station?" he asked, forgetting that Bill couldn't hear him. He had expected a domed settlement, but all he could see was a wide place by the side of the road, circled by boulders that appeared to have been whitewashed.

Bill didn't answer him. Ford looked at him in annoyance. He studied the controls on the inside of the hatch. When he thought he knew which one opened it, he slipped his mask on. Then he leaned over and punched Bill in the shoulder.

"Mask up," he yelled. "I'm going out."

Bill had his mask on before Ford had finished speaking, and Ford saw his eyes going wide with alarm as he activated the hatch. It sprang open; Ford turned and slid into a blast of freezing air.

He hit the ground harder than he expected to, and almost fell. Gasping, hugging himself against a cold so intense it burned, he stared in astonishment at the dawn.

There was no ceiling. There were no walls. There was nothing around the freighter, as far as the limits of his vision, but limitless space, limitless sky of the palest, chilliest blue he had ever seen, stretching down to a limitless red plain of sand and rock. He turned, and kept turning: no domes, no Tubes, nothing but the wide open world in every direction.

And here was a red light appearing on the horizon, red as blood or rubies, so bright a red it dazzled his eyes, and he wondered for a moment if it was the eye of Marswife. Long purple shadows sprang from the boulders and stretched back toward his boots. He realized he was looking at the rising sun.

So this is where the lights were going to, he said to himself, *all those nights they were going away into the dark. They were coming out here. This is the most wonderful thing I have ever seen.*

Somehow he had fallen into the place he had always wanted to be.

But the cold was eating into his bones, and he realized that if he kept on standing there he'd freeze solid in his happy dream. He set off toward the nearest boulder, fumbling with the fastening of his pants.

Someone grabbed his shoulder and spun him around.

"You *idiot!*" Bill shouted at him. "Don't you know what happens if you try to pee out here?"

From the horror on Bill's face, even behind the mask, Ford realized that he'd better get back in the cab as fast as he could.

When they were safely inside and the seals had locked, when Bill had finished yelling at him, Ford still sat shivering with more than cold.

"You mean it boils and *then* it explodes?" he said.

"You are such an idiot!" Bill repeated in disbelief.

"How was I supposed to know?" Ford said. "I've never been Outside before! We use the reclamation conduits at home—"

"This isn't the Long Acres, dumbbell. This is the middle of frozen Nowhere and it'll kill you in two seconds, okay?"

"Well, where can you go?"

"In the lavatory!"

"But I didn't want to wake up your dad."

"He'll sleep through anything," said Bill. "Trust me."

Red with humiliation, Ford crawled into the back and after several tries figured out how to operate the toilet, as Billy snored away oblivious. Afterward he crawled back up front, carefully closed the door and said:

"Er . . . so, where does somebody have their bath?"

Bill, who had turned his Gamebuke on again, did not look up as he said:

"At the Empress."

"No, I mean . . . when somebody has a bath out here, where do they have it?"

Bill lifted his eyes. He looked perplexed.

"What are you on about? Nobody bathes out here."

"You mean, you only wash when you're at the Empress?"

Now it was Bill's turn to flush with embarrassment.

"Yeah."

Ford tried to keep his dismay from showing, but he wasn't very good at hiding his feelings. "You mean I can't have a bath until we get back?"

"No. You can't. I guess people wash themselves every day in the Long Acres, huh?" said Bill angrily.

Ford nodded. "We have to. It stinks too bad if we don't. Because there's, er, manure and algae and, er, the methane plant, and . . . we work hard and sweat a lot. So we shave and wash every day, see?"

"Is *that* why the MAC haven't got any hair?"

"Yeah," said Ford. He added, "Plus my dad says hair is a vanity. Means being a showoff, being flash."

"I know what it means," said Bill. He was silent a moment, and then said:

"Well, you won't be sweating much out here. Freezing is more like it. So you'll have to cope until we get back to the Empress. It'll only be two weeks."

Two weeks? Ford thought of what his dad and mum would say to him when he turned up again, after being missing for so long. His mouth dried, his heart pounded. He wondered desperately what kind of lie he might tell to get himself out of trouble. Maybe that he'd been kidnapped? It had almost really happened. Kidnapped and taken to work in the iron mines, right, and . . . somehow escaped, and . . .

Billy retreated to his Gamebuke again, as Ford sat there trying to imagine what he might say. The stories became wilder, more unbelievable as they grew more elaborate; and gradually he found himself drifting away from purposeful lies altogether, dreamily wondering what it might be like if he never went back to face the music at all.

After all, Sam was going to do it; Sam was clever and funny and brave, and he was walking away from the Collective to a new life. Why couldn't Ford have a new life too? What if he became a Hauler, like Billy, and lived out the rest of his life up here where there were no limits to the world? Blatchford the MAC boy would vanish and he could be just Ford, himself, not part of anything. *Free.*

FIVE

It took them most of a week to get to Depot South. Ford enjoyed every minute of it, even getting used to the idea of postponing his bath for two weeks. Mostly he rode up front with Billy, as Bill stayed in the back sulking. Billy told him stories as they rocketed along, and taught him the basics of driving the freighter; it was harder than driving a tractor but not by as much as Ford would have thought.

"Look at you, holding our Evelyn on the road!" said Billy, chuckling. "You are one strong kid, for your age. Li'l Bill can't drive her at all yet."

"I'm a better navigator than you are!" yelled Bill from the back, in tones of outrage.

"He is, actually," said Billy. "Best navigator I ever saw. Half the time I have to get him to figure coordinates for me. You ever get lost in a storm or anything, you'll wish you had li'l Bill there with you." He looked carefully into the back to see if Bill was watching, and then unzipped a pouch in his psuit and took out a small bottle. Quickly he shook two tiny red pills into his palm and popped them into his mouth.

"What're those?" Ford asked.

"Freddie Stay-awakes," said Billy in a low voice. "Just getting ready for another night shift. We're going to set a new record for getting to the Depot, man."

"We don't have to hurry or anything," said Ford. "Really."

"Yeah, we do," said Billy, looking uncomfortable for the first time since Ford had known him. "Fun's fun, and everything, but . . . your people must be kind of wondering where you are, you know? I mean, it was a good idea to get you away from Mother's Boys and all, but we don't want people thinking you're dead, huh?"

"I guess not," said Ford. He looked sadly up at the monitor, at the wide open world. The thought of going back into the Tubes, into the reeking dark of the cowsheds and the muddy trenches, made him despair.

∘ ∘ ∘

Depot South loomed ahead of them at last, a low rise of ice above the plain. At first Ford was disappointed; he had expected a gleaming white mountain, but Billy explained that the glacier was sanded all over with red dust from the windstorms. As the hours went by and they drew closer, Ford saw a low-lying mist of white, from which the glacier rose like an island. Later two smaller islands seemed to rise from it as well, one on either side of the road.

"There's old Jack and Jim!" cried Billy. "We're almost there, when we see Jack and Jim."

Ford watched them with interest. As they drew near, he laughed; for they looked like a pair of bearded giants hacked out of the red stone. One was sitting up, peering from blind hollow eyes and holding what appeared to be a mug clutched to his stomach. The other reclined, with his big hands folded peacefully on his chest.

"How'd they get there?" he exclaimed, delighted.

"The glacier deposited them," said Bill, who had come out of the back to see.

"No! No! You have to tell him the story," said Billy gleefully. "See, Jack and Jim were these two Haulers, come up from Australia. So they liked their beer cold, see? Really cold.

"So they go into the Empress, and Mother, she says, Welcome my dears, have a drop of good cheer, warm buttery beer won't cost you dear. But Jack and Jim, both he and him, they liked their beer cold. Really cold.

"Says one to the other, like brother to brother, there must be a place in this here space where a cobber can swill a nice bit of chill, if he likes his beer cold. Really cold.

"So they bought them a keg, and off they legged it for the Pole, the pole, where it's nice and cold, and they chopped out a hole in the ice-wall so, and that keg they stowed in the ice, cobber, ever so nice. And it got cold. Really cold.

"So they drank it down and another round and another one still and they drank until they set and they sot and they clean forgot, where the white mists creep they fell asleep, and they got cold. Really cold.

"In fact they froze, from nose to toes, and there they are to this very day, and the moral is, don't die that way! 'Cause what's right for Oz ain't right on Moz, 'cause up here it's cold. Really cold!"

Billy laughed like a loon, pounding his fist on the console. Bill just rolled his eyes.

"They're only a couple of boulders," he said.

"But you used to love that song," said Billy plaintively.

"When I was three, maybe," said Bill, turning and going into the back. "You'd better get him out one of your extra psuits. He won't fit in any of mine."

"He used to sing it with me," said Billy to Ford, looking crestfallen.

◔ ◔ ◔

They pulled into Depot South and once again Ford had expected to see buildings, but there were none; only a confused impression of tumbled rock on the monitor. He looked up at it as Billy helped him into a psuit.

"Is it colder out there?" he asked.

"Yeah," said Bill, getting down three helmets from a locker. "You're at the South Pole, dummy."

"Aw, now, he's never been there, has he?" said Billy, adjusting the fit of the suit for Ford. "That feel okay?"

"I guess it—whoa!" said Ford, for once the fastenings had been sealed up the suit seemed to flex, like a hand closing around him, and though it felt warm and snug it was still a slightly creepy sensation. "What's it doing?"

"Just kind of programming itself so it gets to know you," Billy explained, accepting a helmet from Bill. "That's how it keeps you alive, see? Just settles in real close and puts a couple of sensors places you don't notice. Anything goes wrong, it'll try to fix you, and if it can't, it'll flash lights at you so you know."

"Like that?" Ford pointed at the little red light flashing on Billy's psuit readout panel. Billy looked down at it.

"Oh. No, that's just a short circuit or glitch or something. It's been doing that all the time lately when nothing's wrong."

"Some people take their suits into the shop when they need repair, you know," said Bill, putting on his own helmet. "Just an idea, Dad. Hope it's not too radical for you."

As Billy helped him seal up his helmet, Ford looked at Bill and thought: *You're a mean little twit. I'd give anything if my dad was like yours.*

But when they stepped Outside, he forgot about Bill and even about Billy. He barely noticed the cold, though it was so intense it took his breath away and the psuit helpfully turned up its thermostat for him. Depot South had all his attention.

They were surrounded on three sides by towering walls, cloudy white swirled through with colors like an Ice Pop, green and blue blue blue and lavender, all scarred and rough, faceted and broken. Underneath his feet was a confusion of crushed and broken rock, pea-sized gravel to cobbles, ice mixed with grit and stone, and a roiling mist swirled about his ankles.

Here and there were carvings in the ice wall, roughly gouged and hacked: HAULERS RULE OK and BARSOOM BRUCE GOT HERE ALIVE and one that simply said THANKS MARSWIFE, over a niche that had been scraped from the ice where somebody had left a little figurine like the one on Beautiful Evelyn's console. There were figures carved too; on a section of green ice, Ford noticed a four-armed giant with tusks.

Behind him, he became aware of a clatter as Billy and Bill opened a panel in the freighter's side and drew out something between them. He turned to see Billy hoisting a laser-saw, and heard the *hummzap* as it was turned on.

"Okay!" said Billy, his voice coming tinnily over the speaker. "Let's go cut some ice!"

He went up to the nearest wall, hefted the laser and disappeared in a cloud of white steam. A moment later a great chunk of ice came hurtling out of the steam, and bounced and rolled to Bill's feet. He picked it up, as another block bounded out.

"Grab that," said Bill. "If we don't start loading this stuff, Dad will be up to his neck in ice."

Ford obeyed, and followed Bill around to the rear of the freighter, where a sort of escalator ramp had been lowered, and watched as Bill dropped the block to the ramp. It traveled swiftly up the ramp to a hopper at the top of Beautiful Evelyn's tank, where it vanished with a grinding roar, throwing up a rainbowed shatter of ice-shards and vapor against the sunlight. Fascinated, Ford set his block on the ramp and watched as the same thing happened.

"What's it doing?"

"Making carbon dioxide snowcones, what do you think?" said Bill. "And we take the whole lot back to Settlement Base, and sell it to the MAC."

"You do?" Ford was astonished. "What do we need it for?"

"Hel-LO, terraforming, remember?" said Bill. "Making Mars green like Earth? What the MAC was brought up here to do?"

He turned and trudged back around the side of the freighter, and Ford walked after him thinking: *I'll bet you wouldn't hold that nose so high up in the air if I bashed it with my forehead.*

But he said nothing, and for the next hour they worked steadily as machines, going back and forth with ice blocks to the ramp. The tank was nearly full when they heard the drone of ice-cutting stop.

"That's not enough, Dad," Bill called, and nobody answered. He turned and ran. Ford walked around the side of the freighter and saw him kneeling beside Billy, who had fallen and lay with the white mist curling over his body.

Ford gasped and ran to them. The whole front of Billy's psuit was lit with blinking colors, dancing over a readout panel that had activated. Bill was bending close, waving away the mist to peer at it. Ford leaned down and saw Billy's face slack within the helmet, his eyes staring and blank.

"What's wrong with him?" said Ford.

"He's had a blowout," said Bill flatly.

"What's blowout?"

"Blood vessel goes bang. Happens sometimes to people who go Outside a lot." Bill rested his hand on his father's chest. He felt something in one of the sealed pouches; he opened it, and drew out the bottle of Freddie Stay-awakes. After staring at it for a long moment, his face contorted. He hurled the bottle at the ice-wall, where it popped open and scattered red pills like beads of blood.

"I knew it! I knew he'd do this! I knew this would happen someday!" he shouted. Ford felt like crying, but he fought it back and said:

"Is he going to die?"

"What do you think?" said Bill. "We're at the bloody South Pole! We're a week away from the infirmary!"

"But—could we maybe keep him alive until we get back?"

Bill turned to him, and a little of the incandescent rage faded from his eyes. "We might," he said. "The psuit's doing what it can. We have some emergency medical stuff. You don't understand, though. His brain's turning to goo in there."

"Maybe it isn't," said Ford. "Please! We have to try."

"He'll die anyway," said Bill, but he got Billy under the shoulders and tried to lift him. Ford came around and took his place, lifting Billy easily; Bill grabbed his father's legs, and between them they hoisted Billy up and carried him into the cab.

There they settled him in his bunk and Bill fumbled in a drawer for a medical kit. He drew out three sealed bags of colored liquid with tubes leading from one end and hooks on the other. The tubes he plugged into ports in the arm of Billy's psuit; the hooks fitted into loops on the underside of the upper bunk, so the bags hung suspended above Billy.

"Should we get his helmet off him?" Ford asked. Bill just shook his head. He turned and stalked out of the compartment. Ford took a last look at Billy, with the glittering lights on his chest and his dead eyes staring, and followed Bill.

"What do we do now?"

"We get the laser," said Bill. "We can't leave it. It cost a month's pay."

SIX

The freighter was a lot harder to handle now, full of ice, than it had been on the way out when Billy had let him drive. It took all Ford's strength to back her around and get her on the road again, and even so the console beeped a warning as they trundled out through Jack and Jim, for he nearly swerved and clipped one of the giants. At last he was able to steer straight between the boulders and get up a little speed.

"We really can't, er, send a distress signal or anything?" he asked Bill. Bill sat hunched at his end of the cab, staring at the monitors.

"Nobody'll hear us," he said bitterly, "There's half a planet between Mons Olympus and us. Did you notice any relay towers on the way out here?"

"No."

"That's because there aren't any. Why should Areco build any? Nobody comes out here except Haulers, and who cares if Haulers die? We do this work because nobody else wants to do it, because it's too dangerous. But Haulers are a bunch of idiots; *they* don't care if they get killed."

"They're not idiots, they're brave!" said Ford. Bill looked at him with contempt. Neither of them said anything for a long while after that.

~ ~ ~

By the time it was beginning to get dark, Ford was aching in every muscle of his body from the sheer effort of keeping the freighter on the road. The approaching darkness was not as fearful as he'd thought it might be, because for several miles now someone had daubed the lines of boulders with photoreflective paint, and they lit up nicely in the freighter's high-beams. But Beautiful Evelyn seemed to want to veer to the left, and Ford wondered if there was something wrong with her steering system until he saw drifts of sand flying straight across the road in front of her, like stealthy ghosts.

"I think the wind's rising," he said.

"You think, genius?" Bill pointed to a readout on the console.

"What's it mean?"

"It means we're probably driving right into a storm," said Bill, and then they heard a shrill piping alarm from the back. Bill scrambled aft; Ford held the freighter on the road. *Please don't let that be Billy dying! Please, Marswife, if you're out there, help us!*

Bill returned and crawled into his seat. "The air pressure's dropping in here. The psuit needed somebody to okay turning it up a notch."

"Why's the air pressure dropping?"

Bill sounded weary. "Because this is going to be a really bad storm. You'd better pull over and anchor us."

"But we have to get your dad to an infirmary!"

"Did you think we were going to drive for a whole week without sleeping?" Bill said. "We don't have any Freddies now. We have to sit out the storm no matter what happens. Five-Fifty-K is coming up soon. Maybe we can make it that far."

It was in fact twelve kilometers away, and the light faded steadily as they roared along. Ford could hear the wind howling now. He remembered a story Billy had told him, about people seeing dead Haulers in their high-beams, wraiths signaling for help at the scenes of long-ago breakdowns. The whirling sand looked uncannily like figures with streaming hair, diving in front of the freighter as though waving insubstantial arms. He was grateful when the half-circle of rocks that was Five-Fifty-K Station appeared in her lights at last, and she seemed eager to swerve away from the road.

Bill punched in the anchoring protocol, and Beautiful Evelyn gave a lurch and dropped abruptly, as though she were sitting down. Ford cut the power; the drives fell silent. They sat there side by side in the silence that was filled up steadily by the whine of blowing sand, and a patter of blown gravel that might have sounded to them like rain, if they had ever heard rain.

"What do we do now?" said Ford.

"We wait it out," said Bill.

They went into the back to check on Billy—no change—and heated something frozen and ate it, barely registering what it was. Then they went back into the cab and sat, in their opposite corners.

"So we really are on our own?" said Ford at last. "Areco won't send Security looking for us?"

"Areco doesn't send Mother's Boys anyplace," said Bill, staring into the dark. "Mother hired 'em."

"Who's Mother, anyway?"

"The lady who found the diamond and got rich," said Bill. "And bought Mons Olympus, and everybody thought she was crazy, because it was just this big volcano where nobody could grow anything. Only, she had a well drilled into a magma pocket and built a power station. And she leased lots to a bunch of people from Earth, and that's why Mons Olympus makes way more money than Areco and the MAC."

"The MAC isn't supposed to make money," said Ford. "We're supposed to turn Mars into a paradise. Our contract says Areco is going to give it to us for our own, once we've done it."

"Well, you can bet Areco isn't going to come rescue us," said Bill. "Nobody looks out for Haulers except other Haulers. And their idea of help would be giving Dad a big funeral and getting stinking drunk afterward."

"Oh," said Ford. Bill gave him an odd look.

"People in the MAC look out for each other, though, don't they?"

"Yeah," said Ford wretchedly. "There's always somebody watching what you do. Always somebody there to tell you why what you want to do is wrong. Council meetings go on for hours because everybody has to say something or it isn't fair, but they all say the same thing anyway. Blah blah blah. I *hate* it there," he said, surprising himself by how intensely he felt.

"What's it supposed to be like, when Mars is a paradise?"

Ford looked at Bill to see if he was being mocking, but he wasn't smiling.

"Well, it'll be like . . . there'll be no corruption or oppression. And stuff. They say water will fall out of the sky, and nobody will ever have to wear a mask again." Ford slumped forward and put his head on his knees. "I used to imagine it'd be . . . I don't know. Full of lights."

"People would be safe, if Mars could be made like that," said Bill in a thoughtful voice. "Terraformed. Another Earth. No more big empty spaces."

"I *like* big empty spaces," said Ford. "Why does Mars have to be just like Earth anyway? Why can't things stay the way they are?"

"You like this?" Bill swung his arm up at the monitors, that showed only the howling night and a blur of sand. "'Cause you can have it. I hate it! Tons of big nothing waiting to kill us, all my whole life! And Dad just laughed at it, but he isn't laughing now, huh? You know what's really sick? If he dies—if we get back alive—I'll be better off."

"Oh, shut up," said Ford.

"But I will," said Bill, with a certain wonderment. "Lots better off. I can sell this freighter—and Dad paid into the Hauler's Club, so there'd be some money coming in there—and . . . wow, I could afford a *good* education. Maybe University level. I'll be able to have everything I've always wanted, and I'll never have to come out here again."

"How can you talk like that?" Ford yelled. "You selfish pig! You're talking about your own dad dying! You don't even care, do you? Your dad's the bravest guy I ever met!"

"He got himself killed, after everything I told him. He was stupid," said Bill.

"He isn't even dead yet!" Ford, infuriated, swung at him. Bill ducked backward, away from his flailing fists, and got his legs up on the seat and kicked Ford. Ford fell sideways, but scrambled up on his knees and kept coming, trying to back Bill into the corner. Bill dodged and hit him hard, and then again and again, until Ford got so close he couldn't get his arms up all the way. Ford, sobbing with anger, punched as hard as he could in the cramped space, but Bill was a much better fighter for all that he was so small.

By the time they had hurt each other enough to stop, both of them had bloody noses and Ford had the beginning of a black eye. Swearing, they retreated into their separate corners of the cab, and glared at each other until the droning hiss of the wind and the pattering of gravel on the tank lulled them to sleep.

SEVEN

When they woke, hours later, it was dead quiet.

Ford woke groaning, partly because his face was so sore and partly because he had a stiff neck from sleeping curled up on the seat. He sat up and looked around blearily.

He realized that he couldn't hear anything. He looked up at the monitors and realized that he couldn't see anything, either; the screens were black. Frightened, he leaned over and shook Bill awake. Bill woke instantly, staring around.

"The power's gone out!" Ford said.

"No, it hasn't. We'd be dead," said Bill. He punched a few buttons on the console and peered intently at figures that appeared on the readout. Then he looked up at the monitors. "What's that?" He pointed at the monitor for the rear of the freighter, where there was a sliver of image along the top. Just a grayish triangle of light, shifting a little along its lower edge, just like . . .

"Sand," said Bill. "We're buried. The storm blew a dune over us."

"What do we do now?" said Ford, shivering, and the psuit thought he was cold and warmed up comfortingly.

"Maybe we can blow it away," said Bill. "Some, anyway." He switched on the drives and there was a shudder and a jolt that ran the whole length of the freighter. With a *whoosh,* Beautiful Evelyn rose a few inches. The rear monitor lit up with an image of sand cascading past it; some light showed on her left-hand monitor too.

"Okay!" said Bill, shutting her down again. "We're not going to die. Not here, anyway. We can dig out. Get a helmet on."

They went aft to get helmets—Billy still stared at nothing, though his psuit blinked at them reassuringly—and, when they had helmeted up, Bill reached past Ford to activate the hatch. It made a dull muffled sound, but would not respond. He had to try three more times before it consented to open out about a hand's width. Sand spilled into the cab, followed by daylight.

Bill swore and climbed up on the seat, pushing the hatch outward. "Get up here and help me!"

Ford scrambled up beside him and set his shoulder to the hatch. A lot more sand fell in, but they were able to push it open far enough for Bill to grab the edge and pull himself up, and worm his way out. Ford climbed after, and in a moment was standing with Bill on the top of the dune that covered the freighter.

Bill swore quietly. Ford didn't blame him.

They stood on a mountain of red sand and looked out on a plain of red sand, endless, smooth to the wide horizon, and the low early sun threw their shadows far out behind them. The sky had a flat metallic glare, polished by the storm; the wind wailed high and mournful.

"Where's the road?" cried Ford.

"Buried under there," said Bill, pointing down the slope in front of them. "It happens sometimes. Come on." He turned and started down the slope. Ford stumbled after him, slipped, and fell, rolling ignominiously to the bottom. He picked himself up, feeling stupid, but Bill hadn't noticed; he was digging with his hands, scooping away sand from the freighter.

Ford waded in to help him. He reached up to brush sand from the tank, but at his touch the sand puckered out in a funny starred pattern. Startled, he drew his hand back. Cautiously he reached out a fingertip to the tank; the instant he touched it, a rayed star of sand formed once again.

"Hey, look at this!" Giggling, he drew his finger along the tank, and the star spread and followed it.

"It's magnetic," said Bill. "Happens sometimes, when the wind's been bad. My dad said it's all the iron in the sand. It fries electronics. Hard to clean off, too."

Ford brushed experimentally at the tank, but the sand stuck as though it were a dense syrup.

"This'll take us forever," he said.

"Not if we get to the tool chest," said Bill. "We can scrape off most of it."

They worked together and after ten minutes had cleared a panel in the freighter's undercarriage; Bill pried it open and pulled out a couple of big shovels, and after that the work went more quickly.

"Wowie. Sand spades. All we need is buckets and we could make sand castles, huh?" said Ford, grinning sheepishly.

"What's that mean?"

"It's something kids do on Earth. Sam says, before we emigrated, our dad and mum took him to this place called Blackpool. There was all this blue water, see, washing in over the sand. He had a bucket and spade and he made sand castles. So here we are in the biggest Blackpool in the universe, with the biggest sand spades, yeah? Only there's no water."

"How could you make castles out of sand?" Bill said, scowling as he worked. "They'd just fall in on you."

"I don't know. I think you'd have to get the sand wet."

"But why would anybody get sand wet?"

"I don't know. I don't think people do it on purpose; I think it just happens. There's all this water on Earth, see, and it gets on things. That's what Sam says."

Bill shook his head grimly and kept digging. They cleared the freighter's rear wheels, and Ford said:

"Why do you reckon the water's blue on Earth? It's only green or brown up here."

"It's not blue," said Bill.

"Yes, it is," said Ford. "Sam has holos of it. I've seen 'em. It's bluer than the sky. Blue as blue paint."

"Water isn't any color really," said Bill. "It just looks blue. Something about the air."

Ford scowled and went around to the other side of the freighter, where he dug out great shovelfuls of sand and muttered, "It *is* blue. They wouldn't have that Blue Room if it wasn't blue. All the songs and stories say it's blue. So there, you little know-it-all."

He had forgotten that Bill could hear him on the psuit comm, so he was quite startled when Bill's voice sounded inside his helmet:

"Songs and stories? Right. Go stick your head in a dune, moron."

Ford just gritted his teeth and kept shoveling.

It took them a long while to clear the freighter, because they only made real progress once the wind fell a little. Eventually, though, they were able to climb back into the cab and start up Beautiful Evelyn's drives. She blasted her way free of the dune and Ford strained to steer her up, over and down across the rippled slope below.

"Okay! Where's the road?" he said.

"There," said Bill, pointing. "Don't you even know directions? We anchored at right angles to the road. It's still there, even if we can't see it. Just take her straight that way."

Ford obeyed. They rumbled off.

They drove for five hours, over sand and then over rocky sand and at last over a cobbled plain, and there was no sign of the double row of boulders that should have been there if they had been on the High Road.

Bill, who had been watching the readouts, grew more and more pale and silent.

"We need to stop," he said at last. "Something's wrong."

"We aren't on the High Road anymore, are we?" said Ford sadly.

"No. We're lost."

"What happened?"

"The storm must have screwed up the nav system," said Bill. "All that magnetic crap spraying around."

"Can we fix it?"

"I can reset it," said Bill. "But I can't recalibrate it, because I don't know where we are. So it wouldn't do us any good."

"But your dad said you were this great navigator!" said Ford.

Bill looked at his boots. "I'm not. He just thought I was."

"Well, isn't that great?" said Ford. "And here you thought *I* was such an idiot. What do we do now, Professor?"

"Shut up," said Bill. "Just shut up. We're supposed to go north, okay? And the sun rises in the east and sets in the west. So as long as we keep the setting sun on our left, we're going mostly in the right direction."

"What happens at night?"

"If the sky's clear of dust clouds, maybe we can steer by the stars."

Ford brightened up at that. "I used to watch the stars a lot," he said. "And we ought to be able to see the mountain after a while, right?"

"Mons Olympus? Yeah."

"Okay then!" Ford accelerated again, and Beautiful Evelyn plunged forward. "We can do this! Billy wouldn't be scared if he was lost, would he?"

"No," admitted Bill.

"No, because he'd just point himself at the horizon and he'd just *go*, zoom, and he wouldn't worry about it."

"He never worried about anything," said Bill, though not as though he thought that was especially smart.

"Well, it's dumb to worry," said Ford, with a slightly rising note of hysteria in his voice. "You live or you die, right? The main thing, is . . . is . . . to be really alive before you die. I could have lived my whole life walking around in the Tubes and never, ever seen stuff like I've seen since I ran away. All this sky. All that sand. The ice and the mist and the different colors and everything! So maybe I don't get to be old like Hardie Stubbs's granddad. Who wants to be all shriveled up and coughing anyway?"

"Don't be stupid," said Bill. "I'd give anything to be down in the Long Acres right now, and I wouldn't care what work I had to do. And you wish you were there too."

"No, I don't!" Ford shouted. "You know what I'm going to do? As soon as we get back, I'll go see my dad and I'll say: 'Dad, I'm leaving the MAC. Sam did it and so can I. Only I'm not going back to Earth. Mars is *my* place! And I'm going to be a Hauler, and stay Outside all the rest of my life.'"

Bill stared at him.

"You're crazy," he said. "You think your dad will just let you go?"

"No," said Ford. "He'll grab my ear and about pull it off. It doesn't matter. Once I'm nine, the MAC says I have a right to pick whatever job I want."

"Once you're *nine*?"

Ford turned red. "In MAC years. We have one for every two Earth years."

"So . . . you're how old now?" Bill began to grin. "Six?"

"Yeah," said Ford. "And you can just shut up, okay?"

"Okay," said Bill, but his grin widened.

EIGHT

They drove all the rest of that day, but when night fell they were so tired they agreed to pull over to sleep. Ford stretched out in the cab and Bill went back to crawl into the bunk above Billy, who lay there still, unresponsive as a waxwork.

◔ ◔ ◔

He was still alive when morning came. Bill was changing his tube-bags when Ford came edging in, yawning.

"You wait and see," said Ford, in an attempt to be comforting. "He'll be fine if we can get him to the infirmary. Eric Chetwynd's dad fell off a tractor and fractured his skull, and *he* was in this coma, see, for days, but then they did surgery on him and he was opening his eyes and talking and everything. And your dad hasn't even got any broken bones."

"It's not the same," said Bill morosely. "Never mind. Let's get going. Sun's on our right until noon, got it?"

They drove on. Ford's muscles ached less now; he was beginning to feel more confident with Beautiful Evelyn. He watched the horizon and imagined Mons Olympus rising there, inevitable, the red queen on the vast chessboard of the plain. She *would* come into view soon. She had to. And someday, when he had a freighter of his own and drove this route all the time, a little thing like going off course wouldn't bother him at all. He'd know every sand hill and rock outcropping like the palm of his hand.

He thought about getting a tattoo on his face. Deciding what it ought to look like occupied his thoughts for the next couple of hours, as Bill sat silent across from him, staring at the monitors and twisting his hands together in his lap.

Then:

"Something's moving!" said Bill, pointing at the backup cam monitor.

Ford spotted it: something gleaming, sunlight striking off a vehicle far back in their dust-wake.

"Yowie! It's another Hauler!" he said. "Billy's saved!"

He slowed Beautiful Evelyn and turned her around, so the plume of dust whirled away and they could see the other vehicle more clearly.

"It's not a Hauler," said Bill. "It's just a cab. Who is that? That's nobody I know."

"Who cares?" said Ford, pounding on the console in his glee. "They'll know how to get back to the road!"

"Not if they're lost too," said Bill. The stranger was barreling toward them quite deliberately and they could see it clearly now: a freighter's cab with no tank attached, just the tang of the hookup sticking out behind, looking strange as some tiny insect with an immense head. It pulled up alongside them. Bill hit the comm switch and cried, "Who's that?"

There was a silence. Then a voice crackled through the speakers, distorted and harsh: "Who's that crying who's that? Sounds like a youngster."

Ford leaned over and shouted, "Please, we're lost! Can you show us how to get back to the road?"

Another silence, and then:

"Two little boys? What're you doing out here, then? Daddy had a mishap, did he?"

Bill gave Ford a furious look. Ford wondered why, but said:

"Yes, sir! We need to get him to the infirmary, and our nav system went out in the storm! Can you help us?"

"Why, sure I can," said the voice, and it sounded as though the speaker were smiling. "Mask up now, kids, and step Outside. Let's talk close-up, eh?"

"You jackass," muttered Bill, but he pulled on his mask.

When they slid down out of the cab they saw that the stranger had painted his cab with the logo CELTIC POWER and pictures of what had been celtic knots and four-leafed clovers, though they were half scoured away. The hatch swung up and a man climbed out, a big man in a psuit also painted in green and yellow patterns. He looked them over and grinned within his mask.

"Well, hello there, kids," he said. "Gwill Griffin, at your service. Diamond prospector by trade. What's the story?"

"Bill's dad had a blowout," said Ford. "And we were trying to get him back, but we've lost the road. Can you help us, please?"

"A blowout?" The man raised his eyebrows. "Now, that's an awful thing. Let's have a look at him."

"You don't need—" began Bill, but Mr. Griffin had already vaulted up into Beautiful Evelyn's cab. Bill and Ford scrambled after him. By the time they had got in he was already in the back, leaning down to peer at Billy.

"Dear, dear, he's certainly in trouble," he said. "Yes, you'd better get him back to Mons Olympus, and no mistake." He looked around the inside of the cab. "Nice rig he's got here, though, isn't it? And a nice full tank of CO_2, I take it?"

"Yeah," said Ford. "It happened right as we were finishing up. Do you know how to, er, recalibrate nav systems?"

"No trouble at all," said Mr. Griffin, shoving past them and into the seat at the console. Bill watched him closely as he punched it up and set in new figures. "Poor little lads, lost on your own Outside. You're lucky I found you, you know. The road's just five kilometers east of here, but you might have wandered around forever without finding it."

"I knew we had to be close," said Ford, though he did not feel quite the sense of relief he might have, and wondered why.

"Yes; terrible things can happen out here. I saw your rig in the middle of nowhere, zigzagging along, and I said to myself: 'Goddess save me, that must be Freeze-Dried Dave!' I've seen some strange things out here in my time, I can tell you."

"Who's Freeze-Dried Dave?" asked Ford.

"Him? The Demon Hauler of Mare Cimmerium?" Mr. Griffin turned to him, pushing his mask up. He was beardless and freckled, though he wore a wide mustache, and was not as old as Ford had thought him to be at first.

"Nobody knows who Freeze-Dried Dave was; just some poor soul who was up here in the early days, and they say he died at the console whilst on a run, see? And his cab's system took over and went on Autopilot. They think it veered off the road in a storm and just kept rovering on, and every time the battery'd wear out it'd sit somewhere until another storm scoured the dust off the solar cells. Then it'd just start itself up again."

Ford realized what was making him uneasy. The man sounded like an actor in a holo, like somebody who was speaking lines for an effect.

"Some prospectors found it clean out in the middle of nowhere, and went up to it and got the hatch to open. There was Freeze-Dried Dave still sitting inside her, shriveled up like; but no sooner had they set foot to the ladder than she roared to life and took off, scattering 'em like bowling pins. And what do you think she did then? Only swerved around and came back at 'em, that's what she did, and mashed one into the sand while the others ran for their lives.

"*They* made it home to tell the tale. There's many a Hauler since then who's seen her, thundering along on her own business off the road, with that dead man rattling around inside. Some say it's Dave's ghost driving her, trying to find his way back to Settlement Base. Some say it's the freighter herself, that her system's gone mad with sorrow and wants to kill anyone gets close enough, so they don't take her Dave away. You'll never find a prospector like me who'll go anywhere near her. Why, it's bad luck even to see her." He winked broadly at Ford.

"We need to get my dad to the infirmary," said Bill, clearing his throat. "Thanks for helping us. Let's go, okay?"

"Right," said Mr. Griffin, masking up again. "Only you'd best let me do a point-check on your freighter first, don't you think? That was quite a storm; could be all sorts of things gummed up you don't know about. Wouldn't want to have a breakdown out here, eh?"

"No, sir," said Ford. Mr. Griffin jumped down from the cab. Bill was preparing to jump after him, but he held up his hand.

"Now, I'll tell you what we'll do," he said. "You lads sit in there and watch the console. I'm going to test the tread relays; that's the surest thing will go wrong after a storm, with all those little magnetic particles getting everywhere and persuading the relays to do things they shouldn't. Could cause all your wheels to lock on one side, and you don't want that to happen at speed! You'd roll and kill yourselves for sure. I'll just open the panel and run a quick diagnostic; you can give me a shout when the green lights go on."

"Okay," said Bill, and climbed back in and closed the hatch. As soon as it was closed, he swore, and kept swearing. Ford stared at him.

"What are you on about?" he demanded. "We're safe now."

"No, we bloody aren't," said Bill. "Gwill Griffin, my butt. I know who that guy is. His name's Art Finlay. He was one of Mother's Boys. She fired him last year. He liked to go into the holding cell and slap guys around. He thought nobody was looking, but the cameras caught him. So all that old-diamond-prospector-with-his-tall-tales stuff was so much crap. So's the PanCeltic accent; he emigrated up here from some place in the Americans on Earth."

"So he's a phony?" Ford thought of the inexplicably creepy feeling the stranger had given him.

"Yeah. He's a phony," said Bill, and reached over to switch on the comm unit. "How are those relays?" he said.

"Look fine," was the crackly answer. "Your daddy took care of this rig, sure enough. Look at the console, now, lads; tell me when the green lights go on."

They stared at the panel, and in a moment: "They're on," chorused Bill and Ford.

"Then you're home and dry."

"Thanks! We're going to go on now, okay?" said Bill.

"You do that. I'll just follow along behind to be sure you get home safe, eh?"

"Okay," said Bill, and shut off the comm. "Get going!" he told Ford. "Five kilometers due east. We ought to be able to see it once we get over that rise. Let's leave this guy way behind us."

Ford started her up again, and Beautiful Evelyn rolled forward. She picked up speed and he charged her at the hill, feeling a wonderful sense of freedom as she zoomed upward. Bill cut into his reverie by yelling:

"The camera's been changed!"

"Huh?"

"Look," said Bill, pointing up at the left-hand monitor. It was no longer showing Beautiful Evelyn's port side and a slice of ground, as it had been; now there was only a view of the northern horizon. "He moved the lens. Move it back!"

"I don't know how!" Ford leaned in, flustered, as Bill jumped up and reached past him to stab at the controls that would align the camera lenses. Beautiful Evelyn's side came back into view.

"She looks all right," said Ford. "And, hey! There's the High Road! Hooray!"

"No, she doesn't look all right!" said Bill. "Look! He left the relay panel open! How come the telltale warning isn't lit?"

"I don't know," said Ford.

"Of course *you* don't know, you flaming idiot," said Bill, shrill with anger. "And here he comes!"

Ford looked up at the backup cam and saw Mr. Griffin's cab advancing behind the freighter; then the image switched to the left hand camera, as it moved up on Beautiful Evelyn's port side. It drew level with the open panel. They watched in horror as the cab's hatch swung down. They saw Mr. Griffin, masked up, leaning out.

"He's going to do something to the panel!" shrieked Bill.

"Oh, no, he won't," said Ford, more angry than he had ever been in his life. Without a second's hesitation he steered Beautiful

Evelyn sharply to the left. She more than sideswiped Mr. Griffin; with a terrific crash she sent his cab spinning away, rolling over and over, and they saw him go flying out of it. Beautiful Evelyn lurched and sagged. They rumbled to a stop. They sat for a moment, shaking.

"We have to go see," said Bill. "Something's wrong."

They masked up and went Outside.

NINE

Beautiful Evelyn's foremost left tire had exploded. There was a thick crust of polyceramic around the wheel, but nothing else. It must have sent pieces flying in all directions when it burst. Ford gaped at it while Bill ran down to the open panel. Ford heard a lot of swearing. He turned and saw Bill tearing something loose, and holding it up.

"Duct tape," said Bill. "He put a piece of duct tape over the warning sensor."

"Did he damage the, whatzis, the relays?" Ford looked in concern at the open panel, with no idea what he was seeing inside.

"No. You nailed him in time. But if he'd bashed them with something once we'd come up to speed, we'd have flipped over, just like he said. Then all he'd have had to do was move in and pick over the wreck. Help himself to the tank. Tell anybody who asked questions a story about some 'poor little dead lads' he'd found out here." Bill looked over at the dust rising from the wreck of Griffin's cab.

He bent and picked up a good-sized rock.

Ford followed his gaze.

"You think he's still alive?" he said, shuddering.

"Maybe," said Bill. "Get a rock. Let's go find out."

But he wasn't alive. They found him where he'd fallen, nine meters from his cab. His mask had come off.

"Oh," said Ford, backing away. "Oh—"

He turned hastily and doubled up, vomiting into his mask. Turning, he ran for the freighter. Scrambling in and closing the hatch, he groped his way to the lavatory and pulled his mask off. He vomited again, under Billy's blank gaze.

He had cleaned himself up a little and stopped crying by the time he heard Bill coming back.

"Can you mask up?" Bill asked him, over the commlink.

"Yeah—" said Ford, his voice breaking on another sob. Hating himself, he pulled the mask on and heard the hatch open. Bill climbed in.

"We might be okay," said Bill. "I had a look at his rig. Same size tires as ours. Maybe we can change one out."

"Okay," said Ford. Bill looked at him.

"Are you going to be all right? You're green."

"I killed a guy," said Ford.

"He was trying to kill us," said Bill. "He deserved what he got."

"I know," said Ford, beginning to shiver again. "It's just—the way it looked. The face. Oh, man. I'm going to see it when I close my eyes at night, for the rest of my life."

"I know," said Bill, sounding tired. "That was how I felt, the first time I saw somebody die like that."

"Does it happen a lot?"

"To Haulers? Yeah. Mostly to new guys." Bill stood up. "Come on. Blow your nose and let's go see if we can change the tire."

Walking out to the wreck, Ford began to giggle weakly.

"We really blew *his* nose for him, huh?"

⬮ ⬮ ⬮

The cab had come to rest upright. Its hatch had been torn away, and the inside was a litter of tumbled trash and spilled coffee that had already frozen. Ford made a step of his hands so Bill could climb up and in.

"I don't see any lug nuts," Ford said, looking at the nearest tire. "How do we get them off?"

"They're not like tractor tires," said Bill crossly, punching buttons on the console. "Crap. All the electronics are fried. There's supposed to be an emergency release, though. Ours is under the console, because it's a Mitsubishi. This is a Toutatis. Let me look around in here . . ."

Ford glanced over his shoulder in the direction in which the dead man lay. He looked back hurriedly and gave an experimental tug at the tire. It felt as immovable as a ten-ton boulder. He reached in and got his arms around it, and pulled as hard as he could.

"I think maybe this is it," said Bill, from inside the cab. "Stand clear, okay?"

Ford let go hastily and tried to scramble away, but the tire shot off the axle as though it had been fired from a cannon.

It caught him in the stomach. He was thrown backward two meters, and fell sprawling on the ground, too winded to groan.

"Dumbass," said Bill, looking down. He jumped from the cab and pushed the tire off Ford. "I *said* stand clear. Why doesn't anybody ever listen to me?"

Ford rolled over, thinking he might have to throw up again. He got painfully to his hands and knees. Bill was already rolling the tire toward Beautiful Evelyn, so Ford struggled to his feet and followed.

He held the tire upright, standing well clear of the axle when Bill fired off the burst one. It shot all the way over to the wreck. Then Bill got back down, and together they lifted the tire up and slammed it into place. They drove down to the road, between two boulders, and turned north again.

●　●　●

"Look, you need to get over it," said Bill, who had been watching Ford. "It's not like you meant to kill him."

"It's not that," said Ford, who was gray-faced and sweating. "My stomach really hurts, is all."

Bill leaned close and looked at him.

"Your psuit says something's wrong," he said.

"It does?" Ford looked down at himself. How had he missed that flashing yellow light? "It's like it's shrinking or something. It's so tight I can almost not breathe."

"We have to stop," said Bill.

"Okay," said Ford. Beautiful Evelyn coasted to a stop and sat there in the middle of the road, as Bill climbed over and stared intently at the diagnostic panel on the front of Ford's psuit. He went pale, but all he said was:

"Let's trade places."

"But you can't drive her," Ford protested.

"If we're on the straightaway and there's no wind, I can sort of drive," said Bill. He dove into the back, as Ford crawled sideways into his seat, and came out a moment later with one of the little tube-bags. "Stick your arm up like *this,* okay?"

Ford obeyed, and watched as Bill plugged the tube into the psuit's port. "So that'll make me feel better?"

"Yeah, it ought to." Bill swung himself into the console seat and sent Beautiful Evelyn trundling on.

"Good." Ford sighed. "What's wrong with me?"

"Psuit says you've ruptured something," said Bill, staring at the monitor. He accelerated.

"Oh. Well, that's not too bad," said Ford, blinking. "Jimmy Linton got a rupture and he's okay. Better than okay, actually. The medic said he couldn't work with a shovel anymore. So . . . they made him official secretary for the Council, see? All he has to do is record stuff at meetings and post notices."

"Really."

"So if I have a rupture, maybe my dad won't take it so hard that I want to be a Hauler. Since that way I get out of working in the methane plant and the cow sheds. Maybe."

Bill gave him an incredulous look.

"All this, and you still want to be a Hauler?"

"Of course I do!"

Bill just shook his head.

☞ ☞ ☞

They drove in a dead calm, at least compared to the weather before. Far off across the plains they saw dust devils here and there, twirling lazily. The farther north they drove, the clearer the air was, the brighter the light of the sun, shining on standing outcroppings of rock the color of rust, or milk chocolate, or tangerines, or new pennies.

"This is so great," said Ford, slurring his words as he spoke. "This is more beautiful than anything. Isn't the world a big place?"

"I guess so," said Bill.

"It's *our* place,' said Ford. "They can all go back to Earth, but we never will. We're Martians."

"Yeah."

"Did you see, I have hair growing in?" Ford swung his hand up to pat his scalp. "Red like Mars."

"Don't move your arm around, dude, okay? You'll rip the tube out."

"Sorry."

"That's all right. Maybe you should mask up, you know? You could probably use the oxygen."

"Sure . . ." Ford dragged his mask into place

After a while, he smiled and said: "I know who I am."

He murmured to himself for a while, muffled behind the mask. The next time Bill glanced over at him, he was unconscious.

And Bill was all alone.

Billy wasn't there to be yelled at, or blamed for anything. He might never be there again. He couldn't be argued with, he couldn't be shamed or ignored or made to feel anything Bill wanted him to feel. Not if he was dead.

But he'd been like that when he'd been alive, too, hadn't he?

The cold straight road stretched out across the cold flat plain, and there was no mercy out here, no right or wrong, no lies. There was only this giant machine hurtling along, that took all Bill's strength to keep on the road.

If he couldn't do it, he'd die.

Bill realized, with a certain shock, how much of his life he'd wanted an audience. Someone else to be a witness to how scared and angry he was, to agree with him on how bad a father Billy had been.

What had he thought? That someday he'd stand up in some

kind of giant courtroom, letting the whole world know how unfair everything had been from the day he'd been born? Out here, he knew the truth.

There was no vast cosmic court of justice that would turn Billy into the kind of father Bill had wanted him to be. There was no Marswife to swoop down from the dust clouds and guide a lost boy home. The red world didn't care if he sulked; it would casually kill him, if it caught him Outside.

And he had always known it.

Then what was the point of being angry about it all the time?

What was the point of white-knuckled fists and a knotted-up stomach if things would never change?

His anger would never force anybody to fix the world for him. But . . .

There were people who tried to fix the world for themselves. Maybe he could fix his world, just the narrow slice of it that was his.

He watched the monitors, watched the wind driving sand across the barren stony plain, the emptiness that he had hated ever since he could remember. What would it take to make him love it, the way Billy or Ford loved it?

He imagined water falling from the sky, bubbling up from under the frozen rock. Maybe it would be blue water. It would splash and steam, the way it did in the bathhouse. Running, gurgling water to drown the dust and irrigate the red sand.

And green would come. He couldn't get a mental image of vizio acres over the whole world, tenting in greenness even up here; that was crazy. But the green might creep out on its own, if there was enough water. Wiry little desert plants at first, maybe, and then . . . Bill tried to remember the names of plants from his lesson plans. Sagebrush, right. Sequoias. Clover. Edelweiss. Apples. A memory came back to him, a nursery rhyme he'd had on his Buke once: *I should like to rise and go, where the golden apples grow . . .*

He blurred his vision a little and saw himself soaring past green rows that went out forever, that arched over and made warm shade and shelter from the wind. Another memory floated up, a picture from a lesson plan, and his dream caught it and slapped it into place: cows grazing in a green meadow, out under a sky full of white clouds, clouds of water, not dust. And, in the most sheltered places, there would be people. Families. Houses lit warm at night, with the lights winking through the green leaves. Just as he had always imagined. One of them would be his house. He'd live there with his family.

Nobody would give him a house, or a family, or a safe world to live in, of course. Ever. They didn't exist. But . . .

Bill wrapped it all around himself anyway, to keep out the cold and the fear, and he drove on.

At some point—hours or days later, he never knew—his strength gave out and he couldn't hold Beautiful Evelyn on the road anymore. She drifted gently to the side, clipping the boulders as she came, and rumbled to a halt just inside Thousand-K Station.

Bill lay along the seat where he had fallen, too tired and in too much pain to move. Ford still sat, propped up in his corner, most of his face hidden by his mask. Bill couldn't tell if he was still alive.

He closed his eyes and went down, and down, into the green rows.

●━●━●

He was awakened by thumping on the cab, and shouting, and was bolt upright with his mask on before he had time to realize that he wasn't dreaming. He crawled across the seat and threw the release switches. The hatch swung down, and red light streamed in out of a black night. There stood Old Brick, granddaddy of the Haulers, with his long beard streaming sideways in the gale and at least three other Haulers behind him. His eyes widened behind his mask as he took in Bill and Ford. He reached up and turned up the volume on his psuit.

"CONVOY! WE GOT KIDS HERE! LOOKS LIKE TOWNSEND'S RIG!"

TEN

Bill was all right after a couple of days, even though he had to have stuff fed into his arm while he slept. He was still foggy-headed when Mother came and sat by his bed, and very gently told him about Billy.

Bill mustn't worry, she said; she would find Billy a warm corner in the Empress, with all the food and drink he wanted the rest of his days, and surely Bill would come talk to him sometimes? For Billy was ever so proud of Young Bill, as everyone knew. And perhaps take him on little walks round the Tubes, so he could see Outside now and again? For Billy had so loved the High Road.

○ ○ ○

Ford wasn't all right. He had to have surgery for a ruptured spleen, and almost bled to death once they'd cut his psuit off him.

He still hadn't regained consciousness when Bill, wrapped in an outsize bathrobe, shuffled down to the infirmary's intensive care unit to see him. *See him* was all Bill could do; pale as an egg, Ford lay in the center of a mass of tubes and plastic tenting. The only parts of him that weren't white were his hair, which was growing in red as Martian sand, and the greenish bruise where Bill had punched him in the eye.

Bill sat there staring at the floor tiles, until he became aware that someone else had entered the room. He looked up.

He knew the man in front of him must be Ford's father; his eyes were the same watery blue, and his ears stuck out the same way. He wore patched denim and muddy boots, and a stocking cap pulled down almost low enough to hide the bandage over his left eyebrow. There was a little white stubble along the line of his jaw, like a light frost.

He looked at Ford, and the watery eyes brimmed over with tears. He glanced uncertainly at Bill. He looked down, lined up the toes of his boots against a seam in the tile.

"You'd be that Hauler's boy, then?" he said. "I have to thank you, on behalf of my Blatchford."

"Blatchford," repeated Bill, dumfounded until he realized whom the old man meant. "Oh."

"That woman explained to me," said Ford's dad. "Wasn't my Blatchford's fault. Poor boy. Don't blame him for running off scared. Your dad did a good thing, taking him in like that. I'm sorry about your dad."

"Me, too," said Bill. "But For—Blatchford'll be all right."

"I know he will," said Ford's dad, looking yearningly at his son. "He's a strong boy, my Blatchford. Not like his brother. You can raise somebody up his whole life and do your best to teach him what's right, and—and overnight, he can just turn into a stranger on you.

"My Sam did that. I should have seen it coming, him walking out on us. He never was any good, really. A weakling.

"Not like my little Blatchford. Never a word of complaint out of *him*, or whining after vanities. *He* knows who he is. He'll make the Collective proud one day."

Bill swallowed hard. He knew Ford would never make the Collective proud; Ford would be off on the High Road as soon as he could, in love with the wide horizon, and the old man's angry heart would break again.

The weight of everything that had happened seemed to come crashing down on Bill at once. He couldn't remember when he'd felt so miserable.

"Would you tell me something, sir?" he said. "What does it take to join the MAC?"

"Hm?" Ford's dad turned.

"What do you have to do?"

Ford's dad looked at him speculatively. He cleared his throat. "It isn't what you do. It's what you *are,* young man."

He came and sat down beside Bill, and threw back his shoulders.

"You have to be the kind of person who believes a better world is worth working for. You can't be weak, or afraid, or greedy for things for yourself. You have to know the only thing that matters is making that better world, and making it for everyone, not just for you.

"You may not even get to see it come into existence, because making the world right is hard work. It'll take all your strength and all your bravery, and maybe you'll be left at the end with nothing but knowing that you did your duty.

"But that'll be enough for you."

His voice was thin and harsh; he sounded as though he was reciting a lecture he'd memorized. But his eyes shone like Ford's had, when Ford had looked out on the open sky for the first time.

"Well—I'm going to study agriculture," said Bill. "And I thought, maybe, when I pass my levels, I'd like to join the MAC. I want that world you talk about. It's all I've ever wanted."

"Good on you, son," said Ford's dad, nodding solemnly. "You study hard, and I'm sure you'd be welcome to join us. You're the sort of young man we need in the MAC. And it does my heart good to know my Blatchford's got a friend like you. Gives me hope for the future, to think we'll have two heroes like you working in our cause!"

He shook Bill's hand, and then the nurse looked in at them and said visiting hours were over. Ford's dad went away, down the hill. Bill walked slowly back to his room.

He didn't climb back into bed. He sat down in a chair in the corner, and looked out through Settlement Dome at the cold red desert, at the far double line of boulders where the High Road ran off into places Billy would never see again. He began to cry, silently, tears burning as they ran down his face.

He didn't know whether he was crying for Billy, or for Ford's dad.

The world was ending. The world was beginning.

A BILLION EVES

by Robert Reed

Robert Reed was born in Omaha, Nebraska, in 1956. He has a bachelor of science degree in Biology from the Nebraska Wesleyan University, and has worked as a lab technician. He became a full-time writer in 1987, the same year he won the L. Ron Hubbard Writers of the Future Contest, and has published eleven novels, including The Leeshore, The Hormone Jungle, *and the far future science fiction novels* Marrow *and* The Well of Stars. *An extraordinarily prolific writer, Reed has published over 140 short stories, mostly in* Fantasy & Science Fiction *and* Asimov's, *which have been nominated for the Hugo, James Tiptree Jr. Memorial, Locus, Nebula, Seiun, Theodore Sturgeon Memorial, and World Fantasy awards, and have been collected in* The Dragons of Springplace *and* The Cuckoo's Boys. *His most recent book is the novella* Flavors of My Genius. *Nebraska's only SF writer, Reed lives in Lincoln with his wife and daughter, and is an ardent long-distance runner.*

1

Kala's parents were thrifty, impractical people. They deplored spending money, particularly on anything that smacked of luxury or indulgence; yet, at the same time, they suffered from big dreams and a crippling inability to set responsible goals.

One spring evening, Father announced, "We should take a long drive this summer."

"To where?" Mom asked warily.

"Into the mountains," he answered. "Just like we've talked about doing a thousand times."

"But can we afford it?"

"If we count our coins, and if the fund drive keeps doing well. Why not?" First Day celebrations had just finished, and their church, which prided itself on its responsible goals, was having a successful year. "A taste of the wilderness," he cried out at the dinner table. "Doesn't that sound fun?"

To any other family, that would have been the beginning of a wonderful holiday. But Kala knew better. Trouble arrived as soon as they began drawing up lists of destinations. Her brother Sandor demanded a day or two spent exploring the canyon always named Grand. Father divulged an unsuspected fondness for the sleepy, ice-caked volcanoes near the Mother Ocean. When pressed, Kala admitted that she would love walking a beach beside the brackish Mormon Sea. And while Mom didn't particularly care about scenery—a point made with a distinctly superior tone—she mentioned having five sisters scattered across the West. They couldn't travel through that country and not stop at each of their front doors, if only to quickly pay their respects.

Suddenly their objectives filled a long piece of paper, and even an eleven-year-old girl could see what was obvious: Just the driving was going to choke their vacation. Worse still, Mom announced, "There's no reason to pay strangers to cook for us. We'll bring our own food." That meant dragging a bulky cooler everywhere they went, and every meal would be sloppy sandwiches, and every day would begin with a hunt for fresh ice and cheap groceries to replace the supplies that would inevitably spoil.

Not wanting to be out-cheaped by his wife, Father added, "And we'll be camping, of course." But how could they camp? They didn't have equipment. "Oh, we have our sleeping sacks," he reminded his doubting daughter. "And I'll borrow gear from our friends at church. I'm sure I can. So don't worry. It's going to be wonderful! We'll just drive as far as we want every day and pull over at nightfall. Just so long as it costs nothing to pitch a tent."

To Kala, this seemed like an impossible, doomed journey. Too many miles had to be conquered, too many wishes granted, and even under the best circumstances, nobody would end up happy.

"Why don't you guys ever learn?" Kala muttered.

"What was that, darling?"

"Nothing, Father," she replied with a minimal bow. "Nothing."

● ● ●

Yet luck occasionally smiles, particularly on the most afflicted souls. They were still a couple hundred miles from the mountains when the radiator hose burst. Suddenly the hot July air was filled with hissing steam and the sweet taste of antifreeze. Father invested a few moments cursing God and the First Father before he pulled onto the shoulder. "Stay inside," he ordered. Then he climbed out and lifted the long hood with a metallic screech, breathing deeply before vanishing into the swirling, superheated cloud.

Sandor wanted to help. He practically begged Mom for the chance. But she shot a warning stare back at him, saying, "No, young father. You're staying with me. It's dangerous out there!"

"It's not," Kala's brother maintained.

But an instant later, as if to prove Mom correct, Father cried out. He screamed twice. The poor man had burned his right hand with the scalding water. And as if to balance his misery, he then blindly reached out with his left hand, briefly touching the overheated engine block.

"Are you all right?" Mom called out.

Father dropped the hood and stared in through the windshield, pale as a tortoise egg and wincing in misery.

"Leave that hood open," Sandor shouted. "Just a crack!"

"Why?" the burnt man asked.

"To let the air blow through and cool the engine," the boy explained. He wasn't two years older than Kala, but unlike either parent, Sandor had a pragmatic genius for machinery and other necessities of life. Leaning toward his little sister, he said, "If we're lucky, all we'll need is a new hose and fluid."

But we aren't lucky people, she kept thinking.

They had left home on the Friday Sabbath, which meant that most of the world was closed for business. Yet despite Kala's misgivings, this proved to be an exceptional day: Father drove their wounded car back to the last intersection, and through some uncommon fluke, they found a little fix-it and fuel shop that was open. A burly old gentleman welcomed them with cornbread and promises of a quick repair. He gave Father a medicating salve and showed the women a new Lady's Room in back, out of sight of the highway. But there wasn't any reason to hide. Mom had her children late in life, and besides, she'd let herself get heavy over the last few years. And Kala was still wearing a little girl's body, her face soon to turn lovely, but camouflaged for the moment with youth and a clumsy abundance of sharp bone.

Sharing the public room, the mother and daughter finished their cornbread while their men stood in the garage, staring at the hot, wet engine.

Despite being the Sabbath, the traffic was heavy—freight trucks and tiny cars and everything between. Traveling men and a few women bought fuel and sweet drinks. The women were always quick to pay and eager to leave; most were nearly as old as Mom, but where was the point in taking chances? The male customers lingered, and the fix-it man seemed to relish their company, discussing every possible subject with each of them. The weather was a vital topic, as were sports teams and the boring district news. A glum little truck driver argued that the world was already too crowded and cluttered for his tastes, and the old gentleman couldn't agree more. Yet the next customer was a happy salesman, and, in front of him, the fix-it man couldn't stop praising their wise government and the rapid expansion of the population.

Kala mentioned these inconsistencies to her mother.

She shrugged them off, explaining, "He's a businessman, darling. He dresses his words for the occasion."

Kala's bony face turned skeptical. She had always been the smartest student at her Lady's Academy. But she was also a serious, nearly humorless creature, and perhaps because of that, she always felt too sure of herself. In any situation, she believed there was one answer that was right, only one message worth giving, and the good person held her position against all enemies. "I'd never dress up my words," she vowed. "Not one way or the other."

"Why am I not surprised?" Mom replied, finding some reason to laugh.

Kala decided to be politely silent, at least for the present time. She listened to hymns playing on the shop's radio, humming along with her favorites. She studied her favorite field guide to the native flora and fauna, preparing herself for the wilderness to come. The surrounding countryside was as far removed from wilderness as possible—level and open, green corn stretching to every horizon and a few junipers planted beside the highway as windbreaks. Sometimes Kala would rise from her chair and wander around the little room. The shop's moneybox was locked and screwed into the top of a long plastic cabinet. Old forms and paid bills were stacked in a dusty corner. A metal door led back into the Lady's Room, opened for the moment but ready to be slammed shut and locked with a bright steel bolt. Next to that door was a big sheet of poster board covered with photographs of young women. Several dozen faces smiled toward the cameras. Returning to her chair, Kala commented on how many girls that was.

Her mother simply nodded, making no comment.

After her next trip around the room, Kala asked, "Were all of those girls taken?"

"Hardly," Mom replied instantly, as if she was waiting for the question. "Probably most are runaways. Bad homes and the wrong friends, and now they're living on the street somewhere. Only missing."

Kala considered that response. Only missing? But that seemed worse than being taken from this world. Living on the street, without home or family—that sounded like a horrible fate. Guessing her daughter's mind, Mom added, "Either way, you're never going to live their lives." Of course she wouldn't; Kala had no doubt about that.

Sandor appeared abruptly, followed by Father. Together they delivered the very bad news. Their old car needed a lot of work. A critical gasket was failing, and something was horribly wrong in the transmission. Repairs would take time and most of their money, which was a big problem. Or maybe not. Father had already given this matter some thought. The closest mountains weren't more than three hours away. Forced into a rational corner, he suggested camping in just one location. A base camp, if you would. This year, they couldn't visit the Grand Canyon or the Mormon Sea, much less enjoy the company of distant sisters. But they could spend ten lazy days in the high country, then return home with a few coins still rattling in their pockets.

Mom bowed to her husband, telling him, "It's your decision, dear."

"Then that's what we'll do," he said, borrowing a map from the counter. "I'll find a good place to pitch the tent. All right?"

Full of resolve, the men once again left. But Mom remained nervous, sitting forward in her chair—a heavy woman in matronly robes, her hair grayer than ever, thick fingers moving while her expression was stiff and unchanging.

Kala wanted to ask about her thoughts. Was she disappointed not to see her sisters? Or was she feeling guilty? Unless of course Mom was asking herself what else could be wrong with a car they had bought for almost nothing and done nothing to maintain.

The sudden deep hissing of brakes interrupted the silence. A traveler had pulled off the highway, parking beside the most distant gas pump. Kala saw the long sky-blue body and thought of a school bus. But the school's old name had been sanded off, the windows in the front covered with iron bars, while the back windows were sealed with plywood. She knew exactly what the bus was. Supplies were stuffed in the back, she reasoned. And a lot more gear was tied up on the roof—bulky sacks running its full length, secured with ropes and rubber straps and protected from any rain with yellowing pieces of thick plastic.

A man stepped out into the midday glare. He wasn't young, or old. The emerald green shirt and black collar marked him as a member of the Church of Eden. Two pistols rode high on his belt. He looked handsome and strong, and, in ways Kala couldn't quite define, he acted competent in all matters important. After glancing up and down the highway, he stared into the open garage. Then he pulled out a keychain and locked the bus door, and he fed the gas nozzle into the big fuel tank, jamming in every possible drop.

Once again, the fix-it man had stopped working on their car.

But unlike the other interruptions, he started to walk out toward the pump, a long wrench in one hand. The always-friendly face was gone. What replaced it wasn't unfriendly, but there was a sense of caution, and perhaps a touch of disapproval.

"No, sir," the younger gentleman called out. "I'll come in and pay."

"You don't have to—"

"Yeah, I do. Keep your distance now."

The fix-it man stopped walking, and after a moment, he turned and retreated. The younger man hit the bus door once with the flat of his hand, shouting, "Two minutes."

By then, everybody had moved to the public room. Father glanced at the Lady's Room but then decided it wasn't necessary. He took his position behind Mom's chair, his sore red hands wrapped in gauze. Sandor hovered beside Kala. The fix-it man stood behind the counter, telling the women, "Don't worry," while opening a cupboard and pulling something heavy into position.

"It was a gun," Sandor later told his sister. "I caught a glimpse. A little splattergun. Loaded and ready, I would bet."

"But why?" Kala would wonder aloud.

"Because that green-shirt was leaving us," her brother reminded her. "Where he was going, there's no fix-it shops. No tools, no law. So what if he tried to steal a box of wrenches, you know?"

Maybe. But the man had acted more worried about them, as if he was afraid somebody would try to steal his prized possessions. Entering the room carefully, he announced, "My brother's still onboard."

"Good for him," said the fix-it man.

"How much do I owe?"

"Twenty and a third."

"Keep the change," he said, handing over two bills. The green-shirted man tried to smile, only it was a pained, forced grin. "Tell me, old man: Anybody ask about me today?"

"Like who?"

"Or anybody mention a bus looking like mine? Any gentlemen come by and inquire if you've seen us . . . ?"

The fix-it man shook his head, nothing like a smile on his worn face. "No, sir. Nobody's asked about you or your bus."

"Good." The green-shirted man yanked more money from the roll, setting it on the plastic countertop. "There's a blonde kid. If he stops by and asks . . . do me a favor? Don't tell him anything, but make him think you know shit."

The fix-it man nodded.

"He'll give you money for your answers. Take all you can. And then tell him I went north from here. Up the Red Highway to Paradise. You heard me say that. 'North to Paradise.'"

"But you're going somewhere else, I believe."

"Oh, a little ways." Laughing, the would-be Father turned and started back to his bus. That's when Sandor asked, "Do you really have one?"

"Quiet," Father cautioned.

But the green-shirted man felt like smiling. He turned and looked at the thirteen-year-old-boy, asking, "Why? You interested in these things?"

"Sure I am."

Laughing, the man said, "I bet you are."

Sandor was small for his age, but he was bold and very smart about many subjects, and in circumstances where most people would feel afraid, he was at his bravest best. "A little Class D, is it?"

That got the man to look hard at him. "You think so?"

"Charged and ready," Sandor guessed. He named three possible manufacturers, and then said, "You've set it up in the aisle, I bet. Right in the middle of the bus."

"Is that how I should do it?"

"The rip-zone reaches out what? Thirty, thirty-five feet? Which isn't all that big."

"Big enough," said the man.

Just then, someone else began pulling on the bus horn. Maybe it was the unseen brother. Whoever it was, the horn was loud and insistent.

"You're not taking livestock," Kala's brother observed.

This time, Mom told Sandor to be quiet, and she even lifted a hand, as if to give him a pop on the head.

"Hedge-rabbits," the man said. "And purple-hens."

Both parents now said, "Quiet."

The horn honked again.

But the green-shirted man had to ask, "How would you do it, little man? If you were in my boots?"

"A Class-B ripper, at least," Sandor declared. "And I'd take better animals, too. Milking animals. And wouldn't bother with my brother, if I had my choice."

"By the looks of it, you don't have a brother."

"So how many of them do you have?" Sandor asked. Just the tone of his voice told what he was asking. "Six?" he guessed. "Eight? Or is it ten?"

"Shush," Mom begged.

The green-shirted man said nothing.

"I'm just curious," the boy continued, relentlessly focused on the subject at hand. "Keep your gene pool as big as possible. That's what everybody says. In the books, they claim that's a good guarantee for success."

The man shook his longest finger at Sandor. "Why, little man? You think I should take along another? Just to be safe?"

In an instant, the room grew hot and tense.

The green-shirted man looked at both women. Then with a quiet, furious voice, he snarled, "Lucky for you ladies, I don't have any more seats." Then he turned and strode out to the bus and unlocked the door, vanishing inside as somebody else hurriedly drove the long vehicle away from the pump.

For several moments, everybody was enjoying hard, deep breaths.

Then the fix-it man said, "I see a pretty miserable future for that idiot."

"That's not any way to leave," Father agreed. "Can you imagine making a life for yourself with just that little pile of supplies?"

"Forget about him," Mom demanded. "Talk about anything else."

Alone, Kala returned to the poster displaying photographs of all the lost women. It occurred to her that one or two of those faces could have been onboard the bus, and perhaps not by their own choice. But she also understood that no one here was going to call the proper authorities. The men would throw their insults at the would-be Father, and Mom would beg for a change in topics. But no one mentioned the idiot's poor wives. Even when Kala touched the prettiest faces and read their tiny biographies, it didn't occur to her that some strong brave voice should somehow find the words to complain.

2

No figure in history was half as important as the First Father. He was the reason why humans had come to this fine world, and every church owed its existence to him. Yet the man remained mysterious and elusive—an unknowable presence rooted deep in time and in the imagination. No two faiths ever drew identical portraits of their founder. A traditional biography was common to all schoolbooks, but what teachers offered was rather different from what a bright girl might find on the shelves of any large library. The truth was that the man was an enigma, and when it came to his story, almost everything was possible. The only common features were that he was born on the Old Earth in the last days of the twentieth century, and, on a Friday morning in spring, when he was a little more than twenty-nine years of age, the First Father claimed his destiny.

Humans had only recently built the first rippers. The machines were brutal, ill-tempered research tools, and physicists were using them to punch temporary holes in the local reality. Most of those holes led to hard vacuums and a fabulous cold; empty space is the standard state throughout most of the multiverse. But quantum effects and topological harmonics showed the way: If the ripper cut its hole along one of the invisible dimensions, an island of stability was waiting. The island had separated from the Now two billion years ago, and on the other side of that hole were an infinite number of sister-earths, each endowed with the same motions and mass of the human earth.

Suddenly every science had a fierce interest in the work. Large schools and small nations had to own rippers. Biologists retrieved microscopic samples of air and soil, each sample contaminated with bacteria and odd spores. Every species was new, but all shared the ingredients of earth-life: DNA coded for the same few amino acids that built families of proteins that were not too unlike those found inside people and crabgrass.

The Creation was a tireless, boundless business. That's what human beings were learning. And given the proper tool and brief jolts of titanic energy, it was possible to reach into those infinite realms, examining a minuscule portion of the endlessness.

But rippers had a second, more speculative potential. If the same terrific energies were focused in a slightly different fashion, the hole would shift its shape and nature. That temporary disruption of space would spread along the three easiest dimensions, engulfing the machine and local landscape in a plasmatic bubble, and that bubble would act like a ship, carrying its cargo across a gap that was nearly too tiny to measure and too stubborn to let any normal matter pass.

Whoever he was, the First Father understood what rippers could do. Most churches saw him as a visionary scientist, while the typical historian thought he was too young for that role, describing him instead as a promising graduate student. And there were always a few dissenting voices claiming that he was just a laboratory technician or something of that ilk—a little person armed with just enough knowledge to be useful, as well as access to one working ripper.

Unnoticed, the First Father had absconded with a set of superconductive batteries, and, over the course of weeks and months, he secretly filled them with enough energy to illuminate a city. He also purchased or stole large quantities of supplies, including seeds and medicines, assorted tools, and enough canned goods to feed a hundred souls for months. Working alone, he crammed the supplies into a pair of old freight trucks, and, on the perfect night in April, he drove the trucks to a critical location, parking beside No Parking signs and setting their brakes and then flattening their tires. A third truck had to be maneuvered down the loading dock beside the physics laboratory, and, using keys or passwords, the young man gained access to one of the most powerful rippers on the planet—a bundle of electronics and bottled null-spaces slightly larger than a coffin.

The young man rolled or carried his prize into the vehicle, and with quick, well-rehearsed motions, he patched it into the fully charged batteries and spliced in fresh software. Then before anyone noticed, he gunned the truck's motor, driving off into the darkness.

Great men are defined by their great, brave deeds; every worthy faith recognizes this unimpeachable truth.

According to most accounts, the evening was exceptionally warm, wet with dew, and promising a beautiful day. At four in the morning, the First Father scaled a high curb and inched his way across a grassy front yard, slipping between an oak tree and a ragged spruce before parking tight against his target—a long white building decorated with handsome columns and black letters pulled from a dead language. Then he turned off the engine, and perhaps for a moment or two, he sat motionless. But no important doubts crept into his brave skull. Alone, he climbed down and opened the back door and turned on the stolen ripper, and, with a few buttons pushed, he let the capacitors eat the power needed to fuel a string of nanosecond bursts.

Many accounts of that night have survived; no one knows which, if any, are genuine. When Kala was eleven, her favorite story was about a young student who was still awake at that early hour, studying hard for a forgotten examination. The girl thought it was odd to hear the rumbling of a diesel motor and then the rattling of a metal door. But her room was at the back of the sorority house; she couldn't see anything but the parking lot and a tree-lined alley. What finally caught her attention was the ripper's distinctive whine—a shriek almost too high for the human ear—punctuated with a series of hard little explosions. Fresh holes were being carved in the multiverse, exposing the adjacent worlds. Tiny breaths of air were retrieved, each measured against a set of established parameters. Hearing the blasts, the girl stood and stepped to her window. And that's when the ripper paused for a moment, a hundred trillion calculations made before it fired again. The next *pop* sounded like thunder. Every light went out, and the campus vanished, and a sphere of ground and grass, air and wood was wrenched free of one world. The full length of the house was taken, and its entire yard, as well as both supply trucks and the street in front of the house and the parking lot and a piece of the alley behind it. And emerging out of nothingness was a new world—a second glorious offering from God, Our Ultimate Father. The girl was the only witness to a historic event, which was why the young Kala found her tale so appealing.

The First Father saw nothing. At the pivotal moment of his life, he was hunkered over the stolen ripper, reading data and receiving prompts from the AI taskmaster. The girl started to run. By most accounts she was a stocky little creature, not pretty but fearless and immodest. Half-dressed, she dashed through the darkened house, screaming for the other girls to wake up, then diving down the stairs and out the front door. Kala loved the fact that here was the first human being to take a deep breath on another earth. The air was thick and unsatisfying. Out from the surrounding darkness came living sounds. Strange creatures squawked and hollered, and flowing branches waved in a thin moonlight. The girl thought to look at the sky, and she was rewarded with more stars than she had ever seen in her life. (Every sister world is a near-twin, as are the yellow sun and battered moon. But the movement of the solar system is a highly chaotic business, and you never know where inside the Milky Way you might end up.) Standing on sidewalk, the girl slowly absorbed the astonishing scene. Then she heard pounding, and, when she turned, she saw the long truck parked against a tangle of juniper shrubs. On bare feet, she climbed into the back end and over a stack of cold black batteries. The First Father was too busy to notice her. One job was finished, but another essential task needed his undivided attention. Having brought a hundred young women to an empty, barely livable world, the man had no intention of letting anyone escape now. Which was why he wrenched open the hot ripper, exposing its intricate guts, and why he was using a crowbar to batter its weakest systems—too consumed by his work to notice one of his future wives standing near him, wearing nothing but pants and a bra and a slightly mesmerized expression.

3

For more than a week, Kala's family lived inside a borrowed tent, and without doubt, they never enjoyed a better vacation than this. The campground was a rough patch of public land set high on a mountainside. Scattered junipers stood on the sunny ground and dense spruce woods choked an adjacent canyon. A stream was tucked inside the canyon, perfect for swimming and baths. A herd of semi-tame roodeer grazed where they wanted. Rilly birds and starlings greeted each morning with songs and hard squawks. Their tent was in poor condition, ropes missing and its roof ripped and then patched by clumsy hands. But a heat wave erased any danger of rain, and, even after the hottest days, nights turned pleasantly chilly, illuminated by a moon that was passing through full.

Kala was the perfect age for adventures like these: Young enough to remember everything, yet old enough to explore by herself. Because this wasn't a popular destination, the woods felt as if they belonged to her. And best of all, higher in the mountains was a sprawling natural reserve.

Where her brother loved machinery, Kala adored living creatures.

By law, the reserve was supposed to be a pristine wilderness. No species brought into this world could live behind its high fences. But of course starlings flew where they wanted, and goldweed spores wandered on the softest wind, and even the best intentions of visitors didn't prevent people from bringing seeds stuck to their clothing or weaknesses tucked into their hearts.

One morning they drove into the high alpine country—a risky adventure, since their car still ran hot and leaked antifreeze. The highway was narrow and forever twisting. A shaggy black forest of native trees gave way to clouds, damp and cold. Father slowed until the following drivers began to pull on their horns, and then he sped up again, emerging onto a tilted, rock-strewn landscape where black fur grew beside last winter's snow. Scenic pullouts let them stop and marvel at an utterly alien world. Kala and her brother made snowballs and gamely posed for pictures on the continental divide. Then Father turned them around and drove even slower through the clouds and black forest. In the same instant, everyone announced: "I'm hungry!" And because this was a magical trip, a clearing instantly appeared, complete with a wide glacial stream and a red granite table built specifically for them.

Lunch was tortoise sandwiches and sour cherries. The clouds were thickening, and there were distant rumblings of thunder. But if there was rain, it fell somewhere else. Kala sat backwards at the table, smelling the stream and the light peppery stink of the strange trees. Despite a lifetime spent reading books and watching documentaries, she was unprepared for this divine place. It was an endless revelation, the idea that here lived creatures that had ruled this world until the arrival of humans. If the local climate had been warmer and the soil better, this reserve couldn't have survived. She was blessed. In ways new to her, the girl felt happy. Gazing into the shadows, she imagined native rock-lambs and tomb-tombs and the lumbering Harry's-big-days. In her daily life, the only animals were those that came with the Last Father— the roodeer and starlings and such. And their crops and a few hundred species of wild plants came here as seeds and spores that people had intentionally carried along. But these great old mountains wore a different order, a fresh normalcy. The shaggy black forest looked nothing like spruce trees, bearing a lovely useless wood too soft to be used as lumber, and always too wet to burn.

A narrow form suddenly slipped from one shadow to the next.

What could that have been?

Kala rose slowly. Her brother was immersed in a fat adventure novel. Her parents glanced her way, offering smiles before returning to the subject at hand: What, if anything, would they do with the afternoon and evening? With a stalker's pace, Kala moved into the forest—into the cool spicy delicious air—and then she paused again, eyes unblinking, her head cocked to one side while she listened to the deep booming of thunder as it curled around the mountain flanks.

A dry something touched Kala on the back of the calf.

She flinched, looking down.

The housefly launched itself, circling twice before settling on her bare arm. Kala never liked to kill, but this creature didn't belong here. It was one of the creatures humans always brought—by chance, originally, and now cherished because maggots could be useful disposing of trash. With the palm of her right hand, she managed to stun the creature, and then she knelt, using eyes and fingers to find its fallen body, two fingertips crushing the vermin to an anonymous paste.

Sitting nearby, studying Kala, was a wild cat. She noticed it as she stood again—a big male tabby, well fed and complacent, caught in a large wire trap. Cat-shaped signs were posted across the reserve, warning visitors about feral predators. These animals were ecological nightmares. During its life, a single killing machine could slaughter thousands of the native wisp-mice and other delicate species; and a male cat was the worst, since it could also father dozens of new vermin that would only spread the carnage.

Kala approached the cat, knelt down and looked into its bright green eyes. Except for the tangled fur, nothing about the animal looked especially wild. When she offered her hand, the cat responded by touching her fingertips with the cool end of its nose. Exotics like this were always killed. No exceptions. But maybe she could catch it and take it home. If she begged hard enough, how could her parents refuse? Kala studied the mechanism of the trap and found a strong stick and slipped it into a gap, and then with a hard shove, she forced the steel door to pop open. The cat had always been wild, and it knew what to do. As soon as the door vanished, Kala reached for its neck, but her quarry was quicker. It sprinted back into the dark shadows, leaving behind a young girl to think many thoughts, but mostly feeling guilt mixed with a tenacious, unexpected relief.

"Find anything?" Father asked on her return.

"Nothing," she lied.

"Next time," he advised, "take the camera."

"We haven't seen a tomb-tombs yet," her mother added. "Before we leave, I'd like to have a close look at them."

Kala sat beside her brother, and he glanced up from his book, investing a few moments watching her as she silently finished her sandwich.

Later that day, they visited a tiny museum nestled in a wide black meadow. Like favored students on a field trip, they wandered from exhibit to exhibit, absorbing little bits of knowledge about how these mountains were built and why the glaciers had come and gone again. Display cases were jammed with fossils, and in the basement were artifacts marking these last centuries when humans played their role. But the memorable heart of the day was a stocky, homely woman who worked for the reserve—a strong, raspy-voiced lady wearing a drab brown uniform complete with a wide-brimmed hat and fat pockets and an encyclopedic knowledge on every imaginable subject.

Her job was to lead tourists along the lazy trail that circled her museum grounds. Her practiced voice described this world as well as each of its known neighbors. From the First Father to the Last, seventeen examples of the Creation had been settled, while another fifty worlds had been visited but found unsuitable. The Old Earth and its sisters belonged to one endless family, each world sharing the same essential face: There was always a Eurasia and Africa, an Australia and two Americas. The North Pole was water, while islands or a single continent lay on the South Pole. Except for the fickle effects of erosion, landmasses were constant. Two billion years of separation wasn't enough to make any earth forget which family it belonged to.

But where stone and tectonics were predictable, other qualities were not. Minuscule factors could shift climates or the composition of an atmosphere. Some earths were wet and warm. Kala's earth, for instance. Most had similar atmospheres, but none were identical to any other. A few earths were openly inhospitable to humanity. Oxygen cycles and methane cycles were famously temperamental. Sometimes life generated enough greenhouse gas to scorch the land, lifting the oceans into a cloudborn biosphere. Other earths had been permanently sterilized by impacting comets or passing supernovae. Yet those traps were easy to spot with a working ripper; little bites of air warned the Fathers about the most deadly places. What the woman lecturer discussed, and in astonishing depth, were worlds that only seemed inviting. Everyone knew examples from history. After a hard year or two, or in the case of Mattie's House, a full ten years of misery, the reigning Father had realized there was no hope, and, gathering up his pioneers, he used the ripper's remaining power to leap to another, more favorable world.

"We have a wonderful home," the woman declared, leaning against one of the native trees. "A long Ice Age has just released this land, giving us a favorable climate. And the northern soils have been bulldozed to the warm south, making the black ground we always name Iowa and Ohio and Ukraine."

Her praise of their world earned grateful nods from tourists.

"And we're blessed in having so much experience," she continued. "Our ancestors learned long ago what to bring and how to adapt. Our culture is designed to grow quickly, and by every measure. Ten centuries is not a long time—not to a world or even to a young species like ours—but that's all the time we needed here to make a home for five billion of us." Smiles rode the nodding faces.

"But we're most blessed in this way," she said. Then she paused, letting her wise old eyes take their measure of her audience. "We are awfully lucky because this world is extremely weak. For reasons known and reasons only guessed at, natural selection took its sweet time here. These native life forms are roughly equivalent to the First Earth during its long ago Permian. The smartest tomb-tombs isn't smart at all. And as any good Father knows, intelligence is the first quality to measure when you arrive at a new home."

Kala noticed the adults' approval. Here was the central point; the woman was speaking to the young men in her audience, giving them advice should they ever want to become a Father. One hand lifted, begging to be seen.

"Yes, sir," said the lecturer. "A question?"

"I could ask a question, I suppose." The hand belonged to an elderly gentleman with the pale brown eyes of the First Father as well as his own thick mane of white hair. "Mostly, I was going to offer my observations. This morning, I was hiking the trail to Passion Lake—"

"A long walk," the woman interjected, perhaps trying to compliment his endurance.

"I was bitten by mosquitoes," he announced. "Nothing new

about that, I suppose. And I saw rilly birds nesting in one of your false-spruces." The rillies were native to the Second Father's world. "And I'm quite sure I saw mice—our mice—in the undergrowth. Which looked an awful lot like oleo-weed when it's gone wild."

Oleo-weed was from the First Father's world, and it had been a human companion for the last twenty thousand years.

The lecturer adjusted her big-brimmed hat as she nodded, acting unperturbed. "We have a few exotics on the reserve," she agreed. "Despite our rules and restrictions—"

"Is this right?" the white-haired man interrupted.

"Pardon me?"

"Right," he repeated. "Correct. Responsible. What we are doing here . . . is it worth the damage done to a helpless planet . . . ?"

More than anything, the audience was either puzzled by his attitude or completely indifferent. Half of the tourists turned away, pretending to take a burning interest in random rocks or the soft peculiar bark of the trees.

The lecturer pulled the mountain air across her teeth. "There are estimates," she began. "I'm sure everybody here has seen the figures. The First Father was the first pioneer, but he surely wasn't the only one to lead people away from the Old Earth. Yet even if you count only that one man and his wives, and if you make a conservative estimate of how many Fathers sprang up from that first world . . . and then you assume that half of those Fathers built homes filled with young people and their own wandering hearts . . . that means that by now, millions of colony worlds have been generated by that first example. And each of those millions might have founded another million or so worlds—"

"An exponential explosion," the man interjected.

"Inside an endless Creation, as we understand these things." She spoke with a grim delight. "No limit to the worlds, no end to the variety. And why shouldn't humanity claim as much of that infinity as he can?"

"Then I suppose all of this has to be moral," the white-haired man added, the smile pleasant but his manner sarcastic. "I guess my point is, madam . . . you and those like you are eventually going to discover yourselves without employment. Because there will be a day, and soon, when this lovely ground is going to look like every other part of our world, thick with the same weeds and clinging creatures we know best, and exactly the same as the twenty trillion other human places."

"Yes," said the woman, her satisfaction obvious. "That is the future, yes."

The lecturer wasn't looking at Kala, but every word felt as if it had been aimed her way. For the first time in her life, she saw an inevitable future. She loved this alien forest, but it couldn't last. An endless doom lay over the landscape, and she wanted to weep. Even her brother noticed her pain, smiling warily while he asked, "What the hell is wrong with you?"

She couldn't say. She didn't know how to define her mind's madness. Yet afterwards, making the journey back to the parking lot, she thought again of that wildcat; and with a fury honest and pure, she wished that she had left the creature inside that trap. Or better, that she had used that long stick of hers and beaten it to death.

4

The most devoted wives left behind written accounts of their adventures on the new world—the seven essential books in the First Father's Testament. Quite a few churches also included the two Sarah diaries, while the more progressive faiths, such as the one Kala's family belonged to, made room for the Six Angry Wives. Adding to the confusion were the dozens if not hundreds of texts and fragmentary accounts left behind by lesser-known voices, as well as those infamous documents generally regarded to be fictions at best, and, at worst, pure heresies.

When Kala was twelve, an older girl handed her a small, cat-eared booklet. "I didn't give this to you," the girl warned. "Read it and then give it to somebody else, or burn it. Promise me?"

"I promise."

Past Fathers had strictly forbidden this testament, but someone always managed to smuggle at least one copy to the next world. *The First Mother's Tale* was said to be a third-person account of Claire, the fifty-year-old widow whose job it had been to watch over the sorority house and its precious girls. Claire was a judicious, pragmatic woman—qualities missing in her own mother, Kala realized sadly. On humanity's most important day, the housemother woke to shouts and wild weeping. She threw on a bathrobe and stepped into slippers before leaving her private ground-floor apartment. Urgent arms grabbed her up and dragged her down a darkened hallway. A dozen terrified voices were rambling on about some horrible disaster. The power was out, Claire noticed. Yet she couldn't find any trace of cataclysms. The house walls were intact. There was no obvious fire or flood. Whatever the disturbance, it had been so minor that even the framed photographs of Delta sisters were still neatly perched on their usual nails.

Then Claire stepped out the front door, and hesitated. Two long trucks were parked in the otherwise empty street. But where was the campus? Past the trucks, exactly where the Fine Arts building should be, a rugged berm had been made of gray dirt and gray stone and shattered tree trunks. Beyond the berm was a forest of strange willowy trees. Nameless odors and a dense gray mist were drifting out of the forest on a gentle wind. And illuminated by the moon and endless stars was a flock of leathery creatures, perched together on the nearest limbs, hundreds of simple black eyes staring at the newcomers.

The First Father was sitting halfway down the front steps, a deer rifle cradled in his lap, a box of ammunition between his feet, hands trembling while the pale brown eyes stared out at the first ruddy traces of the daylight.

Women were still emerging from every door, every fire escape. Alone and in little groups, they would wander to the edge of their old world, the bravest ones climbing the berm to catch a glimpse of the strange landscape before retreating again, gathering together on the damp lawn while staring at the only man in their world.

Claire pulled her robe tight and walked past the First Father.

No life could have prepared her for that day, yet she found the resolve to smile in a believable fashion, offering encouraging words and calculated hugs. She told her girls that everything would be fine. She promised they'd be home again in time for classes. Then she turned her attentions to the third truck. It was parked beside the house, its accordion door raised and its loading ramp dropped to the grass. Claire climbed the ramp and stared at the strange, battered machinery inside. The young woman who had heard the ripper in operation—the only witness to their leap across invisible dimensions—was telling her story to her sisters, again and again. Claire listened. Then she gathered the handful of physics majors and asked if the ripper was authentic. It was. Could it really do these awful things? Absolutely. Claire inhaled deeply and hugged herself, then asked if there was any possible way, with everything they knew and the tools at hand, that this awful-looking damage could be fixed?

No, it couldn't be. And even if there was some way to patch it up, nobody here would ever see home again.

"Why not?" Claire asked, refusing to give in. "Maybe not with this ripper-machine, no. But why not build a new one with the good parts here and new components that we make ourselves . . . ?"

One young woman was an honor student—a senior ready to graduate with a double major in physics and mathematics. Her name, as it happened, was Kala—a coincidence that made one girl's heart quicken as she read along. That ancient Kala provided the smartest, most discouraging voice. There wouldn't be any cobbling together of parts, she maintained. Many times, she had seen the ripper used, and she had even helped operate it on occasion. As much as anyone here, she understood its powers and limitations. Navigating through the multiverse was just this side of impossible. To Claire and a few of her sisters, the First Kala explained how the Creation was infinite, and how every cubic nanometer of their world contained trillions of potential destinations.

"Alien worlds?" asked Claire.

"Alternate earths," Kala preferred. "More than two billion years ago, the world around us split away from our earth."

"Why?"

"Quantum rules," said Kala, explaining nothing. "Every world is constantly dividing into a multitude of new possibilities. There's some neat and subtle harmonics at play, and I don't understand much of it. But that's why the rippers can find earths like this. Two billion years and about half a nanometer divide our home from this place."

That was a lot for a housemother to swallow, but Claire did her best.

Kala continued spelling out their doom. "Even if we could repair the machine—do it right now, with a screwdriver and two minutes of work—our earth is lost. Finding it would be like finding a single piece of dust inside a world made of dust. It's that difficult. That impossible. We're trapped here, and Owen knows it. And that's part of his plan, I bet."

"Owen?" the First Mother asked. "Is that his name?"

Kala nodded, glancing back at the armed man.

"So you know Owen, do you?"

Kala rolled her eyes as women do when they feel uncomfortable in a certain man's presence. "He's a graduate student in physics," she explained. "I don't know him that well. He's got a trust fund, supposedly, and he's been stuck on his master thesis for years." Then with the next breath, she confessed, "We went out once. Last year. Once, or maybe twice. Then I broke it off."

Here was a staggering revelation for the living Kala: The woman who brought her name to the new world had a romantic relationship with the First Father. And then she had rejected him. Perhaps Owen still loved the girl, Kala reasoned. He loved her and wanted to possess her. And what if this enormous deed—the basis for countless lives and loves—came from one bitter lover's revenge?

But motivations never matter as much as results.

Whatever Owen's reasons, women sobbed while other women sat on the lawn, knees to their faces, refusing to believe what their senses told them. Claire stood motionless, absorbing what Kala and the other girls had to tell her. Meanwhile a sun identical to their sun rose, the air instantly growing warmer. Then the winged natives swept in low, examining the newcomers with their empty black eyes. A giant beast not unlike a tortoise, only larger than most rooms, calmly crawled over the round berm, sliding down to the lawn where it happily began to munch on grass. Meanwhile, houseflies and termites, dandelion fluff and blind earthworms, were beginning their migrations into the new woods. Bumblebees and starlings left their nests in search of food, while carpenter ants happily chewed on the local timber. Whatever you believe about the First Father, one fact is obvious: He was an uncommonly fortunate individual. The first new world proved to be a lazy place full of corners and flavors that earth species found to their liking. Included among the lucky colonists were two stray cats. One was curled up inside a storage shed, tending to her newborn litter, while the other was no more than a few days pregnant. And into that genetic puddle were three kittens smuggled into the sorority house by a young woman whose identity, and perhaps her own genetics, had long ago vanished from human affairs.

On that glorious morning, two worlds were married.

Each Testament had its differences, and every story was believable, but only to a maybe-so point. Claire's heretical story was the version Kala liked best and could even believe—a sordid tale of women trapped in awful circumstances but doing their noble best to survive.

"Hello, Owen," said Claire.

The young man blinked, glancing at the middle-aged woman standing before him. Claire was still wearing her bathrobe and a long nightgown and old slippers. To Owen, the woman couldn't have appeared less interesting. He nodded briefly and said nothing, always staring into the distance, eyes dancing from excitement but a little sleepiness creeping into their corners.

"What are you doing, Owen?"

"Standing guard," he said, managing a tense pride.

With the most reasonable voice possible, she asked, "What are you guarding us from?"

The young man said nothing.

"Owen," she repeated. Once. Twice. Then twice more.

"I'm sorry," he muttered, watching a single leather-wing dance in the air overhead. "There's a gauge on the ripper. It says our oxygen is about 80 percent usual. It's going to be like living in the mountains. So I'm sorry about that. I set the parameters too wide. At least for now, we're going to have to move slowly and let our bodies adapt."

Claire sighed. Then one last time, she asked, "What are you guarding us from, Owen?"

"I wouldn't know."

"You don't know what's out there?"

"No." He shrugged his shoulders, both hands gripping the stock of the rifle. "I saw you and Kala talking. Didn't she tell you? Yeah, I saw you two chatting. There's no way to tell much about a new world. The ripper can taste its air, and if it finds free oxygen and water and marker molecules that mean you're very close to the ground—"

"You kidnapped us, Owen." She spoke firmly, with a measured heat. "Without anyone's permission, you brought us here and marooned us."

"I'm marooned too," he countered.

"And why should that make us feel better?"

Finally, Owen studied the woman. Perhaps for the first time, he was gaining an appreciation for this unexpected wildcard.

"Feel how you want to feel," he said, speaking to her and everyone else in range of his voice. "This is our world now. We live or die here. We can make something out of our circumstances, or we can vanish away."

He wasn't a weak man, and, better than most people could have done, he had prepared for this incredible day. By then, Claire had realized some of that. Yet what mattered most was to get the man to admit the truth. That's why she climbed the steps, forcing him to stare at her face.

"Are you much of a shot, Owen? Did you serve in the military? In your little life, have you even once gone hunting?"

He shook his head. "None of those things, no."

"I have," Claire promised. "I served in the Army. My dead husband used to take me out chasing quail. When I was about your age, I shot a five-point whitetail buck."

Owen didn't know what to make of that news. "Okay. Good, I guess."

Claire kept her eyes on him. "Did you bring other guns?"

"Why?"

"Because you can't look everywhere at once," she reminded him. "I could ask a couple of these ladies to climb on the roof, just to keep tabs on things. And maybe we should decide who can shoot, if it actually comes to that and we have to defend the house."

Owen took a deep, rather worried breath. "I hope that doesn't happen."

"Are there more guns?"

"Yes."

"Where?"

His eyes tracked to the right.

"In that truck?" Claire glanced over her shoulder. "The women checked the doors. They're locked, aren't they?"

"Yes."

"To keep us out? Is that it?"

He shifted his weight, and with a complaining tone said, "I can't see much, with you in the way."

"I guess not," Claire responded. Then she pushed closer, asking, "Do you know the combinations of those padlocks?"

"Sure."

"Are you going to open them?"

Silence.

"All right," she said. "I guess that's just a little problem for now."

Owen nodded, pretending to be in complete control, set his rifle to one side, looked at her, and said, "I guess it is."

"You're what's important. You are essential."

"You bet."

"And for reasons bigger than a few locks."

The young man had to smile.

"What's inside the trucks?"

He quickly summarized the wealth brought from the old world, then happily added, "It's a great beginning for our colony."

"That does sound wonderful," Claire replied, her voice dipped in sarcasm.

Owen smiled, hearing the words but not their color.

"And if you could please tell me . . . when do you intend to give us this good food and water? Does your generosity have a timetable?"

"It does."

"So tell me."

Owen offered a smug wink, and then he sat back on the hard steps, lifting a hand, showing her three fingers.

"Excuse me?"

"Three girls," he explained. Then the hand dropped, and he added, "You know what I mean."

Here was another revelation: In every official Testament, the First Father unlocked every door and box in the first few minutes. Without exception, he was gracious and caring, and the girls practically fought one another for the chance to sleep with him.

"You want three of my ladies . . . ?"

"Yes."

Rage stole away Claire's voice.

Again, Owen said, "Yes."

"Are you going to select them?" the housemother muttered. "Or is this going to be a job for volunteers?"

Every face was fixed on Owen, and he clearly enjoyed the attention. He must have dreamed for months about this one moment, imagining the tangible, irresistible power that no one could deny . . . and because of that strength, he could shrug his shoulders, admitting, "It doesn't matter who. If there's three volunteers, then that's fine."

"You want them now?"

"Or in a week. I can wait, if I have to."

"You don't have to."

The smile brightened. "Good."

"And you get just one woman," Claire warned, grabbing the belt of her bathrobe and tightening the sloppy knot. "Me."

"No."

"Yes." Claire touched him on a knee. "No other deal is on the table, Owen. You and I are going inside. Now. My room, my bed, and afterwards, you're going to get us into those trucks, and you'll hand over every weapon you brought here. Is that understood?"

The young man's face colored. "You're not in any position—"

"Owen," she interrupted. Then she said, "Darling," with a

bite to her voice. And she reached out with the hand not on his knee, grabbing his bony chin while staring into the faint brown eyes that eventually would find themselves scattered across endless worlds. "This may come as news to you. But most men of your age and means and apparent intelligence don't have to go to these lengths to get their dicks wet."

He flinched, just for an instant.

"You don't know very much about women. Do you, Owen?"

"I do."

"Bullshit."

He blinked, biting his lower lip.

"You don't know us," she whispered to him. "Let me warn you about the nature of women, Owen. Everyone here is going to realize that you're just a very ignorant creature. If they don't know it already, that is. And if you think you've got power over us . . . well, let's just say you have some very strange illusions that need to die . . ."

"Quiet," he whispered.

But Claire kept talking, reminding him, "In another few weeks, a couple months at most, you will be doomed."

"What do you mean?"

"Once enough girls are pregnant, we won't need you anymore."

All the careful planning, but he hadn't let himself imagine this one obvious possibility. He said as much with his stiff face and the backward tilt of his frightened body.

"You can have all the guns in the world—hell, you do have all the guns—but you're going to end up getting knifed in bed. Yes, that could happen, Owen. Then in another few years, when your sons are old enough and my Deltas are in their late thirties . . . they'll still be young enough to use those boys' little seeds . . ."

"No," he muttered.

"Yes," she said. Her hand squeezed his knee. "Or maybe we could arrive at a compromise. Surrender your guns and open every lock, and afterwards, maybe you can try to do everything in your power to make this mess a little more bearable for us . . ."

"And what do I get?"

"You live to be an old man. And if you're an exceptionally good man from here on, maybe your grandchildren will forgive you for what you've done. And if you're luckier than you deserve to be, perhaps they'll even like you."

5

When Kala was fourteen, her church acquired the means to send one hundred blessed newlyweds off to another world. United Manufacturing had built a class-B ripper specifically for them. Tithes and government grants paid for the machine, while the stockpiles of critical supplies came through direct donations as well as a few wealthy benefactors. A standard hemispherical building was erected in an isolated field, its dimensions slightly smaller than the ripper's reach. Iron and copper plates made the rounded walls, nickel and tin and other useful metals forming the interior ribs, and secured to the roof were a few pure gold trimmings. The ground beneath had been excavated, dirt replaced with a bed of high-grade fertilizer and an insulated fuel tank set just under the bright steel floor. No portion of the cavernous interior was wasted: The young couples were taking foodstuffs and clean water, sealed animal pens and elaborate seed stocks, plus generators and earth-movers, medicine enough to keep an entire city fit, and the intellectual supplies necessary to build civilization once again.

On the wedding day, the congregation was given its last chance to see what the sacrifices had purchased. Several thousand parishioners gathered in long patient lines, donning sterile gloves and filter masks, impermeable sacks tied about their feet. Why chance giving some disease to the livestock or leaving rust spores on the otherwise sterile steel floor? The young pioneers stood in the crisscrossing hallways, brides dressed in white gowns, grooms in taut black suits, all wearing masks and gloves. One of the benefits born from the seventeen previous migrations was that most communicable diseases had been left behind. Only sinus colds and little infections born from mutating staph and strep were a problem. Yet even there, it was hoped that this migration would bring the golden moment, humanity finally escaping even those minor ailments.

The youngest brides were only a few years older than Kala, and she knew them well enough to make small talk before wishing them good-bye with the standard phrase, "Blessings in your new world."

Every girl's mask was wet with tears. Each was weeping for her own reason, but Kala was at a loss to guess who felt what. Some probably adored their temporary fame, while other girls cried out of simple stage fright. A few lucky brides probably felt utter love for their husbands-to-be, while others saw this mission as a holy calling. But some of the girls had to be genuinely terrified: The smartest few probably awoke this morning to the realization that they were doomed, snared in a vast and dangerous undertaking that had never quite claimed their hearts.

Standing near the burly ripper—a place of some honor—was a girl named Tina. Speaking through her soggy mask, she said to Kala, "May you find your new world soon."

"And bless you in yours."

Kala had no interest in emigrating. But what else could she say? Tina was soon to vanish, and the girl had always been friendly to Kala. Named for the first wife to give a son to the First Father, Tina was short and a little stocky, and, by most measures, not pretty. But her father was a deacon, and more important, her grandmother had offered a considerable dowry to the family that took her grandchild. Was the bride-to-be aware of these political dealings? And if so, did it matter to her? Tina seemed genuinely thrilled by her circumstances, giggling and pulling Kala closer, sounding like a very best friend when she asked, "Isn't this a beautiful day?"

"Yes," Kala lied.

"And tomorrow will be better still. Don't you think?"

The mass marriage would be held this evening, and come dawn, the big ripper would roar to life.

"Tomorrow will be different," Kala agreed, suddenly tired of their game.

Behind Tina, wrapped in thick plastic, was the colony's library. Ten thousand classic works were etched into sheets of

tempered glass, each sheet thin as a hair and guaranteed to survive ten thousand years of weather and hard use. Among those
works were the writings of every Father and the Testaments of the
Fifteen Wives, plus copies of the ancient textbooks that the Deltas
brought from the Old Earth. As language evolved, the texts had
been translated. Kala had digested quite a few of them, including
the introductions to ecology and philosophy, the fat histories of
several awful wars, and an astonishing fable called *Huckster Finn.*

Tina noticed her young friend staring at the library. "I'm not
a reader," she confided. "Not like you are, Kala."

The girl was rather simple, it was said.

"But I'm bringing my books too." Only the bride's brown
eyes were visible, dark eyebrows acquiring a mischievous look.
"Ask me what I'm taking."

"What are you taking, Tina?"

She mentioned several unremarkable titles. Then after a dramatic pause, she said, "*The Duty of Eve.* I'm taking that too."

Kala flinched.

"Don't tell anybody," the girl begged.

"Why would I?" Kala replied. "You can carry whatever you
want, inside your wedding trunk."

The Duty was popular among conservative faiths. Historians
claimed it was written by an unnamed Wife on the second new
world—a saintly creature who died giving birth to her fifth son,
but left behind a message from one of God's good angels:
Suffering was noble, sacrifice led to purity, and if your children
walked where no one had walked before, your life had been
worth every misery.

"Oh, Kala. I always wanted to know you better," Tina continued. "I mean, you're such a beautiful girl, and smart. But you
know that already, don't you?"

Kala couldn't think of a worthwhile response.

With both hands, Tina held tight to Kala's arm. "I have an extra copy of *The Duty.* I'll let you have it, if you want."

She said, "No."

"Think about it."

"I don't want it—"

"You're sure?"

"Yes," Kala blurted. "I don't want that damned book." Then she yanked her arm free and hurried away.

Tina stared after her, anger fading into subtler, harder to name emotions.

Kala felt the eyes burning against her neck, and she was a little bit ashamed for spoiling their last moments together. But the pain was brief. After all, she had been nothing but polite. It was the stupid girl who ruined everything.

According to *The Duty*, every woman's dream was to surrender to one great man. Kala had read enough excerpts to know too much. The clumsy, relentless point of that idiotic old book was that a holy girl found her great man, and she did everything possible to sleep with him, even if that meant sharing his body with a thousand other wives. The best historians were of one mind on this matter: *The Duty* wasn't a revelation straight from God, or even some second-tier angel. It was a horny man's fantasy written down in some lost age, still embraced by the conniving and believed by every fool.

Kala walked fast, muttering to herself.

Sandor was standing beside the ripper, chatting amiably with the newly elected Next Father. Her brother had become a strong young man, stubborn and charming and very handsome, and, by most measures, as smart as any sixteen-year-old could be. He often spoke about leaving the world, but only if he was elected to a Next Father's post. That was how it was done in their church: One bride for each groom, and the most deserving couple was voted authority over the new colony.

"It's a good day," Sandor sang out. "Try smiling."

Kala pushed past him, down the crowded aisle and out into the fading sunshine.

Sandor excused himself and followed. He would always be her older brother, and that made him protective as well as sensitive to her feelings. He demanded to know what was wrong, and she told him. Then he knew exactly what to say. "The girl's as stupid as she is homely, and what does it matter to you?"

Nothing. It didn't matter at all, of course.

"Our world's going to be better without her," he promised.

But another world would be polluted as a consequence: A fact that Kala couldn't forget, much less forgive.

*   *   *

The marriage was held at dusk, on a wide meadow of mowed spring fescue. The regional bishop—a charming and wise old gentleman—begged God and His trusted angels to watch over these good brave souls. Then with a joyful, almost giddy tone, he warned the fifty new couples to love one another in the world they were going to build. "Hold to your monogamy," he called out. "Raise a good family together, and fill the wonderland where destiny has called you."

A reception was held in the same meadow, under temporary lights, the mood slipping from celebration to grief and back again. Everyone drank more than was normal. Eventually the newlyweds slipped off to the fifty small huts standing near the dome-shaped building. Grooms removed the white gowns of their brides, and the new wives folded the gowns and stored them inside watertight wooden trunks, along with artifacts and knick-knacks from a life they would soon abandon.

Kala couldn't help but imagine what happened next inside the huts.

A few sips of wine made her warm and even a little happy. She chatted with friends and adults, and she even spent a few minutes listening to her father. He was drunk and silly, telling her how proud he was of her. She was so much smarter than he had ever been, and prettier even than her mother. "Did I just say that? Don't tell on me, Kala." Then he continued, claiming that whatever she wanted from her life was fine with him . . . just so long as she was happy enough to smile like she was smiling right now . . .

Kala loved the dear man, but he didn't mean those words. Sober again, he would find some way to remind her that Sandor was his favorite child. Flashing his best grin, he would mention her brother's golden aspirations and then talk wistfully about his grandchildren embracing their own world.

Kala finally excused herself, needing a bathroom.

Abandoning the meadow, walking alone in darkness, she considered her father's drunken promise to let her live her own life. But what was "her life"? The question brought pressure, and not just from parents and teachers and her assorted friends. Kala's own ignorance about her future was the worst of it. Such a bright creature—everyone said that about her. But when it came to her destiny, she didn't have so much as a clue.

As Kala walked through the oak woods, she noticed another person moving somewhere behind her. But she wasn't frightened until she paused, and an instant later, that second set of feet stopped too.

Kala turned, intending to glance over her shoulder.

Suddenly a cool black sack was dropped over her head, and an irresistible strength pushed her to the ground. Then a man's voice—a vaguely familiar voice—whispered into one of her covered ears. "Fight me," he said, "and I'll kill you. Make one sound, and I'll kill your parents too."

She was numb, empty and half-dead.

Her abductor tied her up and gagged her with a rope fitted over the black sack, and then he dragged her in a new direction, pausing at a service entrance in back of the metal dome. She heard fingers pushing buttons and hinges squeaking, and then the ground turned to steel as her long legs were dragged across the pioneers' floor.

Her numbness vanished, replaced with wild terror.

Blindly, Kala swung her bound legs and clipped his, and he responded with laughter, kneeling down to speak with a lover's whisper. "We can dance later, you and me. Tonight is Tina's turn. Sorry, sorry."

She was tied to a crate filled with sawdust, and by the smell of it, hundreds of fertile tortoise eggs.

When the service door closed, Kala tugged at the knots. How much time was left? How many hours did she have? Panic gave her a fabulous strength, but every jerk and twist only tightened the knots, and after a few minutes of work, she was exhausted, sobbing through the rope gag.

No one was going to find her.

And when they were in the new world, Tina's husband—a big

strong creature with connections and a good name—would pretend to discover Kala, cutting her loose and probably telling everyone else, "Look who wanted to come with us! My wife's little friend!" And before she could say two words, he would add, "I'll feed her from share of the stores. Yes, she's my responsibility now."

Kala gathered herself for another try at the ropes.

Then the service door opened with the same telltale squeak, and somebody began to walk slowly past her, down the aisle and back again, pausing beside her for a moment before placing a knife against her wrists, yanking hard and cutting the rope clear through.

Off came her gag, then the black sack.

Sandor was holding a small flashlight in his free hand, and he touched her softly on her face, on her neck. "You all right?"

She nodded.

"Good thing I bumped into that prick out there." Her brother was trying to look grateful, but his expression and voice were tense as could be. "I asked him, 'Why aren't you with your bride?' But he didn't say anything. Which bothered me, you know." He paused, then added, "I've seen him stare at you, Kala."

"You have?"

"Haven't you?" Sandor took a deep breath, then another, gathering himself. "So I asked if he'd seen you come this way. And then he said, 'Get away from me, little boy.'"

Sandor began cutting her legs free. In the glare of his light, she saw his favorite pocket knife—the big blade made sticky and red, covered as it was with an appalling amount of blood.

"Did you kill him?" Kala muttered.

In a grim whisper, Sandor said, "Hardly."

"What happened?"

"I saved you," he answered.

"But what did you do to that man?" she demanded.

"Man?" Sandor broke into a quietly, deathly laugh. "I don't know, Kala. You're the biologist in the family. But I don't think you could call him male anymore . . . if you see what I mean . . ."

6

In a personal ritual, Kala brought *The First Mother's Tale* out of hiding each spring and read it from cover to cover. She found pleasure in the book's adventures and heroisms, and the tragedies made her reliably sad, and even with whole tracts memorized, she always felt as if she was experiencing Claire's story for the first time. That strong, determined woman did everything possible to help her girls while making Owen behave. She made certain that every adult had a vote in every important decision—votes that were made after her console, naturally. Claire always spoke for the dead at funerals, and she oversaw a small feast commemorating the anniversary of their arrival. Hard famine came during their third winter. The local tortoises had been hunted to extinction while the earthly crops never prospered. It was Claire who imposed a ration system for the remaining food, and after six Wives were caught breaking into the last cache of canned goods, Claire served as judge in the bitter trial. Each girl claimed to have acted for the good of a hungry baby or babies. But there were dozens of children by then, and whose stomach wasn't growling? Twelve other girls—some Wives, some not—served as the jury. In a ritual ancient as the species, they listened to the evidence before stepping off by themselves, returning with a verdict that found each defendant guilty as charged.

The housemother had no choice but order a full banishment.

The original Tina was one of the criminals. After some rough talk and vacuous threats, she and the other five picked up their toddlers and started south, hoping to hike their way to fresh pastures and easy food.

There was no doubt that the Six Angry Wives existed. But no consistent tale of crimes was told about them, and no Testament mentioned Claire as the presiding judge. What was known was that six women wandered through the wilderness, and when they returned ten years later, they brought blue-hens and fresh tortoise eggs as well as their four surviving children—including one lovely brown-eyed boy, nearly grown and eager to meet his father.

The truth was, no important church recognized Claire's existence, which was the same as never existing. Even the oddest offshoot faiths denied her any vital role in their history. According to *The First Mother's Tale*, the housemother lived another seven years and died peacefully in her sleep. Owen borrowed one of his Wives' Bibles to read prayers over her grave. With the relief of someone who had escaped a long burden, he thanked the woman's soul for its good work and wise guidance. And then *The First Mother's Tale* concluded with a few hopeful words from its author, the brilliant and long-dead Kala.

Except of course nothing is ever finished, and considering everything that had happened since, most of the story had barely begun.

According to most researchers, it took a full century for the pioneers to find their stride. Owen lived to be eighty—a virile man to the end—and borrowing on his godly status, he continued sleeping with an assortment of willing, fertile granddaughters. Claire's grave was soon lost to time, or she never even existed. But Owen's burial site became the world's first monument. Limestone blocks were dragged from a quarry and piled high, and the structure was decorated with a lordly statue and praising words as well as the original, still useless, ripper. Worshippers traveled for days and weeks just for a chance to kneel at the feet of the great man's likeness, and sometimes an old wound felt healed or some tireless despair would suddenly lift, proving again the powers of the First Father.

Four centuries later, enough bodies and minds were wandering the world to allow a handful to become scientists.

Inside a thousand years, humanity had spread across the warm, oxygen-impoverished globe, keeping to the lowlands, erasing the native species that fit no role. Cobbler-shops became factories, schools became universities, and slowly, the extraordinary skills necessary to build new rippers came back into the world.

In 1003, a wealthy young man purchased advertisement time on every television network. "The bigger the ripper, the better the seed," he declared to the world. And with that, he unveiled a giant Class-A ripper as well as the spacious house that would carry him and a thousand wives to a new world, plus enough frozen sperm from quality men to ensure a diverse, vital society.

He found no shortage of eager young women.

What actually became of that colony and its people, no one could say. To leave was to vanish in every sense of the word. But thousands of rippers were built during the following centuries. Millions of pioneers left that first new world, praying for richer air and tastier foods. And after six centuries of emigration, Kala's descendants gathered around a small class-B, read passages from the Bible as well as from the Wives' Testaments, and then together they managed their small, great step into the unknown.

7

At nineteen, Kala applied with the Parks Committee, and through luck and her own persistence, she was posted to the same reserve she once visited as a youngster. She was given heavy boots and a wide-brimmed hat as well as an oversized brown uniform with a Novice tag pinned to her chest. Her first week of summer was spent giving tours to visitors curious about the native fauna and flora. But the assignment wasn't a rousing success, which was why she was soon transferred to exotic eradications—an improved posting, as it happened. Kala was free to drive the back roads in an official truck, parking at set points and walking deep into the alien forest. Hundreds of traps had to be checked every few days. Native animals were released, while the exotics were killed, usually with air-driven needles or a practiced blow to the head. At day's end, she would return to the main office and don plastic gloves, throwing the various carcasses into a cremation furnace— fat starlings and fatter house mice, mostly. If they died in the trap, the bodies would stink. But she quickly grew accustomed to the carnage. In her mind, she was doing important, frustrating work. Kala often pictured herself as a soldier standing on the front lines, alone, waging a noble struggle for which she expected almost nothing: A little money, the occasional encouragement, and, of course, the chance to return to the wilderness every morning, enjoying its doomed and fading strangeness for another long day.

One July afternoon, while Kala worked at the incinerator, another novice appeared. They had been friendly in the past. But today, for no obvious reason, the young man seemed uncomfort-

BEST SHORT NOVELS: 2007

able. As soon as he saw Kala, his face stiffened and his gait slowed, and then, perhaps reading her puzzlement, he suddenly sped up again. "Hello," he offered with the softest possible voice.

Kala smiled while flinging a dead cat into the fire. "Did you hear?" she began. "They found a new herd of Harry's-big-days. Above Saint Mary's Glacier."

The young man hesitated for an instant. Then with a rushed voice, he sputtered, "I've got an errand. Bye now."

Long ago, Kala learned that she wasn't as sensitive to emotions as most people. Noticing something was wrong now meant there was a fair chance that it really was. Why was that boy nervous? Was she in trouble again? And if so, what had she screwed up this time?

When Kala was giving tours, there was an unfortunate incident. A big blowhard from the Grandfather Cult joined the other tourists. His personal mission was to commandeer her lecture. One moment, she was describing the false spruces and explaining how the tomb-tombs depended wholly on them. And suddenly the blowhard interrupted. With an idiot's voice, he announced that the native trees were useless as well as ugly, and all the local animals were stupid as the rocks, and their world's work wouldn't be finished until every miserable corner like this was turned into oak trees and concrete.

Kala's job demanded a certain reserve. Lecturers were not to share their opinions, unless those opinions coincided with official park policy. Usually she managed to keep her feelings in check. She endured three loud interruptions. But then the prick mentioned his fifteen sons and twelve lovely daughters, boasting that each child would end up on a different new world. Kala couldn't hold back. She was half his age and half his size, but she stepped up to him and pushed a finger into his belly, saying, "If I was your child, I'd want to leave this world too."

Most of the audience smiled, and quite a few laughed.

But the blowhard turned and marched to the front office, and by day's end, Kala was given a new job killing wildcats and other vermin.

The last carcasses were burning when her superior emerged from the station. He was an older fellow—a life-long civil servant who probably dreamed of peace and quiet until his retirement, and then a peaceful death. Approaching his temperamental novice, the man put on a painful smile, twice saying her name before adding, "I need to talk to you," with a cautious tone. A headless starling lay on the dirt. With a boot, Kala kicked it into the incinerator and again shut the heavy iron door. Then with a brazen tone, she said, "Listen to my side first."

The man stopped short.

"I mean it," she continued. "I don't know what you've heard. I don't even know what I could have done something wrong. But I had very good reasons—"

"Kala."

"And you should hear my explanation first."

The poor old gentleman dipped his head, shaking it sadly, telling her, "Kala, sweetness. I'm sorry. All I want to say . . . to tell you . . . is that your brother called this morning. Right after you drove off." He paused long enough to breathe, and then informed her, "Your father died last night, and I'm very, very sorry."

◔ ◔ ◔

Thrifty and impractical: Father was the same in death as in life.

That was an uncharitable assessment, but it happened to be true. Father left behind a long list of wishes, and Mother did everything he wanted, including the simple juniper box and no official funeral procession. The tombstone was equally minimal, and because cemeteries were expensive, he had mandated a private plot he had purchased as soon as he fell sick—a secret illness kept from everyone, including his wife of thirty-one years. But the burial site had drawbacks, including the absence of any road passing within a couple hundred yards. Kala's parents hadn't been active in any church for years, which meant it was their scattered family that was responsible for every arrangement, including digging the grave to a legal depth, finding pallbearers to help carry the graceless casket, and then after the painful service, filling in the hole once again.

"It's a lovely piece of ground," Sandor mentioned, and not for the first time. Then he dropped a load of the dry gray earth, watching it scatter across a lid of tightly fitted red planks, big clods thumping while the tiny clods scattered, rolling and shattering down to dust, making the skittering sound of busy mice.

"It is pretty," Mother echoed, sitting on one of forty folding chairs.

Everyone else had left. Barely three dozen relatives and friends had attended the service, and probably only half of them had genuinely known the deceased. If Father died ten years ago, Kala realized, two hundred people would have been sitting and standing along this low ridge, and the church would have sent at least two ministers—one to read Scripture, while the other sat with the grieving family, giving practiced comfort. But the comfort-givers abandoned them soon after that terrible wedding night. For maiming one of the grooms, Sandor had been shunned. And once Kala and her parents didn't follow suit, the congregation used more subtle, despicable means to toss them away.

For months, Kala continued meeting old friends in secret. A little too urgently, they would tell her that nothing was her fault. But then they started asking how Kala could live with a person who had done such an awful thing. After all, Sandor had neutered one of the leading citizens of their congregation—an act of pure violence, too large and far too wicked not to be brought to the attention of the police. It didn't matter that he was protecting his only sister, which was normally a good noble principle. And it didn't matter that decent men always defended their women, or that if a girl was abducted when she's fourteen, some family member was required to send a message to those horny fools lurking out there: Hurt her, and I'll take your future generations from you!

None of that meant anything to her friends. And once Kala admitted that she felt thankful for her brother's actions, those same friends stopped inventing tricks to meet her on the sly. Of course her brother wasn't the only person needing blame. Parents were always culpable for the sins of their children, it was said. Didn't Sandor's father and mother give him their genes and some portion of their dreams? He was technically still a child when the crime occurred, still possessed by them, and supposedly answering first to God and then to them. Wasn't that how it was supposed to be?

The kidnapping was an unfortunate business, said some. The new husband shouldn't have done what he did, and particularly with one of their own. But even in a faith that cherished monogamy, his actions were understandable. Twenty thousand years of history had built this very common outlook. One deacon—a younger man devoid of charm or common sense—visited their house after Sunday service. Sitting in the meeting room with Kala's father, the deacon asked, "Where lies the difference? A young man takes two brides to a fresh world, while another lives with his first wife for twenty years, then holds a painless divorce and starts a new family with a younger woman?"

"There's an enormous difference," Father had responded, his voice rising, betraying anger Kala had rarely heard before. She was sitting in her bedroom upstairs, listening while her other great defender said, "My daughter is a young girl, first of all. And second, she had no choice in this matter. None. She was tied up like a blue-hen and abused like cargo, thrown into a situation where she would never see her family or world again. Is that fair? Or just? Or at all decent? No, and no, and no again."

"But to cut the groom like he was cut—"

"A little cut, from what I've heard."

Which was the greater surprise: Father interrupting, or insulting the penis of another man?

The deacon groaned and then said, "That vicious animal . . . your darling Sandor . . . he deserves to sit in jail for a few years."

"Let the courts decide," Father replied.

"And you realize, of course." Their guest hesitated a moment before completing his thought. "You understand that no worthy group of pioneers will let him into their ranks. Not now. Not with his taste for violence, they won't."

"I suppose not."

"Which is a shame, since your son always wanted to be a Father."

Kala heard silence, and when she imagined her father's face, she saw a look of utter shame.

Then the stupid deacon had to share one last opinion. With a black voice, he announced, "I came here for a reason, sir. I think you should appreciate what other people are saying."

"What others?"

"Women as well as the men."

"Tell me," Father demanded.

"The girl looks older than fourteen. Her body is grown, and that voice of hers could be a woman's. Any healthy man would be interested. But there's a problem in the words that Kala uses . . . and that smart, sharp tone of hers . . ."

"What are you telling me?"

"Many of us . . . your very best friends . . . we believe that somebody should knock your daughter down a notch or two. And give her some babies to play with, too."

Father's chair squeaked—a hard defiant sound.

"Go," Kala heard him say. "Get out of my house."

"Gladly," the deacon replied. "But just so you know my sense of things, realize this: Your daughter had an opportunity that night. It might not seem fair or just to us. But if she and that brother of hers had a wit between them, she'd be living today on a better world. But as things stand, I can't imagine any reputable group will accept trouble like her. Her best bet for the future is a sloppy abduction by a single male who simply doesn't know who she is." There was a pause—a gathering of breath and fury. Then for the only time in her life, Kala heard her father saying, "Fuck you."

That moment, and the entire nightmare . . . all of it returned to her at the gravesite. The intervening years suddenly vanished, and her lanky body was left shaking from nerves and misery. Sandor and their mother both noticed. They watched her fling gouts of earth into the hole, and misunderstanding everything, Mom warned, "This isn't a race, sweetness."

Kala felt as if she had been caught doing something awful. She couldn't name her crime, but shame took hold. Down went the shovel, and she knelt over the partly filled grave, staring at the last two visible corners of her father's casket.

Sandor settled beside her.

With what felt like a single breath, Kala confessed the heart of her thoughts: A single night had torn apart their lives, and despite believing she was blameless, she felt guilty. Somehow all the evil and poor luck that had followed them since was her fault. Because of her, they had lost their church and friends. Father died young, and now their mother would always be a widow. And meanwhile, her brother was a convicted criminal, stripped from what he had wanted most in life—the opportunity to become a respectable Father to some great new world. After a difficult pause, Mom broke in. "I wouldn't have liked that at all," she maintained, "losing you without the chance to say, 'Good-bye.'"

Kala had hoped for more.

"You're being silly, sweet," would have been nice. "You aren't to blame for any of this at all," would have been perfect.

Instead, the old woman remarked, "These last years have been hard. Yes. But don't blame yourself for your father's health."

Sandor drove his shovel into the earth pile behind Kala. Then with a weighty sigh, he said, "And don't worry about me. I'm doing fine."

Hardly. Because of his stay in prison, her brother had missed his last years at school. The boy he had been was gone, replaced by a hard young man with self-made tattoos and muscles enough for two athletes.

Kala disagreed.

"You're wrong," she said with a shake of her head.

Then Sandor laughed at her, kicking a clod or two into the hole and staring down at their father, quietly reminding everyone, "'Respectable' is just a word." His face was tight, his eyes were enormous, and his voice was dry and slow when he added, "And there's more than one route to reach another world."

8

Kala's world was settled by a confederation of small and medium-sized churches. Two million parishioners had pooled their resources, acquiring a powerful class-A ripper—a bruising monster capable of stealing away several city blocks. Each congregation selected their best pioneers, and the Last Father was elected to his lofty post, responsible for the well being of more than a thousand brave souls, plus three stowaways and at least fifteen young women kidnapped on the eve of departure. A farm field on the

Asian continent was selected, in a region once known as Hunan. Where wheat and leadfruit normally grew, a huge, multi-story dome was erected. Every pioneer plugged his ears with foam and wax. The giant ripper shook the entire structure as it searched across Creation, and, with a final surge, machine and humans were dragged along the hidden dimensions, covering the minuscule distance.

Rippers had no upper limit to their power, but there were practical considerations. Entering another world meant displacing the native air and land. With its arrival, that class-A ripper shoved aside thousands of tons of dirt and rock, erecting a ring-shaped hill of debris instantly heated by the impact. Wood and peat caught fire, and deep underground, the bedrock was compressed until it was hot enough to melt. The Last Father ordered everyone to remain indoors for the day, breathing bottled air and watching the fires spread and die under an evening thunderstorm. Then the survey teams were dispatched, racing over the blackened ground, finding pastures of black sedge-like grass where they caught the native mice and pseudoinsects as well as a loose-limbed creature with a glancing resemblance to the lost monkeys in the oldest textbooks.

Experience promised this: If intelligence evolved on a new world, chances are it would live in Asia. Competition was stiffest on large landmasses. That's how it had been on the original earth. Australia was once home to opossums and kangaroos, and dimension-crossing pioneers might have been tempted to linger there, unaware that lying over the horizon were continents full of smart, aggressive placental creatures, including one fierce medium-sized ape with some exceptionally mighty plans.

But the vermin brought home by the survey teams had simple smooth brains, while the monkey-creature proved to be an intellectual midget next to any respectable cat. The Last Father met with his advisors and then with his loving wife, and following a suitable period of contemplation and prayer, he announced that this was where God wished them to remain for the rest of their days.

The new colony expanded swiftly, in numbers and reach.

The Last Father died with honor, six of his nine children carrying his body into a granite cathedral built at the site of their arrival.

By then villages and little cities were scattered across a thousand miles of wilderness. Within ten generations, coal-fired ships were mapping coastlines on every side of the Mother Ocean, while little parties were moving inland, skirting the edges of the Tibetan Plateau on their way to places once called Persia and Turkey, Lebanon and France.

The original churches grew and split apart, or they shriveled and died.

And always, new faiths were emerging, often born from a single believer's ideals and his very public fantasies.

The original class-A ripper served as an altar inside the Last Father's cathedral. A cadre of engineers maintained its workings, while a thousand elite soldiers stood guard over the holy ground. The symbols were blatant and unflinching: First and always, this world would serve as a launching point to countless new realms. Human duty was to build more rippers—a promise finally fulfilled several centuries ago. By Kala's time, the thousand original pioneers had become five billion citizens. Tax codes and social conventions assured that rippers would always be built. Experts guessed that perhaps fifteen billion bodies could live on these warm lands, and with luck and God's blessing, that would be the day when enough rippers were rolling out of enough factories to allow every excess child to escape, every boy free to find his own empty, golden realm, and every girl serving as a good man's happy Wife.

9

Sandor hated that his sister traveled alone. Every trip Kala took was preceded by a difficult conversation, on phone or in person. It was his duty to remind her that the open highway was an exceptionally dangerous place. Sandor always had some tale to share about some unfortunate young woman who did everything right—drove only by day, spoke to the fewest possible strangers, and slept in secure hotels that catered to their kind. Yet without exception, each of those smart ladies had vanished somewhere on the road, usually without explanation.

"But look at the actual numbers," Kala liked to counter. "The chance of me being abducted twice in my life—"

"Is tiny. I know."

"Dying in a traffic accident is ten times more likely," she would add.

But eventually Sandor analyzed the same statistics, ambushing her with a much bleaker picture. "Dying in a wreck is three times as likely," he informed Kala. "But that's for all women. Old and young. Those in your subset—women in their twenties, with good looks and driving alone—are five times as likely to disappear as they are to die in a simple, run-of-the-mill accident."

"But I have to travel," she countered. Her doctorate involved studying the native communities scattered across a dozen far flung mountaintops. Driving was mandatory, and since there was barely enough funding as it was, she had no extra money to hire reliable security guards. "I know you don't appreciate my work—"

"I never said that, Kala."

"Because you're such a painfully polite fellow." Then laughing at her own joke, she reminded him, "I always carry a registered weapon."

"Good."

"And a gun that isn't registered."

"As you damn well should," Sandor insisted.

"Plus there's a thousand little things I do, or two million things I avoid." She always had one or two new tricks to offer, just to prove that she was outracing her unseen enemies. "And if you have any other suggestions, please . . . share them with your helpless little sister . . ."

"Don't tease," he warned. "You don't understand what men want from women. If you did, you'd never leave home."

Kala had a tidy little apartment on a women's floor, set ten stories above the street—far too high to be stolen away with even the biggest ripper. On this occasion, Sandor happened to be passing through, supposedly chasing a mechanic's job but not acting in any great hurry to leave. His main mission, as far as she could tell, was to terrify his little sister. As always, he came armed with news clippings and Web sites. He wanted her to appreciate the fact that her mountains were full of horny males, each one more dangerous than the others, and all the bastards fighting for their chance to start some new world. As it happened, last week a large shipment of class-C rippers had just been hijacked from an armed convoy, and now the Children of Forever were proclaiming a time of plenty. And just yesterday, outside New Eternal, some idiot drove a big freight truck through two sets of iron gates before pulling up beside the classroom wing of a ladies' academy. Moments later, a large class-B ripper fired off, leaving behind a hemispherical hole and a mangled building, as well as a thousand scared teenage girls, saved only because they had been called into the auditorium for a hygiene lecture from the school's doctor.

Kala shrugged at the bad news. "Crap is a universal constant. Nothing has changed, and I'm going to be fine."

But really, she never felt good about driving long distances, and the recent news wasn't comforting. Nearly a hundred stolen rippers were somewhere on the continent, which had to shift the odds that trouble would find her. Kala let herself feel the fear, and then with a burst of nervous creativity, she blurted out a possible solution.

"Come with me," she said.

Sandor was momentarily stunned.

"If you're that especially worried about me, ride along and help me with my work. Unless you really do have some plush mechanic's job waiting."

"All right then," he answered. "I'd like that."

"A long family vacation," she said with a grin.

And he completed her thought, adding, "Just like we used to do."

☙ ☙ ☙

More than ten years had passed since they last spent time together, and the summer-long journey gave them endless chances to catch up. But for all the days spent on the road, not to mention the weeks hiking and working on alpine trails, they shared remarkably little. Kala heard nothing about life in prison and very little about how Sandor had made his living since his release. And by the same token, she never felt the need to mention past boys and future men—romantic details that she always shared with her closest friends. For a time, the silences bothered her. But then she decided siblings always had difficulty with intimacy. Sharing genetics and a family was such a deep, profound business that no one felt obliged to prove their closeness by ordinary routes. Sandor revealed himself only in glimpses—a few words or a simple gesture—while in her own fashion, Kala must have seemed just as close-mouthed. But of course these secrets of theirs didn't matter. This man would always be her brother, and that was far larger than any other relationship they might cobble together while driving across the spine of a continent.

Sandor relished his job as protector. At every stop, he was alert and a little aggressive, every stranger's face deserving a quick study, and some of them requiring a hard warning stare. She appreciated the sense of menace that seemed to rise out of him at will. In ways she hadn't anticipated, Kala enjoyed watching Sandor step up to a counter, making innocent clerks flinch. His tattoos flexed and his face grew hard as stone, and she liked the rough snarl in his voice when he said, "Thank you." Or when he snapped at some unknown fellow, "Out of our way. Please. Sir."

If anything, empty wilderness was worse than the open road. It made him more suspicious, if not out-and-out paranoid.

Kala's work involved an obscure genus of pseudoinsects. She was trying to find and catalog unknown species before they vanished, collecting data about their habitat and specimens that she froze and dried and stuck into long test tubes. One July evening, on the flank of a giant southern volcano, she heard a peculiar sound from behind a grove of spruce trees. A rough hooting, it sounded like. "I wonder what that was," she mentioned. Sandor instantly slipped away from the fire, walking the perimeter at least twice before returning again, one hand holding a long flashlight and the other carrying an even longer pistol equipped with a nightscope. "So what was it?" she asked.

"Boys," he reported. "They were thinking of camping near us."

"They were?"

"Yeah," he said, sitting next to the fire again. "But I guess for some reason they decided to pull up their tent and move off. Who knows why?"

Moments like that truly pleased Kala.

But following her pleasure was a squeamish distaste. What kind of person was she? She thought of herself as being independent and self-reliant, but on the other hand, she seemed to relish being watched over by a powerful and necessarily dangerous man.

Two days later, driving north, Sandor mentioned that he had never gotten his chance to visit the Grand Canyon. "Our vacation never made it," he reminded her. "And I haven't found the time since."

Kala let them invest one full day of sightseeing.

The canyon's precise location and appearance varied on each world. But there was always a river draining that portion of the continent, and the land had always risen up in response to the predictable tectonics. Since their earth was wetter than most, the river was big and angry, cutting through a billion years of history on its way to the canyon floor. Kala paid for a cable-car ride to the bottom. They ate hard-boiled blue-hen eggs and mulberries for lunch, and afterwards, walking on the rocky shoreline, she pointed to the rotting carcass of a Helen-trout. The First Father didn't bring living fish with him, but later Fathers realized that fish farming meant cheap protein. The Helen-trout came from the fifth new world—indiscriminate feeders that could thrive in open ocean or fresh water, and that adored every temperature from freezing to bathwater. No major drainage in the world lacked the vermin. "They die when they're pregnant," she explained. "Their larvae use the mother as food, eating her as she rots, getting a jump on things before they swim away."

Sandor seemed to be listening. But then again, he always seemed to pay attention to his surroundings. In this case, he gave a little nod, and after a long pause said, "I'm curious, Kala. What do you want to accomplish? With your work, I mean."

He asked that question every few days, as if for the first time.

At first Kala thought that he simply wasn't hearing her answers. Later, she wondered if he was trying to break her down, hoping to make her admit that she didn't have any good reason for her life's investment. But after weeks of enduring this verbal dance, she began to appreciate what was happening. To keep from boring herself, she was forced to change her response. Inside the canyon, staring at the dead fish, she didn't bother with old words about the duty and honor that came from saving a few nameless bugs. And she avoided the subject of great medicines that probably would never emerge from her work. Instead, staring down at the rich bulging body, she offered a new response.

"This world of ours is dying, Sandor."

The statement earned a hard look and an impossible-to-read grin. "Why's that?" he asked over the roar of the water.

"A healthy earth has ten or twenty or fifty million species. Depending on how you count them." She shook her head, reminding him, "The Last Father brought as many species as possible. Nearly a thousand multicellular species have survived here. And that's too few to make an enduring, robust ecosystem."

Sandor shrugged and gestured at the distant sky. "Things look good enough," he said. "What do you mean that it's dying?"

"Computer models point to the possibility," she explained. "Low diversity means fragile ecosystems. And it's more than just having too few species. It's the nature of these species. Wherever we go, we bring weed species. Biological thugs, essentially. And not just from the original earth but from seventeen distinct evolutionary histories. Seventeen lines that are nearly alien to one another. That reduces meaningful interactions. It's another factor why there will eventually come a crunch."

"Okay. So when?"

She shrugged her shoulders.

"Next year?"

"Not for thousands of years," she allowed. "But there is a collapse point, and after that, the basic foundations of this biosphere will decline rapidly. Phytoplankton, for one. The native species are having troubles enduring the new food chains, and if they end up vanishing, then nobody will be making free oxygen."

"Trees don't make oxygen?"

"They do," she admitted. "But their wood burns or rots. And rotting is the same reaction as burning, chemically speaking."

Sandor stared at the gray mother fish.

"You know how it is when you turn on a ripper?" Kala asked. "You know how the machine has to search hard for a world with a livable atmosphere?"

Her brother nodded, a look of anticipation building in the pale brown eyes.

"Do you ever wonder why so many earths don't have decent air for us? Do you?" Kala gave him a rough pat on the shoulder, asking, "What if a lot of pioneers have been moving across the multiverse? Humans and things that aren't human, too. And what if most of these intrepid pioneers eventually kick their worlds out of equilibrium, killing them as a consequence?"

"Yeah," he said.

Then after a long thoughtful moment: "Huh."

And that was the last time Sandor ever bothered to doubt the importance of Kala's work.

10

The heart of every ripper was a cap-shaped receptacle woven from diamond whiskers, each whisker doctored with certain rare-earth elements and infused with enough power to pierce the local brane. But as difficult as the receptacle was to build, it was a simple chore next to engineering the machines to support and control its work. Hard drives and the capacitors had to function on the brink of theoretical limits. Heat and quantum fluctuations needed to be kept at a minimum. The best rippers utilized a cocktail of unusual isotopes, doubling their reliability as well as tripling the costs, while security costs added another 40 percent to the final price. Twice that summer, Kala and her brother saw convoys of finished rippers being shipped across country. Armored trucks were painted a lush emerald green, each one accompanied by two or three faster vehicles bristling with weapons held by tough young men. Routes and schedules were supposed to be kept secret. Since even a small ripper was worth a fortune, the corporations did whatever they could to protect their investments. Which made Kala wonder: How do the Children of

Forever learn where one convoy would be passing, and what kind of firepower would it take to make the rippers their own?

Sandor was driving when they ran into one of the convoys. A swift little blister of armor and angry faces suddenly passed them on the wrong side. "Over," screamed every face. "Pull over."

They were beside the Mormon Sea, on a highway famous for scenery and its narrow, almost nonexistent, shoulders. But Sandor complied, fitting them onto a slip of asphalt and turning off the engine, then setting the parking brake and turning to look back around the bend, eyes huge and his lower lip tucked into his mouth.

For a moment or two, Kala watched the bright water of the inland sea, enjoying the glitter stretching to the horizon. Then came the rumble of big engines, and a pair of heavy freight trucks rolled past, followed by more deadly cars, and then another pair of trucks.

"Class-Cs," Sandor decided. "About a hundred of them, built down in Highborn."

The trucks had no obvious markings. "How can you tell?"

"The lack of security," he said. "Cs don't get as much. It's the As and Bs that bandits can sell for a fortune. And I know the company because each truck's got a code on its side, if you know how to read it."

The convoy had passed out of sight, but they remained parked beside the narrow road.

"When are we moving again?" she asked.

"Wait," he cautioned.

She shifted in her seat and took a couple meaningful breaths.

Reading the signs, Sandor turned to her. "You don't want to trail them too closely. Someone might get the wrong idea. Know what I mean?"

And with that, her brave, almost fearless brother continued to sit beside the road, hands squeezing the wheel.

"You gave somebody the wrong idea," she said.

"Pardon?"

"Sandor," she said. "In your life, how many convoys have you followed?"

Nothing changed about his face. Then suddenly, a little smile turned up the corner of his mouth, and with a quiet, conspiratorial voice, he admitted, "Fifty, maybe sixty."

She wasn't surprised, except that she didn't expect to feel so upset. "Is that how badly you want it? To be a Father . . . you're willing to steal a ripper just to get your chance . . . ?"

He started to nod. Then again, he looked at his sister, reminding her, "I'm still here. So I guess I'm not really that eager."

"What went wrong? The work was too dangerous for you?"

His expression looked injured now. Straightening his back, he started the car and pulled out, accelerating for a long minute, letting the silence work on Kala until he finally told her, "You know, there were thirty-two security men on that other convoy. The one hit by the Children of Forever. Plus a dozen drivers and three corporate representatives. And all were killed during the robbery."

"I know that—"

"Most of those poor shits were laid down in a ditch by the road and shot through the head. Just so motorists wouldn't notice the bodies when they drove past." He squeezed the steering wheel until it squeaked, and very carefully, he told Kala, "That's when I gave up wanting it. Being a Father to the very best world isn't enough reason to murder even one poor boy who's trying to make some money and keep his family fed."

＊ ＊ ＊

A pair of mountain ranges stood as islands far out in the Mormon Sea, and they spent a few days walking the tallest peaks. Then they drove north again, up to the Geysers, enjoying a long hike through the mountains north of that volcanic country. Then it was late August, and they started back toward Kala's home. One stop remained, kept until now for sentimental reasons.

"Our best vacation," she muttered.

Sandor agreed with his silence and a little wink.

They stayed in a reserve campground meant for employees, and Kala introduced her brother to the few rangers that remained from her days here. The mood was upbeat, on the whole. Old colleagues expressed interest in her studies, asking knowledgeable questions, and in some cases, offering advice.

One older gentleman—a fellow who had never warmed much to her before—nodded as he listened to her description of her work. Then he said, "Kala," with a sweet, almost fatherly voice. "I know a place with just that kind of bug. I can't tell you the species, but I don't think it's quite what you've found before."

"Really? Where?"

He brought out a map and pointed at a long valley on the other side of the continental divide. "It looks too low in altitude, I suppose. And a lot of junipers are moving in. But if you get up by this looping road here—"

Sandor pushed in close to watch.

"There's a little glen. I've seen that blue bug there, I'm sure."

"Thank you," Kala told him.

"Whatever I can do to help," the old ranger said. Then he made a show of rolling up the map, asking, "I can take you up myself. If your brother wants to stay here and rest for a bit."

Sandor said, "No thanks."

But he said it in an especially nice way. For the time being, neither one of them could see what was happening.

11

As promised, juniper trees were standing among the natives. Rilly birds and starlings must have eaten juniper berries outside the reserve. Since their corrosive stomach acids were essential for the germination process, wherever they relieved themselves, a new forest of ugly gray-green trees sprouted, prickly and relentless. Most biologists claimed that it was an innate, mutualistic relationship between species. But Kala had a different interpretation: The birds knew precisely what they were doing. Whenever a starling took a dump, it sang to the world, "I'm planting a forest here. And I'm going to be the death of you, you silly old trees."

Sandor squatted and stuck his thick fingers into the needle litter, churning up a long pink worm. After a summer spent watching Kala, he was now one of the great experts when it came to a single genus of pseudoinsects. "Not all that promising," he announced.

Earthworms were another key invader from their home world. And no, nightcrawlers didn't usually coexist with her particular creepy-crawlies.

"Maybe higher up," he offered.

But the old ranger told her this was the place, which implied that her subjects were enduring despite worms and trees: A heroic image that Kala wanted to cling to for a little while longer.

"You wander," she said. "If I don't find anything, I'll follow."

Sandor winked and stepped back into the black shadows.

Twenty minutes later, Kala gave up the hunt. Stepping into a little clearing, she sat on a rock bench, pulling a sandwich from her knapsack and managing a bite before a stranger stepped off the trail behind her.

"Excuse me?"

Startled, Kala wheeled fast, her free hand reaching for the pistol on her belt. But the voice was a girl's, and she was a very tiny creature—big-eyed and fragile, maybe ten years younger than Kala. The girl looked tired and worried. Her shirt was torn, and her left arm wore a long scrape that looked miserably sore.

"Can you help me, ma'am? Please?"

Carefully, Kala rose to her feet while pushing the sandwich back inside her bag, using that same motion to make certain that her second pistol was where she expected it to be. Then with a careful voice, she asked, "Are you lost, sweetie?"

"That too," the girl said, glancing over her shoulder before stepping away from the forest's edge. "It's been days since I've been outside. At least."

Kala absorbed the news. Then she quietly asked, "Where have you been?"

"In the back end."

"The end of what?"

"The bus," the girl snapped, as if Kala should already know that much. "He put me with the others, in the dark—"

"Other girls?"

"Yes, yes." The little creature drifted forward, tucking both hands into her armpits. "He's a mean one—"

"What sect?"

"Huh?"

"Does he belong to a sect?"

"The Children of Forever," the strange girl confessed. "Do you know about them?"

With her right hand, Kala pulled the pistol from her belt while keeping the bag on her left shoulder. Nothing moved in the trees. Except for the girl and her, there might be no one else in this world.

"He's collecting wives," the girl related. "He told me he wants ten of us before he leaves."

"Come closer," Kala told her. Then she asked, "How many girls does he have so far?"

The girl swallowed. "Three."

"And there's just him?"

"Yeah. He's alone." The girl's eyes were growing larger, unblinking and bright. "Three other girls, and me. And him."

"Where?"

"Down that way," said the girl. "Past the parking lot, hiding up in some big old grease trees."

Kala's car lay in the same direction. But Sandor had gone the opposite direction. Whispering, she told the stranger, "Okay. I can help you."

"Thank you, ma'am!"

"Quiet."

"Sorry," the girl muttered.

"Now," Kala told her. "This way."

The girl fell in beside her, rubbing her bloodied arm as she walked. She breathed hard and fast. Several more times, she said, "Thank you." But she didn't seem to look back half as often as Kala did, and maybe that was what seemed wrong.

After a few minutes of hard walking, Kala asked, "So how did you get free?"

The girl looked back then. And with a nod, she said, "I crawled up through the vent."

A tiny creature like that: Kala could believe it.

"I cut my arm on a metal edge."

The wound was red, but the blood had clotted some time ago. Even as Kala nodded, accepting that story, a little part of her was feeling skeptical.

"If he finds me, he'll hurt me."

"I won't let him hurt you," Kala promised.

"There's three other girls in the bus," she repeated. Then she put her hands back into her armpits, hugging herself hard, saying, "We should save them, if we can. Sneak up to the bus while he's hunting for me and get them free, maybe."

But Kala wanted to find Sandor. She came close to mentioning him to the girl, but then she thought better of it. Her brother's presence was a secret that made her feel better. It gave her the confidence to tell the girl, "Later. First I have to make sure that you're safe."

The girl stared up at her protector, saying nothing.

"Come on," Kala urged.

"I want to be safe," the girl said.

"That's what I'm doing—"

"No," she said. Then her hands came out from under her arms, one of them empty while the other held a little box with two metal forks sticking from one end, and the forks jumped out and dove into Kala's skin, and suddenly a hot blue bolt of lightning was rolling through her body.

The girl disarmed Kala and stole her bag and tied her up with plastic straps pulled from her back pocket. Then she vanished down the path. The pain subsided enough to where Kala could sit up, watching uphill, imagining her brother's arrival. But this wasn't the path he had taken, and he still hadn't shown by the time the girl and a New Father appeared. A stubby automatic weapon hung on his shoulder. He was forty or forty-five years old, a big, strong, and homely creature with rough hands and foul breath. "She is awfully pretty," was his first assessment, smiling at his latest acquisition. Then he offered a wink, adding, "He promised I'd like you. And he was right."

The old ranger had set this up.

"I didn't see any brother," said the tiny girl.

"That would be too easy," the man cautioned. Then he handed his weapon to the girl and grabbed Kala, flinging her over a shoulder while saying, "I don't think he'll be any problem. But come on anyway, sweet. Fast as we can walk."

They entered the open glade, crossing the parking lot and

passing Kala's tiny car before they climbed again, entering a mature stand of native trees. Hiding in the gloom was a long bus flanked by a pair of fat freight trucks, each vehicle equipped with wide tires and extra suspension. And there were many more brides than three, Kala saw. Twelve was her first count, fourteen when she tried again. Each girl was in her teens. They looked like schoolgirls on a field trip, giggling and teasing the newest wife by saying, "Too old to walk for herself," and, "Fresh blood in the gene pool, looks like."

Three young men silently watched Kala's arrival. Sons, by the looks of them. In their early twenties, at most.

"Beautiful," said one of the boys.

The other two nodded and grinned.

With the care shown to treasured luggage, the older man set Kala beneath a tree, her back propped against the black trunk, arms and legs needing to be retied, just to make sure. Kala quickly looked from face to face, hoping for any sign of empathy. There was none. And the girl who had been sent out as bait stood over Kala for several minutes, wearing the hardest expression of all.

"He will come for me," Kala said.

"Your brother probably will," said the New Father. "But I've been watching you two. He's carrying nothing bigger than that long pistol, and we've got artillery here he wouldn't dare face."

As if to prove their murderous natures, the sons retrieved their own automatic weapons from the bus.

"What next?" one son asked.

"Stay here with me," their father advised.

But the oldest son didn't like that tactic. "We could circle around, pick him off when shows himself."

"No," he was told.

"But—"

"What did I say?"

The young man dropped his face.

"God led us to this place," the wiser man continued. "And God has seen to give us a sticky hot day. Pray for storms. That's my advice. Then we can punch a hole in the clouds and get power enough to finally leave . . ."

Lightning, he was talking about. Kala had heard about this

technique: With a proper rocket and enough wire following like a tail, it was possible to create lightning during a thunderstorm. A channel of air supplied the connection to the charged earth below. The bolt would strike a preset lightning rod . . . up in the tree on the other side of camp, she realized. She noticed the tall black spike and the heavy wires leading down into the ripper that was probably set in the center of the bus, a class-C that was hungry and waiting for its first and only meal. Kala could guess why these people had come into the mountains. They liked solitude and cheap energy, and besides, the police were hunting everywhere else for those who had murdered the security guards.

Sandor was somewhere close, Kala told herself.

Watching her.

She almost relaxed, imagining her brother hunkered low in the shadow of some great old tree, waiting for a critical mistake to be made. Hunting for an opening, a weakness. Any opportunity. She went as far as picturing his arrival: Sandor would wait for afternoon and the gathering storms, and maybe the rain would start to fall, fat drops turning into a deluge, and while the devout boys and girls watched for the Lord in that angry sky, her brother would sneak up behind her and neatly cut her free.

Obviously, that's what would happen.

Kala thought so highly of the plan that she was as surprised as anyone when a figure emerged from the shadows—a man smaller than most were, running on bare feet to keep his noise to a minimum. He was quick, but something in his stride seemed unhurried. Untroubled. He looked something like a hiker who had lost his way but now had found help. Perhaps that was what Sandor intended. But his face was grim and focused, and no motion was wasted.

Everybody—grooms and brides and even their captive—stared for a moment, examining the stranger in their midst. Then the newcomer reached beneath his shirt and lifted a long pistol, and the first hollow point removed the top of the father's head and the second one knocked the small girl flat. Then Sandor was running again, slipping between brides, and one of the sons finally lifted his weapon, spraying automatic gunfire until three girls had dropped and another brother had pushed the barrel into the forest floor, screaming, "Stop, would you . . . just stop!"

Sandor had the third brother by the neck, slamming him against the broad black trunk of a tree. Then he stared out at the cowering survivors, pressing the barrel of the pistol into the man's ass, and with a voice eerily composed, he said, "Put your guns down. Do it now. Or I'm going to do some painting over here . . . with a goddamn pubic hair brush . . ."

12

The matronly gray robes of middle age had vanished, replaced by an old woman's love for gaudy colors. She was wearing a rich slick and very purple dress with a purple hat with a wide gold belt and matching shoes. Diet and exercise had removed enough weight to give her a stocky, solid figure. She nicely filled the station of her life—that of the fit, well-rested widow. Seeing her children standing at her doorway, Mom smiled—a thoroughly genuine expression, happy but brief. Then she found something alarming in their faces. "What's happened?" With concern, she said, "Darlings. What's wrong?"

Kala glanced at her brother and then over her shoulder.

In the street sat a plain commercial van. Nothing about the vehicle was remarkable, except that its back end was being pressed down by the terrific, relentless weight of a class-C ripper and a powerful little winch.

The van was their fourth vehicle in three days, and Sandor would replace it tomorrow, if he thought it would help.

"I was just leaving," their mother offered. And when no one else spoke, she added, "I don't normally dress like this—"

"Don't go," said her son.

"Are you meeting friends?" Kala asked. "If you don't show, will somebody miss you?"

Mom shook her head. "I just go the tea parlor on Fridays. I know people, but no, I doubt if anybody expects me."

It was the Sabbath today, wasn't it?

"Can I park the van inside your garage?" Sandor asked.

Mom nodded. "You'll have to pull my car out—"

"Keys," he said.

She fished them from a purse covered with mock jewelry, and Sandor started down the front stairs.

Kala gratefully stepped inside. All these years, and the same furnishings and carpet populated the living room, although every surface was a little more worn now. Immersed in what was astonishingly familiar, she suddenly relaxed. She couldn't help herself. All at once it was impossible to stand under her own power, and as soon as she sat, a deep need for sleep began to engulf her.

"What's happened?" Mom repeated. "What's wrong?"

"We're going to explain everything, Mom."

"You look awful, sweetness. Both of you do." The old woman sat beside Kala on the lumpy couch, one hand patting her on the knee. "But I'm glad to see you two, together." Sometime in these last few moments, Kala had begun to cry.

"Tell me, dear."

In what felt like a single breath, the story emerged. For the second time in her life, Kala had been kidnapped, but this time Sandor killed two people while freeing her. A second bride died in random gunfire, and two more were severely injured. "But we had to leave them," Kala confessed. "After we disarmed the brothers and brides, we left them with first aid kits and two working trucks . . . except Sandor shot out the tires before we drove off in their bus, just to make sure we would have a head start . . ."

Her mother held herself motionless, mouth open and no sound worth the effort.

"It was a big long bus with a ripper onboard. Sandor drove us through the mountains. Fast. I don't know why we didn't crash, but we didn't. We stopped at a fix-it shop and he made calls, and a hundred miles after that, we met a couple friends of his . . . men that he met inside prison, I think . . ."

"When was this?"

"Wednesday," she answered. "Those friends helped Sandor pull the ripper from the bus. They gave us a new truck and kept the capacitors and the other expensive gear for themselves. Then he and I drove maybe two miles, and that's when Sandor stole a second truck. Because he didn't quite trust his friends, and what if they decided to come take the ripper too?" She wiped at her eyes, her cheeks. "After that, we drove more than a thousand miles, but never in a straight line. By then, we'd finally decided what we were going to do, and he stole the van before we came here."

Mom was alert, focused. She was sitting forward with her hand clenched to her daughter's knee. Very quietly, she asked, "Is it one of the stolen rippers? From that convoy?"

Kala nodded. "The ID marks match."

"Have you thought about giving it back to its rightful owners?"

"We talked about that. Yes."

But then Mom saw what had eventually become obvious to Kala. "Regardless what you tell the owners, they'll think your brother had something to do with the robbery and murders. And what good would that do?"

"Nothing."

Then her mother gathered up Kala's hands, and without hesitation, she said, "God has given you a gift, darling."

She didn't think about it in religious terms. But the words sounded nice.

"A great rare and wonderful gift," her mother continued. "And you know, if there is one person who truly deserves to inherit a new world, it has to be—"

"My brother?"

"No," Mom exclaimed, genuinely surprised. Then as the front door swung open and Sandor stepped inside, she said brightly, "It's you, sweetness. You deserve the best world. Of course, of course, of course . . . !"

◦ ◦ ◦

Their frantic days had only just begun. The Children of Forever would have learned their names from the old ranger, or maybe from Kala's abandoned car. And people who had murdered dozens to steal the ripper would undoubtedly do anything to recover what was theirs and avenge their losses. Obviously, it was best to vanish again, this time taking their mother with them. Old lives and treasured patterns had to be avoided, yet even on the run, they still had to find time and energy to make plans for what was to come next.

Sandor knew the best places to find machinery and foodstuffs and the other essential supplies. But Kala knew where to find people—the right people—who would make this business worthwhile. And it was their mother who acted as peacemaker, calming the water when her two strong-willed children began fighting over the details that always looked trivial the next day. Suddenly it was winter—the worst season to migrate to another world. But that gave them the gift of several months where they could make everything perfect, or nearly so.

Years ago, the old fix-it man who once worked on their family car had retired, and the next owner had driven his shop out of business. The property was purchased from the bank for nothing and reconnected to the power grid, and with Kala's friends supplying labor and enough money, Sandor managed to refit the building according to their specific needs. Medical stocks were locked in the lady's room. The garage was jammed with canned and dried food and giant water tanks, plus the rest of their essential goods, including a fully charged class-C ripper that would carry away the little building.

On a cold bleak day in late March—several weeks before their scheduled departure—a stranger came looking for gasoline. He parked beside one of the useless pumps and pulled on his horn several times. Then he climbed out of the small, nondescript car, and, ignoring the CLOSED signs painted on the shuttered windows, walked across the cracked pavement in order to knock hard on both garage doors and the front door.

"Hey! Anybody there?" he shouted before finally giving up.

As he returned to his car, Kala asked her brother, "What is he? Children of Forever, or some kind of undercover cop?"

"Really," Sandor replied, "does it matter?"

Kala set her splattergun back in its cradle.

"I think it's time," their mother offered.

It was too early in the season to be ideal. But what choice did they have? Kala lifted the phone and made one coded call to the nearest town. And within the hour, everybody had arrived. Those who weren't going with them offered quick tearful good-byes to those who were, showering those blessed pioneers with kisses and love. But then the pioneers had enough, and with quick embarrassed voices, they said, "Enough, Mommy. Daddy. That's enough. Good-bye!"

⊸ ⊸ ⊸

Kala had come too far and paid too much of a price not to watch what was about to happen. She opened all of the shutters in the public room, letting the murky gray flow inside, and then she sat between two six-year-olds, one of whom asked, "How much longer now?"

"Soon," she promised. "A minute or two, at most."

Sandor and several other mechanically minded souls were in the garage, watching the ripper power up. Sharing the public room with Kala were a handful of grown men and a dozen women, plus nearly forty children sitting on tiny folding chairs, the oldest child being a stubborn twelve-year-old boy—the only son of colleagues who were staying behind.

Kala's mother was one of the women, and she wasn't even the oldest.

"We're not making everybody else's mistakes," Kala had explained to her, sitting in the old living room some months ago. "We're taking grandparents and little kids, but very few young adults. I don't want virility and stupidity. I want wisdom and youth."

"What seeds are you taking?" her mother had asked.

"None."

"Did I hear you say—?"

"No seeds, and no animals. Not even one viable tortoise shell. And before we leave, I want to make sure every mouse in the building is dead, and every fly and flea, and if there's one earthworm living under us, I'll kill it myself when it pops up in the new world."

Nobody was leaving this world but humans.

And even then, they were traveling as close to empty-handed as they dared. They had tools and a few books about science and mechanics. But everyone had taken an oath not to bring any

Bibles or odd Testaments, and, as far as possible, everything else that smacked of preconceptions and fussy religion had to be left behind on their doomed world.

The children came from families who believed as Kala believed.

It was amazing, and heartening, how many people held opinions not too much unlike hers. And sometimes in her most doubting moments, she found herself wondering if maybe her home world had a real chance of surviving the next ten thousand years.

But there were many parents who saw doom coming–ecological or political or religious catastrophes–and that's why they were so eager to give up a young son or daughter. They were there now, standing out near the highway, surely hearing the ripper as it began to hammer hard at reality.

From inside the cold garage, Sandor shouted, "A target's acquired!"

Will this madness work? Kala asked herself one last time. Could one species arrive on an alien world, with children and old people in tow, and find food enough to survive? And then could they pass through the next ten thousand years without destroying everything that that world was and could have become . . . ?

And then it was too late to ask the question.

The clouds of one day had vanished into a suddenly blue glare of empty skies, a green-blue lawn of grassy something stretching off into infinity . . . and suddenly a room full of bright young voices shouted, "Neat! Sweet! Pretty!"

Then the boy on her right tugged at her arm, adding, "That's fun, Miss Kala. Let's do it again!"

THE VOYAGE OF
NIGHT SHINING WHITE

by Chris Roberson

Chris Roberson was born in Memphis, Tennessee, in 1970. He attended the University of Texas at Austin, and worked as a baker, taught middle school history, was a product support engineer, and gave change at an arcade. Roberson's work is heavily influenced by the pulp adventure classics of the 1940s and 1950s. An exciting new writer, he has published six novels, including Set the Seas on Fire; Here, There & Everywhere; *and* Paragaea: A Planetary Romance. *His first short story, "Lord Peter Midnight and the Goblin King," appeared in* The Clockwork Reader, Volume 1, *in 2001. His short story "O One," part of the Celestial Empire alternate history sequence, was nominated for the World Fantasy Award and won the Sidewise Award in 2004. A publisher and editor, Roberson also runs Monkeybrain Books with business partner and spouse, Allison Baker, and edited the anthology* Adventure, Volume 1, *in 2005. He is currently working on Celestial Empire novels* The Dragon's Nine Sons *and* Iron Jaw and Hummingbird, *and the cross-time Arthurian science fantasy* End of the Century. *He lives in Austin, Texas, with his wife and daughter.*

1

Hexagram 45
Ts'ui: Lake Above Earth
Gathering Together (Massing)

ZHENG YI STOOD at the panoramic window, looking out across the blue-green curve of the Earth below him, at the silhouette of the ship in the near distance. It glittered like an ornamental fish caught in sunlight against the dark black of space, seeming fragile and small. Zheng felt as though he could reach out and take it in his hand, but that it would break at the slightest touch. So delicate a thing. The ship would be Zheng's home for the next year and more. *Night Shining White.*

The rotation of Diamond Summit beneath Zheng's feet continued, and the ship slipped slowly out of sight. Zheng's mouth was dry, and he wiped his sweating palms against the fabric of his tunic. A page, fawning and insincere, touched him gingerly on the elbow, and indicated that the transport was ready to receive him. Zheng shouldered his bag, and followed the page to the docking area.

Onboard the Cloud Flyer, Zheng sat strapped in his seat, looking out the viewport. The docking clamps released with a distant clanging noise, and the little shuttle slipped out into space, carried first by inertia, then guided by slight firings of the attitude thrusters. The orbital city of Diamond Summit filled the viewport window, then slowly dwindled as they moved further and further away. The faint line of the orbital elevator tether, the Bridge of Heaven, traced from Diamond Summit down to the planet's surface below.

Zheng gripped the arms of his chair, and squeezed his eyes tightly shut. He never adjusted easily to zero gravity in the best of circumstances, and with his anxiety these were far from the best of circumstances. Diamond Summit had been his home for the last six months, and in that time he'd come to feel somewhat secure there, on solid ground. To see it teetering so delicately on top of a spider's strand of bundled steel and ceramics was unsettling. That he was going from such a position to one even more precarious only made matters worse.

Zheng finally opened his eyes as their destination hove into view, the Cloud Flyer drawing near for the docking procedure. The rest of the crew was already onboard, and only scant hours remained before they would be leaving Earth orbit for their six month long journey to the red planet. Zheng Yi would be the last to join them.

Zheng looked upon the ship, and realized he would not see it again from this vantage for many long months. He'd know the small shell of ceramic and steel from the inside only, his whole universe reduced to those bare few square meters. So delicate a thing. His hands trembled, almost imperceptibly.

The ships docked with a shuddering thud, and the pilot invited Zheng to disembark. Zheng secured the strap of his luggage around his arm, and guided himself awkwardly through the cabin to the exit, his bag floating like a dark cloud over his head. The pressurize door hissed open and, fighting his rising gorge, Captain Zheng Yi made his way through the docking umbilicus to his first command, *Night Shining White.*

☞ ☞ ☞

Night Shining White was the least of the ten ships in the Treasure Fleet of the Dragon Throne. It would be the last to leave Earth orbit, the last to reach Fire Star, and the first to return from the red planet. A water-tender, its hold contained large collapsible tanks that would be transferred to the other ships in the flotilla on their arrival at the red planet, freeing the cargo space for the return trip. Once enough samples of mineral and ore and soil had been retrieved from the red planet's surface to fill the holds of *Night Shining White,* the ship would begin the six month journey back to Earth. Theirs would be the smallest share of glory, theirs the smallest portion of the Emperor's favors.

☞ ☞ ☞

The Minister of Rites was on hand to greet Captain Zheng when he boarded, as protocol demanded.

"Captain Zheng," the Minister began, bobbing his head in deference while clinging lightly to the handholds riveted to the bulkhead. "The crew is finishing their morning meal, as First Watch has only just begun, while Physician Xiang Du is in the ship's surgery making his final preparations for our journey. If you will accompany me to the Command Center, I can call the crew to attendance, and we can begin the invocations."

Zheng Yi swallowed hard, conscious that a captain's first words onboard should not be spoken in a wavering voice.

"As you say, Minister Bao," Zheng said, trying to find a secure position, his limbs refusing to cooperate in zero gravity. "If you will lead the way . . ." Zheng motioned for the minister to proceed, but at the end of his arm's arc his hand bumped the bulkhead, which sent the rest of his body spiraling slowly in the opposite direction.

The minister, for his part, bowed his head again briefly, averting his eyes and pretending not to notice the new captain bobbing like a lost balloon against the ceiling. The minister turned, and with a slight touch against the handholds glided his hefty bulk expertly through the hatch. The captain followed, awkwardly, slowly.

◦ ◦ ◦

There had not yet been time for introductions, so Captain Zheng knelt in the middle of the Command Center surrounded by strangers. The steering console was before him, like a podium, with the reactor controls arrayed on panels just beyond. A candle was secured to the casing of the steering console, a stick of incense burning on either side. The candle's flame was a perfect sphere in zero gravity, a miniature sun perched at the head of the taper, while the smoke from the burning incense drifted outwards in all directions in complex shapes and curls, driven by minute currents in the ship's air, dancing to the beat of the crewmen's exhalations and slight movements.

Captain Zheng knelt on the deck, his legs held in place by

straps bolted to the plates. He bowed his head for a moment, then lifted his eyes to the candle's tiny sphere, arms outstretched, ready to continue.

"As the divine smoke rises, as the candle burns, we bow down with hearts pure and true and beseech the messengers of merit to convey by means of these offerings in this year, in this month, on this day, at this hour; we respectfully entreat the patriarchs of the imperially created reactor throughout the ages, to the ancient geomancers and astrologers: Yellow Emperor, Duke of Zhou, immortal masters of former ages divinely knowledgeable about yin-yang, Dark Raven, immortal White Crane master."

Captain Zheng paused, and glanced around the cabin at the other six men, knelt against straps on the deck, their heads and hands in attitudes of supplication.

"And patriarchs of the ages who have traversed the seas and skies; who know the solar winds, the asteroids, the gravity wells, the moon; who are conversant with the orbital paths, the constellations and the guiding stars; those from past times to the present day, those who first transmitted it and those who later taught it."

A crewman, the youngest of them, whispered something to the older man at his side, but was quickly silenced by a hiss and glare from the Minister of Rites. The young crewman, cowed, shrank into himself, eyes averted.

"And the great guardian spirits of the reactor; the great guardian spirit of the isotope, the page boy who sets the free neutron in motion, the spirit of the water coolant, the lord of fission, the strongman who cleaves the isotope in two, the spirit soldiers who drive the free neutrons in their courses, the guardian spirits of the control rods, the master of the reaction, and all the other immortal masters and spirit soldiers and divine emissaries—All the efficacious spirits of the incense and candle."

Minister Bao gently released the straps from his legs, and drifted to the captain's side, a bulb of wine held in one hand.

"And the protectress of our ships, the Celestial Consort, Tianfei, brilliant, divine, marvelous, responsive, mysterious force, protector of the people, guardian of the country."

The minister gently screwed the top of the wine bulb open, and handed it to the captain. "Come down one and all to this incense feast, partake of this sagely vessel; Come riding on auspicious clouds from the ends of the earth; Come down and grace our incense table; Let us seat you in your respective places that we might reverentially offer the immortal masters a flagon of wine, beseeching them to protect our ships and valuables."

Captain Zheng held the the wine bulb near the candle's flame, and squeezed. A single drop burped through the pressurized mouth, and drifted gracefully towards the candle's spherical flame.

"We are your servants."

The drop of wine, like a miniature liquid moon, plunged into the tiny sun. The flame guttered, and was extinguished. The rite was complete.

⊸ ⊸ ⊸

Minister Bao made cursory introductions once the invocations were concluded, but Zheng scarcely managed to connect the names he'd studied back on Diamond Summit with the faces before him. They were all good sailors, if the reports were to be believed, all of them exemplars in their fields. Of everyone on the ship, only Zheng himself was out of place. He'd been appointed to the Ministry of Celestial Excursion as a reward for a dead man's service, and Zheng had been in no position to object. It was not the place of a palace servant to refuse an order from the Dragon Throne, not Zheng's place to defy the Emperor's will. Zheng was just grateful that the ship's proper functioning and success did not depend on his ability to understand its workings, only his ability to remember which of the crewmen were responsible for what tasks.

The minister led Zheng from the Command Center to the captain's quarters in Compartment Three. He offered to give the captain a tour of the ship, but Zheng politely declined for the moment, requesting a short while to grow accustomed to the lack of gravity before making his rounds. With another abbreviate bow, the minister left Zheng to situate himself in his cabin.

As soon as he was left alone, Zheng drew a jar of reinforced ceramic from his luggage, and guided himself gracelessly to a high shelf where he began to secure the jar with straps and buckles. His every concentration on the task, he was startled by a rapping on the steel door of the hatch.

"Your pardons for this interruption, my captain, but I wanted to offer you my services."

The straps were not yet fastened in place and, when Zheng turned, the jar began to drift away from the bulkhead like an errant cloud. Panicked, Zheng scrambled to get his hands around it.

When the jar was safely back in his grasp, Zheng turned his attention to the open door. Floating just beyond was a slender man, with delicate mustaches and thin hair that swam around him in the low gravity like an anemone, dressed like all the crewmen in a simple white tunic and trousers, feet shod in soft-soled slippers. He had a high forehead, a narrow face, and long, graceful fingers. Zheng was not a terribly large man, round but not given to fat, with muscle beneath his soft skin, but beside this thin rail of a man he seemed like a mountain.

"Physician . . . Xiang?" the captain replied, searching to match the face with the name.

"Yes, my captain," the man replied with a slight smile and a nod, a circumscribed bow. "Xiang Du, Physician in Imperial Service."

"What is it I can do for you, physician?"

"Oh, no sir, I'm afraid you misunderstand. It is more along the lines of what I can do for you." Xiang gestured to the open door with a flick of his slender fingers. "May I enter?"

The captain nodded in response, and the physician gripped the edge of the hatch and gently propelled himself inside. The physician left his hand on the hatch door, and with raised eyebrows requested permission to close it behind him. Zheng, clutching the ceramic jar with one hand, waved him to proceed with the other.

Once the hatch door was securely shut, the physician arranged himself in the corner, and looked sidelong at the captain.

"Well?" Zheng asked.

"You'll pardon my speaking bluntly, my captain, but it is the prerogative of a ship's physician to ascertain the health of all those onboard, not least of which the man in charge. I am merely attempting to determine whether you are ill, or merely ill at ease. I'd hoped to keep this discussion confidential . . ." He trailed off, and motioned towards the closed hatch.

"I understand," the captain replied, forcing himself to relax. "I assure you, physician, I am in perfect health. The Ministry of Celestial Excursion's staff surgeons at Diamond Summit gave me a clear report just yesterday." He paused, and then added, "And I should note that their examinations included maladies of the nerves and emotions as well as those of blood, bone and muscle. My humors are in balance, my yin and yang in proper proportion."

"That is gratifying to hear, my captain," the physician replied, still looking at him through narrowed eyes. "This is your . . ." the physician paused, momentarily, ". . . first command, I take it?"

"And what of it?" Zheng asked, defensively, narrowing his eyes.

"Nothing, nothing at all," the physician responded. "I myself have spent the last two years providing medical services at the orbital shipyards beyond Diamond Summit, at the top of the Bridge of Heaven, and have perforce spent much of that time without the benefit of gravity, whether real or simulated by rotation. Your pardon for mentioning it, but you seem somewhat tense, your mien a trifle pale. Is it safe to assume that you are unaccustomed to low gravity environments?"

Zheng nodded in response.

"You'll get your legs below you soon enough," the physician said. "And from what the steersman tells me, we'll be deploying the counterweight and beginning rotation almost immediately after leaving Earth orbit, so you've not too much longer to go before you feel the tug of gravity on your bones again." The physician's eyes trailed to the ceramic jar clutched against the captain's chest, and then his gaze darted momentarily below the captain's waist and the smooth expanse of fabric between his legs. "If my asking does not offend, is that the captain's . . ." The physician paused, searching for the appropriate word.

"We call it 'The Treasure'," the captain answered. "We carry it with us always, in the hopes that it can be buried alongside us in death, and that we will be made whole men in the world to come." Zheng suppressed a shiver, remembering the sudden chill of the blade against his skin, and the sharp red pain that followed.

The physician's eyes darted past the captain's waist again, flickering back to meet his gaze in less than a heartbeat.

"I've never actually seen one before," Physician Xiang said, impressed. "One of the 'Treasures,' that is."

The captain took hold of a railing along the bulkhead, and pulled himself back to the high shelf. He carefully strapped the jar in place, and then pushed off the wall, angling back to his luggage fixed to the deck.

An awkward silence followed as the captain withdrew a slender leather case from his bag, a silence in which neither man seemed to know quite what to say. The captain did not want to dismiss the physician too hastily, but he had nothing more to say, while the physician kept glancing at the jar strapped to the high shelf, an uncomfortable look on his narrow face. When the captain unhooked the latches on the leather case and withdrew the long, two-stringed fiddle, the physician's entire manner changed. His face lit up, and he clapped his hands like a child opening a long desired gift.

"An *erhu*!" the physician said, using the proper name for the instrument. "Do you play?"

The captain ran his fingers along the narrow neck of the fiddle, lovingly.

"I was a member of an imperial ensemble in the Forbidden City for the last four years, conductor of the ensemble for nearly half that time. Despite the space and mass requirements for the voyage, I insisted to the Ministry chiefs that I be allowed to bring at least one instrument along with me."

"As did I!" the physician replied, his excitement growing. "I play the *dizi* flute myself, and very nearly needed to smuggle my flute in as a piece of medical equipment, when it came time to mass out my belongings on Diamond Summit. Luckily, I don't weigh as much as my height allows, so I was granted this small indulgence. Oh, I'm delighted to have another musician onboard. Do you suppose I might hear you play, at your convenience naturally?"

The captain smiled.

"Of course," he answered.

"Well, with your permission, I'll take my leave," the physician said. He pushed himself out of the corner and drifted through the room towards the hatch. "I've some final arrangements to make in the surgery. Engineer Hong insists that the reactor will be ready in time for us to depart on schedule, and I don't want all of my equipment jarring loose and drifting through the ship."

"Is there some problem with the reactor?"

"Nothing serious, I'm given to understand. Some final adjustments to the casing, I believe. Hong or the Engineer's Mate could explain it better than I."

The captain returned his fiddle to the case, and then secured it to a shelf with another set of straps.

"I will ask him. Thank you, physician."

Physician Xiang rested his hand on the door's handle, and paused. Over his shoulder, he said, "My captain, another moment of your time?"

"Certainly."

"I am, by inclination, a Daoist. Might I share with you a thought which might be pertinent to your current situation? Purely in the realm of the philosophical, meaning no disrespect."

"By all means."

"Lao-tzu speaks about the nature of the ideal leader. Such a man holds no prejudice, harbors no fear, and allows his followers to be guided by their own best natures." The physician paused, watching the captain's face closely. "No fears, my captain. Men will excuse anger before they will accept fear. Better that followers should assume their leader is a man of temper than conclude he is afraid."

The captain nodded slowly.

"I understand," Zheng said. "Thank you, Physician Xiang."

"Your service, my captain. The health of this ship and all on her, body and mind, is my duty."

The physician swung open the door, and drifted into the hallway beyond, out of view.

👁 👁 👁

It was the Third Watch and time for the midday meal when the
Minister of Rites returned to take the captain on his tour of the
ship. When underway, the officers and crew would gather in their
respective mess areas, the crew in their Common Room and the
officers in the Captain's Mess. The morning and midday meals
were light, usually no more than a bowl of rice doused in some
simple stock, with green tea and bits of salted fish or pork served
alongside. The evening meal was more elaborate, prepared and
served by the Engineer's Mate, first to the officers, then to the
crew, the Mate himself able to sit and eat only when the others
had been fed. The viands, including foodstuffs, condiments and
ingredients, were all kept in the lower deck of the Second
Compartment, beneath the Command Center.

Today, with the final preparations for leaving Earth orbit underway, the crew had been asked to forgo the standard midday
meal, and to sup on rice balls and green tea in bamboo vacuum-
flasks as they worked. Physician Xiang had elected to skip the
Midday altogether, busying himself in the surgery, and Minister
Bao had brought the captain the same rough fare enjoyed by the
crew.

Once the captain had finished, the minister waiting patiently
at his side while he ate, the ship's tour began. The ship was divided into six compartments numbered from bow to stern, separated from each other by steel bulkheads. Each compartment
could be sealed off and pressurized by heavy airtight doors, so
that an explosive decompression in one compartment would not
cripple the entire ship. The compartments were divided into two
or three decks each, with ladders and hatches allowing access between decks. Running the length of the ship was a central passageway, starting with the docking area in Compartment One and
ending just short of the reactors in Compartment Six, with smaller
passages and hallways branching off along its length.

The tour began at the nose of the ship, in the bow, with
Compartment One. This was the forward-most point in the ship,
and the narrowest, housing navigational equipment, sensors, and
radio receivers and transmitters. Through the long voyage to the
red planet, *Night Shining White* would be able to stay in contact

not only with the Ministry chiefs back on Earth, but also with the other ships in the Treasure Fleet flotilla.

The next, Compartment Two, was divided into two decks. The first was dominated by one large room, the Command Center. From navigation to steering to propulsion, all of the ship's systems were controlled from this large cabin. Reinforced leaded glass viewports at the front of the Command Center looked out over the tapering nose of the ship's bow, allowing an unobstructed view ahead. The second, lower deck was given over entirely to the ship's stores, viands, victuals, and medicinal supplies.

Compartment Three primarily housed the officers' quarters. There were three decks in all, the first occupied by the captain's quarters and the captain's mess, the second by the quarters of the Minister of Rites and a small cabin set aside for matters of protocol, and the third by the physician's quarters and the ship's surgery.

Compartment Four's first two decks were divided into the crew's quarters and Common Room, with the space for a third deck occupied by cargo holds.

Compartment Five housed the ship's generators, compressors, heating and refrigeration units, air purifiers and circulators, and the balance of the cargo holds.

Compartment Six, finally, was dominated by the ship's reactor, the tanks of hydrogen used for propulsion, and the thrust mechanisms.

●　●　●

In the course of his tour, Zheng came upon Steersman Fei and Navigator Liu in the Command Center, each at his station, making their final checks of the ship's systems. Each bowed his head for a fraction of a second, deferential but preoccupied, but when Bao began to chastise them for their inappropriate behavior, Zheng waved him away.

"They are busy men at their tasks, minister," Zheng said. "Surely protocol allows for gradations."

Minister Bao tensed, but nodded reluctantly.

"There are degrees of observation, certainly, my captain," the minister answered. "But surely the highest virtue can be attained only by adhering to the highest degree?"

Zheng tried to compose a diplomatic response. The minister was a hard-line Confucian, and held his position by dint of his strict nature. Zheng had no wish to offend. While Zheng was the master and commander of the ship in all regards, ultimately even he would be judged by his adherence to the rules and protocols imposed by the Dragon Throne. Zheng had even heard rumors that some ships carried among their crew Embroidered Guards, secret policemen from the Eastern Depot, the Emperor's eyes and ears and hands, deadly even thousands of miles away from the Imperial Palace. It would be an inauspicious beginning to their journey to offend the protocol minister before even leaving Earth orbit, an even less auspicious beginning to rouse the suspicion of a hidden enforcer.

"You are wiser than I in such matters, minister," Zheng finally answered, then feigned interest in the navigator's calculations.

The two men, steersman and navigator, were as different as two individuals could reasonably be, the embodiment of the dual nature of yin-yang. Liu was a wisp of a man, short and slight, with a low forehead and a round face. He was always smiling, a gap-toothed grin, and his hair was shorn short, with a short fuzzy beard on his chin. Fei, on the other hand, was tall and well mus-cled, like an athlete or martial artist. His expression was severe, his face sharp like an ax blade, his chin and scalp shaved clean and gleaming.

Zheng turned his attention to the steersman's console, where a red light was flashing beneath Steersman Fei's hand.

"Is there some trouble, steersman?" Zheng asked, dangling from a handhold in the bulkhead.

"Some minor trouble in Compartment Six, my captain," the steersman answered, averting his eyes in deference. "Engineer Hong is addressing it as we speak."

Zheng nodded, and pushed off the wall towards the doorway to the next compartment. "Carry on, men," he called over his shoulder, and followed Minister Bao on the tour.

They encountered the balance of the crew in the junction between Compartments Five and Six. Engineer Hong was crouched against the ceiling, wiping his red face with a soiled cloth, his expression weary. Hong was fat but muscled, a bear of a man, red faced, his hair going from gray to white, with wispy mustaches and beard. His fingernails, Zheng saw, were cracked and torn, with a crescent of grime under each.

On the deck, a collection of tools held awkwardly in his narrow arms, sat Engineer's Mate Chen. Thin, tall but slight, Chen was like a stalk of bamboo transformed into a man. His face was still hairless, his chin not yet sprouting its first beard, and his hair was shaved back and braided in a Manchurian queue at the neck.

"Is there a problem, Engineer Hong?" Captain Zheng asked as he drifted through the passageway towards the junction, coming into view. "You seem . . . frustrated?"

"Not at all, my captain," Engineer Hong replied, wiping his face as clean as possible and maneuvering himself into a bowed position. "Chen and I were just making some last minute adjustments when we encountered, what you might call, an issue."

"An issue," Zheng repeated. "And that is distinguished from a problem how, precisely?"

"Well sir, my captain, begging your pardon, I suppose you might say that an issue is a problem that comes with its own solution ready made. It isn't a problem, rightly, if there's a way to fix it close to hand."

"So we don't have a problem, then, we have an issue, as you have a solution to the problem in the works?"

The engineer nodded, briskly.

"Even though the solution is not yet in place?"

Again came the brisk nod.

"That's it exactly, my captain, sir."

Beneath him, the Engineer's Mate looked up at his immediate superior with an expression nothing short of reverential.

"Engineer Hong," Zheng answered, "might I say that you have an impressive ability to circumvent the accepted definitions of language?"

The engineer grinned proudly.

"Thank you, sir," he said.

A long and awkward silence followed. The captain eyed the engineer expectantly, as though waiting for a particular response.

"And the issue?" the captain finally said.

"Ah, yes, sorry," the engineer answered, swabbing at his sweating red face with the cloth. "It's the reactor cooling loop, sir. We were doing some final pressure tests on the Nuclear Thermal Rocket, and found a small crack in one of the gaskets. Nothing terribly serious, just the result of expansion and compression when the parts were assembled at the shipyards, I imagine. We flushed the system, and replaced the gasket, and now we're just waiting for the system to repressurize so we can make sure the seal is solid. We should be done by Fifth Watch, I imagine."

"So you anticipate this solution will prove adequate, Engineer Hong? There's no way the new gasket could develop the same crack given time?"

"Well, the only way that could happen would be if the design is defective. And if it was, we'd surely have run into the problem before, or the Ministry's quality inspectors would have identified the flaw."

The captain glanced at the young engineer's mate, who was still looking on the engineer with reverential awe, nodding his head slowly.

"Engineer's Mate Chen, have you anything to add?" Captain Zheng asked, pleasantly.

The mate began to stammer a reply, unable to form a complete word, much less a thought. His eyes were glued to the deck, unable to meet the captain's gaze.

"B-b-b . . ."

Minister Bao shot forward, kicking off the deck plate and angling expertly to the captain's side.

"My captain," the minister said, whispering into Zheng's ear. "Protocol demands that a strict chain of command be observed. While the captain may, of course, address any member of his crew, a crewman of the mate's rank may not speak directly to the captain, addressing his response instead to his immediate superiors, such as Engineer Hong."

Captain Zheng flinched.

"My apologies," Zheng said, his eyes on Minister Bao but his words intended for all in earshot. "Well, if there are no further concerns, I think I'll return to my quarters to review our orders."

Minister Bao's shoulders relaxed, and he bobbed a quick bow in midair.

"As you wish, my captain."

◓ ◓ ◓

The other nine ships in the Treasure Fleet had departed Earth orbit on a staggered schedule over the course of the previous two months, at a rate of one launch every five days. All of the ships had been, like *Night Shining White,* constructed in orbit, though most were far larger and more powerful than the small watertender. Even the closest in size, *Jade Maiden,* was almost half again as large as *Night Shining White;* it was a livestock carrier, its holds divided into stalls full of grunting, shitting beasts—goats, cattle, and pigs. Next in size was the serene greenhouse ship, *The Nameless Origin of Heaven and Earth,* full of quiet steaming plants scrubbing oxygen from the crew's exhalations, bottling it away for transfer to the other ships on their arrival at the red planet Fire Star. The largest of the ships, the twin frigates *The Five Classics* and *The Six Virtues,* carried Cloud Flyer shuttles, landing vehicles, rugged six wheel self-driven wagons and habitats for use on the planet's surface. The remaining four ships were of middling size, *The Deer and Cauldron, Yellow Emperor, Celestial Consort,* and *Water Margin,* and primarily carried men and light equipment.

It had been the dream of the last three emperors to extend the reach of the Dragon Throne beyond the confines of Earth, out into the stars. The first of the space-reaching emperors had overseen the first launches to Earth orbit, and the initial construction of the Bridge of Heaven, the orbital elevator that grew from Gold Mountain on the island of Fragrant Harbor to stretch beyond the reaches of the atmosphere. His son and successor had surpassed his father's reach, ordering the construction of a small fleet of launch vessels, the assemblage of the first elements of the orbital city of Diamond Summit. The third and current emperor of the space dynasty, then, had driven for the completion of the orbital city, the establishment of the Cold Palace base on the surface of the moon, and mounted plans to reach the Earth's nearest planetary neighbor. The red planet, fourth from the sun. Fire Star.

There was competition to reach the red planet first. The Aztecs of Mexica, never comfortable under the banner of the Dragon Throne, had shrugged off the imperial yoke a century before, and successfully resisted all attempts by the Army of the Green Standard to reintegrate them into the empire. The Aztecs had launched a few crude rockets into orbits in the decades previous, and were rumored to harbor plans to establish a presence on the red planet before the emperor. The agents of the Eastern Depot had been able to find no evidence that they had the technical wherewithal to accomplish their goals. The Aztecs were, the Ministry of Celestial Excursion had concluded, a backwards and benighted people, savages who felt that blood sacrifice was necessary for the smooth operation of their machinery. They presented no significant threat to the ambitions of the Dragon Throne.

When *Night Shining White* left Earth orbit at First Watch the following day, the final element of the Treasure Fleet would be in motion, and the dream of three emperors to conquer the heavens would be that much closer to fruition.

◦ ◦ ◦

After the conclusion of the morning meal, the Minister of Rites gathered the crew together once more in the Command Center. Navigator Liu and Steersman Fei were at their posts, while Engineer Hong and his mate Chen were strapped into gravity chairs near the reactor controls. The captain, physician, and minister had secured themselves in three chairs bolted to the deck, facing the array of viewports overlooking the bow.

"Navigator, do we have the course plotted and calculated?" Captain Zheng asked, following the standard script.

Navigator Liu made a final sweep across his abacus, the magnetic beads sliding along the frictionless greased rods, clicking into one another rhythmically.

"Yes, my captain," the navigator replied, checking the results against the sums recorded on his wipe-board.

"Steersman, has the appropriate thrust and directional values been selected?"

Pro forma, Steersman Fei made a show of checking the toggled switches on his station.

"Yes, my captain," he replied with a flourish.

"Engineer, is the reactor prepared and ready for operation?"

Without hesitation, Engineer Hong raised his red face proudly and crossed his arms over his chest.

"Yes, my captain."

"In that case, Engineer Hong," the captain answered, "withdraw the cooling rods one quarter, release the liquid hydrogen into the heating chamber, and prepare to iris open the aperture for thrust."

"Yes, my captain," the engineer replied, and he and the mate began to work a row of knobs and switches before them.

It was only a matter of moments before the engineer turned in his seat, and gave the captain the sign that all was in readiness.

"Minister, will you perform the final invocation?"

The minister dipped his head to the captain, and then raised his eyes to the viewports before them.

"Tianfei, Celestial Consort and guardian of the country, keep us in your hand."

The captain muttered a quick Amida Buddha of his own just in case, and saw the Engineer thumbing a small icon of Tianfei worn on a chain around his neck. The physician beside him was smiling almost beatifically, while the Navigator grinned nervously.

"Engineer," the captain said with a tone of finality. "Begin thrust."

A slow vibration rumbled through the skeleton of the ship, a low harmonic frequency buzzing their bones and teeth. The earth's moon, visible out of the corner viewport, shifted incrementally out of view, glacially slow. The field of stars beyond was unchanged, unwavering, too distant to change perspective.

Captain Zheng's hands tightened in white knuckled fists on the arms of his chair. *Night Shining White* was underway.

2

Hexagram 35
Chin: "Fire Above Earth"
Progress

Captain Zheng Yi and Physician Xiang Du harmonized in the captain's quarters after the evening meal, Zheng with his two-stringed *erhu* fiddle and Xiang with his six-holed *dizi* flute. It had become a nightly ritual the past three months, the pair of them playing classic duets well into the watches of the morning.

Minister Bao sometimes lingered for a short while, listening in, but usually excused himself quickly, insisting he had some matter of protocol or ritual to which to attend. Captain and physician were both convinced the minister had grown uncomfortable with the easy manner with which they addressed one another, which drifted well beyond the bounds of shipboard propriety in Bao's view.

Zheng never minded Bao's departure. His music had always been more for himself and the other musicians, not for the audience. Though he'd performed daily during his years with the palace ensemble, he'd played before the emperor only once, the rest of his time spent performing for the Imperial Mothers, or other members of the extended royal family or palace staff, most of them too busy with gossips and intrigues to attend to the music. In Xiang Du, he'd found the perfect accompaniment and audience in one, and needed no other.

During a pause between selections, Zheng sat cross-legged on the sleeping pallet, tuning the strings on the fiddle between his knees. Xiang knelt on the deck plates in the simulated gravity, his gaze drifting up to the ceramic jar lashed to the high shelf.

"Tell me, Yi," the physician said, cocking his head to one side.

"Mmm?"

"Do you ever miss it. Being . . . whole, that is?"

It took a moment for the captain to get Xiang's meaning, but he followed his gaze to the shelf and understood.

"It's hard to say, really," Zheng answered. "I was so young when the procedure was performed, I scarcely recall how things were different before. And it wasn't as though I'd made much use of the equipment before the age of eight, as it was."

"So young," Xiang said, his voice low. "And your father didn't even ask before things began?"

"He'd arranged for me to come and work at the palace, and that meant that I would become a eunuch. He saw no two ways about it. He'd undergone the procedure as an adult, when he'd been invited to come and serve the young emperor as tutor, and he saw no better life for his son than to join him." The captain paused, a wry grin on his face. "A eunuch and son of a eunuch. Is it hereditary, do you think?"

Xiang could not muster much of a grin in response.

"I've not often known the company of a woman since my wife died, Yi," the physician answered, "but to never have had that experience . . . It seems hard to fathom."

"You are the Daoist among us, Du," the captain said, his grin widening. "Surely this is a case of the usefulness of the useless, and the uselessness of the useful? We all are what we must be, what our true nature dictates. There is no tragedy in that."

Xiang smiled slyly.

"Spoken like a man who doesn't know what he is missing, I'm afraid," the physician said, raising the flute to his lips and beginning to play.

● ● ●

Night Shining White was just over halfway through her journey, more than ninety days in all. The ship had been running in silence for a week, a silence that would persist until the sun subsided. Solar flares had disrupted radio communications, both with the other ships in the flotilla and with the Ministry of Celestial Excursion chiefs back on Earth. It was just as well. The other ships hadn't had much interesting to say in weeks, and the only word from Earth were requests for endless reports on the crew's efficiency. To make matters worse, since *Night Shining White* had such a small crew, without a designated communications man, the crewmen had to take turns at the radio as it was, diverting their attentions away from their own tasks. Granted, their tasks were fairly light at this stage of the journey. Minor course corrections and small repairs were the order of the day, with the rest of the time spent lounging in the Common Room, telling jokes and stories, or just exercising, a benefit of the ship's simulated gravity.

Once they'd cleared Earth orbit, the captain had ordered the counterweight deployed. A spent fuel tank from a decommissioned launch vehicle, the massive counterweight was tethered to the ship by means of a long steel cable attached to the ship's spine just outside the first deck of Compartment Three. Then, attitude thrusters on the ship, and additional ones on the counterweight controlled by remote, set the ship and counterweight rotating around one another, spinning end over end through space. Though they spun at a leisurely rate, it was sufficient to impart artificial gravity to the ship by means of centrifugal force. The gravity was lower than Earth normal, but only by a fraction, and made living in the ship considerable more agreeable than zero gravity had done. The crewmen could sleep on their pallets without needing to strap blankets around their bodies, could climb ladders rather than bounce off the walls like errant balloons, and best of all could use the toilet facilities just as if they were back home, rather than suctioning fluids and wastes away from their bodies with noxious hoses.

For the officers and crew, the ship had finally begun to feel like home.

● ● ●

Late nights, when their duets had come to an end and Physician Xiang had returned to his quarters, Captain Zheng lay on his sleeping pallet with his head near the open hatch, listening to the sounds of the crewmen echoing down the passageway from the Common Room in Compartment Four. They told stories from their home villages, parochial legends and tall tales, things they had seen and jokes they had heard. They drank their ration of rice wine from bamboo flasks, and clattered their magnetic mah jong tiles against the steel deck plates.

Zheng was always reminded of the whispered amusements of the eunuchs in the Forbidden City, their jibes and japes, long nights in dark shadows or by candle flame after the palace had put itself to bed. From the age of eight onwards, it had been as though Zheng was part of a family of hundreds, surrounded on all sides by his fellows.

Here, at the heart of this silent beast of ceramic and steel, his only social interaction was with the other officers, Physician Xiang and Minister Bao. He was often tempted to rise out of bed and make his way below decks to the Common Room, to share the jokes and stories of his own youth with the crew. But while Minister Bao might turn a reluctantly blind eye to the easy friendship that had grown between captain and physician, he would never allow the captain to fraternize with the crew. Captain Zheng had long ago given up the suspicion that the minister was a secret policeman from the Eastern Depot, but in matters of protocol his word held sway, and it would go badly for Zheng on their return to Earth were Bao to come out against him. So night after long night, Zheng laid with his head by the open hatch door, listening to the laughter that remained just out of reach.

❧ ❧ ❧

Minister Bao grew increasingly uncomfortable onboard ship as the journey progressed. He was raised in Zhili province, near the city of Northern Capital, and entered the bureaucracy at a young age. He had looked upon his appointment to the Ministry of Celestial Excursion as an honor, but the idea of journeying so far had never sat well with him.

The physician had asked him once, over the midday meal of rice and fish head stew, why he was so discomfited, when he had been relatively at ease before their departure.

"My parents still live," Minister Bao had answered, and resisted any requests from the physician to clarify further, politely excusing himself, his hands tucked into his sleeves and his head bowed.

A long silence followed, in which Captain Zheng and the physician both kept the eyes on the door through which the minister had retreated, their thoughts their own.

"If *you* had asked him, he would have been *forced* to answer," Physician Xiang said finally.

Captain Zheng sipped his tea.

"Oh, but he *did* answer, physician," the captain said.

The physician looked at his friend, his face overwritten with confusion.

"You neglect the classics, Du," Zheng went on. "Confucius said that when one's parents are still living, one shouldn't travel far away. If one has no choice but to travel, he should let his parents know his whereabouts so that they won't worry. It would be easier for Bao, I think, were his parents in the ground; then he wouldn't be betraying his filial responsibilities." Xiang laughed, mirthlessly.

"He should pity me, then," the physician said, "or else revile me. When I left my home in the Changsha province, my father barely bestirred himself beyond his front door to see me off. I was a disappointment to him, I think, in not following in the family business." Xiang drew a long breath, and sighed. "And you, my captain. What did your parents make of your journeying beyond the heavens?"

A cloud passed over Zheng's face.

"My father died on the day I departed, and my mother died a-birthing." His eyes drifted shut, and a long pause followed. "My filial duties have been performed, as best as I was able."

Xiang nodded, slowly, and turned his attention back to the stew.

⇒ ⇒ ⇒

There were moments of levity when the officers and crew were on duty, brief shining flashes of laughter amidst the tedium of their daily routine, usually when Minister Bao was elsewhere. So far as the captain knew, the minister had the respect of the crewmen, but none seemed comfortable in his presence. They had all had protocol and procedure drummed into them by Ministers of Rites since they first came into the emperor's service, whether they were impressed into duty or volunteered for the tasks, and Minister Bao no doubt served to remind them of less pleasant days.

On the ninety-second day of the journey, while Minister Bao was in his quarters reviewing the five classics, the rest of the crew were at their posts in the Command Center, looking out at the slowly changing stars.

"Any course corrections, Liu?" Steersman Fei asked of the navigator.

"No, the same course as yesterday, I'm afraid."

"Is any day different than the last?" Engineer Hong asked, looking up from reactor controls.

"M-my uncle," Engineer's Mate Chen offered, a rare contribution, "said that it was a curse to live in interesting times."

Hong clapped him on the shoulder, encouraging.

"Then, my boy, I think we must be blessed," the engineer said.

"I don't know," Steersman Fei answered. "A little interest from time to time wouldn't be so bad. I sometimes wish I could erase my memory of the days previous."

"W-why?" Engineer's Mate Chen asked.

"If all days are the same, but I couldn't remember them, then at least I'd have a bit of variety."

"You should be careful what you wish for," Navigator Liu said, leaning back in his seat, knitting his fingers behind his head.

The captain and the physician, a few meters behind the rest in the officers' chairs, cast quick glances at one another. They'd overheard the crew's discussions often enough to recognize the navigator's posture and tone. When he adopted this attitude, it meant that he was cooking up some sort of treat.

"Oh, is that so?" Engineer Hong said, egging him on. "How do you mean?"

"Well," Liu said, "back home in Henan province, there was a man who had no memory at all. If he closed his eyes, he forgot what he'd been looking at before he opened them again. If he went to sleep, when he awoke he forgot where he was. In time, this became a burden to his family and friends, and his wife sought help. She got word of a sage in the next village, on the far side of a mountain pass, that could cure her husband's condition. So she saddled their horse, wrote out directions for her husband to follow, gave him a bag of silver *taels,* and armed him with a bow and a quiver of arrows. 'Husband,' she told him, 'on the other side of the mountain is a man who can cure you, but you must be careful. There are brigands in the mountains, who will try to steal your purse from you. Use the bow to defend yourself if you must, but don't stop unless you can't help it.' The man listened attentively, kissed his wife, and rode off down the road."

Navigator Liu paused for a moment, glancing around the cabin at his fellow crewmen, gauging their response.

"Well," Liu continued, "by the time the forgetful man was on the mountain pass, he felt the call of nature tugging on him fiercely. He'd eaten a hearty meal the night before, and things had run their course. So he dismounted, tied his horse to a tree, stuck the bundle of arrows point first in the ground for safe keeping, and went about his business. When he'd finished, he stood up, belted his robes around him, and forgot completely where he was.

"Looking to his side, he saw the bunch of arrows stuck tip down in the soil. 'Oh, my, that was a narrow escape,' he said. 'Those brigands just missed me.'

"Then he saw his horse, tied to the tree. 'But look at my good fortune,' he said. 'One of the bandits has lost his horse, and the spoils of war are mine.'

"The forgetful man started for the horse, and stepped heavily in his own waste, piled steaming on the ground. 'Oh, no,' he said, 'some dog has done their business just here, and I've stepped square in it.'

"He wiped his feet clean on the ground as best he could, climbed on the back of the horse, and rode down the mountain pass the way he had come. He finally came to his own house, and marveled. 'What a fine house,' he said. 'Practically a mansion. This sage must be truly wise to afford such a grand home.' His wife came out to greet him, and was happy he had returned safely, if not at least in a better condition."

The men laughed long and hard, Engineer Hong loudest of

all, and even the captain could not refrain from a long bout of chuckling. The physician, for his part, only smiled slightly, stroking his long mustaches.

"Navigator Liu," the physician finally said, steepling his fingers, his elbows rested on the chair's arms.

The men's laughter abruptly stopped, and all but the navigator tried to look busy, unsuccessfully stifling their giggles. The navigator turned around in his chair, sitting up straighter, not sure what to expect.

"Yes, Physician Xiang?"

"Even in Changsha, we had heard of the forgetful man of Henan," the physician said. "But the story we had was of the day he was finally cured. Have you heard it?"

The navigator, suppressing a grin, shook his head.

"No, physician, I don't believe I have."

"I doubt I can relate it with your level of skill, but I will attempt," the physician said. "It seems that on some later occasion the sage from the other side of the mountain, hearing of the distress of the forgetful man's wife, came to offer his services. And, as the wife had hoped, he was able to cure the disorder, returning the man's memory to him. How do you suppose the man responded?"

The navigator, his smile scarcely hidden, shook his head again.

"I don't know, physician."

Physician Xiang's mouth spread into a sly grin.

"He cursed the sage, naturally. When his senses had been restored, the formerly forgetful man stood before the scholar and his family, and tore his clothing, bemoaning his fate. 'In my forgetfulness I was a free man,' he told them, 'unaware if heaven or earth existed. But now I remember all that has passed, and all that remains, all that was gained or lost, all that brought sorrow or joy, all that was loved or hated. I remember the ten thousand vexations of my life, and I fear that the same things will disturb my mind no less all the days of my life. Where shall I find another moment's peaceful oblivion?' "

The smile played across the physician's face. He drew himself up, and left the Command Center, returning to his quarters. When he had gone, the captain covered his mouth with his hands, watching the confused or disquieted expressions of the navigator and the rest. Finally, he could bear it no longer and burst into laughter, loud as gunfire.

"That will teach you, poor Liu," the captain said through his laughter, "not to tell jokes to a Daoist, unless you want a lesson in philosophy."

⊖ ⊖ ⊖

The first sign of trouble came during the Fourth Watch. A warning light flashed on the reactor controls, a faint blue against the cold gray of the instrument panel, and a warning bell began to chime softly.

"Engineer Hong?" Captain Zheng asked from his chair, leaning forward with interest. The engineer and his mate were gathered near the reactor controls in the Command Center, doing their routine checks.

"Yes, my captain," Hong answered, moving over to inspect the indicators. "We've nearly finished our daily checks, and nothing is out of place, so this may just be a false reading."

"Nothing serious?" the captain asked.

"Too soon to say for certain," Hong answered, guardedly, leaning close to the gauges. "Let me do a visual inspect and report back. Chen, come with me."

Wasting no time, Hong and Chen made their way through the central passageway back to Compartment Six, and the small service area behind the main hydrogen tanks. From this vantage point, they could inspect the primary reactor systems.

The gauges and dials in the service area bore out the readings Hong had taken in the Command Center.

"Engineer?" Chen said, looking over his shoulder. "What does that moving needle mean?" He pointed to a quickly dropping gauge.

"It means that the pressure in the reactor cooling loop has started to drop."

Chen's face fell.

"Th-that doesn't sound good," he said.

"It isn't," Hong answered. "No question. It most certainly isn't."

Hong's fingers flew over the reactor controls, but the warnings continued to ping, and spread beyond his reach.

There were two coolant pumps in the system. Engineer Hong shouted for Chen to man the standby feed pump. At his command, Hong would monitor the primary pump and Chen would bring the secondary pump online. The audible hum of the primary pump was already winding down, a slow decrescendo towards silence.

Hong gave the signal, and Chen began twisting the valve handles, cutting in steam to drive the pump's impeller.

Nothing happened. Hong raced to Chen's side to see for himself that the valves were fully open. He cursed under his breath, and lashed out at the pump with his foot, barking his shin against the manifold.

"We just tested this pump," Hong shouted. He turned to Chen, his face growing redder with every passing second. "Didn't we just test this pump, Chen?"

Chen's eyes were wide and startled. He tried to compose a response but failed, only stammering out meaningless staccato syllables.

"Run through the cycle again!" Hong shouted, and returned to the primary pump controls. "Now!"

Chen closed the secondary valves shut, and then wrenched them open full again. Nothing again.

Hong wiped his deeply creased forehead with a soiled rag.

"You keep at it, Chen. I'll report the situation to the Command Center. Don't stop! Keep at it!"

Before leaving, Hong's eyes drifted back to the primary pump. It was slowing more rapidly now, wheezing and clanking like a dying asthmatic trying to draw one final breath. Steam hissed out around the main crank shaft. In his years of service in the imperial fleets, he'd never seen these symptoms, but he knew the root cause in the marrow of his bones.

"There's a leak in the primary coolant line, my captain,"

Hong reported in the Command Center. "Neither the primary nor the back-up pumps can attain a head of pressure."

"Is this an issue, Engineer Hong?" the captain asked.

"No, my captain," Hong answered. "This is most definitely a problem."

◦ ◦ ◦

As the pressure in the cooling loop continued to drop, the temperature gauges measuring the core temperatures in the reactor itself began steadily to climb. The sudden drop in pressure indicated that the Nuclear Thermal Rocket system was losing coolant, and that meant that the heat from the nuclear fission process within the reactor itself could not be removed and transferred to the secondary coolant flowing within the heat exchangers. The immediate impact would be that the liquid hydrogen in the heating array could not be made to expand, and the ship would lose its forward thrust. In the longer term, it meant that the flow would have to be renewed, or the fission process in the reactor core would continue unchecked, the control rods alone not sufficient to limit the cascading reactions, and if things progressed too long, it could lead to the meltdown of the nuclear fuel itself, causing a catastrophic nuclear explosion.

They were more than halfway to the red planet, too far to turn back, and the solar flares had not subsided in days, all communication still silenced. No one was coming to their aid.

◦ ◦ ◦

"What are our options, Engineer Hong?" the captain asked.

The officers and crew had gathered in the Command Center, each tense and shuffling nervously, their eyes straying to the environmental controls and gauges.

"I don't see as there really are that many, my captain," Hong answered.

Chen, whose sole responsibility was to monitor the readings from the rear compartments, raised his head.

"T-t-temperature in Compartment Six is up twenty degrees, in

Compartment Five is up fifteen, and ten in Compartment Four," he reported. "R-radiation levels in Compartments Six and Five are up almost fifteen percent, and c-climbing."

Captain Zheng received the news with a curt bob of his head.

"Okay, Hong, if you have any solutions in your rear pockets, now would be the time to reveal them."

Engineer Hong's face had gone pale, his mouth drawn into a tight line. Even more surprising, he seemed to have stopped sweating.

"Well, that is, erm," the engineer began, his eyes drifting down to the deck plates.

"What?" Navigator Liu said, jabbing the engineer in the side with an elbow. "Or has Chen's stuttering proved contagious?"

Hong looked sidelong at the navigator, unable even to muster the energy to respond to the jibe.

"There's one possibility," Engineer Hong went on. "There *is* a way to restore cooling to the system without the pumps, but I've never heard of anyone trying it before."

The engineer paused, biting his lower lip. The captain motioned him to continue, impatient.

"Well, we could fabricate a kind of backup system by welding some pipes together." Again the hesitation, but this time the engineer continued without being prompted.

"We could cobble together a device that would cycle water from the ship's cargo tanks into the reactor. A sort of homemade cooling condenser."

The captain looked from the engineer to the other crewmen, taking in the slowly nodding heads.

"This would work, then?" the captain asked. "We could reduce the core temperature and still maintain thrust?"

Engineer Hong glanced around the cabin, and nodded reluctantly.

"Yes," he answered. "But it won't be easy. Someone is going to have to crawl into the shielded area above the reactor, up with the control rods, to weld the leads from the tanks. It's pretty damned hot in there in the best of circumstances, and with the reactor threatening meltdown, it'll be like a kiln."

"And the radiation?" Physician Xiang asked.

Engineer Hong's eyes hooded, his expression falling from bad to worse.

"It'll be pretty damned hot on that count, too," he answered.

Captain Zheng drew a heavy breath, and closed his eyes for a moment, digesting the news. Finally, his lids opened slowly, and he leveled his gaze at the engineer.

"And there's no other option?" he asked.

The engineer crossed his meaty arms over his chest, his mouth set.

"No, my captain," he answered. "It's unorthodox, I'll grant you, but I don't see as we have any choice. May the Celestial Consort bless whichever of us goes into that oven, but we have no choice."

☉ ☉ ☉

Navigator Liu and Steersman Fei were all for drawing lots, to see who would brave the heat and radiation in the reactor chamber, while Engineer Hong insisted that he be allowed to do the job himself. Minister Bao floated the notion that the physician determine the healthiest among the crew, in the hopes that the heartiest crewman would prove most likely to escape the ill effects of the experience. To this, Physician Xiang remained silent, keeping his thoughts to himself. Captain Zheng listened to each suggestion in turn, and then rose from his seat.

"I'll be in my quarters," he said, heading for the door. "You'll have my answer before the end of the Fourth Watch."

The engineer stepped forward, raising his hand, his face deeply lined.

"Whatever we do," Hong said, "and whoever does it, it needs doing quickly. Every minute we waste is one minute closer to meltdown and a runaway nuclear explosion." He paused, and then added, "Meaning no disrespect, my captain."

Zheng paused, and glanced back over his shoulder, his eyes narrowed. "You'll have my answer before the Watch is through," he said, and was gone.

Captain Zheng sat cross-legged on his sleeping pallet, his *erhu* fiddle lying idle in his lap. There came a rapping at his open door, and Physician Xiang's head appeared around the corner.

"Am I disturbing your deliberations, my captain?" Xiang said, his voice level.

Zheng scowled.

"Yes," he barked, waving the physician away with a flick of his wrist.

"Then you have my humblest apologies," Xiang said, and strode into the room.

The physician knelt down opposite the captain, his expression blank.

"You have a difficult decision before you, Yi," he said.

The captain closed his eyes, and buried his face in his hands.

"You think I don't know that, Du?" He drew a ragged breath. "Whatever I decide, I'm likely sending one of the men to his death."

The physician kept silent, dropping his gaze to the deck. The captain lowered his hands, but kept his eyes down. Without looking up, he began to speak.

"This wasn't the life I chose," he said. "Not that I had much voice in any decision along the way. But this was not the path I would have selected. Have I told you about my father?"

The physician shook his head.

"Only that he became a eunuch in later life, and served the emperor as personal tutor." The captain ran his fingers along the neck of his fiddle.

"My father served as Imperial tutor during the early days of the Emperor's reign," Captain Zheng said, "and was a favorite of the Dragon Throne for decades. Zheng Li had been a scholar in Beijing, having traveled from his home in Mongolia to the city called Northern Capital to study, and stayed when he was awarded an instructor's position at the Imperial Academy. He arranged for a marriage to a respectable girl from a local family, and started a family. Zheng Li went on to become one of the most revered instructors at the Academy. An expert in the Classics with a particular love for Sung Dynasty poetry, he developed quite a reputation in the early days of the current emperor's reign. When it came time for the young emperor's regent to select an appropriate tutor for the young ruler, then not yet past his fifth year, Zheng Li was invited to serve at the emperor's pleasure. To be personal tutor meant that he would need to reside full time within the walls of the Forbidden City, which meant further that he would have to sacrifice his manhood and become a eunuch. Zheng Li didn't mind the loss, so much, as he had already sired a son, and his wife had died in childbirth. He had no desire to start another family. So, leaving me in the care of his dead wife's family, Zheng Li paid the six *taels* of silver, surrendered his manhood, and received his treasure preserved in a jar. He crossed through the Gate of Celestial Purity, entered the Inner Court of the Forbidden City, and rarely left it again."

"Did you see him again?"

"I saw my father seldom over the next few years. Every two months, on the day of the new moon, the revered Imperial Tutor would arrive at the house of his dead wife's sister, my aunt. I, always busy with my studies, would stand dutifully while my father inspected my work, briefly glancing over my calligraphy and sums. I would wait for my father to speak. Finally, Zheng Li would ask how I was progressing in my studies, and whether I was displaying appropriate discipline and filial piety." The captain stressed the last words, turning the words into a curse. "I would answer that I was, my father would reach out and touch my shoulder with outstretched fingers, and then the audience would be over. My father returned to the palace, and I would not see him again for another two months. These visits never lasted more than two minutes."

The physician's expression softened.

"That sounds like a hard and lonely life," he said.

"Perhaps," the captain answered. "But it was not to last, in any case. When I was eight years old, my father arrived for his regular visit in the company of another man. The stranger carried a heavy woven bag studded in brass. My father paid the man six silver coins, and then instructed me to disrobe. Trembling with fear, I did as I was told. The man instructed me to lie up on the bench, while removing bottles, knives and straps from the woven bag. Voice wavering, I asked my father what was to happen. My father smiled, a smile which did not quite reach his eyes, and explained that I was going to come and live at the Forbidden City, and serve the emperor. My throat was thick and dry, my eyes on the wicked knife in the man's hand. I asked my father whether I was going to live with him at the palace. My father answered that I was, and told me to be brave. The man with the knife went to work."

The captain paused, his eyes tightly shut, recalling old pains.

"I remember the man's hands as being rough as the canvas of his bag. I remember the sudden chill of the knife blade against my skin, and then the sharp red pain. I remember little else of the day."

The captain looked up, and saw the sympathy in the physician's eyes. He waved away his pity and continued.

"The surgeon was experienced, an expert," Captain Zheng said. "Fewer than five in a hundred of his patients died as a result of his work. The fever was long and painful, and there were moments when I wished for death, but I survived." He paused, rubbing his chin, remembering. "I entered imperial service as a member of the Household Department. My duties varied over the years, from serving food to the emperor's 'Mothers,' the Empress Dowager and the wives and consorts of the emperor's predecessors; to transporting bales of tea from one side of the palace to another; to serving the Eunuchs of the Presence in managing the harem, fetching the tablet to record the date and time of intercourse for those occasions on which the emperor wished to conceive, fetching the 'cold flower' herbs on those occasions when he didn't. Throughout, I continued my studies, but saw my father no more often than before, if not less frequently. Finally, I was appointed as a member of one of the palace ensembles, groups of musicians which played for the emperor's pleasure, during official events, receptions, or just during meals to aid in the digestion. I learned the *erhu*, and came to know it well."

The physician nodded in agreement. He'd often complimented the captain on his playing, saying that it was a rarity to find such skill in one who hadn't made music their profession.

"By the end of two years," the captain continued, "I had risen to a position of leadership among the musicians. I selected the repertoire for the evening, decided who would perform on what occasions, and in what capacity. I was in my early twenties, and had found my place in the world."

The captain tightened his grip on the fiddle in his lap, his expression hardening.

"My world came crashing down when I received word that I'd been selected to serve the Ministry of Celestial Excursion. They said that it was as a result of my youth, my intellectual vigor, my physical stamina, and the leadership I exhibited as part of the imperial ensemble. I was to travel to the island of Fragrant Harbor, across from the Peninsula of Nine Dragons, to the Gold Mountain base of the Bridge of Heaven. I was to ride the carriage to the top, to the Diamond Summit, and undergo training as a captain. Within a year's time, I would be traveling to the Fire Star."

The captain lifted the fiddle into the playing position, and plucked one string with an outstretched finger.

"I didn't believe any of it. I was convinced I only received the appointment because the emperor wanted to reward my father's long years of service. I went to speak to my father, to request his assistance in getting out of the appointment, only to be told that my father had died that morning, shortly before I'd gotten word about the appointment."

The captain shook his head, and then set the fiddle down carefully on the pallet next to him.

"I couldn't go to the Emperor, so I would never know for sure. I had no choice but to obey. I traveled to the base of the Bridge of Heaven, rode the carriage up to the orbital city of Diamond Summit, and began my training, convinced all the while that it was only a matter of time before I would be revealed as a fraud."

The captain glanced to the open door, and closed his eyes, an expression of pain flashing across his face.

"From our discussions these past months," the physician said, finally answering, "I know you learned the rudiments of space travel, avionics, navigation and engineering while studying at Diamond Summit, but in the end expertise is not a factor in command. You need not understand every job on the ship, you need only understand the role of every man on the ship, and be able to drive every man to do his best. Just as you could not play every instrument in the ensemble, but could still conduct them."

The captain looked back at his friend the physician, expression pleading.

"And if I must conduct one of these men to their deaths?" he said. "What then?"

The physician reached out, and laid a comforting hand on the captain's knee.

"We all must follow our own true natures, Yi, and be the men that we must be. That is the way. That is the Dao."

The captain swallowed hard, and squeezed his eyes shut.

"I feel, so often, that I am forced to live some other man's destiny," he said.

"As do all men of greatness," the physician answered. He paused, drawing back his hand. "Have you made your decision?"

The captain nodded slowly, and climbed to his feet.

"Sadly, yes," he answered. "In the end, there is only one choice reason will allow, though my heart is sick to make it."

The physician reached out again, resting his hand for the briefest moment on the captain's shoulder.

"Then let the crew see you make that decision," he said. "The ideal leader is one who looks after his followers as though they were his own children. Children look to their parents to make the decisions they cannot, to display wisdom they lack. Make your choice, and the men will honor it."

The captain's eyes narrowed, and he turned reluctantly to the door.

"I don't worry that they will honor it," he answered. "I only hope they forgive me for it, when the worst is upon us."

3

Hexagram 39
Chien: "Water Above Mountain"
Obstruction

Physician Xiang was helping Engineer's Mate Chen adjust the final straps and buckles on the radiation suit when the young man caught the physician's eye, a worried expression on his face. "Ph-physician Xiang? This is going to keep me s-safe from the heat and the radiation in there, isn't it?"

The physician looked to the captain and the engineer, who stood nearby. Neither man could meet Xiang's gaze.

Physician Xiang turned back to the young man, and laid a gentle hand on his shoulder. "Of course, Chen," he said. "It most certainly will."

The mate's shoulders relaxed, like a great weight had been lifted from them. As the physician lifted the helmet into place, the young man's expression looked relieved through the leaded glass.

Engineer Hong stepped forward, and handed Chen the welding equipment and the length of pipe. They had found it difficult to find a length of pipe suitable for the connection, since whatever was used would have to hold up under extremely high temperature and pressure. Engineer's Mate Chen received the pipe reverentially, like a token bestowed by the Emperor himself.

The captain and physician followed as Hong led the mate to the junction with Compartment Six, and the reactor chamber beyond.

The engineer gripped the mate's upper arm, briefly, his face closed and tense like a father watching a son go off to war.

"Good luck, Chen," the engineer said, and turned away as the mate lumbered through the hatch in the heavy suit.

When Chen had gone, the hatch closed safely behind him, the engineer went to stand beside the captain and physician.

"Well, physician," the captain said, his voice grave. "Will the radiation suit protect young Chen from the dangers posed by the reactor?"

The engineer's face darkened, and he turned away. He already knew the answer.

"No," Physician Xiang said, shaking his head slowly. "The suits were designed to protect crewmen working in the rear compartments, in the event the shielding in the reactor chamber began to fail, but they were not intended to be used within the reactor itself. It is better than nothing, but not by much."

The engineer's hands tightened to fists at his side.

"It should have been me . . ." the engineer began, his voice straining, but the captain waved him silent.

"I've made my decision," the captain said firmly. "Of all the crew, Engineer's Mate Chen is the most . . ." He paused, the next word like nettles in his mouth. "Expendable . . . of all the crewmen. I know you'd prefer it were you in there, but you're simply too valuable to us." The engineer's face darkened further, glowering, and he crossed his meaty arms across his chest.

☞ ☞ ☞

Chen's job was to weld the pressure line from the pump to the pipeline from the reactor's air vent, cutting that pipeline out of the air purging system. Then Engineer Hong, working in Compartment Five's cargo hold, could connect the air system pipeline directly into the water-tanks. Once all the connections had been welded, water could be pumped directly from the tanks into the reactor core.

Without the reactor functioning, all of the ship's systems were running at reduced capacity. When the reactor was working properly, part of the system's heat output was used to convert wastewater to steam, which drove primary and secondary electrical generators. With the system shut down, the generators lay fallow, and the only power available was that leeched off the backup battery reserves. By this point, even if the solar flares had subsided, the communications would have been inoperative.

Navigator Liu and Steersman Fei were in the Command Center, monitoring the temperature and radiation levels by the low emergency lights. Minister Bao, desperate to be of some service, busied himself by ferrying reports from the Command Center to the captain who stood watch in Compartment Five and back again. Physician Xiang, his herbs and unguents prepared and ready, stood by, his anxious eyes never leaving the hatchway to Compartment Six. Engineer Hong was below decks in Compartment Five, welding the air purging system to the water-tanks as quickly as he was able.

Tense moments oozed by. Hong completed his welds, and climbed the ladder halfway to the upper deck, sticking his head through the hatch and asking the captain whether there'd been any word or sign of Chen. The captain said there hadn't been, and the engineer hammered his fist against the deck plates, immediately apologizing to the captain for his outburst.

There came a clattering at the hatch, and the captain and the physician scrambled to help open the heavy reinforced door from their side. The engineer sprang from the ladder, and reached the doorway just as the door clanged open and the engineer's mate appeared. The engineer and the physician helped Chen to remove the heavy mask. He coughed and sputtered, his eyes watering and his skin bright red, as though he'd just been immersed in too hot water, or spent too long under a blazing sun.

"Well, boy?" the engineer asked, grabbing Chen's upper arm in a fatherly gesture of support. "Did it work?"

Chen coughed, and seemed to gag slightly, a splash of bile flecking the corners of his mouth.

"N-no," he managed. "I couldn't get the two pipelines to butt-weld together. There . . . there wasn't enough surface contact."

The captain slammed his fist into his open palm.

"Damn," Zheng spat.

The engineer gripped Mate Chen's arm tightly for a moment, forcing a proud but grim smile on his face.

"I've got an idea, my captain," Engineer Hong said. "I had to cut off a piece of the air pipeline in the cargo hold to make room for the joint, and the bit of pipe that came free is larger in diameter than the ones Chen's been working at. If we put the pipe from the air vent into one end, and insert the pipe from the booster pump into the other, we could weld the larger pipe shut on either side."

"Use it as a kind of coupling, do you mean?" the captain asked.

"Just exactly!" the engineer answered.

"So let's get to it, then," the captain ordered.

The engineer nodded, and turned to retrieve the pipe from below decks, but paused on reaching the ladder.

"Only problem, my captain," he said, his voice low, "is that's too much job for just one man. You'd need a second pair of hands to make it work."

The captain shook his head, resolute.

"I know what you're suggesting, Engineer Hong, but I just can't allow it. We need you too desperately to risk ..." He paused, and cast a glance at the shivering Chen. "That is, we need your expertise on this side to control the reactor systems once the repair is in place."

"Yes, sir," the engineer began, raising his hand to object, "but ..."

"Permission to assist, my captain," came the voice of Steersman Fei from the passageway.

A long silence passed, as each man turned to look at the tall muscular man in the doorway.

"Fei, do you know what you're asking?" the captain asked, taking a half step forward, his expression softening.

Steersman Fei's expression remained unchanged, his mouth drawn into a line.

"I know, my captain," he answered firmly. "Navigator Liu is sufficiently familiar with the steering systems to substitute in my ... absence ... and I've a great deal of experience with welding, from my time spent in the shipyards of Diamond Summit. I helped assemble the first ships to travel to the moon. I think I can manage to weld two pipes together."

The captain reached out, and laid a hand on Fei's shoulder.

"May you follow in the footsteps of the Buddha, Steersman."

"Thank you, my captain," Fei answered, bowing his head.

"And may whatever gods there are keep you in their hands," the captain added, under his breath, as Fei began to climb into the bulky radiation suit. "Perhaps they can protect you where I could not."

⟩ ⟩ ⟩

Fei and Chen were suited and ready to get to work. Engineer's Mate Chen was wavering, unsteady on his knees, but the steersman took his arm to steady him. The engineer and the captain worked the manual controls to slide back the double locking bolts on the hatch door, and reluctantly ushered the two radiation-suited men through the junction into Compartment Six. The passageway beyond the bulkhead was lit dimly from emergency lights, burning low on the battery reserves, but the air seemed suffused with a faint blue haze. To Fei's eyes, it was almost as if he were seeing the room in black and white, the details picked out only in contrasts, not in colors.

Fei hesitated as the passageway narrowed and bifurcated into smaller passages. He'd never been this far astern in the ship before. He turned to Chen, and tried to speak, but their voices were muffled by the heavy shielding and the leaded glass of the helmet, so each only saw the other miming words and syllables. When Chen tried to answer, Fei fancied he could see the boy stutter.

Chen pointed out the branch to their left, curving off to starboard. Fei gave an exaggerated nod, and led the way.

The chamber above the reactor was small and cramped, the ceilings barely tall enough for the men to walk in upright, their shoulders hunched and their legs bowed. The domed lid of the reactor dominated the center of the chamber floor, the unwelded ends of pipe laying nearby, one end jutting from below and the other from above, like broken bones piercing the skin. Blue-violet flames played on the reactor lid, casting strange shadows on the dim walls of the chamber.

Chen recoiled. The steersman reached out a hand to take the young man's elbow, keeping him from retreating. Fei realized the flames must have started since Chen departed.

Fei had spent more than a decade loading cargo in zero gravity, assembling ships in orbit, ferrying equipment from Earth to moon and back again, and had seen more than his share of hardship. It would take more than a small fire to defeat his spirit.

Fei unslung the extinguisher strapped across his back, and released a tight stream of foam at the base of the flames. The shadows on the chamber walls stilled, and the flames diminished to bare sparks.

Fei led Chen forward, and they went to work.

◡ ◡ ◡

Back in Compartment Five, the captain, physician and engineer waited by the closed hatch door. They stood in silence, their eyes rarely drifting from the double-bolted door.

Minister Bao appeared in the passageway, puffing and out of breath.

"Is there any word?" the minister asked, his voice straining. He looked from the three men to the hatch and back again.

None of the three spoke, only shook their heads gravely and returned to their vigil at the hatch.

The minister's shoulders slumped, and he lingered at the doorway, joining the three men in their silent watching.

◡ ◡ ◡

Finally, there came a banging on the other side of the hatch door, sounding like distant thunder, or explosions far off.

"Come on, men," the captain barked, and grabbed for the handles.

The hatch door was massive, and without the electrical systems operational to drive the motors, it was heavy work to move. The engineer joined the captain at the task, and with both men leaning into it, the door finally opened on clanking hinges.

Steersman Fei stumbled through the opening into Compartment Five first. Standing straight, he reached up and unbuckled the clasps on his helmet, wrenching it from his head, and immediately doubled over, vomiting up thick yellowish-white foam. His skin had turned a deep red, and his eyes were swollen and bloodshot.

Engineer's Mate Chen appeared in the doorway, but collapsed to the deck before he'd made it all the way through, his head and shoulders in Compartment Five with his legs still trailing in the blue haze beyond the hatch.

"Chen!" Engineer Hong shouted.

The engineer rushed to help the mate, who collapsed to the deck in the doorway. Once the mate was clear, Physician Xiang surged forward, trying to close the door. Every moment it was open the temperature in Compartment Five rose another degree.

"Minister!" the physician called over his shoulder, struggling fruitlessly with the handles. "Help me!"

The minister hesitated, lingering at the rear of the room, keeping as far from the faint blue glow and heat as possible.

"Bao, damn you!" Xiang shouted. "Show your virtue, you coward."

The minister swallowed hard, took a deep breath, and crossed the floor, coming to the physician's assistance.

The captain was holding Fei up, his grip tight on the steersman's arm.

"Steersman," he said, his voice forceful but level. "Did the coupling hold?"

Fei fought to retain consciousness, obviously awash in pain. He nodded his head, painfully, and croaked out a single word.

"Yes."

The captain turned to the engineer, his expression hard.

"Engineer, open the line from the cargo tanks!"

The door to Compartment Six closed at last, the physician took the engineer's place at Chen's side, leaving Hong free to dive through the hatch to the cargo hold below.

Captain Zheng stood over the open hatch, crouched down, shouting through the opening. "Engineer Hong," the captain called, cupping his hands around his mouth. "Report."

Hong appeared on the ladder, a weary smile cracking his face.

"Pressure is holding, my captain," the engineer answered. "There don't appear to be any leaks."

Navigator Liu appears in the passageway, excited. Then he saw Steersman Fei, hunched over and twitching, yellowish-white sputum down his chin and front, and froze in place, his expression horrified.

"Navigator," the captain called, rising on weary legs. "What news?"

The navigator, reluctantly dragging his gaze from the swollen-eyed Fei, looked back to the captain.

"The temperature levels in the reactor have already dropped five degrees, my captain, and are continuing to fall steadily."

The captain nodded, and ordered the navigator to return to the Command Center and continue monitoring their status.

They had succeeded, but looking at the two men twitching on the deck plates, wracked with shivers and retching, the captain wondered if the price was worth it.

Two days later, Fei and Chen were down in the surgery, strapped to sleeping pallets to prevent their thrashing, displaying symptoms of advanced radiation sickness. Their skin was red and blotchy, tongue thickened so much they could barely speak, their eyes swollen shut and sightless. Ichors ran from their scalps, a yellowish, foul smelling discharge that seeped out from the roots of their hair.

The solar flares appeared to have subsided, but it did *Night Shining White* little good. Working together Engineer Hong and Navigator Liu had restored functionality to the radio receivers, but the electrical shorts attendant to the recent problems with the reactor and generator had fused the circuits of the radio transmitter, leaving them unable to broadcast. The engineer and navigator spent days trying to repair the transmitter, or jury-rig a replacement from the components on hand, but the solution eluded their grasp. No longer deaf, they remained dumb, unable to call for assistance. Their only hope was to continue on, and rendezvous with the rest of the Treasure Fleet in orbit around the red planet Fire Star.

The other crewmen began to exhibit signs of low-level radiation sickness, as well, even those like Liu who had not gone near the reactor. The engineer made close inspections of the radiation readings, using a handheld counter, and found that all the water-tanks in the holds, in Compartments Four and Five, were emitting growing levels of radiation. Particulate fission products had backed up through the makeshift cooling system more than their early estimates had anticipated. Given the massive volume of water, and the shielded tanks, the engineer had made the educated assumption that the possibility of contamination of the storage water was low, the risk of increased radiation negligible. All of those who served on ships driven by nuclear thermal propulsion were exposed to low levels of radiation from the moment they stepped onboard; but the levels registered by the engineer's tests in the rear compartments ranged far beyond the allowed dosages.

They had no choice but to seal off the rear compartments, moving the crewmen into Compartments Three and forward. Luckily, the ship's stores were still uncontaminated, safely tucked away in Compartment Two, so they'd no fear of starvation.

Packed together into the quarters in Compartment Three, the men of *Night Shining White* sailed on, counting the days.

⬭ ⬭ ⬭

The men ate their meals together, gathered in the Command Center, all division between officer and crewmen lost. They were just one body of men now, packed tightly, desperate to forget their troubles.

The captain had doubled each man's daily ration of rice wine. When the minister had objected, the captain drew him and the physician to one side to explain.

"Physician Xiang," the captain said in a hushed whisper, drawing the other men close to him, "has it not been suggested that under the influence of alcohol the elements of the body are less susceptible to radiation?"

The physician nodded, warily.

"Yes, it's certainly true that resistance to external irritants rises under the influence," he answered, "at least on a purely subjective basis."

"Exactly so," the captain said. "I have seen drunk men stand naked in freezing temperatures, with hardly a shiver. If another drop of wine with their midday meals helps the men to weather this storm, and holdfast their courage for another day, then the regiments of protocol will be damned. The men will have their drink, and be welcome to it."

"As you say, my captain," Minister Bao reluctantly acceded.

Even so, the minister's fears that the men would grow boisterous and rowdy while under the influence proved not entirely groundless, as their meals became more and more bouts of frantic cheer, the men desperate for some minor diversion.

"Tell us a story, Liu," Engineer Hong ordered, his tone one of forced merriment but his expression grave. He took a mouthful of rice, and washed it down with a swig of cold wine. "Something to liven our hearts."

Hong's eyes drifted to the junction to Compartment Three, where his mate Chen and the steersman lay swollen and sightless, unable to keep food or liquid inside them, dying by inches.

"Yes, navigator," the captain said, returning to his seat. "You cannot tell us you have run out of anecdotes."

The navigator hunched his shoulders, a pained expression flashing momentarily across his round face.

"All right," he said reluctantly, drawing himself up. "I suppose there is one story of Henan I've not shared with you. My father, as you might recall, was a tax collector for the emperor, and spent his days out among the people, collecting the emperor's due. Well, there was one farmer who, season after season, pulled in bumper crops, growing more than enough to feed his family, make a healthy exchange on the market, and satisfy my father the tax collector as well. So it was a surprise to my father when he arrived one year to find that the farmer had produced not a single bushel in the entire season.

"My father sought out the farmer, who was sitting ragged and alone, in the shade of a knotted old tree. The farmer stared steadfastly at the trunk of the tree, refusing to look away. 'What is this you do,' my father asked him. 'And why have your fortunes fallen so low?'

"The farmer did not look away from the tree, but answered my father thusly. 'Last season,' he said, 'I was toiling in my fields when a rabbit ran out of the underbrush, slammed headlong into the trunk of this tree, and broke his neck. The rabbit died in an instant. So I took its body home to my family, and we made a splendid meal of it. I realized that my long hours of toil in the fields were a waste, if such splendid fare could be had so easily. So I abandoned my crops to the wilds, and kept watch here for another rabbit.'

"My father then asked the farmer, 'And how often has this tree fed you, in this manner?' The farmer shook his head. 'Only that first time, so far, but it happened once, and is sure to happen again.'"

The other men laughed, harder and longer than the story merited, and soon the navigator himself joined in the laughter. These were hard days, and they were glad for any release they could find.

◦ ◦ ◦

Late nights, the captain and the physician serenaded the crew with fiddle and flute. The minister, engineer and navigator would squeeze into the corners of the captain's quarters, and the pair of them would play into the early watches of the night.

As the days had worn on, the men had come to find some comfort in the close quarters, tending to gather more often in the smaller cabins than in the larger chamber of the Command Center. Perhaps it was that the open space of the larger rooms only served to remind them of the absences, of those suffering silently below decks. Their diminished numbers could more comfortably fill the smaller spaces.

When the captain and physician would reach the end of their final piece, lowering their instruments in the gathering gloom, the five men would sit in silence. Reluctant to dispel the mood, or else hesitant to retire for the night, the men would linger on, extending the day as long as they might.

"There's no quiet so deep as that among the stars, my father used to say," Engineer Hong finally spoke, shattering the silence with the voice lowered. He paused, and then added, "But I don't know that I like the quiet so much, in later days. Too much it reminds me of the tomb."

The captain lifted his head, looking at the rugged old engineer.

"I've never heard you mention your father," Captain Zheng said. "What was he like?"

A slight smile crossed the engineer's face, and he rubbed at his broad forehead with a calloused hand.

"What is any father like, sir?" Hong answered. "I remember him as larger than life, with a voice that could drown out the thunder, but was he all of that? No, he was a man, like any other, but he served the emperor, and served him well. You might not know to look at me, but I'm a second generation sailor beyond the heavens. My father was among those who assisted in the first orbital launch, when our emperor's grandfather held the throne, and he helped construct the Bridge of Heaven itself. I was but a babe in arms when the first skeletal frame of Diamond Summit was assembled in orbit, but my father went back up again, his duty not yet fully served. When I was old enough to comprehend, I wanted nothing but to follow my father into space, and when I'd my legs under me and had sprouted my first man's hair, I apprenticed under him as engineer's mate in the Lunar fleet. My father . . ." Hong trailed off, his eyes on the far distance, his mind gone somewhere else. Finally, he continued. "My father was caught in an explosive decompression. It was a Cloud Flyer, shuttling equipment from one ship in the Lunar Fleet to another, and the seams in the hull gave way, and that was all there was for it. Six men died in an instant, that day, their blood boiling in their veins, their skin freezing hard as ice."

Navigator Liu, seated beside the engineer on the deck, laid a comradely hand on the engineer's hunched shoulder.

"All men meet their ends in their own time," the navigator said.

The physician narrowed his eyes, thoughtfully, and crossed his arms over his chest.

"Perhaps," he said in a quiet voice, "death is not the evil we all suppose."

Eyes flashed towards the physician, darkly.

The captain, not sure the others were in a philosophical mood, raised an eyebrow at his friend.

"Xiang," the captain said simply, his tone cautioning.

"No, I mean no disrespect, Yi," Physician Xiang answered, and across the cabin the minister cringed to hear such familiarity before the crewmen. "I'm merely reminded of something the sage Zhuangzi wrote. He told the story of Li Ji, a young woman about to wed. Li Ji, the sage wrote, was wracked with sorrows on her wedding day. She was to marry the prince of Jin against her will, and she was so sad that she drenched her bridal dress in tears. But after she had wed, and had joined the prince's household, she found herself sleeping in a long, soft bed, eating delicacies brought to her from the four corners of the world. Who would believe that she had cried her eyes out on her wedding day, over this 'terrible' fate?" The physician paused, and looked around the room at his fellows. "We all fear dying, but isn't it possible that death will be such a marvel that we will end up regretting ever having lived?"

Navigator Liu, his normal good humor evaporated, scowled, his face darkened.

"I mean you no disrespect, friend physician," Liu said, teeth gritted and eyes narrowed, "but I grow weary of philosophy. Kind words and platitudes to comfort the sick and dying, like a sop to a crying child. They don't make our pains vanish, only befuddle our brains so we forget we were ever hale."

Minister Bao began to rise to his feet, apprehensively.

"Perhaps it is time we all retire," the minister said, his voice uneven. "The watch is late and . . ."

"No," Captain Zheng said, waving the minister to seat himself. "It is still early yet."

The captain glanced around the room. He could feel the tensions rising, and knew they must be allowed to dwindle before the men were dismissed, else they fester in the night and threaten to burst open in the days to follow.

"Navigator Liu," the captain said, forcing a light tone into his voice, "you've often mentioned your father the tax collector. Have you any more stories of his exploits, of the poor comical unfortunates he encountered?"

The navigator glowered from under his brows.

"No, my captain," he said in a strained voice. "I'm afraid I've no humor left to me." The navigator looked from the captain to the physician, his eyes flashing.

"Then how about explaining how a tax collector's son came to travel beyond the heavens," the captain said, his tone trending towards command. "I'm sure you haven't regaled us with that tale, as yet."

The navigator looked back to the captain, and read the order in the captain's eyes. He drew a heavy breath, held it, and then let out a sigh, his shoulders slumped and his chin falling to his chest. The captain recognized these as relaxation techniques. The navigator was drawing upon some specialized training to reduce his levels of internal stress.

Finally, the navigator raised his face to the room and began to speak.

"My father, as you say, was a tax collector, and so I spent the long hours of my childhood watching my father work his abacus, tallying rows of numbers, figuring sums, determining the emperor's share of a farmer's labor, of a miller's work. When I grew to be a man, I found myself shackled to an abacus as well, apprenticed from my teenaged years to the Imperial House of Calculation in the capital city, just beyond the walls of the Imperial Palace, and then selected from among those ranks to learn the art of celestial navigation. I have held the dust of the moon in my open palm, and walked out in the cold blackness between worlds, plotted courses covering a million miles and brought my ship safely back within inches, but in the end, it is all numbers and sums. I find, in the final analysis, that my work is not really so different from my father's, except that he had a home to which to return at day's end, while my abacus is the only home I know."

"Yet you have followed your duty!" Minister Bao broke in, his voice rising. He'd hardly spoken a word all day. "I hear self-pity in our tone, Liu, when I should hear pride. You betray your own virtue. We all do as we must."

The minister pushed himself off the deck, and stood with his arms akimbo, hands on his hips. "Would that all peoples filled their roles as well. As Confucius teaches, the primary principle of governance is that kings should behave as kings, ministers as ministers, fathers as fathers and sons as sons. Your father did his duty, in the benefit of his country and emperor. You do no less. This is virtue, Liu, not some sad fate."

The captain and physician caught each other's eye. They'd rarely seen the minister so animated, and certainly not since the onset of their recent troubles.

"Minister Bao," the physician began, raising his hand. "Perhaps you are correct after all, and the watch grows late."

The minister shook his head.

"My father served the Dragon Throne in the bureaucracy," Bao went on, "just like his father before him, and his father before him. My family knows no greater calling than to serve the Dragon Throne, whether in the capital city or on the far side of the world."

"Or the far side of the solar system," the engineer chimed in, out of the corner of his mouth. He quickly lowered his eyes, refusing to meet the minister's gaze. "Meaning no disrespect, minister."

"None inferred, engineer," the minister answered. He had grown excited, and began to pace the small space at the center of the cabin. "We pity ourselves our circumstances, but perhaps we are wrong. Perhaps we have been given a gift, the opportunity to show our qualities, to test our virtue in adversity, to see precisely the kinds of men we are."

From his quiet corner, Navigator Liu's mouth drew back in his sneer.

"And Fei?" Liu snarled. "And Chen? What kind of men have they proven to be? Dead ones?"

The minister recoiled, as if he'd been struck, his face fallen.

"I . . . that is to say . . . I . . ." Minister Bao stammered, unable to respond.

The captain rose from his sleeping pallet, and made a motion towards the door.

"I think, after all, that the evening has worn thin, and night is well upon us. We should rest ourselves. We've another day of work before us."

By turns sullen and angry and distressed, the men filed from the captain's quarters, out into the passageway.

The physician was the last to leave, turning at the threshold to look back over his shoulder.

"The men hold up better than could be expected, Yi," he said, his voice low, "which I attribute primarily to their captain. Don't lose heart that their wills sometime falter."

Captain Zheng smiled wanly, and nodded.

"My thanks, Du," he said softly. "I will, as always, try to live up to your inflated opinion of my character."

Physician Xiang smiled.

"I would expect nothing less."

The physician departed, leaving the captain alone in the silent gloom. He looked to his sleeping pallet with distaste. No matter how long he stretched the days, the nights were too long for his taste.

☞ ☞ ☞

Engineer's Mate Chen died in the night, surrendering to the illness that had ravaged his young body. Steersman Fei lingered on, in a kind of half-life, though he was lucid for only moments at a stretch, the pains driving him to delirium the rest of the time.

Minister Bao organized impromptu burial rites, and the captain read an invocation to Tianfei as the men gathered around the body in Compartment One. When they had done, and burned a cube of incense to a nub, they wrapped Chen's body in reflective foil and placed him in the docking airlock.

At the captain's direction, Navigator Liu and Engineer Hong worked the release mechanism to iris open the outside hatch. Hong, barely able to see through the mist of tears, rotated the control rod until the door to the outer hull was open fully, the airlock exposed to hard vacuum. As the air still trapped within the lock rushed out into space, it carried the foil-covered form of young Chen with it, tumbling end over end into the gulf between worlds.

Liu and Hong worked the door closed again, and the men returned to their duties without another word.

☞ ☞ ☞

Three days on, still more than a month out from Fire Star, warning lights began to flash in the Command Center. Temperatures were slowly rising in the reactor core, and there were disturbing indications from Compartment Four and Five.

The captain stood nervously by, waiting for Engineer Hong and Navigator Liu to complete their deliberations. They checked and rechecked the readings, confirming radiation levels and temperatures in the rear compartments, and pressure levels from gauges on the water-tanks in the cargo holds. When they turned to deliver their findings to the captain, their faces were bloodless pale, ashen-white.

It was the engineer who finally spoke.

"We . . . we had accounted for a certain amount of boil off of the water in the makeshift system, and the possibility of additional leaks in the core system, but with the tonnage of water on hand we assumed the risks were within reason." He broke off, glancing at Navigator Liu and then at the deck-plates.

"And?" the captain asked, impatiently.

"The calculations were solid," Navigator Liu said, "given the facts on hand. The engineer's decision was the correct one under the circumstances."

The physician, who'd been behind the captain, stepped forward, all thoughts of protocol forgotten.

"But the warning indicators," Physician Xiang spat. "What do they mean?"

Engineer Hong looked up, meeting the captain's gaze, his face set.

"The water level in the tanks has dropped quicker than we'd hoped, through boil off or leakage."

Minister Bao stepped forward now, uncharacteristically speaking out of turn.

"How much water is left?" he asked, his voice quavering.

"The tanks are nearly empty," Navigator Liu answered.

"At this rate," the engineer said, "we've only got a matter of days before we're completely out of coolant, and then a full core meltdown will only be a matter of time."

4

Hexagram 53
Chien: "Sun Above Mountain"
Development (Gradual Progress)

All question of rank or privilege was forgotten, no man higher or lower in rank than any other, save the captain. His were the questions to be answered, whomever could answer them best. He conducted the discussions like a musical performance, calling on each man in turn. The navigator would forward an opinion, a suggestion for a possible course of action, and Captain Zheng would read disapproval in the face of Physician Xiang, and call on him to counter. When Engineer Hong recoiled at the suggestions of the physician, his opinions were next given voice, and so on.

It took only a matter of hours before the men had reduced their situation to a brutal calculus.

They had no way of halting the inevitable meltdown of the reactor core. Once the meltdown began, under the most optimistic of circumstances, they would all be dead within moments, likely less. The heat from the explosion would cook them in their skins, if the radiation did not kill them first. Even sealed away in Compartment One, all wearing pressurized radiation suits, they would last only a matter of heartbeats.

Their only choice lay in jettisoning the core from the ship, disengaging all the clamps and bolts holding the reactor system in place, and then opening wide the thrust chamber to the hard vacuum. The core would tumble out into space, far enough away that the ship could weather the resultant thermonuclear explosion.

This option, though, was not without its risks, or its detractors.

◔ ◔ ◔

"We'd be adrift," Engineer Hong said, when the captain had given him leave to speak. "We're still weeks from Fire Star. We could use the solid fuel attitude thrusters on the counterweight and the ship's outer hull to give us a bit of a boost, but that would last . . . What? No more than a day?"

"We could make it," Navigator Liu said when the captain had nodded his direction. "First we cut loose the counterweight, then reorient the ship for a straight line burn."

"Without the rotation we'd lose gravity," Physician Xiang said, speaking out of turn. "It's hard enough to tend to Steersman Fei as it is, but if my herbs and unguents are going to be drifting in zero gravity, I'm going to be limited to lashing down poultices with bandages, and the friction of the straps against his skin might cause serious dermal abrasion on already damaged tissues."

The captain raised his hand to interrupt the physician.

"Physician," the captain said, his expression grave but his tone insistent, "given the best case scenario, what are Fei's chances of returning to Earth alive at all? Even if we reach the rest of the Treasure Fleet, do they really have the wherewithal to improve his condition beyond what you've already accomplished?"

The physician's face darkened, and he slowly shook his head.

"Steersman Fei's chances at life are slim," he answered, his voice strained, "but he deserves every opportunity. I fear that increasing the risk to him would lessen the likelihood of his survival immeasurably."

"Du," the captain said, "if we don't do something, and quickly, then *all* of our chances of survival will lessen immediately to nil."

"What of the rest of the fleet?" the physician went on. "Have we inadvertently put all the other ships in peril, now that we have lost the better portion of the Treasure Fleet's water reserves?"

"Not serious peril, no," the captain replied, rubbing his chin. "The Ministry of Celestial Navigation so orchestrated matters that the loss of any single ship would not cripple the entire fleet. The other vessels will need to operate under somewhat severe rationing for the remainder of the voyage, and will not be able to return as many samples from the red planet as had been hoped, but there will not be any serious risk added on our account." The captain turned back to the navigator. "Go on, Liu."

The navigator glanced apologetically at the physician, and then continued.

"We're four weeks out from Fire Star, that's true, but if we were able to generate a sufficient velocity before ejecting the reactor core, we could coast along until we were caught in the gravitational attraction of the red planet. At that stage, provided we'd been conservative in their use, we could use the solid fuel attitude adjustment thrusters on the outer hull to steer us into a stable orbit."

"But what about power?" Minister Bao asked when the captain pointed his way. "Without the reactor, we'd be floating dead." He paused, and made a quick motion as though to ward away ill spirits. "Floating powerless, that is to say," he quickly added.

"Not necessarily," Engineer Hong answered at the captain's request. "Our backup batteries are designed to run essential ship systems at full capacity for fourteen days. If we cut the power to the rear compartments, and only provided heat and air circulation to the forward compartments, and restricted usage at that, we could make it stretch."

"How many of the compartments would we have to seal off, engineer?" the captain asked.

"All but One and Two, I expect," the engineer answered, and then glanced over to the navigator, who was working the calculations on his abacus. The navigator looked up from his sums, and nodded grimly. "Yes, everything from Compartment Three back will need to be sealed off and shut down. It will be a mite cramped in the Command Center for the rest of the trip, but I think we could manage it."

Navigator Liu leaned over, and checked one of the readings on the steersman console. "The batteries are currently charged to twenty-five percent," he said, sitting up, "as regulations demand. It'll take some time to charge them to full capacity."

"How long?" the captain asked.

Navigator and engineer looked to one another, and then back to the captain.

"Three days," the engineer said, with a ragged sigh.

"And how long until the temperatures in the core reach critical levels?" the captain asked.

"Three days," the engineer answered, reluctantly.

The captain stood from his chair, and clapped his hands together, sounding like a gunshot.

"In that case, it sounds like there is no time to lose," he said. "To work!"

"Yes, my captain," the navigator and engineer responded in unison.

— ◦ —

Captain Zheng was in his quarters, checking the straps securing his treasure jar, when he heard the thud. Explosive bolts on the outer hull just above his cabin discharged, sounding like distant thunder, and the counterweight went spinning off into space. The reinforced steel cable lashed against the hull once before it spun forever out of reach, sounding a discordant note, a twang like an out of tune harp.

Up in the Command Center, Navigator Liu was at the steersman console, delicately working the attitude thrusters on the outer skin of the ship, slowing the rotations of *Night Shining White* until it hovered motionless and still in space.

The captain was in the passageway, making his way forward when the last of the centrifugal forces bled away. He was at the junction to Compartment Two, and felt a stomach-churning sense of vertigo. When he tried to take another step, he lifted from the deck plates, spinning like a lost kite through the empty air. Zheng fought against the nausea, keeping his eyes on a fixed point, and grabbing for the handholds set in passageway walls.

Swallowing hard against the bile rising in his throat, the captain maneuvered his way into the Command Center.

"I'd forgotten just how much I dislike this," he said to the navigator, drifting near the steersman console.

The engineer followed the captain into the cabin, expertly kicking against the bulkhead and floating directly to the reactor controls.

"Engineer Hong, are we ready to proceed?" the captain asked, steadying himself against the ceiling.

The engineer made some final checks of the indicators and gauges, and nodded.

"All set, my captain."

The captain pushed off the ceiling, angling towards his chair. With some small difficulty, he managed to get himself strapped in. Minister Bao and Physician Xiang appeared in the doorway, and the captain waited until each had secured themselves in their seats.

"Physician, is the . . . surgery squared away?" the captain asked.

His mouth drawn into a tight line, the doctor glanced to Minister Bao and back to the captain.

"Yes," he said, "Steersman Fei is strapped in place, as best as we were able."

The captain nodded curtly.

"Navigator, is our course plotted and laid in?"

"Yes, my captain."

"Very well. Engineer, withdraw the control rods full, and release the hydrogen into the heating chamber."

"Yes, my captain."

In moments, the light indicating maximum pressure in the heating chamber lit under the engineer's hands.

"The thrust chamber is at highest pressure, my captain," the engineer reported.

"In that case, Engineer Hong," the captain answered, "iris the aperture wide, and give us a full burn thrust."

The engineer nodded, and toggled the lever that opened the rocket thrust at the rear of the ship.

"Navigator, are the batteries charging?"

"Yes, my captain. We're already to twenty-seven percent on the primary and secondary backup batteries, and climbing."

The captain relaxed against the straps, letting out a heavy sigh.

"In that case, gentlemen, I believe we have three days of leisure before us. Minister, triple rations of rice wine with today's meals, if you please."

The minister, remarkably, did not object, but smiled a weak smile, and nodded.

⊂ ⊃ ⊂

The captain was transferring his treasure jar from the high shelf to a small padded rucksack when there came a knock at the open door.

"Am I intruding?" Physician Xiang asked, hovering in the doorway.

The captain shook his head in response, and motioned the physician to enter.

"I've asked the others to gather the most prized of their personal possessions before we seal off the rear compartments," the captain explained. "We should have some small storage space left us in the ship's stores, and if the space is lacking, we'll just need to eat and drink faster." He paused, and glanced at the *erhu* fiddle secured to the bulkhead near the head of his sleeping pallet. "Still, we won't have room enough for everything, so some things must be left behind."

The physician followed the captain's gaze, and nodded.

"I'm fortunate that the limitation is one of volume, this time, and not mass," Xiang said, drawing his *dizi* flute from an inner pocket of his tunic. "This is small enough I can carry it with me, if needs must."

The captain smiled in response, and pushing off the bulkhead drifted down towards the deck.

"Care to while the time away with a bit of music, Du?"

The physician grinned, and maneuvered himself into the room.

"I can't imagine what gave you that idea, Yi."

Arranging themselves, the pair began to play, the physician hovering in midair, the captain in the corner, bracing himself between bulkhead and deck, the fiddle held between his knees.

When the captain had bowed his third dissonant cord, the sound setting the physician's teeth to rattling, the playing paused. The physician, lowering his flute, looked to his friend, concerned.

"I don't suppose I need mention that your heart doesn't appear to be in it?" he said.

The captain, laying the fiddle across his legs, shook his head.

"No, I'll admit my thoughts are . . . preoccupied."

"But why?" the physician asked, forcing a cheery disposition. "According to Liu and Hong, everything is going to plan. We're building sufficient velocity to get us to the red planet well before the batteries are drained of all power. It will have been a long, difficult journey, but we will have made it."

The captain looked sharply at the physician.

"Not all of us."

The physician averted his eyes.

"Yes, despite my best efforts, I don't know that Fei will survive the journey, or even the night."

The captain shook his head.

"No, not Fei, mores the pity. I mean whomever has to release the clamps on the reactor."

The physician looked up, confused.

"I thought that the reactor could be ejected from the Command Center."

"No," the captain said, his voice low. "That was my initial impression, too, but I asked Hong to clarify the matter for me in secret. The release mechanisms involved are located back in Compartment Five. One of the crew must go back into the sealed off areas of the ship to work the controls, and they'll run the inescapable risk of . . ."

The captain broke off, his gaze falling to the deck.

"Of ending up like Steersman Fei," the physician finished for him.

"Or Mate Chen," the captain answered. "Wrapped in a blanket of foil and buried out among the heavens."

The physician's eyes closed tightly, and a pained expression flashed across his face.

"So who will you select to go?" the physician asked in a low voice.

The physician set the fiddle to one side, securing it carefully to straps against the bulkhead.

"I will select no one," the captain answered. "I will do it myself."

◦ ◦ ◦

They had reached the third day of burn, and the batteries were fully charged. It was time to proceed.

Steersman Fei, unconscious now for over two days, was strapped to a stretcher and maneuvered through the halls and passageway from the ship's surgery to the Command Center. With Engineer Hong's assistance, Physician Xiang secured the stretcher to the deck plates at the rear of the cabin, and made Fei as comfortable as was possible.

Navigator Liu made final calculations at his station, and then moved to the steersman console to check their rate of speed and trajectory. When he was satisfied that their course and velocity were sufficient, he turned and nodded to the captain.

The captain sat perched on his chair at the rear of the Command Center, a grave expression on his face. He paused, drawing a long, steady breath, and then motioned for the crew's attention. The others stopped their activities, and turned to listen.

"We are near the culmination of our plans," the captain began. "But what some of you may not know is that, for one of us at least, the risks are not yet through."

Engineer Hong's brows knitted, and he averted his eyes.

"The final element of our plan requires that the reactor be jettisoned from the ship," the captain went on, "which necessitates one of our number entering the contaminated rear compartments. The controls are manual, and are located in Compartment Five, where the temperature has risen steadily for the last three days, and where the radiation levels now far exceed those faced by Steersman Fei and Engineer's Mate Chen in the reactor chamber." The captain crossed his arms over his chest.

"I have decided that this task should fall to me," he said. The men eyed him warily, their expressions ranging from shock to confusion. "My role on this ship has been that of a conductor, to coordinate the efforts of other men. With this final task complete, there will be no more effort to coordinate. This will be the final leg of the journey of *Night Shining White*, as it coasts gently to Fire Star and safety. As a result, my role will no longer be required."

The men looked to one another, eyes wide. Neither Navigator Liu nor Minister Bao had been aware such a sacrifice would be required, while Engineer Hong had silently expected he would be to go himself. Physician Xiang, for his part, kept his gaze fixed on the captain, his expression closed.

"No, my captain," Engineer Hong began, stepping forward. "It should be me that goes. Mine is the authority over the reactor, the task my responsibility."

"No, Hong," the captain answered, shaking his head slowly. "You are the only one of us here with the expertise to man the reactor controls from the Command Center, to insert the control rods at the crucial moment and allow the core to be ejected."

The engineer opened his mouth to object, but then slowly closed it again, glancing back to the complex reactor controls at the front of the cabin. He looked to the captain, then averted his gaze.

"Navigator Liu is needed to control the attitudinal thrusters," the captain went on, "and to ensure that you reach the red planet as intended. The physician must remain healthy, since there's every chance the symptoms of radiation sickness among the rest of you will continue. You will need him at your side to see you through the coming weeks. Minister Bao, for his part . . ."

The minister surged forward, head back and jaw set.

"For my part," Bao said, interrupting, "my duty here is abandoned. Mine is the ritual and protocol, the proper governance of the ship's society. In this abbreviated space," he indicated the Command Center with a wave of his arm, "there is no protocol left to keep, no ritual to observe, only men following their true natures and hoping to survive. These men need their captain, more than they could ever need a hundred political officers like me. No, captain, it should be I who goes."

The captain released the straps holding him in his seat, and drifted free.

"My orders, minister, are that you stay here with the men," he said firmly. "As Minister of Rites, I expect that you will recognize my authority in this matter, and obey my will."

A long pause followed, the captain and the minister locking eyes. The minister seemed to deflate, his shoulders slumping, and he drifted back and away. Something flashed across his eyes, then, his chest expanding, and he raised his head. He pushed forward, and grabbed hold of the captain's arm.

"No," the minister said simply. "I will not. You will stay, and I will go."

The captain wrenched his arm free of the minister's grip, and tried to shove past him to the passageway.

"Let me go, damn you," the captain said. "This is my decision to make."

The minister reached forward with both hands, grabbing the captain around the waist from behind.

"This is mutiny, Minister Bao!" the captain shouted.

In the confusion, Navigator Liu reached beneath the navigator's console, then propelled himself up to the ceiling, then bounced back to the deck plates like a ricocheting ball, ending up directly in front of the captain.

The navigator held a small, shining pistol, which he leveled at the captain's chest.

"Mutiny, my captain?" he said with a hint of irony. "Yes, I believe it is."

⚬ ⚬ ⚬

The other men in the cabin all froze in place, looking at the navigator in shocked amazement.

"Where did you get that?" the captain asked, glaring at the navigator through narrowed eyes.

All firearms were expressly forbidden on imperial ships. It was as much a matter of avoiding explosive decompression from errant shots shattering viewport windows or hulls, as it was a matter of forestalling insurrection. Only agents of the Dragon Throne could carry firearms and escape a death sentence.

Navigator Liu offered a lopsided grin, and held the shining, ornate pistol up as if inspecting it for the first time. It was silver in color, acid-etched with complex curlicues along the barrel and revolving chamber, with jade inlays in the handle.

"This?" Navigator Liu said through his grin. "It was presented to me by the head of the Eastern Depot himself."

The captain's eyes widened, as the other men drew instinctively back.

"Eastern Depot," the captain repeated. "Then you . . . *you* are a secret policeman."

The navigator gave a little bow in midair, the gun still trained on the captain's chest. "Yes, that felicity is mine," he answered with a grim smile. "I was recruited as one of the Embroidered Guards out of the ranks of the Ministry of Calculation. They needed men skilled at sums and figures who could be trained as the emperor's eyes and ears in space. It's been largely kept from the fleet, but there have been several mutinies these past years, whole ships lost to mutinous crews, and on missions far less dangerous and taxing than that given to *Night Shining White*. The Eastern Depot placed men in amongst all the ships of the Treasure Fleet to Fire Star. To do otherwise would simply be too great a risk."

The captain's eyes narrowed.

"And yet here you are, with a pistol pointed at your captain's chest," he snarled. "If that is not mutiny, then what is?"

The navigator looked from the gun back up to the captain, and gave a slight shrug, his head cocked to one side.

"I know," Liu answered with a grin. "Ironic, isn't it, that I reveal myself to you only to assist a crewman in refusing your orders. The secret policeman, siding against the captain with the crew." Liu shook his head sardonically. "Life is a strange journey, my captain, with many detours along the way."

The navigator motioned with the pistol for Minister Bao to step forward.

"As much as I loathe sending another man to almost certain death," Liu said, "I am forced to agree with the Minister of Rites. The captain's place is with his crew, not bathing in radiation below decks. You have held these men together this long, and you'll hold them together for more days to come."

Liu motioned Physician Xiang to come forward.

"Physician, will you help the minister into one of the radiation suits?" the navigator commanded by way of request. He turned back to the captain, and added apologetically, "I am sorry about this, my captain."

Captain Zheng looked from the navigator to Minister Bao, lumbering awkwardly into the radiation suit.

"It's my ship, and my authority, Liu," the captain snapped. "I order you to step aside and let me do this thing!"

The navigator proffered a sad smile.

"In that case, my captain, this *is* mutiny after all."

● ● ●

Though their primary radio transmitter array was still fused and inoperative, the engineer had been able to rig the communication equipment to send and receive radio signals over short distances. Working in secret over the two days previous, he'd rigged a small radio transceiver into the radiation suit's helmet, along with a miniature speaker and microphone. He'd intended the device to allow him to radio back success after ejecting the reactor core, but now it would be Minister Bao in the suit, and the engineer waiting helplessly for news in the Command Center. The captain remained in his chair, the navigator standing nearby with his pistol trained on him. Neither man spoke, only darted glances at the far side of the room where the engineer and physician went about the grim business of encasing Minister Bao in the radiation suit.

"You're sure you know what to do, minister?" Engineer Hong asked, the suit's helmet held in his hands. "It's not too late for me to . . ."

Minister Bao shook his head sharply, motioning for Hong to lift the helmet into place. "No, engineer, I remember what you've told me," he answered, his voice coming from somewhere far away.

"If you run into any trouble, just use the radio," the engineer said, sounding like a worried mother. "There's always the other radiation suit if you find you need assistance."

The engineer and the physician rotated the suit's helmet into place, and secured the last of the straps and buckles. The minister reached out and laid a gloved hand on the engineer's shoulder.

"My thanks, friend," Bao said softly, his voice reverberating through the Command Center, picked up by the helmet microphone and broadcast through the speakers at the communications console. The minister flinched back, hearing his own voice echoing back to him, and then laughed.

"I've more to be worried about than echoes, I should think," he said, forcing a hint of good cheer. "Well, no time to waste."

The minister made his way to the passageway, and to the rear compartments beyond. The plan was simple. Once the minister had released the clamps and bolts on the reactor core from the relative safety of Compartment Five, the engineer in the Command Center would open wide the thrust chamber, exposing it to the hard vacuum beyond. When the liquid hydrogen in the propellant tanks was released, it would expand out into the vacuum, carrying the reactor core with it.

The hatches between Compartments Five through Three were to be left open. The rear compartments would remain pressurized until the minister had made it back to Compartment Three, which they would then use as a kind of airlock. Once the minister closed off Compartment Three, the crewmen in the Command Center could open the hatch to allow him to return to Compartment Two. When he was safely back in the Command Center, they could seal off the hatch, and cut air pressure and heat to all of the areas from Compartment Three to stern. They had worked the plan out in detail, to eliminate the risk that the minister would be exposed to a depressurized cabin. The radiation suit, though proof against heat and midrange levels of radiation, was not pressurized, and didn't carry its own air supply. If the minister was exposed to vacuum it would be a close race which would kill him first—a ruptured suit or suffocation.

＊　＊　＊

Once the hatch was shut, and Minister Bao was on his way to the rear of the ship, Navigator Liu tucked the pistol away in an inner pocket, and returned to his station at the navigator's console. The captain, wasting no time with acrimony or recrimination, turned to the physician.

"Du, how long does the minister have before the radiation exposure is critical?" he asked, his voice level but tense.

The physician pushed off the bulkhead and drifted to the reactor controls, and leaned in close to read the indicator gauges.

"Based on the radiation readings in the aft compartments," he

answered, "if the minister makes it to the controls in the anticipated time frame, and returns immediately, then there's a good
chance his exposure will be minimal. He'll get sick, but not much
worse than that." The captain turned his attention to the engineer,
who had maneuvered himself to the radio controls.

"Engineer, do we have an open line to the minister?"

The engineer hunched over the controls, stabbing at a few
switches.

"We do now, my captain," he answered, wheeling around, his
expression grim.

"Minister, can you hear me?" Captain Zheng called out in a
loud voice.

A blast of static followed, then a screech, then the voice of the
minister buzzed through, clear as wind chimes.

"Yes, my captain," the voice of the minister issued from the
speakers. "Though not quite so loud, please. The speaker is quite
close to my ear."

The captain glanced over at the engineer, a slight smile on
his lips.

"My compliments, engineer," he said in a quiet voice, then
raised his volume somewhat and went on. "Minister, what is your
progress?"

A short bark of static, and then the minister's voice again
buzzed from the speakers. "I'm just now in the junction with
Compartment Four, making my way through the passageway. It's
hot, my captain. Damned hot, if you'll forgive the language."

The captain shook his head, chuckling ruefully.

"It's quite all right, minister," he answered. "Now, listen to
me, Bao. The physician says that you'll be fine if you can hurry.
You're making good time so far, so if you can just keep it up, you
should make it through this with little more than an upset stomach and a skin burn." A strange rhythm sound issued from the
speakers, which the captain realized after a moment was the
sound of the minister laughing.

"I'll do my best, my captain," the minister answered. "Just entering Compartment Five now."

The men in the Command Center waited in tense silence,
hearing only static.

"All right, I'm at the primary reactor controls," came the voice through the speakers, at last.

Engineer Hong leaned forward, gripping onto the communications console with both hands and speaking directly into the microphone.

"Do you see the four release levers, minister?"

After a buzz of static, the voice of the minister filled the cabin. "Yes, I see them."

The engineer took a ragged breath.

"Now," he went on, "as I told you, first you must disengage the safety latches, then you can move the levers to the release position. Do you see the safety latches?"

The engineer cocked his head to one side, as if listening for a distant voice.

"I'm releasing the first of the latches now," came the voice of the minister. They could hear him grunting with strain, his breathing labored, and finally a sound of sudden release, like a heavy sigh. "That's one. Moving the lever . . ." Again, a grunt and strain. "Now! Okay, that's one done."

An indicator bulb on the reactor controls lit up, leaving three dark bulbs beside it.

"And three to go," the captain said, evenly. "Keep at it, minister, you're making good time."

"Now the second . . . latch . . . is . . . open," the voice of the minister buzzed. "A-and . . . the lever is done."

The second of the bulbs lit, bright yellow against the cold metal plating, with two more left still dim.

"That's it, minister," the navigator said, his lips drawn tight.

"The third latch . . . is . . . open. And now the lever." A grunt, heavy breathing, and a sigh of relief. The third indicator bulb on the reactor controls winked on. "Okay, the third lever is open. That just leaves the one."

"You're nearly done, minister," the engineer said. "Once you move that lever into place, I can release the hydrogen and open the thrust chamber from here."

"Temperature climbing rapidly in the core," the physician reported, glancing over the reactor controls. "Radiation levels spiking."

The navigator left his console and maneuvered to the physician's side.

"We're drawing near a complete meltdown, my captain," the navigator reported, calling over his shoulder.

"He only needs a few more minutes," the captain said, his eyes fixed to the speakers. "Minister, how is it coming?"

A buzz of static followed.

"Just opening the last . . . latch . . . and now the fourth lever is . . . is . . ." A straining grunt, labored breath, all building to a crescendo, as the minister let out a scream that rattled the fixtures in the Command Center.

"Minister!" the engineer called.

"Bao, report!" the captain ordered.

There was a long pause, as static poured from the speakers.

"The last release lever," the minister finally answered, his voice sounding tinny and distant. "It won't budge."

"Have you tried . . ." the engineer began.

"It won't budge!" came the voice from the speakers, cutting him off. "It might as well have been cast in iron in this position. It isn't moving at all."

The engineer, face red and sweating, looked back to the captain.

"Hong, what are our options?" the captain asked.

"Well, someone could enter the reactor chamber and pry loose the last clamp manually, but it would be suicide to go in there . . ."

"Now entering Compartment Six," buzzed the voice from the speakers.

"Minister!" the engineer shouted, as the captain leapt out of his chair.

"The light is strange in here," Minister Bao said through the growing static. "Blue and violet flames play on the walls and floor. It's much hotter than I would have expected." There was a squeal of static, and then the voice of the minister could be heard again. "I am fortunate to find this opportunity to display my virtue. Thank you, captain, I . . ."

"My captain," called Navigator Liu from the reactor controls.

"The water level in the cargo tanks has dropped to nil. There can't be more than bare mouthfuls of coolant left in the core at this point."

"And the temperature is starting to spike," Physician Xiang added.

"Minister, get out of there!" called the engineer, grabbing the microphone in his hands, his face turned beat red.

The captain kicked towards the communications console, grabbing hold of the engineer's shoulder and pulling him back.

"Bao, can you see the remaining clamp?" he shouted, eyes wide.

A riot of static burst from the speakers.

"The radiation is playing havoc with the transceiver," the navigator said, drifting over to hover behind the captain.

"Bao!" the captain called again.

"I see—" they heard through the static and noise. "—trying to— clamp—"

"Minister, can you hear us?" the captain shouted.

"—about to—"

There was a final wordless shout that sounded through the speakers, and then they were awash with static.

"Yi," called Physician Xiang from the reactor controls.

The captain looked over, and the physician indicated the fourth indicator bulb burning brightly against the gray steel.

"Temperature is critical," the physician added. "Approaching core meltdown."

The captain pushed the engineer aside, and grabbed the microphone in both hands.

"Bao! Can you hear me?"

From the speakers came nothing but static.

"My captain," the navigator said in a low voice. "If we don't jettison the reactor core, his sacrifice will have been for nothing."

The captain's hands tightened into white-knuckled fists at his sides, and he shook with impotent rage.

"Yi," the physician said. "We don't have any choice."

The captain glared at the physician, eyes flashing.

"Don't you think I know that?" he barked. The captain turned to the engineer. "Hong, flush the hydrogen tanks and prepare to iris open the thrust chamber."

"But, sir . . ." the engineer objected.

"Do it," the captain said simply, and pushed off towards his chair.

Long seconds oozed by.

"The chamber is at full pressure, my *captain*," the engineer said, turning the address into a curse.

"Open the aperture full, Engineer Hong," the captain said, sounding defeated.

The engineer stabbed a switch on the controls, praying to all the gods there were for forgiveness.

⊖ ⊖ ⊖

Flushed out in a cloud of boiling hydrogen gas, the reactor and the body of the minister spun out of the rocket exhaust, spinning end over end, like a new born star and its misshapen satellite. With a blinding flash, the reactor core erupted in a thermonuclear explosion, glowing like a miniature supernova as it tumbled out in to the cold blackness, consuming the body of its lone satellite in its fury.

⊖ ⊖ ⊖

The ship made its final days to the Fire Star, drifting in still silence, the men packed cheek to jowl in the Command Center. The engineer and navigator, numbly, rigged an assembly that protruded from the docking array airlock, with electrical controls on the inside and a battery powered light on the other end. The light was powerful enough to be seen for thousands of miles, and by flickering the power to cause flashes of particular lengths and durations, they could communicate using a signaling language that was ancient when sailors first used it in the days of the Yellow Emperor.

Words were seldom spoken in the last weeks of the journey, no songs sung, no jokes related. The men sat in silence, each ensconced in his own thoughts, their grief kept private. Steersman

Fei died within sight of Fire Star, the red planet hanging the size of a melon beyond the Command Center's forward viewport. The men could muster little energy for the burial, wrapping him in a reflective blanket and shoving him out the airlock with little ceremony. There were no rites to observe. They had lost the minister of protocols.

Navigator Liu worked the attitudinal thrusters like a virtuoso, steering them into a stable parking orbit above the red planet. Using the makeshift signaling device, the engineer signaled their distress to the nearest of the ships, *The Six Virtues*. The communications chief of the large transport replied via radio, and the two ships carried on a brief but staggered conversation, with the captain of *The Six Virtues* asking questions that buzzed through the radio speakers in the Command Center of *Night Shining White*, and the smaller ship responded by means of the simple flashing code.

When the ship-to-ship shuttle from the transport maneuvered into position to dock with the water-tender, Navigator Liu and Engineer Hong were waiting in the airlock to receive them. Captain Zheng lingered in the Command Center, the physician at his side. The captain clutched a ceramic jar to his chest.

"I haven't proven much of a captain," Zheng finally said, his voice faint and low. "Pretty useless, in the final analysis."

"Why would you say such a thing?" the physician asked, eyebrow raised.

Zheng turned to his friend, as though shocked that he could ask.

"My ship is a derelict, our cargo lost to the vacuum, and almost half of my crew has died in the voyage. How otherwise would you describe it?"

The physician pursed his lips, thoughtfully, and laid a hand on the captain's shoulder.

"I hadn't seen it in that light, Yi. To my eyes, you are the man who brought more than half of your ship's crew unweathered through the storms. That Fei, Chen and Bao were lost along the way is a tragedy, to be sure, but that the rest of us still live is due only to your leadership. What you call useless is only a matter of perspective. A thing's use can often be overlooked."

The captain looked sidelong at the physician.

"There is nothing, whether humor or tragedy, that you will not turn to your philosophy, is there?" the captain asked, a faint smile playing across his lips.

"We contribute what we can, and must each follow our own natures," the physician answered with a smile.

The physician turned, and pushed himself towards the forward passageway.

"Come on," he called back over his shoulder. "There's nine more ships in this Treasure Fleet, and I'm sure that one of them can find a use for us."

The captain returned his treasured jar to his padded rucksack, and then pushed off the chair, drifting after the physician.

"You don't suppose any of them require a pair of musicians, do you, Du?" he called. "I know of two who are in current need of employment."

The two men made their way through the compartment to the airlock, and from there into the shuttle. The hatch closed behind them, and *Night Shining White* was left empty, its voyage done.

JULIAN: A CHRISTMAS STORY

by Robert Charles Wilson

Robert Charles Wilson was born in California in 1953, but grew up in Canada. His first short story, "Equinocturne," (as Bob Chuck Wilson) was published in 1975; by the mid-1980s, Wilson was being published consistently in numerous places. His short story "The Perseids" was a World Fantasy and Nebula finalist and an Aurora Award winner, and "The Inner, Inner City" was a World Fantasy Award finalist. He has published twelve novels, including A Hidden Place, Mysterium, Darwinia, *and Hugo Award winner* Spin, *and one collection,* World Fantasy Award nominee The Perseids and Other Stories. *The novella* Julian: A Christmas Story *is his most recent book and he has just completed* Axis, *a sequel to* Spin. *Wilson currently lives in Concord, Ontario, north of Toronto.*

1

THIS IS A story about Julian Comstock, better known as Julian the Agnostic or (after his uncle) Julian Conqueror. But it is not about his conquests, such as they were, or his betrayals, or about the War in Labrador, or Julian's quarrels with the Church of the Dominion. I witnessed many of those events—and will no doubt write about them, ultimately—but this narrative concerns Julian when he was young, and I was young, and neither of us was famous.

2

In late October of 2172—an election year—Julian and I, along with his mentor Sam Godwin, rode to the Tip east of the town of Williams Ford, where I came to possess a book, and Julian tutored me in one of his heresies.

It was a brisk, sunny day. There was a certain resolute promptness to the seasons in that part of Athabaska, in those days. Our summers were long, languid, and hot. Spring and fall were brief, mere custodial functions between the extremes of weather. Winters were short but biting. Snow set in around the end of December, and the River Pine generally thawed by late March.

Today might be the best we would get of autumn. It was a day we should have spent under Sam Godwin's tutelage, perhaps sparring, or target-shooting, or reading chapters from the Dominion History of the Union. But Sam was not a heartless overseer, and the kindness of the weather had suggested the possibility of an Outing, and so we had gone to the stables, where my father worked, and drawn horses, and ridden out of the Estate with lunches of black bread and salt ham in our back-satchels.

We rode east, away from the hills and the town. Julian and I rode ahead; Sam rode behind, a watchful presence, his Pittsburgh rifle ready in the saddle holster at his side. There was no immediate threat of trouble, but Sam Godwin believed in perpetual preparedness; if he had a gospel, it was BE PREPARED; also, SHOOT FIRST; and probably, DAMN THE CONSEQUENCES. Sam, who was old (nearly fifty), wore a dense brown beard stippled with wiry white hairs, and was dressed in what remained presentable of his tan-and-green Army of the Californias uniform, and a cloak to keep the wind off. He was like a father to Julian, Julian's own true father having performed a gallows dance some years before. Lately he had been more vigilant than ever, for reasons he had not discussed, at least with me.

Julian was my age (seventeen), and we were approximately the same height, but there the resemblance ended. Julian had been born an aristo; my family was of the leasing class. His skin was clear and pale where mine was dark and lunar. (I was marked by the same Pox that took my sister Flaxie to her grave in '63.) His hair was long and almost femininely clean; mine was black and wiry, cut to stubble by my mother with her sewing scissors, and I washed it once a week or so—more often in summer, when the brook behind the cottage ran clean and cool. His clothes were linen and, in places, silk, brass-buttoned, cut to fit; my shirt and pants were coarse hempen cloth, sewn to a good approximation but obviously not the work of a New York tailor.

And yet we were friends, and had been friends for three years, since we met by chance in the forested hills west of the Duncan and Crowley Estate, where we had gone to hunt, Julian with his fine Porter & Earle cassette rifle and me with a simple muzzle-loader. We both loved books, especially the boys' books written in those days by an author named Charles Curtis Easton.[1] I had been carrying a copy of Easton's *Against the Brazilians,* illicitly borrowed from the Estate library; Julian had recognized the title, but refrained from ratting on me, since he loved the book as much as I did and longed to discuss it with a fellow enthusiast (of which there were precious few among his aristo relations)—in short, he did me an unbegged favor, and we became fast friends despite our differences.

In those early days I had not known how fond he was of blasphemy. But I had learned since, and it had not deterred me. Much.

We had not set out with the specific aim of visiting the Tip; but at the nearest crossroad Julian turned west, riding past cornfields and gourd fields already harvested and sun-whitened split-rail fences on which dense blackberry gnarls had grown up. The air was cool but the sun was fiercely bright. Julian and Sam wore broad-brimmed hats to protect their faces; I wore a plain linen pakul hat, sweat-stained, rolled about my ears. Before long we passed the last rude shacks of the indentured laborers, whose near-naked children gawked at us from the roadside, and it became obvious we were going to the Tip, because where else on this road was there to go? —unless we continued east for many

---

[1] Whom I would meet when he was sixty years old, and I was a newcomer to the book trade—but that's another story.

hours, all the way to the ruins of the old towns, from the days of the False Tribulation.

The Tip was located far from Williams Ford to prevent poaching and disorder. There was a strict pecking order to the Tip. This is how it worked: professional scavengers hired by the Estate brought their pickings from the ruined places to the Tip, which was a pine-fenced enclosure (a sort of stockade) in a patch of grassland and prairie flowers. There the newly arrived goods were roughly sorted, and riders were dispatched to the Estate to make the high-born aware of the latest acquisitions, and various aristos (or their trusted servants) would ride out to claim the prime gleanings. The next day, the leasing class would be allowed to sort through what was left; after that, if anything remained, indentured laborers could rummage among it, if they calculated it worthwhile to make the journey.

Every prosperous town had a Tip; though in the east it was sometimes called a Till, a Dump, or an Eebay.

Today we were fortunate: several wagonloads of scrounge had lately arrived, and riders had not yet been sent to notify the Estate. The gate was manned by a Home Guard, who looked at us suspiciously until Sam announced the name of Julian Comstock; then the guard briskly stepped aside, and we went inside the enclosure.

Many of the wagons were still unloading, and a chubby Tipman, eager to show off his bounty, hurried toward us as we dismounted and moored our horses. "Happy coincidence!" he cried. "Gentlemen!" Addressing mostly Sam by this remark, with a cautious smile for Julian and a disdainful sidelong glance at me.

"Anything *in particular* you're looking for?"

"Books," Julian said promptly, before Sam or I could answer.

"Books! Ordinarily, I set aside books for the Dominion Conservator . . ."

"The boy is a Comstock," Sam said. "I don't suppose you mean to balk him."

The Tipman reddened. "No, not at all . . . in fact we came across something in our digging . . . a sort of *library in miniature* . . . I'll show you, if you like."

This was intriguing, especially to Julian, who beamed as if he had been invited to a Christmas party. We followed the stout Tipman to a freshly arrived canvasback wagon, from which a laborer was tossing bundled piles into a stack beside a tent.

These twine-wrapped bales were books . . . old, tattered, and wholly free of the Dominion Stamp of Approval. They must have been more than a century old; for although they were faded they had obviously once been colorful and expensively printed, not made of stiff brown paper like the Charles Curtis Easton books of modern times. They had not even rotted much. Their smell, under the cleansing Athabaska sunlight, was inoffensive.

"Sam!" Julian whispered. He had already drawn his knife and was slicing through the twine.

"Calm down," suggested Sam, who was not an enthusiast like Julian.

"Oh, but—*Sam*! We should have brought a cart!"

"We can't carry away armloads, Julian, nor would we ever have been allowed to. The Dominion scholars will have all this, though perhaps you can get away with a volume or two."

The Tipman said, "These are from Lundsford." Lundsford was the name of a ruined town thirty or so miles to the southeast. The Tipman leaned toward Sam Godwin, who was his own age, and said: "We thought Lundsford had been mined out a decade ago. But even a dry well may freshen. One of my workers spotted a low place off the main excavations—a sort of *sink-hole*: the recent rain had cut it through. Once a basement or warehouse of some kind. Oh, sir, we found good china there, and glasswork, and many more books than this . . . most were mildewed, but some had been protected under a kind of stiff oilcloth, and were lodged beneath a partially collapsed ceiling . . . there had been a fire, but they survived it . . ."

"Good work, Tipman," Sam Godwin said.

"Thank you, sir! Perhaps you could remember me to the great men of the Estate?" And he gave his name (which I have forgotten).

Julian had fallen to his knees amidst the compacted clay and rubble of the Tip, lifting up each book in turn and examining it with wide eyes. I joined him in his exploration.

I had never much liked the Tip. It had always seemed to me

a haunted place. And of course it *was* haunted: that was its purpose, to house the revenants of the past, ghosts of the False Tribulation startled out of their century-long slumber. Here was evidence of the best and worst of the people who had inhabited the Years of Vice and Profligacy. Their fine things were very fine, their glassware especially, and it was a straitened aristo indeed who did not possess antique table settings rescued from some ruin or other. Sometimes one might find silver utensils in boxes, or useful tools, or coins. The coins were too plentiful to be worth much, individually, but they could be worked into buttons or other adornments. One of the high-born back at the Estate owned a saddle studded with copper pennies all from the year 2032. (I had occasionally been enlisted to polish it.)

But here also was the trash and inexplicable detritus: "plastic," gone brittle with sunlight or soft with the juices of the earth; bits of metal blooming with rust; electronic devices blackened by time and imbued with the sad inutility of a tensionless spring; engine parts, corroded; copper wire rotten with verdigris; aluminum cans and steel barrels eaten through by the poisonous fluids they had once contained—and so on, almost *ad infinitum.*

Here, too, were the in-between things, the curiosities, the ugly or pretty baubles, as intriguing and as useless as seashells. ("Put down that rusty trumpet, Adam, you'll cut your lip and poison your blood!"—my mother, when we had gone to the Tip many years before I met Julian. There had been no music in the trumpet anyway; its bell was bent and corroded through.)

More than that, though, there was the uneasy knowledge that these things, fine or corrupt, had survived their makers—had proved more imperishable than flesh or spirit (for the souls of the secular ancients were almost certainly not first in line for the Resurrection).

And yet, these books . . . they tempted; they proclaimed their seductions boldly. Some were decorated with impossibly beautiful women in various degrees of undress. I had already sacrificed my personal claim to virtue with certain young women at the Estate, whom I had recklessly kissed; at the age of seventeen I considered myself a jade, or something like one; but these images were so frank and impudent they made me blush and look away.

Julian simply ignored them, as he had always been invulnerable to the charms of women. He preferred the larger and more densely written material—he had already set aside a textbook of *biology*, spotted and discolored but largely intact. He found another volume almost as large, and handed it to me, saying, "Here, Adam, try this—you might find it enlightening."

I inspected it skeptically. The book was called *The History of Mankind in Space.*

"The moon again," I said.

"Read it for yourself."

"Tissue of lies, I'm sure."

"With photographs."

"Photographs prove nothing. Those people could do anything with photographs."

"Well, read it anyway," Julian said.

In truth the idea excited me. We had had this argument many times, Julian and I, especially on autumn nights when the moon hung low and ponderous on the horizon. *People have walked there,* he would say. The first time he made this claim I laughed; the second time I said, "Yes, certainly; I once climbed there myself, on a greased rainbow—" But he had been serious.

Oh, I had heard these stories before. Who hadn't? Men on the moon. What surprised me was that someone as well-educated as Julian would believe them.

"Just take the book," he insisted.

"What, to keep?"

"Certainly to keep."

"Believe I will," I muttered, and I stuck the object in my backsatchel and felt both proud and guilty. What would my father say, if he knew I was reading literature without a Dominion stamp? What would my mother make of it? (Of course I would not tell them.)

At this point I backed off, and found a grassy patch a little away from the rubble, where I could sit and eat some of the lunch I had packed, and watch Julian, who continued to sort through the detritus with a kind of scholarly intensity. Sam Godwin came and joined me, brushing a spot on an old timber so he could recline without soiling his uniform, such as it was.

"He sure loves those old books," I said, making conversation.

Sam was often taciturn—the very picture of an old veteran—but he nodded and spoke familiarly: "He's learned to love them. I helped teach him. I wonder if that was wise. Maybe he loves them too much. It might be they'll kill him, one of these days."

"How, Sam? By the apostasy of them?"

"Julian's too smart for his own good. He debates with the Dominion clergy. Just last week I found him arguing with Ben Kreel[2] about God, history, and such abstractions. Which is precisely what he must *not* do, if he wants to survive the next few years."

"Why, what threatens him?"

"The jealousy of the powerful," Sam said, but he would say no more on the subject, only sat and stroked his graying beard, and glanced occasionally, and uneasily, to the east.

—　—　—

The day went on, and eventually Julian had to drag himself from his nest of books with only a pair of prizes: the *Introduction to Biology* and another volume called *Geography of North America.* Time to go, Sam insisted; better to be back at the Estate by supper; in any case, riders had been sent ahead, and the official pickers and Dominion curators would soon be here to cull what we had left.

But I have said that Julian tutored me in one of his apostasies. Here is how it happened. We stopped, at the drowsy end of the afternoon, at the height of a ridge overlooking the town of Williams Ford, the grand Estate upstream of it, and the River Pine as it cut through the valley on its way from the mountains of the West. From this vantage we could see the steeple of the Dominion Hall, and the revolving wheels of the grist mill and the lumber mill, and so on, blue in the long light and hazy with wood smoke, colored here and there with what remained of the autumn foliage. Far to the south a railway bridge crossed the gorge of the Pine like a suspended thread. *Go inside,* the weather seemed to proclaim;

---

[2]Our local representative of the Council of the Dominion; in effect, the Mayor of the town.

it's fair but it won't be fair for long; bolt the window, stoke the fire, boil the apples; winter's due. We rested our horses on the windy hilltop, and Julian found a blackberry bramble where the berries were still plump and dark, and we plucked some of these and ate them.

This was the world I had been born into. It was an autumn like every autumn I could remember. But I could not help thinking of the Tip and its ghosts. Maybe those people, the people who had lived through the Efflorescence of Oil and the False Tribulation, had felt about their homes and neighborhoods as I felt about Williams Ford. They were ghosts to me, but they must have seemed real enough to themselves—must have *been* real; had not realized they were ghosts; and did that mean I was also a ghost, a revenant to haunt some future generation?

Julian saw my expression and asked me what was the matter. I told him my thoughts.

"Now you're thinking like a philosopher," he said, grinning.

"No wonder they're such a miserable brigade, then."

"Unfair, Adam—you've never seen a philosopher in your life." Julian believed in philosophers and claimed to have met one or two.

"Well, I *imagine* they're miserable, if they go around thinking of themselves as ghosts and such."

"It's the condition of all things," Julian said. "This blackberry, for example." He plucked one and held it in the pale palm of his hand. "Has it always looked like this?"

"Obviously not," I said, impatiently.

"Once it was a tiny green bud of a thing, and before that it was part of the substance of the bramble, which before that was a seed inside a blackberry—"

"And round and round for all eternity."

"But no, Adam, that's the point. The bramble, and that tree over there, and the gourds in the field, and the crow circling over them—they're all descended from ancestors that didn't quite re-semble them. A blackberry or a crow is a *form*, and forms change over time, the way clouds change shape as they travel across the sky."

"Forms of what?"

"Of DNA," Julian said earnestly. (The *biology* he had picked out of the Tip was not the first *biology* he had read.)

"Julian," Sam warned, "I once promised this boy's parents you wouldn't corrupt him."

I said, "I've heard of DNA. It's the life force of the secular ancients. And it's a myth."

"Like men walking on the moon?"

"Exactly."

"And who's your authority on this? Ben Kreel? The *Dominion History of the Union*?"

"Nothing is changeless except DNA? That's a peculiar argument even from you, Julian."

"It would be, if I were making it. But DNA *isn't* changeless. It struggles to remember itself, but it never remembers itself perfectly. Remembering a fish, it imagines a lizard. Remembering a horse, it imagines a hippopotamus. Remembering an ape, it imagines a man."

"Julian!" Sam was insistent now. "That's *quite* enough."

"You sound like a Darwinist," I said.

"Yes," Julian admitted, smiling in spite of his unorthodoxy, the autumn sun turning his face the color of penny copper. "I suppose I do."

⌒ ⌒ ⌒

That night, I lay in bed until I was reasonably certain both my parents were asleep. Then I rose, lit a lamp, and took the new (or rather, very old) *History of Mankind in Space* from where I had hidden it behind my oaken dresser.

I leafed through the brittle pages. I didn't read the book. I *would* read it, but tonight I was too weary to pay close attention, and in any case I wanted to savor the words (lies and fictions though they might be), not rush through them. Tonight I wanted only to sample the book; in other words, to look at the pictures.

There were dozens of photographs, and each one captured my attention with fresh marvels and implausibilities. One of them showed—or purported to show—men standing on the surface of the moon, just as Julian had described.

The men in the picture were evidently Americans. They wore flags stitched to the shoulders of their moon clothing, an archaic version of our own flag, with something less than the customary sixty stars. Their clothing was white and ridiculously bulky, like the winter clothes of the Inuit, and they wore helmets with golden visors that disguised their faces. I supposed it must be very cold on the moon, if explorers required such cumbersome protection. They must have arrived in winter. However, there was no ice or snow in the neighborhood. The moon seemed to be little more than a desert, dry as a stick and dusty as a Tipman's wardrobe.

I cannot say how long I stared at this picture, puzzling over it. It might have been an hour or more. Nor can I accurately describe how it made me feel . . . larger than myself, but lonely, as if I had grown as tall as the stars and lost sight of everything familiar. By the time I closed the book the moon had risen outside my window—the *real* moon, I mean; a harvest moon, fat and orange, half-hidden behind drifting, evolving clouds.

I found myself wondering whether it was truly possible that men had visited that celestial body. Whether, as the pictures implied, they had ridden there on rockets, rockets a thousand times larger than the familiar Independence Day fireworks. But if men had visited the moon, why hadn't they stayed there? Was it so inhospitable a place that no one wished to remain?

Or perhaps they *had* stayed, and were living there still. If the moon was such a cold place, I reasoned, people residing on its surface would be forced to build fires to keep warm. There seemed to be no wood on the moon, judging by the photographs, so they must have resorted to coal or peat. I went to the window and examined the moon minutely for any sign of campfires, pit mining, or other lunar industry. But I could see none. It was only the moon, mottled and changeless. I blushed at my own gullibility, replaced the book in its hiding place, chased these heresies from my mind with a prayer (or a hasty facsimile of one), and eventually fell asleep.

3

It falls to me to explain something of Williams Ford, and my family's place in it—and Julian's—before I describe the threat Sam Godwin feared, which materialized in our village not long before Christmas.[3]

Situated at the head of the valley was the font of our prosperity, the Duncan and Crowley Estate. It was a country estate (obviously, since we were in Athabaska, far from the eastern seats of power), owned by two influential New York mercantile families, who maintained their villa not only as a source of income but as a kind of resort, safely distant (several days' journey by train) from the intrigues and pestilences of city life. It was inhabited—ruled, I might say—not only by the Duncan and Crowley patriarchs but by a whole legion of cousins, nephews, relations by marriage, high-born friends, and distinguished guests in search of clean air and rural views. Our corner of Athabaska was blessed with a benign climate and pleasant scenery, according to the season, and these things attract idle aristos the way strong butter attracts flies.

It remains unrecorded whether the town existed before the Estate or vice versa; but certainly the town depended on the Estate for its prosperity. In Williams Ford there were essentially three classes: the Owners, or aristos; below them the leasing class, who worked as smiths, carpenters, coopers, overseers, gardeners, beekeepers, etc., and whose leases were repaid in service; and finally the indentured laborers, who worked as field hands, inhabited rude shacks along the west bank of the Pine, and received no compensation beyond bad food and worse lodging.

My family occupied an ambivalent place in this hierarchy. My mother was a seamstress. She worked at the Estate as had her parents before her. My father, however, had arrived in Williams Ford as a transient, and his marriage to my mother had been controversial. He had "married a lease," as the saying has it, and had been taken on as a stable hand at the Estate in lieu of a dowry.

---

[3] I beg the reader's patience if I detail matters that seem well-known. I indulge the possibility of a foreign audience, or a posterity to whom our present arrangements are not self-evident.

The law allowed such unions, but popular opinion frowned on it. We had few friends of our own class, my mother's blood relations had since died (perhaps of embarrassment), and as a child I was often mocked and derided for my father's low origins.

On top of that was the issue of our religion. We were—because my father was—Church of Signs. In those days, every Christian church in America was required to have the formal approval of the Board of Registrars of the Dominion of Jesus Christ on Earth. (In popular parlance, "The Church of the Dominion," but this was a misnomer, since every church is a Dominion Church if it is recognized by the Board. Dominion Episcopal, Dominion Presbyterian, Dominion Baptist—even the Catholic Church of America since it renounced its fealty to the Roman Pope in 2112— all are included under the Dominionist umbrella, since the purpose of the Dominion is not to *be* a church but to *certify* churches. In America we are entitled by the Constitution to worship at any church we please, as long as it is a genuine Christian congregation and not some fraudulent or satanist sect. The Board exists to make that distinction (also, to collect fees and tithes to further its important work).

We were, as I said, Church of Signs, which was a marginal denomination, shunned by the leasing class, recognized but not fully endorsed by the Dominion, and popular mostly with illiterate indentured workers, among whom my father had been raised. Our faith took for its master text that passage in Mark which proclaims, "In my Name they will cast out devils, and speak in new tongues; they will handle serpents, and if they drink poison they will not be sickened by it." We were snake-handlers, in other words, and famous beyond our modest numbers for it. Our congregation consisted of a dozen farmhands, mostly transients lately arrived from the southern states. My father was its deacon (though we did not use that name), and we kept snakes, for ritual purposes, in wire cages on our back acre, next to the outbuilding. This practice contributed very little to our social standing.

That had been the situation of our family when Julian Comstock arrived as a guest of the Duncan and Crowley families, along with his mentor Sam Godwin, and when Julian and I met by coincidence while hunting.

At that time I had been apprenticed to my father, who had risen to the rank of an overseer at the Estate's lavish and extensive stables. My father loved animals, especially horses. Unfortunately I was not made in the same mold, and my relations with the stable's equine inhabitants rarely extended beyond a brisk mutual tolerance. I did not love my job—which consisted largely of sweeping straw, shoveling ordure, and doing in general those chores the older stable hands felt to be beneath their dignity—so I was pleased when it became customary for a household amanuensis (or even Sam Godwin in person) to arrive and summon me away from my work at Julian's request. (Since the request emanated from a Comstock it couldn't be overruled, no matter how fiercely the grooms and saddlers gnashed their teeth to see me escape their autocracy.)

At first we met to read and discuss books, or hunt together; later, Sam Godwin invited me to audit Julian's lessons, for he had been charged with Julian's education as well as his general welfare. (I had been taught the rudiments of reading and writing at the Dominion school, and refined these skills under the tutelage of my mother, who believed in the power of literacy as an improving force. My father could neither read nor write.) And it was not more than a year after our first acquaintance that Sam presented himself one evening at my parents' cottage with an extraordinary proposal.

"Mr. and Mrs. Hazzard," Sam had said, putting his hand up to touch his cap (which he had removed when he entered the cottage, so that the gesture looked like a salute), "you know of course about the friendship between your son and Julian Comstock."

"Yes," my mother said. "And worry over it often enough—matters at the Estate being what they are."

My mother was a small woman, plump, but forceful, with ideas of her own. My father, who spoke seldom, on this occasion spoke not at all, only sat in his chair holding a laurel-root pipe, which he did not light.

"Matters at the Estate are exactly the crux of the issue," Sam Godwin said. "I'm not sure how much Adam has told you about our situation there. Julian's father, General Bryce Comstock, who was my friend as well as my commanding officer, shortly before his death charged me with Julian's care and well-being—"

"Before his death," my mother pointed out, "at the gallows, for treason."

Sam winced. "True, Mrs. Hazzard, I can't deny it, but I assert my belief that the trial was rigged and the verdict indefensible. Defensible or not, however, it doesn't alter my obligation as far as the son is concerned. I promised to care for the boy, Mrs. Hazzard, and I mean to keep my promise."

"A Christian sentiment." Her skepticism was not entirely disguised.

"As for your implication about the Estate, and the practices of the young heirs and heiresses there, I couldn't agree more. Which is why I approved and encouraged Julian's friendship with your son. Apart from Adam, Julian has no true friends. The Estate is such a den of venomous snakes—no offense," he added, remembering our religious affiliation, and making the common but mistaken assumption that congregants of the Church of Signs necessarily *like* snakes, or feel some kinship with them—"no offense, but I would sooner allow Julian to associate with, uh, scorpions," striking for a more palatable simile, "than abandon him to the sneers, machinations, ruses, and ruinous habits of his peers. That makes me not only his teacher but his constant companion. But I'm almost three times his age, Mrs. Hazzard, and he needs a reliable friend more nearly of his own growth."

"What do you propose, exactly, Mr. Godwin?"

"What I propose is that I take on Adam as a second student, full-time, and to the ultimate benefit of both boys."

Sam was usually a man of few words—even as a teacher—and he seemed as exhausted by this oration as if he had lifted some great weight.

"As a student, but a student of *what*, Mr. Godwin?"

"Mechanics. History. Grammar and composition. Martial skills—"

"Adam already knows how to fire a rifle."

"Pistol work, saber work, fist-fighting—but that's only a fraction of it," Sam added hastily. "Julian's father asked me to cultivate the boy's mind as well as his reflexes."

My mother had more to say on the subject, chiefly about how my work at the stables helped offset the family's leases, and how difficult it would be to do without those extra vouchers at the Estate store. But Sam had anticipated the point. He had been entrusted by Julian's mother—that is to say, the sister-in-law of the President—with a discretionary fund for Julian's education, which could be tapped to compensate for my absence from the stables, and at a handsome rate. He quoted a number, and the objections from my parents grew considerably less strenuous, and were finally whittled away to nothing. (I observed all this from a room away, through a gap in the door.)

Which is not to say no misgivings remained. Before I set off for the Estate the next day, this time to visit one of the Great Houses rather than the stables, my mother warned me not to tangle myself too tightly with the affairs of the high-born. I promised her I would cling to my Christian virtues. (A hasty promise, less easily kept than I imagined.[4])

"It may not be your morals that are at risk," she said. "The high-born conduct themselves by different standards than we use, Adam. The games they play have mortal stakes. You do know that Julian's father was hung?"

Julian never spoke of it, but it was a matter of public record. I repeated Sam's assertion that Bryce Comstock had been innocent.

"He may well have been. That's the point. There has been a Comstock in the Presidency for the past thirty years, and the current Comstock is said to be jealous of his power. The only real threat to the reign of Julian's uncle was the ascendancy of his brother, who made himself dangerously popular in the war with the Brazilians. I suspect Mr. Godwin is correct, that Bryce Comstock was hanged not because he was a *bad* General but because he was a *successful* one."

---

[4]Julian's somewhat feminine nature had won him a reputation among the other young aristos as a sodomite. That they could believe this of him without evidence is testimony to the tenor of their thoughts, as a class. But it had occasionally rebounded to my benefit. On more than one occasion, his female acquaintances—sophisticated girls of my own age, or older—made the assumption that I was Julian's intimate companion, in a *physical* sense. Whereupon they undertook to cure me of my deviant habits, in the most direct fashion. I was happy to cooperate with these "cures," and they were successful, every time.

No doubt such scandals were possible—I had heard stories about life in New York City, where the President resided, that would curl a Cynic's hair. But what could these things possibly have to do with me? Or even Julian? We were only boys.

Such was my naiveté.

4

The days had grown short, and Thanksgiving had come and gone, and so had November, and snow was in the air—the tang of it, anyway—when fifty cavalrymen of the Athabaska Reserve rode into Williams Ford, escorting an equal number of Campaigners and Poll-Takers.

Many people despised the Athabaskan winter. I was not one of them. I didn't mind the cold and the darkness, not so long as there was a hard-coal heater, a spirit lamp to read by on long nights, and the chance of wheat cakes or headcheese for break-fast. And Christmas was coming up fast—one of the four Universal Christian Holidays recognized by the Dominion (the others being Easter, Independence Day, and Thanksgiving). My favorite of these had always been Christmas. It was not so much the gifts, which were generally meager—though last year I had received from my parents the lease of a muzzle-loading rifle of which I was exceptionally proud—nor was it entirely the spiritual substance of the holiday, which I am ashamed to say seldom entered my mind except when it was thrust upon me at religious services. What I loved was the combined effect of brisk air, frost-whitened morn-ings, pine and holly wreaths pinned to doorways, cranberry-red banners draped above the main street to flap cheerfully in the cold wind, carols and hymns chanted or sung—the whole breath-less confrontation with Winter, half defiance and half submission. I liked the clockwork regularity of these rituals, as if a particular cog on the wheel of time had engaged with neat precision. It soothed; it spoke of eternity.

But this was an ill-omened season.

The Reserve troops rode into town on the fifteenth of December. Ostensibly, they were here to conduct the Presidential

Election. National elections were a formality in Williams Ford. By the time our citizens were polled, the outcome was usually a foregone conclusion, already decided in the populous Eastern states—that is, when there was more than one candidate, which was seldom. For the last six electoral years no individual or party had contested the election, and we had been ruled by one Comstock or another for three decades. *Election* had become indistinguishable from *acclamation*.

But that was all right, because an election was still a momentous event, almost a kind of circus, involving the arrival of Poll-Takers and Campaigners, who always had a fine show to put on.

And this year—the rumor emanated from high chambers of the Estate, and had been whispered everywhere—there was to be a movie shown in the Dominion Hall.

I had never seen any movies, though Julian had described them to me. He had seen them often in New York when he was younger, and whenever he grew nostalgic—life in Williams Ford was sometimes a little sedate for Julian's taste—it was the movies he was provoked to mention. And so, when the showing of a movie was announced as part of the electoral process, both of us were excited, and we agreed to meet behind the Dominion Hall at the appointed hour.

Neither of us had any legitimate reason to be there. I was too young to vote, and Julian would have been conspicuous and perhaps unwelcome as the only aristo at a gathering of the leasing class. (The high-born had been polled independently at the Estate, and had already voted proxies for their indentured labor.) So I let my parents leave for the Hall early in the evening, and I followed surreptitiously, and arrived just before the event was scheduled to begin. I waited behind the meeting hall, where a dozen horses were tethered, until Julian arrived on an animal borrowed from the Estate stables. He was dressed in his best approximation of a leaser's clothing: hempen shirt and trousers of a dark color, and a black felt hat with its brim pulled low to disguise his face.

He dismounted, looking troubled, and I asked him what was wrong. Julian shook his head. "Nothing, Adam—or nothing *yet*—

but Sam says there's trouble brewing." And here he regarded me with an expression verging on pity. "War," he said.

"There's always war."

"A new offensive."

"Well, what of it? Labrador's a million miles away."

"Obviously your sense of geography hasn't been much improved by Sam's classes. And we might be *physically* a long distance from the front, but we're *operationally* far too close for comfort."

I didn't know what that meant, and so I dismissed it. "We can worry about that after the movie, Julian."

He forced a grin and said, "Yes, I suppose so. As well after as before."

So we entered the Dominion Hall just as the lamps were being dimmed, and slouched into the last row of crowded pews, and waited for the show to start.

There was a broad stage at the front of the Hall, from which all religious appurtenances had been removed, and a square white screen had been erected in place of the usual pulpit or dais. On each side of the screen was a kind of tent in which the two players sat, with their scripts and dramatic gear: speaking-horns, bells, blocks, a drum, a pennywhistle, *et alia.* This was, Julian said, a stripped-down edition of what one might find in a fashionable New York movie theater. In the city, the screen (and thus the images projected on it) would be larger; the players would be more professional, since script-reading and noise-making were considered fashionable arts, and the city players competed with one another for roles; and there might be a third player stationed behind the screen for dramatic narration or additional "sound effects." There might even be an orchestra, with thematic music written for each individual production.

Movies were devised in such a way that two main characters, male and female, could be voiced by the players, with the male actor photographed so that he appeared on the left during dialogue scenes, and the female actor on the right. The players would observe the movie by a system of mirrors, and could follow scripts illuminated by a kind of binnacle lamp (so as not to cast a distracting light), and they spoke their lines as the photographed actors spoke, so that their voices seemed to emanate from the screen. Likewise, their drumming and bell-ringing and such corresponded to events within the movie.[5]

"Of course, they did it better in the secular era," Julian whispered, and I prayed no one had overheard this indelicate comment. By all reports, movies had indeed been spectacular during the Efflorescence of Oil—with recorded sound, natural color rather than black-and-gray, etc. But they were also (by the same reports) hideously impious, blasphemous to the extreme, and routinely pornographic. Fortunately (or *unfortunately,* from Julian's point of view) no examples have survived; the media on which they were recorded was ephemeral; the film stock has long since rotted, and "digital" copies are degraded and wholly undecodable. These movies belonged to the twentieth and early twenty-first centuries—that period of great, unsustainable, and hedonistic prosperity, driven by the burning of Earth's reserves of perishable oil, which culminated in the False Tribulation, and the wars, and the plagues, and the painful dwindling of inflated populations to more reasonable numbers.

Our truest and best American antiquity, as the *Dominion History of the Union* insisted, was the nineteenth century, whose household virtues and modest industries we have been forced by circumstance to imperfectly restore, whose skills were practical, and whose literature was often useful and improving.

But I have to confess that some of Julian's apostasy had infected me. I was troubled by unhappy thoughts even as the torchieres were extinguished and Ben Kreel (our Dominion representative, standing in front of the movie screen) delivered a brief lecture on Nation, Piety, and Duty. *War,* Julian had said, implying not just the everlasting War in Labrador but a new phase of it, one that might reach its skeletal hand right into Williams Ford—and then what of me, and what of my family?

"We are here to cast our ballots," Ben Kreel said in summa-

---

[5]The illusion was quite striking when the players were professional, but their lapses could be equally astonishing. Julian once recounted to me a New York movie production of Wm. Shakespeare's *Hamlet,* in which a player had come to the theater inebriated, causing the unhappy Denmark to seem to exclaim "Sea of troubles–(an unprintable oath)–I have troubles of my own," with more obscenities, and much inappropriate bell-ringing and vulgar whistling, until an understudy could be hurried out to replace him.

tion, "a sacred duty at once to our country and our faith, a country so successfully and benevolently stewarded by its leader, President Deklan Comstock, whose Campaigners, I see by the motions of their hands, are anxious to get on with the events of the night; and so, without further adieu, etc., please direct your attention to the presentation of their moving picture, *First Under Heaven*, which they have prepared for our enjoyment–"

The necessary gear had been hauled into Williams Ford under a canvas-top wagon: a projection apparatus and a portable Swiss dynamo (probably captured from the Dutch forces in Labrador), powered by distilled spirits, installed in a sort of trench or redoubt freshly dug behind the church to muffle its sound, which nevertheless penetrated through the plank floors like the growl of a huge dog. This vibration only added to the sense of moment, as the last illuminating flame was extinguished and the electric bulb within the huge black mechanical projector flared up.

The movie began. As it was the first I had ever seen, my astonishment was complete. I was so entranced by the illusion of photographs "come to life" that the substance of the scenes almost escaped me . . . but I remember an ornate title, and scenes of the Second Battle of Quebec, recreated by actors but utterly real to me, accompanied by drum-banging and shrill penny whistling to represent the reports of shot and shell. Those at the front of the auditorium flinched instinctively; several of the village's prominent women came near to fainting, and clasped the hands or arms of their male companions, who might be as bruised, come morning, as if they had participated in the battle itself.

Soon enough, however, the Dutchmen under their cross-and-laurel flag began to retreat from the American forces, and an actor representing the young Deklan Comstock came to the fore, reciting his Vows of Inauguration (a bit prematurely, but history was here truncated for the purposes of art)–that's the one in which he mentions both the Continental Imperative and the Debt to the Past. He was voiced, of course, by one of the players, a *basso profundo* whose tones emerged from his speaking-bell with ponderous gravity. (Which was also a slight revision of the truth, for the genuine Deklan Comstock possessed a high-pitched voice, and was prone to petulance.)

The movie then proceeded to more decorous episodes and scenic views representing the glories of the reign of Deklan Conqueror, as he was known to the Army of the Laurentians, which had marched him to his ascendancy in New York City. Here was the reconstruction of Washington, DC (a project never completed, always in progress, hindered by a swampy climate and insect-borne diseases); here was the Illumination of Manhattan, whereby electric streetlights were powered by a hydroelectric dynamo, four hours every day between 6 and 10 pm; here was the military shipyard at Boston Harbor, the coal mines and foundries and weapons factories of Pennsylvania, the newest and shiniest steam engines to pull the newest and shiniest trains, etc., etc.

I had to wonder at Julian's reaction to all this. This entire show, after all, was concocted to extol the virtues of the man who had contrived the death by hanging of his father. I could not forget—and Julian must be constantly aware—that the current President was a fratricidal tyrant. But Julian's eyes were riveted on the screen. This reflected (I later learned) not his opinion of contemporary politics but his fascination with what he preferred to call "cinema." This making of illusions in two dimensions was never far from his mind—it was, perhaps, his "true calling," and would culminate in the creation of Julian's suppressed cinematic masterwork, *The Life and Adventures of the Great Naturalist Charles Darwin* . . . but that tale remains for another telling.

The present movie went on to mention the successful forays against the Brazilians at Panama during Deklan Conqueror's reign, which may have struck closer to home, for I saw Julian wince once or twice.

As for me . . . I tried to lose myself in the moment, but my attention was woefully truant.

Perhaps it was the strangeness of the campaign event, so close to Christmas. Perhaps it was *The History of Mankind in Space*, which I had been reading in bed, a page or two at a time, almost every night since our journey to the Tip. Whatever the cause, I was beset by a sudden anxiety and sense of melancholy. Here I was in

the midst of everything that seemed familiar and ought to be comforting—the crowd of the leasing class, the enclosing benevolence
of the Dominion Hall, the banners and tokens of the Christmas
season—and it all felt suddenly *ephemeral,* as if the world were a
bucket from which the bottom had dropped out.

Perhaps this was what Julian had called "the philosopher's
perspective." If so, I wondered how the philosophers endured it.
I had learned a little from Sam Godwin—and more from Julian,
who read books of which even Sam disapproved—about the discredited ideas of the Secular Era. I thought of Einstein, and his insistence that no particular point of view was more privileged than
any other: in other words his "general relativity," and its claim
that the answer to the question "What is real?" begins with the
question "Where are you standing?" Was that all I was, here in the
cocoon of Williams Ford—a Point of View? Or was I an incarnation of a molecule of DNA, "imperfectly remembering," as Julian
had said, an ape, a fish, and an amoeba?

Maybe even the Nation that Ben Kreel had praised so extravagantly was only an example of this trend in nature—an imperfect
memory of another century, which had itself been an imperfect
memory of all the centuries before it, and so back to the dawn of
Man (in Eden, or Africa, as Julian believed).

Perhaps this was just my growing disenchantment with the
town where I had been raised—or a presentiment that it was about
to be stolen away from me.

● ● ●

The movie ended with a stirring scene of an American flag, its
thirteen stripes and sixty stars rippling in sunlight—betokening,
the narrator insisted, another four years of the prosperity and
benevolence engendered by the rule of Deklan Conqueror, for
whom the audience's votes were solicited, not that there was any
competing candidate known or rumored. The film flapped
against its reel; the electric bulb was extinguished. Then the deacons of the Dominion began to reignite the wall lights. Several of
the men in the audience had lit pipes during the cinematic display, and their smoke mingled with the smudge of the torchieres,

a blue-gray thundercloud hovering under the high arches of the ceiling.

Julian seemed distracted, and slumped in his pew with his hat pulled low. "Adam," he whispered, "we have to find a way out of here."

"I believe I see one," I said, "it's called the door—but what's the hurry?"

"Look at the door more closely. Two men of the Reserve have been posted there."

I looked, and what he had said was true. "But isn't that just to protect the balloting?" For Ben Kreel had retaken the stage and was preparing to ask for a formal show of hands.

"Tom Shearney, the barber with a bladder complaint, just tried to leave to use the jakes. He was turned back."

Indeed, Tom Shearney was seated less than a yard away from us, squirming unhappily and casting resentful glances at the Reserve men.

"But after the balloting—"

"This isn't about balloting. This is about conscription."

"Conscription!"

"Hush!" Julian said hastily, shaking his hair out of his pale face. "You'll start a stampede. I didn't think it would begin so soon . . . but we've had certain telegrams from New York about setbacks in Labrador, and the call-up of new divisions. Once the balloting is finished the Campaigners will probably announce a recruitment drive, and take the names of everyone present and survey them for the names and ages of their children."

"We're too young to be drafted," I said, for we were both just seventeen.

"Not according to what I've heard. The rules have been changed. Oh, you can probably find a way to hide out when the culling begins—and get away with it, considering how far we are from anywhere else. But *my* presence here is well known. I don't have a mob or family to melt away into. In fact it's probably not a coincidence that so many Reserves have been sent to such a little village as Williams Ford."

"What do you mean, not a coincidence?"

"My uncle has never been happy about my existence. He has

no children of his own. No heirs. He sees me as a possible competitor for the Executive."

"But that's absurd. You don't *want* to be President—do you?"

"I would sooner shoot myself. But Uncle Deklan has a jealous bent, and he distrusts the motives of my mother in protecting me."

"How does a draft help him?"

"The entire draft is not aimed at me, but I'm sure he finds it a useful tool. If I'm drafted, no one can complain that he's excepting his own family from the general conscription. And when he has me in the infantry he can be sure I find myself on the front lines in Labrador—performing some noble but suicidal trench attack."

"But—Julian! Can't Sam protect you?"

"Sam is a retired soldier; he has no power except what arises from the patronage of my mother. Which isn't worth much in the coin of the present realm. Adam, is there another way out of this building?"

"Only the door, unless you mean to break a pane of that colored glass that fills the windows."

"Somewhere to hide, then?"

I thought about it. "Maybe," I said. "There's a room behind the stage where the religious equipment is stored. You can enter it from the wings. We could hide there, but it has no door of its own."

"It'll have to do. If we can get there without attracting attention."

But that was not too difficult, for the torchieres had not all been re-lit, much of the hall was still in shadow, and the audience was milling about a bit, and stretching, while the Campaigners prepared to record the vote that was to follow—they were meticulous accountants even though the final tally was a foregone conclusion and the ballrooms were already booked for Deklan Conqueror's latest inauguration. Julian and I shuffled from one shadow to another, giving no appearance of haste, until we were close to the foot of the stage; there we paused at an entrance to the storage room, until a goonish Reserve man who had been eyeing us was called away by a superior officer to help dismantle the projecting equipment. We ducked through the curtained door into near-absolute darkness. Julian stumbled over some obstruction (a piece of the church's tack piano, which had been disassembled for cleaning in 2165 by a traveling piano-mechanic, who had died of a stroke before finishing the job), the result being a woody "clang!" that seemed loud enough to alert the whole occupancy of the church, but evidently didn't.

What little light there was came through a high glazed window that was hinged so that it could be opened in summer for purposes of ventilation. It was a weak sort of illumination, for the night was cloudy, and only the torches along the main street were shining. But it registered as our eyes adjusted to the dimness. "Perhaps we can get out that way," Julian said.

"Not without a ladder. Although—"

"What? Speak up, Adam, if you have an idea."

"This is where they store the risers—the long wooden blocks the choir stands on when they're racked up for a performance. Perhaps those—"

But he was already examining the shadowy contents of the storage room, as intently as he had surveyed the Tip for ancient books. We found the likely suspects, and managed to stack them to a useful height without causing too much noise. (In the church hall, the Campaigners had already registered a unanimous vote for Deklan Comstock and had begun to break the news about the conscription drive. Some few voices were raised in futile objection; Ben Kreel was calling loudly for calm—no one heard us rearranging the unused furniture.)

The window was at least ten feet high, and almost too narrow to crawl through, and when we emerged on the other side we had to hang by our fingertips before dropping to the ground. I bent my right ankle awkwardly as I landed, though no lasting harm was done.

The night, already cold, had turned colder. We were near the hitching posts, and the horses whinnied at our surprising arrival and blew steam from their gaping nostrils. A fine, gritty snow had begun to fall. There was not much wind, however, and Christmas banners hung limply in the frigid air.

Julian made straight for his horse and loosed its reins from the post. "What are we going to do?" I asked.

"You, Adam, will do nothing but protect your own existence as best you know how; while I—"

But he balked at pronouncing his plans, and a shadow of anxiety passed over his face. Events were moving rapidly in the realm of the aristos, events I could barely comprehend.

"We can wait them out," I said, a little desperately. "The Reserves can't stay in Williams Ford forever."

"No. Unfortunately neither can I, for Deklan Conqueror knows where to find me, and has made up his mind to remove me from the game of politics like a captured chess piece."

"But where will you go? And what—"

He put a finger to his mouth. There was a noise from the front of the Dominion Church Hall, as of the doors being thrown open, and voices of congregants arguing or wailing over the news of the conscription drive. "Ride with me," Julian said. "Quick, now!"

We did not follow the main street, but caught a path that turned behind the blacksmith's barn and through the wooded border of the River Pine, north in the general direction of the Estate. The night was dark, and the horses stepped slowly, but they knew the path almost by instinct, and some light from the town still filtered through the thinly falling snow, which touched my face like a hundred small cold fingers.

⊸ ⊸ ⊸

"It was never possible that I could stay at Williams Ford forever," Julian said. "You ought to have known that, Adam."

Truly, I should have. It was Julian's constant theme, after all: the impermanence of things. I had always put this down to the circumstances of his childhood, the death of his father, the separation from his mother, the kind but aloof tutelage of Sam Godwin.

But I could not help thinking once more of *The History of Mankind in Space* and the photographs in it—not of the First Men on the Moon, who were Americans, but of the Last Visitors to that celestial sphere, who had been Chinamen, and whose "space suits" had been firecracker-red. Like the Americans, they had planted their flag in expectation of more visitations to come; but the End of Oil and the False Tribulation had put paid to those plans.

And I thought of the even lonelier Plains of Mars, photographed by machines (or so the book alleged) but never touched by human feet. The universe, it seemed, was full to brimming with lonesome places. Somehow I had stumbled into one. The snow squall ended; the uninhabited moon came through the clouds; and the winter fields of Williams Ford glowed with an unearthly luminescence.

"If you must leave," I said, "let me come with you."

"No," Julian said promptly. He had pulled his hat down around his ears, to protect himself from the cold, and I couldn't see much of his face, but his eyes shone when he glanced in my direction. "Thank you, Adam. I wish it were possible. But it isn't. You must stay here, and dodge the draft, if possible, and polish your literary skills, and one day write books, like Mr. Charles Curtis Easton."

That was my ambition, which had grown over the last year, nourished by our mutual love of books and by Sam Godwin's exercises in English Composition, for which I had discovered an unexpected talent.[6] At the moment it seemed a petty dream. Evanescent. Like all dreams. Like life itself. "None of that matters," I said.

"That's where you're wrong," Julian said. "You must not make the mistake of thinking that because nothing lasts, nothing matters."

"Isn't that the philosopher's point of view?"

"Not if the philosopher knows what he's talking about." Julian reined up his horse and turned to face me, something of the im-

---

[6]Not a talent that was born fully-formed, I should add. Only two years previously I had presented to Sam Godwin my first finished story, which I had called "A Western Boy: His Adventures in Enemy Europe." Sam had praised its style and ambition, but called attention to a number of flaws: elephants, for instance, were not native to Brussels, and were generally too massive to be wrestled to the ground by American lads; a journey from London to Rome could not be accomplished in a matter of hours, even on "a very fast horse"–and Sam might have continued in this vein, had I not fled the room in a condition of acute auctorial embarrassment.

periousness of his famous family entering into his mien. "Listen, Adam, there is something important you can do for me—at some personal risk. Are you willing?"

"Yes," I said immediately.

"Then listen closely. Before long the Reserves will be watching the roads out of Williams Ford, if they aren't already. I have to leave, and I have to leave tonight. I won't be missed until morning, and then, at least at first, only by Sam. What I want you to do is this: go home—your parents will be worried about the conscription, and you can try to calm them down—but don't allude to any of what happened tonight—and first thing in the morning, make your way as inconspicuously as possible into the Estate and find Sam. Tell him what happened at the Church Hall, and tell him to ride out of town as soon as he can do so without being caught. Tell him he can find me at Lundsford. That's the message."

"Lundsford? There's nothing at Lundsford."

"Precisely: nothing important enough that the Reserves would think to look for us there. You remember what the Tipman said in the fall, about the place he found those books? A low place near the main excavations. Sam can look for me there."

"I'll tell him," I promised, blinking against the cold wind, which irritated my eyes.

"Thank you, Adam," he said gravely. "For everything." Then he forced a smile, and for a moment was just Julian, the friend with whom I had hunted squirrels and spun tales: "Merry Christmas," he said. "Happy New Year!"

And wheeled his horse about, and rode away.

5

There is a Dominion cemetery in Williams Ford, and I passed it on the ride back home—carved stones sepulchral in the moonlight—but my sister Flaxie was not buried there.

As I have said, the Church of Signs was tolerated but not endorsed by the Dominion. We were not entitled to plots in the Dominion yard. Flaxie had a place in the acreage behind our cottage, marked by a modest wooden cross, but the cemetery put me in mind of Flaxie nonetheless, and after I returned the horse to the barn I stopped by Flaxie's grave (despite the shivery cold) and tipped my hat to her, the way I had always tipped my hat to her in life.

Flaxie had been a bright, impudent, mischievous small thing—as golden-haired as her nickname implied. (Her given name was Dolores, but she was always Flaxie to me.) The Pox had taken her quite suddenly and, as these things go, mercifully. I didn't remember her death; I had been down with the same Pox, though I had survived it. What I remembered was waking up from my fever into a house gone strangely quiet. No one had wanted to tell me about Flaxie, but I had seen my mother's tormented eyes, and I knew the truth without having to be told. Death had played lottery with us, and Flaxie had drawn the short straw.

(It is, I think, for the likes of Flaxie that we maintain a belief in Heaven. I have met very few adults, outside the enthusiasts of the established Church, who genuinely believe in Heaven, and Heaven was scant consolation for my grieving mother. But Flaxie, who was five, had believed in it fervently—imagined it was something like a meadow, with wildflowers blooming, and a perpetual summer picnic underway—and if that childish belief soothed her in her extremity, then it served a purpose more noble than truth.)

Tonight the cottage was almost as quiet as it had been during the mourning that followed Flaxie's death. I came through the door to find my mother dabbing her eyes with a handkerchief, and my father frowning over his pipe, which, uncharacteristically, he had filled and lit. "The draft," he said.

"Yes," I said. "I heard about it."

My mother was too distraught to speak. My father said, "We'll do what we can to protect you, Adam. But—"

"I'm not afraid to serve my country," I said.

"That's a praiseworthy attitude," my father said glumly, and my mother wept even harder. "But we don't yet know what might be necessary. Maybe the situation in Labrador isn't as bad as it seems."

Scant of words though my father was, I had often enough relied on him for advice, which he had freely given. He was fully aware, for instance, of my distaste for snakes—for which reason, abetted by my mother, I had been allowed to avoid the sacraments of our faith, and the venomous swellings and occasional amputations occasionally inflicted upon other parishioners—and, while this disappointed him, he had nevertheless taught me the practical aspects of snake-handling, including how to grasp a serpent in such a way as to avoid its bite, and how to kill one, should the necessity arise.[7] He was a practical man despite his unusual beliefs.

But he had no advice to offer me tonight. He looked like a hunted man who has come to the end of a cul-de-sac, and can neither go forward nor turn back.

I went to my bedroom, although I doubted I would be able to sleep. Instead—without any real plan in mind—I bundled a few of my possessions for easy carrying. My squirrel-gun, chiefly, and some notes and writing, and *The History of Mankind in Space;* and I thought I should add some salted pork, or something of that nature, but I resolved to wait until later, so my mother wouldn't see me packing.

○ ○ ○

Before dawn, I put on several layers of clothing and a heavy pakul hat, rolled down so the wool covered my ears. I opened the window of my room and clambered over the sill and closed the glass behind me, after I had retrieved my rifle and gear. Then I crept across the open yard to the barn, and saddled up a horse (the gelding named Rapture, who was the fastest, though this would leave my father's rig an animal shy), and rode out under a sky that had just begun to show first light.

Last night's brief snowfall still covered the ground. I was not the first up this winter morning, and the cold air already smelled of Christmas. The bakery in Williams Ford was busy making na-

---

[7]"Grasp it where its neck ought to be, behind the head; ignore the tail, however it may thrash; and crack its skull, hard and often enough to subdue it." I had recounted these instructions to Julian, whose horror of serpents far exceeded my own: "Oh, I could never do such a thing!" he had exclaimed. This surfeit of timidity may surprise readers who have followed his later career.

tivity cakes and cinnamon buns. The sweet, yeasty smell filled the northwest end of town like an intoxicating fog, for there was no wind to carry it away. The day was dawning blue and still.

Signs of Christmas were everywhere—as they ought to be, for today was the Eve of that universal holiday—but so was evidence of the conscription drive. The Reservists were already awake, passing like shadows in their scruffy uniforms, and a crowd of them had gathered by the hardware store. They had hung out a faded flag and posted a sign, which I could not read, because I was determined to keep a distance between myself and the soldiers; but I knew a recruiting-post when I saw one. I did not doubt that the main ways in and out of town had been put under close observation.

I took a back way to the Estate, the same riverside road Julian and I had traveled the night before. Because of the lack of wind, our tracks were undisturbed. We were the only ones who had recently passed this way. Rapture was revisiting his own hoof-prints.

Close to the Estate, but still within a concealing grove of pines, I lashed the horse to a sapling and proceeded on foot.

The Duncan-Crowley Estate was not fenced, for there was no real demarcation of its boundaries; under the Leasing System, everything in Williams Ford was owned (in the legal sense) by the two great families. I approached from the western side, which was half-wooded and used by the aristos for casual riding and hunting. This morning the copse was not inhabited, and I saw no one until I had passed the snow-mounded hedges which marked the beginning of the formal gardens. Here, in summer, apple and cherry trees blossomed and produced fruit; flowerbeds gave forth symphonies of color and scent; bees nursed in languid ecstasies. But now it was barren, the paths quilted with snow, and there was no one visible but the senior groundskeeper, sweeping the wooden portico of the nearest of the Estate's several Great Houses.

The Houses were dressed for Christmas. Christmas was a grander event at the Estate than in the town proper, as might be expected. The winter population of the Duncan-Crowley Estate was not as large as its summer population, but there was still a number of both families, plus whatever cousins and hangers-on had elected to hibernate over the cold season. Sam Godwin, as Julian's tutor, was not permitted to sleep in either of the two most luxurious buildings, but bunked among the elite staff in a white-pillared house that would have passed for a mansion anywhere but here. This was where he had conducted classes for Julian and me, and I knew the building intimately. It, too, was dressed for Christmas; a holly wreath hung on the door; pine boughs were suspended over the lintels; a Banner of the Cross dangled from the eaves. The door was not locked, and I let myself in quietly.

It was still early in the morning, at least as the aristos and their elite helpers calculated time. The tiled entranceway was empty and still. I went straight for the rooms where Sam Godwin slept and conducted his classes, down an oaken corridor lit only by the dawn filtering through a window at the long end. The floor was carpeted and gave no sound, though my shoes left damp foot-prints behind me.

At Sam's particular door, I was confronted with a dilemma. I could not knock, for fear of alerting others. My mission as I saw it was to deliver Julian's message as discreetly as possible. But nei-ther could I walk in on a sleeping man—could I?

I tried the handle of the door. It moved freely. I opened the door a fraction of an inch, meaning to whisper, "Sam?"—give him some warning.

But I could hear Sam's voice, low and muttering, as if he were talking to himself. I listened more closely. The words seemed strange. He was speaking in a guttural language, not English. Perhaps he wasn't alone. It was too late to back away, however, so I decided to brazen it out. I opened the door entirely and stepped inside, saying, "Sam! It's me, Adam. I have a message from Julian—"

I stopped short, alarmed by what I saw. Sam Godwin—the same gruff but familiar Sam who had taught me the rudiments of history and geography—was practicing *black magic,* or some other form of witchcraft: on *Christmas Eve!* He wore a striped cowl about his shoulders, and leather lacings on his arm, and a boxlike implement strapped to his forehead; and his hands were upraised over an arrangement of nine candles mounted in a brass holder that appeared to have been scavenged from some ancient Tip.

The invocation he had been murmuring seemed to echo through the room: Bah-*rook*-a-*tah*-atten-*eye*-hello-*hey*-noo . . .

My jaw dropped.

"Adam!" Sam said, almost as startled as I was, and he quickly pulled the shawl from his back and began to unlace his various unholy riggings.

This was so irregular I could barely comprehend it.

Then I was afraid I *did* comprehend it. Often enough in Dominion school I had heard Ben Kreel speak about the vices and wickedness of the Secular Era, some of which still lingered, he said, in the cities of the East—irreverence, irreligiosity, skepticism, occultism, depravity. And I thought of the ideas I had so casually imbibed from Julian and (indirectly) from Sam, some of which I had even begun to believe: Einsteinism, Darwinism, space travel . . . had I been seduced by the outrunners of some New Yorkish paganism? Had I been duped by Philosophy?

"A message," Sam said, concealing his heathenish gear, "what message? Where is Julian?"

But I could not stay. I fled the room.

Sam barreled out of the house after me. I was fast, but he was long-legged and conditioned by his military career, strong for all his forty-odd years, and he caught me in the winter gardens—tackled me from behind. I kicked and tried to pull away, but he pinned my shoulders.

"Adam, for God's sake, settle down!" cried he. That was impudent, I thought, invoking God, *him*—but then he said, "Don't you understand what you saw? I am a Jew!"

A Jew!

Of course, I had heard of Jews. They lived in the Bible, and in New York City. Their equivocal relationship with Our Savior had won them opprobrium down the ages, and they were not approved of by the Dominion. But I had never seen a living Jew in the flesh—to my knowledge—and I was astonished by the idea that Sam had been one all along: *invisibly,* so to speak.

"You deceived everyone, then!" I said.

"I never claimed to be a Christian! I never spoke of it at all. But what does it matter? You said you had a message from Julian—give it to me, damn you! Where is he?"

I wondered what I should say, or who I might betray if I said it. The world had turned upside down. All Ben Kreel's lectures on patriotism and fidelity came back to me in one great flood of guilt and shame. Had I been a party to treason as well as atheism?

But I felt I owed this last favor to Julian, who would surely have wanted me to deliver his intelligence whether Sam was a Jew or a Mohammedan: "There are soldiers on all the roads out of town," I said sullenly. "Julian went for Lundsford last night. He says he'll meet you there. Now *get off of me!*"

Sam did so, sitting back on his heels, deep anxiety inscribed upon his face. "Has it begun so soon? I thought they would wait for the New Year."

"I don't know *what* has begun. I don't think I know anything at all!" And, so saying, I leapt to my feet and ran out of the lifeless garden, back to Rapture, who was still tied to the tree where I had left him, nosing unproductively in the undisturbed snow.

◠ ◠ ◠

I had ridden perhaps an eighth of a mile back toward Williams Ford when another rider came up on my right flank from behind. It was Ben Kreel himself, and he touched his cap and smiled and said, "Do you mind if I ride along with you a ways, Adam Hazzard?"

I could hardly say no.

Ben Kreel was not a pastor—we had plenty of those in Williams Ford, each catering to his own denomination—but he was the head of the local Council of the Dominion of Jesus Christ on Earth, almost as powerful in his way as the men who owned the Estate. And if he was not a pastor, he was at least a sort of shepherd to the townspeople. He had been born right here in Williams Ford, son of a saddler; had been educated, at the Estate's expense, at one of the Dominion Colleges in Colorado Springs; and for the last twenty years he had taught elementary school five days a week and General Christianity on Sundays. I had marked my first letters on a slate board under Ben Kreel's tutelage. Every Independence Day he addressed the townsfolk and reminded them of the symbolism and significance of the Thirteen Stripes and the Sixty Stars; every Christmas, he led the Ecumenical Services at the Dominion Hall.

He was stout and graying at the temples, clean-shaven. He wore a woolen jacket, tall deer hide boots, and a pakul hat not much grander than my own. But he carried himself with an immense dignity, as much in the saddle as on foot. The expression on his face was kindly. It was always kindly. "You're out early, Adam Hazzard," he said. "What are you doing abroad at this hour?"

"Nothing," I said, and blushed. Is there any other word that so spectacularly represents everything it wants to deny? Under the circumstances, "nothing" amounted to a confession of bad intent. "Couldn't sleep," I added hastily. "Thought I might shoot a squirrel or so." That would explain the rifle strapped to my saddle, and it was at least remotely plausible; the squirrels were still active, doing the last of their scrounging before settling in for the cold months.

"On Christmas Eve?" Ben Kreel asked. "And in the copse on the grounds of the Estate? I hope the Duncans and Crowleys don't hear about it. They're jealous of their trees. And I'm sure gunfire would disturb them at this hour. Wealthy men and Easterners prefer to sleep past dawn, as a rule."

"I didn't fire," I muttered. "I thought better of it."

"Well, good. Wisdom prevails. You're headed back to town, I gather?"

"Yes, sir."

"Let me keep you company, then."

"Please do." I could hardly say otherwise, no matter how I longed to be alone with my thoughts.

Our horses moved slowly—the snow made for awkward footing—and Ben Kreel was silent for a long while. Then he said, "You needn't conceal your fears, Adam. I know what's troubling you."

For a moment I had the terrible idea that Ben Kreel had been behind me in the hallway at the Estate, and that he had seen Sam Godwin wrapped in his Old Testament paraphernalia. Wouldn't that create a scandal! (And then I thought that it was exactly such a scandal Sam must have feared all his life: it was worse even than being Church of Signs, for in some states a Jew can be fined or

even imprisoned for practicing his faith. I didn't know where
Athabaska stood on the issue, but I feared the worst.) But Ben
Kreel was talking about conscription, not about Sam.

"I've already discussed this with some of the boys in town,"
he said. "You're not alone, Adam, if you're wondering what it all
means, this military movement, and what might happen as a result of it. And I admit, you're something of a special case. I've
been keeping an eye on you. From a distance, as it were. Here,
stop a moment."

We had come to a rise in the road, on a bluff above the River
Pine, looking south toward Williams Ford from a little height.

"Gaze at that," Ben Kreel said contemplatively. He stretched
his arm out in an arc, as if to include not just the cluster of buildings that was the town but the empty fields as well, and the murky
flow of the river, and the wheels of the mills, and even the shacks
of the indentured laborers down in the low country. The valley
seemed at once a living thing, inhaling the crisp atmosphere of
the season and breathing out its steams, and a portrait, static in
the still blue winter air. As deeply rooted as an oak, as fragile as a
ball of Nativity glass.

"Gaze at that," Ben Kreel repeated. "Look at Williams Ford,
laid out pretty there. What is it, Adam? More than a place, I think.
It's a way of life. It's the sum of all our labors. It's what our fathers
have given us and it's what we give our sons. It's where we bury
our mothers and where our daughters will be buried."

Here was more Philosophy, then, and after the turmoil of the
morning I wasn't sure I wanted any. But Ben Kreel's voice ran on
like the soothing syrup my mother used to administer whenever
Flaxie or I came down with a cough.

"Every boy in Williams Ford—every boy old enough to submit
himself for national service—is just now discovering how reluctant
he is to leave the place he knows best. Even you, I suspect."

"I'm no more or less willing than anyone else."

"I'm not questioning your courage or your loyalty. It's just
that I know you've had a little taste of what life might be like elsewhere—given how closely you associated yourself with Julian
Comstock. Now, I'm sure Julian's a fine young man and an excellent Christian. He could hardly be otherwise, could he, as the

nephew of the man who holds this nation in his palm. But his experience has been very different from yours. He's accustomed to cities and movies like the one we saw at the Hall last night (and I glimpsed you there, didn't I? Sitting in the back pews?)—to books and ideas that might strike a youth of your background as exciting and, well, *different*. Am I wrong?"

"I could hardly say you are, sir."

"And much of what Julian may have described to you is no doubt true. I've traveled some myself, you know. I've seen Colorado Springs, Pittsburgh, even New York City. Our eastern cities are great, proud metropolises—some of the biggest and most productive in the world—and they're worth defending, which is one reason we're trying so hard to drive the Dutch out of Labrador."

"Surely you're right."

"I'm glad you agree. Because there is a trap certain young people fall into. I've seen it before. Sometimes a boy decides that one of those great cities might be a place he can *run away to*—a place where he can escape all the duties, obligations, and moral lessons he learned at his mother's knee. Simple things like faith and patriotism can begin to seem to a young man like burdens, which might be shrugged off when they become too weighty."

"I'm not like that, sir."

"Of course not. But there is yet another element in the calculation. You may have to leave Williams Ford because of the conscription. And the thought that runs through many boys' minds is, if I *must* leave, then perhaps I ought to leave on my own hook, and find my destiny on a city's streets rather than in a battalion of the Athabaska Brigade . . . and you're good to deny it, Adam, but you wouldn't be human if such ideas didn't cross your mind."

"No, sir," I muttered, and I must admit I felt a dawning guilt, for I had in fact been a little seduced by Julian's tales of city life, and Sam's dubious lessons, and *The History of Mankind in Space*—perhaps I *had* forgotten something of my obligations to the village that lay so still and so inviting in the blue near distance.

"I know," Ben Kreel said, "that things haven't always been easy for your family. Your father's faith, in particular, has been a trial, and we haven't always been good neighbors—speaking on behalf of the village as a whole. Perhaps you've been left out of some activities other boys enjoy as a matter of course: church activities, picnics, common friendships . . . well, even Williams Ford isn't perfect. But I promise you, Adam: if you find yourself in the Brigades, especially if you find yourself tested in time of war, you'll discover that the same boys who shunned you in the dusty streets of your home town become your best friends and bravest defenders, and you theirs. For our common heritage ties us together in ways that may seem obscure, but become obvious under the harsh light of combat."

I had spent so much time smarting under the remarks of other boys (that my father "raised vipers the way other folks raise chickens," for example) that I could hardly credit Ben Kreel's assertion. But I knew little of modern warfare, except what I had read in the novels of Mr. Charles Curtis Easton, so it might be true. And the prospect (as was intended) made me feel even more shame-faced.

"There," Ben Kreel said: "Do you hear that, Adam?"

I did. I could hardly avoid it. The bell was ringing in the Dominion church, calling together one of the early ecumenical services. It was a silvery sound on the winter air, at once lonesome and consoling, and I wanted almost to run toward it—to shelter in it, as if I were a child again.

"They'll want me soon," Ben Kreel said. "Will you excuse me if I ride ahead?"

"No, sir. Please don't mind about me."

"As long as we understand each other, Adam. Don't look so downcast! The future may be brighter than you expect."

"Thank you for saying so, sir."

❧ ❧ ❧

I stayed a while longer on the low bluff, watching as Ben Kreel's horse carried him toward town. Even in the sunlight it was cold, and I shivered some, perhaps more because of the conflict in my mind than because of the weather. The Dominion man had made me ashamed of myself, and had put into perspective my loose ways of the last few years, and pointed up how many of my native beliefs I had abandoned before the seductive Philosophy of an agnostic young aristo and an aging Jew.

Then I sighed and urged Rapture back along the path toward Williams Ford, meaning to explain to my parents where I had been and reassure them that I would not suffer too much in the coming conscription, to which I would willingly submit.

I was so disheartened by the morning's events that my eyes drifted toward the ground even as Rapture retraced his steps. As I have said, the snows of the night before lay largely undisturbed on this back trail between the town and the Estate. I could see where I had passed this morning, where Rapture's hoof prints were as clearly written as figures in a book. (Ben Kreel must have spent the night at the Estate, and when he left me on the bluff he would have taken the more direct route toward town; only Rapture had passed this way.) Then I reached the place where Julian and I had parted the night before. There were more hoof prints here, in fact a crowd of them—

And I saw something else written (in effect) on the snowy ground—something which alarmed me.

I reined up at once.

I looked south, toward Williams Ford. I looked east, the way Julian had gone the previous night.

Then I took a bracing inhalation of icy air, and followed the trail that seemed to me most urgent.

6

The east-west road through Williams Ford is not heavily traveled, especially in winter. The southern road—also called the "Wire Road," because the telegraph line runs alongside it—connects Williams Ford to the railhead at Connaught, and thus sustains a great deal of traffic. But the east-west road goes essentially nowhere: it is a remnant of a road of the secular ancients, traversed mainly by Tipmen and freelance antiquarians, and then only in the warmer months. I suppose, if you followed the old road as far as it would take you, you might reach the Great Lakes, or somewhere farther east, in that direction; and, the opposite way, you could get yourself lost among washouts and landfalls in the Rocky Mountains. But the railroad—and a parallel turnpike farther south—had obviated the need for all that trouble.

Nevertheless, the east-west road was closely watched where it left the outskirts of Williams Ford. The Reserves had posted a man on a hill overlooking it, the same hill where Julian and Sam and I had paused for blackberries on our way from the Tip last October. But it is a fact that the Reserve troops were held in Reserve, and not sent to the front lines, mainly because of some disabling flaw of body or mind; some were wounded veterans, missing a hand or an arm; some were too simple or sullen to function in a disciplined body of soldiers. I cannot say anything for certain about the man posted as lookout on the hill, but if he was not a fool he was at least utterly unconcerned about concealment, for his silhouette (and that of his rifle) stood etched against the bright eastern sky for all to see. But maybe that was the intent: to let prospective fugitives know their way was barred.

Not *every* way was barred, however, not for someone who had grown up in Williams Ford and hunted everywhere on its perimeter. Instead of following Julian directly I rode north a distance, and then through the crowded lanes of an encampment of indentured laborers (whose ragged children gaped at me from the glassless windows of their shanties, and whose soft-coal fires made a smoky gauze of the motionless air). This route connected with lanes cut through the wheat fields for the transportation of harvests and field-hands—lanes that had been deepened by years of use, so that I rode behind a berm of earth and snake rail fences, hidden from the distant sentinel. When I was safely east, I came down a cattle-trail that reconnected me with the east-west road, on which I was able to read the same signs that had alerted me back at Williams Ford, thanks to the fine layer of snow still undisturbed by any wind.

Julian had come this way. He had done as he had intended, and ridden toward Lundsford before midnight. The snow had stopped soon thereafter, leaving his horse's hoof prints clearly visible, though softened and half-covered.

But his were not the only tracks: there was a second set, more crisply defined and hence more recent, probably set down during the night; and this was what I had seen at the crossroads in Williams Ford: evidence of pursuit. Someone had followed Julian, without Julian's knowledge. This had dire implications, the only redeeming circumstance being the fact of a single pursuer rather than a company of men. If the powerful people of the Estate had known that it was Julian Comstock who had fled, they would surely have sent an entire brigade to bring him back. I supposed Julian had been mistaken for a simple miscreant, a labor refugee, or a youngster fleeing the conscription, and that he had been followed by some ambitious Reservist. Otherwise that whole imagined battalion might be right behind me . . . or perhaps soon *would* be, since Julian's absence must have been noted by now.

I rode east, adding my own track to these two.

Before long it was past noon, and I began to have second thoughts as the sun began to angle toward an early rendezvous with the southwestern horizon. What exactly did I hope to accomplish? To warn Julian? If so, I was a little late off the mark . . . though I hoped that at some point Julian had covered his tracks, or otherwise misled his pursuer, who did not have the advantage I had, of knowing where Julian meant to stay until Sam Godwin could arrive. Failing that, I half-imagined *rescuing* Julian from capture, even though I had but a squirrel rifle and a few rounds of ammunition (plus a knife and my own wits, both feeble enough weapons) against whatever a Reservist might carry. In any case these were more wishes and anxieties than calculations or plans; I had no fully formed plan beyond riding to Julian's aid and telling him that I had delivered my message to Sam, who would be along as soon as he could discreetly leave the Estate.

And then what? It was a question I dared not ask myself—not out on this lonely road, well past the Tip now, farther than I had ever been from Williams Ford; not out here where the flatlands stretched on each side of the path like the frosty plains of Mars, and the wind, which had been absent all morning, began to pluck at the fringes of my coat, and my shadow elongated in front of me like a scarecrow gone riding. It was cold and getting colder, and soon the winter moon would be aloft, and me with only a few ounces of salt pork in my saddlebag and a few matches to make a fire if I was able to secure any kindling by nightfall. I began to wonder if I had gone quite insane. At several points I thought: I could go back; perhaps I hadn't yet been missed; perhaps it wasn't too late to sit down to a Christmas Eve dinner with my parents, raise a glass of cider to Flaxie and to Christmases past, and wake in time to hear the ringing-in of the Holiday and smell the goodness of baked bread and Nativity apples drenched in cinnamon and brown sugar. I mused on it repeatedly, sometimes with tears in my eyes; but I let Rapture continue carrying me toward the darkest part of the horizon.

Then, after what seemed endless hours of dusk, with only a brief pause when both Rapture and I drank from a creek which had a skin of ice on it, I began to come among the ruins of the secular ancients.

Not that there was anything spectacular about them. Fanciful drawings often portray the ruins of the last century as tall buildings, ragged and hollow as broken teeth, forming vine-encrusted canyons and shadowy cul-de-sacs.[8] No doubt such places exist—most of them in the uninhabitable Southwest, however, where "famine sits enthroned, and waves his scepter over a dominion expressly made for him," which would rule out vines and such tropical items[9]—but most ruins were like the ones I now passed, mere irregularities (or more precisely, *regularities*) in the landscape, which indicated the former presence of foundations. These terrains were treacherous, often concealing deep basements that could open like hungry mouths on an unwary traveler, and only Tipmen loved them. I was careful to keep to the path, though I began to wonder whether Julian would be as easy to find as I had imagined—"Lundsford" was a big locality, and the wind had already begun to scour away the hoof prints I had relied on for navigation.

I was haunted, too, by thoughts of the False Tribulation of the last century. It was not unusual to come across desiccated human remains in localities like this. Millions had died in the worst dislocations of the End of Oil: of disease, of internecine strife, but mostly of starvation. The Age of Oil had allowed a fierce inten-

---

[8] Or "culs-de-sac"? My French is rudimentary.
[9] Though Old Miami or Orlando might begin to fit the bill.

sity of fertilization and irrigation of the land, which had fed more people than a humbler agriculture could support. I had seen photographs of Americans from that blighted age, thin as sticks, their children with distended bellies, crowded into "relief camps" that would soon enough be transformed into communal graves when the imagined "relief" failed to materialize. No wonder, then, that our ancestors had mistaken those decades for the Tribulation of prophecy. What was astonishing was how many of our current institutions—the Church, the Army, the Federal Government—had survived more or less intact. There was a passage in the Dominion Bible that Ben Kreel had read whenever the subject of the False Tribulation arose in school, and which I had committed to memory: *The field is wasted, the land mourns; for the corn is shriveled, the wine has dried, the oil languishes. Be ashamed, farmers; howl, vine keepers; howl for the wheat and the barley, for the harvest of the field has perished . . .*

It had made me shiver then, and it made me shiver now, in these barrens which had been stripped of all their utility by a century of scavenging. Where in this rubble was Julian, and where was his pursuer?

It was by his fire I found him. But I was not the first to arrive.

◔ ◔ ◔

The sun was altogether down, and a hint of the aurora borealis played about the northern sky, dimmed by moonlight, when I came to the most recently excavated section of Lundsford. The temporary dwellings of the Tipmen—rude huts of scavenged timber—had been abandoned here for the season, and corduroy ramps led down into the empty digs.

Here the remnants of last night's snow had been blown into windrows and small dunes, and all evidence of hoof prints had been erased. But I rode slowly, knowing I was close to my destination. I was buoyed by the observation that Julian's pursuer, whoever he was, had not returned this way from his mission: had not, that is, taken Julian captive, or at least had not gone back to Williams Ford with his prisoner in tow. Perhaps the pursuit had been suspended for the night.

It was not long—though it seemed an eternity, as Rapture short-stepped down the frozen road, avoiding snow hidden pitfalls—before I heard the whickering of another horse, and saw a plume of smoke rising into the moon-bright sky.

Quickly I turned Rapture off the road and tied his reins to the low remnants of a concrete pillar, from which rust-savaged iron rods protruded like skeletal fingers. I took my squirrel rifle from the saddle holster and moved toward the source of the smoke on foot, until I was able to discern that the fumes emerged from a deep declivity in the landscape, perhaps the very dig from which the Tipmen had extracted *The History of Mankind in Space.* Surely this was where Julian had gone to wait for Sam's arrival. And indeed, here was Julian's horse, one of the finer riding horses from the Estate (worth more, I'm sure, in the eyes of its owner, than a hundred Julian Comstocks), moored to an outcrop . . . and, alarmingly, here was another horse as well, not far away. This second horse was a stranger to me; it was slat-ribbed and elderly-looking; but it wore a military bridle and the sort of cloth bib—blue, with a red star in the middle of it—that marked a mount belonging to the Reserves.

I studied the situation from behind the moon-shadow of a broken abutment.

The smoke suggested that Julian had gone beneath ground, down into the hollow of the Tipmen's dig, to shelter from the cold and bank his fire for the night. The presence of the second horse suggested that he had been discovered, and that his pursuer must already have confronted him.

More than that I could not divine. It remained only to approach the contested grounds as secretively as possible, and see what more I could learn.

I crept closer. The dig was revealed by moonlight as a deep but narrow excavation, covered in part with boards, with a sloping entrance at one end. The glow of the fire within was just visible, as was the chimney hole that had been cut through the planking some yards farther down. There was, as far as I could discern, only one way in or out. I determined to proceed as far as I could without being seen, and to that end I lowered myself down the slope, inching forward on the seat of my pants over ground that was as cold, it seemed to me, as the wastelands of the Arctic north.

I was slow, I was cautious, and I was quiet. But I was not slow, cautious, or quiet *enough;* for I had just progressed far enough to glimpse an excavated chamber, in which the firelight cast a kaleidoscopic flux of shadows, when I felt a pressure behind my ear—the barrel of a gun—and a voice said, "Keep moving, mister, and join your friend below."

◦ ◦ ◦

I kept silent until I could comprehend more of the situation I had fallen into. My captor marched me down into the low part of the dig. The air, if damp, was noticeably warmer here, and we were screened from the increasing wind, though not from the accumulated odors of the fire and the stagnant must of what had once been a basement or cellar in some commercial establishment of the secular ancients.

The Tipmen had not left much behind: only the rubble of broken bits of things, indistinguishable under layers of dust and dirt. The far wall was of concrete, and the fire had been banked against it, under a chimney hole that must have been cut by the scavengers during their labors. A circle of stones hedged the fire, and the damp planks and splinters in it crackled with a deceptive cheerfulness. Deeper parts of the excavation, with ceilings lower than a man standing erect, opened in several directions.

Julian sat near the fire, his back to the wall and his knees drawn up under his chin. His clothes had been made filthy by the grime of the place. He was frowning, and when he saw me his frown deepened into a scowl.

"Go over there and get beside him," my captor said, "but give me that little bird rifle first."

I surrendered my weapon, modest as it was, and joined Julian. Thus I was able to get my first clear look at the man who had captured me. He appeared not much older than myself, but he was dressed in the blue and yellow uniform of the Reserves. His Reserve cap was pulled low over his eyes, which twitched left and right as though he were in constant fear of an ambush. In short he seemed both inexperienced and nervous—and maybe a little dim, for his jaw was slack, and he was evidently unaware of the dribble of mucous that escaped his nostrils as a result of the cold weather. (But as I have said before, this was not untypical of the members of the Reserve, who were kept out of active duty for a reason.)

His weapon, however, was very much in earnest, and not to be trifled with. It was a Pittsburgh rifle manufactured by the Porter & Earl works, which loaded at the breech from a sort of cassette and could fire five rounds in succession without any more attention from its owner than a twitch of the index finger. Julian had carried a similar weapon but had been disarmed of it; it rested against a stack of small staved barrels, well out of reach, and the Reservist put my squirrel rifle beside it.

I began to feel sorry for myself, and to think what a poor way of spending Christmas Eve I had chosen. I did not resent the action of the Reservist nearly as much as I resented my own stupidity and lapse of judgment.

"I don't know who you are," the Reservist said, "and I don't care—one draft-dodger is as good as the next, in my opinion—but I was given the job of collecting runaways, and my bag is getting full. I hope you'll both keep till morning, when I can ride you back into Williams Ford. Anyhow, none of us shall sleep tonight. I won't, in any case, so you might as well resign yourself to your captivity. If you're hungry, there's a little meat."

I was never less hungry in my life, and I began to say so, but Julian interrupted: "It's true, Adam," he said. "We're fairly caught. I wish you hadn't come after me."

"I'm beginning to feel the same way," I said.

He gave me a meaningful look, and said in a lower voice, "Is Sam—?"

"No whispering there," our captor said at once.

But I divined the intent of the question, and nodded to indicate that I had delivered Julian's message, though that was by no means a guarantee of our deliverance. Not only were the exits from Williams Ford under close watch, but Sam could not slip away as inconspicuously as I had, and if Julian's absence had been noted there would have been a redoubling of the guard, and

perhaps an expedition sent out to hunt us. The man who had captured Julian was evidently an outrider, assigned to patrol the
roads for runaways, and he had been diligent in his work.

He was somewhat less diligent now that he had us in his control, however, for he took a wooden pipe from his pocket, and
proceeded to fill it, as he made himself as comfortable as possible
on a wooden crate. His gestures were still nervous, and I supposed the pipe was meant to relax him; for it was not tobacco he
put into it.

The Reservist might have been a Kentuckian, for I understand the less respectable people of that State often form the habit
of smoking the silk of the female hemp plant, which is cultivated
prodigiously there. Kentucky hemp is grown for cordage and
cloth and paper, and as a drug is less intoxicating than the Indian
hemp of lore; but its mild smoke is said to be pleasant for those
who indulge in it, though too much can result in sleepiness and
great thirst.

Julian evidently thought these symptoms would be welcome
distractions in our captor, and he gestured to me to remain silent,
so as not to interrupt the Reservist in his vice. The Reservist
packed the pipe's bowl with dried vegetable matter from an oilcloth envelope he carried in his pocket, and soon the substance
was alight, and a slightly more fragrant smoke joined the effluvia
of the campfire as it swirled toward the rent in the ceiling.

Clearly the night would be a long one, and I tried to be patient in my captivity, and not think too much of Christmas matters, or the yellow light of my parents' cottage on dark winter
mornings, or the soft bed where I might have been sleeping if I
had not been rash in my deliberations.

7

I began by saying this was a story about Julian Comstock, and I
fear I lied, for it has turned out mainly to be a story about myself.

But there is a reason for this, beyond the obvious temptations
of vanity and self-regard. I did not at the time know Julian nearly
as well as I thought I did.

Our friendship was essentially a boys' friendship. I could not help reviewing, as we sat in silent captivity in the ruins of Lundsford, the things we had done together: reading books, hunting in the wooded foothills west of Williams Ford, arguing amiably over everything from Philosophy and Moon-Visiting to the best way to bait a hook or cinch a bridle. It had been too easy, during our time together, to forget that Julian was an aristo with close connections to men of power, or that his father had been famous both as a hero and as a traitor, or that his uncle Deklan Comstock, the President, might not have Julian's best interests at heart.

All that seemed far away, and distant from the nature of Julian's true spirit, which was gentle and inquisitive—a naturalist's disposition, not a politician's or a general's. When I pictured Julian as an adult, I imagined him contentedly pursuing some scholarly or artistic adventure: digging the bones of pre-Noachian monsters out of the Athabaska shale, perhaps, or making an improved kind of movie. He was not a warlike person, and the thoughts of the great men of the day seemed almost exclusively concerned with war.

So I had let myself forget that he was *also* everything he had been before he came to Williams Ford. He was the heir of a brave, determined, and ultimately betrayed father, who had conquered an army of Brazilians but had been crushed by the millstone of political intrigue. He was the son of a powerful woman, born to a powerful family of her own—not powerful enough to save Bryce Comstock from the gallows, but powerful enough to protect Julian, at least temporarily, from the mad calculations of his uncle. He was both a pawn and a player in the great games of the aristos. And while *I* had forgotten all this, Julian had *not*—these were the people who had made him, and if he chose not to speak of them, they nevertheless must have haunted his thoughts.

He was, it is true, often frightened of small things—I still remember his disquiet when I described the rituals of the Church of Signs to him, and he would sometimes shriek at the distress of animals when our hunting failed to result in a clean kill. But tonight, here in the ruins, I was the one who half-dozed in a morose funk, fighting tears; while it was Julian who sat intently still, gazing with resolve from beneath the strands of dusty hair that strag-gled over his brows, as coolly calculating as a bank clerk.

When we hunted, he often gave me the rifle to fire the last lethal shot, distrusting his own resolve.

Tonight—had the opportunity presented itself—I would have given the rifle to him.

⬱ ⬱ ⬱

I half-dozed, as I said, and from time to time woke to see the Reservist still sitting in guard. His eyelids were at half-mast, but I put that down to the effect of the hemp flowers he had smoked. Periodically he would start, as if at a sound inaudible to others, then settle back into place.

He had boiled a copious amount of coffee in a tin pan, and he warmed it whenever he renewed the fire, and drank sufficiently to keep him from falling asleep. Of necessity, this meant he must once in a while retreat to a distant part of the dig and attend to physical necessities in relative privacy. This did not give us any advantage, however, since he carried his Pittsburgh rifle with him, but it allowed a moment or two in which Julian could whis-per without being overheard.

"This man is no mental giant," Julian said. "We may yet get out of here with our freedom."

"It's not his *brains* so much as his *artillery* that's stopping us," said I.

"Perhaps we can separate the one from the other. Look there, Adam. Beyond the fire—back in the rubble."

I looked.

There was motion in the shadows, which I began to recognize.

"The distraction may suit our purposes," Julian said, "unless it becomes fatal." And I saw the sweat that had begun to stand out on his forehead, the terror barely hidden in his eyes. "But I need your help."

I have said that I did not partake of the particular rites of my father's church, and that snakes were not my favorite creatures. This is true. As much as I have heard about surrendering one's volition to God—and I had seen my father with a Massassauga

Rattler in each hand, trembling with devotion, speaking in a tongue not only foreign but utterly unknown (though it favored long vowels and stuttered consonants, much like the sounds he made when he burned his fingers on the coal stove)—could never entirely assure myself that I would be protected by divine will from the serpent's bite. Some in the congregation obviously had not been: there was Sarah Prestley, for instance, whose right arm had swollen up black with venom and had to be amputated by Williams Ford's physician . . . but I will not dwell on that. The point is, that while I *disliked* snakes, I was not especially *afraid* of them, as Julian was. And I could not help admiring his restraint: for what was writhing in the shadows nearby was a nest of snakes that had been aroused by the heat of the fire.

I should add that it was not uncommon for these collapsed ruins to be infested with snakes, mice, spiders, and poisonous insects. Death by bite or sting was one of the hazards routinely faced by Tipmen, including concussion, blood poisoning, and accidental burial. The snakes, after the Tipmen ceased work for the winter, must have crept into this chasm anticipating an undisturbed hibernation, of which we and the Reservist had unfortunately deprived them.

The Reservist—who came back a little unsteadily from his necessaries—had not yet noticed these prior tenants. He seated himself on his crate, scowled at us, and studiously refilled his pipe.

"If he discharges all five shots from his rifle," Julian whispered, "then we have a chance of overcoming him, or of recovering our own weapons. But, Adam—"

"No talking there," the Reservist mumbled.

"—*you must remember your father's advice,*" Julian finished.

"I said keep quiet!"

Julian cleared his throat and addressed the Reservist directly, since the time for action had obviously arrived: "Sir, I have to draw your attention to something."

"What would that be, my little draft dodger?"

"I'm afraid we're not alone in this terrible place."

"Not alone!" the Reservist said, casting his eyes about him nervously. Then he recovered and squinted at Julian. "I don't see any other persons."

"I don't mean persons, but vipers," said Julian.

"Vipers!"

"In other words—snakes."

At this the Reservist started again, his mind perhaps still slightly confused by the effects of the hemp smoke; then he sneered and said, "Go on, you can't pull that one on me."

"I'm sorry if you think I'm joking, for there are at least a dozen snakes advancing from the shadows, and one of them[10] is about to achieve intimacy with your right boot."

"Hah," the Reservist said, but he could not help glancing in the indicated direction, where one of the serpents—a fat and lengthy example—had indeed lifted its head and was sampling the air above his bootlace.

The effect was immediate, and left no more time for planning. The Reservist leapt from his seat on the wooden crate, uttering oaths, and danced backward, at the same time attempting to bring his rifle to his shoulder and confront the threat. He discovered to his dismay that it was not a question of *one* snake but of *dozens,* and he compressed the trigger of the weapon reflexively. The resulting shot went wild. The bullet impacted near the main nest of the creatures, causing them to scatter with astonishing speed, like a box of loaded springs—unfortunately for the hapless Reservist, who was directly in their path. He cursed vigorously and fired four more times. Some of the shots careened harmlessly; at least one obliterated the midsection of the lead serpent, which knotted around its own wound like a bloody rope.

"Now, Adam!" Julian shouted, and I stood up, thinking: My father's advice?

My father was a taciturn man, and most of his advice had involved the practical matter of running the Estate's stables. I hesitated a moment in confusion, while Julian advanced toward the captive rifles, dancing among the surviving snakes like a dervish. The Reservist, recovering somewhat, raced in the same direction; and then I recalled the only advice of my father's that I had ever shared with Julian:

Grasp it where its neck ought to be, behind the head; ignore the tail,

---

[10]Julian's sense of timing was exquisite, perhaps as a result of his theatrical inclinations.

however it may thrash; and crack its skull, hard and often enough to subdue it.

And so I did just that—until the threat was neutralized.

Julian, meanwhile, recovered the weapons, and came away from the infested area of the dig.

He looked with some astonishment at the Reservist, who was slumped at my feet, bleeding from his scalp, which I had "cracked, hard and often."

"Adam," he said. "When I spoke of your father's advice—I meant the *snakes.*"

"The snakes?" Several of them still twined about the dig. But I reminded myself that Julian knew very little about the nature and variety of reptiles. "They're only corn snakes," I explained.[11] "They're big, but they're not venomous."

Julian, his eyes gone large, absorbed this information.

Then he looked at the crumpled form of the Reservist again. "Have you killed him?"

"Well, I hope not," I said.

8

We made a new camp, in a less populated part of the ruins, and kept a watch on the road, and at dawn we saw a single horse and rider approaching from the west. It was Sam Godwin.

Julian hailed him, waving his arms. Sam came closer, and looked with some relief at Julian, and then speculatively at me. I blushed, thinking of how I had interrupted him at his prayers (however unorthodox those prayers might have been, from a purely Christian perspective), and how poorly I had reacted to my discovery of his true religion. But I said nothing, and Sam said nothing, and relations between us seemed to have been regularized, since I had demonstrated my loyalty (or foolishness) by riding to Julian's aid.

It was Christmas morning. I supposed that did not mean any-

---

[11]Once confined to the southeast, corn snakes have spread north with the warming climate. I have read that certain of the secular ancients used to keep them as pets—yet another instance of our ancestors' willful perversity.

thing in particular to Julian or Sam, but I was poignantly aware of the date. The sky was blue again, but a squall had passed during the dark hours of the morning, and the snow "lay round about, deep and crisp and even." Even the ruins of Lundsford were transformed into something soft-edged and oddly beautiful. I was amazed at how simple it was for nature to cloak corruption in the garb of purity and make it peaceful.

But it would not be peaceful for long, and Sam said so. "There are troops behind me as we speak. Word came by wire from New York not to let Julian escape. We can't linger here more than a moment."

"Where will we go?" Julian asked.

"It's impossible to ride much farther east. There's no forage for the animals and precious little water. Sooner or later we'll have to turn south and make a connection with the railroad or the turnpike. It's going to be short rations and hard riding for a while, I'm afraid, and if we do make good our escape we'll have to assume new identities. We'll be little better than draft dodgers or labor refugees, and I expect we'll have to pass some time among that hard crew, at least until we reach New York City. We can find friends in New York."

It was a plan, but it was a large and lonesome one, and my heart sank at the prospect.

"We have a prisoner," Julian told his mentor, and he took Sam back into the excavated ruins to explain how we had spent the night.

The Reservist was there, hands tied behind his back, a little groggy from the punishment I had inflicted on him but well enough to open his eyes and scowl. Julian and Sam spent a little time debating how to deal with this encumbrance. We could not, of course, take him with us; the question was how to return him to his superiors without endangering ourselves unnecessarily.

It was a debate to which I could contribute nothing, so I took a little slip of paper from my back-satchel, and a pencil, and wrote a letter.

It was addressed to my mother, since my father was without the art of literacy.

You will no doubt have noticed my absence, I wrote. *It saddens me to be away from home, especially at this time (I write on Christmas Day). But I hope you will be consoled with the knowledge that I am all right, and not in any immediate danger.*

(This was a lie, depending on how you define "immediate," but a kindly one, I reasoned.)

In any case I would not have been able to remain in Williams Ford, since I could not have escaped the draft for long even if I postponed my military service for some few more months. The conscription drive is in earnest; the War in Labrador must be going badly. It was inevitable that we should be separated, as much as I mourn for my home and all its comforts.

(And it was all I could do not to decorate the page with a vagrant tear.)

Please accept my best wishes and my gratitude for everything you and Father have done for me. I will write again as soon as it is practicable, which may not be immediately. Trust in the knowledge that I will pursue my destiny faithfully and with every Christian virtue you have taught me. God bless you in the coming and every year.

That was not enough to say, but there wasn't time for more. Julian and Sam were calling for me. I signed my name, and added, as a postscript:

Please tell Father that I value his advice, and that it has already served me usefully. Yrs. etc. once again, Adam.

"You've written a letter," Sam observed as he came to rush me to my horse. "But have you given any thought to how you might mail it?"

I confessed that I had not.

"The Reservist can carry it," said Julian, who had already mounted his horse.

The Reservist was also mounted, but with his hands tied behind him, as it was Sam's final conclusion that we should set him loose with the horse headed west, where he would encounter more troops before very long. He was awake but, as I have said, sullen; and he barked, "I'm nobody's damned mailman!"

I addressed the message, and Julian took it and tucked it into the Reservist's saddlebag. Despite his youth, and despite the slightly dilapidated condition of his hair and clothing, Julian sat tall in the saddle. I had never thought of him as high-born until that moment, when an aspect of command seemed to enter his body and his voice. He said to the Reservist, "We treated you kindly—"

The Reservist uttered an oath.

"Be quiet. You were injured in the conflict, but we took you prisoner, and we've treated you in a more gentlemanly fashion than we were when the conditions were reversed. I am a Comstock—at least for the moment—and I won't be spoken to crudely by an infantryman, at any price. You'll deliver this boy's message, and you'll do it gratefully."

The Reservist was clearly awed by the assertion that Julian was a Comstock—he had been laboring under the assumption that we were mere village runaways—but he screwed up his courage and said, "Why should I?"

"Because it's the Christian thing to do," Julian said, "and if this argument with my uncle is ever settled, the power to remove your head from your shoulders may well reside in my hands. Does that make sense to you, soldier?"

The Reservist allowed that it did.

* * *

And so we rode out that Christmas morning from the ruins in which the Tipmen had discovered *The History of Mankind in Space*, which still resided in my back-satchel, vagrant memory of a half-forgotten past.

My mind was a confusion of ideas and anxieties, but I found myself recalling what Julian had said, long ago it now seemed, about DNA, and how it aspired to perfect replication but progressed by remembering itself imperfectly. It might be true, I thought, because our lives were like that—*time itself* was like that, every moment dying and pregnant with its own distorted reflection. Today was Christmas: which Julian claimed had once been a pagan holiday, dedicated to *Sol Invictus* or some other Roman god; but which had evolved into the familiar celebration of the present, and was no less dear because of it.

(I imagined I could hear the Christmas bells ringing from the Dominion Hall at Williams Ford, though that was impossible, for we were miles away, and not even the sound of a cannon shot could carry so far across the prairie. It was only memory speaking.)

And maybe this logic was true of people, too; maybe I was already becoming an inexact echo of what I had been just days before. Maybe the same was true of Julian. Already something hard and uncompromising had begun to emerge from his gentle features—the first manifestation of a new Julian, a freshly *evolved* Julian, called forth by his violent departure from Williams Ford, or slouching toward New York to be born.

But that was all Philosophy, and not much use, and I kept quiet about it as we spurred our horses in the direction of the railroad, toward the rude and squalling infant Future.

THE LINEAMENTS OF GRATIFIED DESIRE

by Ysabeau S. Wilce

Ysabeau S. Wilce is a new writer whose first story, "Metal More Attractive," was published in The Magazine of Fantasy and Science Fiction *in 2004. Like all of her work to date, it was set in "Alta Califa," an alternate California, and is heavily influenced by Wilce's military history studies. A second story, "The Biography of a Bouncing Boy Terror," appeared in 2005 and "The Lineaments of Gratified Desire" appeared in 2006. Wilce's first novel, a young adult fantasy with a preposterously long title,* Flora Segunda: Being the Magickal Mishaps of a Girl of Spirit, Her Glass-Gazing Sidekick, Two Ominous Butlers (One Blue), a House with Eleven Thousand Rooms, and a Red Dog, *was published to considerable acclaim earlier this year. She currently lives with her husband, a dog, and a large number of well-folded paper-towels in Chicago, Illinois.*

> *"Abstinence sows sand all over*
> *The ruddy limbs & flowing hair*
> *But Desire Gratified*
> *Plants fruit of life & beauty there."*
> —*William Blake*

I: STAGE FRIGHT

Here is Hardhands up on the stage, and he's cheery cherry, sparking fire, he's as fast as a fox-trotter, stepping high. Sweaty blood dribbles his brow, bloody sweat stipples his torso, and behind him the Vortex buzz saw whines, its whirling outer edge black enough to cut glass. The razor in his hand flashes like a heliograph as he motions the final Gesture of the invocation. The Eye of the Vortex flutters, but its perimeter remains firmly within the structure of Hardhands' Will and does not expand. He *ululates* a Command, and the Eye begins to open, like a pupil dilating in sunlight, and from its vivid yellowness comes a glimpse of scales and horns, struggling not to be born.

Someone tugs at Hardhands' foot. His concentration wavers. Someone yanks on the hem of his kilt. His concentration wiggles, and the Vortex wobbles slightly like a run-down top. Someone tugs on his kilt-hem and his concentration collapses completely, and so does the Vortex, sucking into itself like water down a drain. There goes the Working for which Hardhands has been preparing for the last two weeks, and there goes the Tygers of Wrath's new drummer, and there goes their boot-kicking show.

Hardhands throws off the grasp with a hard shake, and looking down, prepares to smite. His lover is shouting upward at him, words that Hardhands can hardly hear, words he hopes he can hardly hear, words he surely did not hear a-right. The interior of the club is toweringly loud, noisy enough to make the ears bleed, but suddenly the thump of his heart, already driven hard by the strength of his magickal invocation, is louder.

Relais, pale as paper, repeats the shout. This time there is no mistaking what he says, much as Hardhands would like to mistake it, much as he would like to hear something else, something sweet and charming, something like: you are the prettiest thing ever born, or the Goddess grants wishes in your name, or they are killing themselves in the streets because the show is sold right out. Alas, Relais is shouting nothing quite so sweet.

"What do you mean you cannot find Tiny Doom?" Hardhands shouts back. He looks wildly around the congested club, but it's dark and there are so many of them, and most of them have huge big hair and huger bigger boots. A tiny purple girl-child and her stuffy pink pig have no hope in this throng; they'd be trampled under foot in a second. That is exactly what Hardhands had told the Pontifexa earlier that day; no babysitter, he, other business, other pleasures, no time to take care of small children, not on this night of all nights: The Tygers of Wrath's biggest show of the year. Find someone else.

Well, talkers are no good doers, they say, and talking had done no good, all the yapping growling barking howling in the world had not changed the Pontifexa's mind: it's Paimon's night off, darling, and she'll be safe with you, Banastre, I can trust my heir with no one else, my sweet boy, do your teeny grandmamma this small favor and how happy I shall be, and here, kiss-kiss, I must run, I'm late, have a wonderful evening, good luck with the show, be careful with your invocation, cheerie-bye my darling.

And now see:

Hardhands roars: "I told you to keep an eye on her, Relais!"

He had too, he couldn't exactly watch over Tiny Doom (so called because she is the first in stature and the second in fate), while he was invoking the drummer, and with no drummer, there's no show (no show damn it!) and anyway if he's learned anything as the grandson of the Pontifexa of Califa, it's how to delegate.

Relais shouts back garbled defense. His eyes are whirling pie-plates. He doesn't mention that he stopped at the bar on his way to break the news and that there he downed four Choronzon Delights (hold the delight, double the Choronzon) before screwing up the courage to face his lover's ire. He doesn't mention that he can't exactly remember the last time he saw Little Tiny Doom except that he thinks it might have been about the time when she said that she had to visit El Casa de Peepee (oh cute) and he'd taken her as far as the door to the loo, which she had insisted haughtily she could do alone, and then he'd been standing outside, and gotten distracted by Arsinoë Fyrdraaca, who'd sauntered by, wrapped around the most gorgeous angel with rippling red wings, and then they'd gone to get a drink, and then another drink, and then when Relais remembered that Tiny Doom and Pig were still in the potty and pushed his way back through the crush, Tiny Doom and Pig were not still in the potty anymore.

And now, here:

Up until this very second, Hardhands has been feeling dandy as candy about this night: his invocation has been powerful and sublime, the blood in his veins replaced by pure unadulterated

Magickal Current, hot and heavy. Up until this very second, if he clapped his hands together, sparks would fly. If he sang a note, the roof would fall. If he tossed his hair, fans would implode. Just from the breeze of the Vortex through his skin, he had known this was going to be a charm of a show, the very pinnacle of bombast and bluster. The crowded club still hums with cold fire charge, the air still sparks, cracking with glints of magick: yoowza. But now all that rich bubbly magick is curdling in his veins, his drummer has slid back to the Abyss, and he could beat someone with a stick. Thanks to an idiot boyfriend and a bothersome five-year-old his evening has just tanked.

Hardhands' perch is lofty. Despite the roiling smoke (cigarillo, incense, and oil), he can look out over the big big hair, and see the club is as packed as a cigar box with hipsters eager to see the show. From the stage Hardhands can see a lot, his vision sharpened by the magick he's been mainlining, and he sees: hipsters, b-boys, gothicks, crimson-clad officers, a magistra with a jaculus on a leash, etc. He does not see a small child or a pink pig or even the tattered remnants of a small child and a pink pig or even, well, he doesn't see them period.

Hardhands sucks in a deep breath and uses what is left of the Invocation still working through his veins to shout: "✘◎!"

The syllable is vigorous and combustible, flowering in the darkness like a bruise. The audience erupts into a hollering hooting howl. They think the show is about to start. They are ready and geared. Behind Hardhands, the band also mistakes his intention, and despite the lack of drummer, kicks in with the triumphant blare of a horn, the delirious bounce of the hurdy-gurdy.

"✘◎!" This time the shout sparks bright red, a flash of coldfire that brings tears to the eyes of the onlookers. Hardhands raises an authoritative hand towards the band, crashing them into silence. The crowd follows suit and the ensuing quiet is almost as ear shattering.

"✘◎.." This time his words provide no sparkage, and he knows that his Will is fading under his panic. The club is dark. It is full of large people. Outside it is darker still and the streets of South of the Slot are wet and full of dangers. No place for a Tiny Doom and her Pig, oh so edible, to be wandering around, alone.

Outside it is the worst night of the year to be wandering alone anywhere in the City, particularly if you are short, stout, and toothsome.

"✗◎!" This time Hardhands' voice, the voice which has launched a thousand stars, which has impregnated young girls with monsters and kept young men at their wanking until their wrists ache and their members bleed, is scorched and rather squeaky:

"Has anyone seen my wife?"

II: HISTORICAL NOTES

Here's a bit of background. No ordinary night, tonight, not at all. It's Pirate's Parade and the City of Califa is afire—in some places actually blazing. No fear, tho', bucket brigades are out in force, for the Pontifexa does not wish to lose her capital to revelry. Wetness is stationed around the things that the Pontifexa most particularly requires not to burn: her shrines, Bilskinir House, Arden's Cake-O-Rama, the Califa National Bank. Still, even with these bucket brigades acting as damper, there's fun enough for everyone. The City celebrates many holidays, but surely Pirates' Parade ranks as Biggest and Best.

But why pirates and how a parade? Historians (oh fabulous professional liars) say that it happened thusly: Back in the day, no chain sealed the Bay of Califa off from sea-faring foes and the Califa Gate sprang wide as an opera singer's mouth, a state of affairs good for trade and bad for security. Chain was not all the small city lacked: no guard, no organized militia, no bloodthirsty Scorchers regiment to stand against havoc, and no navy. The City was fledgling and disorganized, hardly more than a village, and plump for the picking.

One fine day, Pirates took advantage of Califa's tenderness, and sailed right through her Gate, and docked at the Embarcadero, as scurvy as you please. From door to door they went, demanding tribute or promising wrath, and when they were loaded down with booty they went well satisfied back to their ships to sail away.

But they didn't get far. While the pirates were shaking down the householders, a posse of quiet citizens crept down to the docks and sabotaged the poorly guarded ships. The pirates arrived back at the docks to discover their escape boats sinking, and when suddenly the docks themselves were on fire, and their way off the docks was blocked, and then they were on fire too, and that was it.

Perhaps Califa had no Army, no Navy, no Militia, but she did have citizens with grit and cleverness, and grit and cleverness trump greed and guns every time. Such a clever victory over a pernicious greedy foe is worth remembering, and maybe even repeating, in a fun sort of way, and thus was born a roistering day of remembrance when revelers dressed as pirates gallivant door to door demanding candy booty, and thus Little Tiny Doom has muscled in on Hardhands' evening. With Grandmamma promised to attend an euchre party, and Butler Paimon's night off, who else would take Tiny Doom, (and the resplendently costumed Pig) on candy shakedown? Who but our hero, as soon as his show is over and his head back down to earth, lucky boy?

Well.

The Blue Duck and its hot dank club-y-ness may be the place to be when you are tall and trendy and your hearing is already shot, but for a short kidlet, big hair and loud noises bore, and the cigarillo smoke scratches. Tiny Doom has waited for Pirates' Parade for weeks, dreaming of pink popcorn and sugar squidies, chocolate manikins and jacknsaps, praline pumpkin seeds and ginger bombs: a sackful of sugar guaranteed to keep her sick and speedy for at least a week. She can wait no longer.

Shortness has its advantage; trendy people look up their noses, not down. The potty is filthy and the floor yucky wet; Tiny Doom and Pig slither out the door, right by Relais, so engaged in his conversation with a woman with a boat in her hair that he doesn't even notice the scram. Around elbows, by tall boots, dodging lit cigarettes and drippy drinks held low and cool-like, Tiny Doom and Pig achieve open air without incident and then, sack in hand, set out for the Big Shakedown.

"Rancy Dancy is no good," she sings as she goes, swinging Pig,

who is of course, too lazy to walk, *"Chop him up for firewood . . . When he's dead, boil his head and bake it into gingerbread . . ."*

She jumps over a man lying on the pavement, and then into the reddish pool beyond. The water makes a satisfying SPLASH and tho' her hem gets wet, she is sure to hold Pig up high so that he remains dry. He's just getting over a bad cold and has to care for his health, silly Pig he is delicate, and up past his bedtime, besides. Well, it is only once a year.

Down the slick street, Tiny Doom galumphs, Pig swinging along with her. There are shadows ahead of her and shadows behind, but after the shadows of Bilskinir House (which can sometimes be *grabby*) these shadows: so what? There's another puddle ahead, this one dark and still. She pauses before it, and some interior alarum indicates that it would be best to jump over, rather than in. The puddle is wide, spreading across the street like a strange black stain. As she gears up for the leap, a faint rippling begins to mar the mirror-like surface.

"Wah! Wah!" Tiny Doom is short, but she has lift. Holding her skirt in one hand, and with a firm grip upon Pig, she hurtles herself upward and over, like a tiny tea cosy levering aloft. As she springs, something wavery and white snaps out of the stillness, snapping towards her like the crack of a whip. She lands on the other side, and keeps scooting, beyond the arm's reach. Six straggly fingers, like pallid parsnips, waggle angrily at her, but she's well beyond their grip.

"Tell her, smell her! Kick her down the cellar," Tiny Doom taunts, flapping Pig's ears derisively. The scraggly arm falls back, and then another emerges from the water, hoisting up on its elbows, pulling a slow rising bulk behind it: a knobby head, with knobby nose and knobby forehead and a slowly opening mouth that shows razor sharp gums and a pointy black tongue, unrolling like a hose. The tongue has length where the arms did not, and it looks gooey and sticky, just like the salt licorice Grandmamma loves so much. Tiny Doom cares not for salt licorice one bit and neither does Pig, so it seems prudent to punt, and they do, as fast as her chubby legs can carry them, further down the slickery dark street.

III: IRRITATING CHILDREN

Here is Hardhands in the alley behind the club, taking a deep breath of brackish air, which chills but does not calm. Inside, he has left an angry mob, who've had their hopes dashed rather than their ears blown. The Infernal Engines of Desire (opening act) has come back on stage and is trying valiantly to suck up the slack, but the audience is not particularly pacified. The Blue Duck will be lucky if it doesn't burn. However, that's not our hero's problem; he's got larger fish frying.

He sniffs the air, smelling: the distant salt spray of the ocean; drifting smoke from some bonfire; cheap perfume; his own sweat; horse manure. He closes his eyes and drifts deeper, beyond smell, beyond scent, down down down into a wavery darkness that is threaded with filaments of light which are not really light, but which he knows no other way to describe. The darkness down here is not really darkness either; it's the Magickal Current as his mind can envision it, giving form to the formless, putting the indefinable into definite terms. The Current bears upon its flow a tendril of something familiar, what he qualifies, for lack of a better word, as a taste of obdurate obstinacy and pink plush, fading quickly but unmistakable.

The Current is high tonight, very high. In consequence, the Aeyther is humming, the Aeyther is abuzz; the line between In and Out has narrowed to a width no larger than a hair, and it's an easy step across—but the jump can go either way. Oh this would have been the very big whoo for the gig tonight; musickal magick of the highest order, but it sucks for lost children out on the streets. South of the Slot is bad enough when the Current is low: a sewer of footpads, dollymops, blisters, mashers, cornhoes, and others is not to be found elsewhere so deep in the City even on an ebb-tide day. Tonight, combine typical holiday mayhem with the rising magickal flood and Goddess knows what will be out, hungry and yummy for some sweet tender kidlet chow. And not even regular run of the mill niblet, but prime grade A best grade royalty. The Pontifexa's heir, it doesn't get more yummy than that—a vampyre could dare sunlight with that bubbly blood zipping through his veins, a ghoul could pass for living after gnawing on that sweet flesh. It makes Hardhands' manly parts shrivel to think upon the explanation to Grandmamma of Tiny Doom's loss and the blame sure to follow.

Hardhands opens his eyes, it's hardly worth wasting the effort of going deep when everything is so close to the surface tonight. Behind him, the iron door flips open and Relais flings outward, borne aloft on a giant wave of disapproving noise. The door snaps shut, cutting the sound in a brief echo which quickly dies in the coffin narrow alley-way.

"Did you find her?" Relais asks, holding his fashionable cuffs so they don't trail on the mucky cobblestones. Inside his brain is bouncing with visions of the Pontifexa's reaction if they return home minus Cyrenacia. Actually, what she is going to say is the least of his worries; it is what she might do that really has Relais gagging. He likes his lungs exactly where they are: inside his body, not flapping around outside.

Hardhands turns a white hot look upon his lover and says: "If she gets eaten, Relais, I will eat you."

Relais' father always advised saving for a rainy day and though the sky above is mostly clear, Relais is feeling damp. He will check his bankbook when they get home, and reconsider Sweetie Fyrdraaca's proposition. He's been Hardhands' leman for over a year now: blood sacrifices, coldfire singed clothing, throat tearing invocations, cornmeal gritty sheets, murder. He's had enough. He makes no reply to the threat.

Hardhands demands, not very politely: "Give me my frock-coat."

Said coat, white as snow, richly embroidered in white peonies and with cuffs the size of tablecloths, well, Relais had been given that to guard too, and he now has a vague memory of hanging it over the stall door in the pisser, where hopefully it still dangles, but probably not.

"I'll get it—" Relais fades backward, into the club, and Hardhands lets him go. For now.

For now, Hardhands takes off his enormous hat, which had remained perched upon his gorgeous head during his invocation via a jeweled spike of a hairpin, and speaks a word into its up-turned bowl. A green light pools up, spilling over the hat's capacious brim, staining his hand and the sleeve below with drippy magick. Another commanding word, and the light surges upward and ejects a splashy elemental, fish-tail flapping.

"Eh, boss—I thought you said I had the night off," Alfonso complains. There's lip rouge smeared on his fins and a clutch of cards in his hand. "It's Pirates Parade."

"I changed my mind. That wretched child has given me the slip and I want you to track her."

Alfonso grimaces. Ever since Little Tiny Doom trapped him in a bowl of water and fed him fishy flakes for two days, he's avoided her like fluke-rot.

"Why worry your good luck, boss—"

Hardhands does not have to twist. He only has to look like he is going to twist. Alfonzo zips forward, flippers flapping and Hardhands, after draining his chapeau of Current and slamming it back upon his grape, follows.

IV: WHO'S THERE?

Here is The Roaring Gimlet, sitting pretty in her cozy little kitchen, toes toasting on the grate, toast toasting on the tongs, drinking hot ginger beer, feeling happily serene. She's had a fun-dandy evening. Citizens who normally sleep behind chains and steel bolts, dogs a-prowl and guns under their beds, who maybe wouldn't open their doors after dark if their own mothers were lying bleeding on the threshold, these people fling their doors widely and with gay abandon to the threatening cry of "Give us Candy or We'll Give you the Rush."

Any other night, at this time, she'd still be out in the streets, looking for drunken mashers to roll. But tonight, all gates were a-jar and the streets a high tide of drunken louts. Out by nine and back by eleven, with a sack almost too heavy to haul, a goodly load of sugar, and a yummy fun-toy, too. Now she's enjoying her happy afterglow from a night well-done. The noises from the cellar have finally stopped, she's finished the crossword in *The Alta Califa,* and as soon as the kettle blows, she'll fill her hot water bottle and aloft to her snuggly bed, there to dwell the rest of the night away in kip.

Ah, Pirates Parade, best night of the year.

While she's waiting for the water to bubble, she's cleaning the tool from whence comes her name: the bore is clotted with icky stuff and the Gimlet likes her signature clean and sharply shiny. Clean hands, clean house, clean heart, the Gimlet's pappy always said. Above the fireplace, Pappy's flat representation stares down at his progeny, the self-same gimlet clenched in his hand. The Roaring Gimlet is the heir to a fine family tradition and she does love her job.

What's that a-jingling? She glances at the clock swinging over the stove. It's almost midnight. Too late for visitors, and anyway, everyone knows the Roaring Gimlet's home is her castle. Family stays in, people stay out, so Daddy Gimlet always said. Would someone? No, they wouldn't. Not even tonight, they would not.

Jingle jingle.

The cat looks up from her perch on the fender, perturbed.

Heels down, the Gimlet stands aloft, and tucks her shirt back into her skirts, ties her dressing gown tight, bounds up the ladder-like kitchen stairs to the front door. The peephole shows a dimly lit circle of empty cobblestones. Damn it all to leave the fire for nothing. As the Gimlet turns away, the bell dances again, jangling her into a surprised jerk.

The Roaring Gimlet opens the door, slipping the chain, and is greeted with a squirt of flour right in the kisser, and a shrieky command:

"Give us the Candy or We'll give you the Rush!"

The Gimlet coughs away the flour, choler rising, and beholds before her, knee-high, a huge black feathered hat. Under the hat is a pouty pink face, and under the pouty pink face, a fluffy far-thingale that resembles in both color and points an artichoke, and under that, purple dance shoes, with criss-crossy ribbands. Riding on the hip of this apparition is a large pink plushy pig, also wear-ing purple criss-crossy dance shoes, golden laurel leaves perched over floppy piggy ears.

It's the Pig that the Gimlet recognizes first, not the kid. The kid, whose public appearances have been kept to a minimum (the

Pontifexa is wary of too much flattery, and as noted, chary of her heir's worth) could be any kid, but there is only one Pig, all Califa knows that, and the kid must follow the Pig, as day follows night, as sun follows rain, as fortune follows the fool.

"Give us the CANDY or we'll GIVE YOU THE RUSH!" A voice to pierce glass, to cut right through the Gimlet's recoil, all the way down to her achy toes. The straw-shooter moves from *present* to *fire;* while Gimlet was gawking, reloading had occurred, and another volley is imminent. She's about to slam shut the door, she cares not to receive flour or to give out yum, but then, door-jamb held halfway in hand, she stops. An idea, formed from an over-abundance of yellow nasty novellas and an under-abundance of good sense, has leapt full-blown from Nowhere to the Somewhere that is the Roaring Gimlet's calculating brain. So much for sugar, so much for swag: here then is a price above rubies, above diamonds, above chocolate, above, well, Above All. What a pretty price a pretty piece could fetch. On such proceeds the Gimlet could while away her elder days in endless sun and fun-toys.

Before the kid can blow again, the Gimlet grins, in her best granny way, flour feathering about her, and says, "Well, now, chickiedee, well now indeed. I've no desire to be rushed, but you are late and the candy is—"

She recoils, but not in time, from another spurt of flour. When she wipes away the flour, she is careful not to wipe away her welcoming grin. "But I have more here in the kitchen, come in, tiny pirate, out of the cold and we shall fill your sack full."

"Huh," says the child, already her husband's Doom and about to become the Roaring Gimlet's, as well. "GIVE ME THE CANDY—"

Patience is a virtue that the Roaring Gimlet is well off without. She peers beyond the kid, down the street. There are people about but they are: drunken people, or burning people, or screaming people, or carousing people, or running people. None of them appear to be observant people, and that's perfecto. The Gimlet reaches and grabs.

"Hey!" says the Kid. The Pig does not protest.

Tiny Doom is stout, and she can dig her heels in, but the

Gimlet is stouter and the Gimlet has two hands free, where Tiny Doom has one, and the Pig is too flabby to help. Before Tiny Doom can shoot off her next round of flour, she's yanked and the door is slammed shut behind her, bang!

V: BAD HOUSEKEEPING

Here is Hardhands striding down the darkened streets like a colossus, dodging fire, flood, and fighting. He is not upset, oh no indeedy. He's cool and cold and so angry that if he touched tinder it would burst into flames, if he tipped tobacco it would explode cherry red. And there's more than enough ire to go around, which is happy because the list of Hardhands' blame is quite long. Firstly: the Pontifexa for making him take Cyrenacia with him. What good is it to be her darling grandson when he's constantly on doodie-detail? Being the only male Haðraaða should be good for: power, mystery, free booze, noli me tangare, first and foremost, the biggest slice of cake. Now being the only male Haðraaða is good for: marrying small torments, kissing the Pontifexa's ass, and being bossed into wife-sitting. He almost got Grandmamma once; perhaps the decision should be revisited.

Secondly: Tiny Doom for not standing still. When he gets her, he's going to paddle her, see if he doesn't. She's got it coming, a long time coming and perhaps a hot hinder will make her think twice about, well, think twice about everything. Didn't he do enough for her already? He married her, to keep her in the family, to keep her out of the hands of her nasty daddy, who otherwise would have the prior claim. Ungrateful kidlet. Perhaps she deserves whatever she gets.

Thirdly: Relais for being such an utter jackass that he can't keep track of a four year old. Hardhands has recently come across a receipt for an ointment that allows the wearer to walk through walls. For which, this sigil requires three pounds of human tallow. He's got a few walls he wouldn't mind flitting right through and at last, Relais will be useful.

Fourthly: Paimon. What need has a domicilic denizen for a night off anyway? He's chained to the physical confines of the

House Bilskinir by a sigil stronger than life. He should be taking care of the Heir to the House Bilskinir, not doing whatever the hell he is doing on his night off which he shouldn't be doing anyway because he shouldn't be having a night off and when Hardhands is in charge, he won't, no sieur.

Fifthly: Pig. Ayah, so, well, Pig is a stuffy pink plush toy, and can hardly be blamed for anything, but what the hell, why not? Climb on up, Pig, there's always room for one more! And ire over all: his ruined invocation, for which he had been purging starving dancing and flogging for the last two weeks, all in preparation for what would surely be the most stupendous summoning in the history of summoning. It's been a stellar group of daemons that Hardhands has been able to force from the Aeyther before, but this time he had been going for the highest of the high, the loudest of the loud, and the show would have been sure to go down in the annals of musickoly and his name, already famous, would become gigantic in its shadow. Even the Pontifexa was sure to be impressed. And now . . .

The streets are full of distraction but neither Hardhands nor Alfonso are distracted. Tiny Doom's footprints pitty-patter before them, glowing in the gloam like little blue flowers, and they follow, avoiding burning brands, dead horses, drunken warblers, slithering servitors, gushing water pipes, and an impromptu cravat party and, because of their glowering concentration, they are avoided by all the aforementioned, in turn. The pretty blue footprints dance, and leap, from here to there, and there to here, over cobblestone and curb, around corpse and copse, by Cobweb's Palace and Pete's Clown Diner, by Ginger's Gin Goint and Guerrero's Helado, and other blind tigers so blind they are nameless also, dives so low that just walking by will get your knickers wet. The pretty prints don't waver, don't dilly-dally, and then suddenly, they turn towards a door, broad and barred, and they stop.

At the door, Hardhands doesn't bother knocking, and neither does Alfonso, but their methods of entry differ. Alfonso zips through the wooden obstruction as though it is neither wooden nor obstructive. Hardhands places palm down on wood, and via a particularly loud Barbarick exhortation, blows the door right off its hinges. His entry is briefly hesitated by the necessity to chase after his chapeau, having blown off also in the breeze of Barbarick, but once it is firmly stabbed back on his handsome head, onward he goes, young Hardhands, hoping very much that something else will get in his path, because, he can't deny it: exploding things is Fun. The interior of the house is dark and dull, not that Hardhands is there to critique the décor. Alfonso has zipped ahead of him, coldfire frothing in his wake. Hardhands follows the bubbly pink vapour, down a narrow hallway, past peeling paneling, and dusty doorways. He careens down creaky stairs, bending head to avoid braining on low ceiling, and into a horrible little kitchen.

He wrinkles his nose. Our young hero is used to a praeterhuman amount of cleanliness, and here there is neither. At Bilskinir House even the light looks as though it's been washed, dried and pressed before hung in the air. In contrast, this pokey little hole looks like the back end of a back end bar after a particularly festive game of Chew the Ear. Smashed crockery and blue willow china crunches under boot, and the furniture is bonfire ready. A faint glow limns the wreckage, the after-reflection of some mighty big magick. The heavy sour smell of blackberries wrinkles in his nose. Coldfire dribbles from the ceiling, whose plaster cherubs and grapes look charred and withered.

Hardhands pokes at a soggy wad of clothes lying in a heap on the disgusting floor. For one testicle shriveling moment he thought that he saw black velvet amongst the sog; he does, but it's a torn shirt, not a puffy hat.

All magickal acts leave a resonance behind, unless the magician takes great pains to hide: Hardhands knows every archon, hierophant, sorceress, bibliomatic, and avatar in the City, but he doesn't recognize the author of this Working. He catches a drip of coldfire on one long finger and holds it up to his lips: salt-sweet-smoky-oddly familiar but not enough to identify.

"Pigface pogo!" says our hero. He has put his foot down in slide and almost gone face down in a smear of glass and black goo—mashy blackberry jam, the source of the sweet stench. Flailing un-heroically he regains his balance, but in doing so grabs at the edge of an overturned settle. The settle has settled backwards, cock-eyed on its back feet, but Hardhands' leverage rocks it forward again, and, hello, here's the Gimlet—well, parts of her anyway. She is stuck to the bench by a flood of dried blood, and the expression on her face is doleful, and a little bit surprised.

"Pogo pigface on a pigpogopiss! Who the hell is that?"

Alfonzo yanks the answer from the Aethyr. "The Roaring Gimlet, petty roller and barn stamper. You see her picture sometimes in the post office."

"She don't look too roaring to me. What the hell happened to her?"

Alfonzo zips closer, while Hardhands holds his sleeve to his sensitive nose. The stench of metallic blood is warring with the sickening sweet smell of the crushed blackberries, and together a pleasuring perfume they do not make.

"Me, I think she was chewed," Alfonzo announces after close inspection. "By something hungry and mad."

"What kind of something?"

Alfonso shrugs. "Nobody I know, sorry, boss."

As long as Doom is not chewed, Hardhands cares naught for the chewy-ness of others. He uneasily illuminates the fetid shadows with a vivid Barbarick phrase, but thankfully no rag-like wife does he see, tossed aside like a discarded tea-towel, nor red wet stuffy Pig-toy, only bloody jam and magick bespattered walls. He'd never admit it, particularly not to a yappy servitor, but there's a warm feeling of relief in his toes that Cyrenacia and Pig were not snacked upon. But if they were not snacked upon, where the hell are they, oh irritation.

There, in the light of his sigil—sign: two dainty feet stepped in jammy blood, hopped in disgust, and then headed up the back stairs, the shimmer of Bilskinir blue shining faintly through the rusty red. Whatever got the Gimlet did not get his wife and pig, that's for sure, that's all he cares about, all he needs to know, and the footprints are fading, too: onward.

At the foot of the stairs, Hardhands poises. A low distant noise drifts out of the floor below, like a bad smell, a rumbly agonized sound that makes his tummy wiggle.

"What is that?"

A wink of Alfonzo's tails and top-hat and here's his answer:

"There's some guy locked in the cellar, and he's—he's in a bad way, and I think he needs our help—"

Hardhands is not interested in guys locked in cellars, nor in their bad ways. The footprints are fading, and the Current is still rising, he can feel it jiggling in his veins. Badness is on the loose—is not the Gimlet proof of that?—and Goddess Califa knows what else, and Tiny Doom is alone.

VI: Sugar Sweet

Here is Hardhands, hot on the heels of the pretty blue footsteps skipping along through the riotous streets. Hippy-hop, pitty-pat. The trail takes a turning, into a narrow alley and Hardhands turns with it, leaving the sputtering street lamps behind. Before the night was merely dark: now it's darkdarkdark. He flicks a bit of coldfire from his fingertips, blossoming a ball of luminescence that weirdly lights up the crooked little street, broken cobbles and black narrow walls. The coldfire ball bounces onward, and Hardhands follows. The foot prints are almost gone: in a few more moments they will be gone, for a lesser magician they would be gone already.

And then, a drift of song:

"Hot corn, hot corn! Buy my hot corn!
Lovely and sweet, Lovely and Warm!"

Out of the shadow comes a buttery smell, hot and wafting, the jingling of bells, friendly and beckoning: a Hot Corn Dolly, out on the prowl. The perfume is delightful and luscious and it reminds Hardhands that dinner was long since off. But Hardhands does not eat corn (while not fasting, he's on an all meat diet, for to clean his system clear of sugar and other poisons), and when the Hot Corn Dolly wiggles her tray at him, her green ribboned braids dancing, he refuses.

The Corn Dolly is not alone, her sisters stand behind her, and their wide trays, and the echoing wide width of their farthingale skirts, flounced with patchwork, jingling with little bells, form a barricade that Hardhands, the young gentleman, cannot push through. The Corn Dolly skirts are wall-to-wall and their ranks are solid and only rudeness will make a breach.

"I cry your pardon, ladies," he says, in feu de joie, ever courteous, for is not the true mark of a gentleman his kindness towards others, particularly his inferiors? "I care not for corn, and I would pass."

"Buy my hot corn, deliciously sweet,
Gives joy to the sorrowful and strength to the weak."

The Dolly's voice is luscious, ripe with sweetness. In one small hand she holds an ear of corn, dripping with butter, fragrant with the sharp smell of chile and lime, bursting up from its peeling of husk like a flower, and this she proffers towards him. Hardhands feels a southerly rumble, and suddenly his mouth is full of anticipatory liquid. Dinner was a long long time ago, and he has always loved hot corn, and how can one little ear of corn hurt him? And anyway, don't he deserve some solace? He fumbles in his pocket, but no divas does he slap; he's the Pontifexa's grandson, and not in the habit of paying for his treats.

The Dolly sees his gesture and smiles. Her lips are glistening golden, as yellow as her silky hair, and her teeth, against the glittering, are like little nuggets of white corn.

"A kiss for the corn, and corn for a kiss, one sweet with flavor, the other with bliss," she sings, and the other dollies join in her harmony, the bells on their square skirts jingling. The hot corn glistens like gold, steamy and savory, dripping with yum. A kiss is a small price to pay to sink his teeth into savory. He's paid more for less and he leans forward, puckering.

The dollies press in, wiggling their oily fingers and humming their oily song, enfolding him in the husk of their skirts, their hands, their licking tongues. His southerly rumble is now a wee bit more southerly, and it's not a rumble, it's an avalanche. The corn rubs against his lips, slickery and sweet, spicy and sour. The chili burns his lips, the butter soothes them, he kisses, and then he licks, and then he bites into a bliss of crunch, the squirt of sweetness cutting the heat and the sour. Never has he tasted anything better, and he bites again, eagerly, butter oozing down his chin, dripping onto his shirt. Eager fingers stroke his skin, he's engorged with the sugar-sweetness, so long denied, and now he can't get enough, each niblet exploding bright heat in his mouth, his tongue, his head, he's drowning in the sweetness of it all.

And like a thunder from the Past, he hears ringing in his head the Pontifexa's admonition, oft repeated to a whiny child begging for hot corn, spun sugar, spicy taco or fruit cup, sold on the street, in marvelous array but always denied because: YOU NEVER KNOW WHERE IT'S BEEN. An Admonition drummed into his head with painful frequency, all the other kidlets snacked from the street vendors with reckless abandon, but not the Pontifexa's grandson, whose tum was deemed too delicate for common food and the common bugs it might contain.

Drummed well and hard it would seem, to suddenly recall now, with memorable force, better late than never. Hardhands snaps open eyes and sputters kernels. Suddenly he sees true what the Corn Dollies' powerful glamour has disguised under a patina of butter and spice: musky kernels and musky skin. A fuzz of little black flies encircles them. The silky hair, the silky husks are slick with mold. The little white corn teeth grin mottled blue and green, and corn worms spill in a white wiggly waterfall from gaping mouths.

"Arrgg," says our hero, managing to keep the urp down, heroically. He yanks and flutters, pulls and yanks, but the knobby fingers have him firm, stalk to stalk. He heaves, twisting his shoulders, spinning and ducking: now they have his shirt, but he is free.

"✕↣☞◆✋♂❖☉!" he bellows, at the top of his magickal lungs. The word explodes from his head with an agonizing aural thud. The Corn Dollies sizzle and shriek, but he doesn't wait around to revel in their popping. Now he's a fleet footed fancy boy, skedaddling as fast as skirts will allow; to hell with heroics, there's no audience about, just get the hell out. He leaves the shrieking behind him, fast on booted heels, and it's a long heaving pause later, when the smell of burned corn no longer lingers on the air, that he stops to catch breath and bearings. His heart, booming with Barbarick exertion, is starting to slow, but his head, still thundering with a sugary rush, feels as though it might implode right there on his shoulders, dwindle down a pinprick of pressure, diamond hard. The sugar pounds in his head, beating his brain into a ploughshare of pain, sharp enough to cut a furrow in his skull.

He leans on a scaly wall and sticks a practiced finger down his gullet. Up heaves corn, and bile, and blackened gunk, and more gunk. The yummy sour-lime-butter taste doesn't have quite the same delicious savor coming up as it did going down, nor is his shuddering now quite so delightful. He spits and heaves, and heaves and spits, and when his inside is empty of everything, including probably most of his internal organs, he feels a wee bit better. Not much, but some. His ears are cold. He puts a quivery hand to his head; his hat is gone.

The chapeau is not the only thing to disappear, Tiny Doom's tiny footprints, too, have faded. Oh for a drink to drive the rest of the stale taste of rotting corn from his tonsils. Oh for a super duper purge to scour the rest of the stale speed of sugar from his system. Oh for a bath, and bed, and deep sweet sleep. He's had a thin escape, and he knows it: the Corn Sirens could have drained him completely, sucked him as dry as a desert sunset, and Punto Finale for the Pontifexa's grandson. Now it's going to take him weeks of purifications, salt-baths and soda enemas to get back into whack. Irritating. He's also irked at the loss of his shirt; it was brand-new, he'd only worn it once, and the lace on its sleeves had cost him fifty-eight divas in gold. And his hat, bristling with angel feathers, its brim bigger than an apple pancake. He's annoyed at himself, sloppy-sloppy-sloppy.

The coldfire track has sputtered and no amount of Barbarick kindling can spark it alight; it's too late, too gone, too long. Alfonzo, too, is absent of summoning and when Hardhands closes his eyes and clenches his fists to his chest, sucks in deep lungs of air, until the Current bubbles in his veins like the most sparkling of red wines, he knows why: the Current has flowed so high now that even the lowliest servitors can ride it without assistance, is strong enough to avoid constraint and ignore demand. He'd better find the kid soon, with the Current this high, only snackers will now be out, anyone without skill or protection—the snackees—will have long since gone home, or been eaten. Funtime for humans is over, and funtime for Others just begun.

Well, that's fine, Alfonzo is just a garnish, not necessary at all.

Is not Tiny Doom his own blood? Does not a shared spark run through their veins? He closes eyes again, and stretches arms outward, palms upward and he concentrates every split second of his Will into a huge vaporous awareness which he flings out over Califa like a net. Far far at the back of his throat, almost a tickle, not quite a taste, he finds the smell he is looking for. It's dwindling, and it's distant, but it's there and it's enough. A tiny thread connecting him to her, blood to blood, heat to heat, heart beat to heart beat, a tiny threat of things to come when Tiny Doom is not so Tiny. He jerks the thread with infinitesimal delicacy. It's thin, but it holds. It's thin, but it can never completely break.

He follows the thread, gently, gently, down darkened alleys, past shuttered facades, and empty stoops. The streets are slick with smashed fruit, but otherwise empty. He hears the sound of distant noises, hooting, hollering, braying mule, a fire bell, but he is alone. The buildings grow sparser, interspaced with empty lots. They look almost like rows of tombstones, and their broken windows show utterly black. The acrid tang of burning sugar tickles his nose, and the sour-salt smell of marshy sea-water; he must be getting closer to the bay's soggy edge. Cobblestones give way to splintery corduroy which gives way to moist dirt, and now the sweep of the starry sky above is unimpeded by building facades; he's almost out of the City, he may be out of the City now, he's never been this far on this road and if he hadn't absolute faith in the Haðraaða family bond, he'd be skeptical that Tiny Doom's chubby little legs had made it this far either. But they have. He knows it.

Hardhands pauses, cocking his head: a tinge suffuses his skin, a gentle breeze that isn't a breeze at all, but the galvanic buzz of the Current. The sky above is now obscured by wafts of spreading fog, and, bourne distantly upon that breeze, a vague tune. Musick.

Onward, on prickly feet, with the metallic taste of magick growing thicker in the back of his throat. The music is building crescendo, it sounds so friendly and fun, promising popcorn, and candied apples, fried pies. His feet prickle with these promises, and he picks up the pace, buoyed on by the rollicking music, allowing the musick to carry him onward, towards the twinkly lights now beckoning through the heavy mist.

Then the musick is gone, and he blinks, for the road has come to an end as well, a familiar end, although unexpected. Before him looms a giant polychrome monkey head, leering brightly. This head is two stories high, it has flapping ears and wheel-size eyes, and its gaping mouth, opened in a silent howl, is large enough for a gaggle of school children to rush through, screaming their excitement.

Now he knows where he is, where Tiny Doom has led him to, predictable, actually, the most magical of all childhood places: *Woodward's Garden, Fun for All Occasions, Not Occasionally but Always.*

How oft has Hardhands been to Woodward's (in cheerful daylight), and ah the fun he has had there, (in cheerful daylight): The Circular Boat and the Mystery Manor, the Zoo of Pets, and the Whirla-Gig. Pink popcorn and strawberry cake, and Madam Twanky's Fizzy Lick-A-Rice Soda. Ah, Woodward's Garden and the happy smell of sun, sugar, sweat and sizzling meat. But at Woodward's, the fun ends at sundown, as evening's chill begins to rise, the rides begin to shut, the musick fades away and everyone must go, exiting out the Monkey's Other End. Woodward's is not open at night.

But here, tonight, the Monkey's Eyes are open, although his smile is a grimace, less Welcome and more Beware. The Monkey's Eyes roll like red balls in their sockets, and at each turn they display a letter: "F" "U" "N" they spell in flashes of sparky red. Something skitters at our boy's ankles and he jumps: scraps of paper flickering like shredded ghosts. The Monkey's Grin is fixed, glaring, in the dark it does not seem at all like the Gateway to Excitement and Adventure, only Digestion and Despair. Surely even Doom, despite her ravenous adoration of the Circular Boat, would not be tempted to enter the hollow throat just beyond the poised glittering teeth. Despite the promise of the Monkey's Rolling Eyes there is no Fun here.

Or is there? Look again. Daylight, a tiara of letters crowns the Monkey's Head, spelling Woodward's Garden in cheery lights. But not tonight, tonight the tiara is a crown of spikes, whose glittering red letters proclaim a different title: *Madam Rose's Flower Garden.*

Hardhands closes his eyes against the flashes, feeling all the blood in his head blushing downward into his pinchy toes. Madam Rose's Flower Garden! It cannot be. Madam Rose's is a myth, a rumour, an innuendo, a whisper. A prayer. The only locale in Califa where entities, it is said, can walk in the Waking World without constraint, can move and do as their Will commands, and not be constrained by the Will of a magician or adept. Such mixing is proscribed, it's an abomination, against all laws of nature, and until this very second, Hardhands thought, mere fiction.

And yet apparently not fiction at all. The idea of Tiny Doom in such environs sends Hardhands' scalp a-shivering. This is worse than having her out on the streets. Primo child-flesh, delicious and sweet, and plump full of such energy as would turn the most mild mannered elemental into a rival of Choronzon, the Daemon of Dispersion. Surrounded by islocated elementals and egregores, under no obligation and bound by no sigil, indulging in every depraved whim. Surely the tiresome child did not go forward to her own certain doom.

But his burbling tum, his swimming head, knows she did.

If he were not Banastre Haðraaða, the Grand Duque of Califa, this is the point where he'd turn about and go home. First he might sit upon the ground, right here in the dirt, and wallow for a while in discouragement, then he'd rise, dust, and retreat. If he were not himself, but someone else, someone lowly, he might be feeling pretty low.

For a moment, he is not himself, he is cold and tired and hungry and ready for the evening to end. It was fun to be furious, his anger gave him forward motion and will and fire, but now he wants to be home in his downy-soft bed with a yellow nasty newsrag and a jorum of hot wine. If Wish could be made Will in a heart-beat, he'd be lying back on damask pillows, drowning away to happy dreamland.

Before he can indulge in such twaddle, a voice catches his attention.

"Well, now, your grace. Slumming?"

Then does Hardhands notice a stool, and upon the stool a boy sitting, legs dangling, swinging copper-toed button boots back and forth. A pocketknife flashes in his hand; shavings flutter downward. He's tow-headed, and blue-eyed, freckled and tan, and he's wearing a polka-dotted kilt, a redingcote, and a smashed bowler. A smoldering stogie hangs down from his lips.

"I beg your pardon?"

"Never mind, never mind. Are you here for the auction?"

Hardhands replies regally: "I am looking for a child and a pink pig."

The boy says, brightly, "Oh yes, of course. They passed this way some time ago, in quite a hurry."

Hardhands makes move to go inside, but is halted by the red velvet rope which is action as barrier to the Monkey's mouth.

"Do you have a ticket? It's fifteen divas, all you can eat and three trips to the bar."

Remembering his empty pockets, Hardhands says loftily: "I'm on the List."

The List: Another powerful weapon. If you are on it, all to the good. If not, back to the Icy Arrogance. But when has Hardhands not been on the list? Never! Unthinkable!

"Let me see," says the Boy. He turns out pockets, and thumps his vest, fishes papers, and strings, candy and fish-hooks, bones and lights, a white rat, and a red rubber ball. "I know I had something—Ahah!" This ahah is addressed to his hat, what interior he is excavating and out of which he draws a piece of red foolscap. "Let me see . . . um . . . Virex the Sucker of Souls, Zigurex Avatar of Agony, Valefor Teller of Tales, no, I'm sorry your grace, but you are not on the list. That will be fifteen divas."

"Get out of my way."

Hardhands takes a pushy step forward, only to find that his feet cannot come off the ground. The Boy, the Gatekeeper, smells like human but he has powerful praeterhuman push.

"Let me by."

"What's the magick word?"

"⊙⊁▢◆⌇● ⟰◆♎♏■♌⌇⧗⌖⫐"

This word should blossom like fire in the sultry air, it should spout lava and sparks and smell like burning tar. It should shrink the Boy down to stepping-upon size.

It sparks briefly, like a wet sparkler, and gutters away.

He tries again, this time further up the Barbarick alphabet, heavier on the results.

“☪♓❏⬥♋● ☜♐♋❐⬧♏.”

This word should suck all the light out of the world, leaving a blackness so utter that it will leave the Boy gasping for enough breath to scream.

It casts a tiny shadow, like a gothick’s smile, and then brightens.

“Great accent,” says the Boy. He is grinning sympathetically, which enrages Hardhands even more, because he is the Pontifexa’s grandson and there’s nothing to be sorry about for THAT. “But not magickal enough.”

Hardhands is flummoxed, this is a first, never before has his magick been stifled, tamped, failed to light. Barbarick is tricky, it is true. In the right mouth the right Barbarick word will explode the Boy into tiny bits of bouncing ectoplasm, or shatter the air as though it were made of ice, or turn the moon into a tulip. The right word in the wrong mouth, a mouth that stops when it should glottal or clicks when it should clack, could turn his tummy into a hat, roll back time, or turn his blood to fire. But, said right or said wrong, Barbarick never does nothing. His tummy is, again, tingling.

The Boy is now picking his teeth with the tip of his knife. “I give you a hint. The most magickal word of them all.”

What more magick than ✠✠✠✠✠✠ or ⚐⚐⚐⚐⚐? Is there a more magickal word that Hardhands has never heard of? He’s an adept of the sixth order, he’s peeked into the Abyss, surely there is no Super Special Magickal Word hidden from him yet—he furrows his pure white brow into unflattering wrinkles, and then, a tiny whiny little voice in his head says: *what’s the magick word, Bwannie, what’s the magick word?*

“Please.” Hardhands says. “Let me pass, please.”

“With pleasure,” the Boy says, “But I must warn you. There are ordeals.”

“No ordeal can be worse than listening to you.”

"One might think so," the boy says, "You have borne my rudeness so kindly, your grace, that I hate to ask you for one last favour, but I fear I must."

Hardhands glares at the boy, who smiles sheepishly.

"Your boots, your grace. Madama doesn't care for footwear on her clean carpets. I shall give you a ticket, and give your boots a polish and they'll be nice and shiny for you, when you leave."

Hardhands does not want to relinquish his heels, which may only add an actual half an inch in height, but are marvelous when it comes to mental stature, who cannot help but swagger in red-topped jackboots, champagne shiny and supple as night?

He sighs, bending. The grass below is cool against our hero's hot feet, once liberated happily from the pinchy pointy boots (ah vanity, thy name is only sixteen years old) but he'd trade the comfort, in a second, for height.

He hops and kicks, sending one boot flying at the kid (who catches it easily) and the other off into the darkness.

"Mucho gusto. Have a swell time, your grace."

Hardhands stiffens his spine with arrogance and steps into the Monkey's Mouth.

VII: TIME'S TRICK

Motion moves in the darkness around him, a glint of silver, to one side, then the other, then in front of him: he jumps. Then he realizes that the form ahead of him is familiar: his own reflection. He steps forward, and the Hardhands before him resolves into a Hardhands behind him, while those to other side, move with him, keeping pace. For a second he hesitates, thinking to run into a mirror, but an outstretched arm feels only empty air, and he steps once, again, then again, more confidently. His reflection has disappeared; ahead is only darkness.

So he continues on, contained with a hollow square of his own reflections, which makes him feel a bit more cheerful, for what can be more reassuring but an entire phalanx of your own beautiful self? Sure, he looks a bit tattered: bare chest, sticky hair, blurred eyeliner, but it's a sexy tattered, bruised and battered, and slightly forlorn. He could start a new style with this look: *After the Deluge,* it could be called, or, *A Rough Night.*

Of course Woodwards' has a hall of mirrors too, a horrifying place where the glasses stretch your silver-self until you look like an emaciated crane, or squash you down, round as a beetle. These mirrors continue, as he continues, to show only his perfect self, disheveled, but still perfect. He laughs, a sound which, pinned in on all sides as it is, quickly dies. If this is the Boy's idea of an Ordeal, he's picked the wrong man. Hardhands has always loved mirrors, so much so that he has them all over his apartments: on his walls, on his ceilings, even, in his Conjuring Closet, on the floor. He's never met a reflection of himself he didn't love, didn't cherish, cheered up by the sight of his own beauty—what a lovely young man, how blissful to be me!

He halts and fumbles in his kilt-pocket for his favorite lip rouge (*Death in Bloom,* a sort of blackish pink) and reapplies. Checks his teeth for color, and blots on the back of his hand. Smoothes one eyebrow with his finger-tip, and arranges a strand of hair so it is more fetchingly askew—then leans in, closer. A deep line furrows behind his eyes, a line where he's had no line before, and there, at his temple, is that a strand of gray amidst the silver? His groping fingers feel only smoothness on his brow, he smiles and the line vanishes, he grips the offending hair and yanks: in his grasp it is as pearly as ever. A trick of the poor light then, and on he goes, but sneaking glances to his left and right, not from admiration, but from concern.

As he goes, he keeps peeking sideways and at each glance, he quickly looks away again, alarmed. Has he always slumped so badly? He squares his shoulders, and peeks again. His hinder, it's huge, like he's got a caboose under his kilt, and his chin, it's as weak as custard. No, it must just be a trick of the light, his hinder is high and firm, and his chin as hard and curved as granite, he's overstressed and overwrought and he still has all that sugar in his system. His gaze doggedly forward, he continued down the silver funnel, picks up his feet, eager, perhaps for the first time ever, to get away from a mirror.

The urge to glance is getting bigger and bigger, and Hardhands has, before, always vanquished temptation by yielding to it, he looks again, this time to his right. There, he is as lovely as ever, silly silly. He grins confidently at himself, that's much better. He looks behind him and sees, in another mirror, his own back looking further beyond, but he can't see what he's looking at or why.

Back to the slog, and the left is still bugging him, he's seeing flashes out of the corner of his eye, and he just can't help it, he must look: his eyes, they are sunken like marbles into his face, hollow as a sugar skull, his skin tightly pulled, painted with garish red cheekbones. Blackened lips pull back from grayish teeth–his pearly white teeth!–he chatters those pearly whites together, his bite is firm and hard. He looks to the right and sees himself, as he should be.

Now he knows, don't look to the left, keep to the right and keep focused, the left is a mirage, the right is reality. The left side is a horrible joke and the right side is true, but even as he, increasing his steps to almost a run (will this damn hallway never end?), the Voice of Vanity in his head is questioning that assertion. Perhaps the right side is the horrible joke, and the left side the truth, perhaps he has been blind to his own flaws, perhaps–

This time: he is transfixed at the image which stares back, as astonished as he is: he's an absolute wreck. His hair is still and brittle, hanging about his knobby shoulders like salted sea grass. His ice blue eyes look cloudy, and the thick black lines drawn about them serve only to sink them deeper into his skull. Scars streak lividly across his cheeks. Sunken chest and tattoos faded into blue and green smudges, illegible on slack skin. He's too horrified to seek reassurance in the mirror now behind him, he's transposed on the horror before him: the horror of his own inevitable wreckage and decay. The longer he stares the more hideous he becomes. The image blurs for a moment, and then blood blooms in his hair, and dribbles from his gaping lips, his shoulders are scratched and smudged with black, his eyes starting from his skull. He is surrounded by swirling snow, flecks of which sputter on his eyelashes, steam as they touch his skin. The shaft of an arrow protrudes from his throat.

"Oh how bliss to me," the Death's Head croaks, each word a bubble of blood.

With a shout, Hardhands raises his right fist and punches. His fist meets the glass with a nauseous jolt of pain that rings all the way down to his toes. The glass bows under his blow but doesn't crack. He hits again, his corpse reels back, clutching itself with claw-like hands. The mirror refracts into a thousand diamond shards, and Hardhands throws up his other arm to ward off glass and blood. When he drops his shield, the mirrors and their Awful Reflection are gone.

He stands on the top of stairs, looking out over a tumultuous vista: there's a stage with feathered denizens dancing the hootchy-coo. Behind the hootchie-coochers, a band plays a ferocious double-time waltz. Couples slide and twist and turn to the musick, their feet flickering so quickly they spark. The scene is much like the scene he left behind at the Blue Duck, only instead of great big hair, there are great big horns, instead of sweeping skirts there are sweeping wings, instead of smoke there is coldfire. The musick is loud enough to liquefy his skull, he can barely think over its howling sweep.

The throng below whirls about in confusion—denizens, demons, egregores, servitors—was that a Bilskinir-Blue Bulk he saw over there at the bar, tusks a-gleaming, Butler Paimon on his damn night-off? No matter even if it is Paimon, no holler for help from Hardhands, oh no. Paimon would have to help him out, of course, but Paimon would tell the Pontifexa for sure, for Paimon, in addition to being the Butler of Bilskinir, is a suck-up. No thanks, our hero is doing just fine on his own.

A grip pulls at Hardhands' soft hand, he looks down into the wizened grinning face of a monkey. Hardhands tries to yank from the grasp, the monkey has pretty good pull, which he puts into gear with a yank, that our hero has little choice but to follow. A bright red cap shaped like a flower pot is affixed to Sieur Simian's head by a golden cord, and he's surprisingly good at the upright; his free hand waves a path through the crowd, pulling Hardhands behind like a toy.

The dancers slide away from the monkey's push, letting Hardhands and his guide through their gliding. By the band, by the fiddler, who is sawing away at his fiddle as though each note was a gasp of air and he a suffocating man, his hair flying with sweat, his face burning with concentration. Towards a flow of red velvet obscuring a doorway, and through the doorway into sudden hush, the cessation of the slithering music leaving sudden silence in Hardhands' head.

Now he stands on a small landing, overlooking a crowded room. The Great Big Horns and Very Long Claws and etc. are alert to something sitting upon a dais at the far end of the room. Hardhands follows their attention and goes cold all the way to his bones.

Upon the dais is a table. Upon the table is a cage. Within the cage: Tiny Doom.

VIII: Cash & Carry

The bidding has already started. A hideous figure our hero recognizes as Zigurex the Avatar of Agony is flipping it out with a dæmon whose melty visage and dribbly hair Hardhands does not know. Their paddles are popping up and down, in furious volley to the furious patter of the auctioneer:

". . . unspoiled untouched pure one hundred percent kid-flesh plump and juicy tender and sweet highest grade possible never been spanked whacked or locked in a closet for fifty days with no juice no crackers no light fed on honey dew and chocolate sauce . . ."

(Utter lie, Tiny Doom is in a cheesy noodle phase and if it's not noodles and it's not orange then she ain't gonna eat it, no matter the dire threat.) Tiny Doom is barking, frolicking about the cage happily, she's the center of attention, she's up past her bedtime and she's a *puppy*. It's fun!

The auctioneer is small, delicate and apparently human, although Hardhands is willing to bet that she's probably none of these at all, and she has the patter down: "Oh she's darling oh she's bright she'll fit on your mantel, she'll sleep on your dog-bed, she's compact and cute now, and ah the blood you can breed from her when she's older. What an investment, sell her now, sell her later, you're sure to repay your payment a thousand times over and a free Pig as garnish can you beat the deal–and see how bright she does bleed."

The minion hovering above the cage displays a long length of silver tipped finger and then flicks downward. Tiny Doom yelps, and the rest of the patter is lost in Hardhands' roar as he leaps forward, pushing spectators aside: "THAT IS MY WIFE!"

His leap is blocked by bouncers, who thrust him backwards, but not far. Ensues: rumpus, with much switching and swearing and magickal sparkage. Hardhands may have Words of Power, and a fairly Heavy Fist for one so fastidious but the bouncers have Sigils of Impenetrableness or at least Hides of Steel, and one of them has three arms, and suction cups besides.

"THAT IS MY WIFE!" Hardhands protests again, now pinned. "I demand that you release her to me."

"It's careless to let such a tempting small morsel wander the streets alone, your grace." Madam Rose cocks her head, her stiff wire headdress jingling, and the bouncers release Hardhands.

He pats his hair; despite the melee, still massively piled, thanks to Paimon's terrifically sticky hair pomade. The suction cups have left little burning circles on his chest and his bare toes feel a bit tingly from connecting square with someone's tombstone-hard teeth, but at least he solaces in the fact that one of the bouncers is dripping whitish ooze from puffy lips and the other won't be breeding children anytime soon; just as hard a kick, but much more squishy. The room's a wreck, too, smashed chairs, crumpled paper, spilled popcorn, oh dear, too bad.

"She's my wife to be, as good as is my wife, and I want her back." He makes movement towards the cage, which is now terribly quiet, but the bouncers still bar the way.

Zigurex upsteps himself, then, looming over Hardhands who now wishes he had been more insistent about the boots: "Come along with the bidding; it's not all night, you see, the tide is rising and the magick will soon sail."

The other dæmon, who is both squishy and scaly, bubbles his opinion, as well. At least Hardhands assumes it is his opinion, impossible to understand his blubbering, some obscure dialect of Barbarick, or maybe just a very bad accent, anyway who cares what he has to say anyway, not Hardhands, not at all.

"There is no bidding, she's not for sale, she belongs to me, and Pig, too, and we are leaving," he says.

"Do you bid?" Madam Rose asks.

"No I do not bid. I do not have to bid. She is my wife."

"One hundred fifty!" Zigurex says, last-ditch.

The Fishy Thing counters the offer with a saliva spray glug.

"He offers two hundred," says Madam Rose, "What do you offer?"

"Two hundred!" says Hardhands, outraged. "I've paid two hundred for a pot of lip rouge. She's worth a thousand if she's worth a diva—"

Which is exactly of course the entirely wrong thing to say but his outrage has gotten the better of his judgment, which was already impaired by the outrage of being manhandled like a commoner to begin with, and which also might not have been the best even before then.

Madam Rose smiles. Her lips are sparkly pink and her teeth are sparkly black. "One thousand divas, then, for her return! Cash only. Good night good night and come again!" She claps her hands, and the bouncers start to press the disappointed bidders into removing.

"Now look here—" says Hardhands. "You can't expect me to buy my own wife, and even if you could expect me to buy my own wife, I won't. I insist that you hand her over right this very second and impede me no longer."

"Is that so?" Madam Rose purrs. The other bidders retreat easily, perhaps they have a sense of where this is all going and decide it's wise to get out of the way whilst there is still a way to get out of. Even Sieur Squishy and Zigurex go, although not without several smoldering backways looks on the part of the Avatar of Agony, obviously a sore loser. Madam Rose sits herself down upon a velvet covered chair, and waves Hardhands to do the same, but he does not. A majordomo has uprighted the brazier and repaired the smoldering damage, decanted tea into a brass teapot and set upon a round brass tray. Madam Rose drops sugar cubes into two small glasses and pours over: spicy cinnamon, tangy orange.

Hardhands ignores the tea; peers into the cage to access damage.

"Pig has a tummy ache, and wants to go home, Bwannie." The fat little lip is trembling and despite himself, Hardhands is overwhelmed by the tide of adorableness, that he should, being a first rate magician and poet, be inoculated against. She is so like her mother, oh his darling sister, sometimes it makes him want to cry.

He retreats into gruff. "Ayah, so well, Pig should not have had so much candy. And nor should Pig have wandered off alone."

"He is bad," agrees Doom. "Very bad."

"Sit tight and do not cry. We will go home soon. Ayah?"

"Ayah." She sniffs, but holds the snuffle, little soldier.

Madam Rose offers Hardhands a seat, which he does not sit upon, and a glass, which he waves away, remembering anew the Pontifexa's advice, and also not trusting Madam's sparkle grin. He's heard of the dives where they slide sleep into your drink; you gulp down happily and wake up six hours later minus all you hold dear and a splitting headache, as well. Or worse still, ginjoints that sucker you into one little sip, and then you have such a craving that you must have more and more, but no matter how much you have, it shall never be enough. He'll stay dry and alert, thank you.

"I have no time for niceties, or social grace," he says, "I will take my wife and pig, and leave."

"One thousand divas is not so great a sum to the Pontifexa's grandson," Madam Rose observes. "And it's only right that I should recoup some of my losses—look here, I shall have to redecorate, and fashionable taste, as your grace knows, is not cheap."

"I doubt there is enough money in the world to buy you good taste, madama, and why should I pay for something that is mine?"

"Now who owns who, really? *She* is the Heir to the House Haðraaða, and one day she'll be Pontifexa. *You* are just the boy who does. By rights all of us, including you, belong to her, in loyalty and in love. I do wish you would sit, your grace." Madam Rose pats the pillow beside her, which again he ignores.

This statement sets off a twinge of rankle because it is true. He answers loftily, "We are all the Pontifexa's obedient servants, and are happy to bend ourselves to her Will, and her Will in the matter of her Heir is clear. I doubt that she would be pleased to know of the situations of this night."

Madam Rose sets her red cup down. An ursine-headed minion offers her a chocolate, gently balanced between two pointy bear-claws. She opens red lips, black teeth, long red throat and swallows the chocolate without a chew.

"I doubt," she says, "that the Pontifexa shall be pleased at tonight's situation at all. I do wish you would sit, your grace. I feel so small, and you so tall, so high above. And do sample, your grace. I assure you that my candy has no extra spice to it, just wholesome goodness you will find delicious. You have my word upon it."

Hardhands sits, and takes the chocolate he is offered. He's already on the train bound for Purgelandia, he might as well make the journey worth the destination. The Minion twinkles azure bear eyes at him. Bears don't exactly have the right facial arrangement to smirk, but this bear is making a fine attempt, and Hardhands thinks what a fine rug Sieur Oso would make, stretched out before a peaceful fire. In the warmth of his mouth, the chocolate explodes into glorious peppery chocolate yum. For a second he closes his eyes against the delicious darkness, all his senses receding into sensation of pure bliss dancing on his tongue.

"It is good chocolate, is it not?" Madam Rose asks. "Some say such chocolate should be reserved for royalty and the Goddess. But we do enjoy it, no?"

"What do you want?" Hardhands asks, and they both know that he doesn't just mean for Tiny Doom.

"Putting aside, for the moment, the thousand divas, I want nothing more to be of aid to you, your grace, to be your humble servant. It is not what I may want from you but what you can want from me."

"That I have told you."

"Just that?"

In the cage, Tiny Doom is silent and staring, she may be a screamer, but she does, thankfully, know when to keep her trap shut.

"I can offer you no other assistance? Think on it, your grace.

You are an adept, and you traffic with denizens of the deep, through the force of your Will. I am not an adept, I also have traffic with those same denizens."

The second chocolate tangs his tongue with the sour-sweet brightness of lime. "Contrary to all laws of Goddess and nature," he says thickly, when the brilliant flavour has receded enough to allow speech. "Your traffic is obscene. It is not the same."

"I didn't say it was the same, I said we might compliment each other, rather than compete. Do you not get tired of your position, your grace? You are so close, and yet so far. The Pontifexa's brightest boy, but does she respect you? Does she trust you? This little girl, is she not the hitch in your git-along, the sand in your shoe? Leave her with me, and she'll never muss your hair again, or wrinkle your cravat."

"I don't recall inviting you to comment upon my personal matters," says Hardhands, a la prince. "And I don't recall offering you my friendship either."

"I cry your pardon, your grace. I only offer my thoughts in the hope—"

He's tired of the game now, if he had the thousand divas he'd fork them over, just to be quit of the entire situation, it was fun, it was cool, it's not fun it's not cool, he's bored, the sugar is drilling a spike through his forehead and he's done.

"I'll write you a draft, and you'll take it, and we shall leave, and that's the end of the situation," Hardhands says loftily.

Madam Rose sighs, and sips her tea. Another sigh, another sip.

"I'm sorry your grace, but if you cannot pay, then I must declare your bid null, and reopen the auction. Please understand my position. It is, and has always been, the policy of this House to operate on a cash basis; I'm sure you understand why—taxes, a necessary evil, but perhaps more evil than necessary," Madam Rose smiles at him, and sips again before going on. "My reputation rests upon my policies, and that I apply them equally to all. Duque of Califa or the lowliest servitor, all are equal within my walls. So you see, if I allow you license I have refused others, how shall it appear then?"

"Smart," answers our hero. "Prudent. Wise."

Madam Rose laughs. "Would that others might consider my actions in that light, but I doubt their charity. No, I'm sorry, your grace. I have worked hard for my name. I cannot give it up, not for you or for anyone."

She puts her tea glass down and clicks her tongue, a sharp snap that brings Sieur Bear to her side. "The Duque has decided to withdraw his bid; please inform Zigurex that his bid is accepted and he may come and claim his prize."

Hardhands looks at Doom in her cage, her wet little face peers through the bars. She smiles at him, she's scared but she has confidence that Bwannie will save her, Bwannie loves her. Bwannie has a sense of déjà vu; hasn't he been here before, why is it his fate to always give in to her, little monster? Tiny Doom, indeed.

"What do you want?" he repeats.

"Well," Madam Rose says brightly. "Now that you mention it. The Pontifexina is prime, oh that's true, but I know one more so. More mature, more valuable, more ready."

Now it's Hardhands' turn to sigh, which he does, and sip, wetting parched throat, now not caring if the drink be drugged, or not. "You'll let her go? Return her safe and sound?"

"Of course, your grace. You have my word on it."

"Not a hair on her head or a drop from her veins or a tear from her eye? Not a scab, or nail, or any part that might be later used against her? Completely whole? Untouched, unsmudged, no tricks?"

"As you say."

Hardhands puts his glass down, pretending resignation. "All right then. You have a deal." Of course he don't really give in, but he's assessed that perhaps it's better to get Doom out of the way. He can play rough enough if it's only his own skin involved, but why take the chance of her collateral damage? When she's out of the way, he calculates, and Madam Rose's guard is down, then we'll see, oh yes, we'll see.

Madam Rose's shell-white hand goes up to her lips, shading them briefly behind two slender fingers. Then the fingers flip down and flick a shard of spinning coldfire towards him. Hardhands recoils, but too late. The airy kiss zings through the air like an arrow of outrageous fortune and smacks him right in the middle of Death in Bloom. The kiss feels like a kick to the head, and our hero and his chair flip backwards, the floor rising to meet his fall, but not softly. The impact sends his bones jarring inside his flesh, and the jarring is his only movement for the sigil has left him shocked and paralyzed.

He can't cry out, he can't flinch, he can only let the pain flood down his palate and into his brain, in which internal shouting and swearing is making up for external silence. He can't close his eyes either, but he closes his outside vision and brings into inside focus the bright sharp words of a sigil that should suck all the energy from Madam Rose's sigil, blow it into a powder-puff of oblivion.

The sigil burns bright in Hardhands' eyes, but it is also trapped and cannot get free. It sparks and wheels, and he desperately tries to tamp it out, dumping colder, blacker sigils on top its flare, trying to fling it outward and away, but it's stuck firmly inside his solar plexus, he can fling it nowhere. It's caught in his craw like a fish bone, and he's choking but he can't choke because he cannot move. The sigil's force billows through him: it is twisting his entrails into knots, his bones into bows, it's flooding him with a fire so bright that it's black, with a fire so cold that it burns and burns and burns, his brain boils and then: nothing.

IX: THY BAITED HOOK

Here is Hardhands, returning to the Waking World. His blood is mud within his veins, he can barely suck air through stifled lungs and there's a droning in his ears, no not droning, humming, Tiny Doom:

"Kick her bite her that's the way I'll spite her! Kick her bite her that's the way I'll spite her! Kick her bite her that's the way I'll spite her!"

The view aloft is raven-headed angels, with ebony black wings swooping loops of brocade across a golden ceiling. Then the view aloft is blocked by Tiny Doom's face; she still has the sugar mustache, and her kohl has blurred, cocooning her blue eyes in smoky blackness. Her hat is gone.

"Don't worry, Bwannie," she pats his stiff face with a sticky hand, "Pig will save us."

His brain heaves but the rest of him remains still. The frame of his body has never before been so confining. Diligent practice has made stepping his mind from his flesh an easy accomplishment, are there not times when a magician's Will needs independence from his blood and bones? But never before has he been stuck, nor run up against someone else's sigils as harder and more impenetrable than his own. Lying in the cage of his own flesh he is feeling helpless, and tiny, and it's a sucky feeling, not at all suited to his stature of Pontifexa's grandson, first rate magician and—

"I will bite you," says Doom.

"I doubt that," is the gritty answer, a deep rumble: "My skin is thick as steel and your teeth will break."

"Ha! I am a shark and I will bite you."

"Not if I bite you first, little lovely, nip your sweet tiny fingers, crunch crunch each one, oh so delicious, what a snack. Come here, little morsel."

The weight of Tiny Doom suddenly eases off his chest, but not without kicking and gripping, holding on to him in a vise-like grip, oww, her fingers dig like nails into his leg but to no avail. Tiny Doom is wrenched off of him, and in the process he's wrenched side-ways, now he's got a nice view of the grassy floor, a broken teapot, and, just on the edge, someone's feet. The feet are shod in garish two-tone boots: magenta upper and orange toe-cap. Tiny Doom screams like a rabbit, high and horrible.

"You'll bruise her," says a voice from above the feet. "And then the Pontifexa will be chuffed."

"I shall not hurt her one jot if she's a good girl, but she should shut her trap, a headache I am getting."

Good for her, Tiny Doom does not shut her trap, she opens her trap wider and shoots the moon, with a piercing squeal that stabs into Hardhands' unprotected ears like an awl, slicing all the way down to the center of his brain. With a smack, the shriek abruptly stops.

Two pretty little bare feet drift into Hardhands' view, "Stop it you two. She must be returned in perfect condition, an' I get my deposit back. It's only the boy that the Pontifexa wants rid of; the girl is still her heir. Leave her alone, or I shall feed you both into my shredder. Chop chop. The guests are waiting and he must be prepared."

"She squirms," complains the Minion.

Madam Rose, sternly: "You, little madam, stop squirming. You had fun being a puppy, and cupcakes besides, and soon you shall be going home to your sweet little bed. How sad Grandmamma and Paimon shall be if I must give them a bad report of your behavior."

Sniffle, sniff. "But I want Bwannie."

"Never you mind Bwannie for now, here have a Choco-Sniff, and here's one for Pig, too."

Sniff, sniffle. "Pig don't like Choco-Sniffs."

Hardhands kicks, but it's like kicking air, he can feel the movement in his mind, but his limbs stay stiff and locked. And then his mind recoils: What did Madam Rose say about the Pontifexa? Did he hear a-right? Deposit? Report?

"Here then is a jack snap for Pig. Be a good girl, eat your candy and then you shall kiss Bwannie good-bye."

Whine: "I want to go with Bwannie!"

"Now, now," Madam Rose's cheery tone tingles with irritation, but she's making a good show of not annoying Tiny Doom into another session of shrieking. "Now, Bwannie must stay here, and you must go home—do not start up with the whining again, it's hardly fitting for the Pontifexa's heir to cry like a baby, now is it? Here, have another Choco-Sniff."

Then more harshly, "You two, get the child ready to be returned and the boy prepared. I shall be right back."

The pretty feet float from Hardhands' view and a grasp attaches to Hardhands' ankle. Though his internal struggle is mighty, externally he puts up no fuss at all. Flipped over by rough hands, he sees above him the sharp face of a Sylph, pointy eyes, pointy nose, pointy chin. Hands are fumbling at his kilt buckles; obscurely he notices that the Sylph has really marvelous hair, it's the color of fresh caramel and it smells, Hardhands notices, as the Sylph bends over to nip at his neck, like new-mown grass. A tiny jolt of pretty pain, and warm wetness dribbles down his neck.

"Ahhh . . ." the Sylph sighs. "You should taste this, first rate knock-back."

"Madama said be nice."

"I am being nice, as nice as pie, as nice as he is. Nice and sweet." The Sylph licks at Hardhands' neck again; its tongue is scrape-y, like a cat's, and it hurts in a strangely satisfying way. "Sweet sweet darling boy. He is going to bring our garden joy. What a deal she has made. Give the girl, but keep the boy, he's useful to us, even if she don't want him anymore. A good trick he'll turn for Madama. Bright boy."

Hardhands is hoisted aloft, demon claws at his ankles and his wrists, slinging him like a side of beef on the way to the barbeque pit. His eyes are slitted open, his head dangling downward, he can see only a narrow slice of floor bobbing by. A carpet patterned with entwined snakes, battered black and red tiles, white marble veined with gold. He's watching all this, with part of attention, but mainly he's running over and over again what Madam Rose had said about the Pontifexa. Was it possible to be true? Did Grandmamma set him up? Sell him out? Was this all a smoke-screen to get him out of her hair, away from her treasure? He cannot believe it, he will not believe it, it cannot be true.

Rough movement drops Hardhands onto the cold floor, and metal clenches his ankles. The bracelets bite into his flesh as he is hoisted aloft, and all the blood rushes to his head in an explosion of pressure. For a second, even his slit of sight goes black, but then, just as suddenly, he finds he can open his eyes all the way. He rolls eyeballs upward, and seeing retreating minion backs. He rolls eyes downward and sees polished marble floor and the tangled drape of his own hair, Paimon's pomade having finally given up. The gryves are burning bright pain into his ankles, and he's swaying slightly from some invisible airflow, but the movement is kind of soothingly and his back feels nice and stretched out. If it weren't for being the immobilization, and obvious bait, hanging upside down could be kind of fun.

Our hero tries to wiggle, but can't, tries to jiggle but is still stuck. He doesn't dare try another sigil and risk blowing his brains out, and without the use of his muscles he cannot gymnastic himself free. He closes his internal eyes, slips his consciousness into darkness, and concentrates. His Will pushes and pushes against the pressure that keeps him contained, focuses into a single point that must burn through. After a second, a minute, an eternity, all bodily sensation—the burn of the gyres, the stretch of his back, the pressure of his bladder, the breeze on his face—slips away, and his Will floats alone on the Current.

Away from the strictures of his body, Hardhands' consciousness can take any form that he cares to mold it to, or no form at all, a spark of himself drifting on the Currents of Elsewhere. But such is his fondness for his own form, even Elsewhere, that when he steps lightly from the flesh hanging like a side of beef, he coalesces into a representation of himself, in every way identical to his corporeal form, although with lip rouge that will not smudge, and spectacularly elevated hair.

On Elsewhere feet, Hardhands' fetch turns to face its meaty shell, and is rather pleased with the view; even dangling upside down, he looks pretty darn good. Elsewhere, the sigil that has caged Hardhands' motion is clearly visible as a pulsating net of green and gold, interwoven at the intercises with splotches of pink. A Coarctation Sigil, under normal circumstances no stronger than pie, but given magnitude by the height of the Current, and Hardhands' starchy condition. The fetch, however, is not limited by starch, and the Current just feeds its strength. Dismantling the constraint is the work of a matter of seconds, and after the fetch slides back into its shell, it's a mere bagatelle to contort himself down and free.

Casting free of the gyres with a splashy Barbarick command, Hardhands rubs his ankles, and then stands on tingly feet. Now that he has the leisure to inspect the furnishings, he sees there are no furnishings to inspect because the room, while sumptuously paneled in gorgeous tiger-eye maple, is empty other than a curvy red velvet chase. The only ornamentations are the jingly chains dangling from the ceiling. The floor is bare stone, cold beneath his bare feet. And now, he notices that the flooring directly under the dangle is dark and stained, with something that he suspects is a combination of blood, sweat and tears.

Places to go and praterhuman entities to fry, no time to linger to discover the truth of his suspicions. Hardhands turns to make his exit through the sole door, only to find that the door is gone, and in its place, a roiling black Vortex, as black and sharp as the Vortex that he himself had cut out of the Aeyther, only hours before. He is pushed back by the force of the Vortex, which is spiraling outward, not inward, thus indicating that Something is coming, rather than trying to make him go.

The edges of the Vortex glow hot-black, the wind that the Vortex is creating burns his skin; he shields his eyes with his hand, and tries to stand upright, but his tingly feet cannot hold against the force, and he falls. The Vortex widens, like a surprised eye, and a slit of light appears pupil-like in its darkness. The pupil widens, becomes a pupae, a cocoon, a shell, an acorn, an egg, growing larger and larger and larger until it fills the room with unbelievable brightness, with a scorching heat that is hotter than the sun, bright enough to burn through Hardhands' shielding hand. Hardhands feels his skin pucker, his eyes shrivel, his hair start to smolder, and then just as he is sure he is about to burst into flames, the light shatters like an eggshell, and Something has arrived.

Recently, Hardhands' Invocations have grown quite bold, and, after some bitter tooth and nails, he's pulled a few large fish into his circle. But those are as like to. This as a fragment of beer bottle is to a faceted diamond. He knows, from the top of his pulsating head to the tips of his quivering toes that this is no servitor, no denizen, no elemental. Nothing this spectacular can be called, corralled or compelled. This apparition cannot be nothing but the highest of the high, the blessed of the blessed: the Goddess Califa herself.

How to describe what Hardhands sees? Words are too simple, they cannot do justice to Her infinite complexity, she's Everything and Nothing, both fractured and whole. His impressions are blurred and confused, but here's a try. Her hair is ruffled black feathers, it is slickery green snakes, it is as fluffy and lofty as frosting. Her eyes—one, two, three, four, maybe five—are as round and polished as green apples, are long tapered crimson slits, they are as flat white as sugar. She's as narrow as nightfall, She's as round as winter, She's as tall as moonrise, She's shorter than love.

Her feet do not crush the little flowers, She is divine, She is fantastic.

She simply is.

Hardhands has found his footing only to lose it again, falling to his knees before her, her fresh red smile as strong as a kick to the head, to the heart. Hardhands is smitten, no not smitten, he's smote, from the tingly tingly top of his reeling head to the very tippy tip of his tingling toes. He's freezing and burning, he's alive, he's dying, he's dead. He's hypmooootized. He gapes at the Goddess, slack-jawed and tight-handed, wanting nothing more than to reach out and grasp at her perfection, bury himself in the ruffle of her feathers. Surely a touch of Her hand would spark such fire in him that he would catch alight and perish in a blaze of exquisite agony but it would be worth it, oh it would be worth every cinder.

The Goddess's mouth opens, with a flicker of a velvet tongue and the glitter of a double row of white teeth. The Barbarick that flows from Her mouth in a sparkly ribband is as crisp and sweet as a summer wine, it slithers over Hardhands' flushed skin, sliding into his mouth, his eyes, his ears, and filling him with a dark sweet rumble.

"Georgiana's toy," the Goddess purrs. He didn't see Her move but now She is poured over the chaise like silk, and the bear-head minion is offering bowls of snacks, ice cream sundaes, and magazines. "Chewable and sweet, ah lovely darling yum."

Hardhands has forgotten Georgiana, he's forgotten Tiny Doom, he's forgotten Madam Rose, he's forgotten himself, he's forgotten his exquisite manners—no not entirely, even the Goddess's splendor cannot expunge good breeding. He toddles up onto sweaty feet, and sweeps the floor with his curtsy.

"I am your obedient servant, your grace," he croaks.

The Goddess undulates a languid finger and he finds himself following Her beckon, not that he needs to be beckoned, he can barely hold himself aloof, wants nothing more than to throw himself forward and be swallowed alive. The Goddess spreads Her wings, Her arms, Her legs, and he falls into Her embrace, the prickle of the feathers closing over his bare skin, electric and hot.

X: Doom Acts

Here is Tiny Doom howling like a banshee, a high pitched shriek that usually results in immediate attention to whatever need she is screaming for: more pudding, longer story, hotter bath, bubbles. The Minion whose arm she is slung under must be pitch deaf because her shrieks have not the slightest impact upon him. He continues galumphing along, whistling slightly, or perhaps that is just the breeze of his going, which is a rapid clip.

She tries teeth, her fall-back weapon and always effective, even on Paimon whose blue skin is surprisingly delicate. The Minion's hide is as chewy as rubber and it tastes like salt licorice. Spitting and coughing, Tiny Doom gives up on the bite. Kicking has no effect other than to bruise her toes and her arms are too pinned for hitting, and, down the stairs they go, bump bump, Bwannie getting further and further away. Pig is jolting behind them, she's got a grip on one dangly ear, but that's all, and his bottom is hitting each downward stump, but he's too soft to thump.

An outside observer might think that Doom is wailing for more candy, or perhaps is just over-tired and up past her bedtime. Madam Rose certainly thought that her commotion was based in over-tiredness, plus a surfeit of sugar, and the Bouncer thinks it's based in spoiled-ness, plus a surfeit of sugar, but they are both wrong. Sugar is Doom's drug of choice, she's not allowed it officially, but unofficially she has her ways (she knows exactly in what drawer the Pontifexa's secretary keeps his stash of Crumbly Crem-O's and Jiffy-Ju's, and if that drawer is empty, Relais can be relied upon to have a box of bon-bons hidden from Hardhands in the bottom of his wardrobe), and so her system can tolerate massive quantities of the stuff before hyper-activity and urpyness sets in.

No. She is wailing because every night, at tuck-in time, after the Pontifexa has kissed her, and kissed Pig and together they have said their prayers, then Paimon sits on the edge of Tiny Doom's big white frilly bed and tells her a story. It's a different story every night, Paimon's supply of fabulosity being apparently endless, but always with the same basic theme:

Kid is told what To Do.

Kid does Not Do what Kid is told To Do.

Kid gets into Bad Trouble with various Monsters.

Kid gets Eaten.

The End, yes you may have one more drink of water, and then no more excuses and it's lights out, and to sleep. Now.

Tiny Doom loves these stories, whose Directives and Troubles are always endlessly inventively different, but which always turn out the same way: with a Giant Monstrous Burp. She knows that Paimon's little yarns are for fun only, that Kids do not really get eaten when they do not do what they are told, for she does not do what she is told all the time, and she's never been eaten. Of course, no one would dare eat her anyway, she's the Heir to the Pontifexa, and has Paimon and Pig besides. Paimon's stories are just stories, made to deliciously shiver her skin, so that afterwards she lies in the haze of the nightlight, cuddled tight to Pig's squishiness, and knows that she is safe.

But now, tonight, she's seen the gleam in Madam Rose's eye and seen the look she gave her minions and Tiny Doom knew instantly that Bwannie is in Big Trouble. This is not bedtime, there is no Paimon, and no nightlight, and no drink of water. This is all true Big Trouble and Tiny Doom knows exactly where Big Trouble ends. Now she is scared, for Bwannie and for herself, and even for Pig, who would make a perfect squishy demon dessert.

Thus, shrieking.

"BWWWWWWWWWWWWANNNNIE!" Doom cries, "BWAAANIE!"

They jump the last step, Tiny Doom jolting bony hip, oww, and then round a corner. Doom sucks in the last useless shriek. Her top half is hanging half over the servitor's shoulder and her dangling down head is starting to feel tight, plus the shrieking has left her breathless, so for a few seconds she gulps in air. Gulping, her nose running yucky yuck. She wiggles, whispers, and lets go of Pig.

He plops down onto the dirty floor, hinder up and snout down, and then they round another corner and he's gone.

She lifts her head, twisting her neck, and there's the hairy interior of a pointy ear.

She shouts: "HEY MINION!"

"I ain't listening," says the Minion. "You can shout all you want, but I ain't listening. Madam told me not to listen and I ain't."

"I GOTTA PEE."

"You gotta wait," the Minion says, "You be home soon and then you can pee in your own pot. And you ain't gotta shout in my ear. You make my brain hurt, you loudness little bit, you."

"I GOTTA PEE NOW!" Doom, still shouting, anyway, just in case there are noises behind them. "I'M GONNA PEE NOW!"

The Minion stops and shifts Tiny Doom around like a sack full of flour, and breathes into her face. "You don't pee on me, loudness."

Like Paimon, the Minion has tusks and pointy teeth but Paimon's tusks are polished white and his teeth sparkle like sunlight, and his breath smells always of cloves. The Minion's tusks are rubbed and worn, his teeth yucky yellow and he's got bits of someone caught between them.

Doom wrinkles her nose and holds her breath and says in a whine: "I can't help it, I have to go, my hot chocolate is all done." Her feet are dangling and she tries to turn the wiggle into a kick, but she can't quite reach the Minion's soft bits, and her purple slippers wiggle at empty air.

"You pee on me and I snack you up, nasty baby." The minion crunches spiny fangs together, clashing sparks. "Delish!"

"You don't dare!" says Tiny Doom stoutly. "I am the Pontifexina and my grandmamma would have your knobby hide if you munch me!!"

"An' I care, little princess, if you piss me wet, I munch you dry—"

"⌒☞ ☜ e𝓇 𝗑 ▽ 𝗑" whispers Tiny Doom and spits. She's got a good wad going, and it hits the Minion right on the snout.

The Minion howls and drops her. She lands on stingy sleepy feet, falls over, and then scrambles up, stamping. The Minion is also stamping, and holding his hairy hands to his face; under his clawing fingers smoke is steaming. He careens this way and that, Doom dodging around his staggers, and then she scoots by him, and back the way they had just come.

Tiny Doom runs as fast as her fat little legs will run, her heart pounding because she is now in Big Trouble, and she knows if the Minion quits dancing and starts chasing, she's going to be Eaten too. The hot word she spit burned her tongue and that hurts too, and where's Pig? She goes around another corner, thinking she'll see the stairs that they came down, but she doesn't, she sees another long hallway. She turns around to go back, and then the Minion blunders towards her, his face a melt-y mess, and she reverses, speedily.

"I dance around in a ring and suppose and the secret sits in the middle and knows." She sings very quietly to herself as she runs.

Carpet silent under her feet; a brief glimpse of another running Doom reflected off a glass curio cabinet; by a closed door, the knob turns but the door will not open. She can feel the wind of closing in beating against her back, but she keeps going. The demon is shouting mean things at her, but she keeps going.

"You dance around in a ring and suppose and the secret sits in the middle and knows." A door opens and a were-flamingo trips out, stretching its longneck out; Doom dodges around its spindly legs, ignoring yelps. Ahead, more stairs, and there she aims, having no other options, can't go back and there's no where to go sideways.

At the top of the stairs, Doom pauses and finally looks behind. The Minion has wiped most of his melt off, livid red flares burn in his eye sockets and he looks pretty mad. The were-flamingo has halted him, and they are wrangling, flapping wings against flapping ears. The minion is bigger but the were-flamingo has a sharp beak—rapid fire pecking at the minion's head. The minion punches one humongous fist and down the flamingo goes, in a flutter of pink feathers.

"I SNACK YOU, SPITTY BABY!" the Minion howls and other things too mean for Doom to hear.

"We dance around in a ring and suppose and the secret sits in the middle and knows." Doom hoists herself up on the banister, squeezing her tummy against the rail. The banister on the Stairs of Infinite Demonstration, Bilskinir's main staircase, is fully sixty feet long. Many is the time that Doom has swooped down its super-polished length, flying miles through the air, at the end to be received by Paimon's perfect catch. This rail is much shorter, and there's no Paimon waiting, but here we go!

She flings her legs over, and slides off. Down she goes, lickety-split, bumping over splinters, but still getting up a pretty good whoosh. Here comes the demon, waving angry arms, he's too big to slide, so he galumphs down the stairs, clumpty clump, getting closer. Doom hits the end of the banister and soars onward another five feet or so, then ooph, hits the ground, owww. She bounces back upward, and darts through the foyer and into the mudroom beyond, pulling open her pockets as she goes.

Chocosniffs and jacksnaps skitter across the parquet floor, rattling and rolling. Sugarbunnies and beady-eyes, jimjoos and honeybuttons scatter like shot. Good bye crappy candy, good bye yummy candy, good-bye.

"I DANCE AROUND IN A RING AND SUPPOSE AND THE SECRET SITS IN THE MIDDLE AND KNOWS."

Ahead, a big red door, well barred and bolted, but surely leading Out. The bottom bolt snaps back under her tiny fingers, but the chains are too high and tippy-toe, hopping, jumping will not reach them. The Demon is down the stairs, he's still shouting and steaming, and the smell of charred flesh is stinky indeed.

A wall rack hangs by the door, and from coats and cloaks dangle like discarded skins; Doom dives into the folds of cloth and becomes very small and silent. She's a good hider, Tiny Doom, she's learned against the best (Paimon).

Her heart pounds thunder in her ears, and she swallows her panting. When Paimon makes discovery (*if* he makes discovery), it means only bath-time, or mushy peas, or toe-nail clipping. If the demon finds her, Pontifexina or not, it's snicky snack time for sure. She really did have to potty too, pretty bad. She crosses her ankles and jiggles her feet, holding.

In the other room, out of sight, comes yelling, shouting, roaring and then a heavy thud that seems to shake the very walls. The thud reverberates and then fades away.

Silence.

Stillness.

Tiny Doom peeks between the folds. Through the archway she sees rolling candy and part of a sprawled bulk. Then the bulk heaves, hooves kicking. The demon's lungs have re-inflated and he lets out a mighty horrible roar—the nastiest swear word that

Tiny Doom has ever heard. Doom, who had poked her head all the way out for a better view, yanks back, just in time. The Word, roiling like mercury, howls by her, trailing sparks and smelling of shit.

A second roar is gulped off in mid-growl, and turns into a shriek, which is then muffled in thumping and slurping, ripping, and chomping. Doom peeks again: the demon's legs are writhing, wiggling, and kicking. A thick stain spreads through the archway, gooey and green. Tiny Doom wiggles her way out of the velvet and runs happily towards the slurping sound.

XI: Desire Gratified

Inside the Goddess's embrace, Hardhands is dying, he's crying, he's screaming with pleasure, with joy, crying his broken heart out. He's womb-enclosed, hot and smothering, and reduced to his pure essence. He has collapsed to a single piercing pulsing point of pleasure. He has lost himself, but he has found everything else.

And then his ecstasy is interrupted by another piercing sensation: pain. Not the exquisite pain of a well placed needle, or perfectly laid lash, but an ugly pain that gnaws into his pleasurable non-existence in an urgent painful way. He wiggles, tossing, but the pain will not go away, it only gnaws deeper, and with each razor nibble it slices away at his ecstasy. And as he is torn away from the Goddess's pleasure, he is forced back into himself, and the wiggly body-bound part of himself realizes that the Goddess is sucking him out of life. The love-torn spirit part of him does not care. He struggles, trying to dive down deeper into the bottomless divine love, but that gnawing pain is tethering him to the Waking World, and he can't kick it free.

Then the Goddess's attention lifts from him, like a blanket torn away. He lies on the ground, the stones slick and cold against his bare skin. The echo of his loss pounds in his head, farrier-like, stunning him. A shrill noise pierces his agony, cuts through the thunder, a familiar high pitched whine:

"Ya! Ya! Ya!"

His eyes are filled sand; it takes a moment of effort before his nerveless hands can find his face, and knuckle his vision clear. Immediately he sees: Tiny Doom, dancing with the bear headed Minion. Sieur Oso is doing the Mazorca, a dance which requires a great deal of jumping and stamping, and he's got the perfect boots to make the noise, each one as big as a horse's head. Tiny Doom is doing the Ronde-loo, weaving round and round Sieur Oso her circular motion too sick-making for Hardhands to follow.

Then he realizes: no, they are not dancing, Sieur Oso is trying to squash Tiny Doom like a bug, and she, rather than run like a sensible child, is actually taunting him on. Oh Haðraaða!

Dimly Tiny Doom's husband sparks the thought that perhaps he should help her, and he's trying to figure out where his feet are, so as to arise to this duty, when his attention is caught by a whirl, not a whirl, a Vortex the likes of which he has never before seen, a Vortex as black as ink, but streaked hot pink, and furious furious. Though he can see nothing but the cutting blur of the spin, he can feel the force of the fight within; the Goddess is battling it out with something, something strong enough to give her a run for her divas, something tenacious and tough.

"Bwannie! Bwannie!" cries Doom. She is still spinning, and the Minion is starting to look tuckered, his stomps not so stompy anymore, and his jeers turned to huffy puffs. Foam is dribbling from his muzzle, like whipped cream.

Hardhands ignores Tiny Doom.

"Aϖαυντ!" Hardhands grates, trying to throw a Word of encouragement into the mix, to come to his darling's aid. The Word is a strong one, even in his weakened state, but it bounces off the Vortex, harmless, spurned, just as he has been spurned. The Goddess cares nothing for his Hardhands' love, for his desire, he chokes back tears, and staggers to his feet, determined to help somehow, even if he must cast himself into the fire to do so.

Before he can do anything so drastic, there is the enormous sound of suction sucking in. For a split second, Hardhands feels himself go as flat as paper, his lungs suck against his chest, his bones slap into ribbands, his flesh becomes as thin as jerky. The Current pops like a cork, the world re-inflates and Hardhands is round and substantial again, although now truly bereft. The Goddess is gone.

The Vortex has blushed pink now, and its spin is slowing, slower, slower, until it is no longer a Vortex, but a little pink blur, balanced on pointy toes, ears flopping—what the hell? Pig?

He has gone insane, or blind, or both? In one dainty pirouette Pig has soared across the room and latched himself to the Minion's scraggly throat. Suddenly invigorated, Sieur Oso does a pirouette of his own, upward, gurgling.

"What is going on—?" Madam Rose's voice raises high above the mayhem-noises, then it chokes. She has stalled in the doorway, more minions peering from behind her safety. Tiny Doom has now attached to Sieur Oso's hairy ankle and her grip—hands and teeth—are not dislodged by his antic kicking, though whether the minion is now dancing because Tiny Doom is gnawing on his ankle or because his throat is a massive chewy-mess, it's hard to say. Pig disengages from Sieur Oso and leaps to Madam Rose, who clutches him to her bosom in a maternal way, but jerkily, as though she wants less of his love, not more. Her other slaveys have scarpered, and now that the Goddess is gone, Hardhands sees no particular reason to linger either.

He flings one very hard Barbarick word edgewise at the antic bear. Sieur Oso jerks upward, and his surprised head sails backwards, tears through the tent wall, and is gone. Coldfire founts up from the stump of his neck, sizzling and sparky. Hardhands grabs Tiny Doom away from the minion's forward fall, and she grasps onto him monkey-wise, clinging to his shoulders.

"PIG!" she screams, "PIG!"

Madam Rose manages to disentangle Pig, and flings him towards Hardhands and Tiny Doom. Pig sails through the air, his ears like wings, and hits Hardhands' chest with a soggy thud and then tumbles downward. Madam Rose staggers, she is clutching her throat, her hair has fallen down, drippy red. Above her, the tent ceiling is flickering with tendrils of coldfire, it pours down around her like fireworks falling from the sky, sheathing her bones in glittering flickering flesh. The coldfire has spread to the ceiling now, scorching the raven angels, and the whole place is going to go: coldfire doesn't burn like non-magickal fire, but it is hungry and does consume, and Hardhands has had enough consumption for tonight. Hefting Tiny Doom up higher on his shoulder, he turns about to retreat (run away).

"PIG! PIG!" Tiny Doom beats at his head as he ducks under the now flickering threshold, "PIG!"

The coldfire has raced across the roof beyond him and the antechamber before him is a heaving weaving maelstrom of magick, the Current bubbling and sucking, oh it's a shame to let such yummy power go to waste, but now is perhaps not the time to further test his control. Madam Rose staggers out of the flames, the very air around her is bubbling and cracking, spitting Abyss through cracks in the Current, black tendrils that coil and smoke.

Tiny Doom, still screaming: "PIG!"

Hardhands jumps and weaves through the tentacles of flame, flinging banishings as he goes, and the tendrils snap away. He's not going to stop for Pig, Pig is on his own, Hardhands can feel the Current boiling, in a moment there will be too much magick for the space to contain, there is going to be a giant implosion and he's had enough implosions for one night, too. Through the dining room they run, scattering cheese platters, waiters, cocktails and conservationists, crunching crackers underfoot, knocking down a minion with a tray of . . . there, open veranda doors, and beyond those doors, the sparkle of hurdy-gurdy lights. Doom clinging to his head like a pinchy hat, he leaps over the bar, through breaking bottles and scattered ice, and through the doors, into blessed cool air.

The sky above turns sheet white, and the ground shifts beneath his feet in a sudden bass roll. He sits down hard in the springy grass, lungs gasping. Tiny Doom collapses from his grasp and rolls like a little barrel across the springy turf. The stars wink back in, as though a veil has been drawn back, and suddenly Hardhands is limp with exhaustion. The Current is gone. And so, he realizes, when he turns his tired head and looks backwards is Madam Rose's.

Well, good riddance, good bye, adios, farewell. From the space where Madam Rose's used to be, Pig tippy-dances, pirouetting towards Doom, who receives him with happy cries of joy.

Hardhands lies on the grass and stares upward at the starry

sky, and he moves his head back and forth, drums his feet upon the ground, wiggles his fingers just because he can. He feels drained and empty, and sore as hell. The grass is crispy cool beneath his bare sweaty back, and he could just lie there forever. Behind the relief of freedom, however, there's a sour sour taste.

He was set up. The whole evening was nothing but a gag. His grandmother, his darling sweet grandmother whom he did not kill out of love, respect and honour, whom he pulled back from the brink of assassination because he held her so dear, his grandmamma sold him to Madam Rose.

Him, Hardhands, sold him!

The Pontifexa has played them masterfully: Relais' incompetence, Tiny Doom's greed, Madam Rose's cunning, and his own sense of duty and loyalty. He'd gone blindly in to save Tiny Doom and she was the bait and he the stupid stupid prey, all along.

He, Hardhands, expendable!

"Bwannie—get up! Pig wants to go home!"

For a second our hero is wracked with sorrow, he takes a deep breath that judders his bones, and closes his eyes. The darkness is sparked with stars, flares of light caused by the pressure of holding the tears back. But under the surface of his sorrow, he feels an immense longing, longing not for the Pontifexa, or hot water, or for Relais' comforting embrace, or even for waffles. Compared to this longing, the rest of his feelings—anger, sorrow, guilt, love—are nothing. He should be already plotting his revenge, his pay-back, his turn-about-is-fair-play, but instead he is alive with thoughts of sweeping black wings, and spiraling hair, and the unutterable blissful agony of Desire.

"Pig wants a waffle, Bwannie! And I must potty, I gotta potty now!"

Hardhands opens his eyes to a dangly pink snout. Pig's eyes are small black beads, and his cotton stitched mouth is a bit red around the edges, as though he's smeared his lipstick. He smells of salty-iron blood and the peachy whiff of stale coldfire.

"Would you please get Pig out of my face?" he says wearily. The mystery of Pig is beyond him right now; he'll consider that further, later.

Tiny Doom pokes him. She is jiggling and bobbing, with her free hand tightly pressed. She has desires ungratified of her own; her bladder may be full, but her candy sack is empty. "Pig wants you to get up. He says Get Up Now, Banastre!"

Hardhands, thinking of desire gratified, gets up.

LORD WEARY'S EMPIRE

by Michael Swanwick

Michael Swanwick was born in Schenectady, New York, in 1950. His first two short stories were published in 1980, and both appeared on the Nebula ballot that year. One of the major writers working in the field today, he has won the Hugo, Nebula, World Fantasy, Theodore Sturgeon Memorial, and Locus awards. His six novels include In the Drift, *Nebula winner* Stations of the Tide, The Iron Dragon's Daughter, *and* Bones of the Earth. *His short fiction has been collected in* Gravity's Angels, Moon Dogs, *and* Tales of Old Earth. *He is also the author of a Locus Award winning book-length interview with editor Gardner Dozois. Swanwick has recently completed a new "hard fantasy" novel,* The Dragons of Babel, *and a new collection,* The Dog Said Bow-Wow, *is due later this year.*

LIKE A LEAF before a storm, Will fled. The basement corridors of Babel careened and reeled nightmarishly by and still he could not lose his pursuers. Three times the lancers had a clear line of sight and fired, each shot a blow to Will's ringing ears. But then, just beyond a row of overflowing garbage cans, Will saw a steel access door, chained shut but slightly ajar in its frame. He stooped and, grabbing the lower edge of the door, yanked with all his might.

A bullet burned through the air over his head.

The door lurched open, wrenched out of true.

Frantically, Will squeezed through the triangular space and tumbled down a short flight of metal steps. As he stumbled to his feet, he heard the lancers, too large to squeeze through themselves, trying to break down the door.

Blindly, he ran.

Rats scurried away at his approach. Roaches crunched underfoot. He was in a great dark space punctuated by massive I-beams and lit only by infrequent bare bulbs whose light struggled to reach the floor. Somehow, he had made his way into the network of train tunnels that spiraled up through Babel Tower.

Careful to avoid the third rail, Will followed one curving set of tracks into darkness, listening for approaching trains. Sometimes he heard their thunder in the distance, and once a train thundered past, mere inches from where he pressed himself, shivering, against the wall, and left him temporarily blinded. When he could see again, the tunnels were silent. He had lost his pursuers. He was safe now.

And hopelessly lost.

He'd been plodding along for some time when he saw a sewer worker—a haint—in the tunnel ahead, in hip waders and hard hat. "What you doing here, white boy?" the haint asked when Will hailed him.

"I'm lost."

"Well, you best get yourself unlost. They's trouble brewing."

"I can't," Will began. "I don't know—"

"It's your ass," the haint said. He faded through a wall and was gone.

Will spat in frustration. Then he walked on.

●   ●   ●

He knew that he'd wandered into dangerous territory when his left hand suddenly rose up of its own volition to clutch his right forearm. *"Stop!"* he thought to himself. Adrenaline raced through his veins.

Will peered into the claustrophobic blackness and saw nothing. A distant electric bulb cast only the slightest glimmer on the rails. The support beams here were as thick as trees in a midnight forest. He could not make out how far they extended. But by the spacious feel of the air, he was in a place where several lines of tracks joined and for a time ran together.

Far behind him was a lone set of signal lights, unvarying green and red dots.

He was abruptly aware of how easy it would be for somebody to sneak up behind him here. Maybe, he thought, he should turn around and go back.

In that instant, an unseen fist punched him hard in the stomach.

Will bent over almost double, and simultaneously his arms were seized from either side. His captors shoved him forward and forced him down onto his knees. His head was bent almost to the ground.

"Release him." The voice was warm and calm, that of a leader.

The hands let go. Will remained kneeling. Gasping, he straightened and looked about.

He was surrounded.

They—whoever they were—had come up around him in silence. Will's sense of hearing was acute, but even now he couldn't place them by sound. Rather, he felt the pressure of their collective gaze, and saw their eyes, pair by pair, wink into existence.

"Boy, you're in serious trouble now," the voice said, almost mournfully.

For an instant, Will could not speak. But then the speaker's eyes glowed red. "Well? Bast got your tongue? I'm giving you the opportunity to explain why you have invaded the Army of Night's turf. You won't get a second."

Will fought down his fear. There was great danger here, but great opportunity as well—if he had the nerve to grasp it. Speaking with a boldness he did not feel, he said, "This is your territory. I recognize that. It wasn't my intention to trespass. But now that I'm here, I hope you'll allow me to stay."

Calmly, dangerously, the speaker said, "Oh?"

"I'm broke, paperless, and without friends. I'm being pursued and I need someplace to be. This looks as good as any. Let me join your army and I'll serve you well."

"Who's chasing you?"

Will thought of the lancers, of the customs agents before them, and of the political police even earlier, and made a wry grimace. "Who isn't?"

"He kinda cute, Lord Weary," said somebody female. "If he can't fight, maybe we find some other use for him." Several of her comrades snickered.

A third voice said, "Shut the fuck up, Jenny! The Breaknecks sent him here to spy on us. He dies. Simple as that."

"That's not your decision, Tatterwag," Lord Weary said sharply.

"*Siktir git!*" Tatterwag swore. "We know what he is!"

"Are we savages? No, we are a community of brothers. Whatever is done here will be done in accordance with our laws." There was a long pause, during which Will imagined Lord Weary looking from side to side to see if any dared oppose him. When no one did, he went on, "You brought this upon yourself."

Will didn't ask what Lord Weary meant by that. He recognized a gang when he encountered one—he'd run with enough of them as a boy. There was always a leader, always the bright kid who stood at his shoulder advising him, always the troublemaker who wanted to usurp the leader's place. They always had laws, which were never written down. Their idea of justice was inevitably the *lex talionis,* an eye for an eye and a drubbing for an insult. They always settled their differences with a fight.

"Trial by combat," Lord Weary said.

Somebody lit a match. With a soft hiss, a Coleman lantern shed fierce white light over the thronged I-beams, making them leap and then fall as the flame was adjusted down again to near-extinction.

"You may stand now."

Will stood.

A ragged line of some twenty to thirty feys confronted him. They were of varied types and races, tall and short, male and female, but all looked beaten and angry, like feral dogs that know they can never triumph over the village-dwellers but will savage one who is caught alone and without weapons. The lantern shone through several, but dimly, as if through smoked glass, and by this Will knew that they were haints.

Directly before Will stood a tall figure whose air of command made clear that he could only be Lord Weary. He had the pallor, high cheekbones, and almost lanceolate ears of one of high-elven blood, and the noble bearing of a born leader as well. Will could not pick out the owners of the other two voices.

But then a swamp gaunt rushed out of the pack and, pointing a skinny arm at Will, cried, "He's one of the Breakneck Boys! I say we kill him now. Just kill him!"

So he had to be Tatterwag.

Will strode forward, throwing a hard shoulder into the gaunt to knock him aside. "Kill me if you think it possible," he said to Lord Weary. "But I don't think you can. If you doubt me, then name your champion. Make him the biggest, strongest mother you've got, so there won't be any doubt afterwards that I could defeat any one of you if I had to. I do not brag. Then, if you'll take me, I will gladly pledge my loyalty and put my powers at your service."

"That was well spoken," Lord Weary said mildly. "But talk is cheap and times are hard." Raising his voice, he said, "Who shall be our champion?"

"Bonecrusher," somebody said.

There was susurration of agreement. "Bonecrusher . . . 'Crusher . . . The big fella . . . Yeah, Bonecrusher."

The figure that shambled forward was covered with fur, wore no clothing, and carried a length of metal pipe for a club. It was a wodewose—a wild man of the forest.

Will had seen wild men before, out in the Old Forest. In some ways, they were little more than animals, though articulate enough for simple conversations and too cunning to be safely hunted. They were stuck forever in the dawn-times, unable to cope with any way of life more sophisticated than a hunter-gatherer existence nor any tool more complex than a pointed stick. Machines they feared, and they would not sleep in houses, though occasionally an injured one might take shelter in a barn. He could not imagine what twisty path had brought this one so far from his natural habitat.

The wodewose's mouth worked with the effort of summoning

up words. "Fuck you," he said at last. Then, after a pause, "Asshole."

Will bowed. "I accept your challenge, sir. I'll try my best to do you no permanent harm."

A mean grin appeared in the wild man's unkempt beard. "You're bugfuck," he said and then, "Shithead."

This was another thing that every gang Will had ever been in had: Somebody big and stupid who lived to fight.

Lord Weary faded back into darkness and returned bearing a length of pipe, much like the one the wodewose carried. He handed it to Will. "There are no rules," he said. "Except that one of you must die." He raised his voice. "Are the combatants ready?"

"Fuck yeah."

"Yes," Will said.

"Then douse the light."

All in an instant, darkness swallowed Will whole. In sudden fear he cried, "I can't see!"

There was a smile in Lord Weary's voice. "We can."

With a soft scuffle of bare feet, Bonecrusher attacked.

Though Will felt himself as good as blind, there must have been some residual fraction of light, for he saw a pale glint of pipe as it slashed downward at his head. Panicked, he brought up his own pipe just in time to block it.

The force of the blow buckled his knees.

The wodewose raised the pipe again, then chopped it down, trying for Will's shin. Will was barely about to leap back from it in time. There was a *clang* as the pipe bounced off the rail, striking sparks. He found himself panting, though he hadn't even struck a blow yet.

Will knew how to fight with a quarterstaff—every village lad did—but the wild man was not fighting quarterstaff-style but club-style. It was a sweeping, muscular fighting technique the like of which he had never faced before. Back the club slashed, inches from his chest. Had it connected it would have broken Will's ribs. The wild man followed through, as if he were swinging a baseball bat, and brought it smoothly back, hard and level. Will ducked low, saving his skull from being crushed.

Will swung his pipe wildly, and felt it bounce off the wode-wose's ribs. But it didn't even slow the wild man down. His club came down on Will's shoulder.

Just barely, Will managed to twist aside, so that the club only dealt him a glancing, stinging blow to his arm. But that was enough to numb him for an instant and make his fingers involun-tarily release their hold on one end of his weapon. Now it was held only by his left hand.

There was a murmur of admiration from the watchers, but no more. Which meant that Bonecrusher was not popular in the Army of Night, however much they might value his fighting skill.

The pain brought the dragon rising up within Will, a ravening wave of anger that threatened to wash over his mind and drown all conscious thought. He fought it down. Whirling the pipe around his head, he feinted at one shoulder. Then, when the wodewose brought up his own weapon to block it, he shifted his attack. The pipe slammed into Bonecrusher's forehead and bounced off.

Bonecrusher shook his matted dreadlocks and raised his weapon once more.

At that moment, a great noise rose up in the distance. A train! Will tucked his pipe under one arm as if it were a lance and ran full-tilt at his opponent. The pipe struck him in the chest and knocked him stumbling backwards.

The train rounded a bend. Its headlight blossomed like the sun at midnight.

Will retreated to the far side of the track. He pressed himself against the nearest support beam, feeling its cold strength under his back. Across from him, Bonecrusher started forward, hesi-tated, and then turned away, one great hand covering his eyes.

His eyes? Oh.

The locomotive slammed past Will, a wash of air shoving against him like a warm fist. He had a momentary glimpse of as-tonished faces in the passenger car windows before he threw an arm over his eyes to shield himself from the painfully bright light.

Then the train was gone. When he opened his eyes again, he could see nothing.

Bonecrusher chuckled. "Yer blind, aintcha?" he said. "Mother-fucker."

Now Will was truly afraid.

With fear came anger, however, and anger made it easier for him to draw upon the dragon-darkness within him. He felt it rising up in his blood and clamped down tight. He refused to give it control. It struggled against him, a fire running through his veins, an evil song lifting in his throat. It yearned to be let free.

He heard the whisper of Bonecrusher's naked feet on the railroad ties. He backed away.

Now an inner vision seemed to pierce the darkness. All was still shadow within shadow, but he knew that the shifting blackness directly before him was the wodewose padding quietly forward, raising his makeshift club for one final and devastating blow.

The dragon-anger was straining at its leash. So Will let slip his hold a little, allowing the anger to leap forward to meet the attack. He threw aside his own pipe and stepped into the blow. With one hand, he caught the wild man's club and wrested it from his grasp. With the other, he seized the wodewose by the throat.

Flinging away the wodewose's weapon, he stooped and grabbed his opponent by his thigh. The creature's fur was as stiff as an Airedale's, and matted with knots. Will lifted him up over his head. He tried to curse, but Will's hand clutched his throat too tightly for anything meaningful to emerge.

The bastard was helpless now. Will could swing him around and smash his head against a pillar or drop him down over his knee, breaking his spine. It would be the easiest thing in the world, either way.

Well, screw that.

"I don't have anything against you," he told his struggling opponent. "Give me your word of surrender, and I'll set you free."

Bonecrusher made a gurgling noise.

"That's not possible," Lord Weary said with obvious regret. "Our laws say: To the death."

Frustration filled Will. To have come so far, only to be thwarted by a childish warrior's code! Well, then, he would have to run. He doubted the Army of the Night would pursue him with much enthusiasm after seeing how easily he defeated their champion.

"If your laws say that," Will snarled, "then they're not mine." With a surge of anger, he flung the wodewose away from him.

"Fucking bas–!" The word cut off abruptly as the wodewose hit the ground. Electrical sparks flew into the air like fireworks. The wodewose's body arced and crisped. There was a smell of burnt hair and scorched flesh.

Somebody whistled and said, "That's cold."

Will had forgotten entirely about the third rail.

● ● ●

Lord Weary picked out four of his soldiers for a burial detail. "Carry Bonecrusher upstairs," he said, "and leave him some-where he'll be found, so that City Services will take care of the body. Be sure he's lying facing up! I don't want one of my soldiers mistaken for an animal." Then he clapped a hand on Will's shoul-der. "Well fought, boy. Welcome to the Army of Night."

When the burial detail had lugged Bonecrusher's body into oblivion, Lord Weary lined up those who remained and led them the other way. "On to Niflheim," he said. Will joined the line and, shivering, managed to keep pace.

He'd walked for what seemed like forever and no time at all when the smell of urine and feces welled up around him so strong that it made his eyes water. Somebody lived down here. A lot of somebodies. Will found himself stumbling up a crumbling set of stairs and onto a cement platform.

A miniature city arose before him. There were perhaps a hun-dred or so shanties built one on top of the other of wooden crates and cardboard boxes, each one sufficient to hold a sleeping bag and little more. Wicker baskets, large enough to sleep in, hung from the ceiling. There were narrow streets between the shanties down which shadows flitted. The Army wove its way through them into a central plaza, where a cluster of haints and feys sat crouched around a portable television set, its volume turned down to a murmur. Others sat about talking quietly or reading tat-tered paperbacks by candlelight. High on the walls above was a frieze of tiles that showed dwarves mining and smelting and man-ufacturing. Deep runes in the stone arch over a cinder-blocked doorway read: NIFLHEIM STATION. By the newspapers and old clothes strewn about, it had been closed and abandoned long ago.

A hulder (Will could tell from her buxom figure and by the cow's tail sticking out from under her skirt) rose to greet them. "Lord Weary," she said. "You are welcome here, and your army too. I see you have somebody new." Most of those who rose in her wake were haints.

"I thank you, thane-lady Hjördis. Our recruit is so recent he hasn't chosen a name for himself yet. He is our new champion."

"Him?" Hjördis scowled. "This *boy?*"

"Don't be fooled by his looks, the lad's tough. He killed Bonecrusher."

Soft muttering washed over the platform. "By trickery?" somebody asked dubiously.

"In fair and open combat. I saw it all."

There was a moment's tension before the thane-lady nodded, accepting. Then Lord Weary said to her, "We must confer. Serious matters are afoot."

"First we eat," Hjördis said. "You will sit with me at the head table."

To Will's surprise, he was included with Lord Weary in the in-vitation. Apparently the office of champion made him a coun-selor as well. He watched as tables were built in the central square, of boards set over wire milk crates, and then covered with sheets of newspaper in place of linen. A cobbley set out pads of newspaper for seats and paper plates for them to eat from. Another filled the plates with food. The thane-lady's table was set under the wall, beneath the tiled dwarves. She and her favored companions sat with their backs to the wall, so that the rows of lesser-ranked diners faced them.

The food was better than might be expected, some of it scrounged from grocery store dumpsters after passing its sell-by date and the rest of it from upstairs charities. They ate by the light of tuna-can lamps with rag wicks in rancid cooking oil, convers-ing quietly.

Will commented that the tunnels seemed more labyrinthine

and of greater extent than he had thought they would be, and Hjördis said, "You don't know the half of it. There used to be fifteen different gas companies in Babel, six separate sets of steam tunnels, and Sirrush only can say how many subway systems, pneumatic trains, sub-surface lines, underground trolleys, and pedestrian walkways that nobody uses any more. Add to that maintenance tunnels for the power and telephone and plumbing and sewage systems, storm drains, the summer retreats that the wealthy used to have dug for them a century ago, bomb shelters, bootleggers' vaults . . ."

Lord Weary shook his head in agreement. "There is no loremaster of Babel's secret ways. They are too many, and too varied." His sea-green eyes studied Will gravely. "Now. Tell us what drove you here."

Here was another moment of danger. Will knew he must speak carefully and truthfully, or he would not survive the meal. Lord Weary's stern face convinced him of it.

He told his tale:

Long, long ago—though it could scarcely have been more than a year—a war-dragon had crashed in the Old Forest outside Will's village. His fuselage was torn and gashed and its half-elven pilot was dead. Yet he retained enough fuel to crawl into the center square of the village and declare himself its king. None of the elders dare oppose him, for he still had his armament and malice enough to touch it off if he were crossed. Yet he could barely move, and so he had chosen a lieutenant to represent him—male rather than female and young rather than old, for the village hags were far too wily for him to trust.

He had chosen Will.

Then had Will learned the terrible isolation of the collaborator. Though it was none of his choosing, he was despised by all and alienated from those who had been his friends. In the day, he walked about the village, observing. At night, he sat in the pilot's seat and long needles in the armrests slid into his wrists so that the dragon could slither into his mind and access his memories directly, seeing what he had seen and feeling what he had felt. Everybody knew of this, and so they shunned him.

He had thought that things could not get worse. He had been

wrong. A rebellion arose among the younger citizens and to put it down the dragon had entered into Will's mind one evening and not left. Leaving footprints of flame behind him, he had walked through the village, terrorizing all and seizing the rebellion's ringleader.

Puck Berrysnatcher had been Will's best friend. Will had crucified him.

With a cunning and boldness he had not known he possessed, Will had finally managed to killed the dragon and by so doing free the villagers from his tyranny. But that had not changed anybody's minds about him.

"Since that time," Will said, "I have been cast out of my village and ill-fortune has pursued me across Fäerie Minor all the way to the Dread Tower. Perhaps I have been cursed by the dragon's death." He did not say that some fraction of the dragon remained within him yet. On that matter, silence was safest. "All I know is that from that day I have had no place to call home."

"You have a home here now, lad," said Lord Weary. "We shall be a second family to you, if you will have us."

He laid a hand on Will's head, and a great flood of emotion washed over Will. Suddenly, and for no reason he could name, he loved the elf-lord like a father. Warm tears flowed down his cheeks.

When he could speak again, Will asked, "Why do you live down here?"

It was a meaningless question, meant simply to move the conversation to less emotional ground. But graciously, Hjördis explained that though those above dismissed the dwellers in darkness as trolls and feral dwarves, very few of them were subterranean by nature. Most of the thane-lady's folk were haints and drows, nissen, shellycoats, and broken feys—anyone lacking the money or social graces to get along in open society. They had problems with drugs and alcohol and insanity, but they looked after one another as best they could. Their own name for themselves was *johatsu*—"nameless wanderers."

"Are there a lot of communities like this one?"

"There are dozens," Lord Weary said, "and possibly even hundreds. Some are as small as six or ten individuals. Others run much larger than what you see here. No one knows for sure how many live in darkness. Tatterwag speculates there are tens of thousands. But they don't communicate with each other and they won't work together and they are perforce nomadic, for periodically the transit police discover the settlements and bust them up, scattering their citizens. But the Army of Night is going to change all that. We're the first and the only organized military force the johatsu have ever formed."

"How many are in the Army, all told?"

The thane-lady hid a smile under a paper napkin. Stiffly, Lord Weary said, "You've met them all. This is a new idea, and slow to catch on. But it will grow. My dream will bear fruit in the fullness of time." His voice rose. "Look around you! These are the dispossessed of Babel—the weak, the injured, the gentle. Who speaks for them? Not the Lords of the Mayoralty. Not the Council of Magi. His Absent Majesty was their protector once, but he is long gone and no one knows where. Somebody must step forward to fill that void. I swear by the Sun, the Moon, and the Stars, and the Golden Apples of the West, that if the Seven permit it, that somebody shall be me!"

The johatsu froze in their places, not speaking, barely breathing. Their eyes shone like stars.

Hjördis laid a hand over Lord Weary's. "Great matters will wait upon food," she said. "Time enough to discuss these things after we eat."

◉ ◉ ◉

When all had eaten and the dishes been cleared away, Hjördis lit a cigarette and passed it around the table. "Well?" she said at last.

"When last we were here," Lord Weary said, "I left some crates in your keeping. Now we have need of them."

A shadow crossed the thane-lady's face. But she nodded. "I thought as much. So I had my folk retrieve them."

Six Niflheimers stood up, faded into darkness, and returned, lugging long wooden crates between them. The crates were laid down before the table and, at a gesture from Lord Weary, Taggerwag pried open one with his Bowie knife.

Light gleamed on rifle barrels.

Suddenly the taste of death was in the air. Cautiously, Will said, "What do we need these for?"

"There's going to be a rat hunt," Lord Weary said.

"We're hunting rats?"

Lord Weary grinned mirthlessly. "We're not the hunters, lad. We're the rats."

The Niflheimers had been listening intently. Now they crowded around the main table. "We call them the Breakneck Boys," one said. "They come down here once a month, on the day of the Toad or maybe the day of the Labrys, looking for some fun. They got night-goggles and protective spells like you wouldn't believe, and they carry aluminum baseball bats. Mostly, we just slip away from 'em. But they usually manage to find somebody too old or sick or drugged-up to avoid them."

"It's a fucking *hobby* for them," Tatterwag growled.

"Last time, they caught poor old Martin Pecker drunk asleep, only instead of giving him a bashing like usual, they poured gasoline over him and set it on fire."

"I saw the corpse!"

"Long have I argued against this course of action as a mad notion and a dangerous folly," the thane-lady said. "Their sires are industrialists and Lords of the Mayoralty. If even one of their brats dies, they'll send the mosstroopers down here with dire wolves to exact revenge." Then, with obvious reluctance, "Yet the Breaknecks' predations worsen. I see no alternative."

"No!" Will said. He had eaten almost nothing, for his stomach was still queasy from the stench of Niflheim, and Bonecrusher's death weighed heavily upon him. If he closed his eyes, he could see the sparks rising up around the wodewose's body. He hadn't wanted to kill the creature. It had happened because he hadn't thought the situation through beforehand. Now he was thinking very hard and fast indeed. "Put the guns back."

"You're not *afraid?*" Lord Weary drew himself up straight, and Will felt his disapproval like a lash across his shoulders.

"I can take care of the Breaknecks," Will said. "If you want me to, I'll take care of them myself."

There was a sudden silence.

"Alone?"

"Yes. But to pull this off, I'll need a uniform. The gaudier the better. And war paint. The kind that glows in the dark."

Hjördis grinned. "I'll send our best shoplifters upstairs."

"And explosives. A hand grenade would be best, but—no? Well, is there any way we can get our hands on some chemicals to make a bomb?"

"There's a methamphetamine lab up near the surface," Tatterwag said. "The creeps who run it think nobody knows it's there. They got big tanks of ethyl ether and white gasoline. Maybe even some red phosphorus."

"Do we have anybody who knows how to handle them safely?"

"Um . . . there's one of us got a Ph.D. in alchemy. Only, it was back when. Up above." Tatterwag glanced nervously at Lord Weary. "Before he came here. So I don't know whether he wants me to say his name or not."

"You have a doctorate?" Will said. "How in the world did you . . ." He was going to say *fall so low* but thought better of it. ". . . wind up here?"

Offhandedly, Lord Weary said, "Carelessness. Somebody offered me a drink. I liked it, so I had another. Only one hand is needed to hold a glass, so I took up smoking to give the other one something to do. I took to dueling and from there it was only a small step to gambling. I bought a fighting cock. I bought a bear. I bought a dwarf. I began to frequent tailors and whores. From champagne I moved to whisky, from whisky to wine, and from wine to Sterno. So it went until the only libation I had not yet drunk was blood, the only sex untried was squalid, and the only vice untasted was violent revolution.

"Every step downward was pleasant. Every new experience filled me with disdain for those who dared not share in it. And so, well, here I am."

"Is this a true history," Will asked, "or a parable?"

"Your question," Lord Weary said, "is a deeper one than you know—whether the world I sank through was real or illusory. Many a better mind than mine or yours has grappled with this very issue without result. In any event, I'll make your bomb."

It took hours to make the plan firm. But at last Hjördis rose from the table and said, "Enough. Our new champion is doubtless tired. Bonecrusher's quarters are yours now. I will show you where you sleep."

She took Will by the hand and led him to an obscure corner of the box-village. There she knelt before a kind of tent made of patched blankets hung from clotheslines. "In here." She raised the flap and crawled inside.

Will followed.

To his surprise, the interior was clean. Inside, a faded Tabriz carpet laid over stacked cardboard served as floor and mattress. A vase filled with phosphorescent fungi cast a gentle light over the space. Hjördis turned and, kneeling, said, "All that was 'Crusher's is yours now. His tent. His title . . ." She pulled her dress off over her head. "His duties."

Will took a deep, astonished breath. It seemed too awful to kill the wodewose and bed his lover all on the same day. Hesitatingly, he said, "We don't *have* to . . ."

The thane-lady stared at him in blank astonishment. "You're not gay, are you? Or suffering from the fisher king's disease?" She touched his crotch, "No, I can see you're not. What is it, then?"

"I just don't see how you can sleep with me after I killed your . . . killed Bonecrusher."

"You don't think this is *personal,* do you?" Hjördis laughed. "Blondie, you're the most fucked-up champion I ever saw." At her direction, he took off his clothes. She drew him down and guided him inside her. Then she wrapped her legs around his waist and slapped him on the rump.

"Giddy up," she commanded.

Halfway through the night they galloped. In the morning (but he had to take Hjördis's word for it that it was morning), Will went out with two of Lord Weary's scouts to look over possible locales for the plan. Then he returned to the box city and sorted through the heaps of clothing that the Niflheimers brought him, some dug out of old stashes and some fresh-stolen for the occasion. Carefully, he assembled his costume: Biker boots. Mariachi pants. A top hat with a white scarf wrapped around the band, one end hanging free behind like a ghostly fox tail, with a handful of turkey feathers from the meat packing district splayed along the side. A marching band jacket with a white sash. All topped off with a necklace of rat skulls.

With the phosphorescent makeup, he painted two red slashes slanting downward over his eyes, a straight blue line along his nose, and a yellow triangle about his mouth to make a mocking, cartoonish grin: with luck, the effect would be eerie enough to give his enemies pause. More importantly, the elves would see the glowing lines on his face, the top-hat-feathers-and-scarf, and the necklace of skulls, but they wouldn't see *him*. Once he wiped off the makeup and ditched the uniform, he would be anonymous again. He could walk the streets above without fearing arrest.

"I'll just need one last thing," he said when he was done. "A motorcycle."

⚬ ⚬ ⚬

Two days later, the Army of Night's outposts came running up silently with news that the Breakneck Boys had entered the tunnels. Will had already scouted out the perfect place for a confrontation—a vast and vaulted space as large as a cathedral that had been constructed centuries ago as a cistern for times of siege. A far more recent water main cut through it at the upper end, but otherwise it was much as it had been the day it was drained. Now he sent out decoys to lure the Boys there, while he made up his face with phosphorescent war-paint and wheeled his stolen motorcycle into place.

Will waited alone in a niche behind a pillar at the lower end of the cistern. He'd stone-souped the johatsu by asking for first one small thing and then another, each incrementally larger than the one before, because there'd been no alternative. Had he asked for the motorcycle first, he wouldn't have gotten it. But this was as far as bluff would take him. Now he was either going to triumph or to die.

For the longest time there was no noise other than the grumble of distant trains. Then, faintly, he heard drunken elven laughter. He watched as the decoys ran past his station, like two furtive shadows. The voices grew more boisterous and then suddenly boomed as the Breakneck Boys emerged from a doorway near the ceiling at the upper end of the cistern.

They began to descend a long brick stairway along the far wall.

They glimmered in the dark, did the elves, like starlight. They carried Maglites and aluminum bats. Some wore camouflage suits. Some had night goggles. They were nine in number, and uncannily young, little more than children. Their leader drained the last of his beer and threw away the can. It rattled into silence.

Will waited until they were off the stairs and had clambered over the water main and started across the cistern floor. Then he kick-started the motorcycle. It was a stripped-down Kawasaki three cylinder two-stroke, easy to handle and loud as hell. Pulling out of the niche, Will cranked the machine hard left and opened it up. The vault ceiling bouncing the engine's roar back at him, he charged at the elf-pack like a banshee with her ass on fire.

It felt great to be on a cycle again! Puck Berrysnatcher, back when he and Will were best friends, had owned a dirt bike, and they'd practiced on it, turn on turn, until they both mastered such stunts as young males thought important.

Will popped a wheelie and came to a stop not ten yards from the astonished elves.

Throttling down the engine so he could be heard, he cried, "I challenge thee by the *holmgangulog,* if thou hast honor! I am the captain and the rightwise defender of my folk. Present your champion that we may contest at deeds of arms."

A disbelieving look, followed by low, mean laughter passed among the elves. "So you know the politesse of challenge, Master Scarecrow," said the foremost of them. Whatever else he might be, he was no coward. "Very well. I hight Florian of House L'Inconnu." He bowed mockingly. "What is your name and what terms do you propose?"

"Captain Jack Riddle," Will said, choosing the *nom de guerre* almost at random. "High explosives at close quarters."

The elf-brat rubbed his chin, as if amused. "Your proposal is scarce workable." Casually, his hand crept downward between the lapels of his jacket. Doubtless he had a gun there in a shoulder harness. "For, you see, I have no explosives with me."

"Tough titty," Will said.

With a muttered word, he detonated the bomb which earlier he had very carefully placed for maximum effect.

The water main, which was directly behind the Breaknecks, blew open.

A great wave of water struck the Breakneck Boys from behind, knocking them over and tumbling them helplessly before it. But not—and this was the crucial part of Will's plan—killing any of them.

Will, meanwhile, had spun around his bike and opened the throttle wide. He raced down slope ahead of the cascading water, cut a right so sharp he almost lost control, and was out of the cistern and roaring up a narrow electric conduit access tunnel without a single drop getting on him.

He would have liked to have seen the Breaknecks gather themselves together after the water washed them down to the bottom of the cistern. It would have been worth much to have heard their curses and witnessed their dismay as they pulled themselves up and began the long and soggy journey back aboveground. But you couldn't have everything.

Anyway, he was sure to hear of it. There was a slit-gallery near the top of the cistern that had been used for inspections, which was thronged with silent watchers, soldiers from the Army of Night and potential recruits from Niflheim and possibly even Hjördis herself. They'd have seen and heard everything. They'd have witnessed how he had routed their enemies without the least injury to himself. They'd want a share in his glory. They'd boast of his prowess. No longer was he merely their champion.

He was their hero now.

●　●　●

That evening the johatsu migrated several miles deeper into the tunnels. They moved silently and surely, and when they found their destination—an abandoned pneumatic train tube from an experimental line that went bankrupt in the Century of the

Turbine—Lord Weary sent his specialists to tap into the electric and water lines. Even at this distance from the shattered main, the water pressure was lessened. But unlike the citizens above, they'd known to fill plastic bottles beforehand.

"Dockweed," Will said. A hudkin snapped to attention. "Take a couple of likely lads and scout out a good location for latrines. Not too close to the encampment. That's unsanitary." He caught Lord Weary looking at him, and hastily added, "If that's all right with you, sir."

Lord Weary waved a hand, endorsing everything. Then, placing an arm over Will's shoulder, so that it would be ostentatiously obvious to all that they two were conferring with perfect confidence, he murmured, "Dearer art thou to me, after your little escapade today, than meat and drink to a starving man. Stand by me and I shall raise you higher than you can imagine, so that my empire rests upon your shoulders. But if you ever again give orders in my presence without first deferring to me, I'll have you gutted and chained to the bedrock for the rats to eat alive. Do you understand?"

Will swallowed. "Sir."

"I would regret it, of course. But discipline knows no favorites." He released Will. "Tell me something. What exactly have we accomplished today? Other than raising morale, I mean. In a day or three, the main will be rebuilt. The Breakneck Boys are still alive. By now they're probably fast asleep in their feather beds."

"We've cut off an entire neighborhood from water for however long the repairs last. They'll take that seriously up above. If their investigations turn up the Breaknecks' involvement, it will be a political embarrassment for their parents. If not, the Breakneck Boys will still know what a close call it was. The smarter among them will realize they were given a warning. That I could as easily have killed them. We won't be seeing them back again."

"There'll be others."

Will grinned wolfishly. "Bring 'em on."

● ● ●

Will adapted to the darkness. He learned its ways, learned to love the stillness and the silence of it. He grew familiar with the rumor of distant trains, the small dripping and creaking and scurrying sounds that were normal to the tunnels, and the fainter and more furtive noises that were not. He learned how to crouch motionless for hours, his eyes so thoroughly adapted to the dark that when a transit worker or a patrolman went by with a flashlight, he had to narrow them to slits against its glare. He learned how to move silent as a wraith, so that he could follow these intruders from the upper world for hours without them suspecting a thing.

Nighttimes, he went upstairs to dumpster dive and sometimes to steal. Just to keep in touch with his troops. It was important for them to know that he could do the work of any one of them and did not consider it beneath him. On deep patrols, when it was not possible to go topside for food, he learned to catch and roast and eat rats. Whenever they could spare the time, he sent his forces out to explore and to map, until he knew more of Babel's underworld than any individual ever had before. He would interview any wanderer who passed through Lord Weary's territory and those who were capable but solitary by nature he organized into a loose confederation of messengers, so that for the first time, all the johatsu communities were kept informed of each other's goings-on.

Volunteers arrived daily, anxious to serve under the hero of whom they'd heard so much. Most of them were turned away. Nevertheless, the Army of Night grew. Little by little, their territory was expanding. Bindlestiffs, sadistic cops, degenerate trolls, and other predators learned to avoid tunnels marked with the three-lines-and-a-triangle that had become the token of Captain Jack's protection.

Will knew his work was bearing fruit the day he ghosted up behind a transit cop, squeezed his upper arm in one hand, whispered softly in his ear, "My name is Jack Riddle and if you want to live, you'll place your revolver on the ground beside you and leave," and been instantly obeyed.

That same day, one of his runners brought him a wanted poster from up above. It had a crude drawing of a fey with his grinning face-paint, hat, and skull necklace, and read:

WANTED, FOR TERRORIST ACTIVITY, THE DEMON, SPRITE, OR GAUNT KNOWN AS

JACK RIDDLE

Aliases: Captain Jack Riddle, Captain Jack,
Jack the Lucky, Laughing Jack

DESCRIPTION

Date of Birth:	Unknown	Hair:	Blond
Place of Birth:	Unknown	Eyes:	Dark
Height:	Unknown	Sex:	Male
Weight:	Unknown	Complexion:	Pale
Build:	Slim	Citizenship:	Unknown
Scars and Marks:	None known		

Remarks: A flamboyant dresser, Riddle's dramatic persona has
led some to speculate that he may have formerly been involved
in theater. By his bearing, he may once have associated with the
aristocracy, possibly as a servant.

JACK RIDDLE IS BEING SOUGHT FOR HIS ROLE IN
NUMEROUS TERRORIST ACTS PERFORMED IN
CONNECTION WITH HIS LEADERSHIP OF A
SUBTERRANEAN PARAMILITARY FORCE THAT HAS
COMMITTED ASSAULTS UPON AGENTS OF HIS
ABSENT MAJESTY'S GOVERNANCE AS WELL AS UPON
INNOCENT MEMBERS OF THE CITIZENRY OF BABEL.

CAUTION

HE HAS A SAVAGE TEMPER AND SHOULD BE
CONSIDERED ARMED AND EXTREMELY DANGEROUS.

REWARD

His Absent Majesty's Governance is offering the informant's
weight in gold to any citizen in Categories C through G or a
statistically derived equivalent for all others, for information
leading directly to the arrest of Jack Riddle.

"How about that?" Will said, grinning. "And to think that a
couple of months ago I was a nobody!"

"Don't you get cocky, Jack," Hjördis said. "That's a lot of

money. There are plenty who would turn you in for a fraction of that." She fastened her brassiere over her stomach, then slid it right way around, put her arms through the straps and shrugged into it. "I'd be tempted myself, if I didn't have obligations to my people." She wriggled into her dress.

Stung, Will said, "You shouldn't joke like that."

"You think I'm joking? That's enough wealth to buy any-body's way up to the surface."

"We don't need gold to do that. After we've consolidated the underworld, we can rise up from beneath and seize the neighbor-hoods above us. Then we'll take the Dread Tower, one level at a time, all the way to the Palace of Leaves."

"I realize that's Lord Weary's plan," Hjördis said doubtfully. "But how likely is it—really? I fail to understand why you would buy so completely into a fallen elf-lord's delusions of glory."

For a second Will did not speak. Then he said, "I have been driven across Fäerie Minor by chance and events, helpless as a leaf in a storm. Well, no more! I needed a cause to devote myself to, one that would give me the opportunity to strike back against my oppressors, and Lord Weary provided me with one. It's as simple as that."

He returned to the poster. "Innocent citizenry. That would be the Breakneck Boys, you think? Or the drug dealers?" Enough of their soldiers were addicted to various substances that it would be foolish to think that drug trafficking could be stopped. But the dealers were territorial and well-armed, and prone to sudden vio-lence. Johatsu had been gunned down simply because they'd wandered into the wrong tunnel at the wrong time. So the deal-ers had been driven upstairs. Those who cared to sell nickel bags of pixie dust or Mason jars of moonshine close by the commonly known exits were tolerated. But when their goods were tainted—when they killed—they were subject to being snatched and hauled below for a trial by the dead user's peers.

There was a polite cough outside the box's entrance. It was Jenny Jumpup. "Sir. Lord Weary's respects, and he say pull your dick out the lady-thane and assemble your raiders. He wants his horses."

The clanging began in the distance, regular and unrelenting, the sound of somebody hammering on water pipes with a rock. Beyond and fainter, a second set of clangs joined it. Then a third.

"We been spotted," Jenny Jumpup said.

"Good." Will did not slow his pace. "I want them to spot us. I want them to know we're coming. I want them to know that there's nothing they can do to stop us."

"What's to keep them from slipping through the walls?" Tatterwag asked. "They're haints, after all."

"Their horses couldn't follow. We'd get them all. And these guys practically worship their horses." Lord Weary had sent ambassadors to the horse-folk, offering them full membership in his growing empire, immunity from taxation and conscription, a guaranteed supply of food, and other enticements in exchange for a small yearly tribute of horses. His advances had been rejected with haughty scorn, though the horse-folk were the poorest of all who dwelt in darkness, and possessed neither tools nor clothing.

"Then why don't they just saddle up the horses and run? That's what I'd do in their circumstances."

"They *old* haints," Jenny Jumpup said. She was a haint herself, and proud of it. Her hair was done up in a cascade of slim braids, tied in the back in a sort of ponytail, and she wore a brace of pistols butt-forward in her belt. "They ancestors left the Shadowlands before fire was brought down from the sky. They can't farm, they got no weapons, and they can't ride horses."

"So why the fuck do they care if we take them?"

"They're all the horse-folk have." Will called a brief halt to check the map. A muttered word and its lines glimmered like foxfire. The other raiders gathered about him. They were a good group—in addition to his two lieutenants, he had Radegonde de la Cockaigne, Kokudza, the Starveling, and Little Tommy Redcap. "We're on the bottommost level of tracks—but there are tunnels that delve even deeper, some of them natural and others not." He led them some fifty yards down the track. A black opening gaped to one side. Cool air sighed out of it. "This was an aqueduct once, nobody knows how long ago. Looks like dwarven work."

"It's older than dwarves," Jenny Jumpup said scornfully. "My people remember. We built it. And we ain't never been paid for it neither."

"Jenny," Tatterwag said. "Give it a rest."

A train went by and they turned their backs to it. When their eyes had adjusted to the dark once more, they walked some distance into the aqueduct. Will got out the map again. "If everything's gone according to plan, our other troops will be in position *here* and *here*," he said. "That leaves only one way out—right through us. They'll stampede the herd in hopes of trampling us under."

Little Tommy Redcap chuckled nastily. "I'll rip the horses' legs off if they try."

"You were all chosen because you know how to ride," Will said. "Now space yourselves out and let's see if you can climb."

They swiftly scaled the walls. This was a new skill for Will, but one he had picked up easily. There was a narrow ledge just below the vaulted ceiling. The raiders took up positions there, some on one side and some on the other. All save Jenny Jumpup and the Starveling, who swarmed up the ceiling and drove in pitons so they could hang face downward, like bats, waiting.

After a long silence, Kokudza growled, "I don't get it. Horses. Caverns. Call me crazy, but I see a basic conflict here."

"The horses used to be wild," Will said. "Back before Nimrod laid the foundations of Babel, they fed upon the grassy slopes of Ararat. Lord Weary told me he read a paper on this once. Scientists speculate that some of their number would venture into natural caverns to feed upon mosses and lichens. This would have been tens of thousands of years ago, minimum. Something happened, an earthquake maybe, that trapped a small breeding population in the caverns. They adapted to the darkness. You couldn't say they thrived, exactly—there can't be more than a hundred of 'em all told. But they're still here. Albino-pale, short-haired, and high-strung. They won't be easy to catch."

Tatterwag patted his bandolier. "You know what *I* recommend." Now that the Empire was a going concern, they had money enough, extorted from transit workers and the like, to buy materials that had never previously been available underground.

Will had been the first to keep a string of magnesium flares with him always, and a pair of welder's goggles in a breast pocket. Tatterwag, who was not only his second-in-command but a notorious suck-up as well, had followed suit. There was no better indicator of how far and fast Will's star had risen.

Will shook his head. "That won't work on these horses."

"Why not?"

"They're blind," he said. "Now be quiet."

● ● ●

After a while, the clanging stopped. That meant the horses would be coming soon. Some time after that, Will was almost certain that he heard a gentle murmuring noise like the rumor of rain in the distance. It was less a sound than wistful thought. But it was there. Maybe.

"Do not take the lead horse," Lord Weary had told him quietly before they set out.

"Why shouldn't I?" Will had asked. "Surely the leader will be fastest and most desirable."

"Not so. It will be fast but callow. The wiser horses hold back and let the young stallions, their heroes, take the foremost with its attendant risks. They are expendable. The queen-mare, however, will be found at the very center of the herd and it is she you want. Fleetest of all is she and cleverest as well, sure-footed on wet surfaces, cautious on dry, and alert to danger even when all seems safest. Wait and watch. You will know her when you see her."

Far down the tunnel, a gentle luminescence bloomed, faint as the internal glow of the ocean on a moonless night. There was a soft sound, as of many animals breathing deeply in the distance.

"Here they come," Tatterwag said.

Like sea-foam, the horses filled the tunnel. Shadowy figures ran among them, as swiftly as the beasts themselves. These were the old haints, the horse-folk, running naked as the day they were born. Even at a distance, they could be sensed, for with them came fear. Though they could not plant or build or light a fire, the old powers were theirs still, and they were able to generate terror and use it as a weapon. Thus it was that they herded their horses.

Thus it was that they fought, using the great brutes' bodies against their enemies.

"Oh, baby!" Jenny Jumpup moaned. "I gone get me a young stud. I gone wrap my legs around him and never let go. I gone squeeze him so tight he rear up and scream."

"You're making me horny, Jen," Kokudza said. They all laughed softly.

Then the herd was upon them.

The noise of hooves, near-silent a moment before, rose up like thunder. The horses filled the aqueduct like ocean waters surging. One by one, the raiders dropped down upon them, like ripe fruit falling from the trees.

Wait, Will thought. Wait . . . wait . . . not yet . . . And then, just when he felt he could wait no longer, he spotted the queen-mare in the center of the herd, running as quickly as any but clearly not expending herself, holding something extra in reserve.

Will leaped.

Briefly, he flew. Then, one astonishing second later, he *slammed* onto the back of the mare. He grabbed wildly for her neck and scrabbled to keep his legs on either side of her back.

The queen-mare rose up, pawing the air. Will's legs were flung clear, and he was almost thrown. But he clung to her neck, and by the time her forefeet were back on the ground, had managed to get his own legs back in place.

She ran.

Once, twice, she slammed into the horses running to either side of her. Each time, one of Will's legs was crushed briefly between the great beasts. But the impact was not quite enough to numb them, and Will was determined that he would not be stopped by mere pain. He hung on with all his might.

Then the queen-mare had broken free of the herd and was running ahead of them all.

Riding low on her back, concentrating on keeping from falling, Will began to sing the charm he had been taught:

"Your neck is high and straight,
Your head shrewd with intelligence,
Your belly short, your back full,
Your proud chest hard with muscles . . ."

His mount swung her head around and tried to bite him, but he grabbed her mane high on the back of her skull with both hands and was able to keep her teeth from closing on his flesh. And then the charm took hold and she no longer tried to throw him, though she continued to run in a full-out panic.

They were alone now, separated from the herd and galloping wildly down who-knew-which lightless tunnel. Though she was blind, somehow the queen-mare knew where the walls were and did not run into them. Somehow, she never stumbled. Whatever senses she employed in the absence of sight, they were keen and shrewd, and equal to the task. Will understood now, as he had not before, why Lord Weary so desperately wanted these steeds. Will's motorcycle was of only limited utility belowground; it could not be ridden along the ties of the train tracks, nor could it leap over a sudden gap in the floor of a tunnel if Will did not spot it in time. This beast could travel swiftly anywhere. It could traverse the distance between settlements in a fraction of the time a pedestrian could.

"Joy of princes, throne of warriors,
Hoof-fierce treasure of the rich,
Eternal comfort to the restless . . ."

There were hundreds of lines to this charm, and if Will were to skip even a one, it would not work. He had labored hard to memorize them all. Now, as he neared the final stanzas, Will felt the thoughts of the queen-mare like a silvery brook flowing alongside his own. They were coming together now, moving as one, muscle upon muscle, thought on thought, a breath away from being a single shared essence in two bodies.

"Riding seems easy to he who rests indoors
But courageous to he who travels the high-roads
On the back of a sturdy horse."

She was breathing hard now. Horses could only run at a full gallop for brief periods of time, though those who did not know them imagined them continuing thus for hours on end. The queen-mare was winded—Will could feel a sympathetic pain in his own chest—and if she did not stop soon and walk it off, she would run until her great heart burst within her.

This was the moment of crisis. Will had to convince her that accepting him as a rider was preferable to death.

Laying his cheek alongside her neck, still singing, he closed his eyes and entered her thoughts. There was neither color nor light in the queen-mare's world, but her sensorium was wider and more varied than his own, for she was possessed of a dozen fractional senses. Riding her mind, he felt the coolness coming off of the walls, and the dampness or dryness of the ground before them. Tiny electrical charges lying dormant in the conduits and steel catwalks that flashed past tickled faintly against his awareness. Variant densities in the air slowed or sped sounds passing through it. Smells arrived in his nostrils with the precise location of their origins. Braids of scent and sound and feel wound together to give him a perfect picture of his surroundings.

Now Will thought back to the farmlands outside his old village, and recalled the dusty green smell of their fields and the way that in late afternoon the sun turned the seeded tops of the grasses into living gold. He pictured the cold, crystalline waters of a stream running swiftly through a tunnel of greenery and exploding under the hooves of his borrowed mount. He called up the flickering flight of butterflies among the wild flowers in a sudden clearing, and then an orchard with gnarled old apple trees and humble-bees droning tipsily among the half-fermented windfalls. This was something the queen-mare had never experienced, nor ever could. But the desire for it was in her blood and her bones. It was written into her genes.

He sang the last words of the charm. Now, he found himself murmuring into the queen-mare's ear.

"Ohhhh, sweet lady," Will crooned. "You and I, mother of horses . . . we were meant to be. Share your strong back with me, let me ride you, and I will show you such sights every time we travel together."

He could feel the tug of his words on her. He could feel her resolve weakening.

"I'll take good care of you, I promise. Oats every day and never a saddle nor a bit. I'll rub you down and comb your mane and plait your tail. No door shall ever lock you in. You'll have fresh water to drink, and clean straw to sleep on."

He was stroking the side of her neck with one hand now. She was skittish still, but Will could feel the warmth of feeling welling up within her. "And this above all," he whispered: "No one shall ever ride you but me."

Gently, tentatively, he felt her pleasure at the thought. Joyously, confidently, he showed her his own pleasure that she felt thus about him. Self flowed into self, so that the distinction between fey and horse, he and her, dissolved.

They were one now.

Will discovered that he was weeping. It had to be for joy because the emotion that filled him now and that threatened to burst his chest asunder was anything but unhappiness. "What's your name, darling?" he whispered, ignoring the tears running down his cheeks. "What should I call you, my sweet?" But horses had no names, either true or superficial, for themselves. They lived in a universe without words. For them, there could be no lies or falsehoods, because things were simply *so*. Which meant that the task of naming her fell upon Will.

"I shall call you Epona," he said, "Great Lady of Horses."

For the first time since he could not remember when, he felt completely happy.

Will was in no hurry to return to the Army of Night's current bivouac. Epona was the swiftest of her breed; he would not arrive last. "Take me where I need to be," he whispered in her ear. "But slowly." Then he gave the queen-mare her head.

They made their way home through pleasant and winding paths. Occasionally, a lone electric bulb or a line of fluorescent tubes flickered weakly to life before them, floated silently by, and then faded to nothing behind them. Once, Epona daintily picked her way up a long-forgotten marble staircase with crystal chandeliers that loomed from the shadows overhead like the ghosts of giant jellyfish. They went down a long passage of rough stone so low that Epona had to bow her head to get through. Twice the ceiling brushed against Will's back, as he clung tightly to her. Yet, though their path seemed roundabout, Will was the first to return to camp. He had but to picture their destination in his mind, and the queen-mare knew the fastest and safest way there.

They emerged from the catacombs under Battery Park and were home.

Radegonde de la Cockaigne arrived second. She had come from the contested lands of the West, as had Will, but a little of the blood of *les bonnes meres* flowed in her veins and she had grown up privileged. She had been taught to ride, rather than learning on stolen time, and as a result her horse-craft was far superior to his. He was not surprised to see that she had wooed and won a particularly mettlesome steed. After her came Kokudza and Jenny Jumpup, also mounted, and then the Starveling and Little Tommy Redcap, both afoot. Some time later, Tatterwag limped in, looking embarrassed. They had gained four horses and lost not a single life.

● ● ●

Lord Weary came out of Hjördis's box, buckling his belt.

Will made his report.

"Any fatalities?" Lord Weary asked. Then, when Will shook his head, he said, "Let's see the horses."

Will had commandeered a space that was said to have been used once as a holding pen for slave smugglers, and then sent forces aboveground to steal, scavenge, or, in last resort, buy straw to spread on the floor. Lord Weary touched the steel-jacketed door that Will hadn't yet ordered taken off its hinges and muttered, "Good. It'll need a bar, though."

Then Weary saw the horses and a rare smile spread over his pale face.

"They're magnificent!" he said. "I had hoped for five, and been willing to settle for three. *Felicitas in media est,* eh? It's a sign."

Seen together, it was obvious that the four steeds were from the same genetic line. The heads were gaunt and narrow, with large blue veins under pale, translucent skin. Their eyes bulged like tennis balls under lids that had grown together and would never open. All glowed faintly in the darkness. Yet equally clear was it that the one was queen and the others her subjects.

Lord Weary went straight to Epona and peeled back her lips

to examine her teeth. "This one is best," he said at last. "She shall be mine."

Will trembled, but said nothing.

"First things first. Measure her for a saddle and bit."

"Sir!" His aide-de-camp, a haint named Chittiface, clicked his heels and saluted.

"The others too, of course. They're still as wild as so many winds, and will need training. Have them broken and gentled. But take care to use no more force than is necessary. For they are my own precious children and I'll not have them scarred or disfigured." He turned on Will and said, "Captain Riddle, I perceive that I have in some way offended you."

"How can a lord offend his captain?" Will said carefully. "One might as well declare that I have offended my hand, or that I act against the best wishes of my left leg. Can the liver and entrails resent the wise leadership of King Head? 'Tis beyond my imagining."

The stables-to-be were swarming with soldiers, many busy, but the greater number merely curious to see the horses. Will noted that all of his fellow raiders were here as well. And every man-jack and lady-jill of them was pretending not to listen.

"Oh, glib, most monstrous glib indeed!" Lord Weary turned a stern face upon Will. "And yet such a litany of sighs and shudders and tics, of soft gasps and shakes of the head, of sudden winces and tightened lips and suppressed retorts have I seen from you as speaks louder than mere words ever could. You are displeased. With me."

"If so, milord, then I apologize most humbly."

"Humbly, sirrah? You defy me to my teeth and plead humility? I'll not have it. Lie to me a third time at your peril."

"But—"

"Kneel!" Weary said, and then, when Will obeyed, "Both knees!"

Lord Weary was Will's liege, and Will had knelt before him often. But always, as became one of his officers, on a single knee. The ground here was wet and unclean, and the damp filth soaked through the cloth where the knee touched it. There was only one reason for Will to be made to kneel on two knees, and that was so that he might be humiliated.

"Now," Lord Weary said. "As I am your liege and you owe me obedience, speak. Tell me what I have done."

"Lord, these words are nothing I would willingly say. But as you command, so must I obey." Simply, then, and without recrimination, Will explained what promises he had made to Epona, and concluded, "What touches my honor is mine alone, and cannot entail yours. I ask only that you consider these matters seriously."

Lord Weary heard him through. Then he said, "Seize him."

Rough hands gripped Will by either arm. The soldier to his left was a new recruit, but the one to his right was Jenny Jumpup. She did not meet his eyes.

"Strip him to the waist," Lord Weary commanded. "Give him five lashes for insolence."

◖ ◖ ◖

Will lay on his stomach, eyes closed, marveling at the intensity of his own pain. He had retreated to his spare and soldierly nest, built of stacked cardboard, clothesline, and charity blankets on a rarely used catwalk that swayed and rattled every time a train passed underneath. It vibrated now as footsteps noisily clanged up the metal rungs from below.

"We brought you water." A refilled two-liter Pepsi bottle thumped down by Will's chest. Tatterwag sat down at the tent's entrance, folding his long legs beneath him. Jenny Jumpup sat down beside him. "I couldn't come see you sooner because Weary gave me double-shift guarding his new horses. I was dead on my feet by the time I was relieved, so I just crawled in my box and collapsed."

With a groan, Will sat up. He took a swig from the bottle and waited.

At last Jenny Jumpup blurted, "He got no right to do that to you!"

"He has every right. But he was wrong to employ those rights in this instance."

Jenny snorted and looked away dismissively. Tatterwag's mouth moved silently as he worked out the implications of that statement. Then, quietly, he said, "It's war."

"Eh?"

"Lord Weary has closed the underworld to everyone but jo-hatsu. Not just the police—transit, sewage, water, gas, and electrical workers too. If they refuse to leave, Lord Weary says, they're to be beaten. Orders are to mark them up good, so that if they return we'll know to kill 'em."

"That's crazy. We've always kept on good terms with the maintenance crews. They can come and go as they wish. Even the cops we don't kill. We let them know who runs things down here, but we don't threaten their safety. That's been the keystone of our polity."

"Not any more," Jenny Jumpup said. "Lord Weary say once we seize control of their transit and utilities, the uplanders ain't got no choice but to negotiate a peace."

"They'll have no choice but to exterminate us." Closing his eyes made Will's head spin. When he opened them, he was still dizzy. "Has Lord Weary gone mad?"

"Maybe so." Tatterwag leaned forward, lowering his voice. "Some of us think that. And if he's mad, what loyalty do we owe him? None! Maybe this is an opportunity. Some of us think that maybe it's time for a regime change."

"Regime change?"

"A *coup d'etat*. You think, Will! You're close enough to him. He trusts you. Slide a knife between his ribs and the problem goes away."

"It *sounds* simple," Will said carefully. Particularly, he did not say, for those who need have nothing to do with the deed but to urge him on to it. "But I doubt its practicality. Lord Weary's troops would tear me apart if I pulled a stunt like that."

"You've got backing among the officers. We talked this through, didn't we, Jenny?"

She nodded.

"They're prepared to acclaim you. This is your moment, Will. You call the Army of Night together and give 'em a speech—you're good with words, they'll listen to you—and Lord Weary is done and forgotten."

Will shook his head. He was about to explain that Tatterwag's idea wouldn't work because Lord Weary had just started a war and consequently was more popular now than he'd ever been before or would ever be again. But then a train slammed by underfoot, making speech impossible. By the time the catwalk stopped shivering and the diesel fumes had begun to dissipate, he found that he had slumped down onto his bed again and his eyes were closed and his mouth would not form words at his command.

A random thought went by and he followed it into the realm of dreams.

●　●　●

In his dreams, the commanders of the mosstroopers were gathered around a table, staring down at a map of the underworld that was nowhere near so detailed or accurate as his own, though reliable enough, he could see, on the major and more recent excavations. One of them indicated the mouth of the tunnel where the sub-surface route broke into the outer world and became a trolley line. "We'll enter here—" his hand skipped lightly down the map tapping three of the larger subway stations—"and at Bowling Green, Tartarus, and Third Street Stations. The stations in between we can lock down to prevent Lord Weary's riffraff from retreating to the surface."

"That still leaves his rats a thousand bolt-holes, most of which are unknown to us."

"Let them break and run, so long as we shatter their army and account for their leaders."

They all bent over the map, their granite faces as large as cathedrals, their moustaches the size of boxcars. "What of Jack Riddle? He looks feverish."

Lying helpless beneath their stony gazes, pinned between parallel lines of ink, Will saw a hand come down out of the darkness, growing larger and larger until it filled his sight and then continued to swell so that it disappeared from his ken, all save one enormous finger. It was wreathed with blue flames so that the air about it wavered and snapped like a flag in a gale. "This bug?" said its owner contemptuously.

The finger touched the map and Will felt flames engulf him.

⚬ ⚬ ⚬

Will's eyes flew open. Tatterwag and Jenny Jumpup were gone and Hjördis knelt by his side. With hands sure and familiar she rubbed balm over his wounds. The pain flared up like fire where she touched him, and sank down to an icy residue where her hands had passed. The smell, flowery and medicinal, lingered.

"You are so good to me," Will murmured.

"It's nothing personal," Hjördis replied.

"Why do you always *say* things like that?"

"Because they're true. There is nothing special or privileged about our relationship. You are our hero and so I have body-rights over you, as I did with Bonecrusher before you, and as I have over Lord Weary even now. You in turn take tribute from each new community you conquer, yes? A lei of orchids, freely offered and freely taken. Settle for that."

Will stayed silent until Hjördis finished applying the balm. Then he said, "They say there's going to be war."

"Yes, I know. Lord Weary came for the crates of rifles we were holding for him. This time there was no brash young stranger to offer an alternative. So it's war. If you care to call it that."

"What else would you call it?"

"Idiocy. But I will not be here to see it. The johatsu are leaving. The tunnels are emptying out as all the communities up and down their lengths desert them for the upper world. I have sent ahead as many of my own folk as have the sense to leave. Now I am visiting the last holdouts, the obstinate and demented, one by one. When I have spoken to them all I will leave myself."

"Where will you go?"

"There are shelters above. Some will sleep in stairwells. Others in the streets. Come with me."

"You can't leave just because there is danger," Will said. "This is your nation!"

"I have never believed in Lord Weary's fantasies. My folk are not warriors, but the weak and the broken who fled down below to find some semblance of safety," Hjördis said. "As their thane, I cannot forget that."

"Tatterwag wants me to lead a revolt against Lord Weary." Said aloud, it sounded unreal. "He wants me to kill Weary, win over the troops with a speech, and then take control of the Army of Night and lead them upward against our oppressors."

"Yes, Tatterwag would, wouldn't he? It's how he thinks."

"Perhaps I should give his plan some thought. It could be tweaked."

"You're overheated." Hjördis rose. "I will leave the balm here; use it when the pain returns. Don't wear a shirt until the welts have healed. Avoid alcohol. Leave before Lord Weary's war begins."

"I can't abandon my troops. I've fought alongside them, I've–"

"My work here is done," Hjördis said. "You will not see me again." She started down the ladder. Before the sound of her feet on the rungs had echoed into silence, Will was asleep.

 ❧ ❧ ❧

When he awoke, Lord Weary was sitting beside him, smoking. His pale, shrewd face looked oddly detached. Groggily, Will sat up.

"You could kill me," Lord Weary said. "But what advantage would it bring you?"

He passed his cigarette to Will, who took a long drag and passed it back. His back still burned terribly, but the balm Hjördis had applied took some of the edge off the pain.

"You're only a hero, after all. I am a conqueror and someday I may yet be an emperor. I know how to rule and you don't. That's the long and the short of it. Without me, the Army of Night would fall apart in a week. The alliances I have formed and the tributes I demand are all imposed by force of my own personality. Kill me and you lose everything that we have built together."

"I don't think I could kill you."

"No," Lord Weary said. "Not in cold blood, certainly."

It was true. Inexplicably, Will's heart still went out to Lord Weary. He thought he could gladly die for the old elf. Yet the anger remained. "Why did you have me whipped?"

"It was salutary for the troops to see you punished. You drew my Army's admiration and then their loyalty. Therefore it was necessary for me to establish who was liege and who his hound. Had you not defied me on the horse, I would have found another excuse. This is *my* delusion, not yours."

"Excuse me?"

"You asked me once how I came to this sad estate, living in darkness, eating rats and stale donuts, and bedding gutter-haints, and you did not like my answer then. Allow me to try again. Anyone can see I'm high-elven. Most of my soldiers think my title was self-assumed, but I assure you it was mine by birth. How could one of my blood and connections ever end up," he gestured, ". . . here?"

"How?"

"It began one morning in the Palace of Leaves," Lord Weary said. "I awoke early to find that the servants had opened all the windows, for it was a perfect day whose breezes were as light and comfortable upon the skin as the water of a sun-warmed lake. I slipped quietly from my bed so as not to disturb my mistresses and, donning a silk kimono, went out onto the balcony. The sun lay low upon the horizon, so that half the land was in light and half in shadow, and at the very center of the world, its focus and definition, was . . . me.

"A vast and weightless emptiness overcame me then, a sensation too light to be called despair but too pitiless to be anything else. The balcony had only a low marble railing–it barely came up to my waist–and it was the easiest thing imaginable to step atop it. I looked down the tapering slope of Babel at the suburbs and tank farms below, hidden here and there by patches of mist, marveling that I could see them at all from such a height. It would be too strong a word to say that I felt an urge to step off. Call it a whim.

"So I did.

"But so illusory did the world seem to me in the mood I was

in that it had no hold upon me whatsoever. Even gravity could not touch me. I stepped into the air and there I stood. Unmoving.

"And in that instant I faced my greatest peril, for I felt my comprehension expanding to engulf the entire world."

"I don't understand," Will said.

"There is a single essence that animates all that lives, from the tiniest mite eking out a barren existence upon the desert-large shell of another mite too small to see with the naked eye, to the very pinnacle of existence, my own humble and lordly self. It informs even inanimate matter, a simple *I am* that lets a boulder know that it is a boulder, a mountain that it is a mountain, a pebble that it is a pebble. Otherwise, all would be flux and change.

"The body, you know, is ninety percent water, and there are those who will tell you that life is only a device which water employs to move itself about. When you die, that water returns to the earth and via natural processes is drawn up into the air, where it eventually joins up with waters that were once snakes, camels, emperors . . . and rains down again, perhaps to join a stream that becomes a river that flows into the sea. Sooner or later, all but your dust will inevitably return to world-girding Oceanus.

"Similarly, when you die your life-force combines with that of everyone else who has ever died or is yet to be born. Like so many lead soldiers being melted down to form a molten ocean of potential."

Will shook his head. "It is a difficult thing to believe."

"No, it is easy to believe. But it is hard, impossibly hard, to *know*. For to recognize the illusory nature of your own being is to flirt with its dissolution. To become one with everything is to become nothing specific at all. Almost, I ceased to be. I experienced then an instant of absolute terror as fleeting and pure as the flash of green light at sunset.

"In that same instant, I spun on my heel and took two steps down to the balcony. I left the Palace of Leaves and went to a bar and got roaring drunk. For I had seen beneath the mask of the world and *there was nothing there!* Since which time, I have distracted myself with debauchery and dreams. I dreamt up the Army of Night and then I dreamt a world for it to conquer. Finally, I dreamt for it a champion—you."

"With all respect, sir, I had a life before we met."

"You were chased into my arms," Lord Weary said, lighting a new cigarette from the butt of the old one. "Didn't it seem strange to you how you were pursued by one anonymous enemy after another? What had you done to deserve such treatment? Can you name your crime?" He flicked the butt out into the air over the tracks. "I have been, I fear, your persecutor-general and the architect of all your sorrows. I am the greatest villain you have ever known."

"If you are a villain," Will said, "then you are a strange one indeed, for I still love you as if you were my own uncle." Even now, he was not lying. "I hate much about you—your power, your arrogance, your former wealth. I despise the way you use others for your own amusement. And yet . . . I cannot deny my feelings for you."

For an unguarded instant, Lord Weary looked old and jaded. His fingers trembled with palsy and his eyes were vacant. Then he cocked his head and a great and terrible warmth filled him again. "Then I shall swear here and now that when I come to power, you shall be paid for all. What is it you want? Think carefully and speak truly, and it shall be yours."

"I want to see you sitting on the Obsidian Throne."

"That is an evasion. Why should that be more important to you than money or power?"

"Because in order for you to reach such a height would require a great slaughter among the Lords of the Mayoralty, such that the Liosalfar and the Dockalfar and even the Council of Magi would be depopulated."

"Again, why?"

Will ducked his head. In a small voice, he said, "My parents were in Brocieland Station when the dragons came and dropped golden fire on the rail yards. My life was destroyed by a war-machine that may have been on that very run. After I was driven out of it, my village was torched by the Armies of the Mighty. All these forces were in the employ of the Lords of Babel and the war itself the result of their mad polity." He looked up, eyes brimming with hatred. "Kill them all! Destroy those responsible, and I shall ask for not a scintilla more from you."

"My dear, sweet Jack." Lord Weary took Will in his arms and stroked his hair caressingly. "I can deny you nothing." He rose to his feet. "Now my war has begun and whether it is real or not, you have your part to play in it. Stand."

"Yes, sir," Will said. Painfully he stood. Bright spots swam in his eyes.

"Put your shirt and jacket on. I'll have the medic shoot you up with witchwart and lidocaine so you can fight."

᎐ ᎐ ᎐

Lord Weary established his headquarters in the catacombs. In a small room lined with bone-filled vaults and smokily lit by ancient lamps filled with recycled motor oil, he went over the maps with his captains, utilizing a cyclops skull as a makeshift table. They'd placed scouts at all the places where the mosstroopers might profitably begin their attack. There were countless ways in and out of the subterranean world, of course, but very few that would admit military forces in any number.

While the troops assembled rifles, made Molotov cocktails, and folded bandanas and soaked them in water so they could be tied about their faces as a defense against tear gas, their superiors planned an ambush and counterattack. Will had his doubts about the effectiveness of their forces, for he had seen soldiers snorting pixie dust and smoking blunts even as they prepared their weapons. Worse, the more he heard of his commander's plans, the less he trusted them. The tunnels were perfect for guerrilla warfare— wait for the enemy to be overextended and bored, then strike swiftly from the darkness and flee. Direct confrontation meant giving up that advantage. But Lord Weary's compulsion was strong upon him, and in the end Will had no choice but to obey.

So it was that Will found himself upon his motorcycle as part of a small advance force that watched from the shadows as the mosstroopers poured down from the Third Street platform and onto the tracks. The station had been closed, the trains redirected, and the power to the third rail cut. The troopers took up their positions in what looked to Will to be a thoroughly professional manner. They were every one of them Tylwyth Teg—disciplined, experienced, and well-trained. They wore black helmets and carried plexi shields. Gas grenades hung from their belts and holstered pistols as well.

The mosstroopers advanced in staggered ranks, with the dire wolves in the front row, straining at their leashes. It looked for all the world as if the wolves were pulling the troopers forward.

Will watched and waited.

Then, in his distant catacomb sanctum, where he sat scrying the scene in a bowl of ink, Lord Weary spoke a Word which Will could feel in the pit of his stomach.

A sorcerous wind came blowing up from the throat of the earth. It lifted the newspapers and handbills littering the ground and gave them wings, so that they flapped wildly and flew directly into the faces of the mosstroopers like so many ghostly chickens and pelicans. Ragged items of discarded clothing picked themselves up and began to stagger toward the invaders. Coming up out of nowhere as they had, the sorcerous nothings must have looked like a serious magical attack.

Two soldiers, both combat mages by the testimony of their uniforms, stepped forward and raised titanium staves against the oncoming paper birds and cloth manikins. As one, they spoke a Word of their own.

All in an instant, the wind died and the newspapers and old clothes burst into powder.

That was Will's cue. He held a magnesium flare ready in one hand and his lighter in the other. Now, before the mages' staves could recharge, he flipped open his Zippo one-handed and struck a light. Then he pulled the welder's goggles over his eyes and shouted, "Heads down!"

The snipers, who did not have goggles of their own, covered their eyes with their arms. The five cavalry lit and threw their flares.

"Go!" Will screamed.

He opened the throttle too fast and his Kawasaki stalled out. Cursing, he kick-started it back to life.

The plan of attack was simplicity itself: In the instant that their defenses were depleted, hit the mosstroopers and their wolves with magnesium flares, then charge the center of their line while they were still blinded. There, the powerful bodies of the horses would break a way through, spreading confusion in their wake. They were to continue onward without stopping and around the bend beyond Third Street Station, disappearing up the tunnel. This would leave the enemy easy targets for Will's sharpshooters. Or so it was planned.

In practice, it didn't work out that way.

Will had lost only seconds by stalling his bike. But in that delay, the horses had outpaced him. Now he saw them overwhelmed by the dire wolves that the blinded mosstroopers had released. Relying on scent rather than sight, those fierce predators met the horses in the air, snarling and snapping, sinking their great teeth into pale throats and haunches.

The first to fall was Epona.

He heard her scream, and saw both horse and rider buried in black-furred furies. The rider, a nonentity named Mumpoker, died almost immediately but his noble steed bit and kicked even as she went down. Not far behind her, Hengroen and Holvarpnia were also overwhelmed. Will saw Jenny Jumpup leap free of Embarr, collide with a dire wolf in mid-air and fall with the wolf beneath her and both her hands at its throat.

Will opened the throttle wide. Yelling, he drove toward Epona and the fallen riders hoping to achieve he knew not what. But then tear-gas canisters fell clattering to the ground and a wall of chemical mist rolled forward and into his troops. The bandana that Will wore provided little protection. Fiery tears welled up, and he could not see. Desperately, he tried to spin his motorcycle about. The bike skidded on its side and almost slid out from under him. His Zippo flew skittering away.

Will struggled to right the motorcycle.

All about him the dire wolves were fighting and hunting. Though the brutes could not see and their sense of smell had been neutralized by the tear gas, they were yet deadly to any combatant they chanced to stumble into.

A wolf's paws landed on Will's handlebars. All in a panic he raised his pistol and squeezed the trigger. Nothing happened.

He had forgotten the safety.

The dire wolf grinned, baring sharp white fangs. "If you're going to piss yourself, best do it now," it said. "Because you're about to die."

The hideous jaws were about to close on Will's face when the wolf abruptly grunted and half its head disappeared in red spray.

"Some fun, huh, Captain?" Jenny Jumpup grinned madly at Will, then stuffed her pistol in her belt and reached out a hand toward him.

Will pulled her up behind him on the motorcycle. "Let's get the fuck out of here!" he shouted.

They did.

◄ ◄ ◄

That was the war's first action. Will's snipers had retreated in disarray before the advancing mosstroopers without firing a single shot. The horses entrusted him were dead and their riders, all but one, dead or captured. It was a fiasco and, worse, it deserved to be one. Lord Weary's soldiers were only half-trained and their tactics were makeshift at best. They couldn't go up against a disciplined military force like the mosstroopers and expect anything but defeat. That was obvious to Will now.

The guttering flares died to nothing behind them and the dire wolves were called back to their handlers. Will pocketed his goggles. The mosstroopers would continue to advance, he knew, but at a cautious pace. Since they were no longer in immediate danger, he throttled down his bike to a less dangerous speed. Thus, he was able to react in time when Jenny Jumpup murmured, "I think I gone pass out now," and started to slide from the pillion.

Will twisted around to grab Jenny Jumpup with one arm, while simultaneously slamming on the brake. Somehow, he managed to bring the Kawasaki to a stop without dropping her.

Pushing down the kickstand with his heel, Will dismounted and lowered his lieutenant to the ground. Semicircles of blood soaked through her blouse and trousers, more than he could count.

"Oh, shit," he muttered.

Jenny Jumpup's eyes flickered open. She managed a wan

smile. "Hey. You should see the wolf." Then her eyes deadened and her face went slack.

He bandaged her as best he could and then, mating her belt with his, improvised a pistol-belt carry. Bent over beneath her weight, he staggered onto the cycle and got it going again. He dared not stay in the path of the mosstroopers, and he would not leave her behind.

Into the dark they rode.

Once, briefly, Jenny Jumpup regained consciousness. "I got something to confess, Captain," she said. "When Lord Weary whipped you? I enjoyed it."

Shaken, Will said, "I'm sorry if I—"

"Oh, I didn't mean that in a bad way." Jenny Jumpup was silent for a long time. Then she said, "It kinda turned me on. Maybe when this is all over, we can . . ." Then she was out again. Will twisted around and saw that her skin was grey.

"Hang in there. I'll have you to a medic soon."

Will rode as fast and furious as ever he had before.

Some distance down the tunnel, Tatterwag stepped out of the gloom in front of the Kawasaki. And so Will was reunited with those of his snipers who had not simply thrown away their rifles and fled but had retreated with some shred of order. Besides Tatterwag, they were Sparrowgrass, Drumbelo, the Starveling, and Xylia of Arcadia.

Carefully, Will lowered Jenny Jumpup's body to the ground. "See to her wounds," he said. "They were honorably gotten."

Xylia of Arcadia knelt over Jenny. Then she stood and touched her head, heart, and crotch. "She's dead."

Will stared down at the corpse. It was a grey and pathetic thing. Jenny Jumpup's clothes were dark with blood and, deprived of her personality, her face was dull and ordinary. Had he not carried it here on his back, Will would have sworn the body was not hers.

After a long silence, Tatterwag stooped over the body. "I'll take her pistols for a keepsake." He stuck them in his belt.

"I'll take her boots," Xylia of Arcadia said. "They won't fit me, but I know somebody they will."

One by one they removed Jenny Jumpup's things. Will took

her cigarettes and lighter and Drumbelo her throwing knife. The Starveling took her trousers and tunic. That left only a small silver orchid hung on a chain about her neck, which Sparrowgrass solemnly kissed and stuffed into a jeans pocket. They looked at one another uneasily, and then Will cleared his throat. *"From the south she came."*

"The bird, the warlike bird," said Xylia of Arcadia.

"With whirring wings," said Drumbelo.

"She wishes to change herself," said the Starveling.

"Back to the body of that swift bird," said Tatterwag.

"She throws away her body in battle," Sparrowgrass concluded.

Already, freed of her elan vital and any lingering attachment to her possessions, Jenny Jumpup's body was sinking into the ground. Slowly at first, and then more quickly, it slid downward into the darkness of the earth from which it had come and to which all would someday inevitably return. Haints more literally than others, perhaps, but the truth was universal.

❍ ❍ ❍

The staging area, when they finally got there, was in an uproar. The platforms swarmed with haints, feys, and gaunts, carrying crates, barrels, and railroad ties to add to the growing barricades, and moving guns and munitions to hastily improvised emplacements. One leather-winged night gaunt flew up the tunnel from which Will's company had just emerged, with a dispatch box in its claws. Will's heart sank to see how amateurish it all looked.

Porte Molitor Station had seemed a good base because it was located where the A, C, and E lines split from Routes 1, 2, and 3 and was not far downline from the sub-surface exit, thus giving easy access to all four potential war zones. But Porte Molitor was a ghost station, built but never used, and so it did not open to the surface. Now, with retreating soldiers converging from every front and scouts reporting that the enemy was advancing through all three tunnels, it seemed to Will like nothing so much as a trap.

"Who's in charge here?" Will shouted. "What are all these soldiers doing on the tracks? Isn't anybody in charge?"

"Lord Weary has placed Captain Hackem in command of the

defenses for the left Uptown tunnel," a weary-looking hulder said. "Chittiface is responsible for the right Uptown tunnel. And he himself commands the forces defending the Downtown tunnel. Hello, Jack."

"Hjördis!" Will cried in astonishment. "You're back."

"Everybody's back. All the johatsu who fled the tunnels have returned, without exception."

"But *why?*" Earlier, Will had urged the lady-thane not to abandon Lord Weary's cause. Now he knew his counsel had been wrong. She had left and been right to do so. She should have stayed away.

"I don't know." Hjördis looked stricken. "It defies all reason. Perhaps there is a compulsion on us. But if so, it is of a force greater than any I have ever known or heard rumor of, for it drives a multitude."

"Where is Lord Weary? If anybody understands this mystery, it will be he."

"Lord Weary charges you to consult with him before the battle begins. On what matter, he does not say." Hjördis turned away. "Now I must leave. I have a field hospital to oversee."

Will watched her leave. Then he turned to Tatterwag and held out a hand. "Give me your combat knife."

Knife in hand, Will clambered over the barricade and kick-started his bike. Then, though it broke his heart to do so, he plunged the knife into the fuel tank. Gasoline sprayed into the air and drenched the ground. Up and down the tracks he rode. The ties made it a teeth-rattling ride and spread the gasoline from wall to wall before the Kawasaki sputtered to a stop.

"There!" he roared when he was done. "Now, when the hell-hounds come sniffing after us, this will render them nose-deaf!"

That done, he strode off to confront Lord Weary, Tatterwag in tow.

The Downtown tunnel fortifications were simpler than the Uptown barricades—a single barrier that reached almost to the ceiling, without crenels or even a walkway along its top—but correspondingly more massive. He found Little Tommy Redcap overseeing the work there in Lord Weary's place. Johatsu carried box after box to the I-beams and duct-taped them to the foot of the supports. Others ran electrical wires from box to box. They could only be explosive devices.

"What the fuck are you doing?" Will demanded.

"What the fuck does it look like I'm doing?" Little Tommy Redcap lifted his voice: "Yo! I need more primers here!"

"It looks like you're preparing to bring half the buildings in the Bowery crashing down on our heads."

The haint who came running up with the box of primers was puffing on a lit cigar. Little Tommy Redcap snatched it from the johatsu's mouth and started to fling it away. Then he stopped and stuck it in his own mouth instead. "If you knew, why did you ask?"

"If this is done by Lord Weary's orders, then he's crazy," Will said. "If you touch those things off, you'll kill us all."

"You think I'm afraid of dying?" Little Tommy Redcap laughed and then tapped the ashes from his cigar onto the primers for emphasis. "It's a good day to die!"

"You're crazy too."

"Maybe so, but I still got things to do. You got any complaints—" Little Tommy Redcap jerked a thumb upward—"take 'em up with the Big Guy."

High overhead was a gallery which Will did not remember seeing before, in a wall that was taller than it could possibly be. (The station seemed larger too—but he had no time to worry on it.) Lord Weary's face was a pale oval afloat in the darkness like an indifferent moon gazing down upon the wickedness of the world. "I will," he said. "How do I get up there?"

There was a stairwell that Will had never seen before. Two insect-headed guards in green leather armor uncrossed their pikes for him but recrossed them when Tatterwag tried to follow. Leaving his lieutenant behind to argue, Will took the steps two and three at a time. Heart pounding—when had he last rested?—he burst into the gallery.

Lord Weary was leaning over a marble balustrade, contemplating the scene below. He glanced up briefly. "Join me."

A strange lassitude overcame Will and all sense of urgency left him. It was as if in the presence of his liege he had no ambitions of his own. Unhurriedly, he joined the elf-lord. Together they gazed down on the scurrying johatsu. A salt breeze blew up, dispelling the stagnant air of the tunnels. It seemed to Will that he caught a hint of flowers as well. An unseen sun was warm upon his back. "What place is this?"

"A memory, and nothing more. My attention wanders, I fear." Suddenly they stood in a clean, empty room of white marble. A light wind flowed through its high windows. A black absence sat at its center. From some angles it looked like a chair.

"Is that—?"

"Yes. You behold the Obsidian Throne." The air darkened and the vision faded, returning Will to the stale smells and staler prospects of his life underground. Briefly, Lord Weary was silent. Then he said, "The final conflict approaches. Can you hear it coming?"

Will could. "What's that sound?" he asked. "That . . . howling."

"Just watch."

The howling grew until it became a quartet of train whistles shrieking almost in synch. Louder they grew, and louder still. The thunder of iron wheels filled the station. The ground underfoot trembled with premonition.

Then the Uptown barricades exploded. Fragments of beams, barrels, and soldiers were flung into the air as locomotives smashed through the hastily assembled defenses.

There were four of the great beasts, running in unison, with plows affixed to the fronts of their cabs and they did not slow as they passed through the station. Shoulder to shoulder they sped, grinding troops under their wheels. At the Downtown tunnel, they crashed through the barricade and its defenders and, with final triumphant howls, rushed headlong into darkness, leaving hundreds dead in their wake.

Will clutched the balustrade, his eyes starting from his head. The screams and shouts of the survivors echoed and re-echoed in his ears like surf. He could not master his thoughts; they tumbled over each other in meaningless cascades. "You knew this would happen," he said finally, fighting back nausea. "You *arranged* this."

Lord Weary smiled sadly. He leaned over the railing and shouted, "Redcap!"

In the wake of the trains had come the mosstroopers. Somebody fired a magnesium flare at the first squadron to arrive, setting afire the gasoline Will had sprayed throughout the tunnel. But it did not stop them. Burning and ravening, the dire wolves entered Porte Molitor and began killing the survivors. Behind them came the mosstroopers, weapons ready.

Yet amid all this confusion, Lord Weary's voice carried to its target. Little Tommy Redcap looked up from the smoldering body of a dying wolf. "Sir?"

"Are the explosives ready?"

"Sir! Yes, sir!"

"Stand by the igniter and await my command."

"Sir!" Little Tommy Redcap turned and disappeared into the fleeing, fighting, panicking mob.

So great was Will's befuddlement then that it did not surprise him to see Tatterwag leap from the stairwell with blood on his jacket and Jenny Jumpup's pistols in his hands. "Traitor!" he cried, and discharged them both point-blank at Lord Weary's head.

"Ah," the elf-lord sighed. "Like so many things, this moment was far more pleasing in the anticipation than in its realization." He opened a hand and there lay the two freshly fired pistol balls.

He let them drop to the floor.

"You bore me."

All color drained from the swamp gaunt's face. Pleadingly, he raised his hands and shook his head. With neither hurry nor reluctance, Lord Weary reached toward him. His fingers closed not upon Tatterwag, however, but around a filthy old greatcoat. With a moue of distaste, he tossed it over the balustrade.

"What did you just do?" Will asked, shocked. "How did you do that?"

Hjördis stepped from the stairwell, as Tatterwag had a minute before. "He's a glamour-wallah," she said. "Aren't you?"

Lord Weary smiled and shrugged. "I was the King's Master of Revels," he said. "Not that His Absent Majesty ever called upon my services, of course. Still . . . I had talent, I kept in practice. More than one member of the Court was of my devising. Once, I threw a masked ball at which half of those attending had no objective reality whatsoever. The next morning, many a lord and lady woke to discover their bed-mates had been woven of naught but whimsy and thin air."

"I don't understand."

"He creates illusions," Hjördis said. "Very convincing ones. For entertainment. When I was living in a shelter near the Battery, the government sent a glamour-wallah down for the winter solstice and he filled the streets with comets and butterflies." Then, sadly, "Was Tatterwag nothing, after all, but one of your creations?"

Lord Weary cocked his head apologetically. "Forgive an old elf his follies. I made him for a grand role, if that makes any difference. He would have shot me just as I was about to ascend to the Obsidian Throne, and then died in reprisal at the hands of our hot-blooded young hero here." He indicated Will. "Then, lying in his arms, I would have begged Jack to ascend the throne in my place. Which, because he was ambitious and because it was my dying wish, he would have done.

"Alas, my interest in this game has flickered to embers long before I thought it would. What can one do?" He turned to Hjördis. "I suppose you are here for some reason."

"Yes. Your munitions teams have planted explosives on the support beams of the buildings above us. If they are set off, all the johatsu and all the Army of Night will die."

"And this bothers you, I suppose?" Lord Weary sighed. "Foolish child. They were never real in the first place."

Abruptly the cries, shouts, and other noises from below ceased. Hjördis stared over the balustrade down at the suddenly empty tracks and platforms. There were no corpses, no shattered barricades, no mosstroopers or burning wolves, no rebel army, nothing but the common litter of an abandoned subway station. "Then . . . they were all, johatsu and troopers alike, your creations? Only Will and I were . . . ?"

Lord Weary raised an eyebrow and she fell silent.

At last, she spoke again. "I had thought I was real," Hjördis said in a monotone. "I had memories. Ambitions. Friends."

"You grow maudlin." Lord Weary reached for her. His fingers

closed about a mop. This, like the greasy overcoat that had been Tatterwag, he tossed lightly away.

"I'm next, I suppose," Will said bitterly. He clenched his fists. "I *loved* you! Of all the cruel and wicked things you've done, that was the worst. I deserved better. I may not be real, but I deserved better."

"You are as real as I am," Lord Weary said. "No more, no less." He was growing older before Will's eyes. His skin was as pink and translucent as a baby's, but loose upon his flesh. His hair was baby-wispy too and white. The tremor in his voice was impossible to ignore. "Take from that what comfort you can. For my part, I sought to put off enlightenment through treason and violent adventure. But now I see the unity of all things, and it seems that senility has come for me at . . ."

Lord Weary's eyes closed and his head sank down upon his chest. Slowly and without fuss, he faded away to nothing. With him went the balustrade, the gallery, and all the light from the air. Will felt the darkness wrap itself about him like the warm and loving arms of Mother Night.

He did not know if he existed or not, nor did he care. Lord Weary's war—if it had ever begun in the first place—was over.

◠ ◠ ◠

Will awoke to find himself lying on the subway tracks. He staggered to his feet and then had to leap madly backwards as a train came blasting down the tunnel at him.

When his vision returned, Will began to walk.

He'd been plodding along for some time when he saw a haint in the tunnel ahead, wearing the hip waders and hard hat of a sewer worker. "What you doing here, white boy?" he asked when Will hailed him.

"I'm lost."

"Well, you best get yourself unlost. You don't belong down here."

"Point me the way out and I'm gone."

The haint had started to fade through a wall. He hesitated,

and leaned back. "Turn around the way you came. Look for a yellow light on the left. They's a door under it that leads out."

So Will did as he said. Vaguely, he remembered encountering this same sewer worker when first he had stumbled into the underground. He had no idea what that meant. Nor did he know how much of what he had seen and felt and done in the past however-many months had actually happened. Friends and foes alike had died—but had they ever existed in the first place? Were Bonecrusher, Epona, Jenny Jumpup and all the rest real? And if not, did that free him of the obligation to care about them and to mourn their deaths? Try though he might, he could make no sense out of what he had been through.

But when he finally spotted the yellow light shining within its metal cage and the steel door beneath it, he felt a stirring and a rumbling deep within his blood and bones. It was the dragon, laughing. Louder and wilder that laughter grew until it filled up all his being and Will could not help but laugh as well. At what he did not know, unless it was the futility and pointlessness of life itself. He laughed until he cried.

In the silence that ensued, for the first time ever, he heard the dragon speak to him not in emotions but in words.

He began to listen.

AFTER THE SIEGE

by Cory Doctorow

Cory Doctorow was born in Toronto, Canada, in 1971. A self-described "renaissance geek," he was raised by Trotskyist school-teachers in the wilds of Canada, attended alternative schools in Toronto, worked at a SF specialty bookstore, dropped out of four universities, and briefly moved to Mexico to write. He has worked as a programmer, web designer, volunteer in Central America, CIO, founder of a software company, and as an advocate, before becoming a full-time writer last year. Doctorow began selling fiction when he was seventeen, and published a small handful of stories through the early and mid-'90s. His story "Craphound" appeared in 1998, and he won the John W. Campbell Award for Best New Writer in 2000. His best known short fiction is a series of stories that use the titles of famous SF short stories, revisiting the assumptions underpinning their narratives. So far "Anda's Game" has been selected for the prestigious Best American Short Stories *and "I, Robot" was nominated for the Hugo Award. His first novel,* Down and Out in the Magic Kingdom, *was followed by the collections* A Place So Foreign and Eight More *and* Overclocked, *and the novels* Eastern Standard Tribe *and* Someone Comes to Town, Someone Leaves Town. *Upcoming are two new novels from Tor, one a YA,* Little Brother, *about hackers, the other about the economic singularity.*

THE DAY THE siege began, Valentine was at the cinema across the street from her building. The cinema had only grown the night before and when she got out of bed and saw it there, all gossamer silver supports and brave sweeping candy-apple red curves, she'd begged Mata and Popa to let her go. She knew that all the children in the building would spend the day there—didn't the pack of them explore each fresh marvel as a group? The week before it had been the clever little flying cars that swooped past each other with millimeters to spare, like pigeons ripping over your head. Before that it had been the candy forest where the trees sprouted bon-bons and sticks of rock, and every boy and girl in the city had been there, laughing and eating until their bellies and sides ached. Before that, the swarms of robot insects that had gathered up every fleck of litter and dust and spirited it all away to the edge of town where they'd somehow chewed it up and made factories out of it, brightly colored and airy as an aviary. Before that: fish in the river. Before that: the new apartment buildings. Before that: the new hospitals. Before that: the new government offices.

Before that: the revolution, which Valentine barely remembered—she'd been a little kid of ten then, not a big girl of thirteen like now. All she remembered was a long time when she'd been always a little hungry, and when everything was grey and dirty and Mata and Popa whispered angrily at each other when they thought she slept and her little brother Trover had cried thin sickly cries all night, which made her angry too.

The cine was amazing, the greatest marvel yet as far as she was concerned. She and the other little girls crowded into one of the many balconies and tinkered with the controls for it until it lifted free—how they'd whooped!—and sailed off to its own little spot under the high swoop of the dome. From there the screen was a little distorted, but they could count the bald spots on the old war heroes' heads as they nodded together in solemn congress, waiting for the films to start. From there they could spy on the boys who were making spitball mischief that was sure to attract a reprimand, though for now the airborne robots were doing a flawless job of silently intercepting the boys' missiles before they disturbed any of the other watchers.

The films weren't very good in Valentine's opinion. The first one was all about the revolution as if she hadn't heard enough about the revolution! It was all they talked about in school for one thing. And her parents! The *quantities*, the positive *quantities* of times they'd sat her down to Explain the Revolution, which was apparently one of their duties as bona fide heroes of the revolution.

This was better than most though, because they'd made it with a game and it was a game that Valentine played quite a lot and thought was quite good. She recognized the virtual city modeled on her own city, the avatars' dance-moves taken from the game too, along with the combat sequences and the scary zombies that had finally given rise to the revolution.

That much she knew and that much they all knew: without the zombies, the revolution would never have come. Zombiism and the need to cure it had outweighed every other priority. Three governments had promised that they'd negotiate better prices for zombiism drugs, and three governments had failed and in the end, the Cabinet had been overrun by zombies who'd torn three MPs to bits and infected seven more and the crowd had carried the PM out of her office and put her in a barrel and driven nails through it and rolled it down the river-bank into the river, something so horrible and delicious that Valentine often thought about it like you poke a sore tooth with your tongue.

After that, the revolution, and a new PM who wouldn't negotiate the price of zombiism drugs. After that, a PM who built zombiism drug factories right there in the city, giving away the drug in spray and pill and needles. From there, it was only a matter of time until everything was being made right there, copies of movies and copies of songs and copies of drugs and copies of buildings and cars and you name it, and that was the revolution, and Valentine thought it was probably a good thing for everyone except the old PM whom they'd put in the barrel.

The next movie was much better and Valentine and Leeza, who was her best friend that week put their arms around each others' shoulders and watched it avidly. It was about a woman who was in love with two men and the men hated each other and there was fighting and glorious kissing and sophisticated, cutting insults, and oh they dressed so *well!* The audio was dubbed over from English but that was OK, the voice-actors they used were very good.

After the second showing, she and her friends allowed their seats to lower and set off for the concessions stand where they found the beaming proprietors of the cinema celebrating their opening day with chocolates and thick sandwiches and fish pies and bottles of brown beer for the adults and bottles of fizzy elderflower for the kids. Valentine saw the cute boy who Leeza liked and tripped him so he practically fell in Leeza's lap and that set the two of them to laughing so hard they nearly didn't make it back to their seats.

The next picture barely had time to start when it was shut off and the lights came up and one of the proprietors stepped in front of the screen, talking into his phone, which must have been dialed into the cine's sound system.

"Comrades, your attention please. We have had word that the city is under attack by our old enemies. They have bombed the east quarter and many are dead. More bombs are expected soon." They all spoke at once, horrified non-words that were like a panic, a sound made Valentine want to cover her ears.

"Please, comrades," the speaker said. He was about sixty and was getting a new head of hair, but he had the look of the old ones who'd lived through the zombiism, a finger or two bent at a funny angle by a secret policeman, a wattle under the chin of skin loosened by some dark year of starvation. "Please! We must be calm! If there are shelters in your apartment buildings and you can walk there in less than ten minutes, you should walk there. If your building lacks shelters, or if it would take more than ten minutes to go to your building's shelter, you may use some of the limited shelter space here. The seats will lower in order, two at a time, to prevent a rush, and when yours reaches ground, please leave calmly and quickly and get to your shelter."

Leeza clutched at her arm. "Vale! My building is more than ten minutes' walk! I'll have to stay here! Oh, my poor parents! They'll think—"

"They'll think you're safe with me, Leeze," Valentine said, hugging her. "I'll stay with you and both our parents can worry about us."

They headed for the shelter together, white-faced and silent in the slow-moving crowd that shuffled down the steps into the first basement, the second basement, then the shelter below that. A war hero was handing out masks to everyone who entered and he had to go and find more child-sized ones for them so they waited patiently in the doorway.

"Valentine! You don't belong here! Go home and leave room for we who need it!" It was her worst enemy, Reeta, who had been her best friend the week before. She was red in the face and pointing and shouting. "She lives across the street! You see how selfish she is! Across the street is her own shelter and she would take a spot away from her comrades, send them walking through the street—"

The hero silenced her with a sharp gesture and looked hard at Valentine. "Is it true?"

"My friend is scared," she said, squeezing Leeza's shaking shoulder. "I will stay with her."

"You go home now," the hero said, putting one of the child-sized masks back in the box. "Your friend will be fine and you'll see her in a few minutes when they sound the all clear. Hurry now." His voice and his look brooked no argument.

So Valentine fought her way up the stairs—so many headed for the shelter!—and out the doors and when she stepped out, it was like a different city. The streets, always so busy and cheerful, were silent. No air-cars flew overhead. It was silent, silent, like the ringing in your ears after you turn your headphones up too loud. It was so weird that a laugh escaped her lips, though not one of mirth, more like a scared laugh.

She stood a moment longer and then there was a sound like far-away thunder. A second later, a little wind. On its heels, a bigger wind, icy cold and then hot as the oven when you open the door, nearly blowing her off her feet. It *smelled* like something dead or something deadly. She *ran* as fast as she could across the street, pounding hell for leather to her front door. Just as she reached for it, there was a much louder thunderclap, one that lifted her off her feet and tossed her into the air, spinning her around. As she spun around and around, she saw the brave red dome of the cine disintegrate, crumble to a million shards that began to rain down on the street. Then the boom dropped her hard on the pavement and she saw no more.

The day after the siege began, the doctor fitted Valentine for her hearing aid and told her to come back in ten years for a battery change. She hardly felt it slide under her skin but once it was there, the funny underwatery sound of everything and everyone turned back into bright sound as sharp as the cine's had been.

Now that she could hear, she could speak, and she grabbed Popa's hands. "The cine!" she said. "Oh, Popa, the cine, those poor people! What happened to them?"

"The work crews opened the shelter ten hours later," Popa said. He never sugar-coated anything for her, even though Mata disapproved of talking to her like an adult. "Half of them died from lack of air—the air re-circulators were damaged by the bomb, and the shelter was air-tight. The rest are in hospital."

She cried. "Leeza—"

Mata took her hands. "Leeza is fine," she said. "She made sure we told you that."

She cried harder, but smiling this time. Trover was on her mother's hip, and looking like he didn't know whether to stay quiet or pitch one of his famous tantrums. Automatically, Valentine gave him a tickle that brought a smile that kept him from bursting out in tears.

They left the hospital together and walked home, though it was far. The Metro wasn't running and the air-cars were still grounded. Some of the buildings they passed were nothing but rubble, and there robots and people labored to make sense of them and get them reassembled and back on their feet.

It wasn't until the next day that she found out that Reeta had been killed under the cine. She threw up the porridge she'd had for breakfast and shut herself in her room and cried into her pillow until she fell asleep.

Three days after the siege began, Mata went away.

"You can't go!" Popa shouted at her. "Are you crazy? You can't go to the front! You have two small children, woman!" He was red-faced and his hands were clenching and unclenching. Trover was having a tantrum that was so loud and horrible that Valentine wanted to rip her hearing aids out.

Mata's eyes were red. "Harald, you know I have to do this. It's not the 'front'–it's our own city. My country needs me–if I don't help to fight for it, then what will become of our children?"

"You never got over the glory of fighting, did you?" Her father's voice was bitter in a way that she'd never heard before. "You're an addict!"

She held up her left hand and shook it in his face. "An addict! Is *that* what you think?" Her middle finger and little finger on that hand had never bent properly in all of Valentine's memory, and when Valentine had asked her about it, she'd said the terrible word *knucklebreakers* which was the old name for the police. "You think I'm addicted to *this?* Harald, honor and courage and patriotism are *virtues* no matter that you would make them into vices and shame our children with your cowardice. I go to fight now, Harald, and it's for *all* of us."

Popa couldn't find another word to speak in the two seconds it took for Mata to give her two children hard kisses on the foreheads and slam out the door, and then it was Valentine and Popa and Trover, still screaming. Her father fisted the tears out of his eyes, not bothering to try to hide them, and said, "Well then, who wants pancakes?"

But the power was out and he had to make them cereal instead.

● ● ●

Two weeks after the siege began, her mother didn't come home and the city came for her father.

"Every adult, comrade, every adult fights for the city."

"My children–" he sputtered. Mata hadn't been home all night, and it wasn't the first time. She and Popa barely spoke anymore.

"Your girl there is big enough to look after herself, aren't you honey?" The woman from the city was short and plump and wore heavy armor and was red in the face from walking up ten flights to get to their flat. The power to the elevators was almost always out.

Valentine hugged her father's leg. "My Popa will fight for the city," she said. "He's a hero."

He was. He'd fought in the revolution and he'd been given a medal for it. Sometimes when no one was looking, Valentine took out her parents' medals and looked at their tiny writing, their shining, unscratchable surfaces, their intricate ribbons.

The woman from the city gave her father a look that said, *You see, a child understands, what's your excuse?* Valentine couldn't quite feel guilty for taking the woman's side. Leeza's parents fought every day.

"I must leave a note for my wife," he said. Valentine realized that for the first time in her life her parents were going to leave her *all on her own* and felt a thrill.

⊖ ⊖ ⊖

Two weeks and one day after the siege began, her Mata came home and the city came for Valentine.

Mata was grimy and exhausted, and she favored one leg as she went about the flat making them cold cereal with water—all the milk had spoiled—and dried fruits. Trover looked curiously at her as though he didn't recognize her, but eventually he got in her way and she snapped at him to move already and he pitched a relieved fit, pounding his fists and howling. How that little boy could howl!

She sat down at the table with Valentine and the two of them ate their cereal together.

"Your father?"

"He said he was digging trenches—that's what he did all day yesterday."

Her mother's eyes glinted. "Good. We need more trenches. We'll fortify the whole city with them, spread them out all the way to their lines, trenches we can move through without being seen or shot. We'll take the war to those bastards and slip away before they know we've killed them." Mata had apparently forgotten all about not talking to Valentine like a grownup.

The knock at the door came then, and Mata answered it and it was the woman from the city again. "Your little girl," she said.

"No," Mata said. Her voice was flat and would not brook any contradiction. She'd bossed her nine brothers—Valentine's uncles, now scattered to the winds—and then commanded a squadron in the revolution, and no one could win an argument with her. As far as Valentine knew, no one could win an argument with her.

"No?" The woman from the city said. "No is not an option, comrade."

Mata drew herself up. "My husband digs. I fight. My daughter cares for our son. That's enough from this family."

"There are old people in this building who need water brought for them. There's a creche for the boy underground, he'll be happy enough there. Your little girl is strong and the old people are weak."

"No," her mother said. "I'm very sorry, but no." She didn't sound the least bit sorry.

The woman from the city went away. Mata sat down and went back to eating her cereal with water without a word, but there was another knock at the door fifteen minutes later. The woman from the city had brought along an old hero with one arm and one eye. He greeted Mata by name and Mata gave him a smart salute. He spoke quietly in her ear for a moment. She saluted him again and he left.

"You'll carry water," Mata said.

Valentine didn't mind, it was a chance to get out of the flat. One day of baby-sitting the human tantrum had convinced her that any chore was preferable to being cooped up with him.

She carried water that day. She'd expected to be balancing buckets over her shoulders like in the schoolbooks, but they fitted her with a bubble-suit that distributed the weight over her whole body and then filled it up with a hose until she weighed nearly twice what she normally did. Other kids were in the stairwells wearing identical bubble-suits, sloshing up the steps to old peoples' flats that smelled funny. The old women and men that Valentine saw that day pinched her cheeks and then emptied out her bubble-suit into their cisterns.

It was exhausting work and by the end of the day she had

stopped making even perfunctory conversation with the other water-carriers. The old people she met at the day's end were bitter about being left alone and thirsty all day and they snapped at her and didn't thank her at all.

She picked Trover up from the creche and he demanded that he be carried and she had half a mind to toss him down the stairs. But she noticed that he had a bruise over his eye and his hands and face were sticky and dirty and she decided that he'd had a hard day too. Mata and Popa weren't home when they got there so Valentine made dinner—more cold cereal and some cabbage with leftover dumplings kept cool in a bag hung out the window— and then when they still hadn't returned by bedtime, Valentine tucked Trover in and then fell asleep herself.

⇔ ⇔ ⇔

One month after the siege began, Valentine's mother came home in tears.

"What is it, Mata?" Valentine said, as soon as her mother came through the door. "Are you hurt?" Her mother had come home hurt more than once in the month, bandaged or splinted or covered in burn ointment or hacking at some deep chemical irritation in her throat and nose and lungs.

Her mother's eyes were swollen like they had been the day she'd been caught by the gas and they'd had to do emergency robot field-surgery on them. But there were no sutures. Tears had swollen her eyes.

"New trenchbuster missiles on the eastern front," she said. "The anti-missiles are too slow for them." She sobbed, a terrible terrifying sound that Valentine had never heard from her mother. "The bastards are trading with the EU and the Americans for better weapons, they say they're on the same side, they say we are lawless thieves who deprive them all of their royalties—"

Valentine had heard that the Americans and the EU had declared for the other side, while the Russians and the Koreans and the Brazilians had declared for the city. The war gossip was everywhere. The old people didn't pinch her cheeks when she brought water, not anymore–they told her about the war and the enemies who'd come to drive them back into the dark ages.

"Mata, are you *hurt?*" Her mother was covering her face with her hands and sobbing so loudly it drowned out the tantrum Trover threw every night the second she came through the door.

Her shoulders shook. She gulped her sobs. Then she lowered her wet, snotty, sticky hands and wiped them on the thighs of her jumpsuit. She hugged Valentine so hard Valentine felt her skinny ribs creak.

"They killed your father, Vale," she said. "Your father is dead."

Valentine stood numb for a moment, then pulled free of her mother's hug.

"No," she said, calmly. "Popa is digging away from the front, where it's safe." She'd expected that her *mother* would die, not her *father.* She'd known that all along, since her mother stepped out the door of the flat talking of heroism. Known it fatalistically and never dwelt on it, never even admitted it. In her mind, though, she'd always seen a future where her father and Trover and she lived together as heroes of this war, which would surely be over soon, and visited her mother's memorial four times a year, the way they did the memorials for the comrade heroes who'd been martyred in the revolution.

The death toll was gigantic. Three apartment buildings had disappeared on her street with no air raid warning, no warning of any kind. All dead. Why should her brave mother live on?

"No," she said again. "You're mistaken."

"I saw the body!" her mother said, shrieking like Trover. "I held his head! He is *dead,* Vale!"

Valentine didn't understand what her mother was saying, but she certainly didn't want to hang around the flat and listen to this raving.

She turned on her heel and walked out of the flat. It was full dark out and there was snow on the ground and wet snow whipping along in the wind and she didn't have her too-small winter coat on, but she wasn't going to stay and listen to her mother's nonsense.

On the corner a man from the city told her she was breaking curfew and told her to go home or she'd end up getting herself shot. She shivered and glared at him and ignored him and set off in a random direction. She certainly wasn't going to stand on that corner and listen to his lunacy.

There were soldiers drinking in a cellar on another street and they called out to her and what they said wasn't the kind of thing you said to a little girl, though she knew well enough what it meant. Now she was cold and soaked through and shivering uncontrollably and she didn't know where she was and her father was—

She began to run.

Someone from the city shouted at her to stop and so she pelted through the ruins of a bombed building and then down one of the old streets from before the revolution, one of the streets they hadn't yet straightened out and rebuilt. The enemy hadn't bombed it yet, and she wondered if that was because this was the kind of dark and broken and smelly street they wanted the city to be returned to, so they'd left it untouched as an example of what the defenders should be working towards if they wanted to escape with their lives.

Down the street she ran, and then down an alley and another street. She stopped running when she came to a dead-end and her chest heaved. Running had warmed her up a little, but she hadn't had much to eat except cabbage and cold cereal with water for weeks and she couldn't run like she used to.

The cold stole back over her. It was full dark and the blackout curtains on the windows meant that not a sliver of light escaped. The moonless cloudy night made everything as dark as a cave.

Finally, she cried. She hadn't cried since she found out that Teena had died—she hadn't even *liked* Teena, but to have someone die that soon after your seeing them was scary like you had almost died, almost.

The wizard came on her there, weeping. He appeared out of the mist carrying a little light the size of a pea that he cupped in his hand to muffle most of the light. He was about her father's age, but with her mother's look of having survived something terrible without having survived altogether. He dressed like it was the old days, in fancy, bright-colored clothes, and he was well-fed in a way that no one else in the city was.

"Hello there," he said. He got down on his hunkers so he could look her in the eye. "Why are you crying?"

Valentine hated grownups who patronized her and the wizard sounded like he believed that no little girl could possibly have anything *real* to cry about.

"My dad died in the war today," she said. "In a trench."

"Oh, the American trenchbusters," he said, knowingly. "Lots of children lost their daddies today, I bet."

That made her stop crying. Lots of children. Lots of daddies— fathers, she hated the baby-word "daddy." Mothers, too.

"Let's get you cleaned up, put a coat on you, feed you and send you home, all right?"

She looked warily at him. She knew all about strange men who offered to take you home. But she had no idea where she was and she was dark and shivering and couldn't stop.

"My mother is a hero, and a soldier, and she's killed a lot of men," Valentine said.

He nodded. "I shall keep that in mind," he said.

The wizard lived in the old town, in an old building, but inside it was as new as anything she had ever seen. The walls swooped and curved, the furniture was gaily colored and new, like it had just been printed that day. There was so much *light*— they'd been saving it at her building. There was so much *food!* He gave her hamburgers and fizzy elderflower, then steak-frites, then rich dumplings as big as her fist stuffed with goose livers. He had working robots, lots of them, and they scurried after him doing the dishes and tidying and wiping up the slushy footprints.

And when they arrived and he took her coat, old familiar laser-lights played over her, the kind of everywhere-at-once measuring lasers that they used to have at the clothing stores. By the time dinner was done, there were two pairs of fresh trousers, two wooly jumpers, a heavy winter coat, three pairs of white cotton pants (all her pants had gone grey once she'd started having to

launder them, rather than get them printed fresh on Sundays)
and a—

"A bra?" She gave him a hard look. She had the knife she'd
used on the hamburger in her hand. "My mother taught me to
kill," she said.

The wizard had a face that looked like he spent a lot of time
laughing with it, and so even when he looked scared, he also
looked like he was laughing. He held up his hands. "It wasn't my
idea. That's just the programming. If the printer thinks you need
a bra, it makes a bra."

Leeza had a bra, though Valentine wasn't convinced she
needed it. But she had noticed a certain uncomfortable jiggling
weight climbing the stairs, hadn't she? Running? She hadn't
looked in the mirror in—Well, since the siege, practically.

"There's a bathroom there to change into," he said.

His bathroom was clean and neat and there were six toothbrushes beside the sink in a holder.

"Who else lives here?" she said, coming out in her new
clothes (the bra felt *really* weird).

"I have a lot of friends who come and see me now and again.
I hope you'll come back."

"How come your place is like the war never happened?"

"I'm the wizard, that's why," he said. "I can make magic."

His robots tied up her extra clothes in waterproof grip sheets
for her, then helped her into a warm slicker with a hood. "Tell
your mother that you met someone from the city who fed you
and gave you a change of clothes," he said, holding open the
door. He'd explained to her where to go from there to get out to
the old shopping street and from there she could manage on her
own, especially since he'd given her one of his little pea-lights to
carry with her.

"You're not from the city," she said.

"You got me," he said. "So tell her you met a wizard."

She thought about what her mother would say to that, especially when that was the answer to the question *Where have you
been?* "I'll tell her I met someone from the city," she said.

"You're a clever girl," he said.

＊ ＊ ＊

One week after her father died, Valentine stopped carrying water.

"There's not enough food," her mother said, over a breakfast of nothing but dried fruit—the cereal was gone. "If you—" she swallowed and looked out the window. "If you dig in the trenches, we'll get 150 grams of bread a day."

Valentine looked at Trover. He hadn't had a tantrum in days. He didn't cry or even speak much anymore.

"I'll dig."

She dug.

＊ ＊ ＊

Six months after her father died, Valentine stood in the queue for her bread. It was now the full heat of summer and the clothes the wizard had given her had fallen to bits the way all printer clothes did. She was wearing her father's old trousers, cut off just below the knee, and one of his shirts, with the sleeves and collar cut off. All to let a little of the lazy air in and to let a little of the sluggish sweat out. She was dirty and tired the way she always was at day's end.

She was also so hungry.

She and her mother didn't talk much anymore, but they didn't have to. Her mother was sometimes away on long missions, and increasingly longer. She was harrying the enemy with the guerilla fighters, and living on pine-cone soup and squirrels from the woods.

Trover stayed over at the creche some nights. A lot of the little ones did. Who had the strength to carry a little boy up the stairs at the end of a day's digging, at the end of three days' hard fighting in the woods?

The bread-rations were handed out in the spot where the cine once stood. She couldn't really remember what it had been like, though she remembered Teena, the things Teena had said that had made her leave the shelter, which had probably saved her life. Poor Teena. Little bitch.

She was so hungry, and the line moved slowly. She had her

chit from the boy from the city who oversaw the ditch digging in her part of the ditches. He was only a little older than her but he couldn't dig because his hands had been mutilated when a bomb went off near him. He kept them shoved in his pockets, but she'd seen them and they looked like the knucklebreakers had given them a good seeing-to. Every finger pointed a different direction, except for the ones that were missing altogether. There was also something wrong with him that made him sometimes stop talking in the middle of a sentence and sit down for a moment with his head tilted back.

The chit, though–the boy always gave her her chit, and the chit could be redeemed for bread. If she left Trover in the creche they would feed him. If Mata didn't come home from the fighting again tonight, the bread would be hers, and the cabbage, too.

● ● ●

Eight months after her father died, her mother stayed away in the fighting for three weeks and Valentine decided that she was dead and started sleeping in her mother's bed. Valentine cried a little at first, but she got used to it. She started to negotiate with one of the women who lived on the floor below to sell her narrow little bed for 800 grams of bread, 40 grams of butter and–though she didn't really believe in it–100 grams of ground beef.

She never found out if the woman downstairs had any ground beef–where would you get ground beef, anyway? Even the cats and dogs and rats were all gone! For Valentine's mother came home after three weeks and it turned out that she'd been in hospital all that time having her broken bones mended, something they could still do for some soldiers.

Mata came through the door like an old woman and Valentine looked up from the table where she'd been patiently feeding silent Trover before collapsing to sleep again. Valentine stood and looked at her and her Mata looked at Valentine and then her mother hobbled across the room like an old woman and gave Valentine a fierce, hard, long hug.

Valentine found she was crying and also found that silent little Trover had gotten up from the table and was hugging them both. He was tall, she realized dimly, tall enough to reach up and hug her at the waist instead of the knees, and when had *that* happened?

Her mother ate some of the dinner they'd had, and took a painkiller, the old kind that came in pill form that were now everywhere. Take a few of them and you would forget your problems, or so hissed the boys she passed in the street, though she passed them without a glance or a sniff.

Soon Mata was asleep, back in her bed, and Valentine was back in her bed, too, but she couldn't sleep.

Under her bed she had the remains of her grip sheet parcel, one of the precise robot-knots remaining. In that parcel was her winter galosh, just one, the other had been stolen the winter before while she'd had them both off to rub some warmth back into her toes before going back to the digging.

In the toe of the galosh, there was a pea-sized glowing light. She'd never considered selling it for bread, though it was very fine. Its light seemed too bright in the dark flat, so she took it outside into the hot night, and used it to light her way on a secret walk through the old streets of her dirty city.

⌐ ⌐ ⌐

Nine months after her father died, winter had sent autumn as a threatening envoy. The bread ration was cut to 120 grams, and there were sometimes pebbles in the bread that everyone knew were there to increase the weight.

She was proud that when the bread was bad, she and the other diggers cursed the enemy and not the city. Everyone knew that no one had it any better. They fought and suffered together.

But she was so hungry all the time, and you couldn't eat pride. One day she was in the queue for bread and reached out with her trembling hands to take her ration and then she turned with it and in a flash, a man old enough to be her father had snatched it out of her hands and run away with it!

She chased after him and the shrill cries of the women followed them, but he knew the rubble-piles well and he dodged and weaved and she was so tired. Eventually she sat down and wept.

That was when she saw her first zombie. Zombiism had been eliminated when she was practically a baby, just after the revolution, years and years ago.

But now it was back. The zombie had been a soldier, so maybe zombiism was coming back in the gas attacks that wafted over the trenches. His uniform hung in rags from his loose limbs as he walked in that funky, disco-dancer shuffle that meant zombie as clearly as the open drooling mouth and the staring, not-seeing eyes. They were fast, zombies, though you could hardly believe it when they were doing that funky walk. Once they saw prey, they turned into race horses that tore over anything and everything in their quest to rip and bite and rend and tear, screaming incoherencies with just enough words in them to make it clear that they were angry—so *so* angry.

She scrambled up from the curb she'd been weeping on and began to back away slowly, keeping perfectly silent. You needed to get away from zombies and then tell someone from the city so they could administer the cure. That's how you did it, back in the old days.

The zombie was shambling away from her anyway. It would pass by harmlessly, but she had to *get away* in any event, because it was a *zombie* and it was *wrong* in just the same way that a giant hairy spider was wrong (though if she found something giant and hairy today, she'd take it home for the soup-pot).

She didn't kick a tin or knock over a pile of rubble. She was perfectly stealthy. She hardly breathed.

And that zombie saw her anyway. It roared and charged. Its mouth was almost toothless, but what teeth remained there gleamed. It had been a soldier and it had good boots, and they crunched the broken glass and the rubble as it pelted for her. She shrieked and ran, but she knew even as she did that she would never outrun it. She was starved and had already used all her energy chasing the *bastard*, the *fucking bastard* who'd taken her bread.

She ran anyway, but the sound of the zombie's good boots drew closer and closer, coming up on her, closing on her. A hand thumped her shoulder and scrabbled at it and she spied a piece of steel bar—maybe it had been a locking post for a hover-car in the golden days—and she snatched it up and whirled around.

The zombie grabbed for her and she smashed its wrist like an old-time schoolteacher with a ruler. She heard something crack and the zombie roared again. "Bread fight asshole kill hungry!" is what it sounded like.

But one of its hands was now useless, flopping at its side. It charged her, grappling with her, and she couldn't get her bar back for a swing. Its good hand was in her hair and it didn't stink, that was the worst part. It smelled like fresh-baked bread. It smelled like flowers. Zombies smelled *delicious*.

The part of her brain that was detached and thinking these thoughts was not the part in the front. That part was incoherent with equal parts rage and terror. The zombie would bite her soon and that would be it. In a day, she'd be a zombie too, in need of medicine, and how many more would she bite before she got cured.

In that moment, she stopped being angry at the zombie and became angry at the besiegers. They had been abstract enemies until then, an unknowable force from outside her world, but in that moment she realized that they were *people* like her, who could suffer like her and she wished that they would. She wished that their children would starve. She wished the parents would die. The old people shrivel unto death in their dry, unwatered flats. The toddlers wander the streets until sunburn or cold took them.

She screamed an animal scream and pushed the zombie off her with her arms and legs, even her head, snapping it into the zombie's cheekbone as hard as she could and something broke there too.

The zombie staggered back. They couldn't feel pain, but their balance was a little weak. It tottered and she went after it with the bar. One whack in the knee took it down on its side. It reached with its good arm and so she smashed that too. Then the heaving ribs. Then the face, the hateful, leering, mouth-open-stupid face, three smashes turned it into ruin. The jaw hung down to its chest, broken off its face.

A hand seized her and she whirled with her bar held high and nearly brained the soldier who'd grabbed her. He wasn't a zombie, and he had his pistol out. It was pointed at her. She dropped her bar like it was red hot and threw her arms in the air.

He shoved her rudely aside and knelt beside the zombie–the *soldier zombie* she realized with a sick lurch–that she'd just smashed to pieces.

The soldier's back was to her, but his chest was heaving like a bellows and his neck was tight.

"Please," she said. "After they give him the cure, they can fix his bones. I had to hit him or he would have killed me. He would have infected me. You see that, right? I know it was wrong, but–"

The soldier shot the zombie through the head, twice.

He turned around. His face was streaming with tears. "There is no cure, not for this strain of zombiism. Once you get it, you die. It takes a week. Slower than the old kind. It gives you more time to infect new people. Our enemies are crafty crafty, girl."

The soldier kicked the zombie. "I knew his brother. I commanded him until he was killed by a trenchbuster. The mother and father were killed by a shell. Now he's dead and that's a whole family gone."

The soldier cocked his head at her and examined her more closely. "Have you been bitten?"

"No," she said, quickly. The gun was still in his hand. There was no cure.

"You're sure?" he said. His voice was like her father's had been when she skinned her knee, stern but sympathetic. "If you have, you'd better tell me. Better to go quick and painless than like this thing." He kicked the zombie again.

"I'm sure," she said. "Have you got any bread? A man stole my ration."

The soldier lost interest in her when she asked him for bread. "Goodbye, little girl," he said.

That night, she had a fever. She was so hot. She got them all the time, everyone did. Not enough food. No heat. No vegetables and vitamins. You always got fevers.

But she was so hot. She took off her clothes and let the cool air blow over her skin on her narrow bed. Trover was sleeping on the floor nearby–he had outgrown his crib long since–and he stirred irritably as she felt that air cool her sizzling skin.

She ran her fingertips lightly over her body. She was never naked anymore. If you were lucky, you washed your face and hands every day, but baths–they were cold and miserable and who wanted to haul water for them anyway?

Her breasts were undeniable now. Her blood had started a few months back, then stopped. Starvation, she knew, that's what did it. But there was new hair in her armpits and at her groin.

She crossed her arms over her chest and hugged herself. That's when she found the bite on her shoulder, just where it met her neck. It was swollen like a quail egg–the chocolate quail eggs from before, that had grown on the trees, she could taste them even now–and so hot it felt like a coal. In the middle of the egg, at its peak, the seeping wound left behind by one of the zombie's few teeth.

Now she was cold as ice, shivering nude on her thin ruin of a bed with her thin ruin of a body. She would be dead in a week. It was a death sentence, that bite.

And she wouldn't go clean. She'd shamble and scream and bite. Maybe Trover. Maybe Mata. Maybe she'd find Leeza and give her a hard bite before she went.

Her breath was coming in little pants now. She bit her lip to keep from screaming.

She pulled her clothes back on as quietly as she could and slipped out into the night to find the wizard, clutching her pea light. Many times she'd walked toward his house in the night, but she'd always turned back. Now she had to see him.

She passed three zombies in the dark, two dead on the ground and riddled with bullet holes, one leaning out a fifth-story window and screaming its incoherent rage out at the city.

As she drew nearer to the wizard's door, an unshakable fatal conclusion gripped her: he was long gone, shot or gassed, or simply moved to somewhere else. It had been months and months since he'd given her the printer-clothes and the dumplings and surely he was dead now. Who wasn't?

Her steps slowed as she came to his block. Each step was the work of half a minute or more. She didn't want to see his old door hanging off its hinges, didn't want to see the ruins of the brave curves and swoops of his flat and his furniture.

But her steps took her to the door, and it was shut and silent as any of the doors in the street. Nothing marked it beyond the grime of the city and the scratches and scrapes that no one painted over any longer.

She tried the knob. It was locked. She knocked. Silence. She knocked again, harder. Still silence. Crying now, she thundered on the door with her fists and kicked it with her feet. He was gone, gone, gone, and she would be dead in a week.

Then the door opened. It wasn't the wizard, but a well-fed blonde woman in a housecoat with slippers. She was beautiful, a movie-star, though maybe that was just because she wasn't starved nearly to death.

"Girl, you'd better have a good reason for waking up the whole fucking street at three in the morning." Her voice wasn't unkind, though she was clearly annoyed.

"I need to see—" She dropped her voice at the last moment. "I need to see the wizard."

"Oh," the woman said, comprehension dawning on her face. "Oh, well then, come on in. Any friend of the wizard."

The flat was just as she remembered it from that long ago night. The woman gestured at the kitchen and coffee-smells began to emanate from it. Valentine'd forgotten the smell of coffee, but now she remembered it.

"I'll go wake up his majesty, then," the woman said. "Just sit yourself down."

Valentine sat perched on the edge of the grand divan that twisted and curved along one wall of the sitting room. She knew that the seat of her trousers—filthy even before her tussle with the zombie—would leave black marks on its brave red upholstery.

The conversation from down the corridor was muffled but the tone was angry. Valentine felt her cheeks go hot, even through the fever. This place was still civilized and she'd brought the war to it.

Then the wizard came into the sitting room and waved the lights up to full bright, wincing away from the sudden illumination. He squinted at her.

"Do I know you?" he said.

Her tongue caught in her mouth. In his pajamas with his hair mussed, he still looked every inch the wizard.

"I . . ." She couldn't finish. "I–" She tried again. "You gave me clothes. My mother is a soldier."

He snapped his fingers and grinned. "Oh, the *soldier's daughter*. I remember you now. You counted the toothbrushes. You're a bright girl."

"She's a walking skeleton." The beautiful blonde woman was in the kitchen, tinkering with the cooker. It was the pre-war kind, capable of printing out food with hardly any intervention. Valentine was hypnotized by her fingers.

"You want sandwiches and fish-fingers?"

"Start her with some drinking chocolate, Ana," the wizard said. "Hot and then a milkshake. Little girls love chocolate."

She hadn't tasted chocolate in–she didn't know. Her mouth was flooded with saliva. The woman, Ana, pressed some more buttons and then took down a bottle of rum from a cupboard.

"Will you have rum in yours, little girl?"

"I–"

"She's a little young for rum, Ana," the wizard said. He sat down on one of his curvy sofas and it embraced him and unfurled a foot-rest.

"I'll have rum," she said. She was dying, and she wouldn't die without at least having one drink, once.

"Good girl," Ana said. "There's a war on, after all." She poured a liquid with the consistency of mud into a tall mug and then added a glug or two of rum and pushed it across the counter then fixed one for herself. "Come and get it, no waitress service here."

Valentine took off her too-small shoes and walked over the carpet in her dirty bare feet. It felt like something she barely remembered. Grass?

The chocolate smelled wonderful. Wonderful was the word for it. It made her full of wonder. Rich. Something from another planet–from heaven, maybe.

She lifted the mug and felt its warmth seep into her hands. She took a tentative sip and held it in her mouth.

It was spicy! Was chocolate spicy? She didn't think so! The rum made her tongue tingle and the heat made its fumes rise in her head, carrying up the chocolate taste and the peppers. Her eyes streamed. Her ears felt like they were full of chocolate.

She swallowed and gasped and the wizard laughed. She looked at him.

"Ana's recipe. She adds the chilies. I think it's lovely, don't you? Aztec chocolate, we call it."

She took another mouthful, held it, swallowed. The chocolate was in her tummy too, and there was a feeling there, a greedy feeling, a *more* feeling. She drained the glass. Ana and the wizard both laughed.

Ana handed her a tall frosted metal cup with a mountain of whipped cream on top and a straw sticking out. "Chocolate malted," she said. "The perfect chaser."

Transfixed in her bare feet on the carpet, she drank this. A cold headache hit her between the eyes and that didn't stop her from going on drinking. Wow! Wow! Were there tastes like this? Did things really taste this good?

The straw made slurping noises as she chased down the last of the rich liquid.

"Sit now," the wizard said. "Let that work its magic and then we'll put some food down your gullet."

She walked to the sofa. It was like walking on the deck of a rocking ship, or on the surface of the moon. Everything slid beneath her. *I'm drunk,* she thought. *I'm fourteen years old and I am drunk as a skunk.*

She lowered herself carefully and sat up as straight as she could.

"Now, young lady, what brings you to my home in the middle of the night?"

She remembered the bite on her neck and thought for a panicky second that she would throw up.

"I needed to talk to you," she said. "I needed some help."

"What kind of help?"

She couldn't say it. She had the new kind of zombiism and the soldier had explained it clearly—the cure for zombiism now was a bullet to the head.

Then she knew what she must say. The chocolate helped. Her family would love chocolate. "I'm going away soon and my mother and brother won't be able to take care of themselves. I need help to keep them safe once I go."

"Where are you going?"

The drink made it hard to think, but that was balanced out by that precious and magical feeling of fullness in her belly. Her mind flew over all the possible answers.

"I have found someone who'll take me out of the city and to a safe place."

"Are there safe places?" Ana said.

"Oh, Ana, you cynic," the wizard said. "There are many, many safe places. The world is full of them. They are the exception, not the rule. Isn't that why you've come here?"

"We're not talking about why *I* came here," Ana said. She nodded back at Valentine and made a little scooting hand-gesture at her. Valentine couldn't decide if she liked Ana, though Ana was very pretty.

"I need help for my family," she said.

"And why would I give help?" the wizard said. He was still smiling, but that face of his, the face that looked like he'd been wounded and never quite healed, it was set in an expression that scared her a little. His eyes glittered in the low light of the swooping sitting room. She found that she had slumped against the sofa and now it had her in its soft embrace.

"Because you helped me before," she said.

"I see," the wizard said. "So you assumed that because I'd been generous—very, very generous—to you once before that I'd be generous again? You repay my favor with a request for another one?

Valentine shook her head.

"No?"

"I will find a way to repay it," she said. "I can work for you."

"I don't need any ditches dug around here, thank you."

Somewhere in the flat, a door opened and shut. She heard muffled voices. Lots of them. The flat was full of people, somewhere.

"I can do lots of kinds of work," she said. She attempted a smile. She didn't know what she was offering him, but she knew that she was too young to be offering it. And besides, with zombiism, you shouldn't do that sort of thing. She would be safe, though, and careful, so that he would live to help her family.

Ana crossed past her in a flash and then she smacked the wizard, a crack across the face hard enough to rock his head back. His cheek glowed with the print of her open hand.

"Don't you toy with this little girl," she said. "You see how desperate she is? Don't you toy with her."

She whirled on Valentine, who stood her ground even though she wanted to shrink away. If she was old enough to offer herself to the wizard, she was old enough to stand her ground before this beautiful, well-fed blonde woman.

"And you," Ana said. "You aren't a fool, I can tell. So don't act a fool. There are a thousand ways to survive that don't involve lying on your back, and you must know them or you wouldn't have survived this long. Be smart or be gone. I won't watch you make a tragedy of yourself."

"Ana, what do you know about survival?" the wizard said. He had one hand to his cheek, and he was giving her the same glittering look he'd given to Valentine a moment before.

"Just don't play with her," Ana said. "Help her or get rid of her, but don't play with her."

"Go and see to the others, Anushla," the wizard said. "I will negotiate in the best of faith with our friend here and call you in to review the terms of our deal when it's all done, all right?"

Ana looked toward the corridor where the voices were coming from and back to the wizard, then to Valentine. "Be smart, girl," she said.

The wizard brought her a plate of goose-liver dumplings smothered in white gravy and then took a bite out of a big toasted corned beef sandwich that oozed brown mustard.

"Right," he said. "No playing. If you want to work for me, there are jobs that need doing. Have you ever seen stage magic performed, the kind with tuxedos and white doves?"

She nodded slowly. "Before the war," she said.

"You know how the magician always has a supply of lovely assistants on hand?"

She nodded again. They'd worn flattering, tight-fitting calf-high trousers, cutaway coats, tummy-revealing crop-tops, and feathered confections for hats.

"Everyone who does magic has an assistant or two. I'm the wizard and I do the best magic of all, and so I have need of more assistants than most. I have an army of assistants, and they help me out and I help them out."

"I'm leaving in five days," she said.

"The kind of favor I had in mind from you was the kind of favor that you could perform the day after tomorrow."

"And you'd take care of my family?"

"I would do that," he said. "I always take care of my assistants' families. Do we have an agreement?"

She stuck her hand out and they shook.

"Eat your dumplings," he said. "And then we'll get you some things to take home to your family."

☞ ☞ ☞

Two days after the wizard agreed to take care of Valentine's family, the fever had become her constant companion, so omnipresent that it she hardly noticed it, though it made her walk like an old woman and she sometimes had trouble focusing her eyes.

She arose that morning and feasted on brown rolls with hard crusts, small citrus cakes, green beef tea, porridge with currants and blueberry concentrate and sweet condensed milk, and a chocolate bun to top it off.

Trover ate even more than she did, licking up the crumbs. She saw him hide two of the jackfruits under his shirt and nodded satisfaction—he had learned something about surviving, then.

Her mother had not questioned the food nor the clothes nor her daughter's absence that night. But oh, she had given Valentine a look when she came through the door carrying all her parcels, a look that said, *not my daughter any more.* Not a look that refused what she bore, but a look that refused *her.* Valentine didn't bother trying to explain. She knew what her mother suspected and it was better in some ways than the truth.

Her mother drank the real coffee reverently, with three sugars and thick no-refrigeration cream. She ate sardines on toast, green beef tea, and a heap of fluffy scrambled eggs with minced herring, then she put on her uniform and took up her gun and went out the door, without a look back at Valentine.

By the end of the week, she won't have to worry about me, Valentine thought. The fever made her fingers shake, but she still drank her hot chocolate.

Trover knew his own way to the creche, and so Valentine went forth to earn her family's fortune.

The wizard had given her a small sack of little electronic marbles, and had told her to get them planted in no fewer than three hundred locations at the front and in the places where the fighting was likely to move. They were spy-eyes, the kind of thing that she and her friends had exchanged to keep in one anothers' rooms before the war, so they could sneak midnight conversations in perfect encrypted secrecy.

"If I'm caught," she said.

"You'll be shot," he said. "You *must be.* The alternative is that you'll lead them back to me. And if you do that, the whole game is up—your family's lives, my life, your life, the lives of all my assistants and friends will be forfeit. It will be terrible. They will destroy this place. They will destroy your home, too."

She didn't report for her digging. That was OK. Lots of people didn't show up to dig on the days when they were feeling too weak to hold a shovel. She wouldn't be missed.

She had the fastest shoes that the wizard could print for her on her feet, though she'd carefully covered them in grime and dirt so they wouldn't stand out. And she'd taken an inhaler along that would make her faster still. He'd warned her to keep eating after she took the inhaler, or she'd starve to death before the day was out. The pockets on both thighs of her jumpsuit were stuffed with butterballs wrapped around sugared kidneys and livers, stuff that would sustain her no matter how many puffs she took.

No one challenged her on the way to the front. There were some her age who fought and many more who served those who fought, bringing forward ammunition, digging new trenches right at the front. The pay for this was better than the pay she'd gotten digging in the "safe" trenches. She brought a shovel for camouflage.

The first round of trenches were familiar, the same kinds she'd been digging in for months now. She even saw some of the diggers she'd dug alongside of, nodding to them though her heart was thumping. *You'll be shot,* she thought, and she palmed an electronic eye and stuck it to the wall of a trench.

She moved forward and forward, closer to the fighting. It had always been a dull, distant rattle, the fighting, never quite gone, but not always there, either. Instinctively, she'd kept her distance from it, always moving away from it. Today she moved toward it and her blood sang.

One trench over there came the dread *zizz* sound of a trench-buster and she threw herself down. There were anti-busters in the trenches, too, but they didn't always work. The trenchbusters were mostly up around the front, but they sometimes came back to the diggers, and they had killed one crew she knew of.

There were screams from the next trench, then a sound like a bag of gravel being poured out–that was the anti-buster, she knew–and the trenchbuster soared out overhead of her and detonated in the sky, mortally confused by the counter-logic in the anti-buster.

She realized that she had peed herself. Just a little, just a few drops that must have escaped when she gave her involuntary shriek. She planted her hands in the frozen dirt of the trench-floor and got to her knees. That was when she saw the fingertip, shriveled and frozen, lying just a few inches from her. It had been cleanly severed.

She had seen so much death, but the fingertip, cut off and left here to dry out and be trampled down into the dirt . . . It made her stomach do slow somersaults. She threw up a little, and peed herself a little more, and her eyes watered.

That's when she knew she couldn't complete the wizard's mission. There was death ahead for her that day, much death to see at the front, and she couldn't face that. Not when her pockets were full of spy-eyes and that meant espionage, meant that the wizard was on the other side, the side of the bastards whose old people she would starve in their high flats and whose children she would tear from their beloved parents.

The fever made her shake hard now. Her head swam and the world pitched and yawed like a ship in heavy seas.

She stood up and took a step. It was a funky disco-dancer step. Her next step was, too. Then she was walking normally again.

She reached down into her shirt, between her breasts—she had a bra on again, fresh from the wizard's printer—and withdrew the inhaler he'd given her. She'd be dead in a week.

She put the inhaler to her lips and drew in a deep breath while squeezing it, and then the fever was gone. The horror was gone. The fear and cold were gone. What was left behind was a hard, frenetic grin, something that sharpened her every sense and set her feet alight like the most infectious of dance music.

She ran now, flying through the trenches. The closer she got to the front the worse it smelled, but that was OK, bad smells were fine by her. Body parts—the fingertip had just been a preview, here you could find jawbones and tongues, hands and feet, curled-in cocks and viscera that glistened through its dust-crust—not a problem.

She planted five eyes, then crouched to let a trenchbuster sail over her head. She resisted a mad urge to reach up and stick an eye to it, then planted another eye, palming it and sticking it right under the nose of a gunnery sergeant who was hollering at two old women who were struggling to maneuver a gigantic, multi-part weapon into position. To Valentine, the women looked old enough to be from the same tribe she'd hauled water for, and they were so thin they looked like they were made of twisted-together wires. Their eyes were huge and round and showed the whites.

The sergeant paid her no mind as she slipped forward, her shovel still in one hand. The trench dead-ended ahead of her and she jigged to a side trench, but soon that, too, dead-ended. Dead end after dead end—each got its own eye—and before long she was at the end of the road, no more side tunnels. She would have to turn back and try another path. There were no maps of the trenches, of course.

She had another puff off her inhaler. Her stomach lurched

and then her knees gave way. She was back in the dirt now and she remembered what the wizard had told her about eating when she was on the inhaler or starving to death. Then she went into seizure. Her limbs thrashed, her head shook back and forth, she banged her forehead into the dirt. A gargling escaped her throat, nothing at all like words or any other human sound.

When the seizure passed—and it did pass, though it felt like it never would—she shakily withdrew a fistful of butter-ball and sugared organ meat and shoved it in her mouth. Most of it escaped, but some of it got down her throat and her hands were steadier in a moment, enabling her to eat more. She got to her knees, she got to her feet, she ate some more and had another puff off the inhaler.

God oh god! She felt *marvelous* now. Food and the inhaler were magic together. Dead ends, pah! Who had time to go back through the trenches? She'd be dead in five days. She jammed her fingers in the frozen dirt on the trench-side and hauled herself up to the surface.

In her months and months of digging in the trenches, she had never once peeked over the edge. There were things that watched for snoopy looks over the trenches, laser scanners and sentry guns. You could lose the top of your head zip-zap.

Now she was on the surface. It was like the surface of the moon. Craters, hills, trenches, and great clouds of roiling smoke and dust. Nothing alive. Broken guns and things that might have been body parts. She grinned that hard grin, because there was no one else here and so she was the queen of the surface, the bloody angel of the battlefield. She fisted more sugared liver into her gob and *ran.*

Zizz, zizz, zizz. There were bullets and other materiel around her, as soon as she moved, but the world was so clear now, the grey light so pure, the domain so utterly hers, there was no chance she'd be hit by a bullet.

She leapt a trench and skirted a trench, leapt and skirted, heading further and further toward the lines. She nearly tripped over a sentry gun, then leapt *on top of it* as it tried to swivel around to get her in its sights, and she pasted an eye on it and laughed and leapt away.

She was thinking that she should get back into a trench and was trying to pick one when it was decided for her—she was in mid-leap over a trench when a bullet clipped the heel of her shoe and she tumbled down into the trench. She did a tremendous, jarring face-plant into the planks below and lay stunned for a moment with her mouth filling up with blood. Her tongue throbbed—it had been bitten—and as she carefully rolled it around her mouth, she discovered that she'd knocked out one of her front teeth. Not such a pretty girl anymore, but she'd be dead in less than five days.

She got to her knees again and planted an eye as she looked around.

A soldier was staring at her from the end of her current trench. He was saying something, but here the trenches boomed with artillery and zizzed with gunfire and hearing was impossible. She drew closer to him to hear what he had to say and she was practically upon him when she realized that he was wearing an enemy uniform.

She was quick quick, but he was quicker and he had her arm in an iron grip before she could pull away.

He said something in a language that they often spoke in the movies, back where there was a cine across from her block of flats. She knew a few words of that language.

"Friend!" she said.

He said something in a different language, but she didn't recognize that one. Then he switched to Hindi, but all she knew to say in Hindi was Love Love Love I'm in Love, which was the chorus to all the songs in the Hindi movies.

He shook her arm hard. He was angry with her, and his gun was in his other hand now, a soft, floppy handgun like a length of rope and he was gesturing at her and shouting. He was as well-fed as the wizard, and he was not much older than her. She thought that he didn't want to kill her and was angry because he was going to have to.

She tried smiling at him. He scowled hard. She held her hand out to him and touched his arm softly, placatingly. Then she pointed at her pocket, where the butterballs were. Very slowly, she reached into it. He watched her with suspicious eyes, the handgun trained on her now. She thought that if she was a suicide bomber, he'd be dead now, and that made her feel a little better about the war: if this was what a soldier from the other side was like, they all had a chance after all.

She drew out a butter-ball and took a bite of it, then offered it to the soldier. He looked like he wanted to cry. She held it to his mouth so he wouldn't have to let go of her or the gun in order to eat it. He took a small, polite bite, chewed and swallowed. She had a bite, then gave him one. They ate like that until the butter-ball was gone, and then she drew out another, and another.

She pointed to herself. "Valentine," she said.

He shook his head. He was the picture of moroseness. "Withnail," he said.

"Pleased to make your acquaintance, Withnail," she said in his language, another useful phrase culled from the cine, though she suspected she was pronouncing it all wrong. She held out her hand to shake his. He holstered his handgun and shook her hand.

"I have to go, Withnail." She couldn't say this in his language, but she spoke slowly and as clearly as she could.

He shook his head again. She covered his hand on her arm with her own and gave it a squeeze.

"To save my family," she said. "I'm on a mission for your side anyway. Let me go, Withnail." She gave his hand another squeeze. Slowly, he released her arm.

He was very handsome, she saw now, with a good chin and sensuous lips. She'd never kissed a boy and she'd be dead in four days and a little more. Or maybe she'd be dead that afternoon, if she couldn't get back into her own trenches.

She put her hand on the back of his neck and pulled his face to hers and gave him a dry, hard kiss on those pouting lips. It made her blood sing, and she gave him a hug, too, pressing her body to him. He kissed her back after a moment, surprised. His tongue probed at her closed lips and she pulled away, then for a crazy moment she thought of biting him and giving him a dose of zombiism to spread to his comrades in the trenches with him. But that wouldn't be right. They were friends now.

She stuck her fingers in the trench wall. They hurt—she must have broken a finger before. She hauled herself up and began to run, pawing her pockets for her inhaler. "So long, Withnail!" It was another phrase she knew from the cine.

◦ ◦ ◦

Three days after being bitten by the zombie, Valentine woke up with her hand curled protectively over the huge hot egg on her collarbone. She couldn't move that arm this morning, not without pain like nothing she'd ever felt. Her face ached. Her limbs ached. Her new breasts ached like she'd been punched in them, repeatedly. She got out of bed like an old woman and crept to the table.

She sat gingerly and spooned up some cereal. Her mother sat opposite her, staring over her shoulder. Valentine ate a spoonful of cereal, then spat it out as it came into contact with the raw, toothless spot on her gum.

Her mother looked at her.

"Open your mouth, Vale," she said.

Valentine did as she was bade, showing the gap in her teeth.

"You were hit?" her mother said. Valentine didn't answer. She didn't trust herself to speak with her mother looking at her like that. "They won't want you now you've lost that tooth," she said. "You can go back to digging now."

She stood up from the table without a word and went out of the flat. She was so feverish that she couldn't tell if the stairs went down or up, whether she was descending or ascending.

She tottered out on the street. The way she felt, she couldn't walk properly. Her hips wanted to give way with every step and so she walked like a funky disco dancer through the early, cold streets, toward the wizard's house.

She didn't make it. Less than half way there, she sat down on a pile of rubble and retched. She reached down into her pocket and pulled out the wizard's inhaler, but she fumbled it. She couldn't bend over to get it, so she let herself slowly fall to the street, then she crawled one-armed to it. She fitted it to her mouth and then squeezed it with clumsy fingers.

She dragged herself to her feet, not bothering to take the inhaler with her. Her limbs burned now and wanted to move, no matter how much it hurt, and she lurched to the wizard's door, moaning in the back of her throat.

Ana let her in, eyes wide. "You did it." It might have been a question. Valentine let herself slide to the soft, sweet-smelling carpet and closed her eyes.

● ● ●

An unknowable number of hours or days after Valentine got to the wizard's flat, she woke up in a soft, fluffy bed that was quietly massaging her limbs. She was dressed in loose cotton pajamas, and there was a trolley by the bed piled high with the kind of fruit that wasn't a berry and wasn't an orange, but a little of both and each one had a different smiley face growing in the peel.

The wizard came into the room.

"You'll live," he said. "Probably. It would have been a certainty if you'd fucking told me you had zombiism, you little idiot."

Ana came in behind him. "Do you think she would have done your mission for you if she didn't have zombiism, wizard?"

He waved her off. "You've got your cure," he said.

"It won't cure me," Valentine said. Her voice was like a gravel-mixer. "Not the kind I have. There's no cure."

"Oh ho," the wizard said. "Would you care to make a wager on that? How about this: if you die, I take care of your family. If you live, you work for me—and I'll take care of your family."

"You already must take care of my family," she said.

The wizard's eyes glittered. "I think that curing your zombiism is repayment enough, so I've unilaterally renegotiated the terms of our deal. If you don't like that, I can arrange to have you re-infected and we can go back to the original contract."

"You've cured me?"

Ana said, "There are lots of things we have access to here that you can't get in the city. What you had would have killed you if he hadn't helped."

"Will you take my bet?"

She thought about the mission, about the soldier, about being queen of the battlefield. She thought about the way they'd bombed her city and how she'd just helped them kill the city's soldiers and diggers–like her father.

"I won't betray my city to its enemies ever again." She sat up very straight. "I was a traitor once, but I had a fever and I was dying. You are a traitor every day and what is *your* excuse?"

"A traitor? What the hell are you talking about?"

"The spy-eyes I planted so our enemies can spy on us, the wealth you have around here. How many of our people died because you sold them out?"

"Valentine, you are a smart girl and your mother is a soldier, but you aren't so very smart as all that. You are a stupid girl sometimes. Our little palace here isn't full of spies. We're *documentarians*. We shoot the war and we send it to the outside world so they can see the tragedy they are wreaking here. We have a huge activist movement that we fuel through our pictures. The spy-eyes you planted yesterday are now streaming 24/7 to activist sites in fifty countries. It is being played in the halls of the United Nations."

Ana made a spitting sound. "It's being played as filler on the snowy slopes of upper cable. It's being played as ironic snuff-porn in dorm rooms. It's being used as stock footage for avant-garde performance art. Please, wizard, please. She deserves to know the real situation, not the things you tell yourself when you can't sleep."

"It's—*entertainment?*"

"It's riveting," Ana said, like *riveting* meant *terrible.* "Very highly rated."

"And it raises consciousness," the wizard said. "You cynic, Ana, you can't see anything except the worst. It is the reason that anyone except for a few policy wonks have heard of what's going on here."

"Entertainment?"

"Entertainment," the wizard said. "And more than that."

"They're killing us, they're gassing us, they're bombing us, and you're selling back to them as *entertainment?*"

She climbed out of the bed. She hurt, but not so much as she had before. The fever had broken, at least.

"Am I cured?" she asked. "Do I need anything else, or am I cured?"

The wizard scowled. "Now wait a moment—"

"You're cured," Ana said. "You should rest for a few days and eat well, but you will get better no matter what." The wizard turned and shoved her toward the door, so hard she stumbled and hit the jam. She spat on the floor and walked out of the room.

Valentine pulled herself out of the bed. The wizard took her wrist and without hesitating, she jammed her thumb into his eye-socket, grunting with the effort. He shouted and reeled away and she made her way out of the bedroom and down the corridor to the brave red sitting room. Ana had a couple of grip-sheeted, robot-tied parcels for her. "Clothes," she said. "Food. Don't come back. I'm not from here, but even I know how wrong this is. He— there's no excuse for him. Go." She handed Valentine some shoes—good sturdy work-boots, still warm from the printer.

〰 〰 〰

Six months after she took home the clothes that Ana had given her, Valentine was taken off of ditch-digging and put on corpse-duty. They were dying like flies, and the zombies fed on them, and unless the meat was disposed of, the zombies would multiply like rats.

There was only bread on alternate days now. The hunger was like a playmate or a childhood enemy that taunted her. It woke her in the night like a punch in the gut.

The first body she found was missing its ass-cheeks. You could find the bodies by the smell, and she was on corpse-detail with a boy about her age whose face she never saw, because it was covered by a mask. He had a floppy machine-pistol that she hoped he knew how to use, because the zombies were everywhere. He'd been hauling meat for weeks, and grunted out little bits and pieces to help her get acquainted. Neither of them exchanged names.

"What happened to her—"

"Ever see black-market meat? The ass is the last part to go when they starve. The mafiyehs take the cheeks and grind them up with some filler and add flavoring agent and sell it. They used to kill people and take the meat that way, but they don't need to do that anymore. There's enough meat from natural causes."

The smell was terrible. It was a woman and she'd been dead for some time. It was hot out, too. Valentine's mask didn't really seem to help, but when she stuck a finger under it to scratch her sweaty upper lip, an unfiltered gulp of air went up her nose and she gagged.

They started in the early hours of the morning before the heat got too bad. They slept for a few hours at noon, then started again mid-afternoon. She was so hungry that she was dizzy. The next corpse was on the fifteenth storey of a block of revolutionary-era flats. No lift in the city had worked in more than a year. They climbed and rested, climbed and rested. There was no question of going straight up. She was too weak to consider it for a second.

It was a man. He was big and tall, and even starved out as he was, they could barely lift him. He must have been a giant in life.

"We'll never carry him down all those stairs," the boy said. "Go and open the big window."

Valentine obeyed woodenly. She knew that if you couldn't carry the body, you'd have to get it out of the building some other way. She knew that. She didn't want to think about what it meant, but she knew it. There'd been a corpse one floor down from her flat and it had taken weeks for the city to dispose of it and life had been almost unbearable for everyone in the building. And that had been winter, when the cold kept the smell down some.

So you had to get rid of the body. The window was a revolutionary window. It was marvelous and self-cleaning and it swung easily open. Forty-five meters below, she could see the building's deserted courtyard and the corpse wagon that the boy drove haltingly through the city streets. Under other circumstances she might have felt show-offy and ostentatious riding in a car while everyone else walked, but she knew that no one envied her her ride in the corpse wagon.

"Take his ankles." With the mask on, the boy looked like a horse, and she knew she did, too. On the one chair that hadn't been burned for fuel the previous winter, the boy had stacked up the few possessions the corpse had: a ring, a lighter, a clasp-knife, a little set of headphones with their charge-lights showing red.

She picked up the body by the ankles. The boy had him by the shoulders. When they alley-*oop*ed it up off the floor, the body let loose a tremendous, evil fart. It wasn't the first time a body had done that on that day, but it was the loudest and evilest of all the farts. Its ankles were dirty and the smell of its feet and its fart combined into a grey, fuggy miasma that she could smell through the mask.

"You should smell his feet," she said.

"You should smell his breath," the boy said.

They dragged the body to the window and one, two, three, swung it out into the wide world. She watched it spin away, fascinated and wordless. Then it hit the ground and the sound. And the way it looked. And the splash. And the blood.

There were tears streaming down her face, fouling her mask. She stepped out into the corridor and ripped the mask off and faced the wall, groaning.

"It gets easier later," the boy said, tugging her arm.

He was right.

But they needed shovels to get the body into the corpse wagon. Some of the bits had gone a long way off and she had to carry them before her on the spade-end of the shovel. His viscera glistened like an accusation at her. She lived on the fourteenth floor. When her time came, she'd go out the window too.

⌒ ⌒ ⌒

Two years after the siege began, she awoke deaf. Mata was shaking her vigorously and her lips were moving, but there was no sound. Valentine listened hard and made out a distant, underwater sound that she couldn't place, though it was familiar.

Mata was thin and hard now, and slept with a gun and only came home for a few hours at a time. She was taking lots of different pills, and they made her a little jumpy. Valentine wondered if the pills had rendered her mother mute, before she realized that she couldn't hear *anything.*

She tapped her ear.

"I can't hear," she said.

Her mother didn't appear to understand. She still shook Valentine hard.

"I'm deaf, Mata," she said. She shook her head and tugged her earlobes. She was scared now, and she sat up. She wiggled a finger in her ear, which was very greasy. Not even the sound of her finger in her ear carried back to her mind. Stone deaf.

She was breathing heavily, but that happened a lot. The hunger made her weepy and she sometimes cried for no reason. Sometimes in the middle of a sentence she had to sit down and stare at the sky while her tears rolled down her throat, until she felt able to go on again.

She slowed her breathing. "Mata," she said.

Her mother made a "stay there" gesture, then repeated it and mouthed the words at her slowly and obviously. She nodded to show she understood.

She was supposed to be carrying bodies that day. You could get bread every day if you carried bodies. One piece on alternate days from the city, one piece from the black-market in exchange for the loot you could find in the flats of the starved.

There was a new girl that Valentine was training, too. The boy was long gone. He'd tried to touch her breast, not just once, either, and she'd reported him. When the supervisor confronted him, he went crazy and tried to attack the supervisor and the supervisor sent him to the front to carry ammunition, where, Valentine supposed, he was still working. Unless he was dead. She didn't much care which.

But she wanted bread. The creche had shut down a few months before, but Trover had some little boys he played with and they sometimes came home with a little food that he was always careful to share with her, though she was sure that he didn't share everything. She didn't either. No one did. Mata had a little stash of dried fish under her pillow. Valentine almost never raided it, though she could have.

Trover was looking at her. She tugged her earlobes. "I'm deaf," she said. She thought she might be speaking very loudly, but she couldn't tell.

Trover went out of the flat without looking back at her.

She waited for Mata, but the day crept by and Mata didn't return. The more she didn't return, the more Valentine worried. She cried some, and tried to sleep. She sucked pebbles for the hunger, and drank the cistern dry. She carried the chamber-pot downstairs, but the world in silence was so scary that she practically ran back to the flat once she'd tipped it out into the reeking collection-point.

She had finally gotten to sleep when Mata returned. Mata mouthed something at her in slow, deliberate words, but she couldn't make it out. Mata repeated it, and then again. She didn't get any of it, but Mata's expression was clear. No doctors would help her. She hadn't expected them to.

No doctors could help her, as far as she was concerned. She knew exactly what had gone wrong: her hearing aids had failed. Everything from the golden years after the revolution failed. Old people died when their artificial hearts or kidneys seized up and withered. Lifts didn't work. Printers didn't work—they'd nearly all died the day the siege began. The hospitals couldn't print drugs. The sky-cars fell out of the sky.

Nothing worked. Nothing would ever work again. Everything fell apart. Her hearing aids were of that same magical *stuff* as everything else from the revolution, so it followed that they would die too.

Mata must have known this. That's probably what she was saying. If Valentine concentrated, she could recall her mother's voice and have it say the words.

"It's OK, Mata," she said. She knew she was shouting. "It's OK."

Mata cried and she cried, but she put herself to sleep as soon as she could, and once she thought Trover and Mata were sleeping, she took out her small wizard-light and made her way down the silent stairs, into the silent streets.

She walked cautiously toward the wizard's flat. She was deaf, but it felt like she was a little blind too. Without her hearing, she couldn't see right, or balance right. She thought about a life without ears. She'd probably have to go back to digging, since you couldn't haul bodies without a partner and you needed to be able to talk, even if it was only to say alley-*oop*.

She walked like a drunkard, keeping to the darkest streets where even the night wardens stayed away. She let only the tiniest glow escape from her little light.

She was about to turn into the main shopping street when a strong hand seized her arm and jerked her back into the alley. Her first thought was *zombie* and she screamed involuntarily and a fist connected with her mouth, loosening one of the teeth next to her gap. Her head rang like a bell, the first sound she'd heard since that morning.

The little bead fell out of her hand and rolled into a crack in the pavement, crazily illuminating the scene and her attacker. The alley was filthy and covered in drifts of rubble, and the man who'd hit her was a young civil defense warden with acne that looked chemically induced. He didn't smell good. He smelled very bad. Sick, maybe. Unclean like everyone, and worse. He was no zombie. He didn't smell good enough.

She saw his mouth work and knew he was saying something to her. "I'm deaf" she said and she knew she said it too loud because he recoiled and then he punched her harder in the mouth than before.

She fell down this time and he dragged her roughly by one arm away from the light.

She was cried out, and weak from hunger, and she understood what was coming next when he threw her down and grabbed the collar of her shirt and ripped it away from her, then gave her bra the same treatment. She was dazed from the knocks on the head, but she knew what was coming.

Valentine's mother was a soldier. She'd been taught to kill. She'd taught Valentine to kill. Valentine never left the house without a clasp-knife, the knife she'd taken from the corpse she'd thrown out a fifteenth storey window some unknowable time before.

The knife was in her back pocket. She watched the boy's silhouette work at the fastener of his trousers, while she stole a hand behind her and slowly, slowly took out the knife. She let herself make silent choking dazed sounds.

She knew what was coming next, but the boy didn't.

But as he knelt down and reached out for the snap on her

trousers, she showed him what was next. She took two of his fingers and just missed opening her own belly. He tried to jerk his arm away, but she had him by the wrist before he could, and she pulled him down on top of her, making sure that her knife was free of the clinch, free to slip around behind him and take him once-twice-three times in between his ribs, then again into his kidneys. Seeing the splatted corpses she tossed out of windows had given her a very keen idea of how anatomy worked.

She had never felt so clearheaded as she did at this work, and the boy on her thrashed and got her a couple good knocks on the head, and his blood soaked her bare chest and her face and her short hair. But she worked the knife some more, going for the throat and then the face. She let him go and he rolled away and she pounced on him. She worked with the knife. Soon he stopped moving.

Her shirt was in rags, but the bra-clasp still worked, once she bent it back. The pea-light was easy to find—it glowed like a beacon. She picked it up and made her way to the wizard's.

"I'm deaf," she said to Ana. Ana looked the same, at first. And then Valentine saw that she was holding a cane and leaning on it heavily.

She knew that she was half-naked and covered with gore, but she also knew that Ana would not be phased by this. She squeezed past her and into the brave, swooping, just-printed sitting room. She fixed herself some coffee and poured a glug of rum into it while Ana stared at her in some wordless emotion.

"I'm deaf," she repeated, setting down some coffee and rum for Ana. "I could use a shirt, too. And the wizard, of course."

She remembered how to use the cooker from the revolutionary days, but it was like remembering something from a dream. She poked at it, ignoring Ana, and got it to produce a plate of goose-liver dumplings in white gravy. She rinsed the blood off her fingers and then ate the dumplings with them.

Ana stared at her for a long moment, then limped out of the room and fetched the wizard.

He said something that she couldn't hear. Everyone in the city was old, even the young people—wrinkled with dust in the wrinkles and missing teeth and torn clothes. The wizard was forever young. He was clean and unscarred and well-fed as ever.

"Print me some clothes, wizard," she said. "These ones are covered in blood. And I'm deaf, so don't bother talking to me."

The wizard stared at her. She ate a dumpling and licked the gravy off her fingers. Her stomach had been in flutters since waking up deaf, a not entirely unpleasant counterpoint to her constant, painful hunger. The gravy soothed her stomach, the dumplings settled it, the pain retreated.

She was deaf. She was a murderess. But there was food and it was good. Better than no food, anyway.

The wizard brought her a pile of warm, printer-fresh clothes. "Your printers never stopped working, did they?" she said. She was sure she was talking very loudly and she didn't give a festering shit.

"Our printers stopped working the morning of the siege. Everything did. Everything stops working. That's the infowar. The infowar probably is what did it for my hearing aids. They were supposed to last ten years but it's hardly been two."

"I'm taking a shower now," she said. "You can write me an answer if you'd like. I promise to read it afterward."

She took herself to the bathroom and let the shower wash her. There were some tears in her head somewhere but they couldn't find their way to her eyes. That was all right. It was a war, after all.

She dressed in fine printer-fresh clothes and burped a printer-fresh belch. The gravy taste wafted gassily into her mouth.

The wizard had rolled up one of the sofas and unrolled a big screen in its place, the kind of thing she used to love to play games on, in the dreamlike fantasy of yore.

YOU'RE DEAF?

She nodded. "I have hearing aids, from a bomb. They weren't working when I got out of bed this morning. No warning. They went like that." She snapped her fingers.

Some movement caught the corner of her eye and she spun around. There were four more people in the living room, people she hadn't met before though she assumed that they belonged to the distant voices she'd heard on her earlier visits. They had the well-fed look of Ana and the wizard, and a couple of them were obviously foreign. The documentarians. One of them was pointing a camera at her. She bared her gap-tooth grin at the camera and faked a step toward it. The camera-woman cringed back and she laughed nastily.

"Your cameras work. Your printers work. You're not losing the infowar the way we do. That's because there's a way to build things to resist the infowar agents, right? That's why the enemy trenchbusters don't fail the way our weapons do."

The wizard and Ana conversed briefly, their heads pointed away from her. She grabbed the camera away from the startled camera-woman and pointed it at them.

"I want to get a recording of what you're saying now so once my hearing comes back I'll be able to listen. You don't mind, do you?" She laughed again and poked her tongue out through the gap in her teeth. All her teeth were loose now, and running her tongue along the back of them made them wiggle in a way that was part tickle, part hurt.

The wizard got the idea. He made a keyboard appear on the screen again and prodded at it.

IT'S NOT QUITE WHAT YOU THINK VALENTINE

"Sure, what do I know? But you've got something, don't you?"

Ana nodded.

"You can fix my hearing?"

Ana nodded again.

"You could try to kill me while you performed surgery, couldn't you?"

Neither of them said anything.

"I'm boobytrapped." She wasn't, but it had been known to happen. "When I die, boom!" She realized that this lie might be too extravagant. Who'd booby-trap a starved gap-toothed girl? "My mother arranged it."

She thought back to the cine. The food she'd eaten was helping her think, the way it always did, making her realize what a cloud of fuzz-headed hunger she usually floated through.

"I've left a full description of your operation in a sealed envelope to be opened in the event of my death."

That was better. She should have gone with that in the first place. She couldn't tell if they believed her. Ana was shaking her head.

"You've got a doctor here, or someone like a doctor. Whatever's been done to your leg, Ana, a doctor did that."

Ana pointed at the woman from whom Valentine had snatched the camera. Valentine passed it back to her. "Sorry about that."

◔ ◔ ◔

The day after Valentine killed her first man, her hearing came back. The surgery took about ten minutes and was largely performed remotely, reprogramming the hardware in her head with something that the doctor kept calling "hardened logic." She liked the sound of that.

Her hearing came back slowly, in blips and bloops over the course of a few hours. Then it was back, better than new. She found that she could hear sounds from much farther away. The camera-woman also showed her how she could use a terminal to access the memory in her new ears, which would buffer six months' worth of audio. Valentine didn't think she'd be in a position to make much use of this feature, as interesting as it was. There weren't any working machines in the city.

"I'm going home now," she said.

Ana was waiting by the printer, making it output clothes and food as fast as it could, giving it to robots to tie up in grip-sheets.

"Would you have turned us in if we didn't help you?"

Valentine shook her head and tried not to smile. "No one would have believed me anyway. I'm not boobytrapped, either."

"I didn't think you were," Ana said. She gave Valentine a long hug and kissed her cheek. "Be careful, OK?"

"Why don't you people help us? Why can't you give our army hardened logic for their weapons?"

Ana shook her head. She was crying. "You think I haven't asked this? To do that would be suicide. Your enemies would never forgive us. It's one thing to chide them for their slaughter, another thing to end it."

Valentine had Ana print her some convincing rags with bit-mapped filth right in the weave and wrapped her parcels in them so they wouldn't be suspicious. She stepped out into the bright light of a spring day, every sound sharp as a pin-drop, from distant gunfire to the nearby hungry whimpering of a baby.

She walked slowly through the streets. She passed a spot that she thought was the place where the boy grabbed her, where she'd done her work with the knife. If that was the spot, though, there was no sign of it. The corpse-carriers were efficient.

She walked the stairs to her flat quickly, her full belly supplying her with boundless energy. As she reached for the door, though, she heard something from behind it, some crying. Trover. Once he'd cried nonstop. But he hadn't cried in so long she barely remembered the sound.

She swung open the door and saw what Trover was crying about. Mata was stretched out on the floor beside the one chair they hadn't burned for fuel. She wasn't moving and one of her eyes was wide open, the other squeezed shut. Trover was shaking her shoulder and crying.

"What?" Valentine said to her brother, grabbing and shaking him. "What happened?"

He opened his mouth and let out a howl. He hadn't spoken in a long time.

She knelt at her mother's side. Her mother's cheek was cold. Her arms and hands were stiff. Valentine knew that stiffness. Anyone who worked on the corpse patrol knew that stiffness. The front of her mother's torn trousers were damp with cold piss, Valentine could smell it. In Mata's breast pocket were a couple of inhalers, military grade, the kind of thing you took if you couldn't afford to sleep and if you needed to make your body go.

To Valentine, her mother looked like a skeleton, something long-buried and not freshly dead. Compared to Ana, this woman was very ugly and skinny and hard. Too hard to be a mother. She must have taken the drugs to keep herself going when Valentine didn't come home. Maybe she'd gone looking for Valentine. Maybe she'd gone looking for a doctor. Maybe she'd gone to the front to kill some soldiers. Whatever the cause, Valentine had been the reason. It was for her that Mata had killed herself.

Valentine pulled Trover to her and hugged him. The little boy smelled of his own shit. In her parcels, she had the food he needed so she cut them open and gave him some.

She let him eat and covered Mata with some of the new clothes that she'd brought home. She knew how to go through a corpse's pockets efficiently. She also knew all of Mata's hiding places in the tiny, grimy flat. Soon she had Mata's identification, her sidearm, her inhaler, her rucksack. There were soldiers Valentine's age at the front. She could pass.

"Come on, Trover," she said, getting him into a change of clothes, putting good shoes on him. Good shoes would be important. She didn't know how much walking they'd do, but it would be a lot.

She took him down the stairs, snuffling and weeping a little still, but logy from all the rich food. She led him to the civic patrol office.

"I can win the war," she said.

The woman from the city wasn't so fat anymore, but she still had her armor on. She was the one who'd told father he had to go to the war. She didn't seem to recognize Valentine, though.

She stared at Valentine. "I'm busy," she said.

"I know a—" Valentine searched for the word. "A profiteer who has access to hardened logic that the infowar doesn't work against."

The woman from the city looked at her a little longer this time. "I'm very busy, little girl."

"I can bring you to him. He has working printers."

The woman pretended not to hear her. She stared down at a pile of papers in front of her, and it was clear to Valentine that she was only pretending to read them.

Valentine led Trover to the woman's desk and knocked all the papers off of it.

"It's illegal to be a profiteer. Don't you want to at least arrest him?"

"I'll arrest *you*," the woman from the city said, grabbing her wrist. Valentine was ready for this. Her mother had taught her what to do about this. She bent the woman's thumb back and squeezed it until she tumbled out of the chair and dropped to her knees.

"That's enough," said an old, old hero. He sounded like he was right behind her, but that was just her new ears. When she turned around she saw that he was in the doorway. He was so old now that he looked like a zombie, and his one arm was pointing at her with shaky authority. "Let her go."

Valentine released the woman from the city.

"Do you want to see the profiteer?" Valentine said, approaching the hero. Her mother had respected this man, and Valentine decided she would respect him too.

"I will come with you," he said.

"Will you bring guards? He is armed." She thought for a minute. "I believe he's armed."

"It will be fine," he said. He showed her the heavy pistol he wore on his belt.

"My brother has to come, too," Valentine said.

"That will be fine."

The old hero walked slowly and carefully. The soldiers he passed nodded to him and saluted him. The old people smiled and waved. Valentine came to feel proud to be at his side. Normally she was invisible in the city, just another grey, thin face, but with the old hero, she was a hero too. And she *was* a hero: she was about to end the war.

The old man spoke creakingly to her as they walked. He remembered her mother, and he remembered her father. He told her stories of her mother's bravery in the revolution, when he'd been her commander, and she felt her heart race. Valentine was a hero, like her mother. The wizard would win the war for them.

Then they came to his door. The old man didn't need her to point it out. He went and thumped it three times with the butt of his gun.

Ana answered a moment later. She was dressed in old rags, and had left behind the cast from her leg, limping to the door on a makeshift cane.

"Hello, comrade," she said. She didn't have her usual accent.

The hero nodded to her. "Comrade Ana." He knew her name, without being introduced.

The wizard came to the door. "Comrade hero."

"Comrade Georg." The old hero shook the wizard's hand. The wizard was wearing rags like Ana's. He had a cunning glitter in his eye and he took in the street, took in Valentine. "Hello, Valentine," he said.

"This girl tells me you have contraband," the old hero said. "It's my duty to come in and search your premises for it."

"Valentine," the wizard said, with unconvincing disappointment. "The food you took from here wasn't contraband. It was my savings." To the hero, he added, "She took the food and I didn't blame her. Surely she was hungry. If I had been a little child in her circumstances, I might have done the same."

Valentine squeezed Trover's hand until he whimpered. She didn't trust her tongue enough to say anything.

They went into the vestibule and then turned left into a flat. Now, until this time, she'd always turned right when visiting the wizard, but now on the right there was nothing but a smooth, unbroken wall. And to the left, there was an entirely different flat, barren of furniture as her own flat, small and dirty and smelling of death.

"Search away," the wizard said. He tried to put a hand on Valentine's shoulder and she shied away and dropped her hand to the waistband of the trousers he'd printed for her, where she'd hidden her mother's tiny sidearm. "You'll find nothing, I assure you."

Valentine could see that they'd find nothing. All the furniture in the room couldn't have concealed a single tin of food. This wasn't even the right flat. With her amazing ears, she heard the movement of the wizard's associates, the documentarians, in the next flat over.

"I hear them," she said. "Next door. This isn't the right flat."

"This is the flat you led me to," the old hero said.

"It's through there!" she said, pointing at the blank wall. "It's a false wall!" She thumped it but it was solid and stony. Tears pricked her eyes. "These clothes!" she said, desperately, plucking at her shirt and trousers. "He printed them for me! He has hardened logic printers on the other side of that wall. He could win the war!"

The wizard shook his head and smiled at her again. His eyes glittered. "Oh, if only that were true. To win this war—"

She looked imploringly at Ana. Ana looked away.

The old hero shook the wizard's hand with his one remaining hand. "I'm sorry to have disturbed you, comrade."

"Nonsense," the wizard said. "Anything for the city."

"Come along," the old hero said. "Let's leave these people in peace."

Trover let himself be led silently into the street and stayed at her side even when she let go of his hand to silently palm her mother's sidearm.

"Your mother would be ashamed of you," the old hero said. "She wouldn't have wasted the city's time on her fantasies and vendettas."

She kept silent. She knew a nearby alley where no one ventured except for people who disappeared without a trace. Though she wanted to shout at him that her mother died for the city that the old hero had just betrayed, she kept silent.

When they passed the alley-mouth, she hastily shoved Trover into it. He gave a cry and fell over. She ducked in after him.

"He's tripped! Help me!" she called.

The old hero slowly negotiated his way into the alley and to her side. She was holding Trover down as he struggled to rise, but she hoped it looked like she was helping him up. Maybe it did, for the old hero bent at her side and she stuck the sidearm under his chin and pushed it hard into the wattle of skin there.

"My mother died for this city, you traitorous worm," she said, her jaws clenching with the effort of not shouting the words. "I would kill you right now if I didn't think you could be of use to me."

The old hero's eyes were calm. "Lots of people have tried to kill me, little girl."

"Lots of the enemy have tried. How many from the city?"

"Lots," the old hero said. "Lots of them, and yet here I stand, alive and well."

"I want to go to see the people who fight the infowar. I'll kill you if you don't take me to them."

"You want to do what? You stupid little girl." His tone still wasn't angry. "The wizard there is the city's best friend abroad. He's the only reason our enemies haven't crushed us. You want to betray him?"

"I will win this war," she said. But she faltered. She had thought that he'd just been bought off by the wizard, but maybe it was the case that he supported the wizard's work. Was it possible?

"We will win this war, by cooperating with our friends abroad. We can't afford to expose them to risk. I don't expect you to understand, little girl. This is a very deep game."

The phrase "deep game" enraged her so much that she almost shot him there. It was so—*patronizing.*

She let him lead the way toward the front. Trover was whimpering now—he'd twisted his ankle when she'd shoved him—and she whispered to him to be still.

Her plan was stupid. The old hero was going to lead her into a trap, not to the high command, and she knew it.

"I suppose I should just shoot you," she said.

"Why do you say that?" He was so calm. What kind of man was this?

"You'll lead me to a trap and have me shot or arrested. I have to see the infowar command. I have to win the war."

"You dream big, little girl. I have been persecuting the war on our enemies since before your hero mother was born. The first thing I learned is that war is the art of the possible. It is possible that we will win the siege, given enough time and losses. It is not possible that you will win the war."

"So you'll have me shot rather than try."

"I wouldn't have you shot if I could help it. I owe your mother that much."

"If you keep talking about my mother I will shoot you." She found his calm tone calmed her, too. The soldiers still saluted them, the old people waved, and she supposed that if any of them knew she had the old hero under the gun, she'd be torn to pieces. But she was calm and the day was a sunny one.

"My apologies," the old man said.

"I could have you run away and try to find them on my own."

"You'd never find them."

"I found the wizard. I put a weapon under your chin. I'm fifteen years old and I did that much. I will find them and I'll—"

"You'll what? You'll tell them to go to the wizard's flat to retrieve his technology? I assure you, if that was to come to pass, there would be no technology to get by the time you reached his flat."

They were getting closer to the front. The distant gunfire and zizzing trenchbusters were crystal-clear in her amazing new ears.

"He gave some to me," she said. "My hearing aids failed yesterday and he got them back online with hardened logic. I have it in my head."

"You—" The old man stopped in his tracks. She almost shot him by accident, ploughing into him. He turned around, much faster than she'd seen him move to date. "You have it in your head?"

He reached for her and she jerked the sidearm up. Absently he took it away from her in a single cobra-swift movement and dropped it in his shirt pocket. He reached for her again with his one hand and tilted her head, looking for the small scars beneath her jaw.

"He fixed these?"

"Yesterday. I was deaf yesterday morning."

"You're not lying? If you're lying, I will have you shot."

"She was deaf," Trover said, very quietly. "Now she can hear again. My sister isn't lying."

They both looked at him.

"Come with me, little girl," the old hero said, and he struck off.

⊖ ⊖ ⊖

Six hours after Valentine left her dead mother behind in their grimy, bare flat, she came to the infowar command.

It was far back of the lines, near the old woods at the western side of the city, and the entrance to it was guarded by five checkpoints. They took away the sidearm from the old hero at the last one, along with several other small weapons the old hero was carrying. They searched and wanded Valentine and Trover, and

made Trover turn out his pockets. It turned out that he was carrying Valentine's old clasp-knife, which had disappeared some
months before. He handed it to the soldier solemnly, and she
kissed his cheek and tousled his hair and for a moment, she
looked just like their mother and Valentine felt tears behind her
eyes.

"We're here," the old hero said. "Come with me."

There were three airlocks to pass through, and then they were
put into airtight suits with breathing bottles. They didn't have one
that would fit Trover, but the nice soldier who'd kissed his cheek
promised to look after him.

Beyond the last airlock, it was like something from before the
siege, clean and bold and humming with energy.

"We keep everything that works here," the old hero said.
"This is our last cache of materiel that hasn't been compromised
by the infowar. It's a completely sealed space. If a single strand of
malware got in, it would turn epidemic and wipe out everything."

His voice sounded like it was coming from a million miles
away. Shrouded in her breathing hood, Valentine felt like she was
in the first days of a better nation, a time when everything worked
and smelled of sharp cleanliness, not rot and ruin. Hooded figures
walked past them without a glance.

The old hero led her deep into the maze, then through yet another airlock.

"Comrade," the old hero said. "A word, please."

The hooded figure to whom he spoke looked up from its
workbench and peered through the old hero's hood. Then it
saluted smartly and hurried to the old hero's side.

"General–" The hooded figure had a man's voice, almost as
old as the old hero's voice.

The old hero– the general–touched his hand to his hood and
then pulled a retractable wire out of his helmet and presented it
to the other. The other patched it into his helmet's collar. Even
with her marvelous new ears, Valentine couldn't hear what they
said.

They released their umbilicus a moment later and the other
one turned to Valentine.

"Is it true?" His voice was choked, like he could barely get the words out.

"In my ears," she said. "Hardened logic."

The other man danced from foot to foot. "It can't be true," he said.

She nodded.

The old man rooted through his workbench and came up with a wand that he put against the back of her neck. It was similar to the wand that the doctor/camera-woman at the wizard's house had used to figure out her hearing aids.

"You have it?" the general asked.

"I have it," the other one said. "I have copied it. Whether I can decompile it, whether I can make anything useful from it—well, we'll see."

"Tomorrow, then," the general said.

The other one didn't answer. He was hunched over a terminal on his workbench, fingers punishing his keyboard.

"Now where?" Valentine asked as they shucked their isolation suits, the smell of stink and rot flooding back into her nostrils.

"Now we clean house," the general said. "Get your brother and your gun."

❧ ❧ ❧

Twenty four hours after the wizard cured Valentine's hearing, she helped arrest him.

The general knocked on the wizard's door and it swung open. Ana had her cast off again, had her bad cane.

"Yes, comrade?"

"I have business with you and yours. Bring them out here, please."

Ana took in the line of soldiers in the road before her, carrying weapons from knives to old gunpowder weapons to small, floppy sidearms and she went ashen.

"I knew it would be today," she said. She turned to Valentine. "When you came back this morning, I knew it would be today."

"Call them," the old hero said.

"They already know you're here." Smoke emerged from the

doorway behind her. "It's all destroying itself. There was never a chance of you getting access to it."

The general shrugged with one shoulder. Valentine wondered if his stump was smooth like a billiard ball or angry and wounded or shriveled like dried fruit.

She gripped her mother's sidearm tighter and watched the wizard emerge. The documentarians. The wizard's eyes glittered.

"It's all gone," he said. "You won't get a scrap of it. What a goddamned waste. We were on your side, you know."

"You were very well-fed," the general said.

One of the documentarians sobbed.

"What a pointless goddamned waste. Spiteful, stupid, bone-headed—" The wizard broke off, looking at Valentine. "Her hearing aids."

Valentine smiled. "Yes," she said. "My hearing aids. I'm recording you now. Do you have any words you'd like to say for the microphone?"

The wizard's jaw dropped to his chest and his whole body sort of crumpled, slumping in the grasp of the soldier who held him.

"You little—"

Valentine put a sarcastic finger to her lips and then made a show of covering Trover's ears. She saw Ana smile involuntarily before the woman turned away.

⌐ ⌐ ⌐

Three days after they arrested the wizard, the sky-cars lifted off again. They roared over the enemy lines, dropping intelligent motes that zeroed in on enemy soldiers and burrowed up their nostrils and in their ears and in the corners of their eyes and rattled in their skulls until their brains were paste and goo.

Four days after they arrested the wizard, the printers started to supply food and drugs. Clever wormy robots sought out and inoculated the zombies.

Ten days after they arrested the wizard, the buildings started to repair themselves. The lifts all worked again, all at once, in a synchronized citywide *whirrr* of convenience and civilization.

Fourteen days after they arrested the wizard, the siege ended.

Valentine and Trover were in the civil defense bunkhouse. They'd buried their mother that morning, in the woods, in a perfectly square grave that the robots had excavated for them, amid the ranked hundreds of thousands that the robots were digging through the woods, marking each with a small plaque inset to the soil, bearing a name and a date of birth, and sometimes a day of death, and the legend, HERO OF THE SIEGE.

Trover hadn't spoken all that day, but he had tossed in the first shovel-full of dirt at their mother's grave. Around them, the survivors had wailed and torn their clothes and shoveled at the massed dead.

The soldiers laughed and sang around them, drinking champagne and eating chocolate. The men hugged them and the women kissed them, even the sour woman from the city.

The general saw them sitting in their corner, Trover's hand in Valentine's, and he got them and brought them back into the cells. He handed Valentine a key and gestured toward the wing.

"Go and get them. They're free to go now. Tell them to go far."

Ana and the wizard were sharing a tiny cell, the documentarians were in three other cells. Valentine turned the old metal key in each lock in turn.

"It's over," she said. "Victory. The general says to go far."

Ana hugged her so long Valentine thought she'd never let go, but when she did let go, Valentine wished she'd come back.

Valentine never saw them again.

◦ ◦ ◦

Ten years after the siege, Valentine got her medal.

The ceremony was a small one. They had almost run out of special medals to bestow on the living heroes of the siege, and children came last. The only times she saw Trover these days was at a friend's ceremony. The rest of the time, he was preoccupied with his studies. He was training to be a diplomat. He still had a terrible temper. Apparently this was an asset at the System Trade Union.

Valentine walked there, but she was just about the only one.

Others flew, either in sky-cars or on invisible ground-effect cushions. There were a thousand of them getting their medals today, and she and Trover were placed next to each other in the long queue, which was alphabetical by surname.

"They should have given you the biggest and first medal, Vale," Trover said. His hands were in white fists. "You! You won the war! And *he* knows it!"

On stage, the general shook hands with another medal-recipient. He was up to the C's, and Valentine and Trover's last name started with an X. It would be a while yet.

"His other arm is very convincing," she said.

Trover just fumed.

When they took the stage, the general looked at them and winked. He gave them each a medal, then took her by the shoulders and then hugged her to his breast. He was still thin and fragile, but he was also still quick and his hug was firm. He pressed his palm to hers and her body told her he was sending her some data, which she accepted with surprise but without comment.

Trover led her off of the stage. She examined her new download. An audio file. She played it, and it played in her cochlea.

I found the wizard. I put a weapon under your chin. I'm fifteen years old and I did that much. I will find them and I'll—

You'll what? You'll tell them to go to the wizard's flat to retrieve his technology? I assure you, if that was to come to pass, there would be no technology to get by the time you reached his flat.

He gave some to me. My hearing aids failed yesterday and he got them back online with hardened logic. I have it in my head.

You—You have it in your head?

She'd never forgotten those words, not in ten years, not through the reconstruction or her years abroad, not in school and not in work. Not a day had gone by without her thinking of it. Lots of people had ears that could buffer now, and hers now had a hundred-year buffer along with all the audio ever recorded on tap for her pleasure, but she never bothered to rewind her hearing. Those words, in her mind, were all the rewinding she needed.

She sat down hard, right there, on the sugary grass.

Trover was at her side in a flash, calling her name anxiously.

She was crying uncontrollably, but she was smiling too. Those words, pulled off of her ears ten years ago, when they'd gone to infowar command. Oh, God, those old friends, those words. The wizard and Ana. It had been so long. Where had the time gone?

⟐ ⟐ ⟐

The next day, she met an old face.

"You!" he said. He had a thick accent–the kind of accent that said he'd learned her language the hard way; that he hadn't just installed it.

She looked at him. He was very familiar, but she couldn't place him. Maybe if he didn't have that silly beard, forked into two theatrical points, the way they were wearing them in Catalan that year. She tried to picture him without it. He was grinning like a fool and laughing.

"I can't believe it's you!"

She shook her head slowly. Where the hell did she know this guy from? She was supposed to be going to the cine with friends that night–the new show screened between the trees in the western woods and you walked around through it and drank fizzy elderflower and talked with your friends as the story unfolded around you. It was a warm night and perfect for such things.

"You don't remember me?"

Her tooth tingled. The one that had been knocked out in the trench and re-sprouted after the siege. Then she recognized him.

"Withnail?"

He hopped in place. "Valentine! You remembered!"

She put her hand to her breast and staggered back dramatically, hamming it up. He was still very handsome, and she'd never forgotten her first kiss.

"What the hell are you doing here?"

"I have a layover," he said. "Tokyo tomorrow. But I wanted to stop and see the place–"

"Remember the dead?" she said. He had been the enemy, after all. How many of her countrymen had he shot?

"Remember," he said. "Remember everything."

How many of his comrades had died on the day the death

rained from the sky? Surely they had died in great number on that day.

The woods were full of her dead. Mata was there. And there was the movie tonight. She touched the medal on her lapel. He had no medal. The soldiers who'd persecuted the siege received no medals.

"You're here until when?"

"Tomorrow," he said, "first thing."

"First thing tomorrow. Come and see a movie tonight," she said.

He looked at her and cocked his head. She wasn't beautiful, she knew, but sometimes men looked at her that way. Something about what she'd done, they could see it.

"I'd like that very much," he said.

She played back a little audio as they walked together, for a terrible silence descended on them as they walked, awkward and oppressive.

Would you have turned us in if we didn't help you?

No one would have believed me anyway.

"Valentine?"

"Yes, Withnail?"

"Thank you," he said. "For the food. And the kiss. It was my very first."

"Mine too."

"The finest one, too."

She snorted and punched him in the shoulder.

"Shut up, Withnail," she said.

"Yes, Comrade Hero," he said.

She let him kiss her, but only once.

That night, anyway.

BOTCH TOWN
by Jeffrey Ford

Jeffrey Ford was born in West Islip, New York, in 1955. He worked as a machinist and as a clammer before studying English with John Gardner at the State University of New York. He is the author of six novels, including The Portrait of Mrs. Charbuque, *World Fantasy Award winner* The Physiognomy, *and Edgar Allan Poe Award winner* The Girl in the Glass. *His short fiction is collected in the World Fantasy Award winning collection* The Fantasy Writer's Assistant and Other Stories *and in* The Empire of Ice Cream. *His short fiction has won the World Fantasy, Nebula, and Fountain awards. He is currently working on a new novel,* The Shadow Year, *which will be published next year. Ford lives in southern New Jersey where he teaches writing and literature.*

IT ALL BEGAN in the last days of August when the leaves of the elm in the front yard had curled into crisp, brown tubes and fallen away to litter the lawn. I remember I sat at the curb that afternoon, waiting for Mr. Softee to round the bend at the top of Pine Avenue, listening carefully for that mournful knell, each measured *ding* both a promise of ice cream and a pinprick of remorse. Taking a castoff leaf into each hand, I made double fists. When I opened my fingers, brown crumbs fell and scattered on the road at my feet. Had I been waiting for the arrival of the stranger, I might have understood the sifting debris to be symbolic of the end of something. Instead, I waited for the eyes.

That morning, I'd left the house early under a blue sky, walked through the woods and crossed the railroad tracks away from town, where the third rail hummed and lay in wait, like a snake, for an errant ankle. Then, along the road by the fastener factory, back behind the grocery, and up and down the streets, I searched for discarded glass bottles in every open garbage can, dumpster, forgotten corner. By early afternoon, I'd found three soda bottles and a half-gallon milk bottle. At the grocery store, I turned them in for the refund and walked away with a quarter.

All summer long, Mr. Softee had this contest going. With each purchase of twenty-five cents or more, he gave you a card: on the front was a small portrait of the waffle-faced cream being pictured on the side of the truck. On the back was a piece of a puzzle that, when joined with seven other cards, made the same exact image of the beckoning soft one but eight times bigger. I had the blue lapels and red bow tie, the sugar-cone-flesh lips parted in a pure white smile, the exposed, towering brain of vanilla, cream kissed at the top into a pointed swirl, but I didn't have the eyes.

A complete puzzle won you the Special Softee, like Coney Island in a plastic dish—four twirled Softee loads of cream, choco-late sauce, butterscotch, marshmallow goo, nuts, party-colored sprinkles, raisins, M&M's, shredded coconut, bananas, all topped with a cherry. You couldn't purchase the Special Softee, you had to win it, or so said John, who, through the years, had come to be known simply as Softee.

Occasionally John would try to be pleasant, but I think the pa-per canoe of a hat he wore every day had soured his disposition irreparably. He also wore a blue bow tie, a white shirt, and white pants. His face was long and crooked, and, at times, when the or-ders came too fast and the kids didn't have the right change, the bottom half of it would slowly melt—a sundae abandoned at the curb. His long ears sprouted tufts of hair as if his skull contained a hedge of it, and the lenses of his glasses had internal flaws like diamonds. In a voice that came straight from his freezer, he called my sister, Mary, and all the other girls, "Sweetheart."

Earlier in the season, one late afternoon, my brother, Jim, said to me, "You wanna see where Softee lives?" We took our bikes. He led me way up Higbee Lane, past the shoe store and Paumonok School, up beyond Our Lady of Lourdes. After an hour of riding, he stopped in front of a small house. As I pulled up, he pointed to the place and said, "Look at that dump."

Softee's truck was parked on a barren plot at the side of the place. I remember ivy and a one-story house, no bigger than a good-sized garage. Shingles showed their zebra stripes through fading white. The porch had obviously sustained a meteor shower. There were no lights on inside, and I thought this strange because twilight was mixing in behind the trees.

"Is he sitting in there in the dark?" I asked my brother.

Jim shrugged as he got back on his bike. He rode in big circles around me twice and then shot off down the street, screaming over his shoulder as loud as he could, "Softee sucks!" The ride home was through true night, and he knew that without him I would get lost, so he pedaled as hard as he could.

We had forsaken the ostentatious jingle bells of Bungalow Bar and Good Humor all summer in an attempt to win. By the end of July, though, each of the kids on the block had at least two near-complete puzzles, but no one had the eyes. I had heard from Tim Caliban, who lived in the development on the other side of the school field, that the kids over there got fed up one day and rushed the truck, jumped up and swung from the bar that held the rearview mirror, invaded the driver's compartment, all the while yelling, "Give us the eyes. The fuckin' eyes." When Softee went up front to chase them, Tim's brother, Bill, leaped up on the sill of the window through which Softee served his customers, leaned into the inner sanctum, unlatched the freezer, and started tossing Italian Ices out to the kids standing at the curb.

Softee lost his glasses in the fray, but the hat held on. He screamed, "You little bitches!" at them as they played him back and forth from the driver's area to the serving compartment. In the end, Bill got two big handfuls of cards and tossed them out on the lawn. "Like flies on dogshit," said Tim, describing the scene. By the time they realized there wasn't a pair of eyes in the bunch, Softee had turned the bell off and was coasting silently around the corner.

I had a theory, though, that day at summer's end when I sat at the curb, waiting. It was my hope that Softee had been holding out on us until the close of the season, and then, in the final days before school started and he quit his route till spring, some kid was going to have bestowed upon him a pair of eyes. I had faith like I never had at church that something special was going to happen that day to me. It did, but it had nothing to do with ice cream. I sat there at the curb, waiting, until the sun started to go down and my mother called me in for dinner. Softee never came again, but as it turned out, we all got the eyes.

• • •

My mother was a better painter than she was a cook. I loved her landscape of the snow-covered peak of Mount Kilimanjaro, rising above the clouds while gazelles grazed in the savannah of the foreground, but I wasn't much for her spaghetti with tomato soup.

She stood at the kitchen stove over a big pot of it, glass of cream sherry in one hand, burning cigarette with a three-quarter-inch ash in the other. When she turned and saw me, she said, "Go wash your hands." I headed down the hall toward the bathroom and, out of the corner of my eye, caught sight of that ash falling into the pot. Before I opened the bathroom door, I heard her mutter, "Could you possibly . . ." followed hard by the mud-sucking sounds of her stirring the orange glug.

When I came out of the bathroom, I got the job of mixing the powdered milk and serving each of us kids a glass. At the end of the meal there would be three full glasses of it sitting on the table. Unfortunately, we still remembered real milk. The mix-up kind tasted like sauerkraut, and looked like chalk water with froth on the top. It was there merely for show, a kind of stage prop. As long as no one mentioned that it tasted horrible, my mother never forced us to drink it.

In the dining room where the walls were lined with grained paneling, the knots of which always showed me screaming faces, Jim sat across the table from me, and Mary sat by my side. My mother sat at the end of the table beneath the open window. Instead of a plate she had the ashtray and her wine in front of her.

"It's rib stickin' good," said Jim, and added a knifeful of margarine to his plate. When the orange stuff started to cool, it was in need of constant lubrication to prevent it from seizing.

"Shut up and eat," said my mother.

Mary said nothing. I could tell by the way she quietly nodded her head that she was being Mickey.

"Softee never came today," I said.

My brother looked up at me and shook his head in disappointment. "He'll be out there at the curb in a snow drift," he said to my mother.

She laughed without a sound and swatted the air in his direction. "You've got to have faith," she said. "Life's one long son of a bitch."

She took a drag on her cigarette and a sip of wine, and Jim and I knew what was coming next.

"When things get better," she said, "I think we'll all take a nice vacation."

"How about Bermuda?" said Jim.

In her wine fog, my mother hesitated an instant, not sure if he was being sarcastic, but he knew how to keep a straight face. "That's what I was thinking," she said. We knew that, because once a week, when she hit just the right level of intoxication, that's what she was always thinking. It had gotten to the point that when Jim wanted me to do him a favor and I asked how he was going to pay me back, he'd say, "Don't worry, I'll take you to Bermuda."

She told us about the water, crystal blue. So clear you could look down a hundred yards and see schools of manta rays flapping their wings. She told us about the pure white beaches with palm trees swaying in a soft breeze filled with the scent of wildflowers. We'd sleep in hammocks on the beach. We'd eat pineapples we cut open with a machete. Swim in lagoons. Washed up on the shore, amidst the chambered nautilus, the sand dollars, the shark teeth, would be pieces of eight from galleons wrecked long ago.

That night, as usual, she told it all, and she told it in minute detail, so that even Jim sat there listening with his eyes half-closed and his mouth half-open.

"Will there be clowns?" asked Mary in her Mickey voice.

"Sure," said my mother.

"How many?" asked Mary.

"Eight," said my mother.

Mary nodded in approval and went back to being Mickey.

When we got back from Bermuda, it was time to do the dishes. From the leftovers in the pot, my mother heaped a plate with spaghetti for my father for when he got home from work. She wrapped it in wax paper and put it in the center of the stove where the pilot light would keep it warm. Whatever was left over went to George the dog. My mother washed the dishes, smoking and drinking the entire time. Jim dried, I put the plates and silverware away, and Mary counted everything a few dozen times.

The garage of our house had, five years earlier, been converted into an apartment and my grandparents, Nan and Pop, lived in there. A door separated our house from their rooms. My mother knocked, and Nan called out for us to come in.

Pop took out his mandolin and played us a few songs: "Apple Blossom Time," "Show Me the Way to Go Home," "Good Night Irene." All the while he played, Nan chopped cabbage on a flat wooden board with a one-handed guillotine. My mother rocked in the rocking chair and drank and sang. The trilling of the double-stringed instrument accompanied by my mother's voice was beautiful to me.

Over at the little table in the kitchenette area, Mary sat with the Laredo machine, making cigarettes. My parents didn't buy their smokes by the pack. Instead they got this machine that you loaded with a piece of paper and a wad of loose tobacco from a can. Once it was all set up, there was a little lever you pulled forward and back, and presto. It wasn't an easy operation. You had to use just the right amount to get them firm enough so the tobacco didn't fall out the end.

When my parents had first gotten the Laredo, Mary watched them perform the process and was fascinated. She was immediately expert at measuring out the brown shag and never got tired of it. A regular cigarette factory once she got going; Pop called her R. J. Reynolds. He didn't smoke them, though. He smoked Lucky Strikes, and he drank Old Grand-Dad, which seemed fitting.

Jim and I, we watched the television with the sound turned down. Dick Van Dyke mugged and rubber-legged and did pratfalls in black and white, perfectly synchronized to the strains of

"Shanty Town" and "I'll Be Seeing You in All the Old Familiar Places." Even if they weren't playing music, we wouldn't have been able to have the sound up, since Pop hated Dick Van Dyke more than any other person on Earth.

● ● ●

My room was dark, and though it had been warm all day, a cool end of summer breeze now filtered in through the screen of the open window. Moonlight also came in, making a patch on the bare, painted floor. From outside, I could hear the chug of the Farleys' little pool filter next door, and beneath that, the sound of George's claws, tapping across the kitchen linoleum downstairs.

Jim was asleep in his room across the hall. Below us, Mary was also asleep, no doubt whispering the times tables into her pillow. My mother, in the room next to Mary's, I could picture, lying in bed, her reading light on, her mouth open, her eyes closed, and the thick, red volume of Sherlock Holmes stories with the silhouette cameo of the detective on the spine, open and resting on her chest. All I could picture of Nan and Pop was a darkened room and the tiny, glowing bottle of Lourdes Water in the shape of the Virgin that sat on the dresser.

I was thinking about the book I had been reading before turning out the light—another in the series of adventures of Perno Shell. This one was about a deluge, like Noah's flood, and how the old wooden apartment building he lived in had broken away from its foundation and he and all of the other tenants were sailing the giant ocean of the world, having adventures.

There was a mystery about the Shell books, because they were each published with a different author's name, sometimes by different publishing companies, but all you had to do was read a few pages and it was easy to tell that they were all written by the same person. I would never have discovered this if it wasn't for Mary.

Occasionally, I would read to her, snatches from whatever book I was working through. We'd sit in the corner of the backyard on the lower boards of the fence, in the bower made by forsythia bushes. In there, amidst the yellow flowers one day, I read to her from the first Shell book I had taken out: *The Stars Above* by Mary Holden. There were illustrations in it, one per chapter. When I was done reading, I handed the book to her so she could look at the pictures. While paging through it, she held it up to her face, sniffed it, and said, "Pipe smoke." Back then, my father smoked a pipe once in a while, so we knew the aroma. I took the book from her and smelled it up close, and she was right, but it wasn't the kind of tobacco my father smoked. It had a darker, older smell, something like a horse and a mildewed wool blanket, a captain's cabin. I got an image of the silhouette of Holmes on the binding of my mother's book. His pipe had a stem that dipped in a curve like an S and the bowl had a belly.

When I walked to the library downtown, Mary would walk with me. She usually never said a word during the entire trip, but a few weeks after I had returned *The Stars Above,* she came to me while I was searching through the four big stacks that lay in the twilight zone between the adult and children's sections. She tugged at my shirt, and when I turned around, she handed me a book: *The Enormous Igloo* by Duncan Main.

"Pipe smoke," she said.

Opening the volume to the first page, I read to myself, *"Perno Shell was afraid of heights and could not for the world remember why he had agreed to a journey in the Zeppelin that now hovered above his head."* Another Perno Shell novel by someone completely different. I lifted the book, smelled the pages, and nodded.

I wanted Perno Shell to stay in my imagination until I dozed off, but my thoughts of him soon grew as thin as paper, and then the persistent theme of my wakeful nights alone in the dark, namely *Death,* came clawing through. Jimmy Bonnel, a boy who'd lived up the block, two years younger than me and two years older than Mary, had been struck by a car on Montauk Highway one night in late spring. The driver was drunk and swerved onto the sidewalk. According to his brother, Teddy, who was with him, Jimmy was thrown thirty feet in the air. I always tried to picture that: twice again the height of the basketball rim. We had to go to his wake. The priest said he was at peace, but he didn't look it. Lying in the coffin, his skin was yellow, his face was bloated, and his mouth was turned down in a bitter frown.

All summer, he came back to me from where he lay under the ground. I imagined him suddenly waking up, clawing at the lid as in a story Jim had once told me. I dreaded meeting his ghost on the street at night when I walked George around the block alone. I'd stop under a streetlight and listen hard, fear would build in my chest until I shivered, and then I'd bolt for home. In the lonely backyard at sundown, in the darkened woods behind the school field, in the corner of my night room, he was waiting, jealous and angry.

George came up the stairs and stood beside my bed. He looked at me with his bearded face, eyes glinting in the moonlight, and then jumped aboard. He was a small, schnauzer-type mutt but fearless, and having him there made me less scared. Slowly, I began to doze. I had a memory of riding waves at Fire Island and it blurred at the edges, slipping into a dream. Next I knew, I suddenly fell from a great height and woke to hear my father coming in from work. The front door quietly closed. I could hear him moving around in the kitchen. George got up and left.

I contemplated going down to say hello. The last I saw him was the previous weekend. The bills forced him to work all day. There were three jobs: a part-time machining job in the early morning, then his regular job as a gear cutter, and then nights, part-time as a janitor in a department store. He left the house before the sun came up every morning and didn't return until very near midnight. Through the week, I would smell a hint of machine oil, here and there, on the cushions of the couch, on a towel in the bathroom, as if he were a ghost leaving vague traces of his presence.

Eventually, the sounds of the refrigerator opening and closing and the water running stopped, and I realized he must be sitting in the dining room, eating his pile of spaghetti, reading the newspaper by the light that shone in from the kitchen. I heard the big pages turn, the fork against the plate, a match being struck, and that's when it happened. There came from somewhere outside the house the shrill scream of a woman, so loud it tore open the night.

*   *   *

When I came downstairs the next morning, the door to Nan and Pop's was open. I stuck my head in and saw Mary sitting at the table in the kitchenette where the night before she had made cigarettes. She was eating a bowl of Cheerios. Pop sat in his usual seat next to her, the horse paper spread out in front of him. He was jotting down numbers with a pencil in the margins, murmuring a steady stream of bloodlines, jockeys' names, weights, speeds, track conditions, ciphering what he called the *McGinn System*, named after himself. Mary nodded with each new factor added to the equation.

My mother came out of the bathroom down the hall in our house, and I turned around. She was dressed for work in her turquoise outfit with the big star-shaped pin that was like a stained-glass window. I went to her and she put her arm around me, enveloped me in a cloud of perfume that was too much powder, and kissed my head. We went into the kitchen, and she made me a bowl of cereal with the mix-up milk, which wasn't as bad that way, because we were allowed to put sugar on it. I sat down in the dining room and she joined me, carrying a cup of coffee. The sunlight poured in the window behind her. She lit a cigarette and dragged the ashtray close to her.

"Friday, last day of vacation," she said. "You better make it a good one. Monday is back to school."

I nodded.

"Watch out for strangers," she said. "I got a call from next door this morning. Mrs. Kelty said that there was a prowler at her window last night. She was changing into her nightgown, and she turned and saw a face at the glass."

"Did she scream?" I asked.

"She said it scared the crap out of her. Bill was downstairs watching TV. He jumped up and ran outside, but whoever it was had vanished."

Jim appeared in the living room. "Do you think they saw her naked?" he asked.

"A fitting punishment," she said. And as quickly added, "Don't repeat that."

"I heard her scream," I said.

"Whoever it was used that old ladder Pop keeps in the backyard. Put it up against the side of the Keltys' house and climbed up to the second-floor window. So keep your eyes out for creeps wherever you go today."

"That means he was in our backyard," said Jim.

My mother took a drag of her cigarette and nodded. "I suppose."

Before she left for work, she gave us our list of jobs for the day—walk George, clean our rooms, mow the back lawn. Then she kissed Jim and me, and went into Nan's to kiss Mary. I watched her car pull out of the driveway. Jim came to stand next to me at the front window.

"A prowler," he said, smiling. "We better investigate."

A half-hour later, Jim and Mary and I, joined by David Kelty, sat back amidst the forsythias.

"Did the prowler see your mother naked?" Jim asked David.

David had a hairdo like Curly from the Three Stooges, and he rubbed his head with his fat, blunt fingers. "I think so," he said, wincing.

"A fitting punishment," said Jim.

"What do you mean?" asked David.

"Think about your mother's ass," said Jim, laughing.

David sat quietly for a second and then said, "Yeah," and nodded.

Mary took out a Laredo cigarette and lit it. She always stole one or two when making them. No one would have guessed. Mary was sneaky in a way, though. The favorite song of her life would end up being "Time of the Season" by The Zombies, so that gives you a clue. Jim would have told on me if I'd smoked one. All he did was tell her, "You'll stay short if you smoke that." She took a drag and said, "Could you possibly . . ." in a flat voice.

Jim, big boss that he was, laid it out for us. "I'll be the detective and you all will be my team. Jeff," he said, pointing to me, "you have to write everything down. Everything that happens has to be recorded. I have a notebook upstairs to give you. Don't be lazy."

"Okay," I said.

"Mary," he said. She just kept nodding as she had been. "You count shit. And none of that Mickey stuff."

"I'm counting now," she said in her Mickey voice.

We cracked up, but she didn't laugh.

"David, you're my right-hand man. You do whatever the hell I tell you."

David agreed, and then Jim told us the first thing we needed to do was look for clues.

"Did your mother say what the prowler's face looked like?" I asked.

"She said it was no one she ever saw before. Big eyes, big teeth, and really white, like he hadn't seen the sun all summer."

"Could be a vampire," I said.

"It wasn't a vampire," said Jim, "it was a pervert. If we're going to do this right, it's got to be like Science. There are no such things as vampires."

Our first step was to investigate the scene of the crime. Beneath the Keltys' second-floor bedroom window, on the side of their house next to ours, we found a good footprint. It was big, much larger than any of ours when we measured next to it, and it had a design on the bottom of lines and circles.

"You see what that is?" asked Jim, squatting down and pointing to the design.

"It's from a sneaker," I said.

"Yeah," he said.

"I think it's Keds," said David.

"What does that tell you?" asked Jim.

"What?" asked David.

"Well, it's too big to be a kid, but grown-ups usually don't wear sneakers. It might be a teenager. We better save this for if the cops ever come to investigate."

"Did your dad call the cops?" I asked.

"No, he said that if he ever caught who it was, he'd shoot the son of a bitch himself."

It took us about a half-hour to dig the footprint up, carefully loosening all around it and scooping way down beneath it with the shovel. We went to Nan's side door and asked her if she had a box. She gave us a round, pink hatbox with a lid that had a picture of a poodle and the Eiffel Tower on it.

Jim told David, "Carry it like it's nitro," and we took it into our yard and stored it in the toolshed back by the fence. When David slid it into place on the wooden shelf next to the bottles of bug killer and the shears, Mary said, "One."

● ● ●

Nan made lunch for us when the fire whistle blew at noon. She served it in our house at the dining room table. Her sandwiches always had butter, no matter what else she put on them. Sometimes, like that day, she just made butter and sugar sandwiches. We also had barley soup. Occasionally she would make chocolate pudding for us, the kind with a two-inch vinyl skin on top, but usually dessert was just a sugar-callused digit she called a ladyfinger.

Nan had gray, wire-hair like George's, big bifocals, and a brown mole on her temple that looked like a squashed raisin. Her small stature, her dark and wrinkled complexion, the silken black strands at the corners of her upper lip, her high-pitched laughter made her seem to me at times like some ancient monkey king. When she'd fart while standing, she'd kick her left leg up in the back, and say, "Shoot him in the pants, the coat and vest are mine." Every morning she'd say the rosary, and at night sometimes; in the afternoon when the neighborhood ladies came over to drink wine from teacups, she'd read the future in a pack of playing cards.

Each day at lunch that summer, along with the butter sandwiches, she'd also serve up a story from her life. That first day of our investigation, she chose to tell us one from her childhood, at the turn of the century, in Whitestone. Through the hot high noons of June and July, we had come to know that town out of her distant past where her father was the editor of the local paper, the fire engines were pulled by horses, Moisha Pipick, the strongest man alive, ate twelve raw eggs every morning for breakfast, Clementine Cherenete, whose hair was a waterfall of gold, fell in love with a blind man who could not see her beauty, and John Hardy Farty, a wandering vagrant, strummed a harp and sang, "Damn the rooster crow." All events, both great and small, happened within sight of a much-referred-to landmark, Nanny Goat Hill.

"A night visitor," she said when we told her about the footprint we had found and preserved in the hatbox she had given us. "Once there was a man who lived in Whitestone, a neighbor of ours. His name was Mr. Weeks. He had a daughter, Luqueer, who was in my grade at school."

"Luqueer?" said Jim, and he and I laughed. Mary looked up from her soup to see what was funny.

Nan smiled and nodded. "She was a little odd. Spent all her time staring into a mirror. She wasn't vain but was looking for something. Her mother told my mother that at night the girl would wake up choking, blue in the face, from having dreamt she was swallowing a thimble."

"That wasn't really her name," said Jim.

"As God is my judge," said Nan. "Her father took the train every day to work in the city and did not come home until very late at night. He always got the very last train that stopped in Whitestone, just before midnight, and would walk home through the streets from the station, stumbling drunk and singing in a loud voice. It was said that when he was drunk at a bar, he was happy-go-lucky, not a care in the world, but when drunk at home, he hit his wife and cursed her.

"One night in the fall, around Halloween time, he got off the train onto the platform at Whitestone. The wind was blowing and it was cold. The station was empty but for him. He started walking toward the steps that led down to the street, when from behind him he heard a noise like a voice in the wind. *OOOOoooo* was what it sounded like. He turned around, and at the far end of the platform was a giant ghost, eight feet tall, its white form rippling in the breeze.

"It scared the bejesus out of him. He ran home, screaming. The next day, which was Saturday, he told my father that the train station was haunted. My father printed the story as a kind of joke. No one believed Mr. Weeks because everyone knew he was a drunk. Still, he tried to convince people by swearing to it and saying he knew what he saw and it was real.

"At the end of the following week, on the way into the city on

Friday, he told one of the neighbors, Mr. Hardy, who rode in with him at the same time, that the ghost had been there on both Monday and Wednesday nights. On these occasions it had called his name. Weeks was a nervous wreck, stuttering and shaking while he told of his latest encounters. Mr. Hardy said Weeks was a man on the edge, but before getting off the train in the city, Weeks leaned in close to our neighbor and whispered to him that he had a plan to deal with the phantom. It was eight o'clock in the morning, and Mr. Hardy said he already smelled liquor on Weeks's breath.

"That night, Weeks returned from the city on the late train. When he got off onto the platform at Whitestone, it was deserted as usual. The moment he turned around, there was the ghost, moaning, calling his name, and now, for the first time, coming at him. But that day, in the city, Weeks had bought a pistol for four dollars. That was his plan. He took it out of his jacket, and tried to aim it, even though his hand was wobbling terribly from fear. He shot four times, and the ghost collapsed on the platform."

"How can you kill a ghost?" asked Jim.

"It was eight feet," said Mary.

"It wasn't a ghost," said Nan. "It was his wife in a bed sheet, standing on stilts. Her brother had been a performer, who had a pair of stilts, and she borrowed them from him for the get-up. She wanted to scare her husband into coming home on time and not drinking. But he killed her."

"Did he get arrested for murder?" I asked.

"No," said Nan. "He wept bitterly when he found out it was his wife. When the police investigation was over and he was shown to have acted in self-defense, he abandoned his home and Luqueer, and went off to live as a hermit in a cave in a field of wild asparagus at the edge of town. I don't remember why, but he eventually became known as Bedillia, and kids would go out to the cave and scream, 'Bedillia, we'd love to steal ya!' and run when he chased them. Luqueer got sent to an orphanage and I never saw her again."

"What happened to the hermit?" asked Jim.

"During a bad winter, someone found him in the middle of

the field by his cave, frozen solid. In the spring, they buried him there among the wild asparagus."

☙ ☙ ☙

After lunch, we put George on the leash and took him out in the backyard. Mary didn't go with us because she decided to have a session with her make-believe friends, Sally O'Mally and Sandy Graham, who lived in the closet in her room. Once in a while, she'd let them out and she would become Mickey and they would go to school together down in the cellar.

Jim had the idea that we could use George to track the pervert. We'd let him smell the ladder, he'd pick up the scent, and we'd follow along. David Kelty joined us in our backyard where the ladder again lay propped against the side of the tool shed. For a while, we just stood there waiting for the dog to smell the ladder. Then I told Jim, "You better rev him up." To rev George up all you had to do was stick your foot near his mouth. If you left it there long enough, he'd start to growl. Jim stuck his foot out and made little circles with it in the air near George's mouth. *"Geooorgieeee,"* he sang very softly. When the dog had enough, he went for the foot, growling like crazy, and fake biting all over it–a hundred fake bites a second. He never really chomped down, but he worked a sneaker over pretty thoroughly.

When he was revved, he moved to the ladder, smelled it a few times, and then pissed on it. We were ready to do some tracking. George started walking and so did we. Out of the backyard we went through the gate by Nan's side of the house, over the slates and under the pink blossoms of the prehistoric mimosa tree to the front yard, and then down the block.

Around the corner was Southgate school, a one-story structure of red brick, which was a big rectangle of classrooms with a courtyard of grass at its center. On the right-hand side was an alcove that held the playground for the kindergarten–monkey bars, swings, a seesaw, a sandbox, and one of those round, turning platform things that if you got it circling fast enough, all the kids would fly off. The gym was attached on the left-hand side; a giant, windowless box of brick that towered over the squat main building.

The school had a circular drive in front with an elongated, high-curbed oval of grass at its center. Just west of the drive and the little parking lot there were two asphalt basketball courts; and then a vast field with a baseball backstop and bases, where on windy days the powdered dirt of the baselines would rise in cyclones. At the border of the field was a high barbed-wire-topped fence to prevent kids from climbing down into a crater-like sump. Someone long ago had used a chain cutter to make a slit in the fence that a small person could pass through. Down there in the early fall, among the golden rod stalks and dying weeds, it was a kingdom of crickets.

Behind the school were more vast fields of sunburned summer grass cut by three asphalt bike paths. At the back, the school fields were bounded by another development, but to the east lay the woods: a deep oak forest that stretched well into the next town and south as far as the railroad tracks. Streams ran through it, as well as some rudimentary paths that we knew better than the lines on our own palms. A quarter-mile in, there lay a small lake that we had been told was bottomless.

That day, George led us to the boundary of the woods, near the pregnant swelling of the ground known as Sewer Pipe Hill. We stood on the side of the hill where the round, dark circle of the pipe faced the tree line. Some days a trickle of water flowed from the pipe, but now it was bone dry. Jim walked over to the round opening, three feet in circumference, leaned over, and yelled, *"Helloooooo."* His word echoed down the dark tunnel beneath the fields of the school. George pissed on the concrete facing that held the end of the pipe.

"X marks the spot," said Jim. He turned to David. "You better crawl in there and see if the prowler is hiding underground."

David rubbed his head and stared at the black hole.

"Are you my right-hand man?" asked Jim.

"Yes," said David. "But what if he's in there?"

"Before he touches you, just say you're making a citizen's arrest."

Kelty thought about this for a moment.

"Don't do it," I said.

Jim glared at me. Then he put his hand on David's shoulder and said, "He saw your mom's ass."

David nodded and moved toward the pipe. He bent down, got on his knees at the opening, and then shuffled forward into the dark a little way before stopping. Jim went over and lightly tapped him in the rear end with the toe of his sneaker. "You'll be a hero if you find him. They'll put you in the newspaper." David started crawling slowly forward and in seconds was out of sight.

"What if he gets lost in there?" I said.

"We'll just have everyone in town flush at the same time and he'll ride the wave out into the sump behind the baseball field," said Jim.

Every few minutes, one of us would lean into the pipe and yell to David, and he would yell back. We couldn't make out what he was saying, and his voice came smaller and smaller. Then we called a few times and there was no answer.

"What do you think happened to him?" I asked.

"Maybe the pervert got him," said Jim, and he looked worried. "He could be stuck in there."

"Should I run home and get Pop?" I asked.

"No," said Jim, "go up to that manhole cover on the bike path by the playground and call down through the little hole. Then put your ear over the hole and see if you hear him. Tell him to come back."

I took off running up the side of Sewer Pipe Hill and then across the field as fast as I could. Reaching the manhole cover, I got on all fours and leaned my mouth down to the neat round hole at the edge of it. "Hey," I yelled. I then turned my head and put my ear to it.

His voice came up to me quite clearly but with a metallic ring to it, as if he were a robot. "What?" he said. "I'm here." It sounded as if he was right beneath me.

"Come out," I called. "Jim says to come back."

"I like it in here," he said.

In that moment, I pictured his house, his sister Jean with the crossed eyes, his mother's prominent jaw and horse teeth, her crazy red hair, the little man figures his father fashioned out of the wax from his own enormous ears. "You gotta come back," I said.

A half-minute passed in silence, and I thought maybe he had moved on, continuing through the darkness. Finally his voice sounded. "Okay," he said, and then, "Hey, I found something."

● ◆ ◐

I found Jim sitting on the lip of the sewer pipe, reading a magazine, while George sat at his feet, staring up at him. As I eased down the side of the hill, he said, "Look what George tracked down over by that fallen tree." He pointed into the woods. "There were some crushed beer cans and cigarette butts there too."

I came up next to him and looked over his shoulder at the magazine. It was wrinkled from having been rained on and there was mud on the cover. He turned the page he was looking at toward me, and on it I saw a woman with red hair, black stockings, high heel shoes, a top hat, and an open jacket but nothing else.

"Look at the size of those tits," said Jim.

"She's naked," I whispered.

Jim picked the magazine up to his mouth, positioning it right in the middle of her spread-out legs, where the little hedge of red hair grew over her pussy, and yelled, *"Helllooooooo."*

We laughed.

I forgot to tell Jim that I had made contact with David. Instead, we moved on to the centerfold. Three full pages of a giant blonde, bending over a piano bench.

"Aye, aye, Captain," said Jim, and rapidly saluted her ass four times. Then we flipped the pages quickly to the next naked woman, only to stare and swoon.

As I reached down to pet the dog for his discovery, we heard David inside the pipe. Jim got up and turned around and we both stared into the opening. Slowly, the soles of his shoes appeared out of the dark, then his rear end, as he backed out into daylight. When he stood up and turned to face us, he was smiling.

"What's your report?" asked Jim.

"It was nice and quiet in there," said David.

Jim shook his head. "Anything else?"

David held out his hand and showed Jim what he had found. It was a green plastic soldier, carrying a machine gun in one hand and a grenade in the other. I moved closer to see the detail and noticed that the figure wore no helmet, which was unusual for an army man. He wore strings of big bullets over his shoulders and his mouth was open so that you could see his teeth gritted together.

Jim took the soldier out of David's hand, looked at it for a second, said, "Sergeant Rock," and then put it in his pocket.

David's brow furrowed. "Give it back," he said. His hands balled into fists and he took a step forward as a challenge.

Jim said, "Let me ask you a question. When the prowler saw your mother's ass—"

"Stop saying my mother's ass," said David, and took another step forward.

"—did it look like this?" asked Jim, and flipped the magazine so that the centerfold opened.

David saw it and went slack. He slowly brought his hand up to rest with his palm on his cheek and his fingers partially covering his right eye. "Oh, no," he said, and stared.

"Oh, yes," said Jim, and then took the magazine and ripped off the bottom fold of the center section, the page containing the big ass, and handed the sheet to David. "This is your reward for bravery in the sewer pipe."

David took the torn page in his trembling hands, his gaze fixed on the picture. Then he looked up and said, "Let me see the magazine."

"I can't," said Jim, "it's exhibit A. Evidence. You'll get your fingerprints on it." He rolled it up and put it under his arm the way Mr. Mardinella carried the newspaper as he walked down the street on his way home from work every evening.

We spent another couple of hours looking for clues all around the school fields and through the woods, but George lost the scent and we eventually headed home. Every other driveway we passed, David would take his piece of centerfold out of his back pocket and stop and stare at it. We left him standing in front of

Mrs. Grimm's house, petting the image as if it were flesh instead of slick paper.

When we got home, Jim made me go in first and see if the coast was clear. My mother wouldn't be home for about two hours and Nan and Pop were in their place. I didn't see Mary around, but that didn't matter anyway.

Up in his room, Jim slid the loose floorboard back and stowed the magazine. Then he got up and went to his desk. "Here," he said, and turned around holding a black-and-white-bound composition book. "This is for the investigation." He walked over and handed it to me. "Write down everything that happened so far."

I took the book from him and nodded.

"What are you gonna do with the soldier?" I asked.

Jim took the green warrior out of his pocket and held it up. "Guess," he said.

"Botch Town?" I asked.

"Precisely," he said.

I followed him out of the room, down the stairs, through the living room, to the hallway that led to the first-floor bedrooms. At the head of this hall there was a door. He opened it, and we descended on the creaking wooden steps into the dim, mildew waft of the cellar.

⬤ ⬤ ⬤

The cellar was lit by one bare bulb with a pull string and whatever light managed to seep in from outside through the four window wells. The floor was unpainted concrete, as were the walls. The staircase separated the layout between a right and left side, and there was an area behind the steps that allowed access from one side to the other. Six metal poles, four inches thick and six feet apart, supported the ceiling, positioned in a row across the center of the house.

It was warm in the winter and cool in the summer down there in the underground twilight where the aroma of my mother's oil paints and turpentine mixed with the pine and glittering tinsel scent of Christmas decorations heaped up in one corner. It was a treasure vault of the old, the broken, the forgotten. Stuff lay on shelves or stacked along the walls covered with a thin layer of cellar dust, the dandruff of concrete, and veiled in cobwebs hung with spider eggs.

On Pop's heavy wooden workbench, complete with crushing vise, there sat coffee cans of rusted nuts and bolts and nails, planes, rasps, wrenches, levels with little yellow bubbles encased to live forever. Riding atop this troubled sea of strewn tools, seemingly abandoned in the middle of the greatest home repair job ever attempted, was a long curving Chinese junk carved from the horn of an ox, sporting sails the color of singed paper created from thin sheets of animal bone, and manned by a little fellow, carved right out of the black horn, who wore a field worker's hat and kept a hand on the tiller. Pop told me he had bought it in Singapore, when he traveled the world with the Merchant Marine, from a woman who showed him my mother as a little girl, dancing, years before she was born, in a piece of crystal shaped like an egg.

Leaning against the pipe, that ran along the back wall and then out of the house to connect with the sewer line, were my mother's paintings: *The Snows of Kilimanjaro;* a self-portrait of her standing in a darkened hallway, holding me when I was a baby; the flowering bushes of the Bayard Cutting Arboretum; a seascape and view of Captree Bridge. All of her colors were subdued, and the images came into focus slowly, like a phantom approaching out of a fog.

Crammed into and falling out of one tall bookcase that backed against the stair railing on the right-hand side were my father's math books and used notebooks, every inch filled with numbers and weird signs, in his hand, in pencil, as if through many years he had been working the equation to end all equations. I remember a series of yellow journals each displaying in a circle on the cover the bust of some famous, long-dead genius I would have liked to know more about, but when I pulled one journal off the shelf and opened it that secret language told me nothing.

In the middle of the floor on the right-hand side of the cellar sat an old school desk, with wooden chair attached, and a place to put your books underneath. Around this prop, Mary created the school that her alter ego, Mickey, attended. Sometimes, when I knew she was playing this game, I would open the door in the hallway and listen to the strangely different voices of the teacher, Mrs. Harkmar, her classmates, Sally O'Mally and Sandy Graham, and, of course, Mickey, who knew all the answers.

Back in the shadows where the oil burner clanked and whirred and gibbered, there stood a small platform holding the Extreme Unction box, a religious artifact with hand-carved doors and a brass cross protruding from the top. We had no idea what *unction* was, so could not conceive of it in the extreme state, but Jim told me it was "holy as hell" and that if you opened the door, the Holy Ghost would come out and strangle you, making it look like you just swallowed your tongue the wrong way.

To the left of the stairs, beneath the single bare bulb, like a sun, lay Jim's creation, the sprawling burg of Botch Town. At one point my father was thinking of getting us an electric train set. He went out and bought four sawhorses and the most enormous piece of plywood. He set these up as a train table, but then the financial trouble descended and it sat for quite a while, smooth and empty. One day, Jim brought a bunch of cast-off items home with him from his early morning paper route. It had been junk day and the garbage men had not yet come. With coffee cans, old shoeboxes, pieces from broken appliances, Pez dispensers, buttons, Dixie cups, ice cream sticks, bottles, and anything else you could possibly imagine being pitched out, he began to build a facsimile of our development and the area around it. It became a project that he worked on a little here, a little there, continuously adding details.

He'd started by painting the road (a battleship gray) that came down straight from Higbee Lane and then curved around to the school, which was a shoebox with windows cut in it, a flag pole outside, the circular drive, basketball courts, and fields. Neatly written on the building, in black magic marker above the front doors was *Retard Factory*. The rest of the board he painted green, for grass, of course, with the exception of the lake in the woods, whose blue oval was covered with glitter.

❧ ❧ ❧

I sat at the desk in my room, the open notebook in front of me, a pencil in my hand, and stared out the window, trying to recall all of the details surrounding the prowler. There was the old ladder and the footprint, sitting, like a dirt layer cake, in a pink hatbox in the shed. I could have started with Mrs. Kelty and her ass, or just her scream in the night.

In fact, I didn't know where to start and, although from the time I was six, I had always loved writing and reading, I didn't feel much like recording evidence. Then, through the open window, from over at the Farleys', I heard the back screen door groan open and slam shut. I stood and looked to see what was going on. It was Mr. Farley, carrying a highball in one hand and a towel in the other. He was dressed in his swimming trunks, his body soft and yellow-white. His head seemed too heavy for the muscles of his neck, and it made him look as if he was searching for something he had dropped in the grass.

The Farleys' pool was a child's pool, larger than the kind you blow up but no bigger than three-feet deep and no wider than eight across. He set his drink down on the picnic table, draped his towel over the thickest branch of the cherry tree, shuffled out of his sandals, and then stepped gently over the side into the glassy water.

He trolled the surface, inspecting every inch for beetles and bees that had escaped the draw of the noisy little filter that ran constantly. He fetched up blackened cherry leaves from off the bottom with his toes and tossed them into the yard. Only then did he sit, slowly, cautiously, the liquid rising to accommodate his paunch, his sagging chest, and rounded shoulders, until his head bobbed on the surface. Slowly, he dipped forward, bringing his legs underneath him. His arms stretched out at his sides, his legs straightened behind him, his back broke the surface, and his face slipped beneath the water, leaving one bright bubble behind in its place.

He floated there for a moment or two, his body stretched tautly across the center of the pool, and then there came an instant when the rigid raft of his form gave way to death. His arms floated down, and his body curled like a piece of dough in the deep fry. Mr. Farley could really do the dead man's float. I wondered if he left his eyes open, letting them burn with chlorine, or if he closed them in order to dream more deeply into himself.

I sat back down at my desk, and instead of writing about the investigation, I wrote about Mr. Farley. After describing him getting into the pool and fake drowning on the water, I wrote about two other incidents I remembered about him. The first was about his older son, who had since moved away from home. When the boy was younger, Farley, an engineer who made tools for flights into outer space, tried to get his son interested in astronomy and science. Instead, the kid, Gregory, wanted to become an artist. Mr. Farley didn't approve. Before the kid left home for good, he created a giant egg out of plaster of Paris and set it up in the middle of the garden in the backyard. It sat there through months of wind and rain and sun and eventually turned green. On the day after the astronauts walked on the moon, Mr. Farley sledgehammered the thing into oblivion.

The second incident happened one day when I was raking leaves on the front lawn with my father. Suddenly the door over at the Farleys' opened and there he stood, weaving slightly, highball in hand. My father and I both stopped raking. Mr. Farley started down the steps slowly, and with each step his knees buckled a little more until upon reaching the walkway, he stumbled forward, his knees landing on the grass of the lawn. He remained kneeling for an instant, and then tipped forward, falling face first onto the ground. Throughout all of this, and even when he lay flat, he held his drink up above his head like a man trying to keep a pistol dry while crossing a river. I noticed that not a drop was spilled, as did my father, who looked over at me and whispered, "Nice touch."

I put the pencil down and closed the notebook with a feeling that I had accomplished something. It was hard to believe how much I had enjoyed capturing Mr. Farley on paper. I thought to myself, *Perhaps this writing is something that could be mine.* Jim had Botch Town, Mary had her imaginary world, my mother had her wine, my father, his jobs, Nan, the cards, and Pop, his mandolin. Instead of writing about the footprint or Mrs. Kelty's scream, I planned to fill the notebook with the lives of my neighbors, creating a Botch Town of my own between two covers.

When I went down into the cellar to tell Jim about my decision, I found him holding the plastic soldier up to the light bulb.
He showed me what he had done to the figure. Big white circles
had been painted over his eyes, and his hands, which had once
held the machine gun and grenade, had been chopped off and replaced with straight pins that jutted dangerously point out from
the stubs of his arms.

"Watch this, glow in the dark paint," said Jim, standing the figure upright on the board between our house and the Keltys'. He
then leaned way out over Botch Town and pulled the light bulb
string. The cellar went dark.

"The eyes," he said, and I looked down to see the twin circles
on the soldier's face glowing in the night of the handmade town.
The sight of him there, like a specter from a nightmare, gave me
a chill.

Jim stood quietly, admiring his creation, and I told him what
I had decided to do with the notebook. I thought he would be
mad at me for not following his orders.

"Good work," he said. "Everyone is a suspect."

⊸ ⊸ ⊸

Saturday afternoon, I sat with Mary back amidst the forsythias
and read to her the descriptions of the people I had so far written
about in my notebook. That morning I had gone out on my bike
early, scouring the neighborhood for likely suspects to turn into
words, and had caught sight of Mrs. Ryan, whom I named The
Colossus for her mesmerizing girth, and Mitchell Potaney, a kid
who shared my same birthday and who, for every school assembly and holiday party, played "Lady of Spain" on his accordion.

I doled them out to Mary, starting with Mr. Farley, reading
with the same rapid whisper and grave import as I used when re-
laying a chapter of a Perno Shell adventure. Mary was a good audience. She sat still, only nodding her head occasionally as she
did when sitting with Pop while he figured the horses. Each nod
told me that she had taken in and understood the information up
to that point. She was not obviously saddened when Mrs. Ryan's
diminutive, potato-head husband died nor did she laugh at my

description of Mitchell's simpering smile when bowing to scanty applause. Her nod told me she was tabulating the results of my effort, though, and that was all I needed.

When I was done and had closed the notebook, she sat for a moment in silence. Finally, she looked at me and said, "I'll take Mrs. Ryan to place."

Our mother called us in then. My father had just gotten home from work (Saturdays he only went to the shop until 12:30), and it was time for us to visit our Aunt Laura at the T. B. hospital. We piled into the white Biscayne, Jim and me in the back with Mary between us. My father drove with the window open, his elbow leaning out in the sun, a cigarette going between his fingers. I hadn't seen him all week until just then, and he looked tired. Adjusting the rearview mirror, he peered back at us and smiled. "All aboard," he said.

St. Anselm's was somewhere on the north shore of Long Island, nearly an hour drive from our house. The ride was usually solemn, but my father sometimes played the radio for us, or if he was in a particularly good mood, he'd tell us a story about when he was a boy. Our favorites were about the ancient, swaybacked plough horse, Pegasus, dirty white and ploddingly dangerous, he and his brother kept as kids in Amityville. Those stories had wings and he managed to end them just as we pulled in through the tall iron gates of the place.

This hospital was not a single modern building, painted white inside and smelling vaguely of Lysol and piss. St. Anselm's was like a small town of stone castles set amidst the woods; a fairy tale place of giant granite steps, oaken doors, stained glass, dim, winding corridors that echoed in their emptiness. There was a spot set amidst a thicket of poplars where a curved concrete bench lay before a fountain whose statuary was a pelican piercing its own chest with its beak. Water geysered forth from the wound. And the oddest thing of all—everyone there, save for old, bent Doctor Hasbith of the bushy white sideburns, was a nun.

I'd never seen so many nuns before, all of them dressed in their black flowing robes and tight headgear. When one of them came toward you from out of the cool shadows and your eyes weren't yet adjusted to inside, it was like a disembodied face floating in midair. They moved about in utter silence and only rarely would one smile in passing. The place, haunted by God and his mysteries, was both a dream and a nightmare. I couldn't help thinking that our aunt was being held prisoner there, enchanted like Sleeping Beauty, and that on some lucky Saturday we would rescue her.

As was usual, we were not allowed to accompany our parents to the place where Aunt Laura was being kept. Jim was left in charge, and we were each given a quarter to buy a soda. We knew that if we went down a set of winding steps that led into what I thought of as a dungeon, we would find a small room with a soda machine and two tables and chairs. Our usual routine was to descend, have a drink, and then go and sit on the bench by the fountain to watch the pelican bleed water for two hours. But that day, after we'd finished our sodas, Jim pointed into the shadow off to the left side of the small canteen at a door I'd never noticed before.

"What do you think is in there?" he asked.

"Hell," said Mary.

Jim got up and went over to it. I watched as he turned the knob. He flung the door open and jumped back. Mary and I left our seats and stood behind him. From there, you could see a set of stone steps leading down, walls close on either side like a brick gullet. There was no light in the stairway itself, but a vague glow shone up from the bottom. Jim turned to look at us briefly. "I order you to follow me."

● ● ●

At the bottom of the long flight of steps, we found a room with a low ceiling, a concrete floor, and a row of pews that disappeared into darkness toward the back. Up front, near the entrance to the stairway, was a small altar and above it a huge painting in an ornate gilt frame. The dim light we had seen from above was a single bulb positioned to illuminate the picture, which showed a scene of Jesus and Mary sitting next to a pool in the middle of a forest. The aquamarine of Mary's gown was resilient, and both her and Christ's eyes literally shone. The figures were smiling, and their hair along with the leaves in the background appeared to be moving in a light breeze.

"Let's go back," I said.

Mary inched away toward the stairs, and I started to follow her.

"One second," said Jim. "Look at this, the holy fishing trip."

We heard a rustle of material and something clunk against the heavy wood of one of the pews behind us. I jumped and even Jim spun around with a look of fright on his face.

"It's a lovely scene, isn't it?" said a soft, female voice. Then from out of the dark came a nun, whose face, pushing through the black mantle of her vestments, was so young and beautiful, it confused me. She was smiling and her hands were pale and delicate. She lifted one as she passed by us and climbed onto the altar. "But you mustn't miss the idea of the painting," she said, pointing.

"Do you see here?" she asked, and turned to look at us.

We nodded and followed her direction to gaze into the woods behind where Mary and Jesus were sitting.

"What do you see?"

Jim stepped closer and a few seconds later said, "Eyes and a smile."

"Someone is there in the woods," I said as the figure became evident to me.

"A dark figure, spying from the woods," said the nun. "Who is it?"

"The Devil," said Mary.

"You're a smart girl," said the nun. "Satan. Do you see how much this looks like a scene from the Garden of Eden? Well, the painter is trying to show that just as Adam and Eve were subject to temptation, to Death, so were the Savior and his mother. So are we all."

"Why is he hiding?" asked Jim.

"He's waiting and watching for the right moment to strike. He's clever."

"But the Devil isn't real," said Jim. "My father told me."

She smiled sweetly at us. "Oh, the Devil is real, child. I've seen him. If you don't pay attention, he'll take you."

"Goodbye now," whispered Mary, who took my hand and pulled me toward the steps.

"What does he look like?" asked Jim.

I wanted to flee, but I couldn't move. I thought the nun would get angry, but instead her smile intensified, and that same face went from pleasant to scary.

Mary pulled my arm, and we took off up the stairs. Not bothering to stop in the canteen, we kept going up the next set of steps to the outside and only rested when we made it to the bench by the fountain. We waited there for some time, hypnotized by the cascading water, before Jim finally showed up.

"You chickens should be hung for mutiny," he said as he approached.

"Mary was afraid," I said. "I had to get her out of there."

"Check your own shorts," he said. "Anyway, get this. That nun's name was Sister Joseph."

"You mean she was a guy?"

"I don't know," he said, shaking his head. "But she told me a secret."

"What?" I asked.

"How to spot the Devil when he walks the Earth. That's what Sister Joe said, 'When he walks the Earth,' " said Jim, and started laughing.

"She was the Devil," said Mary, staring into the water.

⌒ ⌒ ⌒

That night, back at home, the wine flowed, and my parents danced in the living room to The Ink Spots on the Victrola. Something dire was up, I could tell, because they didn't talk and there was a joyless gravity to their spins and dips.

Before we turned in, Nan came from next door and told us that while we were out she had heard from Rose across the street that the prowler had struck again. When her husband, Dan, had gone out late on Friday night to throw away the trash, he heard something moving back in their grape arbor. He called out, "Who's there?" Of course there was no answer, but he saw a shadow and a pair of eyes. Dan was an airline pilot who flew all over the world, and one of his hobbies was collecting old weapons. He ran inside and fetched a long knife from Turkey that had a wriggled blade like a flat, frozen snake. Rose had told Nan that he charged out the back door toward the arbor, but halfway there, tripped on a divot in the lawn, fell, and stabbed his own thigh. By the time he was able to hobble back beneath the hanging grapes, the prowler had vanished.

While my mother sat in her rocker, eyes closed, rocking to the music, Jim and I arm-wrestled my father a few times and then Mary danced with him, her bare feet on his shoes. "Bed," my mother finally said, her eyes still closed. At the top of the stairs before Jim and I went into our separate rooms, he said to me, "He walks the Earth." I laughed but he didn't. George followed me to bed and lay at the bottom, falling instantly asleep. He kicked his back leg three times and growled in his dreams. I stayed awake for a while, listening to my parents' hushed conversation down in the living room, but I couldn't make anything out.

I wasn't the least tired, so I got up and went over to my desk. Nan's talking about Rose and Dan gave me the idea to capture them in my notebook before I forgot. What I found interesting was that Dan could only be defined by the things that he owned: the leopard skin rug, the shrunken head, the axes and knives and ancient pistols. Otherwise, he was a pretty blank person, save for his toupee, which sat on his head like a doily. Rose, on the other hand, had been born in Ireland, in the town of Cork, and had the most beautiful way of talking. She had grown up with the actor Richard Harris, who sang the song about the cake in the rain. I could not write about her without recounting some of the ghost stories she had told Jim and me.

In one, her father was coming home from a neighboring town one evening, and just before crossing the bridge into their hometown, he was confronted by a funeral procession. He thought it an odd time for a funeral and he asked each of the long train of mourners preceding the funeral carriage who had died. The strangers, dressed in stiff, black crepe and tall hats, none of whom he recognized, refused to acknowledge him. Only the carriage driver would answer, and he told Rose's father that John Connely had passed away. Her father couldn't believe it, because he had just seen John the night before and he had been drinking and laughing. The eerie procession passed by and he continued over the bridge. Upon arriving home, he saw John coming out of his own house to go to the pub. Rose's father waved and wondered what sort of madness he had been subject to, but later that week, his poor neighbor, John, dropped over stone-cold dead from heart failure at dinner in the middle of a sentence.

I wrote it up in detail and also added the one about the giant black dog that haunted the abandoned abbey. It didn't surprise me that the visit from the prowler had frightened Rose. Nothing ever happened by chance for her. Banshees, little people, fetches, you name it and she'd seen it. She was devoted to the tea leaves, and because Nan could read the cards, Rose respected her more than anyone else on the block.

By the time I was done, it had grown quiet downstairs, and I knew my parents had finally gone to bed. Still, I wasn't tired, and on top of that I was a little spooked by remembering Rose's stories. Any meditation on Death was capable of conjuring the angry spirit of Jimmy Bonnel. To dispel his gathering presence, I got out of bed and tiptoed quietly down the stairs. In the kitchen, I stole a cookie and that's when I decided to descend and review Jim's recent progress with Botch Town.

Every old wooden step on the way to the cellar groaned miserably, but my father's snoring, rolling out from the bedroom at the back of the house, covered my own prowling. Once below, I inched blindly forward and when my hip touched the edge of the plywood world, I leaned way out and grabbed the pull string. The sun came out in the middle of the night in Botch Town. I half-expected the figures to all be moving of their own volition, but no, they must have heard me coming and froze on cue. Jim was right, there was a sense of being God, hovering above the clouds and peering down on the minute lives. It also made me think for an instant about my own smallness.

Scanning the board, I found the prowler, with his straight-pin hands, on the prowl, hiding in the toothpick grape arbor netted with vines of green thread behind the Curdmeyers' house across the street from ours, his clever, glowing eyes, like beacons, searching the dark for lost souls.

❤ ❤ ❤

School started on a day so hot it seemed stolen from the heart of summer. The tradition was that if you got new clothes for school, you wore them the first day. My mother made Mary a couple of dresses on the sewing machine. Because he had outgrown what he had, Jim got shirts and pants from Gertz department store. I got his hand-me-downs, but I did also get a new pair of dungarees. They were stiff as concrete and, after months of nothing but cutoffs, seemed to weigh fifty pounds. I sweated like the Easter pig, shuffling through school zombie style, to the library, the lunchroom, on the playground, and all day long that burlap scent of new denim smelled like the spirit of Work.

Jim was starting junior high and, going to a different school, he had to take a bus to get there. Mary and I were still stuck at the Retard Factory around the corner. None of us were good students. I spent most of my time in the classroom either completely confused or daydreaming. Mary was in a special class, basically because they couldn't figure out if she was really smart or really simple. The kids they couldn't figure out, they put in room X. Although all of the other rooms had numbers, this one just had the letter that signaled something cut-rate, like on the TV commercials: Brand X. When I'd pass by that room, I'd look in and see these wacky kids hobbling around or mumbling or crying, and there would be Mary, sitting straight up, focused, nodding every once in a while. Her teacher, Mrs. Rockhill, whom we called Rockhead, was no Mrs. Harkmar and didn't have the secret to draw the Mickey of all right answers out of her. I knew Mary was really smart, though, because Jim had told me she was a genius.

As for Jim, no one knew what the hell he was up to. He had a history of putting obviously wrong answers down on his tests and homework assignments. "What's 6 apples and 3 apples?" they'd asked him in third grade. Jim's answer: "4 tin cans." In an essay question dealing with the Navajo boy, Joe Mannygoats, we had to read about in fifth grade social studies, Jim ignored the question about Navajo family life, and created a scenario where Joe stole a gun and shot his goats. Then he cooked them and in-

BEST SHORT NOVELS: 2007

vited everyone to a barbecue. How Jim stayed out of room X was a room-X mystery no one could solve.

Once they called him into the psychologist's office and made my mother go over to the school and witness the tests they gave him. They showed him pages of paint blobs and asked him what he saw in them. "I see a spider, biting a woman's lip," he said. "That's a sick, three-legged dog, eating grass." Then they asked him to put pegs of various shapes into appropriate holes in a block of wood. He shoved all the wrong pegs in the wrong holes. Finally my mother smacked him in the back of the head, and then he and she started laughing hysterically. Throughout sixth grade, he incorporated something about Joe Mannygoats into all of his test answers, no matter the subject, and signed all yearbooks with that name. Still, he never failed a grade, and this gave me hope that I too would someday leave Southgate.

My teacher for sixth grade was the fearsome Mr. Krapp. To borrow a phrase from Nan, "as God is my judge," that was his name. He was a short guy with a big nose and a crew cut so flat you could land a helicopter on it. Jim had had him and told me he screamed a lot. My mother had diagnosed Krapp with a Napoleonic complex. "You know," she said, "he's a little general." He assured us on the first day that he "wouldn't stand for any of it." The third time he repeated the phrase, Tim Caliban, who sat behind me, leaned forward and whispered, "He'd rather get down on all fours." Krapp had big ears too, and he heard Tim, who he made get up in front of the classroom and repeat for everyone what he'd said. That day we all learned an important lesson in how not to laugh no matter how funny something is.

School brought a great heaviness to the hours of my days as if they had put on new dungarees. By that year, though, it was business as usual, so I weathered it with a grim resignation. The only thing drastic that happened in that first week was on the way home one afternoon: Will Hickey, a kid with a bulging Adam's apple and big, curly hair, challenged me to a fight. I tried to walk away, but before I knew what was going on, a bunch of kids surrounded us and Hickey started pushing me. The whirl of voices and faces, the evident danger, made me lightheaded and what little strength I had quickly evaporated. Mary was with me and she started crying. I was not popular and had no friends there to help me; instead everyone was cheering for me to get beat up.

After a lot of shoving and name calling and me trying to back out of the circle and getting thrown into the middle again, he hit me once in the side of the head and I was dazed. Putting my hands up, I assumed the position I had seen on TV and when other kids fought, and he circled around me. I tried to follow his movements, but he darted in quickly and his bony knuckle split my lip. There was little pain, just an overwhelming sense of embarrassment, because I felt tears welling in the corners of my eyes.

As Hickey came toward me again, I saw Jim pushing through the crowd. He came up behind Hickey, reached around, and grabbed him by the throat with one hand. In a second, Jim wrestled him to the ground where he proceeded to punch him again and again in the face. When Jim got up, blood was running from Hickey's nose and he was quietly whimpering. All of the other kids had taken off. Jim lifted my book bag and handed it to me.

"You're such a pussy," he said.

"How?" was all I could manage, I was shaking so badly.

"Mary ran home and told me," he said.

"Did you kill him?"

He shrugged.

Hickey lived, and his mother called our house that night complaining that Jim was dangerous, but Mary and I had already told our mother what had happened. I remember her telling Mrs. Hickey over the phone, "Well, you know, you play with fire, you're liable to get burned." When she hung up the phone, she flipped it the middle finger, and then told us she didn't want us fighting anymore. She made Jim promise he would apologize to Hickey. "Sure," he said, but later, when I asked him if he was really going to apologize, he said, "Yeah, I'm going to take him to Bermuda."

＊　＊　＊

In reality, the start of school was an afterthought, because the prowler had surfaced twice again. The Graves's teenage daughter, Marci, spotted him spotting her sitting on the toilet late one night.

The Stutton kid, Kenny, who regularly proclaimed in school that he would someday be president, found the shadow man in their darkened garage, crouching in the corner behind the car when he went out there with the empty milk bottles after dinner. As he told Jim and me later when we went to talk to him about it, "He ran by me so fast, I didn't see him, but his air was cold."

"What do you mean his air was cold?" asked Jim.

"It smelled cold."

"Unlike yours?" said Jim.

Kenny nodded.

That evening, down in the cellar, Jim made tiny, red flags out of sewing needles and construction paper, and stuck them into the turf of Botch Town at all the spots where we knew the prowler had been. When he was done, we stepped back and he said, "I saw this on *Dragnet* once. Just the facts. It's supposed to show the criminal's plan."

"Do you see any plan?" I asked.

"They're all on our block," he said, "but otherwise it's just a mess."

Apparently, we weren't the only ones concerned about the prowler, because somebody called the cops. Thursday afternoon, a police officer walked down the block, knocking on people's doors, asking if they had seen anything suspicious at night or if they had heard someone in their backyard. When he got to our house, he spoke to Nan. As usual, Nan knew everything that happened on the street and she gave him an earful. We hid in the kitchen and listened, and in the process learned a tidbit we had been unaware of. It so happened that the Farleys had found human shit at the bottom of their swimming pool, as if someone had sat on the rim and dropped it.

When the cop was getting ready to leave, Jim stepped out of hiding and told him we had a footprint we thought belonged to the prowler. He smiled at us and winked at Nan, but asked to see it. We led him back to the shed, and Jim went in and brought out the hatbox. He motioned for me to take the lid off and I did. The cop bent over and peered inside.

"Nice job, fellas," he said, and took the box with him, but later on, when I walked George around the block that night, I saw the pink cardboard, the poodle, and the Eiffel Tower jutting out of the Mardinellas' open garbage can at the curb. I went over to it and peeked under the lid. The footprint was ruined, so I decided not to tell Jim.

As George and I continued on our rounds, the autumn came. We were standing at the entrance to Southgate; there was a full moon, and suddenly a great burst of wind rushed by. The leaves of the trees at the boundary of the woods over beyond Sewer Pipe Hill rattled, some flying free of their branches in a dark swarm. Just like that, the temperature dropped, I realized the crickets had gone silent, and I smelled a trace of Halloween.

Down the block a wind chime that had been silent all summer sounded its cowbell call, and I turned and looked over at the Fuscias' house; the last one before the school. Their lighted window brought me a memory of their pet rabbit, Dibby, who had chewed through its wooden crate and then chewed a hole in the wall. It was never found and now either lived or died somewhere inside the darkness behind the walls of their house. Mrs. Farley had announced, at one of the wine-in-a-teacup afternoon gatherings of the ladies, presided over by Nan, that Amy Fuscia, who was in Mary's grade, lived in fear that the creature would crawl out of the wall some night and seek revenge on her, and she wet her bed every night since its escape.

I looked up at the stars and felt my mind start to wander, so I sat down at the curb and George sat next to me. That day in school they had herded us into the cafeteria and showed us a movie, *The Long Way Home from School.* It was about kids playing on the train tracks and getting killed by speeding trains or electrocuted on the third rail. The guy who spoke the stories looked like the father from *Leave It to Beaver.* He told one about kids thinking it was fun climbing onto train cars and running across the tops. Little did they know that the train was about to pull out, and when they showed it start to move, he said, "Oops, Johnny fell in between the cars and was crushed to death by tons of steel. It's not so much fun when you're flat as a pancake." After that came a scene of a kid shooting a slingshot at a moving train, that jumped right into another scene of a little girl on board in a passenger compartment with her hand covering her eye and blood dripping

down across her face while the landscape rolled by. "Nice shooting, Cowboy," the guy said.

After the movie, they made us line up out in the hallway on
our knees with our heads down and pressed into the angle where
the floor met the wall. "Cover the back of your head by locking
your fingers behind it. This will protect you from flying debris,"
said Mr. Tary, the principal, as he rubbed his throat. He was always rubbing his throat. We were led to believe, without anyone
coming right out and making the claim, that this maneuver on the
floor would save us if the Russians dropped an atomic bomb on
our town.

My mother had told us if the air raid siren ever really went
off, I was to get home. She and my father had devised a plan. The
minute the siren sounded someone was supposed to shovel dirt
into the window wells of the cellar and then get all the mattresses
from the house and lay them out on the first floor to block the radiation from seeping down. At one time they had stocked a bunch
of cans of food in the cellar and gallons of water with a drop of
bleach in each one to keep them fresh. But as time went on, the
supplies dwindled to a single can of Spam and a bottle of water
that had gone green. As George and I got up and headed back, I
daydreamed a *Twilight Zone* scenario of us projecting ourselves
into the world of Botch Town to escape the horrible death of
atomic bombs in the wider world.

At home, the wine bottle sat on the kitchen counter, empty,
and my mother had passed out on the couch. There was a cigarette between her fingers with an ash almost as long as a cigarette.
Jim pointed it out to me. Then he went and got an ashtray that
was half a giant clamshell we had found on the beach the previous summer, and Mary and I watched as he positioned it under
the ash. He gave my mother's wrist the slightest tap, and the ash
dropped perfectly into the shell.

I wedged a pillow under her head as Jim took her by the
shoulders and laid her down more comfortably on the couch.
Mary fetched the *Sherlock Holmes.* Jim opened it to "The Hound of
the Baskervilles," the story that obsessed her as a writer, and gently placed the volume, binding up, its wings open like those of a
giant red moth, on her chest.

We went next door to say goodnight to Nan and Pop.

"Where's your mother?" asked Nan.

"She's out cold," said Jim.

Nan's lips did that kissing fish thing, in and out, that they did whenever she was about to try to trick you into ignoring the truth. I noticed it first that past summer on the day the ladies came over and she read the cards for them. The widow, old Mrs. Ripici, who lived by herself next to the Curdmeyers on the left, across the street, drew the ace of spades. Nan's lips started going, and she quickly pulled the card from the table and claimed, "Misdeal." There was a moment where the room went stone quiet and then, like someone flipped a switch, the ladies started chattering again.

"Your mother works hard for you kids and she's very tired," Nan told us the night autumn came.

Mary was always upset when my mother didn't tuck her in at night, so to create a diversion, Pop brought out the band. He collected windup toys that played musical instruments, and he had seven of them. One was an Indian who beat a tom-tom, one, an elephant that blew a horn, a clown that played the tambourine, and more. He took out his mandolin, and Nan and Mary and Jim and I madly wound the toys to get them all ready to play at the same time, but at the same time could not let any of them start to unwind. Then Pop gave the signal and we released the keys at their backs. They banged and tooted and jangled away while he strummed and sang "When the Saints Go Marching In." Somehow that crazy music blended together and it all sounded just right.

☙ ❧ ☙

The first Saturday morning after school started, I followed Pop around the yard, holding a colander, as he harvested the yield of the trees. Before he picked each piece of fruit, he'd take it lightly in his hand as if it were a live egg with the most fragile shell imaginable.

As we moved from tree to tree, he told me things about them. "Never put a peach leaf near your mouth," he said. "They're poisonous." Or when we came to the yellow apple tree: "This tree grew from seeds that no one sells anymore. It's called Miter's Sun, and I bought the sapling from an old coot who told me there were less than a dozen of them left in the world. It's important to take care of it, because if it and the couple of others that remain die, it will be gone from the face of the Earth for all of eternity." He picked a small, misshapen yellow apple from a branch, rubbed it on his shirt, and handed it to me. "Take a bite of that," he said. From that ugly marble came a wonderful, sweet taste.

We continued on to the plum tree, and he said to me, "I heard you were in a fight this week."

I nodded.

"Do you want me to teach you how to box?" he asked.

I thought about it for a while. "No," I said, "I don't like to fight."

He laughed so loud that the crow sitting on the TV antenna atop the house was frightened into flight. I felt embarrassed for a moment, but then he reached down and put his hand on my head. "Okay," he said, and laughed more quietly.

After retiring from the Big A, Aqueduct Race Track, where he had worked in the boiler room for years, Pop took up an interest in trees, especially ones that gave fruit. On our quarter-acre of property, he planted quite a few—a peach, a plum, three apple, a cherry, an ornamental crab apple, and something called a Smoke Bush that kept the mosquitoes away—and spent the summer months tending to them; spraying them for bugs, digging around their bases, pulling up saplings, getting rid of dead branches. I'd never seen him read a book about the subject or study it in any way, he just started one day the first week after he had left his job.

I guess it was something he had done before at some point in his long life. Nan had shown us old, yellowing newspaper clippings from when he was a boxer and photographs of him standing on the deck of a ship with an underwater suit on and a metal diving helmet with a little window in it. Once when my parents thought I was asleep on the couch but I just had my eyes closed, I learned that he had spent time in a mental institution where they had given him electroshock therapy. Supposedly, when he was fifteen, his mother had sent him out around the corner for a loaf of bread. He went and joined the Merchant Marine, lying about his age, and returned home three years later, carrying the loaf of bread. When asked how his mother reacted, his answer was, "She beat the shit out of me."

He was powerfully built with a huge chest and wide shoulders. Even in old age, his biceps took three of my hands to fit around. Every once in a while, we'd ask to see his tattoos, vein-blue drawings he could make dance by flexing his muscle: a naked woman on his left forearm; an eagle on his chest; and a weird, fire-breathing dragon-dog, all curly cue fur and huge lantern eyes, on his back that he had gotten in Java from a man who used whale bone needles to render the design. He told Jim and me that the dog creature was named Chimto, and that it watched behind him for his enemies.

The trees may have been Pop's hobby, a way to fill up the hours of retirement, but his art and his love were the horses. He studied the *Daily Telegraph,* the horse paper, as if it were a sacred text. When he was done with it, the margins would be filled with the scribble of horses' names, jockeys' names, times, claiming purses, stacks of simple arithmetic, and strange symbols that looked like Chinese writing. Whatever it all stood for, it allowed him to pick a fairly high percentage of winners. There was one time when he went to the track and came home in a brand new car, and another when he won so much he took us all on vacation to Niagara Falls. Pop's best friend was his bookie, Bill Pharo, and Pop drove over to Babylon to see him almost every day.

⇌ ⇌ ⇌

Saturday afternoon, when my father returned home from work, he called us kids into the living room and made us sit before him on the love seat. My mother and he sat on the couch across the marble coffee table from us. Before they spoke, my mind raced back through the recent weeks to try to remember if we could be in trouble for something.

All I could think of besides the incident with Hickey, which seemed to have blown over by then, was a night sometime before school started when we made a dummy out of old clothes—shirt and pants—stuffed with newspapers and held together with safety pins. The head was from a big, mildewed doll, an elephant stuffed with sawdust someone had won at a fair or the circus, that had been lying around in the cellar for as long as I could remember. We decapitated it, removed some of the sawdust, tied the neck in a knot, and pinned it to the collar of the shirt. The figure was crude, but we knew it would serve our purposes, especially in the dark and when people were driving in their cars. We got it out of the cellar unseen by lifting it through one of the windows into the backyard.

We'd named our floppy elephant guy, Mr. Blah-blah, and tied a long length of fishing line around his chest under the arms of the shirt. We laid him at the curb on one side of the street and then doled out the fishing line over to the other side of the street and through the bottom of the hedges in front of the empty house that had, until recently, belonged to the Holsters. We knew it wouldn't pay to do what we were planning in front of our own house, and the one we chose had the benefit of having a southern extension of the woods right behind it in the backyard. We could move along the trails in the pitch black and anyone who tried to chase us would have to turn back.

Hiding behind the hedges, we waited until we saw the lights of a car coming down the street. Just when the car got close to where the hedges started, we reeled the bum in, pulling on the line, and in the dark he looked like he was crawling across the road in fits and starts, sort of like he'd already been hit once by a car.

The car's brakes screeched and it swerved, almost driving up on the curb and nearly hitting the telephone pole before it stopped. The instant I heard the brakes, I realized the whole thing was a big mistake. Jim and I ran like hell, bent in half to gain cover from the hedges. We stopped at the corner of the house, in the shadows.

"If they come after us, run back and jump the stream, and I'll meet you at the fork in the main path," Jim whispered.

I nodded.

From where we stood, we had a good view of the car. I was relieved to see it was not one I recognized as belonging to one of our neighbors. It was an old model, from before I was born, shiny white, with a kind of bubble roof and fins that stuck up in the back like a pair of goal posts. The door creaked open and a man dressed in a long, white trench coat got out. It was too dark and we were too far away to see his features, but he came around the side of the car and obviously discovered Mr. Blah-blah in the road. He must have seen the fishing line, because he looked up and stared directly at us. Jim pulled me back deeper into the shadows. The man didn't move for the longest time, but his face was pointing exactly at where we stood. My heart was pounding, and only Jim's hand on the back of my shirt kept me from running. Finally, the man got back in the car and drove away. When we were sure the car was gone, we got Blah-blah and threw him back in the woods.

My father cleared his throat, and I looked at Jim, who sat on the other side of Mary, and he looked at me, and I knew that his memory was stuffed with that mildewed elephant head.

"We just wanted to tell you that we don't think Aunt Laura is going to be with us much longer," said my father. His elbows were on his knees and he was looking more at our feet than at us. He rubbed his hands together as if he were washing them.

"You mean she's going to die?" said Jim.

"She's very sick and weak. In a way, it will be a blessing," said my mother. I could see the tears forming in the corners of her eyes.

We nodded, but I was unsure if that was the right thing to do. That phrase, "a blessing," stuck in my mind, and I wondered how dying could be a good thing. Then my father told us, "Okay, go and play." Mary went over to where my mother was sitting and climbed into her lap. I left before the tears really started rolling.

That afternoon, I took George and my notebook and we traveled far. When I started I felt the weight of a heavy thought in my head. I could feel it roosting, but when I tried to realize it, reach for it with my mind, it proved utterly illusive, like trying to catch a killifish in the shallows with your bare hands. On my way up to Higbee Lane, I witnessed a scene involving Mr. and Mrs. Wilson being screamed at by their ten-year-old tyrant son, Reggie; passed by Nick, the janitor from Southgate, who was fixing his car out in his driveway; saw the lumbering, moon-eyed Milton kid, Peter, big and slow as a mountain, riding a bike whose seat seemed to have disappeared up his ass.

We crossed Higbee Lane and went down the street lined on both sides with giant sycamores; leaves gone yellow and brown. To the left of me was the farm, cows grazing in the field, to the right was a ploughed expanse of bare dirt where they had begun to frame a line of new houses. Beyond that another mile, down a hill, amidst a thicket of trees, next to the highway, we came to a stream I knew about where no one ever went.

I sat with my back to an old telephone pole someone had dumped there and wrote up the neighbors I'd seen on my journey—told about how Mrs. Wilson had Reggie when she was forty-one; told about how the kids at school would try to fool Nick, who was Yugoslavian and didn't speak English very well, and his response to them: "Boys, you are talking dogshit;" told about the weird redneck Miltons, who I had overheard described by Mrs. Kelty once as "incest from the hills."

When I was finished writing, I put my pencil in the notebook and drew George close to me. I petted his head and told him, "It's gonna be okay." The thought I'd been carrying finally broke through, and I saw a figure, like a human shadow, leaning over Aunt Laura's bed in the otherwise empty room at St. Anselm's and lifting her up. He held her to him, pressed her inside of him, into the dark, and then, like a bubble of ink bursting, vanished.

⊸ ⊸ ⊸

That night, my mother, well into her bottle of wine, erupted, spewing anger and fear in loud, slurred tones. During these episodes, she was another person, and when they were done I could never remember what the particulars of her rage were, just that the experience seemed to suck the air out of the room and leave me unable to breathe. The image that came to my mind was of the evil queen gazing into her talking mirror, and I tried to rebuff it by conjuring the memory of a snowy day when I was little and she rode Jim and me to school on the sled, running as fast as she could. We laughed, she laughed, and the world was covered in white.

We kids abandoned our father, leaving him to take the brunt of the attack. Jim fled down the cellar to lose himself in Botch Town. Mary went instantly Mickey, encircled herself with a whispered string of numbers for protection, and snuck next door to Nan's house. As I headed up the stairs to the refuge of my own room, I heard the sound of a smack and then something skittered across the kitchen floor. I knew it was either my father's glasses or his teeth, but I wasn't going back to find out. While he sat there, stoically, waiting for the storm to pass, I shoved off with Perno Shell down the Amazon in search of El Dorado.

Sometime later, just after Shell had taken a curare dart in the neck and paralysis was setting in, there was a knock on my door. I said to come in and Mary entered. She curled up at the bottom of my bed and lay there staring at me.

"Hey," I said, "want me to read you some people from my notebook?"

She sat up and nodded.

So I read her all the ones I had recently added, up to the Milton kid on his bike. I recounted my findings at a slow pace in order to kill time and allow her a long stint of the relief she found in the mental tabulation of my findings. When we finished, the house was silent.

"Any winners in that bunch?" I asked.

"Nick the janitor," she said.

"Go to bed now," I told her.

When she opened the door to leave, George was sitting there, waiting to accompany her to her room.

Sunday morning, at the breakfast table, a phone call came in after we had pretty much finished eating and my father was recounting some of his stories from the army. I wondered if my mother's assault the night before had put him in mind of other conflagrations. My mother, now light and smiling, as if suffering amnesia of her Mr. Hyde nature, answered the phone. When she hung up, she told us the news—Charlie Eddisson, who was in my class at Southgate, had gone out to play on Saturday afternoon and had never returned. At dinnertime, when he didn't appear, his mother started to worry. When night fell and he still hadn't gotten home, his father called the police. My mother said, "Either something has happened to him or he's been abducted." Nan's lips moved in and out, and she said, "Maybe he'll show up for lunch."

Charlie Eddisson was even more weak and meek than me. We'd had the same teachers all the way up from kindergarten. In class photographs, he came across as the runt of the collective litter. His arms were as thin as pipe cleaners, and he was short and skinny with a pencil neck and face that looked like Tommy the Turtle from the old cartoons. His glasses were so big, it was as if he had stolen them from his old man, and every time I tried to picture him, I'd see him pushing those huge specs up on the bridge of his nose with one extended finger. Charlie's daily project was trying to achieve invisibility, because the meaner kids liked to pick on him. My feelings for him were ones of sympathy and also relief that he existed, since without him, those same kids would probably have been picking on me.

For gym, we had a teacher, Coach Cambell, who for some reason always had at least one hand in his sweat pants, and I'm not talking about the pockets. When it rained or the weather was too cold to go outside, we'd stay in the gym and play dodge ball. There were two teams, one on either side of the gym. You couldn't cross the dividing line and you had to bean someone on the other side with one of those hard, red gym balls in order to get them out. If they managed to catch the ball, then you were out and had to sit on the side.

One day, right before Christmas, Cambell got that glint in his eye and called for dodge ball. The usual game ensued, and Charlie managed to hide out and practice his powers of invisibility long enough so he was the last one left on his side of the line. On the other side of the line, the last one left was Jake Harweed. No one knew how many times he'd been left back, but it was certain he'd already been arrested once before he'd made it to fifth grade. His arm muscles were like smooth rocks and he had a tattoo he had given himself with a straight pin and India ink: the word *Shit,* scrawled across the calf of his left leg. When Cambell saw the final match-up, he blew the whistle and instituted a new rule: the two remaining players could go anywhere they wanted, the dividing line no longer mattered.

Charlie had the ball, but Jake stalked toward him, unworried. Charlie threw it with all his might, but it just kind of floated on the air, and Jake grabbed it like he was picking an apple off a tree. That should have been the end of the game, but Cambell didn't blow the whistle. Everyone in the gym started chanting Jake's name. Then Jake wound up, and as he did, Charlie backed away until he was almost to the wall. He brought his hands up to cover his face. When it came, the ball hit him with such force in the chest it knocked the air out of him and slammed him backward so that his head hit the concrete wall. His glasses flew off, cracked in half on the hardwood floor, and he slumped down unconscious. An ambulance was called, and for that Christmas, Charlie got a broken rib.

My father and Pop went out in the car to join the search for Charlie, and Jim and I hooked up George and headed for the woods to see if we could track him there. On the way, we passed a lot of parents and kids from the neighborhood either in their cars or on bikes out looking for him too.

Jim told me, "He must have just gotten lost somewhere and couldn't remember how to get home. You know Charlie."

I didn't say anything as my imagination was spinning with images of myself lost, unable to find my way home, or worse, being tied up and taken away to a place where I would never see my parents or home again. I was frightened, and the only thing that prevented me from running back to the house, besides the daylight, was that we had George with us. My thoughts concerning recent events and the new terror I felt for poor Charlie's situation eventually twined together behind my eyes, and I said, "Maybe the prowler took him."

We were, by then, at the entrance to the school, and Jim stopped walking. He turned and looked at me. "You know what?" he said. "You might be right."

"Do you think they thought of it?"

"Of course," he said, but I remembered the hatbox in the garbage can and had my doubts.

Our tour of the woods was brief. It was a beautifully clear and cool day, the trees all turning red, but the idea that the prowler was now doing more than just looking kept us on edge. We only ventured in as far as the bend in the stream where the sassafras grew, before giving up. Once out from under the trees, we peered in the sewer pipe, inspected the basketball courts, gazed briefly down into the sump, and followed the perimeter of the fence around the schoolyard back to the entrance.

"I have thirty cents," said Jim. "You want to go to the deli and get a soda?"

●　●　●

There were cops all over the neighborhood for the next week or so, interviewing people about the disappearance of Charlie Eddisson and trying to piece together what might have happened to him. The story was on the nightly news, and they showed a shot of Southgate in the report. It looked different in black and white, almost like some other school a kid would want to go to. Then they flashed a photo of Charlie, smiling, from behind his big glasses, and I had to look away, aware of what he'd been through since I'd known him.

There had been honest grief over his absence and the anguish it caused his family, but at the end of the second week, the town started to slip into its old ways as if some strong current was pulling us back to normalcy. It distressed me, though I couldn't so easily put my finger on the feeling then, how readily we were to leave Charlie behind and continue with the business of living. I can't say I was any different. My mind turned to worrying about Krapp's math homework and the tribulations of my own family. I suppose the investigation into Charlie's disappearance continued, but it no longer involved the neighborhood at large.

Even though the hubbub surrounding the tragedy was quickly receding, I'd still get a chill when, at school, I'd look over to Charlie's place and see an empty chair, or when out on my bike, I'd pass by his mother, who had certainly lost her mind when losing her son. Every day she'd wander the neighborhood, traipsing through people's backyards, inspecting the dumpsters behind the stores downtown, staggering along the railroad tracks. She had been one of the youngest mothers on the block, but the loss had drained her overnight and she became haggard; her blonde hair frizzed and her expression blank.

In the evenings, she'd walk around to the schoolyard and stand by the playground, calling Charlie's name. One night, as darkness came and we were sitting, eating dinner, my mother, quite a few glasses of sherry on her way to Bermuda, looked up and saw, through the front window, Mrs. Eddisson heading home from Southgate. She stopped talking and got up, walked through the living room and out the door. Jim and Mary and I went to the window to watch. She met Mrs. Eddisson in the street and said something to her. She then stepped closer and put her arms around the smaller woman and held her. They stood like that for a very long time, swaying slightly, until true night came, and every now and then my mother would lightly pat her back.

Since it involved him going out in the early morning before the sun came up, Jim was made to quit his paper route, and certain precautions were taken as far as now locking the front and back door at night. We weren't allowed to go anywhere off the block without another kid with us, and if I went to the woods, I'd have to get Jim to go with me. Still, I walked George by myself at night, and now had another specter lurking behind the bushes, along with Jimmy Bonnel, to contend with.

On the first really cold night, near the end of September, the wind blowing dead leaves down the block, I went out with George and started around the bend toward the school. As we passed Mrs. Grimm's darkened house, I heard a whisper: "Is that you?" The sudden sound of a voice made me jump and George gave a low growl. I looked over at the yard, and there, standing amidst the barren rosebushes, was Mrs. Eddisson dressed in white.

"Charlie, is that you?" she said, and put her hand out toward me.

The sudden sight of her there scared the hell out of me, and I turned, unable to answer, and ran as fast as I could back to the house. When I got home, my mother was asleep on the couch, so just to be near someone else I went down in the cellar to find Jim. He was there, sitting beneath the sun of Botch Town, fixing the roof on Mrs. Ripici's house. On the other side of the stairs,

Mickey and Sandy Graham and Sally O'Mally were working hard in Mrs. Harkmar's class.

"What do you want?" asked Jim.

My heart was still beating fast, and I realized it wasn't so much the sight of Mrs. Eddisson that had scared me, since we were used to her now popping up anywhere at just about any time, but it was the fact that she thought I was Charlie. I didn't want to tell Jim what was wrong, as if to speak it would make the connection between me and the missing boy a real one.

"I guess the prowler is gone now," I said to him. There had been no reported sightings of him since Charlie's disappearance. I scanned the board to find the shadow man's figure, those painted eyes and straight-pin hands, and found him standing behind the Miltons' shack of a place up near Higbee Lane.

"He's still around, I bet," said Jim. "He's laying low because of all the police on the block in the last couple weeks."

My eyes kept moving over the board as he spoke. Botch Town always drew me in. There was no glancing quickly at it. I followed Pine Avenue down from Higbee and around the corner. When I got to Mrs. Grimm's house on the right side of the street, I was brought up short. Standing in her front yard was the clay figure of Mrs. Eddisson.

"Hey," I said, and leaned out over the board to point, "did you put her there?"

"Why don't you go do something," he said.

"Just tell me, did you put that there?"

I knew he could tell from the tone of my voice that I wasn't kidding.

"No," he said. "Why?"

" 'Cause I was just out with George, and that's exactly where I saw her a few minutes ago."

"Maybe she walked over there after I turned the lights out last night," said Jim.

"Come on," I said, "did you move her?"

"I swear I didn't touch her," he said. "I haven't moved any of them in a week."

We looked at each other, and out of the silence that followed, we heard, from the other side of the cellar, the voice of Mrs.

Harkmar say, "Mickey, you have scored a 100 on your English test."

A few seconds passed and then I called out, "Hey, Mary, come here."

The voice of Sally O'Mally said, "I'll have to do better next time."

Jim got up and took a step toward the stairs. "Mickey, we need you over here," he said.

A moment later, Mary came around the stairs and over to where we were standing.

"I'm not going to be mad at you if you did, but did you touch any of the stuff in Botch Town?" he asked, smiling.

"Could you possibly . . . ?" she said in her Mickey voice.

"Did you move Mrs. Eddisson, here?" I asked, and pointed to where the figure stood.

She stepped up to the board and looked down at the town.

"What do you think?" asked Jim, resting his hand lightly on her shoulder.

She stared intently and then nodded.

◖ ◖ ◖

The next day on the playground at school, I overheard Peter Milton telling Chris Hacket that there had been someone at his mother's window the night before.

"Who was it?" asked Chris. "Batman?"

Peter thought for some time and then laughed so his whole giant body jiggled. "No, course not," he said. "She thought she was lookin' at a full moon, but then it was a face."

"What a dip," said Chris.

Peter thought just as long again, and then said, "Hey," reaching out one of his man-sized hands for Chris's throat. Hacket took off, though, running across the field, yelling, "Your mom's got a fart for a brain." Milton ran four steps and then either forgot why he was running or became winded.

The minute I heard what Peter had said, I thought back to the board the previous night and remembered the shadow man's pins scratching the back wall of the Miltons' house. When I got home that afternoon, I told Jim and we went to find Mary. At first, she was nowhere to be found, but then we saw little clouds of smoke rising from the forsythias in the corner of the backyard. We went back there and crawled in to sit on either side of her.

"How do you know where to put the people in Botch Town?" asked Jim.

Mary flicked the ash off her cigarette exactly the way my mother did and said, "Ciphering the McGinn System."

"You're handicapping them?" I asked.

"From your Morning Line," she said.

"What do you mean?" I asked.

"You read them to me," she said.

"My notebook?"

She nodded.

"A town full of horses," said Jim.

"It's not a race," I said.

"Yes it is, in the numbers," she said, staring ahead.

"Do you figure it in your head or on paper?" I asked.

"Sometimes," she said.

Mary stamped out her cigarette. We sat there quiet for a time, the wind blowing the branches of the bushes around us. Above, the dying leaves of the oak tree scraped together. I tried to understand what she was doing with the information I was giving her, but couldn't stretch my imagination around it.

"Where's Charlie Eddisson?" asked Jim.

"Gone," said Mary.

"But where does he belong on the board?"

"I don't know. You never read him to me," she said.

"I never read you his mother either," I said.

"I saw her," said Mary. "Saw her on the street and saw her with Mommy."

For the next fifteen minutes we told her everything we knew about Charlie Eddisson; all of his trials and tribulations in school, what color bike he rode, what team insignia was on his baseball hat (the Cleveland Indians), and so on. She nodded as we fed her the information. When we were done, she said, "Goodbye, now," and got up and left the forsythias.

Jim started laughing. "It's all luck," he said. "There's only so much space in Botch Town and if you place the figures down, they have to go somewhere. There's a good chance you'll get it right sometimes."

"I don't know," I said.

"You think she's Doctor Strange," he said, and laughed so hard at me, I was convinced I'd been a fool. For my trouble, he gave me a Fonseca Pulverizer in the side muscle of my right arm that deadened it for a good five minutes. As he left me behind in the bushes, he called back, "You'll believe anything."

In silent revenge, I thought back a few winters to the night when my parents told Jim and me that there was no Santa Claus. Just that afternoon, Jim had me next to him out in the backyard. The cellar had been off-limits since a week after Thanksgiving. We were lying on our stomachs in the snow, peering through the cellar window. "I see a bike," said Jim. "Christ, I think I see Robot Commando." But when my mother dropped the bomb that there was no Santa Claus after dinner, I was the one who simply nodded. Jim went to pieces. He sat down in the rocking chair by the front window, the snow falling in huge flakes outside in the dark, and he rocked and sobbed with his hands covering his face for the longest time.

I left the bushes and went inside to dig around in the couch cushions for change. I found a nickel and decided to ride to the store and get a couple pieces of Bazooka. There was still an hour left before my mother got home from work and made dinner. The sun was already setting when I left the house. Night was coming sooner and sooner with each day, and I rode along wondering what I should be for Halloween. I took the back way to the store, down Jean Road, and wasn't paying much attention to what was going on around me, when I suddenly woke up to the scent of a vaguely familiar aroma.

A few feet in front of me, parked next to the curb of the sidewalk I rode along, was a white car. I knew I had seen it before, but couldn't remember where right away. Only when I was next to it, and looked in the open passenger-side window to see a man sitting in the driver's seat, did I remember. The fins, the bubble top, the old curved windshield—it was the car that had stopped the night we dragged Mr. Blah-blah across the street. As I passed by, the man inside, wearing a white trench coat and smoking a pipe, turned and stared at me. His hair was close cut, salt-and-pepper, his face, thin with a thin, sharp nose, and his eyes were squinted as if he was studying me.

I panicked and took off. Behind me, I heard the car start up, and that pushed me to peddle even faster. I made it around the turn that led to the stores, but didn't stop. Instead of heading left to the deli, I made a right on Higbee and rode all the way down to Pine and back home. When I almost got to the house, I was winded. Finally I stopped and turned around to see if he was still behind me. The street was empty all the way to the end, and night was only a few minutes away.

I didn't want to tell Jim about what had happened, because I knew he would laugh at me, but I couldn't shake the memory of the way that guy had stared. It took a lot of effort to put him out of my mind. We had dinner and did our homework and went next door to listen to Pop play the mandolin, and only after a few hours was I able to forget him. When I went to bed, though, and opened the novel about Perno Shell in the Amazon, that face came floating back. Pipe smoke! The same exact scent that had made me look up during the bike ride, now emanated from the pages of my book.

● ● ●

The next day, Pop had to drive over to the school and pick Mary up. She was running a high fever and feeling sick to her stomach. Something was definitely making the rounds at Southgate. When my class was in the library that afternoon, Johnny March, the boy who smelled like ass, puked without warning all over the giant dictionary old Mr. Rogers, the librarian, kept on a pedestal by the window. Johnny was escorted to the nurse's office, and Nick the janitor was called in, pushing his barrel of red stuff and carrying a broom. I don't know what that red stuff was, but in my imagination it was composed of grated pencil erasers and its special properties absorbed the sins of children. He used about two snow-shovels full in the library that day. As Nick disposed of the ruined dictionary, much to Mr. Rogers's obvious sadness, he diagnosed the problem. "It must have been the black olives," he said.

Back in Krapp's classroom, though, after library, Patricia Trepedino puked, and then after watching her, Felicia Barnes puked. Nick and his barrel of red stuff were in hot demand, because reports of more puking came in from all over the school, and his call of the black olives was obviously found to be an instance of his "talking dogshit." Krapp was visibly shaken, his nostrils flaring, his eyes darting. After everything was cleaned up, a lingering vomit funk pervading the room, he opened all the windows and put on a filmstrip for us about the uses of fossil fuels, featuring a talking charcoal briquette. He sat in the last row in the dark, dabbing his forehead with a handkerchief.

When I got home, Doctor Geller was there. He had pulled the rocker over by the living room couch where Mary was sleeping wrapped in a blanket with a bed pillow under her head. A big steel pot we knew as "the puke bucket" was on the floor next to her. He opened his eyes and waved to me when I came through the door. He was smoking a cigar, which he took out of his mouth momentarily to put his finger to his lips and caution me to be quiet.

Doctor Geller was everybody's doctor in town. He was a heavyset man, with a thick wave of black hair, a wide face, and glasses. I never saw him without his black suit on and his black bag sitting next to him or in his hand. He gave us kids all of our shots, choked us on flat sticks, rubber hammered our knees, listened to our hearts, and came when we were really sick and couldn't make it to his office. When my mother first brought Mary, small and weak, home from the hospital, he came every day for a month to help her get used to administering a special medicine and to assure her our sister would live. It was not unusual to find him, morning or night, dozing for a few minutes in the living room rocking chair, his pocket watch in his hand. He was constantly tired, dark circles under his eyes, and always due at another sick neighbor's house.

Once, during a snowstorm, when it was impossible to drive, and my mother thought Jim was having an appendicitis attack because of the pains in his stomach, Geller came the half-mile from his office on foot, trudging through the snow. When the doctor discovered Jim only had a bad case of gas, he shook his head and laughed. Then he went next door to see Pop, with whom he shared an interest in the horses, had a glass of Old Grand-Dad and a cigar, and was off. I watched him through the front window when he left, the dark coming on and the snow still driving down.

He didn't stay long the day Mary was sick, but told Nan, who was in and out from her apartment, leaving the door open to listen, that he had another dozen kids to see, who all had the same thing. When he left, I sat at the end of the couch and watched cartoons on TV with the sound off. Just when I was about to get up and go outside, Mary opened her eyes. She was shivering slightly. Her mouth started to move and she mumbled something to me. I got up and went to the hall closet where the towels were kept. Taking a washrag, I wet it with cold water and placed it on her forehead. She grabbed my hand as I pulled it back and her eyes opened wide.

"The boy," she said. "He's to show. I found him." She pointed one finger down at the floor.

"Okay," I said. "Okay."

She soon returned to a deep sleep and seemed to be more comfortable. I told Nan, who had come to the door every few minutes to check on Mary, that I was going outside. She came in then, her cleaning done, and took my place at the end of the couch. I went out into the yard and looked for something to do. Jim, I knew, would not be home soon, as he had joined the wrestling team and now took the late bus. In the middle of smacking the cherry tree trunk with an old, yellow whiffle-ball bat, it suddenly came to me what Mary was signaling.

I ran back inside and went down into the cellar. Leaning out over Botch Town, I pulled the string for the bulb. I started at Higbee Lane and scanned down the block, looking for the clay figure of Charlie Eddisson. Mrs. Ryan was standing, round as a marble, in her front yard. Nick was turned, facing his house. Mr. Kelty was out of place, standing next to Mrs. Graves in the Graveses' backyard. Mr. Stutton had fallen over in his driveway. I did find Mrs. Eddisson on her way down Pine Street toward the school, but didn't see Charlie anywhere. Most of the characters usually just milled around by their houses, but Charlie was no longer there. I thought maybe Mary or Jim had taken him from the board because he was missing.

I was about to turn the light out and give up my search when I finally saw him. All the way on the other side of the board, beyond the school field and the trees that represented the woods, his figure lay on its side, directly in the center of the glittering blue waters of the lake.

Back upstairs, I put the leash on George and we were out the door in a second. Down the block and around the corner we went, moving quickly toward the school. It was getting late in the afternoon and the temperature had dropped. The woods were somewhat forbidding to me after Charlie had gone missing, and I wasn't supposed to go in them alone, but I only hesitated for a moment before plunging in beneath the trees.

We took the main trail, and ten minutes of fast walking later, stood at the edge of the lake. I'm not sure it was really a lake or just a very large pond, but I know that it was supposed to be very deep in places. All of the kids' parents told them it was bottomless, whatever that meant, but the older I got the more I suspected 'it was a story concocted to keep us from swimming in it or trying to set sail on a raft. My father added to the story for us. He had said that the corpse of someone who had drowned in it once was found months later, floating over in the bay. In circumference the lake could easily have fit the entire structure of the school within its boundaries.

Its surface was littered with fallen leaves, and in those places where just the water showed through, the reflection of the surrounding trees was scattered by the wind moving over its surface. It was so peaceful. I didn't know what I expected to find, maybe a body floating out in the middle, but it merely looked as it always did in autumn. I stood there for quite a while, listening to acorns and twigs falling in the woods around me, until I started thinking about Charlie. An image of him resting lightly on his back at the bottom, his eyes wide, mouth open as if he were crying out, his hands reaching up for the last rays of sunlight that came in over the treetops, cutting the water and revealing the way through his murky nightmare back to the world, spooked me. The gathering dusk chased George and me down the path and back out of the woods.

That night I woke from sleep, shivering. The wind was blowing and the antenna on the roof above my room vibrated with a high-pitched wail, like the very house was moaning. I made it to the bathroom, got sick, and staggered back to bed where I fell into feverish dreams—a tumbling whirl of images punctuated with scenes of the sewer pipe, the lake, the descending brick stairway at St. Anselm's. Jimmy Bonnel paid me a visit. Charlie, his mother, the man in the white car, a pale face at the window, and Perno Shell himself chased me, befriended me, betrayed me, until it all suddenly stopped. I heard the birds singing and opened my eyes to see a hint of red through the window. There was a wet cloth on my forehead, and then I noticed the shadowy form of my father, sitting at the end of my bed, hunched forward, eyes closed, one hand lying atop the covers over my ankle. He must have felt me stir. "It's okay," he whispered, "I'm here. Go back to sleep."

Although the fever had broken, and I was feeling much better by nine o'clock in the morning, the virus bought me a day off from school. Mary didn't go either, and my mother stayed home from work to take care of us. It was like the old days, before the drinking and the money trouble. Nan came in and we all sat for an hour after breakfast at the dining room table, playing cards: Old Maid and Casino. I had a great adventure with my plastic soldiers, which I hadn't bothered with for months, on the windowsill in the living room while the brilliant, cold day shone in around me. We watched a mystery movie on TV with Peter Lorre as the sauerkraut-eating detective, Mr. Motto, and my mother made white spaghetti with butter.

At around three o'clock, I lay back down on the couch and closed my eyes. Mary sat on the floor in the kitchen, putting together a puzzle, my mother sat in the rocker beside me and dozed. All was still save the murmur of the wind from outside making it sound as if the house was breathing.

I thought back to when I was in fourth grade and had stayed

out of school off and on for forty-five days. My mother wasn't working then, and if I didn't feel like going to school, she let me stay home. I had genuinely discovered reading that year, and I lay in bed much of the time, devouring one book after another: *Jason and the Argonauts, Treasure Island, The Martian Chronicles, Charlotte's Web,* to name just a few of my favorites. It didn't matter what type of story it was, the characters were more alive to me than all the students and teachers at Southgate.

At lunchtime I would come out into the living room and she would make the spaghetti, and we would watch an old movie. I was the only fourth grader who could identify Paul Muni or Leslie Howard on sight. I loved the mystery movies, their plots and the sense of suspense. My favorites were the ones with the Thin Man, and my mother, of course, was partial to Basil Rathbone as Holmes. Mr. Tary threatened to keep me from passing fourth grade, but she went over to the school and told him I was passing, and I did.

In remembering that year, I realized how different she was from other parents. That difference was like a light that always shone in the back of my mind no matter how dim things got when she'd drink the dark wine and become a vampire. She scared me and I hated what she became, but that light was like the promise of an eventual return to paradise. These memories protected me when suddenly I fell a thousand stories down into sleep. I didn't struggle or abruptly awaken in the descent, but let myself go, my breathing copying the breathing of the house.

I only woke from that peaceful nap of no dreams because Jim pried open my left eye with his thumb. "This one's dead, Doctor," he said. I came to and noticed twilight at the window, heard the sound of the wine bottle pinging the rim of a glass in the kitchen. The first thought I had was of Charlie at the bottom of the lake. Who could I tell that would believe what I thought I knew?

After dinner, my mother put the Kingston Trio on the Victrola and sat at the dining room table drinking and reading the newspaper. Mary was in roller skates, going round and round, following the outer curve of the braided rug in the living room. Inside her orbit, Jim showed me some of his wrestling moves.

"Could you possibly . . ." I heard my mother say, and then she called us over to her.

Jim and I each went to one side of her chair. She pointed at a small photograph on the page. "Look who that is," she said.

I didn't recognize him at first because he wasn't wearing his paper hat, but Jim finally said, "Hey, it's Softee."

Then that long, haggard face came into focus, and I could just about hear him say, *What'll it be, sweetheart?*

My mother told us that the news story was about him recently being arrested because he was wanted for child molestation in another state. For a while, they suspected him in the disappearance of Charlie Eddisson, but he was cleared of that suspicion.

"What's child molestation?" I asked.

"It means he's a creep," said my mother, and turned the page.

"He gave some kid a Special Softee," said Jim.

My mother lifted the paper and swung it at him, but he was too fast.

"What's the world coming to?" she said, and took a sip of wine.

That night, I couldn't get to sleep, partly because I had slept during the day and partly because my thoughts were full of all the dark things that had burrowed into my world. I pictured a specimen of Miter's Sun fresh from the branch but riddled with wormholes. The antenna moaned in the wind, and it didn't matter how close Perno Shell was to the golden streets of El Dorado, the aroma of pipe smoke made it impossible to concentrate on the book.

I got up and went to my desk, opened the drawer, and took out the stack of Softee cards. The living vanilla cone head now struck me as sinister; leering with that frozen smile. I took them over to the garbage pail and dropped them in. Back in bed, though, all I could think of was the one card that I had never owned. Unable to throw it out, bury it, burn it with the rest of the deck, those eyes gained an illusive power, and they watched me from inside my own head. They were Charlie's drowned eyes, the eyes of the prowler, the eyes of the man in the white car, my mother's eyes when the anger was upon her. I hunkered down under the covers and waited to hear my father come in from work.

Instead, I heard a scream, Mary downstairs, and the sound of George barking. I jumped out of bed and took the steps. Jim was up in a flash, right behind me. When I got to her darkened room, she was sitting upright in bed with a terrified look on her face.

"What?" said Jim.

"Someone is outside," she said. "There was a face at the window."

George snorted and growled.

I felt someone right behind me and turned quickly. It was Nan, standing there in her quilted bathrobe and hairnet, holding a blackjack in her hand. The weapon—a slim sack of stitched leather, like a long, black teardrop, with lead sewn into it—had belonged to her first husband, who had been a motorcycle cop in New York City. She'd told me once that you could break bones with it and leave no bruises.

Jim took George by the collar and led him to the kitchen. "Get 'em, George," he said, and opened the back door. The dog ran out, growling. Mary, Nan, Jim, and I waited to hear if he caught anyone. After some time passed, Nan told us to stay put and went out, holding the blackjack at the ready. A few seconds later, she came back with George following her.

"Whoever it was is gone," she said. She sent Jim and me back to bed and told us she'd sit with Mary until our father got home. My mother had never even opened an eye, and as I passed by her bedroom, next to Mary's, I saw her lying there, mouth open, the weight of *Holmes* holding her down.

☞ ☞ ☞

By the time I was in the kitchen the next morning, fixing a bowl of cereal, Jim had already been out in the backyard, studying the scene of the crime.

"The ladder was up against the house," he said.

"Any footprints?" I asked.

He shook his head.

"Your father is calling the police about it from work today," said my mother from the dining room.

Jim leaned in close to me and whispered, "We gotta catch this guy."

I nodded.

I went to school, my head full of worry, only to learn a piece of information that almost made me laugh with joy. At recess, Tim Caliban told me that he had heard from his father that on the coming Saturday the police were going to dredge the lake for Charlie Eddisson. I couldn't believe how lucky I was. It was as if someone had read my mind, and not only that, they were doing something about it. I suppose it only made sense, given the circumstances of Charlie's disappearance, but for me it was an enormous relief.

That afternoon, Krapp announced that the police were going to be "searching" the lake for Charlie on Saturday, and they had asked him to make an announcement that no kids were allowed near the school field or in the woods. Part of our homework assignment was to tell our parents.

"We'll go into the woods behind the Hossetters' house," Jim said later that day after I'd told him. We were in his room, and he was supposed to be doing his homework. "The cops will have guys at the school field and maybe over on Minerva, but they probably won't be that far into the woods. We'll take the binoculars."

I nodded.

"Can you imagine if they pull him out of the lake?" he said, staring at the floor as if he were seeing it before his eyes. "We'll have to get up and go early."

I wasn't so sure I wanted to see them dredge Charlie up, but I knew I had to go. "If they find him, does that mean he fell in or someone threw him in there?" I asked.

"What do I look like, Sherlock Holmes?" he said.

After that he gave me instructions to rig the ladder the next day after school. "Get two old soda cans and fill them with pebbles," he said. "Tie one to one end of the ladder with fishing line and one to the other end the same way. If he comes at night and tries to take it, we'll hear him, and let George out."

The week dragged in anticipation of the Saturday dredging. Mary sat with me the following afternoon as I worked at setting up the ladder. It lay along the fence on the right-hand side of the yard, near the clothesline. She had counted the number of pebbles I put into the first can and would not let me tie the second one on until I had evened up the number in that one.

"Two more," she said when I tried to add just one extra pebble and leave it at that. I looked over at her, and she lifted her hand. First the index finger came up and then, slowly, the thumb. I laughed and put the other two in.

"So, Charlie's in the lake," I said as I tied the second can in place. I had not yet spoken to her about her Botch Town revelation.

"He'll be in the lake," she said.

"Are you sure?" I asked.

"He'll be in the lake."

I went out on my bike looking for someone to write about and passed Mr. Barzita's yard. He was such a quiet old man, I'd almost forgotten he lived on our block. There he was, though, raking leaves in his front yard. He lived alone since his wife had died back when I was only seven. His property was surrounded by a chain-link fence, and instead of going for the usual open lawn, he had long ago planted rows of fig trees, so that the front of his house was obscured by a small orchard. Even though he lived in solitude, rarely coming out of the front gate, he always smiled and waved to us kids when we rode by on our bikes, and he would come to the fence to talk to grown-ups.

Mr. Barzita was one of those old people who seemed to be shrinking, and would eventually disappear instead of die of old age. During the winter, I never saw him, but in spring, he would emerge from his house shorter, more wizened than the year before. On the hottest days of the summer, he would sit in his chaise longue among the fig trees, sipping wine, holding a loaded pellet pistol in his lap. When the squirrels would invade his yard to get at the figs, he'd shoot them. In passing his house, if you yelled to him, "How many?" he'd hold whatever his kill was up by the tails.

One Sunday when just my father and I were in the car, and we passed the old man's house, I asked what he thought of Barzita killing the squirrels. My father shrugged. He told me, "That old man, he was in the medical corps in the army during the Second

World War. At the place where he was stationed, a very remote mountain base in Europe, there was an outbreak of meningitis—a brain disease, very catching, very deadly. They asked for volunteers to take care of the sick. He volunteered. They put him and another guy in a locked room with fifteen infected soldiers. When it was over, he was the only one who came out alive."

I tried to imagine what it must have been like in that room, the air stale with the last exhalations of the dying, but didn't get very far.

"A lot of these old farts you see scrabbling around town . . ." he said. "You'd be surprised."

⬤ ⬤ ⬤

Jim looked both ways up and down Pine to check for cars or anyone who might be watching, and then he and I ducked into the Hossetters' driveway and behind the hedges. We ran around the side of the house, through the backyard, and down a slope that led to a branch of the stream. Jumping the stream, we moved in under the trees. It was a little before eight o'clock on Saturday morning. The sky was overcast and there was a cold breeze that occasionally gusted, lifting the dead leaves off the floor of the woods and loosing more from the branches above.

We moved along the winding path to where it led back behind Southgate. Jim suggested we not take the most direct route that passed closest to the schoolyard, but that we arc out on the less used trail that went through the moss patches and the low scrub. He had Pop's old binoculars around his neck, and he made me carry the Brownie camera. When we came to the split in the path, one direction leading away south toward the railroad tracks and one directly to the lake, he told me to move quietly and that if we got chased we should split up. He'd head for the tracks, and I was supposed to go back the way we came. I nodded and from that point on we only whispered.

After jumping the snaking stream twice more, from mossy hillock to root bole, from sand bank to solid dirt, we came in view of the lake. Jim motioned for me to get down and I did.

"The cops are there already," he said. "We'll have to crawl."

We made our way to within thirty yards of the southern bank of the lake, and moved in behind a fallen oak with some tall stickers forming a kind of blind between us and the view the police had. My heart was pounding, and my hands were shaking. Jim peeked up over the trunk and put the binoculars to his eyes.

"It looks like they just got started," he said. "There's five guys. Two on the bank and three in a flat-bottom boat with a little electric motor."

I looked and saw what he had described. Coming off the back of the boat were two ropes attached to winches with hand cranks. The boat was moving along slowly, trolling the western side of the lake. Then I noticed that on the opposite bank there stood some of the neighbors. Mr. Eddisson was there, a big man with a bald head and a mustache. He wore his gas station uniform and stood, head down, arms folded across his chest. It was the first I'd seen of him since Charlie had gone missing. Beside him was his next-door neighbor, Mr. Gelimina. There were a few other people I didn't recognize, but when one of them moved to the side, I caught sight of Krapp. There he stood, dressed in his usual short-sleeve white shirt and tie, his hairdo flatter than his personality.

"Krapp's here," I whispered.

Jim turned the binoculars to focus on the crowd I had been looking at. "Jeez, you're right," he said.

"Wonder what he's doing here?" I said.

"I think he's crying," said Jim. "Yeah, he's drying his eyes. Man, I always knew he was a big pussy."

"Yeah," I said, but the thought of Krapp both showing up and crying struck me.

Jim swung the binoculars back to see what the cops were doing. He reported to me that at the ends of those ropes they had these big steel hooks with four claws each. Every once in a while, they'd stop moving and reel them in by turning the hand cranks. He gave me an inventory of what they brought up—pieces of trees, the rusted handlebars of a bike, the partial skeleton of either a dog or fox . . . and it went on and on. They slowly covered the entire lake and then started again.

"He's not down there," said Jim. "So much for Mary's predictions."

I peered back over the fallen trunk and watched for a while, braver now that I probably wasn't going to see Charlie. We sat there in the cold for two straight hours and I was starting to shiver. "Let's go home," I whispered.

"Okay," said Jim. "They're almost done." Still he sat watching, and our hiding and spying reminded me of the prowler.

From out on the lake, one of the cops yelled, "Hold up, there's something here." I stuck my head up to watch. The cop started turning the crank, reeling in the rope. "Looks like clothing," he called to the other cops on the bank. "Wait a second . . ." he said. He reeled more quickly then.

Something broke the surface of the water near the back of the boat. It looked like a soggy body at first, but it was hard to tell. There were definitely pants and a shirt. Then the head came into view, big and gray, with a trunk.

"Shit," said Jim.

"Mr. Blah-blah," I whispered.

"Hand me the camera," said Jim. "I gotta get a picture of this."

He snapped it, handed me back the camera, and then motioned for me to follow him. We got down on all fours and crawled slowly away from the fallen tree. Once our escape was covered by enough trees and bushes, we got to our feet and ran like hell.

We stood behind the Hossetters' place, still in the cover of the woods, and worked to catch our breath.

"Blah-blah," said Jim, and laughed.

"Did you put him in there?" I asked.

"Blah," he said, and shook his head. "Nah, Softee molested him and threw him in there."

"Get out," I said.

"Probably Stutton and his horrible dumpling sisters found him and took him to the lake. They're always back here in the woods," he said. "We should have had Mary predict where Mr. Blah-blah would be."

"But then where's Charlie?" I asked.

He brushed past me and jumped the stream.

I followed him across the stream and stayed close as we moved through the backyard and around the house to the street.

When we arrived home, I was relieved to find that my mother wasn't sitting at the dining room table. We had a chance to stash the camera and binoculars. The door to Nan's was open. I could hear Pop in their figuring his system out loud and, without looking, knew Mary was beside him. Jim took our spying implements upstairs, and I walked down the hallway toward my parents' room to see if my mother was up yet. She wasn't in her bed, but when I passed by the bathroom door, I heard her in there retching.

I knocked once. "Are you okay?" I called.

"I'll be right out," she said.

● ● ●

It had been obvious since the start of the school year that Mr. Rogers, the librarian, had been losing his mind. During his lunch break, when we were usually laboring over math in Krapp's class, the old man would be out on the baseball diamond, walking the bases in his rumpled suit, hunched over, talking to himself, as if he were reliving some game from the distant past. That loose dirt that collected around the bases, the soft brown powder that Stinky Steinmacher ate with a spoon, would lift up in a strong wind, circling around Rogers, and he'd clap as if the natural commotion was really the roar of the crowd. Krapp would look over his shoulder from where he stood at the blackboard and see us all staring out the window, shake his head, and then go and lower the blinds.

The loss of his giant dictionary seemed to be the last straw for Rogers, as if it was an anchor that kept him from floating away. With that gone, as my father would say, "He dipped out." Each week we would be delivered to the library by Krapp and spend a half-hour there with Rogers. Of late, the old man had been smiling a lot like a dog on a hot day, and his eyes were always busy, shifting back and forth. Sometimes he'd stand for minutes on end, staring into a beam of light shining in through the window, and sometimes he'd be frantic, moving here and there, pulling books off the shelves and shoving them into kids' hands.

Jake Harweed was brutal to him, making hand motions behind the librarian's back, coaxing everyone to laugh (and you had to laugh if Jake wanted you to). Jake would knock books off the shelf onto the floor and just leave them there. For Rogers to see a book on the floor was a heart-rending experience, and one day Harweed had him nearly in tears. I secretly liked Rogers, because he loved books and had a sense that there was something alive in them between the covers, but I couldn't let on that I wished the others would just leave him alone. Still, he was beginning to put even me off with his weirdness.

On the Monday morning following the dredging, we had library. Rogers sat in his little office nearly the entire time we were there, bent over his desk with his face in his hands. Harweed started the rumor that he kept *Playboy* magazines in there. When the time was almost up, he came out to stamp the books kids had chosen. Before he sat down at the table with his stamp, he walked up behind where I was standing, put one hand on my shoulder, and then reached up over my head to the top shelf where he pulled a thin volume from the row.

"You'll need this," he said, and handed it to me. He walked away to the table then, the kids lined up with their selections, and he began stamping them.

I looked down at the book he had handed me. On the cover, behind the library plastic, was a drawing of a mean-looking black dog. Above the creature in two rows of words, yellow letters made of lines like saber blades, was the title: *The Hound of the Baskervilles*. I wanted to ask him what he meant, but I never got the chance. News spread quickly through the school the next day that he had been fired because he was so old he went nuts. Having the *Baskervilles* in my possession was, at first, an unsettling experience. It felt like I had taken some personal belonging of my mother's, just as if I had appropriated my father's watch or Nan's hairnet. The book itself had an aura of power around it that prevented me from simply opening the cover and beginning. I hid it in my room, between the mattress and box spring of the bed. For the next few days, I'd take it out every now and then and hold it, look at the cover, gingerly flip the pages. Although by this time my mother only used the big, red volume of *The Complete Sherlock*

Holmes as an anvil in her sleep, there was a time when she had avidly read it over and over. She read a wide range of other books as well, everything from Tchaikovsky's *Letters To His Family* to *The Naked Ape,* but always returned to detective stories. She loved them in every form, and before we went broke, spent Sunday mornings consuming five cups of coffee and a dozen cigarettes, solving the mystery of the *New York Times* crossword puzzle.

Painting, playing the guitar, making bizarre collages were mere hobbies compared to my mother's desire to be a mystery writer. Before work became a necessity for her, she'd sit at the dining room table all afternoon, the old typewriter in front of her, composing her own mystery novel. I remembered her having read me some of it. The title was *Something by the Sea,* and it involved her detective Milo, a farting dog, a blind heiress, and a stringed instrument to be played with different colored glass tubes that fit over one's fingers. Something by the Sea was the name of the resort where the story took place. All the while she wrote it, she kept *Holmes* by her side, opened to "The Hound of the Baskervilles."

My fear of starting the library book lasted nearly a week until one night at dinner when my mother told a story about a friend of hers when she was younger. From the state she was in, I was sure her conversation was headed directly toward Bermuda but instead it veered off into an odd detour about Kenny Boucher. He was a boy in her class in grade school, and he stuttered and was very timid, but she involved him as a co-conspirator in all of her evil plots. One was the distribution of Ex-Lax to the kids in the neighborhood under the false claim that it was free chocolate. "It was a shit storm," she said, laughing into her wine.

Another had to do with a giant box they had found at the curb on junk day. They cut a little door out of it and then strung the inside with wads of chewed gum that they stretched into spider webs. When their work was done, they invited friends to enter their clubhouse. Kids emerged covered in gum, their clothes ruined, their hair matted with it.

When Jim and I asked to hear more of her adventures with Kenny Boucher, she shook her head and looked sad. "He died," she said. "He had this disease called Saint Vitus Dance that would make him spin around out of control every once in a while. He had an attack of it one day, fell down in the street, and drowned in a puddle before anyone found him." She fell into a sullen silence and said nothing else for the rest of the night until she sent us to bed.

Upstairs, I thought about the affect her memory had on her and realized that maybe there was something in *The Hound of the Baskervilles* that could tell me a secret about her. I passed up Perno Shell and pulled the book out from under the mattress. That night I stayed up late and read the first few chapters. In them I met Holmes and Watson. The book was not hard to read. I was used to the British voice in it as my father, when we were younger, read us a lot of books by Kipling and Rider Haggard. I was interested in the story, and liked the character of Watson very much, but Holmes was something else.

The great detective came across to me like a snob, the type my father once described as "believing the sun rose and set from his asshole." The picture of him in my mind was something like a mix between Perno Shell and Phineas Fogg, but his personality was pure Krapp. When told about the demon hound, Holmes replied that it was an interesting story for those who believed in fairy tales. He was obviously, "not standing for it." Still, I was intrigued by his voluminous smoking and the fact that he played the violin.

— — —

The days sank deeper into autumn, rotten to their cores with twilight. The bright warmth of the sun only lasted about as long as we were in school, and then once we were home, an hour later, the world was briefly submerged in a rich, golden aura, a honey glow, that was both beautiful and sad, gilding everything, from the barren branches of willows to the old wreck of a Pontiac parked alongside the Miltons' garage. A minute after that, the tide turned, the sun suddenly appeared a distant star, and in rolled a dim gray wave of neither here nor there that seemed to last a week each day, its shadows enhanced by our steamy exhalations and the smoke of burning leaves.

The wind of this in-between time made me always want to curl up inside a memory and sleep with eyes open. Dead leaves rolled across lawns, scraped along the street, quietly tapped the windows. Jack-o'-lanterns with luminous triangle eyes and jagged smiles turned up on front steps and in windows. Rattle-dry corn-stalks bore half-eaten ears of brown and blue kernels like teeth gone bad, as if they had eaten themselves, the way kids wore and then chewed the ultimately unsatisfying licorice/root beer gunk of wax teeth. Scarecrows hung from lawn lampposts or stoop rail-ings, listing forward, disjointed and drunk, dressed in the rumpled plaid shirts of long-gone grandfathers and jeans tied up with a length of rope. In the true dark, when walking George after din-ner, these shadow figures often startled me when their stitched and painted faces took on the features of Charlie Eddisson or Jimmy Bonnel.

Halloween was close, our favorite holiday because it carried none of the pain-in-the-ass holiness of Christmas and still there was free candy. The excitement of it crowded all problems to the side. The prowler, Charlie, school work were overwhelmed by hours of decision as to what we would be for that one night—something or someone who wasn't us, but who we wished to be, which I suppose ended up being us in some way. I could already taste the candy corn and feel my teeth aching. My father had given me a dollar and with it I'd bought a molded plastic skele-ton mask that smelled like fresh BO and made my cheeks sweat.

At the time, the only thought I had about that leering bone face was that it was cool as hell, but maybe, in the back of my mind, I was thinking of all those eyes out there trying to look into me, and it was a good disguise because it let them think they were seeing deep under my skin even though it was only an illusion. I showed the mask to Jim, and he told me, "This is the last year you can wear a costume. You're getting too old. Next year you'll have to go as a bum." All the older kids went around trick-or-treating as bums—a little charcoal on the face and some ripped up, baggy clothes.

Mary decided she would be the jockey, Willie Shoemaker. She modeled her outfit for Jim and me one night. It consisted of baggy pants tucked into a pair of white go-go boots, a baseball cap, a baggy, patchwork shirt, and a piece of thin curtain rod for a jockey's whip. She walked past us once and then looked over her shoulder. In the high nasal voice of the TV race announcer, she said, "And they're off . . ." We clapped for her, but the second she turned away again, Jim raised his eyebrows and whispered, "And it's Cabbage by a head."

Then, only three days from the blessed event, Krapp threw a wet blanket on my daydreams of roaming the neighborhood by moonlight, gathering, door-to-door, a Santa sack of candy, turning the joyous sparks of my imagination to smoke, which leaked out my ears and mixed with the twilight. He assigned a major report that was to be handed in the day after Halloween. Each of us in the class was given a different country, and we had to write a five-page report about it. Krapp presented me with Greece, as if he were dropping a steaming turd into my open Halloween sack.

I should have gotten started that afternoon when school let out, but instead I just sat in my room staring out the window. When Jim got home from wrestling, he came into my room and found me still sitting there like a zombie. I told him about the report.

"You're going to be doing it on Halloween if you don't get started," he said. "Here's what you do. Tomorrow, right after school, ride down to the library. Get the G volume of the encyclopedia, open it to Greece, and just copy what they have there. Write big, but not too big or he'll be on to you. If it doesn't look like what's written there will fill five pages, add words to the sentences. If the sentence says, 'The population of Greece is one million,' instead you write like, 'There are approximately one million Greeks in Greece. As you can see, there are many, many Grecians.' You get it? Use long words like 'approximately' and say stuff more than once in different ways."

"Krapp warned us about plagiarism, though," I said.

Jim made a face. "What's he gonna do, go read the encyclopedia for every paper?"

The next afternoon I was in the public library, copying from the G volume. With the exception of the fact that it said the people there ate goat cheese, none of the information in the book got into my head, as I had become merely a writing machine, dashing down one word after the next. The further I got into the report, the harder it was to concentrate. My mind wandered for long stretches at a time and I stared at the design of the weave in my balled up sweater that lay on the table in front of me. Then I'd look over at the window and see that the twilight was giving way to night. I was determined to finish even if I got yelled at for coming home late for dinner. When I hit the fourth page, I could tell the information in the encyclopedia was running out, and so I started adding filler the way Jim described. The last page and a half of my report was based on about five sentences from the book and was infused with so much hot air I thought it would float away.

I didn't know how late it was when I finished, but I was so relieved I began to sweat. I rolled up the five written pages and shoved them in my back pocket. Closing the big, green tome, I lifted it and took it back in the stacks to reshelve it. As I was coming out of the stacks, I suddenly remembered my sweater and pencil and looked over at the table by the magazine section where I'd been working. Sitting there in my chair was the man in the white trench coat. My heart instantly began pounding. I was stunned for a second, but as soon as I came to, I ducked out of the aisle in behind the row of shelves to my right.

I raced down the row, and, once in the middle, pulled a book off the third shelf from the top and then reached through and pushed the books on the other side over so I could see what he was doing. He was sitting there, reading a magazine, or pretending to. Every couple of seconds he looked up and turned to scan the library. The woman who'd been reading the newspaper in one of the big chairs while I finished the last pages of my report, got up, laid the paper down on the table, and walked away. The man in the white trench coat looked around and, seeing no one near him, lifted my balled up sweater and sniffed it. His beady eyes closed and his head cocked back a bit as if my sweater funk was crumb cake day at McGill's Bakery. A shiver ran through me. Still clutching it in his hand, he stood up and started heading for me.

I ran down to the center aisle and made for the back of the stacks. I was pretty sure that when he came looking for me, he would head up the center aisle so that he could look down each row. Once I reached the back wall, I moved all the way along it to the side of the building that held the front door. Checking my pocket, I touched the rolled up report. I didn't care about leaving the sweater and pencil behind. I waited, while in my mind I pictured him walking slowly toward me, peering down each row. My breathing was shallow, and I didn't know if I would have the power to scream if he somehow cornered me. Then I saw the sleeve of his trench coat, the sneaker of his left foot, before he came fully into view, and I bolted.

I was down the side aisle and out the front door in a flash. I knew that whereas a kid might run in a library, an adult would be expected not to, which might give me a few extra seconds. Outside, I sprinted around to the side of the building where my bike was chained up. Whatever time I saved was spent fumbling with the lock. Just when I had the bike free and got my ass on the seat, I saw him coming around the side of the building. My only route to Higbee was now cut off. Instead of trying to ride around him, I turned and headed back behind the library, into the woods that led to the railroad tracks.

● ● ●

I carried my bike over the tracks in the dark, listening to the deadly hum of electricity coursing through the third rail and watching both ways for the light of a train in the distance. Although the wind was cold, I was sweating, trying not to lose my balance on the dew-covered wooden ties. All the time I cautiously navigated, grim scenes from *The Long Way Home from School* played in my memory. At any second, I expected to feel upon my shoulder the bony hand of the man in the white coat.

On the other side of the tracks there was another narrow barrier of woods, and I searched along it, walking my bike, until I found a path. I wasn't actually sure what street it would lead me to since I had never gone that way before. We occasionally crossed back and forth over the tracks, but always in daylight and always over on the other side of town behind the woods that started at the schoolyard. This was uncharted territory for me.

I walked clear of the trees onto a road that didn't seem to have any houses. My mind was a jumble, and I was on the verge of tears, but I controlled myself by trying to think through where I was in relation to the library and home. I had an idea I was west of Higbee and just had to follow that street around to find the main road. Getting on my bike, I started off, following my best guess.

No sooner had I pedaled twenty feet before I saw, way up ahead, the lights of a car that had just turned onto the street. It was moving slowly, and I immediately feared it was the man in the white coat, searching for me. At the same time that I saw the car coming toward me, I noticed there was another one parked on the right-hand side only a few more feet up the road. I would have taken to the woods, but there was no path immediately there and it was too dark to find one. Once off my bike, I gave it a good shove and it wheeled into the tall grass and bushes and fell over, pretty well covered from sight. I got low and ran up to hide close against the side of the parked car, which was an old station wagon with wood paneling like our next door neighbor's, Mr. Kelty's.

The headlights of the car approaching drew slowly closer, and the low speed that it traveled at could easily have been an indication that the driver was looking for something or someone. By the time it passed the parked car I was hiding behind, I was hunkered down, my hands covering my head air-raid style, my right leg off the curb and under the station wagon. The vehicle moved very slowly by and then picked up speed, almost disappearing around the bend at the opposite end of the road before I could get a look at it. No mistaking, though, I saw the fins of the old white car. I wasn't sure whether to sit tight in case the stranger reached a dead end somewhere and came back or get on my bike and make a run for it.

Then I felt the car I was next to begin to gently rock. From inside there came a muffled moan. I lifted my head up carefully and peered in the window. Only then did I notice that the glass of all the windows was fogged over. It was dark inside, but the dashboard was glowing. I found a small spot where the glass was clear. Lying on the wide front seat was Mrs. Graves, her blouse open, one big, pale breast visible in the shadows, and one bare leg wrapped around the back of a small man. After observing his grease-slicked hair and flapping ears I didn't have to see his face to know that it was Mr. Kelty.

I ran over to where my bike had fallen in the weeds and lifted it. In a second I was on it and peddling like a maniac up the street.

As it turned out, I found Higbee and made it back to the house safely, never seeing the white car along my way. When I pulled up in the front yard, I knew I was late and would get yelled at, perhaps sent to my room. Luckily, through all of the turmoil, my report on Greece still stuck out of my back pocket, and my hope was that this document could be used as proof that I wasn't just goofing off. I was sweating and dirty from kneeling in the road next to the car. When I opened the front door, and stepped into the warmth of the living room, I remembered that I had left my sweater at the library and had not concocted an excuse for its absence.

The house was unusually quiet, and I was inside no more than a few seconds when I could feel something wasn't normal. The light in the dining room, where my mother usually sat drinking in the evenings, was off. The kitchen was also dark. I walked over and knocked on Nan's door. She opened it, and the aroma of fried pork chops came wafting out around us. Her hairnet was in place and she wore her yellow quilted bathrobe.

"You're mother's gone to bed already," she said.

I knew what she meant by this and pictured the empty bottle in the kitchen garbage.

"She told me to give you a kiss, though," she said. She came close and gave me one of those protracted Nan kisses that sounded like air escaping from the pulled-taut, wet mouthpiece of a balloon. "Jim told me you were at the library doing your home-work. I left food for you in the oven."

And that was it. She went back into her house and closed the door. Like my father, I was left to get my own dinner, alone. It was all too quiet, too stark. I sat in the dining room by myself and ate. Nan wasn't a much better cook than my mother. Every din-ner she made had some form of cabbage in it. Only George hap-pened by while I sat there. I cut him a piece of meat and he looked up at me as if wondering why I hadn't taken him out yet.

When I had finished eating and put my plate in the kitchen sink, Jim came down from upstairs.

"Did you get your paper finished?" he asked.

"Yeah," I said.

"Let me see it," he said, and held his hand out.

I pulled it out of my back pocket and handed the rolled up pages to him.

"You shouldn't have bent it all up. What was your country again?" he said, sitting down at the dining room table in my mother's chair.

"Greece."

He read through it really quickly, obviously skipping half the words. When he got to the end, he said, "This last page is a hundred percent double talk. Nice work."

"The Greece part in the encyclopedia ran out," I said.

"You stretched it like Mrs. Ryan's underwear," he said. "There's only one thing left to do. You gotta spice it up a little for the big grade."

"What do you mean?" I asked.

"Let's see," he said, and went back through it. "It says the exports are cheese, tobacco, olives, and cotton. I saw a kid do this thing once for a paper and the teacher loved it. He taped samples of the exports onto a sheet of paper. We've got all these things. Get me a blank sheet of paper and the tape."

Jim went to the refrigerator and took out a slice of cheese and the bottle of olives. I fetched the tape for him, and then he told me to get a copy of a magazine and start looking for a picture about Greece in it for the cover of the report. Fifteen minutes later, as I sat paging through an old issue of *Life*, he turned the sheet of paper he had been working on around to show me.

"Feast your eyes," he said. The page had the word EXPORTS written across the top in block letters. Below that title, a square of American cheese, a half an olive (with pimento), an old, crumpled cigarette butt from the dining room ashtray, and a Q-tip head were affixed with three pieces of tape for each. Under these items appeared their names.

"Wow," I said.

"No applause, just throw money," said Jim. "Did you find a picture for the cover?"

"There's nothing Greek in here," I said, "but this old woman's face looks kind of Greek." I showed him a picture of a woman who was probably about a hundred years old. She was in profile, wore a black shawl, and her face was a prune with eyes. "She's from Mexico, though," I said.

"It's Joe Mannygoats's grandmother," said Jim. "I heard she was half Greek. Cut her out."

I did, pretty well too, except that I hacked the tip of her nose off. He then told me to tape her face to a piece of paper and write the title of the report coming out of her mouth as if she was saying it. There was a subheading in the encyclopedia entry–The Glory That Was Greece–that he told me to use as the title of my paper. "Do it in block letters," he said. "Then take the whole thing and put six books on top of it to flatten it out and you're all set. Krapp's gonna be caught between a shit and a sweat when he sees this one."

- - -

Mary cried at bedtime because my mother wasn't awake to tuck her in. Instead, Nan sat with her until she dozed off. Jim and I were sent upstairs. After it got quiet downstairs, I got out of bed and snuck over to Jim's room and knocked on the open door. It was dark in there and from the light shining in from the hallway it looked like he was already asleep.

"Yeah?" he said, and opened one eye.

"I think I know who the prowler is," I whispered.

He told me to come in. I sat at the bottom of his bed and told him about the man in the white car and recounted what had happened at the library that night. When I told him about the old man sniffing my sweater, he breathed deeply through his nostrils, rolled his eyes upward, and said, "Delicious."

"I'm telling you, it's him," I said. "He travels around during the daytime in that old white car and then at night he sneaks through the backyards, looking for kids to steal. I bet he took Charlie."

"What's he using him as, an air freshener?" asked Jim.

"Not only that, but I think he might be some kind of evil spirit," I said.

"If he's an evil spirit," said Jim, "I doubt he'd be driving a car."

"Yeah, but remember, the nun said that the evil one walks the Earth. Maybe he gets tired of walking and needs to drive some."

"Hey," said Jim, "you said he always smells like smoke? That the books from the library he probably touched smell like smoke? That's what Sister Joe told me was the secret to knowing him when he came. She said he'd smell like the fires of hell. Fire doesn't smell, though, except for the smoke."

This revelation made me shiver and I felt unsafe, even inside the house with Jim there. The old man could be anywhere, listening at the glass, sneaking in the cellar window, anywhere. I swallowed hard.

"So who is this guy?" asked Jim. "Where's he live?"

"I don't know his name," I said. "Do you remember the night we dragged Mr. Blah-blah across the street? The guy who stopped and got out of his car? That's the guy."

"He was kind of creepy looking," said Jim, "and I never saw him around here before." He yawned and lay back on the pillow. "We'll have to find out who he is."

"How?" I asked. I sat there for a long time, waiting for his answer.

"Somehow," he said, and turned over. I knew he was almost asleep.

The antenna cried mercilessly all night, and I tossed and turned, thinking of the man in the white car, my fear in the library, and spying Mrs. Graves's tit. I could sense the evil as it crept forward day by day, dismantling my world, like a very slow explosion. I woke and slept and woke and slept, and it was still dark. The third time I awoke to the same night, I thought I heard the sound of pebbles jangling in soda cans. The plan had been to let George out after whoever it was taking the ladder, but I didn't move, save to curl up into a ball.

The next day, Halloween, was clear and cool and blue. My mother had to leave for work early, so Nan made us breakfast.

Jim told Mary and me to request oatmeal instead of eggs, so the latter would be there to steal later on and use for ammo on the night streets. I could tell Mary was excited because she wasn't being Mickey and wasn't counting or doing any of her strange antics, but instead pumping Jim for a rundown on how the coming night would be. She had always before gone trick-or-treating with our mother and this was to be her first time on the loose with us. The ugly oatmeal came, lumps of steaming khaki, with raisins in it, no less, and we all forced it down. Meanwhile, Jim held forth on the strategies of the holiday.

"The idea," he told Mary, "is to get as much candy as possible. You want candy, wrapped candy. If you get a candy bar, that's the best—a Hershey bar or a Milky Way. Mary Janes are okay if you don't mind losing a few fillings, little boxes of Good & Plenty, Dots, Chocolate Babies, packs of gum, all good. Then you've got your cheapskate single-wrapped candy—root beer barrels, butterscotches, licorice drops—not bad, usually given out by people who are broke, but what can they do? They're trying.

"You don't eat anything that's not wrapped, except for Mr. Barzita's figs. Some people drop an apple in your bag. You can't eat it, but you can throw it at someone, so that's okay. Once in a while a mother will bake stuff to give out. Don't eat it, you don't know what they put in it. It could be the best-looking cupcake you ever saw, with chocolate icing and a candy corn on top, but who knows, they might have crapped in the batter. I've seen where people will throw a penny in your sack. A penny's a penny.

"You always stay where we can see you. If someone invites you into their house, don't go. When we tell you to run, run, 'cause kids could be coming to throw eggs at us. If you hear someone shout 'Nair bomb,' run like hell—"

"What's a Nair bomb?" asked Mary.

"Nair is that chemical stuff women use to take the hair off their legs. Kids pour that stuff into balloons and then throw it at you. If you get hit on the head with it, all of your hair will fall out. If it gets in your eyes, it could blind you for a while."

Mary nodded.

"I'm going to give you two eggs tonight. Save them until you see someone you really want to get. Aim for the head, cause if it hits their coat, it will probably bounce off and smash on the ground. Or you can throw it at the house of someone you hate. Who do you hate?" Jim asked.

"Will Hickey," Mary said.

"Yeah," I said.

"We'll egg his house tonight for sure," said Jim. "Maybe I'll put one through his front window. One more thing: kids will try to steal your sack of candy. Don't let them. Scream and kick them if they try to. I'll come and help you."

"Okay," said Mary.

Then we went in and said goodbye to Nan before leaving for school. She was at her table in the little dining area. Heaped on the table were three enormous piles of candy—one, rolls of Sweet Tarts, another, Mary Janes, the last, miniature Butterfingers. She took one from each pile, stuffed them in a little orange bag with a picture of a witch on a broomstick on it, and twisted the top. Pop was sitting there in his underwear watching her, chewing a Mary Jane.

School was endless that day. We usually had a holiday party in the classroom on Halloween, but not that year. It was cancelled because Krapp had to give us a series of standardized intelligence tests. It was a day of filling in little bubbles with a number two pencil. The questions started off easy, but soon became impossibly strange. There were passages to be read about sardine fishing off the coast of Chile and math problems where they showed you a picture of a weird shape and asked you to turn it around in your mind 180 degrees before answering questions about it.

I realized right before handing one of the exams in that I'd meant to skip an answer I didn't know, but instead filled that bubble in by mistake, so that all my answers from then on would really be for the following question. I felt a fleeting moment of remorse as I put the test in Krapp's hand.

On the playground at lunch break, Tim Caliban told me his theory of taking those kinds of tests. "I don't even bother reading the questions," he said. "I just guess. I've got to get at least some of them right."

Back in the classroom, in the afternoon, Patricia Trepedino, the smartest girl in the class, referred Krapp to question number four. "It says," she said, "concrete is to peanut butter as . . ."

"Yes," said Krapp, checking his sheet.

"Chunky or plain?" she asked.

He stared at her with the same blank look that Marvin Gompers wore after telling us in third grade he was made of metal and then ran headfirst into the brick wall behind the gym. Finally, Krapp snapped out of it and said, "No talking or I will have to invalidate your test."

❧ ❧ ❧

The lingering twilight finally breathed its last, and that first moment of true night was like a gunshot at the start of a race, for, instantly, frantic kids in costumes streamed from lit houses, beginning their rounds, not to return until they had reached the farthest place they could and still remember how to get home. My mother and Nan stood at the front door and waved to us as Jim led the way, dressed in a baggy flannel shirt, ripped dungarees, a black skullcap, and charcoal beard. Mary followed him in her jockey outfit, and I brought up the rear, stumbling on the curbs and across lawns because the slits in my skull mask drastically limited my view. Even though it was cold and windy, before we had climbed two front stoops and opened our bags, my face was sweating. I could hear every breath I took, and each was laced with the hair-raising stench of molded plastic. Finally, when I walked into a parked car, I decided to only pull the mask down when arriving on a house's front steps.

We traveled door-to-door around the block, joining with other groups of kids, splitting away and later being joined by others. David Kelty, dressed like a swami, with a bath towel wrapped in a turban around his head, eyeliner darkening his eyes, and a long, purple robe, followed along with us for a dozen houses. The Farley girls were angels or princesses, I couldn't tell which, but their costumes, made from flowing white material, glowed in the dark. President Kenny Stutton was dressed in his Communion suit, a button on the lapel that said VOTE FOR KENNY, and his sisters were ghosts with sheets over their heads. Reggie Wilson was a robot, wrapped in silver foil, wearing a hat with a light bulb sticking out the top that went on and off without a switch; and Chris Hacket wore the army helmet of his father, who'd gotten hand grenade shrapnel in his ass and lost three fingers in Korea.

We worked the trick-or-treat with a dedication that rivaled our father's for his three jobs, systematically moving up one side of the street and then down the other. Our pillowcases filled with candy. Old lady Ripici gave out Chinese handcuffs, a kind of tube woven from colored paper strips. You stuck a finger in each side and then couldn't pull them out. That's how we lost David Kelty. He was left behind, standing on the lawn, unable to figure out that you just had to twist your fingers to free them. The slow, the hobbled, the weak were all left behind as we blitzkrieged Pine Avenue, moved on to Sylvia, and covered Manhasset.

When we finished with the last house on the last street in that part of the development, we took the secret trail through the dirt hills, through the waist-high weeds, to the path that led around the high fence of the sump, and came out on the western field of Southgate, just beyond the basketball courts. In the moonlight, a strong wind whipping across the open expanse and driving tatters of dark clouds above, we met up with Tim Caliban and some of his friends. We rested for a while there and stuffed chocolate and licorice into ourselves as sustenance for the next leg of the journey.

Just as we were getting ready to head east toward Minerva Avenue on the other side of the school field over by the woods, we were attacked by Stinky Steinmacher, Justin Wunch, and about twenty other dirt eaters. The eggs flew back and forth. President Stutton took one in the face and went down on his knees in tears. Someone yelled that Wunch had Nair bombs and we fled. Jim had Mary by the hand, and I was right behind them. As we ran around the back of the school, I looked over my shoulder to see the enemy swarming toward Kenny. His sisters, the horrible dumplings, had also abandoned him and were gaining on me. We would learn the next day that they beat him with flour socks until he went albino, split his lip, and stole his sack of treasure. Then Stinky peed on him. Any other night of the year such

BEST SHORT NOVELS: 2007

brutality would have been considered an outrage, but not on Halloween when even our parents sided with Darwin.

We begged our way up Minerva and the street beyond that, and the farther we went away from our own neighborhood, kids would break off and head back toward more familiar ground. Once when we left Mary standing on the sidewalk by herself for a minute, a kid tried to steal her sack, but she was able to keep him off by swinging her curtain rod/jockey whip until Jim got to her and pummeled the kid. We ended up taking his sack and splitting it three ways. Still, the run-in had made Mary nervous and she had to sit down on the curb for a while, mumble some numbers, and have a cigarette. The rest of the group went on without us. While we were waiting for her to relax, a bunch of Jim's junior high friends came by, and, just like that, he left me in charge of Mary and went off with them.

By then it was late, and the street we were on, which I didn't know the name of, was deserted. Many of the houses had turned their lights out as a sign they had either gone to bed or were out of candy. That was the way Halloween always went, one minute it was a colorful celebration of chaos, candy gathering, and cruelty, and the next, when you weren't watching, it had laid back and gone to sleep. It was now far quieter, but more eerie, for in sleep, all that was left on the streets were its nightmares. I told Mary to get up and she did. I vaguely remembered the direction home, and we started off, walking quickly, sticking to the shadows so as not to be noticed. We passed darkened houses whose trees were hung with wind-whipped strands of white toilet paper, smashed jack-o'-lanterns in the road, broken shells and the iridescent film of egg splatter reflected under streetlights where a battle had taken place. The scarecrows again took on a sinister aspect, and every shadowy form startled me, brought to mind the prowler and Charlie and worse.

We traveled back three streets, turning right and left and right, trying to home in on the school as a point of orientation, while the temperature dropped drastically.

Mary hadn't worn a coat or a sweat shirt, having felt that without people seeing her baggy shirt, no one would be able to make out that she was Willie Shoemaker. It hadn't mattered, because kids kept asking me all night, "Hey, what's your sister supposed to be?" The guesses ranged from baseball player to clown to janitor, but no one hit on a jockey, even when she had heard one of them mention it and replied, "They're coming around the back turn . . ." Anyway, I stopped and gave her my hooded sweat shirt.

Crossing the school field was a harrowing event, and we kept to the dark of the perimeter fence, so as to remain inconspicuous. Instead of striking out across the field and the lit basketball courts and front drive, I opted for the path that went around the sump. It took a little longer, but that vision of Kenny Stutton being attacked and the fact that Mary was with me made me cautious. The overgrown weed lot was lonesome enough to make me shiver, and the dirt hills were a strange, barren moonscape, but once I saw the street on the other side, I felt we were going to be okay. It was right then, as we stepped down onto the pavement, that lurching into the glow of the streetlight came a true monster; a hulking form with a red and blistered face, its hair sloughing off, leaving huge bald spots. The creature whimpered as it tottered forward, its hands out in front of it. Mary put her arms around me, pressing her face to my side, and I stood, unable to move, my mouth open. Then I realized it was poor Peter Milton, half-blind and suffering the effects of a Nair attack, trying to grope his way home. We let him pass, and then continued on.

As we came down a side street that opened onto Pine Avenue, I finally relaxed. Mary wasn't holding my hand anymore as she could sense my ease and was more calm herself. All we had to do was get to Pine and turn left and walk down seven houses. I wondered where Jim had gone and what adventures he had met and then gave myself over to thinking about the moment when I would empty my sack onto the dining room table, spilling out all that was right and good into a huge pile.

Mary interrupted me by pulling on my shirt. "Pipe smoke," she said.

I stopped walking and looked up. At that very moment, down on Pine, I could see from the aura of a streetlight no more than twenty yards away, that old white car pull away from the curb in the direction of our house. Grabbing Mary by the arm, I led her through a hole in the hedges we had been passing, and whispered to her, "Don't make a sound." We stood, motionless, and waited. Only when I heard the car turn around and recede into the distance toward Higbee did I motion to Mary to return to the street. "Run," I told her, and took her hand. We sprinted around the corner onto Pine and all the way home. She'd been right: pervading the air at the spot where the two roads intersected was that smoldering scent of the man with the white coat. A relentless spirit, it pursued us to our doorstep.

◐ ◐ ◐

I sat at the dining room table, chewing away like a cow with its cud, on both a Mary Jane and the contents of a miniature box of Good & Plenty, feeling slightly nauseous. My mind was vacant and I was so weary I could hardly keep my eyes open. I had an animal fear that if I closed them, my pile of booty, which formed a small, colorful mountain, might disappear. Mary had already fallen asleep on the living room floor, a melting Reese's cup smearing her outstretched hand. My mother sat across from me, smoking a cigarette and picking through both my pile and Mary's for caramels, which, it was understood, were hers.

Jim finally came home, and my mother took Mary off to bed, telling Jim and me it was time to go up. We gathered all of the candy together and put it in the community pot, a huge serving bowl that otherwise only got used on Thanksgiving. As we headed up the stairs, Jim whispered behind me, "We egged the hell out of Hickey's house, and almost got away without anyone seeing us. But I saw Will's weasel face at the upstairs window. I doubt he'll tell his parents since we'd kick his ass, but watch out for him. I'm sure he saw me."

That was the news I was left with at my bedroom door, and suddenly I was no longer tired. The threat of Hickey's revenge was enough to revive me, but since he wasn't there at that moment with his sharp knuckles it eventually receded, and I lay in bed, reviewing the night, the costumes, the thrill of running away across the field at Southgate, the agonized form of Peter Milton, which had brought a sense of genuine horror to the holiday. Then, of course, I came to the incident with the pipe smoke, and the memory of the white car pulling away from the curb made me realize that something was missing. I got out of bed and quietly made my way down stairs to the dining room. There, I dug through the giant bowl of treats we had all three collected.

What was missing were the plump, ripe figs that each year Mr. Barzita wrapped in orange or black tissue paper and tied at the top with ribbon. I saw in my mind a fleeting image of his knotted old fingers, shaking slightly, making a bow. They were a Pine Avenue tradition, but this year there were none. I thought back through the night, and realized that his house had been dark, and he hadn't been at his front gate to meet us and drop one of his "beauties," as he called them, into our sacks. In the rush and fever of greed we hadn't noticed his absence but simply moved on to the Blairs' house. Then I worked away at a dark spot in my memory, clawing through the sugar haze, the night, the turmoil, trying to remember if the white car had been parked in front of his house when we had first passed it early on in our travels, for it was old man Barzita's place it had pulled away from when Mary and I noticed it this evening. Perhaps I had my mask on, or my thoughts were caught up still with the glittering handful of silver-wrapped Chunkies that Mrs. Ryan had dropped into my sack, but no matter how I tried I couldn't remember those minutes.

Instead, I pictured Barzita as a young man, stepping out of that disease-laden room during the war. I wondered if the prowler, the man in the white coat, who had become for me, Death himself, had appeared on Halloween to finally claim a man who by all accounts should have perished years before in another country, in a mountain base stricken with meningitis. The possibility scared me more than any threat posed by Will Hickey.

For solace, I walked down the hallway to my parents' bedroom, forgetting that my mother had passed out on the living room couch. My heart sank as I viewed the empty room. The light was on, as it always seemed to be, but the bed was unmade, my father's work clothes from earlier in the week lay in a pile on the floor.

As I stood there in the doorway, the weariness that had sway over me earlier returned and I yawned. I tottered forward into the room and crawled into my parents' bed on my mother's side. The mattress was soft and I sunk into it. Immediately I noticed the aromas of machine oil and my mother's deep powder, work perfume and these scents combined, their chemistry making me feel safe. I lifted the red, bug-crushing weight of *The Complete Sherlock Holmes* from the night table and turned to "The Hound of the Baskervilles." The print was very small and in double columns, the pages tissue thin. I found the place where I had left off in my own copy and started reading. Not even a minute went by and the tiny letters began moving like ants. Then gravity took over and my arms couldn't hold the volume up. As the open red book settled onto my chest, I settled into sleep.

I dreamed Halloween and an egg battle on the western field beneath the moon at Southgate. Stinky Steinmacher's little brother, Gunther, hit me in the head with an egg and knocked me over. When I opened my eyes, all the kids from both sides were gone, and the man in the white coat was leaning over me to lift me up. I pretended to still be asleep as he carried me, the wind blowing fiercely, toward his car parked by the basketball court. He said in an angry voice to me, "Come on, open your eyes," and then I did and it was morning and I realized his voice had been Jim's. "You'll be late for school." I was in my own bed, upstairs in my room.

It was a rush to get ready, and all three of us kids were groggy. I remembered at the last second to take my report for Krapp from beneath its tomb of six books. Mary and I made it to school just before the bell rang, and we hurried to our classrooms. I was in my seat no more than five minutes before Krapp stood up from his desk and said, with a grim smile on his face, "Hand me your reports." As soon as he said it, I looked around and could tell all of those who'd let Halloween enchant them into inaction by the flush of red that spread across their faces. "Who doesn't have it?" said Krapp. Five trembling hands went up. He lifted his grade book and recorded the zeros with excruciating precision, saying with each one, "A zero for you and two detentions." Someone behind me started crying, but I didn't dare turn around and look.

Krapp swept down the aisle, taking reports, and I held mine out to him. Just before his fingers closed on it, I noticed on the front cover, I had misspelled Greece. Instead of writing it the right way, I had written *The Glory That Was Grease*. He took it all in in a second, the cut out picture of the old Mexican woman in the shawl, the misspelling, and shook his head in disgust. He added the paper to the stack in his other hand, and what he didn't notice, I did. The back of the bottom page, which held the samples of exports, was completely discolored with huge dark stains.

That paper came back to me the next day, bearing an F grade and the words *plagiarism* and *a stinking mess* written across the woman's wrinkled cheek. Between the molded cheese, rotten olive, and cigarette stench, it smelled like shit. I brought it home and showed it to Jim. He shrugged and said, "That's the breaks." He told me not to tell our parents about it. "They won't even notice, they're so busy with work and—" He tilted his head back and brought his arm up as if drinking from a big bottle. "Take it outside and bury it," he said. "It smells like a dead man's feet." So I did, feeling betrayed and knowing that no good would come of it. Mary watched me dig a hole with the shovel. When I was done laying the foul muddle to rest and had tamped down the dirt, she put a rock on top to mark the grave.

● ● ●

I stood above Botch Town, surveying its length and breadth, and noticed that, since Jim had started wrestling, taken up with a new group of friends, stayed away from the house as much as possible, a thin film of dust had settled on his creation. At first I imagined it to be the result of a minor snow squall, the kind that had already happened in early November, but snow was white and I couldn't ignore that this film was gray. Then I imagined it to be a sleeping powder, like a sprinkling of magic dust from an evil magician in a fairy tale. The town appeared quiet, as if in sleep, and there was a certain loneliness that pervaded the entire expanse. Nothing much had moved since last I had looked down upon it before Halloween. Charlie still lay in the lake, Nick was still at work on his car, Mrs. Ryan, no doubt seized by weariness, had rolled forward onto her stomach to sleep.

The only change I noticed was that Mary, obviously out of fright at having seen the face at her window, put the prowler behind our own house. Of course, in reality he was long gone, and had probably spied on a dozen other families since he'd looked in on her. The repair to Mrs. Ripici's roof had still not been completed, and although the Hossetters had been gone for months, the figure of Raymond, the oldest boy, still lay, sleeping, behind the house. I wondered if this was to be the end of Botch Town. If Jim, getting older now, would forsake it, and it would continue to sleep and slowly decompose until the clay figures cracked and turned to dust and the cardboard houses wilted down and lost their forms. There was some connection between the sorry nature of Botch Town and our family, but whatever that connection was remained unclear to me and no manner of dredging with sharp hooks would bring it up.

I walked over to a corner of the cellar where there was a box of old toys we no longer played with. Searching through it, I found the item I remembered from long ago that I had once seen amidst its jumble. It was a Matchbox car, a reproduction of a hearse—long and black. The back doors opened and there had once been a little coffin that slid inside that you could close the doors on. Using Jim's supplies, I painted this car white and, while still wet, set it down on Pine Avenue, parked in front of Mr. Barzita's place. Then, after taking one more look at the entire board, I reached out over it and turned off the sun.

My father miraculously appeared in his bed Sunday morning. I happened to go down the hall to the bathroom and on my way out noticed him lying there asleep next to my mother. The sight of him startled me, and I went upstairs to tell Jim, who was still sleeping. He got up and followed me down the stairs. I went in and told Mary. Nudging her awake, I said, "Hey, Dad's home." She joined Jim and me, and we took up positions around the bed, staring and waiting. After quite a while, my father suddenly sat up and opened his eyes as if a nightmare had awakened him. He shook his head and breathed out, like a sigh of relief, and smiled at us.

We learned that not only was he there, but he would be home for the entire day. After he got up and had his coffee, he asked us if we wanted to go out for a drive. "Where?" asked Jim.

"I don't know. We'll find out when we get there," he said.

We went out and piled into his car, Jim in the passenger side of the front seat and Mary and me in the back. It was cold out, but they opened the windows up front and we drove along with the radio blaring and the wind blowing wildly around us. No one said anything. My father pulled over at a roadside hot dog stand. We ordered cream sodas and those hot dogs that snapped when you bit them, covered in cooked onions and mustard. Sitting on overturned milk crates a few feet from the hot dog stand, we ate in silence. Then we got back in the car and drove fast, and I had a feeling of freedom, of skipping school, of running away.

When we had gone many miles and there was no hope of turning back, Mary leaned over the front seat and said, "We didn't go to church today."

My father turned and looked at her for a second, smiling, "I know," he said, and laughed out loud.

We wound up at a huge park on the north shore. The parking lots were almost empty even though the day was beautifully clear. We parked in the middle of this concrete expanse, surrounded by woods on three sides.

"Which way will we walk?" my father asked me.

I pointed to the west because it seemed like it would take us the farthest from the road and away from the parking lots.

"Okay," he said, "and they're off . . ."

We got out of the car, zipped up our coats, and started in that direction. Jim moved right up next to our father and tried to match him step for step. I had wanted to be there, next to him, but I didn't make a fuss about it. Mary and I brought up the rear. We left the concrete behind and stepped into the shadows beneath the tall pines. There was a half-foot of fallen oak leaves and brown pine needles on the ground, and Mary and I shuffled our feet, occasionally kicking them into the air. She found a giant, yellow leaf as wide as her face, poked two eyeholes into it and held it up by the stem as a mask.

We walked along a path for quite a while, saw crows above in the treetops, and came to a clearing where my father held his hand up and then put his finger to his lips. We three kids stopped walking, and he crouched down and pointed into the trees on the other side of the clearing. Standing there staring at us was a huge deer with antlers. A whole minute went by, and then Mary said, "Hello," and waved to it. The deer sprang to the side and disappeared back into the woods.

In the clearing, we were standing on a patch of sand. My father looked down. "Tracks," he said. "A lot of them came through here in the last few hours." He then found a fox track and showed it to us as well. After the clearing, we changed direction, unanimously deciding, without saying so, that we'd follow the deer. We never saw it again for the rest of the day, but the trail we took led us to a huge hill. My father took Mary by the hand to help her and we all scrabbled up the hill, slipping on the fallen leaves and resting from time to time against the trunks of trees.

As it turned out, the deer had led us in the right direction, for as we crested the top of the rise, the trees disappeared and we could see out across the Long Island Sound all the way to the shore of Connecticut. The vast expanse of water was iron gray and choppy, dotted with white caps. A strong wind blew in our faces and it was exhilarating. The hill was covered in grass all the way down the other side and devoid of trees. At its base was a little inlet that, farther west, skirted the set of sand dunes between us and the sound. It was as wide as two football fields and as long as four, its surface rippling in the wind. An army of white birds stood along its shore, pecking at the wet sand.

My father sat down at the top of the hill and took out his cigarettes. As he lit a match and cupped it in his hands, catching its spark at the end of his smoke, he said, out of the side of his mouth, "You better go down there and investigate." We didn't need to be told twice, but charged down the hill, whooping, and the birds took off, lifting into the sky in waves. It felt for a second, as we charged downhill, like I could lift into the air, myself. Jim tripped and rolled a quarter of the way down, and, seeing him, Mary followed his lead, fell, and rolled the rest of the way.

We stayed down there, by the water, for a long time, skipping stones, dueling with driftwood swords, watching the killifish swarm in the shallows. An hour or two passed, and when Jim and Mary decided to try to catch one of the fish with an old Dixie cup they found in the sand, I looked up at my father just sitting there. I sidled away from them and went back up the hill. During the climb, I lost sight of him, as I could only see a few feet ahead of me with the steep incline, but when I got to the top and he came into view, I noticed that he had his glasses in his hand. I think he had been crying, because as soon as he saw me coming, he wiped his eyes and put the glasses back on.

"Come here," he said to me. "I need some help."

I walked over and stood next to him. He reached up, and placing a hand lightly upon my shoulder, stood, making believe he was using me as a crutch. "Thanks," he said, and for a brief moment, he put his arm around me and hugged me to him. My face went into the side of his coarse, plaid jacket, and I smelled the machine oil. Then he let go and called for Jim and Mary to come back.

We stopped on the way home and had dinner at a chrome diner. My father ordered meat loaf and we all ordered meat loaf too. No one spoke all through dinner, and when the ice cream came, he said to us, "How are you all doing in school?"

I felt Jim lightly kick my shin under the table as he said, "I'm doing great."

"Good," said Mary.

I said nothing at first, but Jim kicked me again, and I said, "Doing fine."

Mary, in her Mickey voice, said, "Could you possibly . . . ?" But my father didn't notice or chose not to notice and called for the check.

By the time we got back home it was dark out. We got ready for bed, and then sat in the living room. My mother was up and around and feeling good. She played the guitar and sang us a few songs. My father, like in the old days, read some poems to us from his collection of little red books—*The Charge of the Light Brigade, The Ballad of Reading Gaol,* and *Crossing the Bar.* That night, I slept well, no dreams, and the antenna whispered instead of moaned, like the music of a very small violin.

☪ ☪ ☪

I looked up Mr. Barzita's phone number in the book, and began calling his house every day after school, but there was never an answer. I asked Nan and Pop if they had seen him, but they both told me no. Pop asked me why I wanted to know, and I just shrugged and said, "Because I haven't seen him around."

"Do you ever see him during the winter?" asked Nan.

It was true, he rarely showed himself after Halloween, and the weather had really gotten frigid. Mid-November and the temperature had dropped into the teens for a week straight. We prayed for a snowstorm, but it seemed like even the sky was frozen solid. Jim and I rode over to Babylon on our bikes on Saturday afternoon and went skating on Argyle Lake, but otherwise, I just stayed inside, reading and catching up on my journal, filling in those members of our neighborhood I'd yet to capture in words.

There was one old lady who lived over by Southgate, and I always forgot her name. It was written on her mailbox, but on the way home from school I kept forgetting to check it. I had a good story about her occasionally going door-to-door, like trick-or-treating, asking everyone on the block for a glass of gin. Her dog, Tatel, a vicious German shepherd, was worth a few lines, especially concerning the time it chased the mailman up the Grimms' elm tree. I had a fine description of this old woman's white, hag hair, her skeleton body, and how her sallow skin fit her skull like a rubber glove you could pick a dime up while wearing, but no name. The cold snap had broken and the temperature had risen slightly, so, to just get out of the house and get some fresh air, I put George on the leash and we took a quick walk around the block.

I wrote her name in my mind, in script, three times—*Mrs. Homretz*—while George peed on the post of her mailbox. The sky was overcast, and even though the wind blew, it was mild enough to keep my jacket open. When I was sure I had it memorized, I turned to start home. Lucky for me I looked around when I did, because just then, rounding the turn on Pine and heading straight for me were three kids on their bikes—Will Hickey, Stinky Steinmacher, and Justin Wunch.

"There he is!" cried Hickey, and I saw all three of them lift their asses off their seats and press down hard on their peddles for a burst of speed. Even before my heart started pounding, and I felt the fear explode inside me, I ran. They had blocked off my direct escape to home, and were gaining on me too fast for me to take the corner at Sylvia in order to make my way around the block back to Pine. They'd have been on me before I reached Tommy Brown's house in the middle of that street. Instead, I made a beeline for Southgate and the woods, thinking they might stop chasing me once they hit the tree line.

George easily kept pace with me as we made our way across the field and then down the slope of Sewer Pipe Hill. I chose the main path, thinking that if they did come after me, I'd get as far into the woods as possible before cutting into the trees and underbrush. At the last second I would head south toward that spit of woods that extended into the backyards of the Stuttons' and Hossetters'. If I could make it that far, I could get back on to Pine close to my house and be home before they caught me. I stopped on the path to listen for them. The pounding in my ears was too loud at first, but then I heard Stinky give a battle cry. The sound of bikes breaking twigs, rolling over fallen leaves, followed.

We were off again, down the trail, branches whipping my face, ruts stumbling me. I tried not to think about what would happen if they caught us. George would hold his own against them, but just picturing Hickey's fists made me go weak inside.

"He's right in front of us," Wunch yelled, and I knew they could see me. I left the path and cut into the trees. They continued behind me, but the underbrush and fallen logs slowed them down, and it sounded as if they had left their bikes behind. If you were a coward like I was, it was a good thing to be a fast runner, which I also was. I ran for another five minutes at top speed, and then I had to stop, not because I was winded, but the lake spread out in front of me. I'd trapped myself.

I knew that if I had to turn either right or left they would easily catch me. The lake was still frozen from the cold snap, but a thin layer of water covered the top as it had begun to thaw. I put a foot out onto the slippery surface and slowly eased my weight down. It held me. George was uncertain of the ice and I had to drag him along behind. I took slow, careful steps forward. By the time they'd broken through the trees at the edge of the lake, I was about fifteen feet from shore. I didn't look back, although they were calling my name and saying I was a "fairy" and a "scumbag" and a "piece of shit." George didn't like the situation at all and began to growl low in his throat.

"Egg my house?" I heard Hickey scream, and then I saw a rock whiz past my head, hit the ice and slide three quarters of the way to the opposite shore.

"Let's go get him," yelled Steinmacher, and they must have stepped onto the ice together, because I felt the entire surface of the lake undulate and make a growling sound like George just before he got down to business chewing a sneaker. Following that, there came from behind me a cracking noise, like a giant egg hatching, and a splash. I looked over my shoulder and saw Wunch standing three feet from shore, up to his waist in brown water. I kept going forward as they helped him out of his hole and retreated.

Their extra weight on the ice must have made it unstable, because now with each step I took I could hear tiny splintering noises and see fissures grow like veins in the clear, frozen green beneath each sneaker. The wind was blowing fiercely out there in the middle of the open expanse, and my sense of victory that they had turned back suddenly vanished, replaced by the prospect that the lake might, at any moment, open up and swallow me. That's when the rock hit me in the back of the head, and I went down hard on my chest and face. I heard a great fracturing sound and my mind went blank as much from fear as from the concussion.

When I finally opened my eyes, I remained splayed out, listening. I heard the wind, dead leaves blowing through the woods, George quietly whimpering, and a very distant sound of laughter, moving away. Every now and then the ice would make a cracking noise. I was soaked from having fallen in the film of water atop the frozen surface, and it came to me slowly that I was shivering. With the slowest and most cautious of movements, I got to my knees. Once I achieved that position, I rested for a moment, my head still hurting and dizzy. My next goal was to stand, and I told myself I would count to thirty and then just stand up and get to shore.

The moment I started counting, I thought of Mary. When I reached twenty-five, I happened to look down, and staring up at me through the green ice was a pair of eyes. At first I thought it was my reflection. I leaned down closer to the surface to see, and there, beneath the ice, was the pale, partially rotted face of Charlie Eddisson. His hair was fixed solid in a wild tangle, much of the whites of his eyes had gone brown, and they were big and round like fish eyes. His mouth was open in a silent scream. Next to his face was the palm of one hand, and I could barely see past his wrist as the forearm disappeared into the murk below. His glasses were missing and so was the flesh of his right cheek.

When I screamed, I felt as though he was screaming through me. Dropping George's leash, I scrabbled to my feet, and, slipping and sliding, ice cracking everywhere around me, I ran straightforward toward the shore, twenty yards away. In the midst of one step I felt the ice crack and give way beneath my heel, but I was already gone. The dog and I reached the shore at the same moment and we both jumped the last few feet over the thin ice at the edge.

Chattering like mad and half-frozen, I came out of the woods through Hossetters' backyard. My pant legs were stiff as was the front of my shirt. When I walked through the front door of our house, the warmth thawed my fear and I began to cry. My mother was cooking dinner in the kitchen, but she just called, "Hello," and didn't come in. I went upstairs to my room, pulled off the wet things, and got into bed. Until I was called to dinner, I lay under the covers, shivering.

◐ ◐ ◐

I never told anyone except Mary that I'd seen Charlie under the ice of the lake, and when I told her she'd been right the whole time, all she said was, "I know." I told her to keep the secret and she just nodded, which with Mary was as good as a written contract. The reason I never spoke up about it was that I couldn't bear the thought of Charlie's mother seeing him the way he was. I thought she would die on the spot if she did, so I held him in my mind, the way the lake held him, and most times he lay at the dark bottom, but sometimes he'd surface.

Two days later, Mr. Barzita's next-door neighbor, Mrs. Blair, suddenly realized that she'd not seen him since the day before

Halloween and went to his house to check up on him. The doors were locked from the inside, so she looked in all the windows. It was while kneeling on the ground, staring down into one of the window wells, the same way Jim had spied what we'd gotten for Christmas, that she saw his shadowy figure hanging, a rope around his neck, from the ceiling rafters of his cellar.

I figured, after much thought, that the man in the white coat couldn't collect Barzita's soul unless he willingly committed suicide and that Charlie'd been killed because the old man had at first refused. I also realized the stranger had been after me next, the second weakest kid in town, but somehow Barzita had finally found the courage to pay up on the deal he'd made to avoid death in the mountains so long ago. If this all sounds crazy, consider the fact: In the spring, when Barzita's son came to town to sell his father's house, he had a yard sale of all the stuff he'd found in it. I saw, while passing by on my bike, my sweater lying on a table by the curb.

That old white car was never seen again on Pine Avenue and the only smoke we smelled afterward was that of piles of leaves burning in subsequent autumns, not to mention the time Mrs. Kelty found out her husband was having an affair with Mrs. Graves and burned all of his belongings in a big blaze on the front lawn. The pale stranger's face never again showed itself at our night windows, but even though he was gone, I could feel his presence had changed me in some way. Maybe it was because of what I knew and couldn't tell but could only secretly write, which I did through the frozen, snowy days of winter; the antenna moaning above me.

As for Botch Town, it's still there, sitting in the cellar astride the sawhorses. Through the years, the clay citizens have carried on with their lives, and although the wizard's dust is deep and the sun no longer shines, they still, from time to time, stare up into the darkness, half-hoping, half-dreading, they'll see the eyes.